THE EATERS OF TIME

THE EATERS OF TIME

THE CYCLE OF BONES

JP CORWYN

4 Horsemen
Publications, Inc.

4 Horsemen
Publications, Inc.

Published By: 4 Horsemen Publications, Inc.

4 Horsemen Publications, Inc.
PO Box 417
Sylva, NC 28779
4horsemenpublications.com
info@4horsemenpublications.com

Cover by Jeff Brown
Edited by Joseph Mistretta

Library of Congress Control Number: 2023946707

Paperback ISBN-13: 979-8-8232-0328-9
Hardcover ISBN-13: 979-8-8232-0330-2
Audiobook ISBN-13: 979-8-8232-0327-2
Ebook ISBN-13: 979-8-8232-0329-6

DEDICATION

Time is a funny thing. Objectively, we know it's a constant, reliable thing. We know that it moves, for all intents and purposes, at the same speed second after second… that it isn't a thing in flux. Yet things we know are often ignored or cast aside for how we feel. Time may be a constant in the rational, objective world, but more and more, we find ourselves looking at it subjectively. Time seems to speed up or slow down for us based on whatever's going on around us in that moment.

How many times do we look up from reading a good book, diving down a rabbit hole on Wikipedia or Reddit, or a million other activities, only to be shocked by how late it's gotten? How many times do we find ourselves at someone's funeral thinking or saying, "I just wish we'd/ he'd/ she'd/I'd had more time"? This latter has been especially true over the last few years given the pandemic, I grant you. But it was true in The Before Times as well.

This book, and indeed the entire series, is still dedicated to people whom I have never met, and in some cases, never will. Never having met them has still done nothing to diminish the influence they've had over my life. But there are others whom I've known and are now gone. Their losses stopped me in my tracks, as so often happens, and I've since had time to reflect on the impacts they've had on my life. They mattered, and still matter … to me, and to all of the lives they touched whilst they were still among us.

In memory of, and gratitude for, Lundvarr, Rowan, and Hawke. My life is better and richer for having known each of you. Thank you for singing along.

With boundless and grateful thanks to Jocko Willink, Leif Babin, and the men of SEAL Team 3, Task Unit Bruiser.

It is by no means an exaggeration to say that without these men, I would be neither who nor where I am today. Among many other important lessons, they reminded me of a truth I'd always espoused but had lost sight of—yes, that was both accurate and a blind joke.

It doesn't matter that you're off the path. What matters is that you get on it now.

~JP Corwyn
Stoke Gifford, United Kingdom
17 September 2022

Elevate your reading adventure!

Dive Into Skolf's Epic Soundscapes with "The Cycle of Bones" Original Soundtracks.

Experience the full depth of JP Corwyn's creation. Immerse yourself amidst haunting voices and the even thunder of battle rhythms. Each track is a journey through the vibrant landscapes and rich tongues of a world both vast and intimate.

From memorable melodies to choruses 'round campfires, the Original Soundtracks are a unique blend of in-world songs and symphonic scores.

Step beyond the page. Bring the world of Skolf to startling, stunning life

Start your journey now. Scan the QR code to visit JP Corwyn's Spotify artist profile, or find 'The Cycle of Bones' soundtracks (and all of your favourite #BlindIndieRock tracks) on Amazon Music Unlimited, Pandora, Google Play, or wherever you stream the music that moves you.

Remember to like, follow, and share.

Table of Contents

Prelude

-I-

Venzene Duchy of Kovalun
County Jižní Pochod
Barony of Hartscross
3 Gerstesykli: 8 Years prior to the Red Storm at Westsong

Kastan had failed. She'd done all she could. Hells, she'd tried nearly every idea that had come to mind, bar scarring herself or taking her own life … to no avail. Time was short, and young Lord Evzen's interest in her remained maddeningly clear.

In a turn of events that would have been a surprise to only the very young or incurably bright of spirit, the weather had done little to improve her mood. The sky had been threatening real rain for the past three days. Thus far, it'd done little more than threaten. The occasional misting—Hells, even the rare shower of heavy raindrops—hardly touched *her*, though the latter seemed to hammer the narrow leaves of the ash trees like ghostly hail.

The column ambled southward; the trees marched ever closer from the west. Kastan rode her sad, gray palfrey, feeling a wave of frustrated woe swell, then ebb away.

Barely a breath into Gerstesykli and the trees and plants already look skeletal. The rational part of the world's been spending its time harvesting, shoring up, and preparing for winter. And here are we, off to celebrate autumn's ardor, riding the reveler's road.

She found herself having to consciously fight her instinct to sneer.

The season didn't usually bring this sort of frustration out in her, yet here it was. *By tomorrow, things will be in full flower in Hartscross, I've no doubt. Nearly a fortnight of feasting—an excuse for aristocratic excess, really.* She shook her head, the leather of her reins creaking as she tightened her fist around them. *Two more days of travel, a week full of fools pledging sworn brotherhood and meaningless military alliance once we arrive, and then... I've lost. Ten days hence comes the festival of Sigdemane. All doors will slam shut, save one, and I'll have no choice but to walk through it—to accept it with what grace I can muster.* She shook her head. *And I've only myself to blame.*

A part of her tried to push the reality away, tried to dive into memories of when she and her brother, Caros, were still small enough to enjoy the games, costumes, food, and fantasy Gerstesykli always brought. It helped for a few moments. But all too soon, such memory gave way to thoughts of her mother, Klara, dead these five years.

She never would have allowed this—allowed Father to demand a match be made as if I were some prize at the end of a lyst's final round.

That was true. It would've been Klara who orchestrated any such matchmaking. *She'd have done it with forethought, not out of desperation. She certainly wouldn't have forced me to marry against my will.*

That might be wishful thinking, but she didn't think so. At the very least, she didn't *want* to think so. Then again, Mother had been nothing if not pragmatic. She'd been the one who'd kept their lands profitable and their wealth in good order. Had she lived... Beyond that, had Kastan been more dutiful...

More? More dutiful? No, that's serving truth's bitter brew in a hero's chalice. Had I not been so selfish ... so childishly greedy with my wants and desires, I could have had her hand to guide me. I would have been able to stop Father's grief bleeding us dry. Instead, I wasted my time on youth's useless games until she was just ... gone.

Kastan had been allowed to go her own way for most of her life. With so many pleasant diversions on offer, she'd never really taken the time to learn at her mother's elbow. After the wasting sickness had taken Klara from them, however, there'd been little choice. Within less than two sykli, their fortune had nearly disappeared. Once she'd become aware of the problem, Kastan had risen to the occasion, learning all she could about effective finance, negotiation, and the running of her family's lands. Unfortunately, it'd taken her a year and a bit more. By then, Father had already burned through most of the wealth that had been put by.

I had to learn as trouble came … to build shelter even as the rain fell. Blessedly—even as a boy—Caros did his part.

True enough. Her brother had begun to win gold and a fair bit of renown at various tournaments—first in the babe's lysts, then the squire's tourneys. That had brought him to then-Baron Edmund's attention. When Edmund made war against Baron Cyril of Bod Trnu, Caros won even more wealth at Edmund's side. *He'd been too young for war, really. Blessedly, Edmund must've seen that—he kept Caros among his personal guard during battle.*

Again, her brother had given over most of his coin in an effort to help shore up their father's spending. *He did it without being asked—did it with a smile, in fact. He held on to just enough to ensure he could keep up both his gear and the appearance that all was well in his world.* He was, in so many ways, far more their mother's son than their father's.

Count Edmund was now their liege lord, and a relative peace had settled over this last year. Their coffers were, for the moment, almost full enough to pay a year's taxation even if disaster struck. Still, it wouldn't last.

Father should've focused on helping Caros. Her not-so-little brother had already earned an excellent reputation and was well on his way to being called to the line. He simply needed to travel, fight against, and be seen by the other knights of the County to *build* on that reputation. *Instead, Father's obsessed with seeing me married. He's set on securing our future position in Kovalunth society by bartering my body and the children I'll be expected to bear.*

This was hardly a new or outlandish idea. Alliances and expansions had been attained through the sword or sweetness of the marriage bed since time was first tallied. By and large, among the great folk—the middle-classed gentry, or the upper-classed nobility—it was what daughters were for.

Speak the truth and spurn the treasure. I acted decisively to save my family. I did right by my mother's memory, and my father's name—right by my brave brother. By doing so, I proved my worth as a wife and so robbed myself of choices.

Her thoughts grew slow and mean as her party ranged south toward Hartscross. Syr Ondra had set her as near as no matter to the very middle of their column, just in front of the two wagons in their train. That was fair enough. She was, after all, the lady of the party. She simply disliked being on display as the group's centerpiece.

No, that's a lie. I'm glad I'm the centerpiece. Let them see how sullen and heavy I've become. Perhaps that'll curb the interest of that strutting, preening ... prancing... Her thoughts trailed off as she gave up the hunt for a more insulting descriptor for Ondra's heir. It didn't matter. None of those unkind slings *actually* suited Evzen, and she knew it.

Unless someone told him to attend to his hair or his raiment, Lord Evzen of Sunův Dar rarely gave such matters any real thought. What was worse, he was good-natured, good-looking, and from a family that was substantively wealthier than her own. He certainly sat tall in the saddle, his blond hair a pale-yellow wave bouncing over his shoulders and across the muscles of his broad back. Evzen wore neither kontusz nor bolero jacket, choosing instead to greet the day in a long, once-white shirt now faded with age and many washings. It was in fine enough shape, and as one layer among many, the color would have seemed deliberate. As a lone upper garment, however, its weathered reality was obvious. The benefit, most other women might say, was that the shirt clung to him in all of the supposedly *right places.* His physique showed him for the warrior he was, and his wealth showed him for the prized husband he would make ... for the right woman.

What fool would spurn such a suitor? She snorted, taking care to keep the sound soft so as not to draw undue attention to herself.

Looking away, she focused on her brother's slim frame within his dark green kontusz. The black silk of his hair—so like her own—hung in a far less animated fashion between his narrow shoulders.

Riding at Evzen's side, he seems more like the retiring, proper younger cousin—perhaps even Evzen's squire. Yes, she supposed some fool or other might well mistake him for some yoked youth leant into service by one of Syr Ondra's house knights. *Still, while Evzen's older, stronger, and taller than Caros, he's seen nothing of war. Ondra prudently stayed out of the conflict, keeping his sons from getting involved. Why risk life and limb when you can let the world's woes pass you by?* The notion made her anger flare once more. She looked around, away, anywhere but at the front of the column.

"Why don't you want to marry my brother?" the velvet voice of Syr Ondra's younger son spoke from behind her.

Honza was thirteen or fourteen, long-limbed, and as awkward as a new foal's first steps. He was the wagon's only occupant, as its cargo was the coin they'd brought to pay Count Edmund's taxes.

Kastan urged her horse out of line and fell into step beside the wagon he drove. The boy had kept his voice down, but still, the idea that the servants in the wagon behind might overhear their conversation didn't sit well with her. She made her own voice soft as her horse fell into step.

"Honza..."

"Kastan." After a few moments of silence, he repeated his question. "Why don't you want to marry my brother?"

It was one thing for Evzen to decide that *he* didn't want *her*. For the woman to reject a suitor was another matter entirely. If she gained her household a reputation for unearned pride and self-import... Never mind finding a wedding match for either herself or her brother. Such a reputation might well delay or even end Caros's chances of being called to the line. She could not, *would* not, allow that to happen.

"What ... makes you ask such a question?" Hells, if *he* could see that she didn't want to marry him, who else had drawn that conclusion?

Honza rolled his dark eyes, though his smile was soft enough to rob the act of any real scorn.

"Shall I make a list? Surely anything I put on it would just be telling you what you already know."

She considered that for a moment. She'd known him—known them both—for most of her life. Now, she realized, she'd never stopped thinking of him as more than Evzen's little brother. True, he was still young, but he wasn't strictly a child any longer. Hells, when had *that* happened?

He shrugged at her silence as if to say, *so be it.*

"In the years since your mother passed, you've avoided nearly all events—be they tournaments, festivals, or dances."

"I've been seeing to my father's estate, Honza. There's been little time for—"

"When you *have* attended them, you've avoided my brother at every turn—never rudely, mind, but there's ever been some excuse or other not to be around him longer than necessary."

"Honza, no. It's simply that I have far, *far* more duties than I did when we were children. I cannot simply—"

"You spent time seemingly afraid of food, nearly disappearing when you turned sideways." He was gentle, but now that he had begun, he seemed determined to finish his litany. "Now you seem to have started eating again, and you refuse to stop. You must weigh, what, thirteen or fourteen stone, now?"

I don't know whether to be impressed or angry at you, but you haven't missed a trick, Honza. You're right about all of it. I stopped eating when father's first flock of suitors began coming to call. Looking sickly was enough to chase them off, but the next batch seemed to prefer the willowy look. Gorging myself served to make them reconsider. Most of them, but not your Evzen.

"You shouldn't have to marry him if you don't want to. Evzen likes you, but..."

"But?" She furrowed her brow, happy to shift the topic to her soon-to-be intended.

Honza bowed his head before he answered, jutting his chin forward as if making a difficult decision. When he finally spoke, he kept his eyes closed, and his voice almost too soft.

"I don't think *he* enjoyed himself either."

Her heart stopped. She knew what he was referring to but asked the question anyway.

"Enjoyed himself when?"

"I ... was in the loft that night, Kastan. I'd been playing a game with the sons of the other nobles and armsmen. I hid upstairs in the stables ... behind the bales of apple hay."

She tried to force her face to remain expressionless and was fairly certain she'd failed. Blessedly, his eyes were still closed. *That proves nothing, Honza.* There *had* been orchard grass in the loft. Of course there had. From Zlaté Pole in the south to Sädelev Org in the north, orchard grass was part of the diet of all well-bred horses.

"I thought you were *wrestling*." He gave a bitter little laugh. "I almost jumped out to join in. When you two began kissing... When I saw you both undress..." He shook his head.

She sat there, trying to absorb the enormity of it. They'd played together for as long as she could remember—she, Caros, and Evzen. Unlike the other noble children, neither Evzen nor her brother tried to keep her out of their play. Whenever they'd been left alone, she raced and wrestled with the boys as if she were one of them.

She had been about Honza's age on the night in question. She hadn't yet turned fifteen. That much she could say with certainty. *Mother had been gone only a few sykli. We'd traveled northwest to Kovadlina Skála...* It had been the first, and to date, *only* time she could recall. The aging lord—a forgettable man save for his far-too-old wooden teeth—had managed to marry off his equally forgettable son, whose teeth she did not precisely remember. The wedding itself was over, and the majority of its guests were racing toward the stupor that always followed such events. Her social obligations duly met, she'd excused herself for the evening and left the hall.

She'd spent endless, purgatorial hours enduring a procession of highborn strangers at her father's side. They'd come to offer polite consolation with understanding smiles that never reached their eyes. She thanked them with the detached grace her father had made clear was her duty, but the act had taken its toll. She had been only too glad to escape at last.

She'd gone to the stables, intending to spend a few quiet moments among the horses. Like so many girls, she'd always loved their strength and beauty. Now, she'd hoped the warm fragrance of horse flesh would act as something of a balm for her wounded heart and lonely mind. When Evzen had come up behind her a few moments later, she'd thought nothing of it. When he'd kissed her, she'd been surprised, but only for a moment. Then she'd been just as heated as he was. It didn't take long before they were up in the loft, fingers buried in each other's hair as they strove to breathe without breaking their kiss. Each pawed at the other's clothing. Then he was laying her down, their mouths still locked together ... and he was inside of her. At first, she thought she'd caught fire—that it wasn't possible for so many sensations to strike her at once. It'd all been far too new to be accounted anything but magical.

That hadn't lasted. He was certainly enthusiastic, but all too soon she'd found herself... *bored, honestly. The entire affair lost its glamour before he'd even finished.*

Still, the idea that Honza had *seen*? She'd feared, off and on over the years, that Evzen might speak about their encounter, giving her a reputation as *that sort of girl*, but he hadn't. Nor had he tried to reclaim the heat of that night. The idea that Honza had been there... had witnessed them naked and striving?

"He doesn't," Honza trailed off, then tried again. "Evzen *likes* you, Kastan, but he doesn't..."

"Doesn't *what*, exactly?" Was her voice higher than usual? She thought it might be.

"I don't *think* he enjoyed himself, as I say. I know you don't *want* to marry him—that you didn't really, um... enjoy..." He trailed off, shaking his head. "Will you marry ... me?"

She gaped. She felt her jaw drop open and simply hang there, but she could do nothing about it. True, he was only five or six years her junior, but...

He seemed to take her silence as a good sign. "Kastan, I'm smarter than my brother. Hells, smarter than my father. I have money put by, and I'm not likely to die in a tournament. I don't intend to even *fight* in them. I can retain a champion for that sort of thing." He paused, looking to their vanguard, where Evzen was currently riding up to pass a word with

Syr Ondra. "He'll marry you... if you'll consent, but he doesn't *love* you! Not... not as I do." His voice was low but urgent. It broke as he finished this brave confession, though whether that was his age or his emotion was anyone's guess. "I've loved you since that night."

He paused for a moment, looking at her, then closed his eyes once more. "I'm... I'm larger than he is... if it helps."

She had to fight to hold back the laughter. *Still, cti strážce ohně. (Honor the fire keeper).* That final point had been an unexpected gift. It had shocked her back to her right mind. The world had at last resumed its normal speed once more.

How do I answer that without being cruel? The idea that she'd been outmaneuvered by a boy of fourteen, if only for a moment, hadn't been lost on her, either. *One crisis at a time, though.*

"Honza..." That was as far as her mind had gotten before she registered what she'd likely been hearing for some time—laughter, harsh as any crow's song, and getting louder. It was coming from off to their right, not far into the poplar trees.

There were several deep whistling noises, and then the world was a blur of sights, sounds, and smells around her.

Honza had been looking at her, his eyes pleading, though his face was set as he awaited her answer. Then he fell toward her, a ragged sigh escaping his parted lips. As he toppled, seeming to take a whole sykli to do it, she saw the pleading expression fade into a look of surprise. Then the light winked out of his dark dreamer's lamps. A broad arrow—nearly as thick as a child's practice spear—protruded from the middle of his back. Dimly, she realized she couldn't see the arrow's head, but that thought was far away.

The horse that drew the wagon stopped, braying its terror as it reared. She heard screams from behind her, then Evzen's fearful, enraged voice shouting for his father, followed by the sound of thundering hooves.

Her own horse was dancing beneath her, anxious to race away. Kastan held the mare back, though she'd made no conscious decision to do so. She reached for Honza's limp form, even as her gaze bent toward Evzen's voice.

As if she dreamed, she marked Syr Ondra's horse dragging him off to the south. He appeared to have one foot caught in the stirrup, and two arrows jutting from his bright side. She doubted he was still alive.

Syr Ondra wounded or dead, and Honza... I have to get that arrow out of you. She leaned to her right, her bright hand gripping the back of the peak seat.

The world was suddenly in motion. Her legs were simply *gone*. Had she been hit? She didn't think so, but—*Wham*! Her knees impacted the wagon's heavy wooden wheel, her chin slamming down beside Honza's motionless head. Her teeth came together, but there was no click. Instead, she tasted iron from where her teeth had driven into the wet bed of her tongue. For a moment, she knew only pain, both sharp and throbbing.

Mrak ... must've lost control over her. Never mind how—her horse was gone. At least the wagon wasn't moving. She pulled herself to her feet and turned to Honza, reaching for the arrow. That was when his body gave up its waste. She recoiled, giving a pathetic little half-scream—a shrill, yet somehow muted "yeee" sound.

She could hear Evzen's battle cry, and she turned in that direction, glad for the distraction. Drunkenly, she moved toward the—*front? Could it still be considered the front of their ... column? Is it even a column anymore(?)*—line.

Near a dozen men were cheering and jeering from the tree line. Three of them had massive bows. She thought the rest were armed with clubs or hatchets, but she couldn't be certain. Was that a fire off behind them? *There are people on the ground. They cannot simply be sitting there, can they? Or could they?*

She'd found her feet again but thought she might fall onto her backside in another moment if things continued. Her legs seemed unwilling, perhaps even unable, to keep her standing for much longer.

This thought was forced away by the sight of Evzen charging the harriers. He bore down on them like hell's own harbinger. He was young and handsome, hair streaming out behind him, sword held high as he drove his horse toward them. There was no sense of speech in his battle cry. He gave a full-throated shriek of righteous rage as he drew back his arm for the strike.

She knew what would happen next but found herself unable to call out—unable to look away. She could only stare with a kind of sick fascination as passion met patience.

The lead archer nodded as if to say *very well* and dropped his bow. He unslung a massive, bearded axe from somewhere and stepped to the left as he swung. The axe bit deeply into the charging horse's legs, above its knees. It screamed—like a woman; it screamed—and dragged itself along the uneven ground. Evzen went tumbling forward over the heads of his attackers, landing behind them with a snapping sound she could hear even at this distance.

"Kass-tannnn!"

Caros sounded as if he were off to her left and getting closer. She looked back in that direction and saw him riding toward her. He looked afraid but not panicky. He skidded to a halt beside her and reached down.

"Up! Now!"

She obeyed.

"I see your horse. We have to check on Evzen. Grab Mrak's reins as we ride by." His voice was clipped but in control.

But what is he saying? Surely Evzen's gone, as are the poor servant girls. We can't be of any help to them, and we can't be a help to anyone else if we're dead or taken...

"Kastan!"

She snapped back to the moment at hand.

"Can you grab Mrak's reins?"

"I... *Yes.* I will." Her voice came out in a rasping grunt.

He rode toward the grey palfrey a dozen or more yards off. Kastan nearly missed when the time came but managed to hook the tip of her middle finger around the leather reins just in the nick.

"Hold tight. We have to be swift." He rode them wide around the man with the axe, crossing into the woods a few yards north of their apparent encampment.

It was too late. She could see it almost at once. Evzen's head lay twisted beyond a neck's normal range. As if the world itself wanted to be thorough, a broken branch rose out of the place where his right eye once rode.

Ahead, near where the young lord had fallen, there was indeed a small campfire with bound captives arrayed a few feet from it. Some ten feet deeper into the woods stood a tall Sediace oak. Its white trunk was dim beneath the gray sky, but that wasn't what'd drawn her attention. Bound to its lowest, thickest branches were a trio of figures. A man, a woman, and a girl of perhaps five or six hung by their wrists, twisting, naked, and bloody from what she *hoped* were only shallow cuts.

"Evz..." Caros's voice was choked with misery but again—no panic.

She felt him deflate, then tense, shaking his head. "We go. Hold tight!"

"Wait!" Her voice was an urgent hiss. Had she stopped breathing? Her eyes weren't on Evzen's ruined form. She would both mourn and celebrate his passing later. *How could... What manner of men or monsters...* But her thoughts had become a warring, roaring parliament of mingled rage and terror.

"What? Kastan, we—"

Whatever objections he had, Kastan hadn't heard them. She'd drawn Mrak close beside Caros's charger and transferred herself to the palfrey's back. As soon as she was settled, she drove her knees into the animal's flanks and charged.

"What in the hells are you *doing*?" She heard the growl that accompanied this question, but that was alright. She also heard his horse's hooves racing to catch her up.

It wasn't a question she, herself, could've answered. In truth, *she* had precious little idea precisely what she was doing. She only knew that she had to save those folk, if she could. Later, she would muse on the strangeness of that decision. She had been terrified—so much so that she'd been willing to leave Evzen to his fate, as well as the servants Syr Ondra had brought with them. It was a selfish thought... if a forgivable one. Yet upon seeing the family—upon seeing the girl hung like meat waiting to be field dressed after a hunt, something in her had ... snapped.

Arrows whistled by her, but she kept her narrow focus on the oak. She had to get to them—had to cut them down. She heard her brother curse, then the sound of metal entering flesh—a sound like wet fabric being ripped, followed by a thump and a scream.

Not Caros. That was a higher note than Caros can reach, even when he jumps into cold water.

She was there. She stopped below the girl, catching her in one arm and reaching up to slice the heavy hemp of the rope. She had to saw at it. She'd almost gotten through when she heard Caros shout her name, followed by a muted trill from the horse beneath her. Then Mrak tore off, leaving Kastan behind.

For an instant, she dangled there, hanging with the girl in one arm and the rope in the other. Her knife had fallen to the grass below her. It proved too much weight for the remaining strands of hemp. She did her best to protect the child as they fell. She succeeded but landed badly on her dim-side ankle.

Caros had ridden to her, his sword still gleaming red from whomever he'd stabbed.

"We have to go, Kastan! *Now*, if we've any chance of esca—"

Caros's voice cut short as two more arrows pierced the air. One struck his dim-side shoulder, the other his charger. He growled, rolling off to his bright side, keeping the horse between himself and the archers. That gambit didn't last long. No sooner had his feet hit the ground than the

horse bolted.

Off to find Tančící Mrak, no doubt. Well, who can blame either of them?

She looked at the other two figures who hung there. The woman was most assuredly dead. Given the severity and locations of her many wounds, the monsters took their time and their pleasure with her.

Now it was Kastan's turn to growl. Her terror was gone. She had never in her *life* been so full of rage, and with it came courage's good sister—determination.

They need to pay. They need to…

"They need to die."

"No argument, but I can't kill them all, Kastan! They aren't going to fight me single combat…" Caros bowed his head for a moment, then stepped between the foemen and his sister. "I'm going to charge them. When I do, run. Head south, if you can."

"Caros…"

It wasn't only that she was horrified at the prospect of what he might do—of losing him. She didn't *want* to flee. Her blood was up, and she wanted to make these men *pay*. They had ruined and likely raped the woman. Regardless of the miserable, low-bellied details, they had inarguably taken the girl's mother from her. And for what? True, the family was Sheshik, but what of that? They could have been Dračí netopýr, and it would have been monstrous.

Even dragon bats deserve better.

"Kastan? Kastan, I need you to do as I say. I'll be *right* behind you, but you need to be ready to move. One?" His voice was full of that good-natured, dry humor she so loved.

But this is the first time you've ever lied to me. He *would* follow if he could, but she knew he had no plans to do so. There'd be no chance if he meant to buy her time to run with the girl.

"C-cut me down. Please. L-let me f-fi-yeet."

"Two?" Without looking away from the slowly advancing men, Caros took a half-step to his left, then threw an exaggerated back cut—his blade slicing from dim side to bright—up and over his head. It connected with the rope well above where the man's hands gripped. Somehow, the dark-skinned fellow managed to drop into a low crouch, almost cat-like.

"My chi-eld's naam is—" he began, but his speech was so slurred that the name was difficult to understand.

"I cannot say that word." She hefted the child against her hip. "Does she know it? Can *she* say it?"

"Kastan..."

She looked from the Sheshik man toward Caros. *He's right. The archers are keeping their arrows trained on us... Wait. Why haven't they fired?*

She caught sight of their empty quivers and understood in a flash. Of course, they hadn't fired. They had only one arrow each now.

A bitter winter's rage fell over her. It was as if all the years before, every injury she had witnessed, every fear she'd suffered, each of life's laughing, lashing moments of misery now screamed and howled within her, urging her on.

"Caros!" She kept her voice low, despite the urgency. "With me. They're nearly out of—"

She was cut off by the sounds of screams... *male* screams. She saw the men turn their heads toward the sound. Setting the girl down, she retrieved her knife from where it had fallen and charged.

"Now!"

She heard a grunt from both her brother and the girl's father, but she thought she heard their footfalls crushing the grass just behind her. As for the other archers, they turned back—but with a fatal lack of alarm.

Kastan leapt onto the nearest man. It was, she thought, the one who had killed Evzen with his axe before resuming his archery duties. She moved with such ferocious speed that she appeared to almost *materialize* before him, raining rage upon his shocked harrier's head.

Shocked, yes, but he was *far* from fearful. He stumbled back, casting his bow aside to try to grab her flailing limbs. He managed to catch first one of Kastan's slender forearms, then the other, staring at her with a mixture of distant avidity and confused curiosity.

Curiosity? Was she acting out of what he considered *normal*? Well, she would sate that curiosity, and gladly. And if she died? So be it. Let this one act—this one decision—stand for all. She bent her neck back and slammed her forehead into the man's face, crushing his bulbous nose right above his matted black beard.

He released her with a graveled shriek of pain, instinctively raising his hands to his bleeding and broken nose.

She drove forward, punching her dim hand into the fork between his raised arms. Her aim was true. She connected with his throat, though with only enough force to surprise him. Out of reflex, he dropped his hands, grabbing her by her outstretched wrist.

She smiled, even as she wept. Her bright hand came up over her shoulder, plunging her dagger into his right eye, just as the branch had darkened poor Evzen's.

He stood there, quivering, grip tightening on her wrist, but she saw the light wink out within his remaining eye. A moment later, he finally crumpled to the forest floor.

Behind him stood a man in a dark leather gambeson, sword in one hand, short-hafted spear in his other. He sheathed the sword at once, then ran his hand through the length of wild brown hair that crowned his head.

"Are there any others, or were these the last?"

Caros stepped to Kastan's left, breathing heavily.

"I'm ... Lord Caros Percoy. This is my sister, the Lady Kastan..."

The man nodded slowly, cast about, then spoke again.

"Was that an answer, my Lord?"

Caros actually stopped breathing for a moment, then did something she hadn't expected. He began to giggle. Within moments, it had turned into streaming-eyed, wild belly-laughter that somehow lightened the entire area.

Kastan looked around, then stepped forward a pace.

"These were the only ones left *here*. I heard men screaming... probably dying back toward our wagons... Did *you* kill all of them, or... or did some escape?" Her voice sounded strange to her own ears—a cold detachment that was somehow both calming and alarming. Her heart *had* begun to slow at last, though a queer, metallic taste had taken up residence in her mouth. When had that happened?

He nodded, sliding the spear into a brace across his back.

"Aye, lady. Dead or bound up and ready to be marched back to Edmund."

She'd snapped her head around at the sound of movement. It'd come from over her shoulder, back toward the fire. Rather than fearful, she found she was almost ... hopeful. *Hells, do I truly want more?* She thought she did, at that.

"No fear. Just mine freeing the prisoners."

She nodded, bending to remove her knife from the dead man's eye. She found she couldn't pry it loose. A hand closed around hers. Looking up, she saw it was the new arrival.

"I have you, lady. On three?"

She nodded. They counted, and together, the knife came free. Her stomach gave a lurch at the ichor still clinging to the blade.

"Here..." He took the knife from her, albeit gently.

"Thannk you, Lord Caaruss. You aand yo siss-ta risssked yo lives to save my doa-ta and I."

Kastan heard this from over her shoulder but left it to Caros. The man before her had finished cleaning the harrier's filth from her eating dagger, though she doubted she would ever eat with that particular blade again. Was he Eoalunth? She thought so, but couldn't be sure. She waited until he made to hand it back to her before speaking again.

"You have my thanks, and Count Edmund's as well, once I tell him of your good works."

He offered a neutral nod but said nothing.

"What name shall I give him, so that he might know the man patrolling his lands for trouble?"

The newcomer actually smiled at that. It was a warm thing that gave his face a boyish look. "Eobum, Lady. It's a name he knows well, as it belongs to the commander of his scouts."

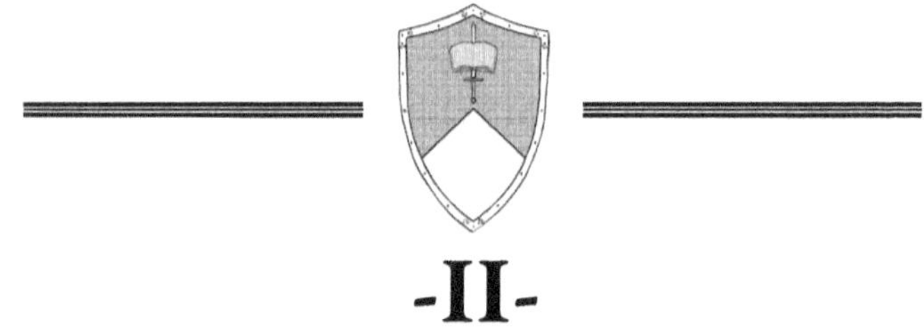

-II-

Thassak Pass
34 Kovsykli: 5 Years prior to the Red Storm at Westsong

Methias wondered if any of his company still lived. His mind kept trying to drag him away from conscious, cogent thought, but he fought against it. There'd been no warning—had been no chance for one, but...

If they're fighting, I have to do my part. I have to get up. Jannon and the others may need... Jannon may... Jannon...

But it was no good. Everything was numb. Even his eyelids refused to obey.

The newly minted Syr Jannon Saysh had stood a watch while the rest of them slept, but he couldn't have known about the creature. Perhaps there had even been more than one. In either case, it didn't much matter. The attack had come without a word of warning, like a sudden summer storm.

No, wait. That can't be right, can it? There was a warning, wasn't there? He recalled Jannon shouting his name, didn't he? He was almost certain of it. Jannon had cried out, calling him ... by *name. That* was what'd

struck him.

He almost never uses my name—hasn't done since he first found me. Unless he's introducing me to someone, it's nearly always Lamlith (Little Fire).

He'd been asleep, though something had been gnawing at the edge of his senses. He'd been fighting to dive back down into Hämärä Meri—the Twilight Sea, where the mind usually wandered during sleep. Then came the jolt of sound, as if he'd been walking atop a frozen pool, and the ice had unexpectedly cracked beneath him.

"Methias! *Methias*!" Jannon's voice, and he had never sounded so afraid. "No! No, Lord, not him! No! I *swear* to you I'll..."

After that, he'd felt that smothering numbness and fallen back into the Twilight Sea once more.

Now Methias drifted in dreams. Oh, there were moments of lucidity, but they were horrid things where he *knew* he was dreaming... could recall *why* he was dreaming.

A line of lore—just a fragment of poetry, really—snagged his mind out of the strange, floating dimness that carried him. It hurt to hear, though even that pain was muted and distant. With a mingled sadness and joy, he allowed himself to focus on the stony, fireside tones of his fallen master, Emil.

> *Adrift in the dark where all things seem still,*
> *Alone, without spark to fight dark or chill,*
> *When light and soft wind come to tempt you away,*
> *That gift is not hope, but the gift of the Grey.*

The Grey? Where did that come from? He felt himself sliding toward the left—felt his hand break out into the open air as if rising above the surface of a pond. He groped with that hand, distantly delighted to feel anything at all. A moment later, he felt his dim-side ear tingle as it, too, found freedom.

...Gift of the Grey? What am I not seeing, Master?

Was he speaking? Had he felt a sense of warmth and movement near his throat? It *may* have been his own voice. It might also have been their healer, Elliata, working to rouse him. *Hells, it may just as easily be my mind playing tricks on me.* He did his best to ignore the sensation, trying to pull himself toward the open air—toward wakefulness.

"The Grey. The Grey. I'm missing something, Emil. The Grey?" He did his best to force his mind back down the Scholar's Road, as his master had taught him. "Sconces on the wall. Sconces down the hall…"

His musings were cut off suddenly as his left eye finally cleared the surface of whatever numbness held him. There was a delicious flash of cold along his nerves. Then came a new sensation—as if a swarm of angry ants crawled beneath his exposed skin. It reminded him of the prickling of a foot or leg after it had fallen asleep and was forced to move.

Again, his mind tried to dive back into the Twilight Sea. Again, he heard his master's voice, and though he couldn't make out the words, the cadence and tones matched that same fragment of half-remembered verse.

With an effort, he opened his newly freed eye and cast about. It was dim, but there was enough light to see by. He was in a clearing that seemed much like the one in which they'd camped.

But no tents… no fire pit. No sign that there's ever been an encampment here. There's light enough to see by, but … there's no source. No fire, no torch…

A line from a much-loved song came back to him, though the situation gave it a rueful sheen. *It's full-moon-bright on a clear Byt night, so our songs won't wake the dreaming.* He tried to shudder but couldn't quite tell if he'd succeeded. *It's too bright, somehow. The moon's only a crescent. I saw it rise as we finished making camp. So where…*

He heard a low, not-quite-animal noise from somewhere behind him, then another from his left. It sounded like a hawk's call trapped behind a wooden door or down a shallow well. *That's almost right, but the size is off. Make the hawk the size of a mastiff or a young pony. That might be about right to match the sound.* Perhaps if he were on his feet, he could face down a *single* predator that size, but in his current state? *And there isn't one single beast. There are at least two of them, whatever they are.*

This realization was followed by another, more immediate one. His slow slide toward his left—toward apparent freedom—was speeding up. It felt like the very ground was being tilted to one side as if to roll him off. Emil's voice was all around him now, echoing, stacking upon itself, though it never changed its timbre or varied its delivery.

"…gift of the Grey, gift of the Grey, the Grey, the Grey, gift, Grey, Grey—"

Perhaps a dozen yards away from him, Methias saw something slide up out of the ground. Its insectoid, triangular head ended in a serrated beak. The creature's scales were a dim, shimmering dun color, contrasting the pale grey stones that served as its eyes. If the head were any indication, the creature would, indeed, be the size of a small horse. It hadn't dug its way free of the soil and scree. It had simply … emerged.

It's as if the ground were the surface of a lake. Why is that familiar?

The creature saw him or perhaps scented him. It cocked its head to one side, gave another of those horrid, trapped-hawk cries, and began swimming toward him. The beast charged *through* the ground, leaving no disturbance in its wake, widening its beak as it came on.

It's grinning at me! I'm sliding toward it, and it's grinning at me in triumph! The inexorable horror of it nearly unmanned him until he saw its eyes once again.

"Grey! The Grey Between!"

The realization was a hammer-blow that brought all the fear and wonder of his earliest lessons back to the fore. The Grey Between was the closest of the Realms Beyond—where haunts were forged out of pain and wrongs done to them. The place where the dead lingered until they at last passed on. And that meant...

"No!" He wasn't sliding toward freedom. He was sliding toward his death.

I refuse! I will not end here! I...

But what could he do? Nothing. That sensation of being dragged toward his left was his sense of self—his actual *soul*—shuffling loose from his body. He could try to pull back into himself, could will himself not to die, but that wouldn't heal him.

"I have you, little wizard." That was Jannon's voice... but changed. It was fuller, projecting an almost physical force. He'd made a simple statement, yet he spoke with a ringing sense of command. Methias saw the creature's head come away from its neck as if it'd run directly into a swinging axe.

Jannon's voice came again, still speaking with that strange resonance. "Here, boy. A gift from the House of Saysh." This was followed by a wave of heat so utter and all-consuming that Methias couldn't breathe. Blessedly, it faded almost as suddenly as it had arrived. His left eye snapped closed, though he hadn't meant for it to. The numbness was fading at last, and while he couldn't move, he could sense the world around him once more.

Jannon spoke anew, some feet farther away from where Methias lay. "Wake. Time is short."

A grunt, then a groan. A soft, clean voice spoke one of the world's oldest questions. "What ... happened?" It was Elliata, their Eodenth healer.

"The encampment was attacked by Isbryd Drayag."

"By ... what?"

"Wraith Dragons, girl. There isn't time to explain, nor does it much matter. I've given you what you need. Heal the others. The boy Methias has already been seen to."

He heard Elliata get to her feet. "You've given me what I... I don't understand."

Jannon's voice came from farther away as he answered. "Concentrate your will, girl. You must cleanse their bodies of the blight they've put into it. If you don't, they die, and any Isbryd Drayag I *didn't* kill will feast on them, spirit and shadow alike. Now, to it." For all the weight his words carried, his tone was calm, approaching casual. It was as if the matter of the company's potential death was of no real concern one way or the other.

Elliata went about doing as she'd been told. She spoke in low, murmured Eodenth—a tongue he could recognize but knew almost none of. He *did* hear her speak the names of their companions, each in turn. She'd finished her work on Naeadne, Wois, and Hakim before Jannon spoke anew.

"Lus rhex. Misda rhex. Taul rryn, t'len sdraliana."

He spoke this vile incantation with calm confidence. The ground shook as if thunder were trapped beneath it. That thunder raced toward them, making the horses scream, to say nothing of the recently awakened men and women.

A moment later, the air was split by a trumpeting sound that was at once pitiful and bone-chilling. A lone horse had loosed a single haunted note as if it were being flayed where it stood. That note shifted, becoming graveled and guttural, full of obvious excitement. It also bore a note of clear affection, despite the sense of unnatural dread it projected.

"I've missed you," Jannon crooned. "Come. We have work." He sounded as if he were swinging up into the saddle.

Methias wept and screamed inside. He recognized the tongue, understood the words, and knew at least some of what they meant for Jannon.

(*Change, blood. Awaken, blood. The Champion calls you to corrupt this shadow.*)

Methias willed his body to respond, trying to force his now throbbing limbs into motion. His fingers danced listlessly amid the grass stems, but he could manage nothing more. Both noise and the noisome rose to meet his misery. There came the sound of what was once a mortal horse pawing at the ground, accompanied by a strong wind full of sour smoke.

"Lord Saysh?" This was Hakim. His normally calm voice was several notes higher than usual. His fear had made it thin and brittle. "What..." He swallowed and tried again. "Why do you mount up when we have wounded to treat? S-surely we should guard them until they can be moved."

For one awful moment, there was silence. Then came what were all but certain to be the last words Jannon Saysh—the *true* Jannon Saysh—would ever utter. Hearing them shattered what remained of Methias's hope. And it *was* Jannon who spoke. The voice Methias had heard every day for more than five years. The voice that had saved him when all others had either betrayed or abandoned him. His words were quiet at first, but as he made his answer, his voice rose full and clear.

"My thanks, Lord Haunek."

Jannon paused after speaking that strange name. *Strange, yes, but familiar somehow.* It gnawed at the back of Methias's mind, teasing out strands of deep dread that went beyond the horror of this miserable moment. *He's entered into a pact with a devil. And that devil's name is Haunek.*

"Look after them, Hakim. This is the end. Our fellowship, our plans... all of it. I ... have to go. I have to hold up *my* end."

"Jannon! Wait! Jan-non!" Naeadne voice rose, even as, by the sound of it, she did. She called after him, her voice betraying anger and fear. Both tones sounded alien in her throat.

It made no difference. With an eruption of hoofbeats, Jannon Saysh, or the devil he had sold his future to in order to save them, was gone.

HOPE, HELP, HOLLOW

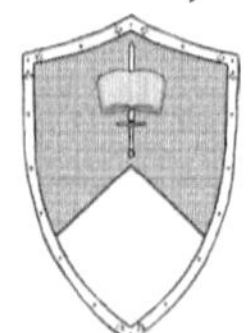

-I-

The Green Lands
42 Gerstesykli: 14 Days after the Red Storm at Westsong

Methias came to a stop, his horse Mezofel following suit beside him. The horse stood easy, paying no heed to the blond boy on his back. Up ahead and to the right, a stand of trees and bushes jutted up from the dark green grasses.

Methias turned, meaning to look up at the boy he'd ransomed from the Hollow Ones. "Do you want help getting down?"

...Apparently not. It was hard not to smile, watching him slide from the saddle and onto the ground with such ease. *He seems to have recovered nicely, so that's something.*

"You've been kind to me. I thank you, my Lord," said the boy. He was smiling again, which was a good sign. He then bowed rather formally, as he'd clearly been taught. The cut of his clothing, his cultured speech, his ease in the saddle...

He's noble-born, then. No surprise, I suppose. For all of its fear and hatred of the Weave, there are very nearly as many casters in Venzene as there are on Nausha. The nobility tends to be the most accomplished, too, despite their oft-vaunted condemnations.

The boy would expect ... what manner of response? A kindly, sagacious nobleman seemed the best fit. Methias made his posture a touch stiffer, keeping his voice neutral at first. "I bid you as safe an evening and as uneventful a life as you're able to find." He ended this neutral formality with a courtly bow to match the boy's own. As he righted himself, he made a conscious effort to adopt a more affable air. "Keep careful watch over your power when you're memorizing rites, or they'll call you the *sleeping sorcerer*."

He appeared to have chosen the right combination of stance and speech pattern. Though no reply was spoken, the boy favored him with a genuine grin and a nod before running off toward the green grove. A moment later and he'd gone through to meet his mistress on the other side—wherever that was.

"Fare you well, boy ... while well still waits."

Methias laid a hand along Mezofel's silky neck, combing his fingers through the charger's mane. He'd made up his mind to stay afoot for the time being. Turning toward the road again, he chuckled.

"No, not unless you're desperate to bear my weight just now." It was to Mezofel he'd spoken as they resumed their walk. The horse kept pace with him without prompting. "Hmm? No, I'm certain you're right. No doubt he'd have made an *excellent* apprentice." He paused, trying to sort out the thoughts as they came, taking care to separate Mezofel's from his own. "No, indeed. Apprentices do not, in fact, grow on trees." He laughed, albeit mildly.

Silence fell for a dozen strides or so. "There's a fine line between fate and fortune, I think. If I see him again without directly seeking him out, we can call *that* fate."

In reply, the horse tossed his proud head, whickering warmly as they walked on.

Methias allowed his mind to lapse into un-thought. The Wilds, as he'd been taught to call them, were a far cry from Skolf, but he'd not been afraid here since he was, well...

Since I was that boy's age, I suppose.

This thought started to lead him, naturally enough, toward memories of his own apprenticeship in Nausha. He'd always found the City of Towers to be impressive, but in the sterile way sculpture or paintings were impressive. They captured the imagination for a moment, but they rarely rolled around in your head or woke you up from a dead sleep. With time and either distance or familiarity, the sense of wonder and awe the great city evoked simply ... faded.

The wilds were more ... omnipresent? That was as close as he could come to finding a word for it. They were like poetry, story, and song. Not the versions written and archived for posterity, but the mundane miracles of raw, living performance. *There's something comforting in the savage actually allowed to be... well, savage. The wilds are unbound, perfectly imperfect. They're—*

His musings were cut off by a single, intense word scraping against his mind's ear.

"Methias!" The sense wasn't that of a shout but of a cracked, rusty whisper seemingly from inside his own skull. He stiffened, acknowledging the voice—making the mental shift to accommodate the speaker's presence.

I could ignore him, of course, but that would only delay the inevitable. I'll need to speak with him eventually.

He ordered his mind, preparing himself. It would be disastrous if he were to allow his face or stance to betray a hasty reaction. *I must be measured in all things. His good will is genuine, but... It's spider silk—strong, but impossibly delicate.*

A moment later—a heartbeat, maybe two—and the wizened, alien form of Ramud Ayumbra faded into existence before him. He floated in the air, seated upon nothing at nearly eye level, and waited. His expression seemed remote and imperious, looking down his nose at Methias's helmeted head.

Ramud Ayumbra was a Meoli... was, it was said, the *first* Meoli reported or recorded. Now he was among the willingly tethered spirits that served on the Borr Gezeol Xec—the Night Song Council of Xecses Merai.

Meoli was polysemous—a word with more than one meaning, dependent on context from speaker or scribe. Most commonly it meant the get of a human and a dwarf. Its second meaning was far kinder. If the "e" were emphasized, the meaning shifted to *the impossible made manifest...* made real. It meant, in other words, *miracle.*

Meoli were either substantively shorter or taller than most dwarves. Ramud Ayumbra was the former. His flesh was a deep, sunbaked brown, like the folk of Northern Shesh. His hair and beard were long, wild, and white like summer clouds—or bleached bone, depending on his facial expressions. His teeth, too, were dazzlingly white, his eyes yellow stars in a clear night sky. He wore a pleated white kilt and grey leather sandals, the coils of which stretched up over his calves. His upper body displayed bare, dusky-brown flesh, save his enormous left arm.

From Winter's Maw to the Singing Sea, smiths across Skolf could be identified by the telltale asymmetry of their arms. Many smiths kept their arms bare whenever work or weather permitted. It was a way to silently display their oft-honored profession. Ramud Ayumbra, first Meoli, seemed unsatisfied with that meager presentation. He'd covered his bright arm in a series of overlapping leather plates of a deep, dark grey. These were reinforced by what looked to be ivory bars along the forearm. The harness ran seamlessly into a well-oiled leather glove of the same dark grey at one end and a bone pauldron covering his left shoulder at the other. This piece was bound to him by means of a wide band of colorless leather across his chest, under his dim arm. The overall effect was both magnificent and disturbing.

Not for the first time, Methias was left with the distinct impression that the fellow took deliberate pride in cultivating his image as something *... other*. It wasn't that he thought the man should conform to meet *his* view of normal. Far from it. Methias was human, after all. *Ramud Ayumbra is ... not.* No, it was simply that he seemed to accentuate the most jagged aspects of everything from his hair to his heritage. While there was certainly nothing intrinsically *wrong* with that...

But it serves to bait the trap. You demand respect in every way, yet in every respect, you seek to force a reaction. And if I yield—as others, apparently, have before me? Then you'll gleefully throw up your hands, say that you tried, and leave another age to fall to the King of the Dead.

Methias stopped walking entirely, knowing full well Mezofel would do the same without needing to be asked. He stepped back and offered a deep nod of his head, fluttering his bright hand to touch his belt, the area just below his ribcage, his lips, and finally his forehead in succession as he righted himself.

How to greet you in this place... The Dwarven tongue would be more forgiving, but the Sheshik ones? The various languages and dialects of Shesh were far more exacting. *Because they're all tonal... and I'm an ill singer. Combining them?* While that task would be less than intuitive, he thought it would be his best course. "Ramud" was Aqdna, the eldest of the Sheshik languages. "Ayumbra" was Eydzul, the lone Dwarven tongue. *Better to acknowledge both in respect, rather than presume he reckons one more important than the other.*

"Rah-mood Ay-*oom*-bra." Methias took pains to roll the first R but only emphasized that single syllable: *oom*. He shifted briefly into Aqdna. "Naum saamreghbel lev mor tiil." Then back to Dwarven. "Gimilxec."

This was a formal greeting if a touch on the warm side. If taken literally, the Sheshik portion translated to *"You I desire that fairness should hunt for."* Sheshik was, however, a poetic language with much of its meaning lost on the casual student. In actuality, its translation was closer to, *"It is my desire that fairness should hunt for you—that great god who is the sun should protect you from the unscrupulous in all things."* The brief return to Eydzul, the Dwarven tongue, offered a simple sign of respect for the Meoli's station, translating to *master, teacher,* or *mentor.*

Ramud Ayumbra remained cross-legged in the air for a long moment, his face an unreadable mask.

He's leaving me rope to hang myself—testing to see if I'll speak further... before he replies. If I do—other than to show weakness by seeking assurance that I have not offended in some way—I break the tenets of both Sheshik and Dwarven courtesy. He resisted the urge to fill the silence.

Ramud Ayumbra, at last, bowed his head, closing his eyes for perhaps a three count.

"Meth-hyoos Ar-thod...zet oal ayom ahg hol Akhdir la Yantahi." The Meoli kept his voice formal, his words carried on a low, stony baritone.

He spoke in Calyari... save his use of "Akhdir la Yantahi." I can hardly fault him for using this place's Sheshik name.

(You have come to the Endless Green.)

Methias nodded. Now that the greetings were properly seen to, it would be safe to revert to the trade tongue. "As you say, and as you instructed."

"I do not instruct, Meth-hyoos. I merely advise."

"As you say, Ramud Ayumbra. I ask that you advise me further, now that I am here."

Ramud's response came without preamble. "You will walk to the ring of Hollow Ones you see atop the hill there." He raised his hand to gesture over his right shoulder, though his focus remained on Methias's eyes. "Pass beyond them and you will find what I promised ... and its guardian."

Methias nodded, saying nothing. He would hold his questions until Ramud Ayumbra invited him to ask them. He didn't have long to wait.

"Speak, while my patience yet wakes."

How to respond... What does he want me to ask? I can't ask what I'll find there. He'll tell me that he's already said, and he has. I cannot ask what he wants me to do. He'll only tell me that I asked him for knowledge that could aid me, and he led me to it.

Methias's mind was swift and agile, which was good. He was able to consider his options at a speed that made others see him as calm, collected, and in control at nearly all times. If his mind worked at the same speed as most seemed to, they would see the truth. It was all a mask.

Most folk observed the way others acted and interacted in their early childhood, and so learned how best to do the same. As they grew, that knowledge developed into a kind of unspoken intuition. Its use came automatically, to one degree or another, just like walking. Most people didn't consciously think about putting one foot in front of the other to cross a room. They simply walked. For Methias, and more than a few of the other casters he'd known in Nausha, communication—social interaction—was anything but automatic.

"Apprentice," his master Emil had said, *"conversation is like drawing a draught of fresh water. Most people live near a creek or river. For them, they walk over, dip their cup or even their whole damned head in the flow, and are sated. You don't live near a creek or river. You live near a deep well. If you need water—if you want to understand and be understood by others, you have to use a force pump, fighting to pull that water out with an act of will. It'll always be work for you. There's nothing you can do to change that."*

And oh how that'd hurt hear. The description was near enough the mark, but the idea that there was nothing he could do… But then Emil had grinned at him—a grin that said plainly that there was more to his tale.

"…Alright then, apprentice. As you know you've work ahead of you, make that work easier. Learn all you can about culture, language, art, and architecture. Learn all that you can about as many things as your head can hold. Use that knowledge to ever improve your arm and the mechanism of your pump. Drawing water will always take more of an effort for you than most, but if you do these things, that effort won't always have to be such hard work or take quite so long. Sconces on the wall…"

So, what did he know about Ramud Ayumbra? He was, or at least presented himself as, a smith. *Yes, but the materials he's used are from animals, not minerals. He's shown that he forges flesh and bone, not just iron and silver…*

"Am I here to gather, or am I here to be made useful?" He paused, then amended. "Made *into* something useful?"

The Meoli's brows rose in surprise at the question. He dipped his chin as he lowered them again, offering a species of nod before he spoke.

"An … unexpectedly astute question, Meth-hyoos."

I've made him revise his opinion of me, at least. Well, no, he may just be trying to find an answer that fits within his intentions. At least Ramud appeared surprised, rather than angry or disgusted with him. That was

something.

"My answer is both. You will gather supplies, certainly. How you proceed once you've seen and heard what lay beyond the Hollow Ones *may* forge you into something useful." He paused, offering a smile that not only failed to reach his eyes but actually seemed to steal the light from them. "Do not forget that a tool may be used by an enemy as easily as by an ally. I look forward to seeing what you make of this place ... or what it makes of you."

Methias took that in, considered for perhaps ten seconds (which was very nearly an age for him), and finally nodded. "Will you be here when I return?"

"*If* you return, I will await you in the Sculptor's Hall in Xecses Merai that was."

Methias bowed his head. "My thanks, Ramud Ayumbra. If I should fail, may you find someone more worthy soon after."

Again came that look of genuine surprise on the Meoli's face. It was dispelled swiftly as he bowed his head in turn. As soon as he'd completed the motion, he winked out of existence.

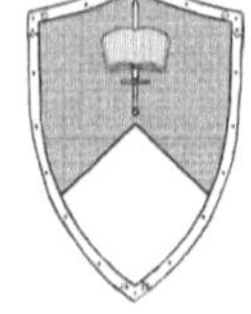

-II-

Methias took a long moment to collect himself, drew a deep breath, and walked on. Just as before, Mezofel fell into step at his side.

As they walked, he gathered what information he could. The hill in question was broad at its base, sloping gently upward. Its crown was utterly hidden by a dense ring of red—the trees, vines, and underbrush possessed by the Hollow Ones.

Yes, but also no. They may ring the hillside, but they don't form a proper circle. Given how they march away from the dirt track I'm on, the hill must be ... long. Can't see how long from this vantage, but ... long, yes. Still, he shook his head, *stone in sky, there are so many trees! Whoever or whatever gathered the Hollow Ones was clearly more worried about defending this place than keeping it hidden.*

Mezofel bent his head, shoving gently at Methias's right arm and whickering softly.

"What about them?" He cocked his head to the side as if listening, then looked toward the looming hill again. "Ahhh, you're right. There *aren't* so many as all that, then." He wondered how he'd missed it. The pines atop the hill clearly were, or had once been, ancient. They stretched well over a hundred feet in height. But the pines were forked near the base of their trunks.

Wise. He paused, considering before he continued their walk. Once the Hollow Ones took possession of vegetation, they only grew when they could find a sufficiency of meat. They didn't need it to survive, but they *did* need it to grow or walk to a new location.

The amount of meat required to move that many would have been ... massive. There are still a good deal more of them gathered here than nature would allow, mind. But you're right. It's not the multitudes I thought I'd seen. For all that, they were so closely packed that they reminded him of the great banyans that were said to have swallowed the ancient cities of the southern springs. He'd seen them only once as he'd fled northward, but they'd made an impact on him, not least because of the wealth of figs they'd provided to a starving boy.

*That was before Traead... before Jannon found me. Before—*The thought flared, then fled like summer lightning.

The base of the hill was still a few yards ahead, but he'd gotten close enough to make out several dashes of white and grey among the red grasses. *Cobbles? Yes! A cobblestone path leading up to ... stairs.* If he'd had any doubts as to the import of this particular hill, this discovery removed it.

"Stay here." Methias's voice—not overly expressive at the best of times—had taken on a flat, dull tone. "I'll be as quick as I can."

Mezofel stomped a single time but otherwise made no noise. Still, it was clear he wasn't happy with his master's choice.

As he gained the first cobbles, Methias caught the strong smell of salt and iron. The Hollow Ones couldn't be active due solely to him, could they? *No. Certainly not. There must be someone or something beyond them— near at hand, though not close enough for the vines to catch.*

He reached back beneath his cloak as he moved. He'd *prepared* for a fight. Only a fool came to the wilds any other way. But if he could *avoid* one...

Once he'd hauled his haversack around to rest on his right hip, he opened its main pocket. *Fresh boar meat,* he thought. *Fresh boar meat from this afternoon's hunt.* Drawing and holding a modest breath, he allowed his hand to pass the pocket's lip.

For an instant, he felt nothing. Oh, there was the mild temperature difference within the bag's commodious main chamber. He could feel that even through his tight leather glove. His splayed fingers, however, found nothing solid. He closed his hand slowly and withdrew it. A thin smile crawled across his lips as he felt the sudden weight of the massive boar steak in his grasp.

Checking back over his shoulder to confirm Mezofel's distance, he moved a few feet farther up the hill. The trees were positively shaking, though their windless movement was without doubt drawing away from him, toward the hill's top. He looked up and addressed himself to the nearest two trees and their attendant shrubs. As he spoke, those same trees turned their leaves and vines toward him with sudden and vicious fervor.

Mezofel gave out a low warning that needed no bond to translate.

"I'd not taunt you. I wish to pass *beyond* you, up the hill, for which I will gladly pay the toll." He waited a moment for Mezofel to deliver the message, then spoke on. "Will you let me pass?"

The trees shook hard enough to nearly uproot themselves. *And if they've drawn in a sufficiency of blood...* Methias felt his stomach turn to lead, his blood growing cold. *No. If they'd had enough blood and meat to charge me, they wouldn't give me warning. But they* have *been kept from slumber. Something must be close ... and bleeding.*

He eyed the way the trees had planted themselves. *There's a gap to the left I could've simply walked through, were they merely trees. If I'm quick...*

Methias hurled the boar steak high. It would land, if it were allowed to land before the Hollow Ones grabbed it, on the right, farthest from the gap. He watched as the tree in question lashed out at its prize, nearly folding itself in half in the process.

He had a moment to feel a mixture of awe and outright horror, then leapt into motion. An awful, creaking groan sounded directly above him as he sprinted toward the widening gap. Another, heavier groan came from above and to his left.

There's a whistling sound, too... like trees in a storm. No wind, just the Hollow Ones striving. That shriller sound's getting louder. It's familiar. It's ... pine song!

He skidded to a halt in the very nick. The ancient tree to the left of the gap—now bent at the nearest of its twin trunks—brought its massive weight down like a falling catapult stone. Methias had an instant to register that, had he not stopped when he did, the impact would have crushed him into jelly in that instant.

To his left, the tree began hauling its trunk back into its upright position. To his right, the Hollow One he'd distracted with the boar steak had apparently finished its main course and decided on Methias for afters. In its haste, its middle branches became momentarily entangled with its neighbor, and the two began to tussle.

Methias could only stare. Two hoary red giants—these massive trees with bifurcated trunks—wrestled mere feet away, and all he could do was stare. It was as much out of awe as it was horror. His perception of time slowed, stretching to a nightmarish crawl.

I'm a child ... watching as the runaway cart hurtles toward me. Yet even recognizing this, he found it impossible to look away, let alone to move.

He felt a fierce pinching in the nerves behind his forehead—heard Mezofel's shrill cry. That broke his torpor. Whether it was the note of obvious panic in his familiar's throat or the painful pinch Mezofel had placed on Methias's Eye of Night, he didn't know.

Nor does it matter. They won't focus on one another forever. If I mean to go...

He dragged iron-laced air into his lungs and bolted, jumping over undulating roots as they ripped out of the ground and the occasional lashing vine. He leapt the last yard, rolling on his dim-side shoulder. A bright brand of sudden pain caused him to snap his teeth together and growl. The sound was short-lived. His teeth had come together so suddenly that he'd managed to bite both sides of his tongue. He tasted blood, but never mind. He had other matters to contend with. A carmine-colored briar vine had wrapped around his leg, trying to pull him back. Its spines had managed to bite into the leather of his boot deeply enough that he could feel their sharp points in his flesh.

He turned to face the vine, staring. He knew he must look a sight, were there anyone to see him just sitting there, but...

Let go... Please! Let go! I don't want to hurt you if I don't have to. Hells, you've suffered enough.

It was no good. The Hollow One wanted him, and that was that. He may as well have wished for winter never to come.

He felt it begin to drag him, trying with maddening slowness to pull him back toward the trees. He squeezed his eyes shut, then raised his bright hand and pointed his little finger at the thorny red rope.

"Zeteek hecn berek ruulth." His voice was low and cold beneath the tumult of the Hollow Ones. His face, however, made no effort to hide

his sadness.

(Your blood burns now.)

At once, the vine stiffened, then lashed backward, releasing his leg. As it withdrew, its surface began to crack and darken—thin ribbons of crimson steam escaping into the open air. The accompanying sound was monstrous... a rising, ephemeral whistle, a fibrous tearing—the defiler's hand as it rips open a victim's bodice.

He refused to look away. His master had battered that instinct out of him early on. *If you'd work the rite, you must own its end.* The vine made it a few yards farther before it simply fell, listless, to the ground. As if in response to this, the trees stopped their warring with one another, though the world had *not* grown silent.

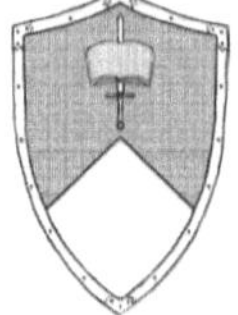

-III-

Methias heard a jumble of sounds some distance behind him. He marked heavy footfalls, cries, and a chorus of voices in a tongue so alien he physically shuddered. It was as if his mind didn't understand how to hear it. Not how to comprehend it, but how to actually process the sound.

He rolled to his feet, turning to take in his surroundings ... and fought the urge to simply gape.

He was on the edge of a sizable, ruined sculpture garden. Its statuary lay shattered and strewn about as if tossed on storm winds. Arms and ruined faces lay between and beneath the few upright stone benches, at the marred feet of marble plinths, or forgotten amid the narrow grass. In the center of this garden stood a tall stone, pale as fresh milk. Though he was sure it was a natural formation, it resembled nothing so much as the middle three fingers of some giant's hand rising from beneath the ground.

Amidst the ruined statuary lay better than half-a-dozen children, freshly butchered by both the claws of some creature and the clear marks of the Weave. His eyes found points of impact where there were burns, discolorations, or, in the case of one young girl, a small sheet of melting ice covering the lower half of her face.

At the far side of the garden, a lone figure stood against a small cadre of shifting shadows. The scene struck Methias as kindling for what would undoubtedly be a lifetime's worth of nightmares.

As he watched, the blackness grew tendrils, a blank, shifty mouth, bolts of shadow fire... There were people within those shadows, moving their limbs to match the leaping, lancing lunacy of the greater blackness.

But their heads! Each of them moves with chin on chest! They move. They react as if they see and know what threatens them, but their heads simply ... loll there.

As for the figure they fought, Methias had at first mistaken it for a dwarven warrior, based not only on size but stance. The truth was far less mundane. The creature's hands were talons. The wretch's face, though surrounded by a mane of rose-red waves, was a mass of dark snakes.

No eyes nor mouth, save those of the serpents themselves, yet there's that ... voice? Can such a thing be called a voice? It's a chorus of bubbling, moaning noise that hurts—physically hurts to hear.

Methias stepped back. With an effort, he *forced* himself to change his field of view. He needed to see the scene as a complete thing unto itself. But his traitor mind did its best to *insist* he look at the creature or the shadows—to focus on the individual players in all of their horrific glory.

No!

He fought to check the urge. His heart felt as if it were about to batter a hole in his chest. His stomach had seized and clenched, which was likely the only reason he hadn't vomited or soiled himself.

"...Battlefield." Methias forced himself to say it. He took pains to keep his voice low, but he had to hear the word aloud. "This is a *battle*field ... and must be viewed as one. Nuth nugosek puav oal ayom, xu lakth puav jhaiyv uundahl, damnit. Puav jhaiyv *uundahl.*"

(Because of mighty hands I am come, and here I shall remain.)

"You *cannot* have her!" The sound came from the shadows or perhaps the folk they puppeteered. It came out in a chorus, a choir of children who sounded not long into their apprenticeships, much like the blond boy he'd rescued. "Go back! The world is tired of your desperate prattling! Go back! You will not take her from me!"

They may bleat in children's voices, but they speak through bearded chins. And her? Her who?

The not-dwarf gabbled in that un-voice again. Methias could feel an altogether unpleasant tingling between his legs and a surge of nausea threatening to overtake him.

The serpents which rode where the not-dwarf's face should have been seemed to curl in on themselves. An instant later, they erupted in a wave of baleful green, like blood spurting from a battlefield wound. It spattered forward, flying past one of the shadows and onto the boy within. Wherever the serpent's spend touched, flesh simply ceased, leaving bone to glitter in its wake. There was no scream, blessedly, but that particular shadow winked out, leaving the body to collapse.

It was then that Methias's eye fell upon the apparent object of this conflict. Laid out on the severed top of a stone bench, he saw the small body of a young girl. She was stocky, broad of shoulder, and well-built for her age, which he hazarded at perhaps eight or nine. She was also unmoving, though he noted she still drew breath, as if in sleep.

The shadows must have scored a hit on the not-dwarf, for there was a spine-scraping, gibbering growl that physically forced Methias to stumble backward, nearly falling. A bright blue scar now glistened where several of the creature's snakes had been a moment before. It leapt into motion, barreling into the remaining shadow puppets, sounding for all the world like a boiling swarm of insects pouring forth from their hive.

"Puav ka vehm hol vel." Methias kept his voice just above a whisper. He would need to move, soon, one way or the other. Whichever side won the contest, the girl was likely to lose, and so was he.

Did he know that? He did not. This rite might show him...

(I will see the Weave.)

He couldn't look for long. The strange light of insanity tried to bore its way past his eyes as they fell upon the not-dwarf's underlying power. Before he looked away, he noted the shadows were not, in fact, *many*. Their light—and indeed it was a light, pale greyish-white—was interconnected as a single source.

His eyes next fell to the girl's motionless form. *Nothing... No taint of the not-dwarf, no tie to the shadow creature. There's ... something off, but whatever it is, she isn't bound to either of those two. If I'm quick...*

He moved as swiftly as he dared, building up speed from a walk to a jog at a steady climb. He had to avoid being a sudden blur in the corners of either creature's eye. He kept his hand on the hem of his cloak so as not to let it make his silhouette too large.

He reached her miserable bower beside a knee-high plinth. Bending down, he tried to shake her awake, his first finger over his own lips in a shushing gesture. No good. Whatever had happened to her, she was utterly unresponsive.

Hells! If she won't wake... If she wouldn't wake, he had only two choices. Leave her behind or...

Methias dismissed his rite, returning his vision to normal, then glanced back at the battle. Both creatures—for he now thought of the children within the shadows as appendages, not individuals—were clearly wounded. Only two of those children were still upright and fighting. The not-dwarf's left arm now hung limply at its side, though it too still strove to win its prize.

Methias nodded to himself, licked his lips as he made up his mind, and picked the girl up. She was heavier than she looked, but he could still manage her with one arm. Her head rolled onto his shoulder as he rose.

"No! You cannot take her! She ... is ... *mine!*" The choir, having been reduced to a duet, did little to make the sound less unnatural. As the shadow children screamed their protests, the not-dwarf turned to look over its wounded shoulder. Its face was now missing half of its serpents, that glistening blue left where they had once been.

One of the shadow children attempted to bolt past their distracted foe, aiming toward Methias with obvious intent. Seeing the girl within running a foot off the ground—as if kicking in a black pool of water—was made even more unsettling by the speed with which she moved.

The not-dwarf called up another eruption of green misery that ate away the shadow girl's face and upper chest. It was an instant of hideous perfection that seared itself into Methias's mind. It would be replayed, he had no doubt, along with the rest of this encounter in countless nightmares to come.

Time for that later. He has one shadow child to kill. Whichever one winds up victorious, this girl is likely to lose.

Methias turned, gazing at the place where he'd broken through the bulwark of the Hollow Ones. *Here's hoping I'm remembering the distance rightly.* He spoke four words and took a single step.

"Puav ka koav *luukth.*" (*I will stand there.*)

His back foot left the ground, and the world blurred past. When it subsided, he was standing ... much closer than he'd intended.

...Miscalculated. I thought my distance would put me just inside the hilltop ring. Not in the very gap.

He had barely enough time to draw breath before the vines above snaked toward him, the roots below beginning to grab at his feet. His gorge began to rise at the overwhelming scent of fresh blood. It seemed to come from every direction. It was the Hollow Ones, of course, moving their loathsome vitality within, in order to move their heavy bulk without.

He drew in an iron-flavored breath as he stepped, trying to get beyond their range. He coughed and gagged instead. Just as he had moments before, he felt a vine snake around his shin.

What can I do? I can see Mezofel. I have the power, can get us free, but I need … air! I'd burn the vines, but have no throat for speaking! The Crown of Stars? No, they're darksome, but not… not hellish or … I… I'd draw War Cry, but how can I fight with the girl in my arms?

His head was swimming. He held the girl tighter, meaning to whisper something to comfort her. She slept on. Wherever her mind wandered, it was beyond his ability to comfort for the moment.

He froze. He could *smell* her—could smell the grass and dirt in her hair.

Before the dizziness overwhelmed him, even as more vines wrapped around his thigh, his waist, his dim-side shoulder, he made his decision. He bent close and buried his face in her brown hair, drawing in a deep draught of sun-sweetened air. Raising his foot, he spoke those same four words and stepped forward.

Again, the world blurred around him, but this time when it was over, he heard a chorus of the damned shrieking its displeasure. He knew why. Even as he stepped to Mezofel, he felt what was left of the vines which had tried to claim him fall to the dirt road beneath his feet.

The horse's ebony ears were perked forward, and he pawed at the ground as he nuzzled Methias's face.

"So was I." Methias's voice sounded ragged and raw. "Believe me, so was I." Shifting the girl's weight slightly, he mounted Mezofel. Once they were settled, the horse turned without prompting and began to walk back the way they'd come.

"Puehv ka zulek puav al luukth." Methias spoke through an exhausted sigh. *(My will takes me beyond here.)*

Between steps, the trio left the wilds behind.

THE DANCING POINT OF NOW

-I-

Venzene Duchy of Kovalun
County Jižní Pochod
Barony of Hartscross–Jižní Lov
3 Korunasykli: 20 Days after the Red Storm at Westsong

Vlk gritted his teeth as he lifted what felt like the hundredth saddle into position. His right side wasn't *screaming* at him anymore. That had been last night when he'd crawled onto his pallet. This morning it merely growled at him and only when he stretched.

The saddle was slightly askew. Shaking his head, he reached out his dim hand to grab for the paddock wall. Without looking, he pulled himself up onto the bottom board there, using his hand to balance. Leaning away from the wall, he used his bright hand to drag the saddle into place, ignoring both the sudden flare of pain and the horse as it tried to nuzzle his chest. He knew her tricks. She wanted to either make him laugh or make him fall. Either outcome would've meant a delay to the saddling process.

"Ne, ne, jablečný dechu." He grinned as he hopped down. "Ty jdeš."

(No, no, apple-breath. You're going.)

The horse offered a rumbled response that sounded suspiciously close to laughter. She stood patiently now, letting him cinch the girth strap into position with no further protests.

"I've finished my own. Can I help?" Andrej's voice drifted in at just the right volume. He sounded awake and ready for the day, but he had the good sense not to sound happy about it. In Vlk's experience, grown men tended to hate happy children in the morning. A moment later, Andrej's face appeared above the wall Vlk had been balancing on.

"Ne," said Vlk. "She's the last. Můj dík." *(My thanks.)*

"Pohoda." Andrej pulled himself up to sit on the low wall, watching. *(Yeah, sure.)*

Vlk finished, turned a touch quicker than he'd intended, and winced.

"That's not from yesterday, is it?" Andrej sounded genuinely concerned.

"It's fiiiine." Vlk led the horse from its stall and waited for Andrej to jump down and walk with him. "Just stings. Besides, I vant a rematch."

Andrej grinned at him, putting a hand on his shoulder as they walked. "I'll give you one, but you won't win it if you keep looking before you step."

Vlk met this pronouncement with a brief glare, then shook his head.

"Nobody else can see vat I'm doing." He didn't much care for the realization of how sulky he sounded. *He'll think I'm vroth vith him. But how to fix it...* Grinning, he elbowed the taller boy. "Iiii think you're a kouzelník." *(A magician).*

Andrej offered a grin in return, but it stopped well short of his eyes.

As they were about to exit the stables, Vlk searched out his friend's face. He had to say ... *something.* The silence had begun to grow fangs. "I vas only throwing snow, Andrej. I know you aren't a vizard. I vouldn't have said it if ve veren't alone..."

The blond boy nodded his acceptance but offered nothing more.

Hells, he thought. *Vhat does he vant me to say? I'm not even sure vhat I said wrong.*

After an awkward few heartbeats, Vlk started them moving again. The sky that greeted them was a pale, pre-sunrise blue-silver. Most of the camp was up and in the doings, or soon would be. Perhaps a dozen yards from the stable entrance, a multi-colored stain marred the early winter grass. It would soon turn into a relatively ordered column of mounted and marching men, but at present, both men and horses seemed sleepy and haphazard.

No, it's just that there are too many small groups. They don't look like a force bound for glory. They look like three forces who have to share the road and really don't vant to.

He supposed he couldn't blame them. He doubted he was the only one who would be glad to see the back of some of these people. If he were forced to ride with them? If he had to stand beside and fight with them?

I'd be trying to keep one eye on the enemy, one on the men beside me.

He did his best not to glare as they approached the knot of riders and footmen. A score or more of the assembled fighting folk were wearing the Bluemark's black kontusze. Others he recognized as those who had *once* worn it. These were now dressed in newly sewn gold bolero coats beneath kontusze of road-roughened brown or tan. They looked ragged and unorganized stood next to the Bluemark, even to Vlk's untrained eye.

Making up the smallest contingent, yet the only one he cared about this morning, were the men of the Percoy household. These wore green kontusze with yellow sashes about their waists. There were only four of them, along with their lord, Caros. His black mane was easy to spot. He seemed to be dancing with his sister—the Lady Kastan—several yards away from the assembled men and horses.

Vlk saw Andrej's face split into a fresh grin as he caught sight of this last detail. His eyes were alight with recognition. It made Vlk wonder if perhaps this sort of thing was common in their encampment. It seemed awfully embarrassing and unmanly to him—having a woman dance with you before riding off to win glory. Still, at least Andrej seemed like himself again. That was something.

Andrej nudged him. "C'mon."

Vlk hesitated. He could see that every one of the Percoy men was either seated on or stood next to a ready mount. "I don't know vich one gets the horse."

"*I* do." With nothing more by way of explanation, Andrej began to walk.

Shrugging, Vlk followed. What else was there to do? He supposed he could stand there waiting for someone to first notice, then shout at him. He could also play catch with an active beehive. It'd pass the time, but it wouldn't win him any goodwill, and it was apt to sting.

Vlk let Andrej lead him over to one of the Percoy men. He'd seen this fellow on occasion, but only at a distance. He was a tall man of Sheshik origin. This made him a rarity in camp but hardly unique. True, none of the children Vlk knew or had grown up with carried Sheshik blood in their veins, but what of that? He did his best to let that question fortify his nerves as he walked. The man was, in a word, intimidating. His face—the only bare skin on display, given the season—was a rich, ruddy brown color. It reminded Vlk of late autumn, somehow—of low, early morning fires.

I don't see vhy he should make me afraid. His brows are thick and black, but my father's are hairier. His eyes are brown, like the forest at dusk. He isn't the tallest man here, nor the strongest looking. So vhy does he... Vhy do I...

Andrej shattered this dramatic thought process as they finished their approach. He walked right up to the man and, grinning widely, threw a punch straight at his belly.

The Sheshik armsman's response was smooth and sure. He lifted his dim arm and rotated it at the elbow, deflecting Andrej's blow with an almost lazy movement. He then swept his foot out, catching Andrej behind his own.

The blond boy began to topple, still grinning—actually starting to giggle. One-handed, the armsman grabbed Andrej's outstretched punching arm, using it to keep the boy from falling. He tangled his other hand into Andrej's long shirt for good measure.

"Bet-tah," the man said. His voice was a ringing baritone, fair and musical. He released Andrej once it was clear that he'd found his balance again.

"I couldn't see your foot move," said Andrej.

"I should-n't won-der. You were fo-cused on your pun-ching." He seemed to make a meal out of longer words, enunciating each syllable with lilting care.

"I know what you mean to say, Kyuma. I was just hoping to surprise you." Andrej didn't sound as if he were being defensive. On the contrary, he sounded as if he were asking—or at least hinting at—a question.

"Then per-haps you need to keep your de-light fur-ther be-neath the sur-fess of your face, Andrej. Happy though I am to see you smile, it did nah-thing to hide your int-tent." The Sheshik man—Kyuma, apparently— grinned broadly. He laid his dim hand on Andrej's shoulder as he spoke. "Your strike was fine and well-aimed. It would have struck just below my ribcage. If that is your tar-get, how-ev-ar, punch *up*, not *out*, yes?" He held up his own bright hand and demonstrated, throwing a slow, imaginary uppercut.

Andrej's grin vanished as he absorbed the lesson. He nodded. Vlk appeared to have been momentarily forgotten.

Kyuma leaned in to touch his forehead to the boy's as he finished. "You have made re-mark-able pro-gress in a very short time, Andrej. You and your fa-ther should be quite proud. While I am on cam-paign with Lord Caros, I want you to learn and prac-tees the second and third stages of Sap Hands." With that, he stepped back, ending the contact.

Andrej stood for a moment as if he needed to digest all of this. Vlk found the entire affair rather odd, although his initial sense of disquiet regarding Kyuma seemed to have winked out. Instead, he felt a touch of jealousy at Andrej's fortune.

At least now I know how he's improved so much, so quickly. I vas beaten for helping Lakkrid and Maksu. Andrej vas rewarded vith a better life.

The jealousy faded swiftly enough. Andrej would teach him what he knew. Their sparring matches were always about picking up tricks from one another.

Always? They'd known each other for, what, a fortnight? Vlk's mind bit into the memory of the day they'd met, and winced. The burst of emotions bound up with that recollection was like biting into a lemon. He reckoned that day would go down as one of his fondest memories. The day itself had been fine. Come sundown, however, its sweetness had been replaced by the bitter taste of pain and embarrassment ... and the salt of his tears.

Vlk had done well in the lyst. He had met two new boys to have adventures with, Andrej and Maksu. Then came that terrifying, glorious moment. Lakkrid—his *friend*, Lakkrid had been in real danger. Albeit in a limited way, Vlk had stood and proven what his friendship was truly worth. Andrej, too, had stood, and he had less of a reason to than almost anyone. He'd only just arrived in camp a day or two before. *He* certainly couldn't have thought of Lakkrid as a friend.

You stood and stayed, though. Everyone else stepped back and kept quiet. But you vere right vith me, protecting Maksu—letting Lakkrid and his uncle fight vithout vorry for him.

Vlk had been sick after, but nobody'd seen it, so that was alright. When he'd come home and told the tale, he'd expected to be praised for it. His mother would fret over him, but Father would be proud, surely.

...But Father vas vroth. He shook his head. *Mother and Father complain at how unfair the vorld is, and how no one is ever given justice ... but Andrej earned his family a place in Lady Kastan and Lord Caros's retinue by doing vhat vas right. My father vanted no reward for me, vishing I'd just minded my own...*

Worse still, Father had commanded Vlk to avoid Lakkrid whenever possible. When all of the children were at play and Lakkrid was in camp, it couldn't be helped. They were not, his father had made it clear, friends. Vlk had plenty of other boys to go about with. Lakkrid was of twice-cursed blood—orc and Eodenth.

He was just thinking of how satisfying it would be to correct his father's mistake, *Gnoerkish and Eodenth blood, Father. Gnoerk, not orc,* when he realized that Kyuma and Andrej were both looking at him.

"I... vhat? Gathering vool. Forgive me," said he.

"Well, I hope you've co-lected enough for now." Kyuma's eyes were dancing.

Vlk pinked at that but smiled and nodded just the same. How had he ever thought this man was frightening?

"I have, yes. I'll need more by day's end, though."

Both Andrej and Kyuma adopted looks of confusion.

"I'm hoping for new shoes soon. I'll need the vool to stuff the toes until I grow into them." Not particularly funny, but it was better than simply standing there looking sheepish. "I have the last horse saddled but don't know who to give it to. Do you, Lord?"

Andrej rolled his eyes, but Vlk could see he was smiling. Kyuma, on the other hand, actually laughed.

"I am no lord, boy. I merely serve as an arms man to the house of Percoy."

"He's Lord Caros's captain," Andrej said. He sounded proud, as if *he* were the captain.

"*Only* where such rank and ti-tle are necessary." Kyuma sounded a touch annoyed at Andrej's words. "Lord Caros and Lady Kastan lead us. I am, at best, first among equals."

Andrej's smile vanished. He bowed his head, apologizing in a small voice.

"I will take the horse," Kyuma said. He stepped forward and offered his hand to Vlk, who dutifully handed him the reins. That accomplished, Kyuma lifted his chin and turned his attention to Andrej. "Go and in-form the Lord Caros that we await his pleasure. We will de-part at his word."

Andrej nodded, turned, and bolted over to where the pair of nobles were still dancing. As Vlk watched, he saw Kastan yank her bright hand away from Caros's dim one and ... jab him in the throat? Vlk had no time to react, for Lord Caros had taken her hand again, resuming their dance as if nothing'd happened.

Vhat in hells?

As Andrej reached them, bowing and beginning to speak, the couple stopped their movement. No, that wasn't true. Their feet had stopped moving, and their heads had turned to regard Andrej. Their hands, how-ever, remained in motion.

Their fingers aren't laced together or even curled. Vhat a strange dance.

As Caros made some response to Andrej, Kastan again tried to yank her hand away, bringing her arm wide as if to strike his face. Though nothing seemed to bind their palms together, Caros moved with the strike, maintaining contact.

She laughed, sounding utterly delighted. Andrej turned, smiling, and walked back toward Kyuma and Vlk. The lord and lady walked behind him, arm in arm.

Vlk sketched a bow as they approached, then righted himself. As he lifted his eyes, he saw Caros lean over to kiss his sister's cheek.

"You'll avoid letting the place burn down whilst we're away winning glory?"

Kastan snorted. "I believe the only talk of burning the encampment down was in relation to your lot returning covered in *ignominy*." She quirked both a grin and a brow, then turned to Kyuma. "You'll do all you can to prevent that, won't you, Kyuma?"

Kyuma bowed, a thin smile playing across his lips. "No fear, my Lady. The men and I are ever vigi-il-ent when it comes to Lord Caros and fire."

"Are you really?" She sounded as if she were fighting the urge to laugh.

"Of course, my lady. Lord Caros has such pretty hair, you see. We would never for-give ourselves if it were to catch fire on our watch."

"There." Caros wore a dry little smile. He swung up into the saddle, taking the reins from Kyuma with a nod of thanks. "Nothing to worry about." He ran two fingers through the black length of his hair as if to underscore his point. "If you change your mind about wintering here..."

"I won't change my mind, Caros."

"*If* you do..."

"I'll see you when the grass is green."

Vlk saw the way the pair grinned at one another and realized *he* was grinning, too. He'd no idea why, but yes. He was grinning. Before he could think too much on that score, however, Kyuma spoke up.

"Lady Kastan?" Once she'd turned to regard him, he continued, "Andrej's spoken of the boy Vlk—the one who stood with him before he and his father came into your service?"

Kastan nodded slowly, then followed Kyuma's eyes as he looked at Vlk.

"Ah!" said she. "I knew I recognized you."

Vlk blinked, blushed, and bowed just to have something to cover those first two up.

"He was watching you and Lord Caros with great interest."

"I... No, my Lady. I..."

Kyuma ignored this. "He wore his confusion on his face. Perhaps you might teach him Sap Hands as well while we are away?"

Kastan looked at Andrej, then Vlk, then Kyuma. She seemed to consider for a long moment before at last speaking.

"I think that can be arranged. Vlk, you work in his Excellency's stables." This wasn't a question.

Andrej must've told her. He made as if to nod, but she'd pressed on before he'd begun the act.

"I will expect you directly after you've finished the stablemaster's morning chores. He'll indulge my request, I'm certain. You'll come to my encampment once you've finished." She paused, giving him a smile that made him tingle from top to toes. "Unless you'd prefer to spend tomorrow with the horses, that is."

"I... I vill, if my master vill allow it." He had no idea what, if anything, could persuade the stablemaster to deny a member of the landed nobility's request, but...

"Excellent. Andrej? Would you be so good as to escort me back to camp?"

She didn't wait for an answer. As she made to offer a final farewell to Kyuma and her brother, Andrej leaned into Vlk to pass a final, murmured word.

"Be easy today. And get good sleep tonight. You'll need all of your strength and wit tomorrow." No sooner had he finished this enigmatic warning then Kastan turned and snaked her arm through Andrej's, leading him away.

Vlk had a moment of burning anger that absolutely could *not* be jealousy, then turned to head back into the stables.

Sap Hands? This thought was utterly eclipsed by another, far more wonderful one. Tomorrow, despite his parents' best efforts, he was going to receive at least *some* goodwill for his stand with Andrej and Lakkrid.

That thought was like a song only he could hear. It kept him smiling through the workday and followed him down into sleep that night.

-II-

**Dereek khn
Kieran Isyl
3 Korunasykli: 20 Days after the Red Storm at Westsong**

Jastar sat alone, absorbing the sounds and smells of the common room. The remnants of his early evening meal lay before him on the small tabletop.

The pottage had been nothing to write songs about, though it'd been satisfying enough for his needs. The fresh bread, on the other hand—a dark, marbled thing he'd been told was rye—had been an utter delight. There was something warm and altogether earthy about it. It made the act of drinking feel twice-blessed, somehow, when paired with any beer, ale, or lager. The flavors seemed to play off of one another.

So far as he knew, rye was a rare and quite expensive crop mainly used for the beautification of manor houses or the parlors of particularly well-to-do merchants. It wasn't good for much else. It was only grown in any quantity in places like Wick and Rockvale, so far as he could recall. The discovery of it here in Dereek khn wouldn't have been much more than a footnote—a sign of the realm's overall wealth.

To them, it's common and must exist in plenty. They serve it with stews at a reasonably common inn and tavern. Just my portion here at table would have been worth, what, the price of a new saddle? At least half of one, surely.

He'd made some polite inquiries as to the source of this apparent wealth, thinking it might prove useful to the forthcoming war effort. To his surprise, he'd learned that, while it had started out much the same way, its use as a food crop had started with a misfortune. Apparently, somewhere back up the hourglass in whatever land Dereek khn's lord had come from, a massive crop of wheat was lost late in the season. A desperate farmer tried planting his fields with a novelty—a small, blueish-green plant prized mainly for its odd coloration. The climate proved ideal for the crop, and it grew in abundance. The tough, resilient grain had since become wildly popular in that land, wherever it was, and consequently, here.

As of yet, he'd been unable to determine where this tale had taken place. It wasn't that the lord's former homeland was considered a secret. It wasn't even an odd question for a newly arrived fighting man to ask.

People were more than willing to shed light on the matter. The problem was that no three people gave the same answer. Some claimed he was from Venzene; others that he was Traeadish. Hysterically, there was even a rumor that the local lord was a disgruntled noble from Thorion.

No matter. I'll solve the mystery, eventually. I just have to choose my words with care. It'd do him no good if his questions drew the wrong kind of attention. His mission was too important to the Thorion Throne to risk seeming overly curious.

Patience... that's what's needed, now. Speed's important, but the wrong information delivered fast just hastens a bad end. He raised his mostly empty mug to his lips, using it to catch a sigh before it drew unwanted attention. *Can't keep letting things slip by me. There's only one cure for that, though... patience. Aye, I can be patient.*

In fact, he'd spent most of this week's daylight hours *patiently* admiring the view. The porch of Kieran Isyl's only inn proved to be a perfect perch from which to mark the comings and goings of this small community. The inn was positioned on the only road, as near as no matter to the settlement's heart. This allowed him to watch the townsfolk and farmsteaders, and the people both great and small, who had business in the keep atop the nearby hill.

He'd recognized folk from Traead, Shesh, and Venzene by their hair and skin tones, and in some rare cases, their accented speech. Others (a great many of them, in fact) were an exotic mystery to him at first. These latter had thick, black hair which was often richly curled the longer it hung. He might have been forgiven for thinking they were from Venzene, at a glance, but looking at them for more than a moment made the differences obvious. Their hair was the right color, but it was somehow too luxuriant. The folk of Venzene were either pale-skinned or baked dark by hours in the sun. These folk had skin he could only describe as shades of olive, ranging from light browns to pale peach. If he'd ever seen their like before, it'd been too brief to register. Given how many of their like made their homes here, his mind had raced to categorize them.

He shook his head, wrinkling his nose briefly as if he'd smelled something unpleasant. *And, like a fool, I just took the simplest answer to hand and moved on without a second thought. They were a curiosity—little more than comely foreign servants, or perhaps slaves.*

Many of them carried or looked after blonde-haired infants and small children. The various hues of blonde and brown were most commonly found crowning the heads of the folk of Thorion, Traead, and parts of

Venzene. Merchants, freeholders, and nobles alike tended both to employ servants and own slaves, so this made a certain amount of sense.

A thing can be sensible without being true, though, can't it? This was a fact he'd long known, but one he'd often found himself forgetting. *Senseless sensibility,* Valad had called such thinking. *An indulgence to be denied whenever possible.*

Blessedly, he'd been quickly disabused of this particular sensible untruth. Over time, he'd noticed many of the children referring to these women as mother, Mama, or Mitéra—a word he hadn't known but had seen enough to understand by context.

So, proven wrong, I leapt to the next conclusion. If they weren't nursemaids, then the children must be bastards. Aye, Jastar, you're so terribly clever, aren't you? Bastards... of course. What else could it possibly have been?

He rolled his eyes at his own idiocy. It was a well-worn fact that men—and not a few women—made liberal use of the slaves and servants they kept to slake their lust. Most thought there was a fine line between use and abuse, but in his estimation, and indeed that of his knight, that was foolish. That particular line only ever really seemed thin from a great height. Jastar had always found the practice pathetic. To his way of thinking, removing a partner's ability to say *no* did more than just abuse that partner. It also sang sagas about the abuser's inability to catch the interest of a willing lover.

I'd just about made up my mind that Dereek khn was, sadly, a place like any other. Then he'd seen them—men who bore the same features and accents as the women he'd noted by day. With them had come older boys whose hair had darkened to a brown that was just next door to black. *Seeing them on the streets—hells, even in the damned inn—made me feel like the Falx's own fool.*

Certainly, *some* of the women he'd seen might be servants or even slaves. It was also absolutely possible that they were—the thought made him angry at his own blindness—just citizens, people who were as bound or as free as any other. Storms be swift, had he really been that dismissive of them... because they were outside of his direct experience? He'd choked down both outrage and pride and stepped down from the high place he'd mentally set himself upon.

It was at that point that he'd finally asked one of the men where he was from.

"Up the hill," the man had said. Smiling, he'd gestured up to the terraces where a town had begun to bloom beneath the stone keep's stern gaze.

He'd asked another where he'd found his pleasant, round-faced wife.

"Dannus's Rest," came the easy reply. This was the name of the largely Traeadish hamlet to the northwest. It was only a few minutes' walk there, and it would likely swallow up Kieran Isyl as a district, eventually.

He'd asked another woman where home was—what nation she'd hailed from.

"Oh, I'm Dereek khnii, Lord. Been here since the beginning."

After that, he'd stopped. He'd been trying to be subtle and direct, simultaneously. It was like trying to throw a sword strike while leaning away from your target. You could do it, but it was a move born of desperation, not patience.

You've been doing far too much of that this week. You're here to gather *information, not go raiding for it.*

The week had been productive enough, all things considered. He supposed he couldn't argue that fact. He'd met the lord's seneschal—a honey-haired and bearded dwarf called Morakogunn Fellhammer—found a new potential food source in the form of rye, and had a reasonable gauge of who the folk of Dereek khn thought they were. Now he just needed to figure out who they *actually* were.

I'm in a forest I don't know, and I have no lantern. If I race, I'm apt to fall or miss a game trail that might lead to something better. Patience, Jast. Patience.

The maid serving him this evening seemed to be of Traeadish heritage. Her hair was a reddish blonde, and she swallowed her Rs when she spoke the trade tongue. As she poured him a fresh mug of beoir Úll—a dry, tart Traeadish apple beer—he took the opportunity to strike up a conversation.

"It's ... Ilimor? Or have I misremembered your name?" He offered her a small and embarrassed smile. It wasn't difficult, given his mood. For her part, she brightened with a smile that managed to be endearing despite the two teeth she was missing.

No. Not missing, just worn down to near nothing. Barring that, she was a pretty thing. Blessedly, she spoke before he'd had the chance to start staring.

"Yor, sure, and that's me, Lord." Her eyes were wide fields of green clover, deep with flecks of black dancing in them. "M-most folk who stay here do their best to convince me m'name's girl, sweets, or koritsi."

Jastar gave a nod of sympathetic amusement but thought he'd seen his chance.

"I ... don't know that last one."

Her smile flashed out again. "Koritsi? Nor'd I, afore comin' here. It's the Naushaii word for girl, or so they tell me."

"Naushaii? Is *that* where they're from? Nausha?" He lifted his chin toward a nearby knot of the folk in question. The group laughed as the eldest among them gesticulated along with whatever he was saying. Jastar couldn't make it out in the overall din, but he thought they were laughing with the man, not at him.

She followed his gaze, then returned her attention to him and nodded, making an *mhm* sound. "City of Towers, sure enough."

Jastar shook his head, bemused. "I should've known that. I'm acquainted with a man whose grandsire, I think, came from there." He was thinking of Sir Trallot, Lord of Rockvale. He was a man Sir Valad had always respected, trusted … but never much cared for. Jastar had never found out why, but he'd been left with the impression it had been something long ago and by the way.

He took a pull from the heavy wooden mug Ilimor had only just refilled. "What's brought so many folk north from Winter's Maw?" He quirked a grin. "Other than Winter's Maw being colder than hearts in the hells, I mean."

She offered a light, somewhat professional smile at that, but answered readily enough. "They came with the Lantatt. He's from Nausha, ain't he." This had been a statement, not a question.

Is he now...? With a grin that made it clear he felt like a fool for not putting that together, he summoned an "Ah, well there's that," before giving her a light salute with his mug.

Chuckling, she excused herself to attend to another patron. That suited him. He had enough on his mind just now.

The realm's leader—this Lantatt—was from Nausha, was he? The impossible island where magic was said to flow like wine? *Well, that explains a few things.* The Countess *had* told him the place was named in the Spell Tongue. He'd been looking out for magics this last week and had seen nothing obvious. Honestly, he'd begun to think the name was little more than an attempt to look tall. If no other sovereign realm were named in that tongue, it would help to legitimize it as a culture to those outside.

Nausha, he mused. *And that links up nicely with why rye is grown in Rockvale and its neighbor, Wick. If the Trallot family came from Nausha and brought the grain to Thorion, albeit before the wheat famine took place, it all lines up. Nausha is where wizards wake. Is that why you didn't care for Sir Trallot, Valad? You feared he was a wizard?*

He shook his head, trying to refocus. Solving the unimportant riddle of why Valad didn't care for the ruling house of Rockvale wasn't his mission, after all.

No, Dereek khn's my mission. If the local lord—this Lantatt—is from Nausha ... that changes ... everything. A wizard, if that was how he styled himself, might've had the punch and power to make the Shivering Song fall silent. *That doesn't mean Her Ladyship's gone, though. Not at all.*

Jastar had learned all he knew of power at the feet of Sir Valad. Perhaps it would be more accurate to say he'd learned it at the man's elbow. Many such lessons were couched as mere conversation at the board, especially during the evening meal. He couldn't speak for the others, but he'd hung on every word.

Power could win a throne or burn a keep, he'd said. *Hit a wild boar with a catapult stone, and you'll be left with the world's foulest jelly for your supper. Hit it with a spear or half a quiver of arrows, and you'll feast like you were at Thorionden's high table. Power can open doors or shatter them. Having it is excellent. Power inexpertly wielded? That's how the mighty usually fall.*

It was too soon to *truly* know how this particular fellow—this ... Lantatt—viewed or wielded power. Still, if Jastar had to guess... if the reports of how rapidly the thorpe along the River had been built were true, and if the Shivering Song were, indeed, made quiet at long last... No, like as not, this man understood power, how to wield it, and perhaps more importantly, *when* to wield it.

This left many questions, but high on Jastar's list was whether her Ladyship had been slain, banished, or...

"Or made an ally of," he muttered.

Yes, that was certainly possible. It was *horrific*, but he'd do better to admit that it *was* possible.

His attention was drawn by Ilimor's easy laughter at a nearby table. A group of soldiers were sitting down to their evening meal. Their livery was a variation on the realm's banner. Upon a black field, a silver mountain sat below a burning silver sword pointed skyward. The sword balanced an open red book just above the crossguard. Two of the soldiers added an upright silver spear to either side of the sword. The third and youngest of the soldiers displayed a pair of burning hammers instead of spears.

He marked them but caught himself smiling at Ilimor's profile. When she laughed again, turning to walk toward the bar, he was struck by how musical the sound was. He wondered, idly, if she was a singer. Perhaps he'd ask her when she refilled his—

"Sir ... Jastar?" The tentative voice of a young soldier pulled his attention away.

"I answer to that name." He'd been too distracted by thoughts of the pretty barmaid to note this youth sidling up to him. He'd have to watch that.

"Ha. Thought as much. Not many with a metal star at the end of a long brown braid, are there?" The young soldier sounded far less tentative now. "I'm sent to you with word from the dwarf of the hour." His voice made it clear that this was a quip he was rather proud of.

Venzene... Eodenth? Eodenth or perhaps Gerstealunth? Even turning bodily to regard the fellow, Jastar still couldn't be certain. If the new arrival had seen twenty Falx Falls, Jastar was Ylspeth in disguise. The youth was shorter than he by almost half a head. His hair was the color of pine-wood, his eyes so light a brown as to be nearly tan. His face bore a cheery smile that somehow managed not to look too earnest. A great blade rested easily against his back, but otherwise, he wasn't dressed for battle. *A sells-word, perhaps?*

"The dwarf of..." *Ahh... As opposed to the man of the hour? Mockery? Sarcasm?* Jastar grinned and saluted with his mug. "That's brave blather. I doubt the throne's seneschal would be impressed with hearing it." Jastar kept his tone light and neutral. Anything could be a test, after all.

He could count the things he knew about dwarves on one hand with fingers to spare. What he did know was that they were reputed to be shrewd, to hold grudges like no other, and to rarely, if ever, mince words. When Jastar had met him the best part of a week ago, Morakogunn had done nothing to disprove any of those presumptions. The throne's chief agent was terse, asked shrewd, probing questions, and left Jastar with the impression that he was not to be taken lightly. The only information he'd come away with was the sense that Fellhammer was protective of either the throne or the human who sat upon it. He couldn't be certain which.

"Aye, well, he's not about, is he? Not unless you're hiding him under your seat." There it was again—that ineffable good humor. "You'll ride out before dawn, south end of town, then the mountains at your back until the sky's well and truly grey."

"I will, will I?" He tried to project the tiniest bite of reproach, but it didn't seem to register.

"Aye, Sir. You'll stop when the sky's grey and check your bearings. When Morning's Gate's lit and lively, put your back to it, and ride 'til you find the Kor."

Jastar had been about to try a stronger method of nudging this man out of his glib demeanor. This *was*, after all, an official message from the realm's seneschal. The man's final word waylaid that plan, however.

"...Core?"

"Aye, Kor." He waved down another of the barmaids and tipped an imaginary mug toward his mouth before continuing. "Kor Kowmor. You're to be there within an hour after sunrise."

"Kowmor's a Traeadish name. *Kor* is something I don't know. A town? A keep?"

"Fortress, I think. Still learning the language, Sir Jast."

Alright, enough was enough. In a mild voice, he asked, "Would you be good enough to give me your name?"

The young man took a moment to display an expression of such comedic disappointment that it almost *had* to be genuine. "Horses run... I *am* sorry. Cr ke Ibhroth, of the Yebu ke."

"Curr... key... Would you repeat that, please?"

That grin returned. "S'hard to learn, Calyari, ain't it? Right, what's an unkind word for a dog?"

"...Cur?"

Ibhroth nodded. "Aye. What d'ya use to open a lockbox?"

"A key." Jastar was smiling in spite of himself.

"Aye. Just so. That means New Guardian or the like. First rank in the Yebu ke. The yay, like you're cheering at a tourney. Boo, like you've jumped out to scare your younger brother..."

"And key for guardian."

"Aye. Yebu means throne, I think. We're the Throne guard."

Jastar nodded, digesting that before pressing on. Truthfully, he'd all but forgotten why he'd been about to chastise Ibhroth.

"Anyroad, I'll be there before you and will meet you when you arrive. This way, there'll be a friendly face before the real romp starts."

"So what, exactly, are we about, Cr ke Ibhroth? What troubles Cur Kowmor?"

Ibhroth laughed, albeit briefly. "Kor, sir. Kor Kowmor." He took a moment to accept the mug he'd finally been brought. After thanking the barmaid—something Jastar realized he'd seen a surprising amount of since his arrival here—Ibhroth continued. "Not much wrong there, but I was told only to offer you *this* if you asked. Before you're given honor and duty befitting your station..." He screwed up his face, clearly trying to remember the exact message. "Aye, be-fitting your station... you must be a-judged by Fyken Presh."

"Alright. Fair enough. I'll tilt the seneschal's quintain." He finished his mug, then turned to stand up. His eyes fell on the soldiers who'd come in just before Ibhroth approached him. The one he'd assumed was the youngest was now, quite clearly, not a young man, but a woman not far from his own age. Her face was full of go-to-hells good humor, shining out from beneath a close-cut crop of dark hair. Now that her gorget was off, seated on the table next to her leather gloves and steel demi-gauntlets, he didn't know how he'd missed it.

"Ibhroth... who are they?"

Ibhroth leaned over, looking, then arched both brows. "That's the Ironbane. The other two are from the Da'shygii—the order of spear and glaivemen."

"Dash... never mind. I'll learn it all, eventually. The... Ironbane?"

"Not my tale to tell. I were at the keep when she earned *that* name."

Jastar nodded and had all but made up his mind to go to the source and ask her himself.

A woman, not a young man. Another dropped detail, Jastar. Well done, you. True, it was a minor detail in the grand scheme, but when the easy things were dropped, it was usually one of two things at the root. It was either the mark of an undisciplined mind or an overtaxed one.

Well, if I'm overtaxed, how can I simplify? What can I do?

The woman was rising, picking up her gear, and saying her farewells. Ibhroth spoke up. "Have you gotten what you need from me, sir?"

Jastar nodded, starting to move forward, making as if to follow the woman, but he stopped himself.

I simplify by sorting priorities. True, any woman who's earned a name on the field is one I'd like to meet, but that can wait. The seneschal's mission... If I miss my mark tomorrow, I risk everything. Best make certain I have tomorrow's route sorted.

"If you would, Cr ke, I'd like to go over it again. There are a few things I don't rightly know." He retook his seat, eyes widening a bit at how close he'd come to overlooking yet *another* detail. Blessedly, he'd caught this one in time to avoid any real trouble. "For instance... what and where is Morning's Gate?"

-III-

Venzene Duchy of Kovalun
County Jižní Pochod
Barony of Hartscross–Jižní Lov
4 Korunasykli: 21 Days after the Red Storm at Westsong

Vlk had needed to fight not to laugh as he crossed the encampment with Andrej. He knew he'd have to find some way to thank Lady Kastan for her kindness, but he had no idea how to go about it.

His father, Liška, had caught him on his way out to meet Andrej. *Caught* him—as if he'd been doing something wrong, but never mind. The stablemaster, Milan Němá-noha, had been his only salvation.

Liška had been a hair's breadth away from striking Vlk for lying—lying, of all things—about being asked to report to the Lady Kastan's encampment after his morning work was done when Milan's short, sharp voice came booming toward them.

"What in hells ya think yer *doing*, man?!" This was followed by the fastest limp Vlk had ever seen. Milan had a heavily lacquered Ashwood prosthetic where the lower half of his left leg had once been. His left side was his dim one, hence the name Němá-noha, which meant Dumb-foot.

"Nothing ta vorry you, Milan. Just teaching Vlk about responsibility... making sure me son do his vork properly."

Milan finished closing the distance and smacked Vlk's father with something that jingled. "If ya don't let go of him and let him be on his way, you'll wind up with less coin in yer pocket at day's end. The boy's done his work for the morning. If you don't let him be, he'll be late getting to the *rest* of the day's work."

Liška kept his glower focused on Vlk, but spoke over his shoulder to the aged stable master. "No fear, Milan. I von't let him drag through the rest of his day."

"Then let him *go*, Liška. And Vlk, don't dare dally as ya make yer way, or one of us'll smart for it." His father obeyed, at last releasing his grip on Vlk's shoulder. Milan's final word caused a look of embarrassed shock to rush onto Liška's normally dour face. "Tell her Ladyship that I'm happy to make you available to her whenever she likes."

"I vill tell her vhen I first see her. Můj vdek." Before his father had time to do more than glare, he'd taken off at a run. Andrej was waiting near the turnoff for Vlk's house.

"I'll just run home and grab my svord," he said. Andrej stopped him with a hand to the shoulder and a shake of the head. "...Vhat?"

"You won't need your sword today. Besides, if I'm wrong, we have more than you have fingers."

"Vhy do you have so many vooden svords? Are they for the children back at Lady Kastan's home? The children of her guards, I mean." He shrugged and fell into step beside Andrej. He could listen and walk at the same time.

"They're for practice. Train with the wooden sword to hone skill and form, practice with the metal one to hold *on* to skill and form." Vlk must have worn his confusion on his face, for Andrej grinned, albeit kindly, and said a little more. "Ever light a fire?"

Vlk nodded. "'Course. My father taught me vhen ve rode vith Lord Alojz last year. Ve vent along to Hartscross vith him to tend to his horses. My father vanted a fire and didn't vant to have to be bothered lighting it himself every night, so he taught me. Vhy?"

Andrej had nodded at that, looking wistful. "I've never seen Hartscross. I hear it's big enough to get lost in." He shook his head. "You... When you make a fire, you need kindling, right?" Vlk nodded. "When you just want to keep a fire going, though, you use actual logs or thick branches." Again, Vlk nodded. "The work before you fight's like fires. The wooden sword's kindling. It gets your fire going, gets your arm and head to do what you want."

Vlk's eyes had grown wide, his smile broad. "Ahhh, Pravda!" *(True!)* "The logs are metal svords—real ones. They keep the fire going... keep the training fresh in your head so your arms don't forget it... That makes sense." He elbowed Andrej in the ribs. "See? I vas right!"

Andrej had blinked at that. "About what?"

"You *are* a kouzelník!" With that, Vlk took off at a dead run. Andrej was close behind, laughing, mock-growling.

They were still laughing as they skidded to a halt before an amused Kastan and half a dozen servant women.

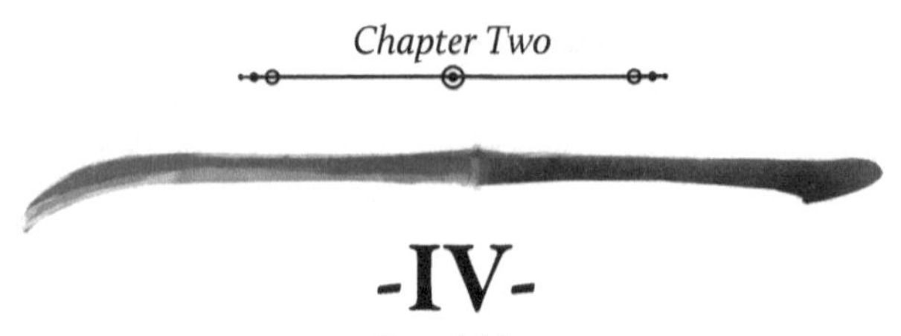

-IV-

Dereek khn
Kor Kowmor
4 Korunasykli: 21 Days after the Red Storm at Westsong

Jastar had risen a touch earlier than usual—five bells past midnight. After finishing his morning exercises, he'd mounted up and hied west. Now he stood next to his pale horse, savoring a draught of the morning's mild air as he looked back toward the mountains. They were, he was all but certain, a spur of the Frost Fangs. This particular section likely had its own name on some map or other, but he hadn't ever come across it.

He forced himself to wait. It shouldn't be much longer, surely...

As he watched, the shy sun glanced out from between two peaks. He turned back to the west, grinning in spite of himself.

There's Morning's Gate, at least. I've managed not to stray too terribly far off course. Ibhroth had been spot on. The shape made by the two peaks did indeed resemble an open town gate. The sun rose into view in as near as no matter to the dead center, making due east impossible to miss.

He reached up to check his saddle a final time. His mace was still firmly affixed to its dim side. His saddlebags, too, remained in place behind, strapped to a ring beneath its seat. The girth strap hadn't loosened overmuch, so all was as well as may be. Hooking his dim side foot into the stirrup, he hauled himself up onto the horse's back and began to ride again.

It was always *the horse*, or *my mare*, or the like. If pressed, he was certain he could pull the beast's name out of his memory, but he'd rarely (if ever) used it. He viewed his relationship with animals as largely transactional and took good care of any he had the keeping of without complaint or malice. His current mare, for example, enjoyed fine food, clean water, regularly-washed saddle blankets, a well-worn, and well-maintained saddle—in short, far more than what was strictly necessary to care for a mount. Still, treat the world well, and most of the time, it'll treat you well in return.

Jastar liked animals well enough. He'd just never felt any abiding affection for them, as others often seemed to. Not that there had ever been any thought of abuse or neglect. Beyond quieting the petty, fleeting flare of frustration when a toe was crushed or the like, what would be the point?

Abuse is an exercise in pride, Valad had taught them. *It's the act of a wretch trying to convince himself that he's still in control. In a desperate desire to prevent his self-import from falling off the tower he's built for it, he lashes out, showing you his weakness.*

Setting the rising sun at his back, Jastar rode west, leaning forward in the saddle as they began climbing a low hill.

"And was it pride that took you from us, Sir?" He spoke to no one in particular—not even his horse. Still, he kept his voice soft and small out of habit.

Those thoughts drew him back to that awful night. It was Valad's duel more than the battle for Westsong that haunted his dreams.

"Yield," Valad had said. He'd barely sounded winded, even after nearly a full minute of defending against Anden's withering attacks.

And Anden? Anden was always a beast in steel skin. Despite that well-earned reputation, you bested him ... without question. Everyone knew it, and none more so than Anden himself.

The lout's face had been a mixed mask of desperate calculation and dawning incomprehension. Plainly this was not how he had envisioned that duel's ending. He should have, but the past was always easier to see, wasn't it? Valad had still been in fine form. He hadn't lost so much as a step. Granted, he was old, but what of that?

"Words in haste need not make wounds that fester." Valad's voice, like the sword he'd held to Anden's neck, had been quite steady. "My ego is not so mountainous that I would see us lose a skilled sword-arm out of hand. Come. Yield and I will grant you parole."

With an effort, Jastar banished the memory. It wasn't that it was too painful to contemplate... Well, no. He'd do better to admit he was avoiding that particular pain. Here and now, however, dwelling—*drowning* in that miserable moment served no purpose other than self-indulgence. He would eventually need to let himself grieve properly, but this was *not* the time for it.

"Keep one eye ever on the dancing point of now," Jastar said in that same, subdued voice. "That was a favorite of yours, Sir."

Valad hadn't repeated the phrase to excess, but there'd been so very many references to it Daydreaming? Blathering at the dinner board over an earlier bout in the sparring ring? "You're abandoning your dancing partner, boys."

Beginning archery practice? "Stop *thinking* about your training, boy. Your arm and eye will recall it without your mind's interference. Instead of straining yourself trying to remember my words, focus on the dancing point of now."

Beating either your chest after a victory or your skull against a wall over a recent failure? The answer was the same whether you were bragging about the past or weeping over it. "Eventually, when you're ready, return from the misty moment of *then*. Come back to the dancing point of *now*."

As he rode, Jastar tried unsuccessfully to push those thoughts away. Finally, he opted for another path. He gave in, heeding Valad's ghost. As was so often the case, it proved to be the path of least resistance. Resigned, yet somehow still smiling about it, he drew in a breath and held it, refocusing on the moment at hand.

The land which now called itself Dereek khn was, officially, the property of the Thorion Throne. In actuality, it had been held by Her Ladyship and her dusk fae for as long as anyone could recount or recall.

Doubts about that fact are rife the farther south you go, but stood here? The idea that these lands were fae-touched... it's hard to dismiss.

He shook his head. He couldn't explain it, not even to himself. These lands were pristine.

No, he thought, *that's drawing it short. Speak the truth and spurn the treasure. These lands are breathtaking.* Every game trail, every rounded bend... He smiled, turning his thoughts into something a touch sweeter, recalling a snippet of song he'd heard someone—probably Rahn—sing. *Every waterfall and forest glen, a perfect, purple passing while my love, she is away.*

This place created a haunting sense that the *memory* of green had long ago faded from true. Being here, seeing such utter vibrance felt like... like you'd only ever had green *described* to you... As if you were only now seeing it for the first time. It wakened something—a forgotten portion of the heart, or perhaps the mind, which had slept for far too long.

A year a'gone, this had been a place of monsters and living cradle-tales. Those days at least *appeared* to be over now. Certainly, there'd been no rumor of the Lady of the Shivering Song or her court. Not since last year's Long Moon. This year's would come in a scant few days, and here was he, Jastar—*Sir* Jastar of Knell's Stone, sleeping north of the Shivering March, and—

He stopped himself, reining up as his mare crested the hill.

"The dancing point of now, Sir. Aye? The dancing point of..." He trailed off, taking in the vista before him. "...now."

Below, perhaps half a mile distant, a conifer grove spilled across the grassy landscape. If he had to give an accurate description of its size—and he knew that he very well might—he would've called it just to the right of *modest*. Beyond the dark and lovely trees, he saw the unmistakable outline of a broad defensive wall in a vast rectangle. The sun was behind him, and while he wasn't accounted especially keen-eyed, his vision was quite clear.

"Aye, the dancing point ... of now." He drew another deep, focusing breath, held it, and let his eyes take in the construction. After a moment, he let himself breathe normally once more. "Stone pillars at regular points... stone troughs running between them with... Those must be timbers."

He lowered his head, trying to concentrate, despite the distraction of the wind shaking the treetops below. Their movement did its best to cause a thrill of wonder to well up in him. Jastar, in turn, did his best to ignore it. The trees were most assuredly *not* beckoning him on, no matter how inviting their shade seemed.

"That's smoke." He could smell it, now. How had he missed that? Given the hour, the tag end of the morning meal should be going on, unless the fortification's lord preferred a leisurely end to his night's fast. As close as Jastar was, he should have smelled the smoke before now, surely. Had he been *that* distracted?

"Well, nevermind." He shook his head, beginning to urge the horse forward again when something stopped him. All at once he smelled the mingled scents of pine and hemlock. His eyes began watering.

Scents? Those weren't scents! They were *screams*... screams that only the nose could hear. His eyes weren't simply watering, they were gushing! His head felt full, as if he had a summer cold. He tried to blink his vision clear, but after a moment, he gave that up, wiping at his streaming eyes like a child.

The horse had started forward again. He must've squeezed his knees as he tended to his dreamer's lamps. He reined up anew, not wanting to ride blind. Blessedly his horse seemed not to mind. He felt her lean her head down, cropping contentedly while she waited for the signal to proceed.

Refocusing took him a moment. He could see again, though his eyes still threatened to water. With an effort, he managed to get this reaction under control. Still, he felt a powerful mixture of woe and wonder, though he couldn't credit either.

Below him, caught in the strong wind, lay that lovely grove. The fort rested just beyond.

"Wait... no." He squinted. The trees were most assuredly *not* caught in the strong wind. They couldn't be. There *was* no strong wind... was there?

No... the wind's all but dropped. Even the grasses are mostly still. What in the hells?

As he watched, each tree appeared to writhe at a different speed and in a different direction from its nearest neighbor. The sound of pine song rose high and shrill. It carried to his ears like whispers in a stone hall. It sounded like...

"Screams!" He drove his heels into his mare's flanks, snatching up the reins as he did so. Surprised, quite happy to leave whatever had startled her rider behind, she bolted hells bent for pudding down the hillside.

The strange screams sounded at once louder and more distant as he rode on. He'd ridden half the span between the hilltop and the tree line when the strange screams reached a crescendo. The sound seemed to rise as it swelled. He couldn't keep from following its progress with his eyes. There was nothing visual to it, save the trees' unnatural shaking, yet he found he couldn't look away.

The sound didn't so much die away as it ... *ceased*. It had swelled, risen, then ... *ceased*. Adding to this sense—underscoring it—was the somehow horrific realization that in that same instant, the trees had grown still. It called to mind the finality of a slamming door or the implacable fall of a headsman's axe.

He reined up, scanning the area for... he wasn't sure. Something, surely. *Birdsong? Aye, small and far, but it's there and growing louder.* As he sat in the saddle, the song was joined by other birds, then squirrels. Finally, as if signifying that whatever had been happening was truly over, he heard the mewing rustle of—he'd swear to it—a *moss cat*.

The world appeared to have been holding its breath. As forest song rose once more, the tension at last began to fade. Jastar felt both his jaw and his bright hand relax. He recalled balling the latter into a fist but had no memory of tightening the former.

The moss cat mewed again. The rasping melody made him smile, even as it made him shiver. It sounded like a large and particularly musical house cat was moving through distant underbrush. The sound was getting closer, too.

He urged his mare forward, hoping to catch a glimpse of the creature. He'd seen only one before, in his fourteenth year, among an overgrown and long-forgotten church yard.

I was ranging with Sir Valad... One of the few times I'd gotten to ride out alone with him. Where were we? Hyrro Hill! That was its name. He smiled as the sweet air of memory blew across him. "Falx-fire! I haven't thought about that place in years…"

Jastar's mare perked her ears forward, whickering as if in response—almost as if she were genuinely happy for him.

He'd allowed her to set the pace, and she'd settled on a slow, easy one. As the velvet rumble of her voice fell silent, however, she stopped altogether. An instant later, he thought he understood why. His own thoughts weren't just cut off, they were obliterated as his eyes fell upon the creature.

It was one of those perfect cradle-tale moments. The moss cat was seated on her haunches in a small clearing. She'd been caught in a shaft of sunlight slanting down through the trees. The size of a young wolf, her coat was a shifting mass of pale moonlight that darkened to the color of summer grass. Her eyes were silver stars tossed on soft seas of green. She regarded him with naked curiosity.

At first, he could only stare, mouth open in a slack-jawed expression of delight. Slowly, however, he felt the intrusion of actual thought. He tried to push it away. Whatever it was, it could wait, surely. Seeing her there, perfectly framed in the sun, surrounded by the dim forest… It was a memory he would surely keep with him for years to come. He would tell his grandchildren about it: The day the world held its breath, and he saw Paníandil, herself.

Wait, what? She? A fair guess, but it could just as easily have been a tomcat. He was certainly no expert. *And Paníandil?* Where had *that* come from? He was certain he'd never heard it before. Was he reaching back to some shred of forgotten memory? *It certainly felt like a word in a Venzene dialect, but… No, the official name for the moss cat's … Makh-something, I think. It's Lesalunth, isn't it?*

Valad had told him what little he'd known about them on the ride back to Knell's Stone. That day had been a jumble of firsts for him. He tried to pour through what he could remember, but it all came dangerously close to memories of Valad. As he tried to untangle the promise of that long-ago day from the pain of more recent ones, another thought struck him.

…A shaft of sunlight? He looked back behind him. Yes, it was indeed just past sunrise. Looking back at the moss cat, there was no mistaking it. There she sat in a soft pillar of sunlight which was spilling down around her from overhead, at a slight angle.

"…How?" It was all he could think to do.

A thought brushed past his mind's ear like a distant whisper.

Machové Mačky.

No sooner had he registered the words than he recalled them from his ride with Valad. He'd had trouble pronouncing the strange words.

"Makh!" Valad's voice came back to him like a cold rain on a burning summer day. *"Makh-ho-vay Mah-ch-key. That's what they were first called by man. They're fae, of course, so they must have names of their own, but that was the first one man ever recorded. You're lucky to have set eyes on one by day."*

"I know!" He'd been absolutely taken by the creature. *It'd come out when I started humming to myself. I turned and there it was atop an old headstone, all blue and silver...*

Jastar was forced back to the present—the dancing point of now—by a strange, looping growl from the creature. Looking up sharply, he could see that she wasn't at all alarmed or angry. She sat there, just as she had thus far. The only mark of difference was that her chin was lifted slightly as if she were projecting.

"Miss-tress?" A man's voice drifted out from deeper in the wood. It was a familiar one, at that.

"Ibhroth?" Jastar tried at once to project his voice ... and to avoid startling the moss cat. He feared he wouldn't see her again once she fled.

"Ha! Told the old man you'd be here with a quickness!" His voice was harsh and unlovely. It threatened to shatter the moment.

"Peace, Cr ke. Step softly. I don't—"

Ibhroth came into view some yards beyond the beam of sunlight. He took a brief look down at the moss cat, his grin widened, and he laughed again.

"Aye, I thought she might find you before I did." Never slowing his stride, he walked up to the cat's right, making a wide circle. "Many thanks, Mistress." He bowed his head toward her, then righted himself, turning to Jastar.

She turned to regard him as he spoke. Cocking her head to the side, she chirruped at him, as if in reply. Turning back to eye Jastar a final time, she sprung away. Her silver gave way to the green of the surrounding woods too quickly for human eyes to mark her.

"Well, let's be off, then," Ibhroth spoke through a smile that was easy to hear.

At that moment Jastar wanted little more than to dismount and strike the man. He'd driven her away!

Almost immediately he recognized how absurd that thought had been. He *did* dismount, urging the horse to follow with a tug on her reins.

"Fair enough, Ibhroth. Let's be about the dwarf's business." As he fell into step beside the man, something occurred to him. "Have you ever heard the word Paníandil?"

Ibhroth grinned, looking over at him. "Aye. One of the soldiers told you after I'd left, did they?"

"Told me ... what?"

"Her name, Sir."

Jastar managed to keep his face neutral, but only just. He nodded as if confirming Ibhroth's guess.

"Nobody can keep a damned secret, can they? Ah well. At least it didn't scare you off. Given what was here when we first settled the place, any whiff of pointed ears makes folk nervous. The few half-men that live here had it rough until the Crown took steps."

Jastar filed that away for a later conversation. His mind was still trying to contend with the fact that, somehow, the moss cat had told him her name.

She... Well, she didn't speak, exactly, but she told me her name! His mind kept repeating it as he walked toward the fort. *Paníandil. Storms be swift... she told me her name...*

-V-

County Thorion
Wick
4 Korunasykli: 21 Days after the Red Storm at Westsong

The sleeping chambers in most strongholds were purpose-built things. Fortresses, castles, towers—it made little difference. The rooms were small, mostly mean compartments built with an eye toward defense and displays of power. It was easy to overlook the cramped quarters if one were asleep. When a body was awake yet had no specific place to be, however, these rooms seemed at once too tall and too narrow for comfort.

Olshnak found himself in just such a situation. He was acting in the robe and office of Herald for Sir Kaith, meaning his room was slightly larger than most. He was also a slave, and a *savage, orcish* one, at that. So dangerous was he that he was kept in line by two jailers wearing the county colors.

He snorted at that notion. It was near enough to the truth, he admitted, but that didn't make it less laughable. Having the two jailers *did* mean he got a slightly larger room than he otherwise would've. After all, one jailer would have to sleep in the chamber with him, while the other took a shift outside.

Have to ensure I won't escape, don't they?

He'd already put in a token appearance downstairs, passing a word with the few servants who would talk to him. He'd even shared some horse bread and breakfast ale with Huron before returning to his chambers. The sun had risen well over an hour ago, though his body all but screamed at him to try to sleep for another few bells. He ignored the urge. It wouldn't be long, and he wanted—needed—to keep his wits about him for what came next.

Seated atop his bed, Olshnak looked over at the room's other pallet. Tomet was, predictably, shamming sleep there. The guard lay as silent and still as usual, breathing slowly with his eyes closed. Olshnak had to admit it was convincing, but he knew better. Tomet was just biding his time.

Aye, and Jek's out in the hall, looking a practiced mix of bored and attentive, I've no doubt. I just wish one of them would get it over with already.

He fetched a sigh, taking no pains to hide it. He wasn't running the risk of waking Tomet, after all.

"You should try to get sleep while you can, Olshnak." Speak of the spark... "When one of us needs you, we'll wake you. No fear." Both his guards spoke in a slow, gruff monotone that was just interesting enough not to lull a listener to sleep.

"I'll wait a touch longer, if it's all the same, Tomet." Then, as an afterthought, "...Unless it's making your beard itch."

This was met with a heavy, awkward silence from the pallet. After a protracted period, Tomet sat up, turning his head to look at Olshnak. "Sarcasm... Or was that meant to be funny? Should I have laughed, Olshnak?" That voice could make a love song sound ominous.

Olshnak let out a slow breath, shaking his head as he rolled onto his side. "Not worth worrying about, Tomet. Can you let it go?"

"...I suppose I can."

An interval of time followed. He couldn't have said how long, for in spite of himself, he'd actually started drifting off. He winced when the door eventually opened. He knew who it would be, of course. Had there been trouble, Jek would have warned them. Like Tomet, he said little, but when violence was on offer, he did nothing to hide the noise.

"Ollllshnak ... wake." Like Tomet, Jek's voice was a gruff near-monotone.

The lone difference was that Jek's was a touch higher in register.

Olshnak lifted his gaze in time to see Tomet head out of the room to take up Jek's former position. Once he'd closed the door, the Gnoerk spoke in scratched resignation.

"Aye, I'm awake."

"Good. We haven't much time before I'm missed. What can you tell me of Sir Kaith's mission?"

Olshnak scratched the area between his nostrils, considering. "You were right to lay your power on him. Lord Ricgerd nearly took him off the field forever, as I expect you know."

There was a modest pause. Jek cocked his head as if considering before responding. "Aye. Yet it was the warden's word, not yours."

Olshnak nodded. "It was. "

"Why?"

The gnoerk had a moment to be confused at the question. "Why... What? Why did—"

"Why did the warden act when you did not? Moreover, why *did* you not?"

"Because if he fell to Ricgerd, you wouldn't have wanted him."

"*That's* a presumptuous statement."

"I think the word you're looking for there is *honest*. It was an *honest* statement."

"Now you seek to correct my words... As if I don't know my own mind?"

Olshnak stood, sighing rather comically.

"Sit down, Olshnak. I've no interest in theatrics." Again the voice came in that stony, short range of notes. As was so often the case, his jailors' speech felt detached from the emotional context of their words. Olshnak had grown accustomed to that oddity, but not so much so that his mind didn't register it. He sat down on the bed once more.

"I've watched him. I expected him to survive against the grieving lord of these lands. If I, personally, had to interfere, then it meant he'd done nothing to inspire loyalty from his men. He'd have proven so drunk on his own woes that he couldn't be counted on to lead a campfire song or catch a sniffle without supervision. You've made it clear that *that's* a thing you most assuredly *don't* want."

This was met with another extended pause before Jek made his reply.

"That much is true. Fine. The service to commend both Sirs Robis and Reginald to history? I realize protocol dictates you won't be in attendance, but do we have any reason to believe Sir Kaith will have further troubles with Ricgerd?"

"Huron tells me that Lord Ricgerd and Sir Kaith have accounted the matter settled between them. Ricgerd embraced him as a brother this morning, it seems. Sir Kaith stopped him from slaying the monstrous stable girl with the sadful song."

"I'm certain there is humor somewhere in there, Olshnak, but I fail to see it from here." There was that sense of looming dread again.

"It's enough to say that Kaith stopped the man from overreacting, which is the outcome you were hoping for when you arranged for him to wind up here, I think."

Another pause, then a nod. "Aye. No argument on that score." Jek lifted his chin as if looking past Olshnak, to the wall behind him. "Did you know Huron? Prior to joining Sir Kaith's retinue, had you met him?"

Olshnak shook his head. "He'd seen me in Thorionden, and I him, but nothing more. One slave tends to mark another when they might otherwise keep their heads down. Not particularly potent influence, I grant, but it made for easy conversation, and a way to further prove my tale to the young knight and his men."

"I see." After a moment, Jek reverted to a posture and expression which at least *approached* politeness. "Olshnak, I cannot overstate how vital Wick is for our intentions. Without it, plans to extend our reach will likely fail. I won't be robbed of the throne over something so preventable as a child's tantrum. See what can be unearthed to speed the process along, or at least guard against its failure."

Olshnak nodded. "I'll do what I can. You'll know more when I do."

Jek nodded. "We'll speak in earnest again tomorrow night, or perhaps the day after, time and guile permitting."

Olshnak nodded again, bowing his head and closing his eyes. "As you wish."

"I'm going to lay down until you've readied yourself for the day," Jek said. A moment later and he'd done just that, leaving Olshnak to sit and think.

It was true. Olshnak didn't want the young knight to die... or to suffer. He wasn't quite certain why he felt that way, but he did. Kaith might have to die, but he'd do what he could to prevent that.

The question is why? He's nothing to me. Granted, the way he'd chosen to intervene on the road with his armsmen... But what of that? So he'd reprimanded his lout before the oaf could embarrass him. What did that matter? It had been satisfying to watch, granted... *Well, mayhap not satisfying. Satisfying would have been Kaith knocking him into the dirt, stripping him of rank, and sending him south wearing a face painted with bewildered, embarrassed misery.* Still, he had to admit, he hadn't expected any sort of correction to Vilmocz's all-too-commonplace behavior.

His mind wandered back to Huron's slender face. That, of course, led him back to Huron's tale. *It's hardly the same thing. Sir Kaith had known Huron since they were boys. He freed a friend—proved their friendship true. Hells, it was likely a friendship that only existed because it was formed with boyhood's sweet suddenness. Likely it was never corrected because Kaith hadn't been expected to attain—to earn station or title. Noble boys don't play with slaves in any way that's not cruel, after all.*

He'd heard more than a few rumors and one actual report of noble gets using slave boys for archery practice, or to take out their frustrations on when they lost a tournament. Of course, their equally noble parents usually provided some form of punishment for *wasting money* by destroying or damaging perfectly good slaves, but...

But that's no help to the slave boys or their families. They don't get anything for their trouble. Even if they did, reparations won't un-cripple a boy, or bring back the dead.

Of course, that was just what was done to the boys. What was done to the girls was often far worse, if they survived the encounters. The closest thing to consolation was that these horrors were visited on people of all bloods, birthplaces, and breeds. Cold comfort, but...

But if Kaith freed Huron... Ahnsiblundeek gi.

(Moon Warden's blood.)

Kaith would, what, somehow wave his banner and *end* the practice of slavery in Thorion? In the wider world? Of course not. Nobody living or in living memory—nobody in the histories and sagas had the power to do that.

He might free ... me. He shook his head. *To what end? If anyone learned the truth and I were a free man, they'd either use me or end me. I'm actually safer as things are now.* Hells, had he really just... *That might be the most cowardly thought you've ever had in your fool head, Olshnak.*

"I need actual sleep," he murmured. *My mind's too muddled.*

He would do his best to see Sir Kaith succeed. That much he could agree to without further internal debate. The rest... *The rest of my musings are for another day.*

Chapter Three

TRAINING TURNS THE TIDE

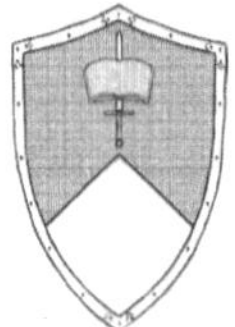

-I-

Dereek khn
Koavahd Kor
4 Korunasykli: 21 Days after the Red Storm at Westsong

Methias sat cross-legged on the marble floor, his back to the cool stone wall. He could feel the linked rings of his hauberk press against him, despite both the robe between it and his flesh and the cloak between it and the stone. He didn't mind. It wasn't painful, merely uncomfortable. That discomfort would serve to ground him somewhat as he cleared his mind.

Besides, within the next few weeks, construction in this wing of the keep will be complete. It'll be wood paneling I'll be leaning against, unless I want to freeze when the snows come.

War Cry lay unsheathed across his lap. As always, the desire to touch the sword—to wield it, even if only against a pel or sparring partner—was strong.

As always? That's drawing it long. Since Khaiyako Dyuma, yes, but not ... always. Regardless, it was a momentary desire easily mastered, given his mind and mood this morning.

I remember a time when I enjoyed the weight of a sword in my hand.

Now it might be more accurate to say it's the sword that enjoys being wielded. Hells, had it been a year already? *Is the long moon a fixed point each winter? No, surely not. I know I've heard farmers speak of both it and the long sun as expected to fall on this day or that in a given year, haven't I?* Well, no matter. No doubt the council would have a record of when he and his company... *If that isn't the very definition of an awkward conversation, I don't know what is. Elder? When was it that my company set you free—the exact date we came to rescue you?* He shook his head. Such a question would make rudeness seem kind by comparison.

Time had long since started slipping past him in fits and starts. Some days flew past like childhood. Others seemed to last forever... *Some nights, as well. It isn't as if I've forgotten where I last left the hourglass. It's more like someone's crept in and stolen it.* Swift or stretched long, work wouldn't wait. With renewed effort, he turned his mind back to it.

The room was still. He'd snuffed out the lone taper he'd used to read over his notes not long up the hourglass. His urge to open his eyes and triple-check himself was strong. Given the unnumbered things he'd been juggling of late, he supposed that was to be expected, but it still rankled.

No, I've done all I can. I have to... have to let it be, else I'll be at this all morning.

True enough. This *had* to be done, and as soon as may be. Putting it off wouldn't remove that need. It would only heighten it.

The chamber was in as total a darkness as he could manufacture, given the sun was already hanging over the nearby peaks. He'd blocked all the light pouring in—shutters and a heavy drape drawn closed over the chamber's only window. The heavy wooden door that led into the hallway had likewise been closed, and a mostly empty chest now lay poised to block the torchlight from sneaking in beneath it.

This wing of the keep was empty and would remain so for at least another hour. *Long enough, I should think.* He caught the fragrant ghost of smoldering wax from the recently doused candle. *Nearly time, then. If I can smell the wax—if my mind's calm enough to mark that scent, then it's nearly time.*

Silence and sightlessness weren't strictly necessary for the rite, but they helped. Such preparations eased the act of channeling both will and the mind's senses toward the task at hand. *It isn't my living eyes or ears I need just now.* No, what he needed for this particular weave work were his *mind's* eye and ear.

Methias drew in a deep breath, pulled it down past his navel, and held it for a three count. He forced his mind to empty itself, refusing to seize on any stray thought or distraction. It took a genuine effort, but that didn't surprise him. It was disappointing. It might've even been a self-fulfilling prophecy, given how things stood. Surprising though? Certainly not. Far too many worries danced into the mental equivalent of arm's reach.

If time didn't much matter—hells, if I just had more of it, I likely wouldn't have needed to perform this little centering rite in the first place. He smiled as he thought of Fyken's oft-repeated saying when it came to such megrims. *"Aye, and if beef were blue, stew would mirror sky. Now to it!"* It was good advice.

The Trade Tongue would serve well enough for this part. He knew the how, where, and why of things. Any other fanfare added to the work would only be an exercise in pride—a chance to prove, if only to himself, that he could overcome additional obstacles and still succeed. There was a time for such training, of course. Now, while time seemed to gleefully stand against them? No, such indulgence would have to wait. His mind was about as clear as he thought he could make it, at least for the moment. He began a low, slow chant.

> *The wind was long. The grass shone gold,*
> *From dawn 'til dusk beyond the hold,*
> *Where beard and braid 'neath burnished sand,*
> *Keep vigils while the endless stand.*

> *Wreathed in beaten iron rings,*
> *Recalling songs few others sing,*
> *A spark to drive the dark away,*
> *And guard the halls of memory.*

His familiar baritone filled the chamber. He could feel it reverberating in his chest as plainly as he could hear it. His mind lunged at the notion of how the sound moved about the room—tried to seize upon how it might be altered by the addition of the paneling that would soon adorn the walls. He pushed the temptation away. Such thought exercises were normally his meat and wine. Now, however, was not the time for such a pleasant diversion.

Not yet... He fought back the urge to open his eyes, choked down the desire to rush out of his reverie and onward toward...

He heard, or perhaps felt, the shape of the room change. In some way he couldn't strictly explain, the ceiling and the walls both before him and to either side seemed to have fallen back from him. It wasn't so much that they *moved*. The gulf between simply ... *was*. The wall behind him remained, but it was somehow cooler. He could feel the temperature shift even through his armored back.

Nearly ... I'm nearly there.

As if his thoughts had summoned it, a light flickered somewhere beyond his closed eyes. There was no accompanying warmth, but the darkness had been replaced by a dim red glow visible even through the drawn shades of his eyelids.

There! His thoughts were mingled relief and triumph. *There—or perhaps it would be better to say here at last.* He'd performed the rite successfully on some three dozen occasions—six of them within the past week. Even so, his every success left him feeling utterly, almost abjectly, delighted. This rite, above nearly all others, kindled a powerful sense of joy and wonder within him, though he hadn't an inkling why.

He willed his eyes to open and sighed. It was a near child-like sound of satisfaction. Everything was as he'd last seen it.

He was sat in a stone hall lit by tiny marble braziers. They'd been set high along its pale, dun length. These were separated by pillars graven in totemic splendor. Each bore the same symbology from floor to high ceiling. He could see the image of an eel, a spider with its mandibles closed and its legs arched to form a heart shape, a square-snouted lizard's head, a bat hung in repose, head toward the floor, wings furled tightly across its chest, and what might have been a diving falcon, or perhaps some other bird of prey he couldn't readily identify. Unlike the totems below it, this carving was either wreathed in too much gloom or was so old that it had worn down to little more than a sketched suggestion.

There were three exits from this massive corridor. A bare aperture lay just to his right. It led upward in a gentle slope, toward darkness. An enormous, arched metal door stood across from him some twenty yards distant. The daunting thing looked either fashioned out of or plated in red-gold. He wasn't certain which, but the answer to that particular riddle didn't much matter, for the door's true value lay elsewhere. The towering portal was nothing short of a masterwork of etching and carving. It bore the image of a line of armored figures with closed-face helms and slender-headed halberds in painstaking detail. Easily overlooked by comparison, a more modest door of heavy, polished wood flanked this showpiece along the left wall.

Methias willed himself to stand, then walked toward the hall's far end. One of the door's decorative sentinels began moving as he closed to perhaps ten paces. It appeared to step forward, growing in size as it exited the surface of the burnished metal. Methias managed all of two more steps. By that point, the armored figure had completed its journey. It now stood blocking the door upon which, or perhaps it would be more accurate to say *within* which, it had lately rested.

The armored figure didn't have to put on an air of intimidation to make his warning clear. He stood somewhere near five feet and a bit more in height with a broad chest and thick arms. He brought the haft of his halberd to a position of guard, hands in a wide grip along its length, the weapon angled diagonally before him.

Not a threat. A line in the proverbial sand. He was unsurprised... if a touch disappointed. *Very well. I'd hoped to have progressed beyond the need for this. Well, never mind. The Eodenth have the right of it. Hope's free.*

He stopped some five paces from the guardian, bowing his head slightly in deference before speaking.

"Peace, my lord silent helm. I only seek Dyith Gimil qha *(the sculptor's hall.)* I am Methias Arthod." He paused for a moment before continuing in a more apologetic tone. "Given you do not speak, nor can I see face, beard, or ought else to separate you from your fellows, I cannot know if you and I have met before, or if this is our first exchange. If we *have*, then I can only ask forgiveness, and hope to do better in the future."

The armored head nodded, waiting.

"May I pass?"

The halberdier nodded once more. The hinges of its armor and the slight scrape of metal on metal, as he did, were the only accompanying noises.

"My thanks."

Methias moved forward, then turned to the left, opening the heavy wooden door and entering the chamber beyond.

-II-

Venzene Duchy of Kovalun
County Jižní Pochod
Barony of Hartscross–Jižní Lov
4 Korunasykli: 21 Days after the Red Storm at Westsong

Vlk made an "oof" sound as Andrej thumped into him from behind. They were both laughing, both out of breath from their run. Andrej threw his arm around the back of Vlk's neck, both leaning on and preventing him from falling. Both boys grinned up as the Lady Kastan approached.

"Well," said she. "I see you managed to find him, Andrej."

Vlk found he was mildly frustrated that Andrej was the one she'd addressed. He understood it, given the taller boy actually slept in this encampment. *More than that. She sent him off to find me and bring me here.* All the same, as Andrej spoke his reply, Vlk wished he had something he could say to drag her attention toward *him*... without making an ass of himself.

"Aye, Lady. I told him we have enough practice swords, though I doubt we'll use them today. So we came straightway here." Andrej's breath seemed to be back under his control.

Wait... There *was* something he could say. Moreover, it was something he'd been *told* to say when he saw the Lady Kastan. Fighting the impulse to grin—why did he feel as if he'd somehow beaten Andrej at some game or other?—he cleared his throat, bowed as formally as he could, and spoke.

"My Lady? My master, Milan Němá-noha, vishes me to give you a message." He hadn't *meant* to draw out the drama of the exchange, but he'd managed to do it, nonetheless. Thinking on it, he found he wasn't a bit sorry. As he righted himself, he noted Lady Kastan was smiling rather warmly at him.

"And what, valiant Vlk, does your master wish you to tell me?"

Havoc's Horn, her voice was so musical! Again, Vlk felt that tingle overtake him from his crown to the calluses on his feet. He wasn't blushing, was he? No! No, of course not. Why would he be blushing?

All at once he realized he was letting far too much time pass without answering her. He shook his head, cleared his throat, and opened his mouth to speak… and nothing came out.

Vhat vas it Milan vanted me to tell her? He shook his head, adding an awkward little laugh for good measure. The action seemed to have knocked something loose, for he suddenly recalled both the message and its subtext.

"Ah, forgive me, Lady. My master *said* to tell you that he vould be happy to lend me to you vhenever you like."

She lifted one corner of her mouth in a shrewd little smile. "And what, valiant Vlk, did he actually *mean,* do you think?"

Vlk gave an open-mouthed grin at that. He felt laughter trying to fight its way out of him, though he had no idea why. What she'd said had been worth a smile, but laughter? That was confusing. It took an effort to keep his voice steady.

"Vell, I expect he hopes you'll fill his pockets now or later. If it's now, he'll be pleased. He vouldn't trust a random guest of the Count's to make good on a favor."

"Because they may not return." She nodded.

"Aye. But you *vill* return. You come into camp at least once a year. He vould trust to your good vill for longer than most, I think."

She was eyeing him—appraising him. It was strange. In one sense, her attention was everything he'd wanted. Yet her gaze was somehow terrible, full of force and, he supposed, nobility. He felt as if he were playing Haunted Forest. *She's it. She's the haunt, and I'm almost sure she's seen vhere I'm hiding. Then again, she might just be looking in my direction. If I run, she'll chase me. If she catches me, I'm dead and have to haunt the forest vith her. If I stay very, very still, I might be safe. She may just pass me by.*

"You're very clever, Vlk. That can be dangerous in certain circles." She seemed to sense his sudden dread at that statement, for she shook her head, voice returning to the warmth it'd worn moments ago. "Nye, Vlk. Some circles, but not *this* circle. Here, we reward cleverness."

He relaxed but nearly jumped as she turned her attention back to Andrej. He'd almost forgotten the other boy was beside him.

"Two buckets each, Andrej. Show Vlk how and where, and perhaps more important, tell him *why.*"

"Yes, Lady." Andrej batted Vlk's bright shoulder. "C'mon. Let's get the boring work done and over."

Vlk nodded, shrugging, then followed the taller boy toward the back of the encampment. He hadn't made it a dozen paces when he stopped short, turning back to regard Lady Kastan.

"Did she say ... *nye?*"

Andrej's footfalls ceased. "What?"

"Lady Kastan said ... *nye,* not *ne.* I'd svear to it."

Andrej came up beside him. "So?"

Vlk shook his head. "I've only ever heard Lakkrid say this—Lakkrid and his father's men." He shrugged, then turned back toward the task at hand. "Vhat must ve do?"

They resumed their walk toward the back end of the encampment, passing a family-sized marquee tent. *Surely that belongs to the Lady Kastan.* A moment later, as the wind dropped, he saw he'd guessed rightly. A heater-shaped banner bearing the Percoy arms—a dancing golden charger on a green field—untwisted itself, looking like a freshly painted shop shingle. He'd seen such signs on the one occasion he'd been to Hartscross township.

"Here," said Andrej from some distance ahead.

Vlk turned his head to look, picking up the pace. His mind was too easily distracted today. He'd no idea why.

Andrej stood in a clearing behind Lady Kastan's tent. He held what looked like a quarterstaff against each shoulder, the butt ends against the ground. As Vlk closed the distance, he caught sight of four wooden buckets to Andrej's right. It looked like they were full of stones, large and small. He thought the smallest might be the size of his closed fist. What was this?

Andrej grinned as if he knew Vlk's thoughts. He tossed him the stave from his dim hand. Vlk caught it easily enough, then closed the remaining few feet between them.

"Hrmmm," Andrej wore a serious look as if he were cross with someone—possibly himself.

"Vhat's vrong?"

"Have you ever driven stakes into the ground? Yes, of course, you have. You must've done when you and your otec rode to Hartscross, yes? Or did you two sleep raw?"

"My *ohhh-tetsss?*" Vlk laughed. "Such respect you show to Liška, Andrej. Do you vant to trade fathers? I vill if you vill." He brightened, turning his voice into an absurdly childish sing-song. He sounded as if he were five, perhaps six. "I'll vager if you put on your best little-boy smile, tatínek might even let you rub his feet after supper!"

He dissolved into laughter, rolling his eyes. *Hells, only grandsires and grand-dames or the smallest of smalls still use Old Kovalunth like that... Usually vhen they're barking at us beside the lyst field. "Your otec vould be ashamed of you," or "Vhen I tell your tatínek vhat filth comes out of your mouth..."* And if the toothless tattlers were traders from abroad? *Then it's "Who's your father, boy?" or "Vhen I find your daddy, I'll see that he beats you!"*

He drew in a breath, laughter still within easy reach, but something struck him as odd. *Vhy isn't he laughing?* He sought Andrej's eyes. When he found them, they were sad and *more* than a little distant.

"Your father's stiff-necked and thick-headed, but he's still your father."

Vlk blinked, all traces of laughter gone. "My father thought I vas telling lies when I vas leaving to come here today, Andrej. He told me I vasn't to spend time with Lakkrid—that I vasn't to be his friend! Don't speak of him as if he vere vorthy." He was scowling now, bordering on true anger. "Ve veren't all so fortunate as you or Lakkrid. Ve don't all have good fathers."

Andrej was quiet for a long moment. He simply looked at Vlk. Finally, when Vlk could take no more—would take no more—he spoke with a sharpness he regretted almost at once.

"*Vhat,* damn you? Vhy don't you speak? You vant to say something, so say it and have done!"

Andrej shook his head. "I don't live there. I've never spoken with your father. He works to put food in your belly, teaches you how to do things, and thinks the same small, mean madness most of the nobles—hells, most of Kovalun does about the Eodenth and the gnoerks. But from all you've told me, it isn't him that beats you. It isn't your father that sent you to bed without supper on the day we met."

That was true, but still... how dare Andrej tell him how to view his fool of a father? Liška complained endlessly about how unfair the world was, yet out of petty lunacy he'd refused fair and willing repayment for Vlk's standing up for Lakkrid and Maksu! Then both of his parents spoke in anger about how unfair it was that a Eoalunth man and his pet orcs soiled Count Edmund's reputation by spilling blood! *This?* This was the man Andrej wanted Vlk to treat with respect?

Andrej's voice shook Vlk out of his raging reverie.

"It doesn't matter. I'm to show you the buckets. Best ... get back to that."

Vlk nodded, albeit slowly. Andrej had taken on a distant, all-business air that Vlk didn't much care for. *Vhy do I feel like I've done something vrong?*

"You don't use your foot or your backside to drive a stake into the ground. You don't hit it with a full water skin either."

"Vhat? Oh. No, of course not." Vlk was glad to have another topic to seize upon. "You use a hammer or an axe handle."

Andrej nodded. "Why?"

Vlk blinked, shaking his head. "Be... because those are the right tools?"

"Aye, but *why?* What do they do that those other things don't?"

"I don't... I don't understand."

Andrej's face still bore that distant, all-business look. "They let you control your strength better."

Vlk tried not to show how idiotic he felt. *I keep getting striped by you, so I know you're not a fool. I just don't know vhat you're trying to get me to say or see.*

Andrej must've seen something of Vlk's incomprehension. The taller boy was smiling. While even this looked to be a surface reaction, at least the smile looked good-natured, rather than born out of pity.

"You don't hunt. You don't know bows."

"Do I *need* to?" As soon as the words had left his mouth, Vlk realized that he sounded affronted. *Vell? Vhat do bows have to do vith buckets?*

Andrej shook his head. "It just makes more sense to me thinking of hunting with a bow than hammering in a tent stake."

"Vhat vas the difference?"

"It takes strength to draw back a bow and have a steady aim. It takes more out of you if you run up and tackle the animal you're hunting and punch it to death. Sure, the animal's still dead and ready to dress, skin, and cook, but you wasted time and trouble. One arrow could've brought him down and had done."

Vlk brightened. "*That* makes sense."

"I should have started there." He shook his head, offering a rueful chuckle. "Right, the buckets are full of rocks. We use the pole to carry a full bucket over our shoulder, or across our back, and move it from one side of this field to the other. We put the bucket down or pick it up *only* with the pole. If we spill any rocks, we have to start that trip again."

Vlk understood the what and how, but... "Vhy?"

"It's supposed to teach us about prz... perz... *precise* use of our strength." Andrej looked relieved to have gotten that strange sounding word out. "It isn't as easy as it sounds. Getting the balance is one thing, but when you walk, the bucket wants to swing on its handle."

Vlk made a slow nod of acceptance, though he had his doubts.

"Right, stand over here." Andrej walked to a space some six or seven paces away from the buckets. "I'll walk my first bucket over with my dim arm keeping the balance. Once I've put it down at your feet, you pick it up and walk it back to the others with your own."

"Vhy only our dim arms?"

"Second bucket's for our brights. You train the same for each side, in case you wind up having to fight with your dim hand or block with your bright one."

Vlk nodded, taking up position where Andrej had indicated, and looked on as the taller boy crossed the field. He watched him dip his blond head down, cocking it to the side as if studying the bucket. Then he seemed to grin, pleased with himself.

Andrej dropped his staff to hip level, then poked one end around the back of the bucket, hooking the wooden handle. He lifted it and threaded perhaps a third of the stave's length through the gap. That done, he crouched, ducked his head beneath the long side of the stave, and stood. The pole now ran behind his neck, the bucket dangling beside his bright shoulder.

Vlk again tried and failed to meet the taller boy's eye. After settling the weight across his shoulders, Andrej dropped his bright arm to his side and began to walk. Vlk couldn't work out if Andrej were attempting to show off, or simply make the task more difficult. *Foolish, either vay.* He watched several small stones shift and skitter toward the pail's edge as it swayed. Admittedly, it never overbalanced. Andrej kept an even, measured pace. In the end, he made a business of lowering slowly to one knee, leaning toward his right, and gently placing the bucket down.

"That vas…" Vlk closed his mouth before he could make things worse between them. He was still angry. He thought he had every right to be, given what Andrej said. Yet for all that, he liked Andrej. He didn't want today to be the end of their friendship.

"Slow?" Andrej stood, smirking. "Slow hurts, but it means I have to do it fewer times. One stone spills, and—"

"I know, I know. You have to do it again." Enough was enough. Vlk just wanted to get this over with. He lifted saddles, sloshing pails of water, and pitchforks full of dung two dozen times a day. This would be nothing special.

"You have to finish the trip, then refill what spilled, then take it again."

This drew him up short. *Vhy don't ve just stop, put the dropped stones in, and start over?* He shook his head. No matter. He copied what Andrej had done to seat the bucket and settle the weight, then stood.

See? The veight vas nothing! He shook his head and started to walk. He hadn't taken his second step before Andrej held up a hand, shaking his head. Vlk looked at him, then at the patch of ground where he pointed. Sure enough, there were four stones behind him in the dirt and grass. He was about to turn his head back to Andrej when another rock struck the grass beside him.

Vlk rolled his eyes. He started to reach for it, then remembered what he'd been told and left them there. Several more fell as he crossed the remaining distance.

He tried twice more in stubborn silence. Each time he walked, dropped stones, and had to finish crossing the short span. Only then could he recover his fallen freight, settle the bucket across his back, and try again. Impossibly, the field seemed to keep getting longer and longer. Finally, out of pure, sore frustration, he asked Andrej to show him again. It took him three more attempts, but eventually he managed it.

"Fiiiinally!" Vlk stood, rubbing his dim-side bicep. "Alright, now vhat?"

Andrej had been smiling, looking genuinely happy for him. At this question, however, his face fell, then grew serious. "You're only half done, Vlk."

Vlk groaned. "Hells. Yeah, ajo." *(right.)* "Bright arm." He shook his head. *No point complaining.* Had he actually been excited about coming here today?

He tightened his grip on the stave, reminding himself that he had, indeed. *Vhat vas I thinking? And you do this every day? You've been doing this since that day?* He didn't know whether to pity Andrej or be jealous of him. After watching him walk the bucket back across the field with maddening ease, he still wasn't sure how he felt. *Vell, nothing for it.* Shrugging—and smarting for it—he made ready to lift.

-III-

Xecses Merai that-was
4 Korunasykli: 21 Days after the Red Storm at Westsong

The—*room? Could you call it a room?*—place in which Methias found himself was one of sensory emptiness. What lay beyond the wooden door wasn't darkness or some poet's idea of oppressive vapidity. A thing must *be* in order to be accounted either one. It was a kind of stasis—an absence of sensation.

The blackness called to mind neither fabric nor fur. There was no sound save his own light breathing. Even that seemed to fade swiftly as if he were in an open field on a still, clear day. Things such as temperature and scent were little more than half-remembered dreams. Stood here, he couldn't help but notice the curious lightness in his limbs, though he was dimly aware of his feet on the steady stone floor.

All of it made him smile. Closing his eyes, he stepped forward and spoke, as if to one at the far end of a long hallway.

"*Ibl, qha thassakl.*" (*Light, Stone Fathers*)

He allowed himself to simply absorb the sudden deluge of sensations. As he'd requested, light, golden and red, blazed just beyond his closed eyelids. A hammer-blow of bouncing sound struck him—the echo of his boots upon the wide stone. His nostrils filled with the blood-like scent of old metal, and the fainter, somehow cleaner smell of carven stone.

He drew his feet level with one another and breathed in—drank in everything with the quiet delight of a blind man returning to the familiar sounds, scents, and sense of home.

"Ibl..." He spoke the word in an undertone, loving the sound—the feel of it, and wondering at its connections. "Ibl... ter-ible, hor-ible, man-age-able, yet we say it to rhyme with the others."

It'd been two days since he'd last set foot in this place, if indeed that was the right way to think of it—*setting foot*. He opened his eyes, and the Sculptor's Hall faded into focus.

Nothing seems out of place. At least, I don't believe so. Stone podia and a seemingly endless series of alcoves either full of or outright made from tablets of stone or metal marched along the walls. Two granite tables broke the massive room's monotony off to his right. Several balconies were set some twenty feet up, each with an alcove and a sitting area of its own. There was no clear source of light, yet the great chamber was as well lit as a clear summer's day.

Methias walked toward the nearest podium and aligned himself behind it, as if about to give a lecture or address a governing assembly.

There's something worth untangling, linguistically, but… but not just now. It won't help with the matter at hand. Yet he couldn't let it go. *Manage-able—able to be done by a man who's come of age, or perhaps within a man's life span? Able is the important part. Are the others, then, able to feel horror and terror, respectively? Or able to cause them, perhaps? In Eydzul, the dwarves translate "ibl" into the trade tongue as … light. Yet their speech is always constructed in a blunt, direct manner. A translation error? A linguistic coincidence?*

"That's enough. I have to put that by for now. If it matters, it'll float back to trouble the surface of my mind before long." He supposed he didn't need to keep his voice low, but this massive chamber felt like a library—*was* a library, after a fashion. *Simply one of carvings, etchings, and the occasional tale-telling pillar, instead of books.*

Acknowledging that well-trodden realization served as a useful focal point. His mind began a concerted effort to filter out most other distractions. Little by little, he found himself returning to the thought which had led him here this morning.

The dwarven girl I pulled from the hilltop.

She hadn't woken or made so much as a note of sound in the week she'd been in his care. Alright, that wasn't strictly true. Her body had given a blessedly brief performance on at least one occasion. He'd visited the chamber in which she rested, speaking with her few caregivers at least twice daily—sometimes more often, but never less. During one such visit, she chanced to break wind before her body released its waste. He hoped not to be present for the demonstration again. It wasn't that he was particularly squeamish. No, she'd been in what passed for a waking period. Her unfocused eyes had been wide and vacant as her body completed this most mundane of chores. Her empty-eyed un-gaze added an eerie, shameful quality to what should have been a necessary but otherwise unimportant act.

It doesn't matter. My discomfiture won't help her. He made a mirthless sound—the sort of chuckle that speaks more of one's own foolishness than genuine humor. "Nor will my arrogance. *My* care? Hardly. Morakogunn has carried out that unhappy chore. He all but insisted on it."

He shook his head, putting his self-recrimination to the side for the time being. "Let's begin with this…" He raised his chin, projecting his voice high, aiming it toward the far reaches of the chamber. "Qha thassak? The wind was long."

The air shifted almost at once. Before him, at the edge of the distant dimness, he saw three lights bloom, white and shimmering. They reminded him of a living version of the stars he'd found gracing the canvases of so many great masters in Nausha.

Three, then. Very well. What was the rest? He found he couldn't recall. The poetry was too fresh a thing. It hadn't taken root in the garden of his memories. That was annoying but not a massive impediment.

"What was the name you gave it?" He raised his voice to its earlier volume. "The song of the dead?" No change.

Wait, I have that reversed. Blunt and direct. The Night Song Council, not the Council of the Song of Night. "The *Death* Song?"

Two of the lights winked out. The third faded more slowly. As it did, a large tablet of beaten iron inlaid with silver began to materialize atop his podium.

"Excellent."

Bending, he examined the intricate etchings and ornamentation. Eydzul letters—all deep lines and squared, blocky shapes—swam before his eyes. After a moment, they were overlaid with twilight-colored letters in the trade tongue.

"The *Grave* Song." He shook his head. Yes, that had been it. He'd simply not heard it enough to commit it to memory yet.

The wind was long. The grass was green,
'Neath stars and moon amidst the sheen,
Of stalwart soldier: Wall of war,
Who stood before our golden door.

Shining helm and burnished mail,
Skillful steel gleamed fair and pale,
With axe and sword both close at hand,
This Soldier stood watch o'er the land.

The grass is grey. The mountains weep.
This soldier will not wake from sleep.
In glory may his memory lay,
And forge lights guide him on his way.

"This looks to be... yes." Methias sighed, closing his eyes. He *had* hoped to see something different—perhaps a missing verse inscribed here, fallen out of favor among the stonebeards. Ah well. Things were rarely that simple.

"Yes, these are, indeed, the same words Morakogunn chanted when we'd felled the last haunt in Khaiyako Dyuma." He scanned it a final time, more out of habit than hope. Morakogunn had been good enough to recite the piece earlier this morning, as well. Khaiyako Dyuma had been nearly a year ago, after all.

He stopped short as his eyes fell upon the fourth and final verse. "No... no, it *isn't* the same. The final quatrain is different. There's no mention of the White Watch Tower. I *know* it, though, don't I?"

The sun has sunk behind the hill,
The river's song is sweet, but still,
When forge sounds shimmer silver light
Find shadow's shrouded road again.

"Why is that familiar to me?" Methias looked up toward one of the balconies as if he might see the answer hung in the air. It was on the very edge of memory—a distinction that didn't hold much help. *In truth, the edge of memory and the endlessly unremembered are as near as no matter to the same thing.*

He looked back down, meaning to file the familiarity away. As with his earlier distraction—if it truly mattered, whatever was pulling at his mind would resurface. It always ... did....

Something had changed. A moment ago, the translation read *The Grave Song.* In the brief time it had taken him to look away, the title had resolved itself into something else altogether.

"The Beacon Song?" He shook his head. Again, that sense of familiarity plucked at his nerves. *Well, if I don't understand, best I take it foot by foot.*

Dwarves begin reciting the verses of their oral history not long after learning to speak. *Hells, that may be a part of how they learn to speak.* Stonebeard oral tradition used its first couplet to describe the framing of the rest—he could think of no examples that broke from that rule. *Admittedly, I only know of a handful of pieces, but still.*

Methias reread the new quatrain and rubbed the space above his nostrils with thumb and forefinger. It was a gesture he'd picked up in Traead, though he couldn't have said why. It had stuck, though, and he found himself employing it whenever he was trying to piece some puzzle or other together.

"If that pattern holds, we can pass over the first two lines for the moment. *Evening, near a river* is enough for now." He re-read the next line. "Forge sound shimmers silver light? Nothing particularly clear there. I know how to bend sound, but I've never studied its effects on light. If I were a dwarf, or perhaps Kovalunth—some other cave-delving culture, this might mean something. Then again, if beef were blue..."

The last line, however—what to make of that? Shadow's shrouded road? *Well, the rote to bring me home speaks of shadows.* "No shadows shake, nor shroud the sheen." Hearing it aloud didn't appear to shake anything loose in his mind.

Nothing useful, anyway. It still makes me think of the Walk.

The Grey Between still held some of that old horror for him. He'd not needed to fear that place for years. It was dangerous, of course... at least for the unwary. The same could be said for cities and untamed wilderness. Still, he'd lost his first friend there. Hells, he'd nearly lost *himself* in the Grey Between. *If I'd slipped sideways—if I'd truly died there—the Isbryd Drayag devour every drop of the untethered. No walk of shadows, no way to...*

He thought back to the girl. It was as if she were dead *inside*, as opposed to physically dead. As if that spark that drove the living...

Her shadow. Her shadow! Hells! What sort of blind, thoughtless—I looked *at her! How did I not* see *it?*

He'd opened his eye of night, trying to detect her bent—her driving urge. In cradle tales, such weave work was framed as seeing or sensing someone's moral fiber or intent. There was both more and a good deal less to it than that.

"She wasn't inclined toward *any* color. No trace of the Red Valley, nor the known hells ... no goodly afterlife, neither the Green, the Grey, *or* the White... Havoc's Horn, she didn't even have the dim, flashing patterns of an *animal*. She was..."

She was empty... as if her shadow had left her, dragging her unguarded mind along behind it. A *caster* could do that—could leave their body, riding their shadow like any other mount while their living flesh lay unattended. Most folk did so unknowingly several times each moon. Dreaming deeply, they rode their shadows like ships on the sea.

"The sea? The sea, yes! Hämärä Meri—the Twilight Sea! *Dwarves* dream... Of *course* they do. I have proof of that from Morakogunn. If she's lost, perhaps she's already begun the..."

His sudden smile outshone every light in the chamber. "The Walk of Shadows. *That* must be the Beacon Song. Find shadow's shrouded road again—that *must* be it, surely."

Methias looked up, speaking to the back of the chamber again. "Qha Thassak? Upon their death, men and gnoerks revert to their purest form and enter the Grey Between. *That* is the first step on their journey back to the dark sea. Is it so with the Qhavok?" *(Stonebeards—the Eydzul word for the dwarven people.)*

No response. Of course not. This place held and presented relevant ancient verses of the Gezeol Merai Qha—the Secluded Stone song. He had asked a broad-scope question, not made a specific, historical request.

I need a title, a line from one of the verses. Ah!

"Qha Thassack? Shadow's shrouded road." Two points of starlight bloomed in the distance. "*Not* the Beacon Song." As before, one winked out. The other faded from the dimness ahead, even as a small pillar materialized on the podium before him. Had it rested upon its back, the pillar would be as long as a man's forearm, and perhaps twice as big around. Its red surface was speckled in various-sized rectangles.

They look like tiny pieces of porcelain. Instead of letting them distract the eye, the sculptor who'd crafted this actually incorporated the oddity into his or her work. *That couldn't have been an easy task.*

The face of the small column was separated into individual panels, each depicting its own symbols and scenes. *Now I just need to figure out how the sculptor meant us to read them ... and in what order.* He allowed himself a long-suffering sigh, then chuckled. "Well, at least there's only this single column. That's something. I can sidestep having to work out its age."

The connections between the stonebeards and the disparate peoples of Shesh weren't widely known, but they were there to be discovered if one took the time to look. Older dwarven symbology followed the Sheshik method used centuries ago, during the Aketra Habuan Ebu—the *Time of the War of Caliphs.* One always read panel by panel from right to left, but earlier works were read floor to ceiling. Sometime later, the stonebeards reverted to Southern sensibilities, their works designed to be read top to bottom. Fine, if Eydzul letters were on offer, but the tales told in art and architecture could be read in either direction and still produce something cogent. In such cases, the age of the work was often the only true determining factor left when attempting to translate.

On *this* pillar, the largest piece of the strange porcelain material took up most of the crowning panel. There was no other hint of craft or technique on that surface. *Wait. Ahhh, I lie. There's a tiny lozenge made out of that same substance in the upper right corner. I mistook that for time eating away at the sculptor's skill and talent.* Even so, the milky surface of the panel itself had been marred.

"It has to be a matter of age, surely. The scratches look random." He turned the piece this way and that, then laughed at his own foolishness. No clear sources of light meant turning something in order to *catch* that light was impossible. "They do look like scars left behind from some scrape or other... or perhaps several scrapes. Some are more deeply gouged on one end, some on the other. Strange..."

He forced himself to put that panel aside for the moment and look at the ones below it. *Best to take in the whole piece before trying to understand any individual mystery.* He raked his eyes down the pillar from top to toe and registered something that nearly prompted him to drop the carving, if not outright fling the thing away.

"*Nine*? Nine panels?"

He forced himself to pause while dread and desire did battle within him. In Dwarven culture, multiples of nine were considered unlucky. The number nine, itself, represented outright calamity.

Dread be damned. Fear of calamity won't stop it from knocking any more than fear of death will stave it off. He bent over the pillar once more... and realized his mistake. *Not nine after all.*

It had been an error born out of his hurried eye, which was really just his racing mind making a meal out of hope. The second panel from the top looked, at a glance, as if it had been split into two smaller ones. The scene was bisected by a horizontal cleft the width of his first two fingers. It was deep and clearly a part of the artist's original intent. A tiny white lozenge ran just below the pane's top, but it was the only one present.

Below that, the next two panels were nearly identical. The first showed another deep channel—this one vertical and as near as no matter to the pane's center. It narrowed as it rose, creating a sense of distance and perspective. At its top, the artist had cleverly left a portion of the pillar's surface uncarved. The result was a clear image of a boulder or series of stones blocking the road. A much smaller path—barely a game trail compared to the road's size—angled off toward the left. He ran a tentative fingertip along the two paths, considering. *Yet the fork is both smooth and even.*

The next scene was that same great road, still carved to show distance and perspective, yet with no blockage. *And with no forking pathway.* He pondered that, forcing his gaze *not* to wander further down for a moment, then gave in.

Below that, he saw something he recognized. A figure stood in the center of the panel. His left side was carved into the stone, whereas his right side was carved in relief.

"The Grey Between."

It had been deftly rendered, but base appreciation wasn't his goal here. He moved on to the last three panels. Though there was no road, the next panel was split vertically as well. The left bore what looked like a grassy field. The right bore a rolling, bare hill.

Next came a deep valley with... "That bird of prey! From the pillars in the entry hall." It was the same shape, rendered in the same position. It was also the same vague suggestion of detail. He'd asked about it, but Morakogunn didn't recognize it, and Ramud Ayumbra was outright dismissive.

"Should it prove relevant to the task at hand, I have no doubt you will discover it for yourself, Meth-hyoos."

He snorted lightly, his momentary thrill of excitement fading almost as swiftly as it had come. Were *all* elders so deliberately dramatic? Surely the answer—the *direct* answer to his question would have taken fewer words to impart.

Shaking his head, his eyes fell on the final panel. For an icy instant, his heart stopped. At first glance, he'd thought he was looking at the hollow's hilltop—the same ring he'd found the dwarven girl in. Almost instantly, he saw his mistake. He was looking at the image of a banyan tree.

It looks sickly. That doesn't make sense, but it does.

He sat back, considering. His mind wandered back to... well, to wandering. His clothes had been little more than rags, save for the massive cloak he'd stolen from his master's house. Emil hadn't needed it any longer—would never need it again.

It'd been days since I'd last eaten. I'd no idea where I was going, other than... south. He let a dry half-chuckle escape into the air. "And, of course—as if I were the child-hero in a cradle tale—the sun was an ominous glow on the horizon, the stars were coming out... and snow had begun to fall."

He recalled the sense of warmth from the banyan, the sense of song—loud enough to hear, but too low to make out. "It blocked the light, constant wind, drawing it and dissipating it through its endless collection of trunks. That same wind dropped a pair of figs on my shoulders." A cold and hungry twelve-year-old boy, however, found the weave at work everywhere. Warmth? Song? Food? "That night, the world was full of ordinary magic."

A knock on the wooden door behind him forced him to jump, scattering the memory the way wind scattered loose parchment.

Someone's near. Fine. Morakogunn wouldn't disturb me without reason.

"My thanks, my lord Silent Helm," he bawled, then proceeded to sit on the floor, his back against the podium.

> *The air is sweet. The sky is pale.*
> *No moonlight dances o'er the vales*
> *No shadows shake, nor shroud the sheen.*
> *Nor in the trees, amidst the green.*
>
> *Keep open door and open eye,*
> *To wary watch the world go by.*
> *Though gold may cover green with sand,*
> *Keep vigils, lest the endless stand.*

-IV-

Dereek khn
Kor Kowmor
4 Korunasykli: 21 Days after the Red Storm at Westsong

When Jastar had passed beneath the fortress's wooden barbican this morning, he'd done so with an open mind, but clearly defined expectations. *It's not terribly old, so it should be in fairly good repair. Somewhere in here, there'll be a pell, perhaps a quintain, and some bales of hay to practice archery against, but more than that...*

He'd realized his error almost instantly. He'd undervalued the place... and by a dangerous margin.

The walls of Kor Kowmor proved a good deal stronger than he'd expected. The fort turned out to be a ringwork. This was a series of baileys—three, in this case—without a grand building to command them. The ground sloped gently downward toward a cluster of small storm drains in the center of the second ward. Thorionden had storm drains, as did Wick, but they were a rare thing—difficult to design, and expensive to have built.

Yet here I find them in a townless outpost, hours from the nearest settlement?

That wasn't the only oddity. The timbers had looked suitably large from the outside. Less than ten paces past the gate, the truth was impossible to ignore. They weren't just large; they were positively *massive*. Each one appeared to have been rammed deep into skolfish earth, then surrounded by pale stone sleeves some four feet high. Stone pillars punctuated this wall of dark wood every few paces, each with an archer's platform atop it.

Far, far more defensible than it looked from the outside. The ward gates, the alures along the walls, and the fortified archery points atop the stone... defending this place would be a pleasure. Taking it—at least if the fort had archers and a sufficiency of arrows put by—would cost an attacker outright lakes of blood.

As for the gear and grounds for training... he'd underestimated that, too. In every outpost, ruin, or peopled fortress he'd seen or read about, the area furthest from the main gate would have housed the grand building— the lord or commander's residence—and audience chamber. Not so in the third and final ward. Here, the ground sloped back upward. It leveled out into a drill yard surrounded by individual sparring rings, a row of wooden pells holding rough shields, and a long strip of land in the northeast corner where actual targets had been painted and mounted. Armed and armored folk chatted together in the drill yard. They made him think of an up-ended ink pot—their black tabard stark against the ground's sandy surface.

Sand? There's no sand for leagues and leagues! It could be purchased, of course, but such an amount would be an absurd expense, given the size of the practice area. He'd tried not to show his wonder—his outright incredulity—at the sheer vanity of such a display, but it took an effort.

Before long, he'd found himself face to face with Kowmor's master—a venerable fellow named Fyken Presh. Most called him Old Man, *The* Old Man, or the strange-sounding Katxsel. This last made Jastar think of someone trying to sell a soldier's bed in the barracks out from under them—cot sell. What was perhaps *more* important was the fact that they didn't call the man *lord*.

Understanding came quickly, but it added yet another to this day's seemingly endless list of surprises. Fyken Presh wasn't called lord because he *was* no lord. He was the senior-most instructor of Dereek khn's army. This wasn't a noble's fort. It was a military base.

The realm has a standardized, professional military... That's something Thorion has never really had, despite Valad's urging. There were simply too many egos at play to allow for uniform training. Not so in Dereek khn, apparently. There was only one pressing question left to answer. Were they trained, or were they trained well?

Before the noon bell had rung for mess, Jastar had both his answer, and the physical aches to show for it. He was sore in places he'd barely recognized as places, was ravenously hungry, and felt as if there weren't enough water or beer in all the world to slake his thirst. He'd loved every moment of it. What was more, he thought Valad would've approved wholeheartedly.

The Old Man had put them through their paces, to be sure. Thirteen men, five women, and Jastar marched, sparred, ran, climbed, practiced *falling* of all things, and rehearsed something Fyken Presh referred to as *Blacktower Rises.*

A combatant started prone—shield to chest, bright arm flung wide, weapon either atop his or her open hand or beside it. One or more foes would press in for the killing blow. The goal was to rise, as the name suggested, but there was a trick to it. The lone defender had to keep his or her shield in position to actively defend against the incoming attacker, while at the same time rising to fight again with weapon in hand.

"I must admit," he murmured to no one in particular, "I liked that one a great deal, in spite of my own performance." He stretched his back, flexed his fingers, and winced as his wrist made a popping noise.

He'd had three chances at the exercise, just as everyone else had. He'd failed all three times. The Old Man had increased the number of foes with each new attempt. Performance didn't appear to temper that in any way. He'd put every one of them through that same gauntlet, increasing the difficulty regardless of previous successes or failures. It hadn't been personal, certainly—the fellow was pitiless, not petty.

That had been yet another surprise, albeit a pleasant one. Often men without standing among the gentry or nobility took what chances they could for petty retribution. It was a way to balance injuries, real or imagined, inflicted upon them by those in power. Not so with Fyken Presh. Rank or station meant nothing to him, save among his direct subordinates. He never failed to use *their* strange titles, and woe betide any among the trainees—Jastar included—should they call their instructors by name alone.

Instead, he addressed those he was training by either their given names or some colorful epithet. These latter almost had to be a taken, perhaps even an earned name for some deed or other. A Sheshik man whose name he hazarded as Kooshoon—something like that at least—had been addressed as *Viper* when he'd gone eight bouts undefeated. Another was Traeadish—Xaithrin-something-Kieran. *That* word was one he knew. After all, the inn he'd called home for the last week was in the settlement of Kieran Isyl, which he'd been told meant Bear Village.

The true revelation, however, hadn't been the new exercise, nor the meaningful misery of genuinely punishing training. It hadn't even been the sense of utter *force* the Old Man radiated. It had been the unexpected and not entirely welcome discovery of a familiar face amongst his fellows.

Storms be swift! That was very nearly one surprise too many. Surprise? That was putting it lightly. *When the Old Man called his name, I was surprised. When I saw the face attached to that name—when I saw Pallith, himself, take the field and knock the Viper into the dirt...*

Pallith of Greenfork might once have been someone Jastar called... *Well, not friend, exactly, but...* But what? He didn't know. Pallith had, along with his late father, Parraj, served as an armsman to Sir Anden's *very own* viper—Sir Dorean.

His father had displeased that puffed-up prattler, somehow. Nobody'd known for certain what the fellow had done, but it'd earned him a death sentence. *Parraj danced for the crows, and you fled. You fled, and there was nothing I could do to help you. Five years at court, feasts, and tournaments together from Southwall to the Northern Marches, and I couldn't* find *you, let alone* aid *you.*

Fair, but this went deeper than the simple sadness or guilt of not being able to help someone who mattered to him. Pallith *knew* Jastar. *Which limits my ability to tell tales, should it come to that. Hells—the mere fact that you're here makes the entire affair more dangerous.*

Threats to Jastar's life were one thing. Every child fears death at some point, but every child in Thorion knows the truth. *The falx comes for us all, in the end. The best you can do is make your life—make your death mean something.*

The larger fear was Pallith's defection. Driven out by a snake-like Dorean or not, Pallith now owed his allegiance to Dereek khn. If he was bitter enough over his treatment in Thorion, he might have given up valuable information on who, what, and where both people and places of import might be. *That* was the true worry.

"Jas-*tarrr*!" Fyken Presh's voice rose as it rolled toward him. It wasn't exceptionally deep, rough, or even loud, yet somehow it overpowered all other sounds in the training yard.

Jastar stood, looking toward the man. Fyken's closely cropped hair might have been whitish-blond, or simply age's earned silver. He was too full of compact muscle, sun-darkened flesh, and scars for Jastar to make a clean guess. He might have been a road-roughened forty, or a world-wise warrior half a sliver shy of his sixties or seventies.

"On me!" The Old Man looked away almost as soon as he'd given the order. He turned back to speak with one of his training cadre—a tall man Jastar hadn't met. That fellow wore a single war-braid, much like his own. The strangeness was in his gear of war. A wide leather band crossed his chest, looping under his right arm. It held a large and intricate bit of kit in place over his left. A metal pauldron covered that shoulder and a series of interlocking leather plates marched down to his wrist, disappearing beneath the bell of a heavy leather gauntlet. He was the only person Jast had seen with such strange armor. The fellow looked like a man from Venzene who'd been out in the sun for too long. That or his heritage was mixed.

As Jastar finished his walk, the other man raised his own voice. "Pallith Melmu! On me!"

Strange. His voice is deeper—even louder. But Fyken's carried more weight, somehow. And Mel-moo? What in hells does Mel-moo mean?

He forced himself to put such questions aside for now. He needed to focus. As he came to a stop, he addressed Fyken in neutral tones.

"Katxsel?"

Fyken Presh kept his voice conversational, though it stayed well apart from any semblance of warmth. "How much unarmed training have you had?"

Jastar blinked, then answered as best he could. "As much as any fighting man, I expect. Grappling, mostly. *Informally,* I've had my share of brawls, so I know how and where to throw a punch. My knight, rest him, taught me *when* to throw one, just as he taught me when to use any other weapon."

Fyken seemed to consider this. As he did, Pallith had made his way over, addressing himself to the strangely armored fellow.

"Lonn-box-sell?" At least that was what it'd sounded like to Jastar's ill-tuned ear. To him, Pallith's voice was the same unreadable, quiet thing it had always been.

Fyken must not have liked what Pallith had said, for without warning, he stepped forward, throwing his bright fist in a cross directly to Pallith's temple. As if this were expected, Pallith dropped into a half crouch, as if sitting in midair, then drove forward toward the Old Man's exposed flank.

What happened after that, Jastar couldn't see. The oddly armored *Lonn-box-sell*—whoever he was—had slipped behind Fyken Presh's back and was now driving his own bright fist up under the shelf of Jastar's chin. The blow was so swift and came with such force that there was no time to react to it. Jastar found himself staggering backward, arms pinwheeling as he tried to keep upright.

That act of rebalancing was far away. The true struggle for equilibrium was in his mind. *Do I hit him back? Is this an actual attack? Have they decided the sons of Thorion County need to be dealt with, or is this merely a lesson?*

He was spared having to think on it for long, for as he lost the battle with that particular patch of Skolfish ground, he felt a steadying hand grip his shoulder.

"No real training in field awareness or reactive defense, Katxsel." The fellow waited until Jast had found his feet in earnest before letting go of his shoulder. "We'll remedy that. Hells, we'll *have* to remedy that if you mean to join the Yebu Ke."

Jastar blinked. *A test, then. How often do those tactics wind up in bloodshed, Lonn-box-sell?*

Aloud, he didn't bother to keep the surprise from his voice. "That's where I'm bound? If I pass your gauntlet, I'm to join the Throne Guard?" It was more than he'd hoped for... and by no small margin. In *that* position, he would have ample opportunity to learn nearly all he could ever want to about Dereek khn's plans, strengths, weaknesses—all of it.

Fyken snorted. "You claim to have earned your spurs, d'you not? Where in hells else would we put someone with skill and training like that?" He shook his head, somewhere between dismissal and bemusement on his weathered face. "I wouldn't get ahead of myself just yet, boy. We have a saying here—a proverb amongst the Dereek khnderath. Nrcarnhecn jhoaz aqan, ruunth hecn. Ariek ayom al—ekhand jhe xi ar."

Jastar merely looked at him, waiting.

Pallith actually grinned, stepping over to put a familiar hand on Jastar's shoulder. "You'll learn before too long, Jast. In the Trader's tongue, it runs: *First ink gets spilled, then blood. Tears come later, with smiles or sobs.* In short? First come your orders, then someone bleeds ... or sweats, or strains. When you've finished, you can be as emotional as you like. For now, though..."

Jastar was grinning in spite of himself. It wasn't simply the news or the fact that Pallith had spoken to him with such obvious warmth. It was the fact that the man had placed his dim hand on Jastar's bright shoulder—shield hand on exposed arm. It was a gesture as old as Thorion, if not older. To those who recognized it, it meant *I have you.*

"Aye. Focus on the dancing point of now."

Fyken offered a wintery smile at that, then nodded toward the Lonn-box-sell. "Go with Lanbachsel Gurin, Jastar. Ink's been spilled. He'll see to the rest. Pallith? You'll find the Mattok putting a unit of Brendek through their paces. Tell her it's *her* turn to try to break the wall."

Pallith's face lit up. Nodding, he made his farewell and headed south toward the gate.

"On me, Jastar." Gurin's voice—he sounded even, but not cold or impatient.

I'm to join the damned Yebu Ke! That'll do for a start. With a nod, Jastar fell into step beside him.

-V-

**Dereek khn
Koavahd Kor
4 Korunasykli: 21 Days after the Red Storm at Westsong**

Methias came back to himself but slowly. He felt as if he'd been asleep for days, and even now hadn't fully returned to wakefulness. Fair enough, had he actually *been* asleep. But traveling into the sword(?)—into Xecses Merai that-was? No. That was an act of projection.

I used a Walking rite, supported by Calling and Sagacite threads. I shouldn't feel tired. If anything, I should feel well-rested. My body should've kept its natural rhythm without my fool thoughts interrupting it every time I hear a gust of wind.

He shook his head. "Unless I returned too swiftly?"

Sighing, he recited a passage from one of his earliest lessons. "The spirit wears the living body as a man wears a heavy woolen tunic or robe in winter. If he pulls the garment over his head too quickly without taking a beat to be sure? He's apt to find he's put it on backward or inside out. So too is it with the walking spirit's return to the waking body."

That theory had been espoused off and on for years. He'd never experienced its purported effects, so he'd dismissed it.

"Still... if I *fell* or *raced* back into my body, I might be misaligned, I suppose." He shook his head. It didn't matter. Not at present, at least.

He made to stand when an echo caught his mind's ear. It wasn't a thing he was hearing *now*. Rather, it was like the ghost of some half-remembered dream. A man—perhaps only a boy—was chanting. It was spoken, not sung, yet it had a rhythm to it that ebbed and flowed like water lapping at the shore.

What do you court when catapults quiet? What do you ask when the arrows aren't aimed? What do you seek when your sword's set aside? Why do you fight? Out of fear, or for fame?

There was more, but it was fading. He'd heard it before, he was quite certain. The King of the Dead had long since started sending dreams to him and the rest of his company. Perhaps it was in one of those?

He rose, walking toward the door. It was a simple enough task, even in the dark. He slid the chest he'd placed to block the light from the hall, then made his way out.

The thin scents of torch oil and candle wax mingled to make their familiar perfume. The stone hall was as dim as he'd expected, but it was notably less empty. A man stood directly across from him. He wore a suit of plate and chain covered by the uniform black tabard of the Yebu Ke. Out of the realm's many military orders, theirs was the closest to the Dereek khnii banner. Only the red tome was missing. The fellow's halberd rested beside him, against the wall. He must've been standing stock still for some time. Methias hadn't heard even the subtle shift of armor against the wall. Then again, he'd been otherwise occupied, hadn't he. Well, no matter.

Here was a man Methias could understand. Waleron wasn't able to think nearly as swiftly or agilely as he was, but his mind worked, or perhaps it would be better to say made *him* work, in much the same way.

"Waleron?"

The man gave a quiet nod of his head, his short black hair barely twitching. "I have word from... from the Fellhammer." He mouthed this last word several times as if chewing on it.

Methias waited, letting a few grains of sand drop through his internal hourglass. When it was clear that he would need to move things along manually, he spoke again.

"Walk with me."

Waleron took up his halberd and fell into step beside him.

"What did Morakogunn say?"

The man held his step for a beat, then answered in an apologetic tone. "Forgive me. I should've said."

"It's fine. You can say *now*." He kept his voice light and unaffected.

"I... he said you've a missive. That Dayf... Day... The Ironbane sends word that you're needed, and soon. That they, that it, or that she is speaking again."

Methias had been content to walk along and let the man tell it any way he needed to. Now he stopped abruptly and turned to face him.

"Repeat that last part, please. Repeat what Daephone said."

Waleron did so willingly enough.

"Nothing more? Nothing about what they, it, or she ... said?"

Waleron shook his head, face apologetic.

Well, your Ladyship, perhaps you aren't done sharing secrets after all. He met Waleron's eyes, confirming he had the man's attention before speaking anew.

"I've instructions for you. Are you ready?"

"I am. What am I meant to do?"

He sounded flat, almost monotone, but Methias knew better than to take that as indifference. This, unless he was very much mistaken, was Waleron's tone of concentration.

"Find Morakogunn and tell him I've left for Yrxa Castle. He'll want to know I've taken someone along. Tell him I'll have Tharus Ire with me. I'll send word when there's word worth sending."

Waleron nodded slowly.

Not good enough, I'm afraid. Then, aloud, he said, "Repeat what you're to tell, and to whom you're to tell it, please?"

Waleron let his eyes slip half-closed, then repeated the message as near to the mark as anyone could hope.

"Good enough. Thank you. Please see that Morakogunn gets the message as soon as you can get it to him."

A moment later and the man was off on his errand.

It's not long past noon… Stone in sky, it's far too early for my day to have been this involved already. He shook his head, chuckling. *First Xecses Merai's talk of the shadowed road, then that strange chant, and now this?*

Yrxa Castle was well and truly occupied by the Dereek khnderath, but that didn't mean it was without very real danger. Blessedly, Daephone was there.

"Well, so be it. Whatever this message portends, either Deaphone's wisdom or her skill at arms will be a match for it." If she couldn't keep the area secure, she would make the decision to withdraw, rather than throw lives away.

His mind began racing through possibilities as to what might *really* be going on—as to what might have woken it, they, or her up. After a moment, he shook his head. "I'm not likely to figure it out stood here, I suppose. Best I find Tharus, mount up, and ride to her Ladyship's seat of power."

WHERE DREAMS AND NIGHTMARES REIGN

-I-

Dereek Khn
Kor Kowmor
Pre-dawn
5 Korunasykli: 22 Days after the Red Storm at Westsong

The moon was impossibly large. It hung low in the sky, stars spilling around it like... like... Jastar had no idea what they were like, but they most assuredly *were* like... The simile kept eluding him.

"The forests and fields swim all around me while moon and stars glow above, and I ... haven't the *faintest* idea what I'm on about!" He fell back onto the grass, laughing. Like a boy he laughed, not stopping until he could feel the weight of his own smile.

The weight of my... What in all the hells that ever were does... He felt fresh laughter fighting to overtake him. *...Does that mean?* The absurdity of that thought sent him off once more, the laughter pouncing on him even as he fled for saner pastures.

He thought he ought to find his feet. Surely he had more important— more pressing things to do than roll amidst the clover like a pup or pony, didn't he?

No! No, I most certainly do not! Pups and ponies are... they're important! Again, he heard himself laughing. "Well?" He had no idea to whom his recrimination was directed, but that didn't matter. "*You* know who you are. And *you* know that pups and ponies are important!"

He heard a giggle somewhere off behind him. It cut through the strange haze of his thoughts, all but shocking him back to himself.

He was on his feet, though he had no memory of actually rising. He meant to turn toward the giggling, but the world seemed to turn around him instead.

He saw her. He saw her and knew her and feared her and loved her. Her dress was the green of summer grass—softly stark, or perhaps starkly soft against the shadowy backdrop of the wild forest around her.

Softly stark? How can something be soft and stark at the same time?

She laughed once more. That laughter was somehow *richer* this time, but it served as his only answer. It was as if those silver eyes had seen his thoughts somehow. Or perhaps those magnificently formed ears had simply *heard* them. Were they pointed? Yes... yes, they *were* pointed, if only slightly.

"Jastar..." She shook her head, face betraying a delighted grin. "Jastar, you're *dreaming!* Surely you know that, don't you?"

He nodded. Of course he knew that.

"Of course I know that, but... but how is it you're here?" Now he was grinning. A fool's grin? Perhaps, but even that seemed absolutely... *right* in this moment.

Her slender brows rose slightly, propelled by the lifting corners of her wide mouth. "Do you know me, then?"

"I do, though I've no idea why."

"Ahhh, so you speak this way to all familiar strangers. I see." She put a tiny hill of sound in that last word, walking up, then sliding down the E sound.

"No. Only you, Lady." Hells, horses, and hammers! He *knew* her. He would swear to it. If he did *not*, it was past time he remedied that.

"So—I'm dreaming, and I dreamt of moon and stars, of grass and green. And finally, as I've wandered, seen the witch, er... woman standing there. Her silver eyes and dusky hair. Then tell me... how I found her there? For if we've met..."

He trailed off, uncertain where the poetry had come from, or where it had fled to. He only knew that he was bitterly angry it departed before he'd damn well *finished* with it!

"...You know not where." Her smile was brighter than any star, her tone soft, warm, and surprised into delight. She reached out her slender hand toward him. "Come, Jastar. There are things you must show me, and perhaps, things *I* must show *you.*"

He had no memory of closing the distance between them. He'd thought to join her, then found himself beside her, taking her arm in his. "Ask," said he. "Ask, and if I can, and if I may, I will."

She squeezed his arm with her own, leaning her cheek against him as they walked on. "Peace, pretty Jastar. I must warn you. You'll recover easily enough, but what I mean to take will sting."

He shook his head. "I don't mind that. A little bite's a little bother. Nothing more than a rose's thorns." Falx's fall! What was he *blathering* about? He felt drunk. His mind wasn't strictly in his control.

No. My mind's my own. It's my tongue... isn't it? It's like I'm having two conversations at once, and only one of them's with the woman I... I...

He froze, turning to look at her—turning *her* to look at *him.* She allowed herself to be moved without resistance, gazing up into his face with a question unspoken on her lips.

Silver eyes. She has silver eyes. Why is that familiar to me?

"We're nearly there, Jastar. Do you need a moment to rest?"

He shook his head, though he barely registered the motion.

"Shall we be off then?" Her face wore a hopeful smile.

He shook his head again, though the negation was directed inward. As if to underscore that, he looked down, wearing a sheepish smile. "Aye, Lady. Lead on. I'm at your side."

She squeezed his arm once more, then returned them to their earlier pace. There were people passing by. He could see them, but he caught no hint of detail. Some rushed past. Others moved as if they were on a crowded market street.

He heard rain... the sounds of battle. His nose caught an acrid wisp of smoke mixed with something fouler.

"I'm with you. I'm here beside you, Jastar. Nothing and no one can harm you here, save yourself. Breathe deeply. Then *you* must lead us. The next step must be yours."

He looked at her, trying to work that out.

"I've led us as far as I can. Only *you* can walk the final few feet. You must show, and I must see."

He tried to speak, but nothing came out. Swallowing, he felt a lump of dread catch in his throat. He took her hand, squeezing it as if needing to know it was real. That accomplished, he closed his eyes and walked on.

The world evaporated, breaking apart. He felt her struggling to hold on to his arm, but she, too, was dissipating.

He screamed, terrified of being parted from her. "No! Wait! No!"

He sat bolt upright. He was in the barracks of Kor Kowmor. It was still dark, but he could hear—could *feel* dawn coming closer. More than that, he could hear someone coughing just outside the door.

He resisted the urge to go and do the wretch an injury. The dream had broken in every way. He recalled it, but only in snatches. *It was important, but I'll be damned if I know why or how. I only know that...*

Falx fire, was he weeping?

I only know that I have to find her again. He shook his head. *I haven't a clue who she was or how to go about it, but I... I have to find her.*

There would be no more sleep for him. His heart was racing, and his blood was up. Resigned, he rose, made up his cot, and headed out to the drill yard for his morning exercises.

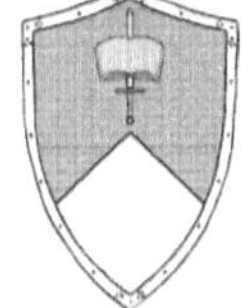

-II-

Dereek khn
Yrxa Castle
5 Korunasykli: 22 Days after the Red Storm at Westsong

Methias was almost adrift—his mind *almost* still. Given where he was, or perhaps more accurately, where his body was, any sense of ease was something of a miracle. He'd managed to quiet the relentless—presence? Could you call such a thing a presence?—cacophony below. Even when he'd woven the rote of silence, he knew it wouldn't last. He was neither powerful nor knowledgeable enough to silence the loathsome... *thing* indefinitely. Peace and rest were gifts to be taken full advantage of.

But no. No, if it cannot be named or categorized, it cannot be contended with. It's an object, or a series of them, making it rooted in Weave fabricant rites. It's also quite clearly death-tied or shadow-tied. The bones and chattering skulls make that plain. That means Calling and Waking threads to support the Fabricant rite. And Sagacite threads, if it actually gathers and reports legitimate information.

That was fair enough, but what of the fear it projected? Anyone who came within earshot of the screaming thing's voice or voice-es grew on edge. Those who drew close enough to hear individual voices or hells be hid, if they somehow managed to make out individual words...

That's not a thing I know. It's an educated guess—something I'd do well to remember. There's horror enough here without my mind conjuring up more.

He shook his head, his hair making rasping noises against the pillow. It was time to put this particular matter by—at least for now. He needed to *clear* his mind, not fill it. Sleep wouldn't come if he allowed his thoughts to stray down the promising path—the path of the solved problem.

That sense of dread may be Weave-work, but it may just as easily be a reflexive response to all of that maddening prattle.

Methias caught himself again, clenching his jaw in annoyance. *I know better.*

With a conscious effort, he forced his body to become rigid—limbs stiff, back straight, toes pointed. Slowly, he allowed his body to relax, and with it, his mind.

Prattle... He loosed a quiet little laugh. That word had once more all but infected his vocabulary over the last year. Its use always lit lanterns down very specific streets of memory—tempting him with the warm weight of what was.

...But never mind. No more strides down that road tonight. With an effort that was almost physically painful, he, at last, pushed both the comforts of memory's mile and The Cage's riddle away.

It was well he was actually tired, both physically and mentally, for he felt his eyes begin to sting. The act of turning away was something he could manage, and one he'd been contending with since he was a boy. Being able to *manage* a thing was hardly the same as being freed from it.

He thought back to his master, Emil. *I'd only been with him for a year. My mind had been particularly difficult to quiet.* He recalled Emil coming into his bedchamber one early spring evening.

He'd wanted to speak with me, but I'd been too overwhelmed to say much. All I could do was shake my head and cry. Hells, even amidst all of it, I remember being terrified of both speaking and remaining silent. "He'll think I'm being silly. He'll think I'm lonely, or homesick, but I don't know how to answer his questions. I don't have words to explain that I'm ... drowning. I can't get air... can't find footing."

The idea that he might've been homesick was laughable, no matter how pervasive it was. He was an orphan, like so many others. He had no memory of a time prior to Emil, outside of the moment he'd been plucked from the orphan train.

At some point, Emil had placed his dim hand on Methias's bright shoulder. He'd squeezed with just enough pressure to draw the boy's gaze upward to meet his own.

"*Gal-ganus Meth-i-as Ar-thod.*" He'd made a rhythm of Methias's name, drawing it out until the words became something luxuriant. "*You've spent too long amidst the noise and heat of crow-ded street. I shall teach you a thing to help you find a moment to rest ... to breathe and to be.*"

It hadn't been a rite, exactly. Rather, it'd served as a method to ground him—a key to a door that only he could find.

Drifting... drifting... drifting... drift. Drift 'neath all skies as wind through the grass sighs, and the pines sing songs of twi-light-ing. Where shadows shape dreams from waking mind's schemes, and we ... call the foes we are fighting. He had been charmed at once—drawn into the riddle and the desire to solve it.

Though many years lay between that day and this, he found the entire affair no less charming, and no less helpful. He had solved most of it. It was a pattern that led down into sleep by its rhyming nature and choice of meter. It had a flow to it that fit well, the way a song might. Employing it now, he found he could almost hear it—could almost see it. The sighing grass... the soughing wind through the trees. Unnumbered stars spilling out above him.

The word *pines* made him think of the twin-trunked Hollow Ones he'd seen around the hilltop, but *that* he could turn away from. Those things were in the Wilds. He would not be traveling there this night. Tonight, he was *drifting... drifting... drifting... drift. Drift 'neath all skies as wind through the grass sighs, and the pines sing songs of twi-light-ing. Where shadows shape dreams from waking mind's schemes, and we ... call the foes we are fighting. Clem-ent, this trip, from a humble boat slip, where the dreaming waves wash clean the day. Cradle and bower hid from star showers where no endless eye's ire can yet stay.*

He was ... not startled, exactly. A species of surprised would be closer to the mark. He'd heard a woman's laughter. *She sounds be-mused, not a-mused—as if she's been caught unawares, and laughter was the only response she could find. She's years past the vapid, attention-seeking giggle of a newly sprouted girl and ages away from sounding shrewish or crone-like. There's only one problem.* He couldn't be certain whether he should join in on the laughter or if it was at his expense.

He heard the fountains bubbling. Could smell the silky sweetness of the white verbena... the twilight-colored wisteria. Their mingled fragrance was heavy but not overpowering. All at once he found himself stood on a familiar marble floor. An instant later, he'd recognized it in earnest. He was in Nausha's royal palace—the inner garden's courtyard. He felt the wind tease its clean fingers through his auburn hair and enjoyed the sensation of being transfixed by the sound of that laughter.

I remember this moment. He fought back the urge to moan aloud. *This, yes, always this. I know I'm dreaming, but I don't care. She terrified me. She'd always terrified me. Seeing her on feast days, at tournaments... hearing her speak, and sing, and laugh. Hells, she still terrifies me, but that hardly matters. This is terror I would face every day, and gladly. Anything to hear her laugh—her true laughter again.*

He resisted the urge to turn toward the sound, to seek it out with his eyes. He knew if he did, he would speed the process along, but though he longed for what came next, he feared giving into that desire too quickly. *Soonest begun, soonest done, after all.* Resigned, therefore, he waited just as he had just over a year ago when this had all been real and new and the truest kind of magic.

"Why ever did you give up your first name?" She was behind him somewhere, walking toward him. "Your master gave you a good name, a strong name, and fair. I mean, stone in sky—you've beaten your accusers and reclaimed your due. Why give over the name you fought so hard to defend?" Her voice drew closer, though there'd been no hint of footfalls.

I recall being delighted by that little mystery—no footsteps on marble flooring.

She pressed on. "You stood, vindicated. And your accuser stalked out of the chamber with his head on fire, if the reports are true, mere moments before the knights of the Magos Astunomía were dispatched to find him." She paused, voice sounding as if she were weighing the possibility. "Of course, given the lord in question, it's more than possible he left with his head *literally* ablaze. Would that such spectacle ended the efforts of he and his supporters, but they never seem to tire of befouling the air with their pointless prattle."

Her voice still held the same power over him, even in dreams such as this. Not that dreams were a requirement. Hells, even awake, he found he could recall this particular moment with near-perfect clarity.

Her sweet scent, distinct from that of the flowers but too subtle to name outright, her sudden proximity, and her clarion voice... He'd felt a sudden rush of heat that seemed to suffuse his body. His skin was still dry, but his neck and face, even his ears had begun to tingle. At the same time, everything *below* his neck had gone positively polar. When she spoke again a moment later, those sensations switched places. His mouth was dry. His stomach clenched as if in preparation for an incoming strike.

There was something about that voice. He didn't think she was consciously trying to sound melodious, but her voice had a natural tone and cadence which projected melody in every single syllable.

And the alliterative phrase... that had nearly undone me. I kept rolling it over in my head—pointless prattle, point-less prat-tle. It'd felt like she'd given my mind a piece of honey cake... a gift from her mind to mine.

He'd tried to speak but found he couldn't. As the silence dragged on, he truly *did* begin to break out in a sweat. He could feel the sea breeze grow colder as it swept across his brow. He was facing away from her still, looking out over the sunset that painted this part of the courtyard garden in odd, bluish hues. It was the crystals adorning the crenellations, he knew, and the stained glass. While such minor miracles were still beautiful to behold, they simply weren't alluring enough to compare with the voice that now, he was almost certain, stood at his shoulder.

"Well? Aren't you going to answer me?" More brief laughter, this little rill as pretty as the rest.

"I..." A new scent. He couldn't place it, but it was certainly new and sharp. He did his best to clear his mind, shaking his head, and drawing in breath to speak when her voice cut in again.

"You what?" Her smile had been an audible thing. "You have no answer? You don't yourself know, as it was only a whim? A passing fancy?"

"I *would* answer if you would keep your tongue behind your teeth for a moment." His voice had been mild, carried on a brief swell of soft laughter. Still, he'd immediately wondered why in the White Veil he'd said such a thing. It wasn't much like him to be glib and sarcastic—to be reactionary in his speech. Yet here he was, being glib to—

"I beg your par-don? Do you have *any* idea whom it is you're addressing?" Her voice was too delightedly shocked to be aloof, though she did her best to rise to the occasion.

"Given you have no entourage, I can only presume that I am addressing a servant. Perhaps one of the scullery maidens?"

"*Scullery* maidens?" *She'd sounded both outraged and amused all at a go.*

He pressed on, smiling in spite of himself. "No... no, perhaps not. Clearly, you're a servant of at least *some* import, given your ability to move around freely from place to place. Still, your *manner* suggests, what, a

Lady's Maid? Perhaps someone serving the Kyria herself?"

"And, like so many other great and noble personages, you refuse to even *acknowledge* servants, let alone deign to *look* at them. I seeee." She sounded intrigued, if not outright *happy* with the turn of conversation. "Ah, my Lord, do forgive this humble woman's ignorance, but I was under the distinct impression that you, in fact, had no land or household, wealth or property of your own. How then is it that you've become so skilled at the spotting of servants? So skilled, in fact, that you were able to see the truth before setting your eyes upon me?"

"Well, you see," said he, "in my years on the road and on the run from the justice the courts of Nausha would surely have been pleased to afford me, I discovered untold gold and jewels, and was offered the hand of many princesses from countless kingdoms along the way."

Where in hells had that come from? I remember saying it, of course, but even now I have no idea what prompted me to speak so.

"Ah, I see!" She did her best to suppress the laughter that insisted on bubbling up to the surface, to no avail. Her voice had modulated up and down, now soft, now full and forceful, as she tried to hold back her hysterics. "So tell me, then, my Lord. Which of these charming foreign princesses have you chosen to marry? What kingdom will you claim and one day rule?"

He'd waved a dismissive hand at that. "Oh, there are so many. I have yet to make my final decision, you see." The smile wouldn't leave his face. His cheeks were actually beginning to hurt. "I shall have to make my decision soon, certainly, but it's very difficult. Each is more beautiful and fabulously wealthy than the last, and each has vast armies and troves of happy, loyal, hard-working peasants. How does one choose?"

"How hard for you!" She'd been so very close to him then. He could almost feel the wind from her speech.

"Yes, it is a burden indeed." He'd done his best to make his voice overly sadful and serious. This, of course, turned it into something of an absurd caricature, just as he'd hoped.

"Well, my Lord Methias, I do hope that whatever kingdom it is you intend to rule will remain a staunch ally of the Nausha throne."

"Oh, I'm afraid that's quite impossible."

"Truly?" She'd lifted the end of that word high enough that it'd finished in something of a *squeak*.

"Oh yes. It is my intent to wage war on these shores. It's past time that the abominations abiding here are dealt with. The Weave, after all, *is* the source of all woe in the world."

She gasped, then. "You mustn't say such things!" Her voice was breathy—full of mock horror and indignation.

"Oh, but I must." His cheeks were burning. The muscles that held his grin in *place* were burning. Every part of him not currently *numb* seemed to be burning! How in hells was he keeping this conversation going without tripping over his tongue?

She once more fought to hold back laughter with limited success. "Surely you fear to speak such bold proclamations *here* of all places, my Lord. Or have you grown so bold that you no longer feel fear?"

That elicited a light snort. "Hardly. I am born and bound to speak only truth. Is that not, after all, the rumor about me now? Galganus the truth-teller? I am now painted as the poor, wronged child, incapable of mistakes or misjudgments, and in desperate need of staunch protection. I am the great symbol of Naushaii justice... a political tool to be wielded." He'd given a dry, rueful little laugh at that. "Is it any wonder I've chosen to leave that name behind?"

"No, I suppose not." She sounded as if she'd ceded that point grudgingly.

An interval of silence fell between them. It had been a moment of anticipation, rather than any sort of normal lull.

Now... now was when I mustered up the courage to see if I'd been right all along. Stone in sky—to be this close to her... to have had such an exchange with... with the Kyria, herself! I'd bumbled and blathered my way into a corner, and this was the only path left to me.

Turning to face her at last, he'd stepped back and bowed.

"Kyria Nybrynci Nausha, it is a decided pleasure to meet you at last." He'd held the bow as he'd finished his speech, eyes locked on her slippered feet. "As you've no entourage, and as I am, at best, a guest in the palace—I should take my leave. Best I not be the cause of your honor being called into question. My company awaits me, in any event." He'd righted himself and took a single step backward, preparing to turn and exit the garden... and was lost.

My eyes fell upon her and I stopped breathing. Rich, olive skin, her hair dark silk, her eyes a dusky mixture of pale brown stretching to violet... I couldn't move. I didn't... want to move.

Before he'd recovered—before he'd realized he'd *needed* to recover —she was upon him. She'd stepped forward so their toes touched, laid a hand upon his chest, tilted her face upward, and stilled herself. She'd left mere inches between her parted mouth and his.

"I… do not want you to go." All humor had evaporated. Her voice had become soft, insistent, and altogether vulnerable in that moment.

He'd been struck dumb. He recalled swallowing hard, his mouth dry. He'd tried to draw in a deep enough gust of air that he might finally give voice to… What? How did one *respond* to a thing like that?

He shook his head, tried to bring up his hands, as if to ward her off. He wound up gripping her shoulders instead. He was shaking.

"Tell me that you'll stay." When his response proved too slow in coming, she spoke more firmly. "You will do me the honor of being my guest at dinner this evening. Say it."

"I… I will…"

His mouth worked, but for a time he could form no words. He was terrified as much of himself in that moment as of her. His mind raced over the thousand things he'd been meant to do that evening. He'd intended to spend time with the Company, thanking them for their efforts to free him. They would want to pack and prepare to leave—to resume the road that Jannon's jailer had left in his wake. He would need sleep so that in the morning he could tackle the necessary legal obstacles and claim what inheritance there was left to him now that he was no longer a suspect in his master's murder. He couldn't stay… *shouldn't* stay. He had no business at such a banquet unless it were the Kyrios himself, or perhaps his father— *their* father—who'd invited him.

"I will do you the honor of being your guest at dinner this evening," he'd heard himself say. He'd not intended to, but now that he had, there'd been nothing for it. "…If I can wait that long to see you again."

It was absurd. I'd just met the woman, and it felt as if the act of separating from her would drive me to madness. Not the poet's version of that word, either. I thought being parted from her might drive me to actual insanity.

"Well, Methias." She'd taken pains to pronounce his name slowly so that each syllable resonated. With an effort, she'd wrenched her eyes away from his. She'd looked down at her hand as it traced his chest. "You were right about one thing. Without an entourage, it would not be appropriate for us to be seen together for very long." She'd swallowed hard, backing away. "I know more about you from this brief interaction than I do about *any* of my would-be suitors, despite hours and hours spent with each of them. Outside of my brother, I think… I think you are the first actual *person* I've ever met." Her voice had grown distant—almost dreamlike. "You're the only one who isn't wearing a mask. I'd … no idea what a powerful thing that would be."

His lips were still parted slightly. His eyes were wide. He could see by the look on her face that she was as confused as he was. They looked at one another, helpless. His eyes searched for some glimmer of falsehood, some hint of subtext... perhaps a note of triumph. She appeared to be doing much the same. For his part, he'd found no such mark of deception, which made matters all the more dangerous.

"One hour," she said. Her face pale except for two burning brands high on her cheeks, she curtsied formally, then turned in a swirl of blue and sped from the garden.

He stood there breathing hard, as if he'd run a race. His heart was pounding, ears thundering as the blood pumped. After a few moments, he got himself under control and turned toward the exit. He would need, at the very least, to go and speak with his company and let them know. They wouldn't be happy, in that they, too, would want to celebrate—or in the case of the brothers—to make preparations to leave the island as quickly as they could.

This isn't now. This isn't happening... now. This isn't Nausha. He'd been lost for a moment, *experiencing*, rather than remembering. *I'm dreaming. This is an island—perhaps a jut of land along the shores of the Twilight Sea.*

That was true, but there was something else. *Dreams are rarely this cogent. This feels more like...*

As if his thoughts had summoned it, he felt a shift in the air, heard the sound of mountain winds from somewhere behind him, and felt the involuntary clenching of his bright fist.

Resigned, he turned to face the source of that ephemeral shift in the air. He was unsurprised to see an archway in the near distance. It floated some twenty feet above, moving toward him at a steady, measured pace. Free-standing, it was some eight feet tall and looked to be carved out of lacquered, yellow bone. Within it, he could see a winding road lined with snow on either side. A scant few evergreens hung in the distance, seeming to float on a snow-covered hillside that nearly matched the color of the cloudy sky.

"All right," he sighed.

As the arch floated down to ground level, he stepped toward it. *No point in waiting until it reaches me. Best to get this over.* With a final thought toward the Kyria's parting words, he stepped through the archway to see what the enemy had in store for him this time.

-III-

Venzene Duchy of Kovalun
County Jižní Pochod
Barony of Hartscross–Jižní Lov
Pre-dawn
5 Korunasykli: 22 Days after the Red Storm at Westsong

Vlk's supper had been a quiet affair. Quieter than usual, in fact, due to an argument his parents were having when he'd come home. They stopped snapping at one another as soon as he opened the door. What followed was an uncomfortably somber evening, each sitting in his or her own corner. Father kept darting nervous, side-long glances at Mother, who sat mending one of Vlk's shirts and pretending not to notice.

Vhatever it is, he vill find a way to apologize to her vithout admitting he vas wrong, and she vill tell him how vise he vas to do vhatever it vas she vanted him to do all along. It was an old, useless, foolish game. Father was the king of their meager castle, but it was Mother who ruled their family.

He finally heard the truth as he was crawling beneath his furs.

"You vere *right* to say what you did to that saf-vage." Mother was speaking in her *we must always be clever* tone. "Doing zo meant ve vere not bound up with his stink." Now came her *we've outsmarted them* voice. "Andt nowwww, Vlk's vorth is *knowun*. The Lady Kastan has paid for his time, andt he still gets his reward for helllping that saf-vages little tushk, eh?"

Father gave a grumbling sigh that Vlk knew all too well. It was his *you win, but I must feel that I still rule this house* voice. "I vill not say I *expected* it, but it vas a possibility. The drunken lord may vell not realize he's lost his purse. If ve happen to find it, honestly of course, vhat harm in profiting from an addled fool, I say."

Mother laughed, affecting a warmth that Vlk knew wouldn't have been reflected in her eyes.

"And whooooo vould argue vith that? You are alvays thing-king, vhich is vhy *ve* have no-thing to vorry about."

This had been followed by the soft sound of first gentle, then more heated kisses. Vlk had rolled his eyes, then rolled over, feeling the first wincing notes of what'd promised to be a never-ending song of discomfort. With every movement, he was given a jarring reminder of just how hard he'd worked today.

He couldn't get or remain comfortable. His arms were sore, but that was alright. All things concerned, that particular pain was relatively quiet. He had other, far more insistent aches. His spine was full of snapping twigs whenever he moved. Worst of all were the bruises on his shoulders. He'd almost swear they were deliberately shifting position. No matter how he rearranged his body and bedding, he always wound up wincing.

And that's not the vorst of it. No, the worst was that he kept hearing *her* laughing, sparring with Andrej, taunting him... *beating* him as if she'd been holding back...

Vlk and Andrej had been playing a version of the willow dance around a woodcutting stump. Andrej had called it a part of their training. Vlk had been doubtful. It was an old game, after all, although it was rarely played by boys their age. Usually racing one another around a tree was only fun for the smalls.

One child was *it*. The other had to try to touch him or her as they moved in a tightish circle around the willow tree—or whatever stood in its stead. It always started out at a casual walk but quickly degenerated into two children racing around the tree at top speed. Sometimes the child who was *it* would catch their fleeing friend, especially if one was more physically active than the other. More often, however, it would end in both children giggling on their backs, covered in sweat, and desperate to get air into their tiny bodies.

Andrej's version of the game was ... different. Both of them would be it. What was more, each could only use their bright hand. A touch with their dims wouldn't count. Being *touched* on their dims wouldn't count. This small shift changed everything.

Vlk thought he'd understood the first time they'd stopped to catch their breaths. He'd been *sure* of it by the time they'd stopped for the noon meal. Andrej had been right. It *was* training. With the need to attack *and* avoid being touched, the entire affair felt more like an unarmed version of a lyst fight.

And then she just ... appeared. I took a pull from my mug. Vhen I lowered it, she vas just ... there, moving past me. She didn't valk. She stalked. She isn't a girl. She vas more like a moss cat.

He'd never actually *seen* a moss cat. They were supposed to have been hunted to extinction in Kovalun centuries a'gone. Still, every child knew, or imagined they knew, how sleek and sure-footed those long-lamented creatures were, just as every child knew about griffins, dragons, vodnik, and Vadātājs.

The *she* in question was a girl not much older than the pair of them. He and Andrej were both thirteen, though annoyingly, Andrej was two sykli his senior. He hazarded the girl's age at fourteen, perhaps fifteen. Old enough—and tall enough, for that matter—to make him feel like a child. Her skin was dark, as were her eyes. Her face was at once inviting and intimidating, which maddened him for reasons he, himself, couldn't fully grasp.

Vhy can she not simply show one or the other? Girls were sweet, or they were sour. He'd known this since the first time a girl had pinched his arm. And why had she pinched his arm? Why, because he had dared to share his cup of water with a *different* girl—one who had seemed friendly and had forgotten her own cup back at home. He'd been no older than six or seven, but he understood the rationale *less* as time went on, not more. *Girls are supposed to be simple. They're smarter than ve are, but the truly pretty ones always seem to make the least sense! Vhy?*

She'd stalked up behind the Lady Kastan, waited in silence until Kastan had been just about to turn, and spoke. Her voice had been familiar—a lilting, modulated melody he couldn't place.

"My lay-dee?" Her smile had been evident in her voice.

Kastan froze for a beat, then spun and drew the girl in. The embrace was brief but warm.

"Welcome back." Kastan drew away, keeping her hands on the girl's upper arms. "I didn't expect to see you until tomorrow... I'd ask if all was well, but the smile on your face is answer enough." She'd beamed down at the girl who stood two or three inches shorter than she.

Vlk had taken an instant dislike to the newcomer, although he had no clear understanding of why.

"Aye, lay-dee. Two great boars are being carried home as we speak. They should be here tomorrow, in time to be cooked for suppa, if you wish it so. One of them would make a fiiine gift to the count for feasting, as well."

Vlk had turned to Andrej, meaning to ask who the girl was. Something on the taller boy's face made his anger redouble. Was he ... *smiling*? His eyes were bright, his cup of ale forgotten and near to spilling, and, yes, he was *smiling* ... at the newcomer's profile.

Vlk tried to sound distant and dismissive—as if he were only asking out of courtesy to Andrej's obvious interest. "Who is she? She embraces Lady Kastan as if she vere her little sister or some other nobleman's daughter."

In answer, Andrej had put his mug down and picked up one of the staves they'd used for the buckets. He took a moment to run his dim-side fingers through his hair before running the back of that same hand beneath his nose.

"There's nothing there, kouzelníku. You've made it disappear vithout even trying." Vlk had delivered this quip in what he'd hoped would be a comedically serious, friendly tone. Andrej didn't seem to notice, for he only nodded and walked off toward the Lady and her guest.

"Fetem?"

Vhat's wrong with his voice? Havoc's Horn, vhy does he sound like he's caught a sore throat in the ten steps between here and there?

The dark-skinned girl turned, eyes half-lidded, mouth in a smile that made Vlk's flesh tingle and his face feel hot.

"Hel-looo, Honeybrow." She eyed the stave he was now leaning against. "Your fa-tha bade me tell you *sleep well to-night*, for tomorrow he will have much work for you to do." Andrej made to nod, drawing breath to speak a reply, but she spoke on. "*All-so...* before we found and felled the boars, we found a pair of bucks figh-ting." She sounded pleased.

"Did you..." Andrej's tone was suddenly hopeful.

"Your fa-tha wounded one, but he managed to bolt away into the trees." She paused as Andrej nodded, shoulders falling. "*I*, on the other hand, brought the second one down." She actually laughed as his head snapped up. "We were boar hunting. I had my boar spear in hand. It may seem strange to you, but I have learned a thing, Honeybrow."

Vlk saw Andrej nearly vibrate with excitement, though he'd had no idea why.

"What did you learn?"

"I learned that a boar spear will bring down a mature buck. The spear does not care *what* kind of animal it's aimed at."

Andrej laughed at this as if it were the funniest thing he'd heard in ages. Vlk didn't know what had gotten into the blond boy, but he blamed this *Fetem* for it.

"So, how large were its horns?"

"Your fa-tha says *large enough*, and so I have given them to him, which means, I believe, that *you* will be getting a new bow very soon."

Andrej threw his head back as if to shout his excitement, but nothing came out. Vlk could see his eyes were closed, and he was smiling in obvious bliss, but no sound slipped past his lips.

When he looked back at Fetem and the Lady Kastan, the newcomer had another question.

"How goes your training?"

Here, Kastan cut in. "He's been bringing Vlk in line with the way we do things today."

"Oh! Come! You should meet him!" Andrej paused—froze, actually, looking up at Kastan. "...If you'll allow it, Lady."

Kastan's bright laughter went a fair bit toward easing Vlk's discomfort.

"Go on, then. We can speak at the evening meal, if not sooner, Fetem."

"As you wish, Lady."

Vlk had stood, grabbing the other stave for reasons he, himself, still didn't understand. He'd offered a polite "Hello" to the girl as she and Andrej drew near.

"Vlk, this is—"

"Fetem. I heard, Andrej." He returned his attention to the taller girl, nodding a further greeting to her. He'd opened his mouth to continue the conversation, his smile starting to bloom, when she spoke. Her words stopped him in mid-motion, the smile only half-formed on his face... which was presently on fire.

"Fetinba is my name. Yours is Vlk, son of Liška. I have heard that you stood with our Andrej when the Bluemark showed their truth to those who cared to see it." Her voice was dark, somehow. She sounded far too much like a grown woman correcting a small child for being rude.

She vas varm just a moment ago. Vhat did I do? This thought was followed almost instantly by another. *Vhere does this girl think she is that she could speak to me so? She's... she's just...* But he didn't know *what* she was just. He only knew that he felt small, foolish, and frustrated.

"I ... must have misheard. I svore I heard both Andrej and the Lady Kastan call you Fetem."

She nodded, expression helpful if a bit detached. Her voice, however, remained that dark, not-quite-flat tone. "You did. I have known the Lady Kastan since I was very small. She may call me whateva she wishes."

Vlk's grip on the stave tightened. "And Andrej?"

She shrugged one languid shoulder. "It is a fair trade. I call him Honeybrow." She ran a hand back through Andrej's hair. "And he calls me the name others close to me do—Fetem."

Vlk opened his mouth several times, but closed it almost at once each time. He could think of nothing to say. He knew only that she didn't seem to like him much, yet she was fond enough of *Honeybrow* to simply run her fingers through his hair. As for Andrej, he was wearing an absurd, yet somehow satisfied, smile on his face.

It wasn't until she'd spoken again that he'd realized the silence had stretched out for too long.

"Well, I've been riding for hours. When you've finished with Vlk, come and find me. If you aren't too tired, we can dance the willow dance for a while before suppa."

Andrej had nodded at that. He'd apparently forgotten where he had last left his voice. She was nearly to what must've been her tent by the time he'd found it again.

"Fetinba?" When she'd looked back at him, he continued. "Welcome home and thank you for the news ... and the buck!"

She bowed her head, smiling that somehow maddening smile Vlk had glimpsed moments before.

He was thinking that he might have to beat Andrej across the head to make him say something useful—to make him return from the Twilight Sea. He was surprised, then, when Andrej had called his name from some feet away.

Vhen did you valk away? He shook his head, trying to clear it. "Yeah, běžím." *(coming.)*

The afternoon's training had kept him too focused to think much on the girl. He'd been making ready to leave as the sun sank behind the hill and had taken a moment to thank the Lady Kastan for arranging it all when he saw her again.

She was holding a stave—likely the one he'd been using, which frustrated him for some reason—and was sparring with Andrej. She was almost utterly defensive, but she looked completely at ease. Andrej, on the other hand, was swinging with a truly frightening look of concentration, and a speed and intensity Vlk couldn't wrap his mind around.

He looks... he looks as if he means to kill her. No, vait. He looks terrified! He does all of the attacking, so vhy does... Vhy does ... he look to be terrified?

As he watched, Fetinba sidestepped and slipped her stave between Andrej's shins, forcing him to the ground. She then brought the stave down toward his head with the speed of a diving hawk!

Vlk had drawn breath to shout a warning, though he knew it would be too late. Incredibly, Andrej had turned, hitting the ground on his shoulder and rolling onto his back. He brought the stave up, his gripping fists set wide so that the incoming blow struck between them with a reverberant *crack!* Rather than rise, he slowly lowered his weapon toward his own chest, Fetinba's inching closer to his face...

Vlk saw Andrej lift both of his legs, bending them back to bring his knees behind hers with sudden ferocity. The strike caught her off balance, driving her forward into a stumble that ended with her on her knees beside him. The sound that followed this was ... odd. *Vhy are they ... laughing?*

Lady Kastan began to laugh as well, which further confused the matter. "Clev-ver! Clever, Andrej!"

Vlk could only shake his head as he left.

Now, as he tried once more to find a comfortable position, he found he was no less confused or frustrated. The girl would have to go. He could accept not being able to defeat Andrej ... *yet.* A tall girl who could outfight both of them? That... That was unfair.

Alright, *she* wasn't unfair. She was, in fact, quite fair, as were almost all the women in Lady Kastan's camp. Come to that, none of them had the warm, plump look most women in the camp carried.

Fair or not, girls are already cleverer than boys. They get to stay home all day and not have to go out in the sun to vork. Vell, not that mother doesn't vork. She vorks ... inside, mostly, and vithout someone telling her vhat to do all day. Still, fair, cleverer, almost always right even if they *weren't* right... *and now one of them can outfight the best varrior I know? That isn't right or fair. Either I have to beat her, or she has to go.*

His last thought as he drifted back into uneasy dreams was the frustrating realization that *all* girls and women seemed to fancy Andrej. *Maybe if I focus on besting you... Honeybrow. Maybe then, if I do it in front of vitnesses on the field...*

-IV-

Dereek khn
Yrxa Castle/adrift upon Hämärä Meri
Pre-dawn
5 Korunasykli: 22 Days after the Red Storm at Westsong

It took Methias a moment to realize where he was, though he supposed he could be forgiven for that. Some part of his mind immediately tried to remind him that he should look behind to see if the arch, the way back, were still visible. That part of him was low, distant, and easily ignored. Instead, he turned in place from left to right in a wide arc, drinking in his surroundings.

What he beheld was something of a winter's marvel. To either side of the road—indeed, it *was* a road, and one freshly cleared at that—snowy hillocks stretched away from one another for some leagues. A disorderly army of scattered pines marched alongside and, in some cases, atop them. At random intervals, thick, deeply green treetops peeked out of the snow, as if checking to see if spring had been sighted. The exposed branches lay less heavy with snow than at first he'd expected. He couldn't be certain, but as far as he could tell, the snow looked freshly fallen.

Until I know how high up in the mountains I am, or how far south, that doesn't offer many clues as to exactly how long ago this is. That was but one of the troubles with these visions. He'd seen things happening as near as no matter to *now* and as far back across the unnumbered centuries as to predate recorded history. There was nothing for it. The dream would spin out, and he would do his best to drag coherence out of the pieces the King of the Dead showed him.

He heard the sounds of battle in the distance and tried to look in that direction. He saw only the wintry landscape strewn atop surfaces both high and lowly.

Battle such as that, especially in the cold, must surely involve fire. Yet I smell no smoke. He looked from one side of this high pass to the other, eyes skyward. If there *were* smoke on the horizon, he couldn't see it from here.

"Somewhere," he said, "the truth of this place is battling with whatever lies the King of the Dead is trying to show me. The question is... how do I find it?"

As if in answer, he became aware of a sound from somewhere behind him, growing closer. *Slow hoofbeats in the snow.*

He didn't turn. He stood and smiled, putting out his dim hand as if about to pat the author of that sound. He was spared having to stand like that for long. The horse's head came into contact with his open palm, dipped, then lifted again, forcing that hand to slide down its neck. He felt strength and focus returning to him almost at once.

"I thought it would be you." He paused, turning to the left to stroke Mezofel's flank before swinging up into the saddle. "I was beginning to feel like I was posing for a painter's pleasure, stood there like that."

He cocked his head to one side as if listening. "No," he chuckled. "I wasn't expecting anyone else in specific. It was just a question of whether *you* would join me here, or if the King of the Dead would *send* someone to join me."

He settled himself into the saddle. As ever, there were no reins to grab. Mezofel wore a halter, of course, but bore neither bit nor bridle.

Once Methias was balanced, Mezofel started to walk. It wasn't long before he'd begun to trot, then canter. Once the road sufficiently widened, he, at last, broke into a gallop. Through it all, Methias simply swayed in the saddle. On Skolf, he would have had to maintain balance with his knees and stirruped feet. In this intrusive dreamscape—this *gift,* as the King of the Dead often portrayed it—only his will was necessary.

Methias smiled. "No, Mezofel," Methias sighed. "Any doubt I had that it was the real and honest you disappeared the moment my..." He paused for a moment, trying to find the right words, then shrugged and pressed on. "The moment my hand touched your flank, I knew. How could I not? Besides, if the King of the Dead has enough power that he can bend the weave to such a degree... If he can make it so our bond is shattered or masked..."

He shook his head. If he had *that* much power, he would have already won, and the world would be so much dust.

The horse whickered and tossed his head.

"I most certainly am *not* taking this lightly." He laughed, albeit briefly. "Did you really not think I'd know you when I saw you?"

The horse trudged on in seeming silence. Methias was about to offer some other platitude or justification to his mount when they crested a hill.

Below, not far distant, he saw precisely the thing he'd feared.

Perhaps a mile—perhaps as far as a league below him—sat a town of brick and oak. It lay like a tumble of colored blocks against the snow and winter grass. In happier times, the chimneys would have had pleasant puffs of smoke rising white and grey before blending with the overcast sky. Individuals and pairs of livestock would've rested in little paddocks beside or behind these houses. The neat and ordered rows of homes and shops would have looked cozy on any other day, especially this time of year. It was tempting to see that pastoral paradise for what one wanted it to be.

To be sure. And the movement I see amounts to nothing more than parents chasing their children through the cobbled streets... just trying to catch them before they do themselves an injury. What other cradle songs should I sing myself, then? If the song's loud enough, perhaps I can block out the screams ... and the soldiers.

Indeed, a legion in gleaming plate was marching into town from the south. He watched as a column of figures in ancient-yet-pristine armor of bronze and steel strode calmly down the street. Most of them wore closed helms, which must have added to the terror. *A faceless foe wields fear as well as fired steel...* Another maxim of Fyken's.

The soldiers below were ruthless and efficient. They wasted no time in slaying literally everything and everyone they came across. With wide, leaf-bladed spears, they ran through men, women, children, and livestock. They did precious little damage to property, however.

They're here for blood, not property.

Reluctantly, Methias reached toward his left hip. He wrapped his hand around War Cry's hilt and made as if to draw it forth.

It's as it was before... as if my hands are numb. It's here, but also ... not here. He added his other hand for good measure. Still no change.

"I'll try one other thing, but I expect I know how this will play out." His voice was distant, calm, and detached. He knew this was a dream, albeit a lucid one. He had little scope to affect it one way or another.

That isn't right, though. If it's a lucid dream, I should be able to take at least some level of control over it or at least of myself within it. Not for the first time, he found himself wondering how in the hells the venerable thing had crafted this rote. It defied reason, but that simply meant Methias didn't have the knowledge to solve the riddle.

Not yet, at any rate. For now, I'm meant only to witness this... whatever it is.

Methias opened his hands wide, splayed his fingers, and positioned his hands and arms as if he were carrying some wide weight. He began to murmur.

"Berfehv... vehm hol berfehv. Puehv ka Berek, xu ruulth... nuth jhaiyv Zet." *(Burning... see the burning. My will burns, and now... so shall you.)*

He felt no use of power. His hands began to glow, and there was a ripple of heat cascading between them, but there was no power here. Still, he made ready, using his knees to guide Mezofel to the edge of the drop. A moment later, he urged them forward as much with his mind's mouth as his knees.

They galloped at full speed down the mountainside. He was out of range by a goodly margin—at this distance, his spell would have done little more than alert the enemy to his presence. It didn't take long to realize that they were making no headway. Out of frustrated disgust, he threw the fiery ball, but it winked out of existence only feet from him.

As I thought.

"You may as well stop, my friend. We're only here to witness, so we might as well see what there is *to* witness." *The King of the Dead will show me what he wants me to see, try to sway me with craven councils, and send me on my way. Then it falls to me to untangle truth from lies, fact from fabrication.*

Now that the urgency was gone—now that he knew intervention was impossible—Methias truly *looked* at the town below him. The place looked familiar to him, though he couldn't place from where. He'd seen so many such villages over the last several years. Still, he couldn't shake the feeling that he'd been here before.

Voices rose off to his right as if in answer to his unasked question.

"Are you satisfied, my Lord?"

He didn't know this voice. No matter. He recognized it for what it was. It sounded as if the speaker were in a shallow cave or the corner of a nearby room with the door swung wide. He, or perhaps *it,* was a creature of bone.

Methias was just turning toward the speaker, hoping to catch some telltale visual marking or affectation to identify him. If nothing else, it would make taking notes an easier task. However, the voice that answered the creature's question utterly obliterated the calm and focus he had regained since Mezofel's arrival.

"I cannot say that it pleases or frustrates me, Loegrem, but yes. I would say that I'm satisfied."

Jannon... Jannon, you live! They have you still, but you live!

A pair of pale warhorses stood stolidly off to one side. Though they were saddled and bore the long, shaggy coats common to Traedish steeds, their flesh hung off them in peeling ribbons. Their eyes were missing, replaced by glassy black stones.

Jannon and Loegrem sat at their ease astride these ghastly mounts. Loegrem wore the same armor as the attacking force below, though his helm bore no bevor. His head was a gleaming skull of either gold or copper—Methias couldn't tell which. The glimmering metal turned what would surely have been bleached bone into something too perverse to simply be called *monstrous*. The fact that he spoke in such a jagged, atonal manner only added to the horror he evoked.

By contrast, Jannon wore the same modest mail he'd worn five years prior. They'd seen him since, but only from afar, across a battlefield or in a crowded market. A great blade rested across his back. The leather of its grip was now a pale white. Methias was fairly certain the blade was the same as before. The pommel certainly was. The white wrapping was a new addition, making the blade look simultaneously righteous and ominous. A single liquor-blond hair peeked out from beneath the iron-crowned helm he still wore.

Haunak's Helm. I opened the way; you claimed the crown, and later, it claimed you.

"I do not suppose anyone accounted *sane* would take much pleasure in this, but it *is* necessary, isn't it?" Loegrem's speech sounded ... *off*. Listening to the once-man evoked a brief sense of vertigo. It was somehow discordant, though his notes and inflections seemed deliberately chosen.

His voice ... draws you in, then makes your flesh crawl. It's... it's like an oboe played purposely out of key.

"It is. Even my host understands why it's necessary, though his opinion on the matter is not *truly* being solicited. It's a simple enough stratagem."

I suppose he's right. This is Longcliffe. I'm almost sure. Destroy places like this, and you strike at the kingdom's very heart. Traead's piety would be a genuine threat to them, were they prepared for the fight. More... Longcliffe is where we found the crown... where I set this all in motion. Perhaps they're covering their tracks?

Methias nodded, mostly to himself. He was fighting back the grief and rage that warred impotently inside him. He could do nothing here. He could only stare at Jannon, trying to find some sign of resistance— some spark of life.

His voice was still so familiar, even changed into that of his jailer.

"I'm not concerned with hunting for anything in specific. Simply gather and stand up all of the men, women, and children that you can find. Is that understood?"

Loegrem nodded. "I've already instructed the men, my Lord. I've added to that instruction that they are to kill any livestock they see. I thought it best to make certain that any survivors do not, well, survive for long."

Methias resisted the urge to shout—to speak some empty child's oath. None of them had given up on the idea of saving Jannon Saysh. Unfortunately, Methias still didn't know how it was possible *to* save him, despite years of research. Exorcising a creature from the hells was easy enough to accomplish. He'd learned how it could be done years up the hourglass now. The problem was that Jannon had made a willing pact. Breaking such a bond—betraying such an oath was...

Jannon spoke again, forcing Methias back to the moment at hand.

"Once Longcliffe has been washed clean, gather the men and the new recruits. The land slopes down the further west we go—the snows won't be so difficult there. We march as soon as may be."

"As you wish, my Lord."

"I want to cleanse the pass in its entirety before the plains feel winter's first breath. We need to take Traead entirely off the field. With that done, the largest of our remaining obstacles is settled."

"Yes, my Lord Haunak." Loegrem nodded only slightly, but then turned and regarded Methias.

This is the part where you address me directly, then. You are the King's vessel this time.

"There is no reason for this to go on any longer." Loegrem's voice had been replaced. It was now deep and sadful—a disappointed father, resigned to watch his errant child do something foolish. Jannon didn't appear to hear him, and Loegrem didn't appear to mind. "I suspect you'll need to persist for a little while longer before you yield the field. I can accept that delay. The truth, however, is simple and honest. We are implacable, and we will make our way, eventually, to every corner of this world, until we finally end it. You can stand against us—stand against me—if you like. I won't stop you until I have to. Send word to every high seat. It makes no difference."

Methias spoke the next few words in unison with the voice issuing from Loegrem's golden skull. He'd heard them many times before.

"You may raise every hand against me, and though every sword and spear are turned to the same purpose, it will ... not ... avail you. You may slow me down for a day... for an age. It will ... not ... avail you. I will return again and again and do battle with the next generation long after you are dust or have become deified. Stand *against* me, stand *out*side, or stand *at* my side. The choice is yours."

With that pronouncement concluded, Methias knew the dream would end. He took one last look at Jannon's stolen face. By force of will alone, he resisted the urge to weep, scream, or yield to the maddeningly calm, hatefully reasonable voice of the enemy. Instead, he tried to take in all that he could before it was too late.

As if thinking it made it so, the dream simply *ceased*. Next he knew, he was alone in his room at Yrxa Castle. He became aware of the warmth of his bed, the sweat on his brow, and the urgent need to find quill, inkpot, and blank page.

CHAPTER FIVE

THE POLITICS OF WAR

-I-

Venzene Duchy of Kovalun
County Jižní Pochod
Barony of Hartscross–The Ash March
5 Korunasykli: 22 Days after the Red Storm at Westsong

Kastan kept her horse walking along at an unhurried pace. Vlasta—her greying Lady's Companion—ambled close behind. They'd ridden in amiable silence beneath the fading trees for the best part of half a bell now.

The air was just this side of crisp—the weather just the other side of dreary—making it one of the last mild days of the year. They'd already been kissed by winter's first claw. All too soon, the snows would come, the lakes and ponds would freeze, and the world would be lulled into a wistful white winter. Opportunities to simply mount up and ride out would be rare, indeed.

My hunting party's returning with meat and to spare, which seems as good an excuse as any. It isn't necessary to ride out to meet them. Of course, it isn't. But the lure of an afternoon ride on such a perfectly painted day was too strong to ignore.

As if to underscore her point, her horse gave a little squeal and jumped a fallen log. He could've easily stepped over it, or gone around it as Vlasta's horse did a moment later, but he, too, was happy to be out and in the doings.

Kastan adjusted her balance in the saddle easily enough, automatically creating slack in the reins, until all four hooves were firmly back on Skolf. She still hadn't quite gotten used to this stallion. He was of Sheshik stock—well-muscled, but smaller than most Kovalunth steeds. He'd proven to be full of a nimble fire that seemed to flare up for no particular reason. Unpredictable fire in a horse meant for battle was, at best, a dangerous delight.

She'd put him through her gauntlet, so to speak. He'd been fine on the quintain and had performed reasonably as she'd practiced with bow and arrow, guiding him with her knees. Unfortunately, he'd proven *less* comfortable with melee combat. He might be reacting to the shadow of her movements more than the sound of her weapon cracking against either pell or partner's shield, but still...

Between that and your tendency to break into a run as often as you can manage it, you and battle may not be well suited for one another. I may wind up either selling or gifting you to someone else.

"Oh, but it'd be a pity to see you ride out of my tale, Jafyl." She spoke in an undertone, though whether she was thinking aloud, or addressing the bold brown beauty, himself, she couldn't have rightly said. Nor did it much matter, for it was Vlasta who made reply.

"Oh, my lady, I'm certain it's just a matter of time."

Kastan grinned, blushing slightly at having been overheard. She'd said nothing untoward, of course. It was just that the knowing, low alto voice riding up on her right always managed to draw guilt out of her—justified or otherwise.

"I hope so. No matter how beautiful he is, I cannot risk being on a horse that's afraid of a fight. Not when we're on the open road, at least."

Vlasta made a tutting sound. The disapproval was robbed of any real bite, however, as Skolf itself seemed to stand against the middle-aged matron. A sudden breeze blew a portion of her yellow headscarf into her face. Rather than becoming affronted, she laughed like a girl. The sound only served to make the mare upon which she rode—a spirited Havalunth Flekket Vind—give a little squeal of surprise as if it were the one being reprimanded. She quieted the horse with a pat and a soft *shushing* sound, then smoothed her errant scarf back down over her black smock. Her normally rigid countenance once more in place, she regarded Kastan with kindly brown eyes.

Kastan did her best to both look and sound reproachful. "That'll teach you to tut at me."

"Will it? I rather doubt it. I've tutted at you for the best part of a decade. D'you think a little thing like capricious wind will stop me now?"

Kastan actually laughed at that. She couldn't help it. It was hard not to laugh when Vlasta became playful. To see her divest herself of her usually dour demeanor felt like catching sight of a long-absent friend in an otherwise crowded room.

Grinning, she met Vlasta's eye and shook her head. "I suppose not. No."

"No, I shouldn't think so. Even Edmund's affection for you won't offer much protection on *that* score, Lady." Vlasta lifted her chin, looking down her nose. Her voice, on the other hand, grew both dry and somehow warmer. "Be glad His Excellency hasn't caught me dressed in one of those beautiful skirts your father continues to send you. You'd never notice it'd gone... until our wedding was announced. Then I'd *tut* you daily. I'd make it a matter of county law..."

Kastan didn't trust herself to speak. She nodded as soberly as she could, though the grin that held back her laughter was beginning to hurt her face.

"I would do *such* things to that man..." Vlasta delivered this in an undertone, but with absolutely no shame.

That did it. Kastan broke. Her laughter seemed to brighten the very air. Jafyl's ears perked about as far forward as she'd ever seen, and he lifted his head as if he would start prancing.

They rode on for a moment longer. Kastan had just about gotten herself under control when Vlasta drew her up short.

"My Lady..."

"Fine. I won't send him off. Well, not without training. I'm certain you're ri—"

"Kastan!" Vlasta's voice was a sharpened hiss. She grabbed her mistress's arm to hold her up. "Listen."

Kastan stopped Jafyl's progress and did as she'd been bidden. Horses.

"That'll be Rákos's hunting party." She looked to the west, peering through the treeline. "Well, better late than never. We *might* make it back in time for—"

"You won't make it back a'tall if you don't open your ears, Lady!" Again her voice was an urgent hiss.

Kastan looked at the woman's stern, grey face, and the first real sense of danger finally penetrated her awareness. *There're too many horses and by quite a lot.*

She blinked, too focused to be afraid. The noise was growing louder. It wasn't just that it was growing closer, though it surely was. No, the sheer volume and reverberation of hooves on hardened winter ground were rapidly increasing in scope and power.

It's like the swelling sound as folk enter an empty hall. The din builds upon itself as their voices fill the chamber until thirty men sound like three score or more.

She drew in a breath and held it. The act helped to refocus her on the task at hand and the training she'd been given. *Name the tasks that need doing. Order them by importance. Take them one at a time. Worry about what you could've done differently when the day is done and there's time to breathe.* She exhaled.

"There'll be fear enough once the fighting starts," said she. "The foemen, whoever they are, will see to that. Chaos, too, if they can manage to create it within our walls."

Realizing Vlasta was still gripping her bright arm, she shook it loose, turning to face her. Kastan found the woman's hazel dreamer's lamps, held her gaze, and spoke. She forced her voice to deliver her words both clearly and calmly, though with a speed and force that offered no room for debate.

"Make for Jižní Lov. Do it at a trot, no faster, unless you've outpaced them or they've spotted you. Edmund must know that they're coming, whoever they are. If you can arrive without them having seen you, Edmund will have time to prepare. If they spot you, they likely won't give him that time. Do you understand?"

"Yes, Lady."

No hesitation. Vlasta was watching Kastan's mouth as she spoke—focusing on absorbing her words and nothing else.

Good.

"When you arrive, Vlk should be at the stables. It's early enough. If he is, send him to tell Fetinba. She can rally the rest of our women. If Vlk isn't there, word will have to wait until you've left Edmund. Do you understand?"

"Yes, Lady."

Again, no hesitation. The matron was clearly scared, but she was still very much in control of her emotions.

"Find Edmund. Tell his guards that you have an urgent message from me. Say whatever you must to get in to see him. *But...*" She held up her forefinger. "*Do not* start a panic by shouting the truth to any who might hear you. Edmund needs as much time as we can give him to take active control of the situation before panic can set in. He must have the chance to organize his defense *before* the people begin to feel real terror. Do you understand all that I've said?"

"Ride for the encampment. Don't be seen. Run if they mark me. Send Vlk to Fetinba, if I can find him swiftly. If not, so be it. Make for Edmund, at any cost. Don't start a panic. Hope that it's enough." Vlasta delivered this with a matter-of-fact rapidity that did Kastan's heart good.

"Hope doesn't hunt for you, Vlasta. Best we give it a helping hand. Now, to it."

She knew the matron would want to ask her questions. She was pleased when, instead, Vlasta turned her spotted steed away and began a steady trot.

Now to find my huntsmen. She'd no sooner finished this thought when another, more horrid one intruded. *Always assuming they've not run afoul of whoever that force belongs to.*

Shaking her head, she urged Jafyl into a trot and rode north.

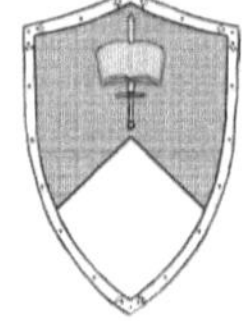

-II-

Dereek khn
Yrxa Castle
5 Korunasykli: 22 Days after the Red Storm at Westsong

Methias moved toward the first chair he'd laid eyes upon. His limbs were heavy and slow to respond. Far more concerning was his beating heart. His pulse was steady enough as it thumped out its usual rhythm, but the *power* behind it was...

I don't know how to even categorize it. Stone in sky but it's fierce! He could feel each pulse in his temples, in the place where the back of his head met his neck, even in his fingertips and the surfaces of his palms.

There has to be a way I'm not seeing. Surely the old singer made use of it. I simply can't work out... how.

He stopped with his bright hand resting on the chair's low back. It was an effort not to grimace at the touch of the somehow-oily wood it'd been carved from. In the ordinary course, all wood was dead by the time it was turned into furniture, building materials, or art. The wood here in Yrxa Castle seemed strangely... alive?

Not exactly. Perhaps aware would be a better word.

He realized he was simply standing there and resisted the urge to let a sigh escape his lips. Daephone was in the chamber still. He could almost feel her eyes on him. Others would come soon enough, once people realized the chamber below had been silenced.

I mustn't sit too heavily. I can be tired. I cannot seem defeated or too done up to continue. If Daephone and the others see me in such a state, their own remarkable wills will begin to fade and fail. From there, it'd only be a matter of time.

He rolled his shoulders back, turned, and alighted upon the padded seat without fanfare.

"My lord?" Daephone's voice. She'd chosen one of her softer tones—a rarity, but hardly winter roses.

He looked up, searching out her eyes—trying to drink in her body language.

Daephone Ironbane's short, nearly black hair—usually neat, tidy, and parted to the left—was uncharacteristically out of place. *The only other time I've seen her so was the morning after we'd taken this place... Dawn, after the Night of the Long Moon.* The look of heavy bruising under her gold-ringed eyes would fade when rest came at last. Until then, she would bear the purple patches without complaint... hells, likely without even noticing them. *A soldier's saddlebags,* they were called. Her shoulders all but sagged beneath the weight of her chain shirt and steel pauldrons. She looked as if she were coming off a long and fitful night's watch.

That last hour took its toll on her, too. She's singed in both mind and will, not that she's noticed either state. Her pale face looks pointed and pensive. Even her armor's leaving its mark. Did I really think she'd be immune simply because she's not a caster?

He'd been sizing her up for too long. It may have only been a few grains of the hourglass, but still. Allowing too many such moments to pass would make him seem distant—perhaps even aloof.

Best I...

Hells but it was hard to redirect his mind. He had to fight not to fall into a more detailed cataloguing of Daephone's appearance, which would be of no help at all. The chattering atonal chorus in the tower's lowest chamber had a way of scraping at the mind.

Enough of that. With an effort, he forced himself to contend with how exactly he should answer her. *Daephone takes great pride in having attained her commission, and rightly so. Hells, she's the only one who's reached that particular height thus far. If I'm to put her at ease, best I address her accordingly.*

"Lankaajh?" *(High captain)*

"I..." She looked away. "Your pardon. It's nothing."

Nothing? So I'm to drag it from you, am I?

He forced that thought away. Anger, especially in this circumstance, was pointless. More than that, it was unwarranted. *She's afraid, or perhaps embarrassed, but doesn't want to tell me why. How do I coax her to... ahhh.*

"Lankaajh." He shook his head. "Daephone."

He saw her look up at him, clearly taken aback by the use of her given name. *Taken aback, but not displeased. That's something.*

"I'm still trying to understand what The Cage is... or represents," said he. "I cannot destroy it until I know that."

"I..." Daephone looked away for a moment. She seemed capable of either meeting his eyes or speaking her mind. Both at once, however... "Why? It's darksome, full of small, chattering skulls, and... *malice*. Surely you *see* that, yes?"

To your credit, you're frustrated with yourself for not being able to follow my line of thought. For not understanding why. You've avoided the simple trap of anger with me—the fool who sees things differently from you. That's a rare way of thinking. Welcome, but rare.

"I *do* see that." He sat back in the chair, palms on his thighs. "You've asked a fair question. I'll try to give as straightforward an answer as I can."

She nodded, then adjusted her stance. She now stood with her hands clasped behind her back, her feet spread to shoulder's width.

She's taken this as a formal explanation, then. Again, he found himself fighting back the urge to sigh. *I'd hoped to have a conversation. Now I must be sure to end with instruction—with a clear directive. Hells.*

"When..." He allowed himself to exhale through his nose, gathering his thoughts. "When you find your foe has a new weapon, has learned and unleashed new weave work, or commands a beast you've not encountered before, you do your best to learn what you can from it, yes?"

"Yes, my Lord."

"If you should find one of those weapons on the battlefield, or recover the foeman's workbook, notes, or beast pens with a few strange creatures still within?"

She cleared her throat, her voice taking on the first hints of her fuller tones. "Yes, my lord. We—or at least *I*—would take those things into custody. I'd learn all I could or pass them onto those best suited to learn from them... such as yourself."

"Why?"

"My lord?"

"Why would you do this? You already have fine weapons, armor, and training. Why take those of the enemy?"

Her expression made it clear that she understood why he was asking. The briefest wrinkling of her nose made it equally clear she thought the question was a touch patronizing.

I'll need to watch that in future. Thank you, Daephone.

"My lord, we would do this to ensure we *remain* armed, armored, and trained in the best way possible. We must learn from our foes if we are to..." Her eyes went wide.

"Defeat them?"

"Yes, my lord, but... but this is different, surely."

"Yes and no. Yes, in that this is—by its very nature and construction—a thing of actual evil and malice. More so given the truth of the Weave and the dead." He noted her confused look and nodded. "Deeper down the well than we need to go just now. You don't need to understand the Weave to know how vile The Cage is. It needs to be destroyed."

"Then ... why have you not destroyed it?"

"I'm still walking the Scholar's Road." He saw her reaction—another brief wrinkling of her nose, as if she'd smelled something unpleasant. "Did anyone ever explain that to you back on Nausha?" He kept his voice conversational. *If I don't, I'm apt to either anger her, or worse, frighten her.*

"Yes, my lord. The path of the scholar—always seeking knowledge." Her voice was flat and affectless as she gave this rather terse definition.

"Not ... exactly." He saw no change in her face, but there was a shallow, sharp intake of breath at his words. Forcing himself to keep that same conversational tone, he pressed on. "Sconces on the wall, sconces down the hall. One pool of torchlight shows the path ahead. You've heard me murmuring this before?" When she'd given him a curt nod, he continued, "The second half of that old mnemonic is ... And as the light fades ... 'neath darkened arcades, the firekeeper sparks the dark instead." He paused for a beat, but she offered no reaction. "The Scholar's Road is a method of how to approach a problem or situation. Torchlight's the knowledge you already know. There are more things *to* know further down the path—the hall, as it were."

Daephone cocked her head to one side, considering. "So... So it grows darker as you move away from what you know, toward what you don't. Is that right?"

Methias grinned, though his eyes were desperate to close. "Exactly so. A reckless mind races into the dark, and nevermind the peril. If there's time to think and plan, however..."

"A wise warrior waits and watches wind," she finished his thought with a note of surprise in her voice.

"Not a proverb I've heard before, but yes. That's just about right, I think." He considered, then nodded, bringing them back to her initial question. "The Cage, then... There are two reasons I don't simply destroy the thing outright. The first is that I don't know what the old singer used it for. I don't know its purpose. The second? I don't know how it may *safely* be destroyed. To simply bludgeon or hack an item like this to bits runs the very real risk that it will shatter with a shockwave of pure power. As potent as this item is, that would be devastation on an order larger than any I could create by deliberate plan or practice. The orbs of power I'm able to generate are measured in strides—yards if you prefer the doctrinal term. The destructive force of The Cage might be measured in *leagues*, should it be mishandled."

The color—what there was of it, for she'd always been pale—drained from her face. For all that, she still managed to keep her expression neutral.

"I... I see."

"Strategically, we need to know what she was doing here, other than holding court with the timeless haunts of her once-kin, that is."

"And you need to uncover how The Cage was used to aid her. Learning *that* will help you uncover how to safely destroy the thrice-cursed thing. I see."

Methias made a "there you are" gesture. He willed himself to add a smile—trying to make the expression climb to eyes that had no interest in participating.

"And I, Thaurus, and anyone else we call into service... we stand guard in case things go badly. We're outside of the chamber door in case you need our aid to ward something off."

Methias shook his head. "Not at all, Lankaajh."

"My lord?"

"You and the others stand outside of the chamber so that you have time to alert the rest of the castle should things go wrong."

She blinked, nodding slowly. "In case you're overthrown, you mean."

"In case I'm taken. My fear isn't that it might kill me, Daephone. This isn't like Oacn Alifehv, nor the battle to take this castle. The risk is that it finds a way to get inside and *control* me. I've seen nothing to suggest it *can*, but death rites loop back on themselves. They aren't a clean, clear path of power. They cross into, over, under, and around many other threads—almost all of them, in fact. Promulgation is one of the more common connections."

She nodded. "I understand." The look in her eyes suggested otherwise.

Methias willed his hands to remain where they were. Any gesture of frustration or dismissal would only serve to alienate her, which would accomplish nothing. "There's nuance it might benefit you to know." When she'd nodded her acceptance, he continued. "The Weave Promulgant works rites that control the actions, emotions, and sometimes very minds of others. With training, a skilled Weave Promulgant can cause panic, love, rage, or woe to bloom inside someone. They aren't *true* or *honest* reactions, so they won't last indefinitely, but often they don't need to. Often a *moment*... a moment is all you need."

Stone in sky. A moment is all you...

Both her expression and her tone showed that this, at least, she understood clearly. "A panic is easy enough to start *without* the Weave. Sometimes it only takes a single word—*fire(!)*—or the like. Shouted in a confined space? People will knock one another into the dirt and charge forward, never mind who they trample in the process. It's miserable, but," she shrugged, "snow will fall."

A moment... A word... A word! Havoc's horn! I'm a fool!

He nearly leapt to his feet. "Daephone, you may have found the very key!"

He didn't wait for a reply. Instead, he tore off toward the tower door. If he was correct...

-III-

Venzene Duchy of Kovalun
County Jižní Pochod
Barony of Hartscross–Jižní Lov
5 Korunasykli: 22 Days after the Red Storm at Westsong

Vlk finished the last of his morning chores with a sigh that was equal parts relief and frustration. It was well past the noon bell, and he counted himself fortunate that Milan Němá-noha was nowhere to be found... to say nothing of his father. Both had departed before high sun to tend to some business or other with the Bluemark's chief groom. This twice-blessed turn of events meant neither his master nor his father could stand behind him to pick at his every action. It also meant they couldn't cuff him over how long it had taken him to get everything settled and sorted.

I've got nine fewer horses to look after in my part of the stables, vhy did it feel like there vas so much more to be done today?

The Count's warband had marched away two days a'gone. All told, there had been nineteen mounted men with Lord Aetanis at their head, and something like a score of footmen. He hated to admit it, given his feelings on the majority of the folk in question, but they'd looked impressive, at least to his unpracticed eye.

Nine horses from the Count's stable... mounts for Lord Caros and his lance of men, Lord Aetanis, the two guards he'd come into camp with, and that sergeant who refused to kill his own men... Stephan vas his name, I think. He shook his head, spitting to one side.

He found his mind returning to thoughts of Lord Aetanis's newly hired footmen. Those same eight men had stood and drawn swords against Lakkrid and his uncle.

Admittedly, Stephan hadn't been there for the fighting, but what of that? They'd been *his* men when they'd meant to kill Lakkrid... *And now they're Lord Aetanis's personal guard? Vhy in the vorld they vere revarded for that is a thing I von't ever understand. They're lowbellies. They'll make the Lord Aetanis and the Count look foolish.*

Beyond all of that, and his frustration at the plodding pace of the day's work, there were other matters to contend with. Rubbing grit out of his eyes, he recognized the truth. He was short-tempered, tired, and troubled all at a go. What sleep he'd gotten had been broken and thin, he was still sore from yesterday's training, and—he'd do better to admit it— he was still thinking angry thoughts about *Honeybrow's* friend Fetinba.

She vill have to go. I'll need to beat her in a sparring match, and I'll need to do it in front of others… especially Honeybrow. Vhen I do that, things vill return to normal, pravdivý jako zítřek.

(True as tomorrow).

He had no intention of using some unfair trick to shame or embarrass her outside of the sparring ring. His mother would have done or planned to do something like that, he had no doubt. And she would easily have roped his father into doing the same. It made a certain amount of sense, as well. It would end the matter without having to fight in the first place. But Vlk refused to sell his honor so cheaply.

If I have to do that, I'm no varrior. I need to best her. Tricking her into looking foolish—making her crawl avay like a vhipped dog—vould mean I von't get to fight her. I can't vin a sparring match I never get to fight. Walking to the water pump, he queued up to clean his hands. *A varrior vants to test himself against other varriors, not to beat his chest and talk about how strong he is. No varrior vorth his svord vould lower himself like that.*

His face split into a dark, snide smile. *The Bluemark vould do such a thing. The count and his men vould not.*

"Pravdivý jako zítřek." he said to no one in particular.

"Vhat is?" The high, clear voice forced him out of his weighty thoughts.

"Nothing, Jitka." Vlk smiled as he turned to see the little girl queue up behind him. Her rich brown waves bounced as she came to a stop. She was carrying a small wooden bucket. It bounced against the dirty wool of her smock—the only clothing she ever wore.

Jitka had been his good luck charm the night they'd last played Zvonění v Jeskyni. She'd been surprised and delighted at having been chosen as his caller. Her voice was sweet, high, and clear. She was *always* singing. Who better to shout "Běh!" for him? She *should* have been shouting *poběž,* but never mind. She was young, and old Kovalunth was complicated. It'd all worked out in the end.

But vait. There's no snow on the ground. You've been barefoot since the last snows melted. Who's gotten you to start veering shoes?

He noticed her gripping her smock along her dim side, hiking it up ever so slightly to reveal her feet. Those she seemed unable to stop tapping as if a song were trapped in her tousle-haired head.

It was his turn at the water pump. He stepped around it so that he could face her as he cleaned his hands and face.

"Those shoes are a pretty pair. Vhen did you get them?"

She'd wanted him to ask, and badly. Her broad grin and wide eyes made that fact endearingly clear.

"Artem made them for me." She was bouncing again. "I vas to tell Daryna that he did and show her."

Daryna was one of his Excellency's cooks. She'd taken responsibility for the little girl when the Count's men had brought her in. They'd found her wandering in the woods—filthy, sickly, and nearly feral, some nine or ten sykli a'gone.

"Vlk? Do you think Artem vill take her to vife?"

His hands and face now cold, and reasonably clean, Vlk leaned back, gesturing Jitka toward him. She obliged willingly enough, but looked up into his face, trying to read his thoughts.

With freshly numbed fingers, he took her bucket from her as gently as he could, placing it under the spout. With his other hand, he worked the force pump once more, filling the bucket but slowly.

"Vell... he's always talking vith her." He shrugged. "Does he talk vith you a lot, too?"

She nodded, hopping from foot to foot.

"Is he nice to you?"

She didn't answer for a long moment. Vlk began to grow concerned, but she seemed only to be lost in thought. Her face was distant, but not clouded with any sort of worry.

"If they wed, vill that mean I have to find a new place to sleep?"

Vlk laughed. *Vell, maybe a little vorry.* "Vhy vould you have to do that?"

"Vell... vhen it gets cold, I sometimes sleep vith Daryna to keep varm. I *like* Artem, but..." She wrinkled her nose. "His breath is..." She shook her head and made flapping gestures as if to ward off a bad smell.

Vlk laughed. He couldn't help it. A moment later, she joined in.

As he stopped the flow of water, he hefted the small bucket, thinking of his first lesson with Andrej. That led him to thoughts of Fetinba, magically transforming Andrej into *Honeybrow*. He made an effort to banish those thoughts. Turning to Jitka, he asked what, to him, were the obvious questions.

"Vhere are you meant to take this? Is it for Artem or Daryna?"

Her face lit up in that smile again. It was a perfect antidote for his frustrations. Somehow, she managed to smile with her entire body, which made it hard to lump her in with most of the other children her age. Being around Jitka made people, well, happy.

"No! Come! Come and see!" With that, she began to run off.

Vlk shook his head. Apparently, he was carrying her water for her. *Vell, at least she asked nicely.* He snorted and walked after her.

What he found beyond the entrance to Maker's Row was at once annoying and amazing. At a small camp table sat Andrej, Fetinba, Pavel, and a man wearing the Count's livery. A moment later, he recognized the man, too. He'd taken Pavel away after Lakkrid faced down the Bluemark. They looked as if they were playing cards—a thing his parents refused to let him do, let alone teach him *how* to do.

He felt a wave of embarrassed rage begin to roll toward him. Here was yet another thing Andrej had been given. It wasn't Andrej's *fault,* of course, and indeed Andrej would almost certainly be willing to teach Vlk how to play. Still, here were Pavel, the dull-witted baker's boy, Andrej, and *Fetinba* sitting with one of the Count's men, playing *cards* as if it were the most natural thing in the world.

Then he saw it.

Jitka had bolted over, crouched down behind the man's camp stool, and began crooning. As she did, she started sliding her hand along what at first he'd taken for a dark red log, before it raised its head and licked her small face. She giggled, stroking the massive hound's sleek crimson head with one hand, and made frantic *hurry up* gestures to Vlk with the other.

"Is that..." He shook his head, speechless for the moment. *Please don't let it be Fetinba's.* If the dark-skinned girl had a Karmínové Srdce—a Crimson Heart—it would be the final... the final... what?

He walked the short distance to where Jitka crouched with the hero's hound. As he did, both Andrej and Pavel nodded in his direction, though they kept their minds focused on their game.

Jitka gestured for him to put the bucket down in front of the Karmínové Srdce, which he did gladly. He'd never actually seen one, but every child knew their description. Blood red fur. Ears that hung down beside their dark faces. Eyes like warmth and wisdom brought to life. As he met the beast's eyes, resisting the urge—the almost physical *need* to pet the massive, friendly-looking creature—he suddenly knew why he feared that it was Fetinba's.

If she has a hero's hound, that makes her a hero. I can help her train, maybe even help her fight, but if I stand against her, I'm the monster. I'm the foe. It voud mean she's the varrior, and I'm the vile thing setting himself in her vay.

He sat on his knees and asked the question, bracing himself for the answer he so dreaded... bracing himself to make peace he didn't want to make.

"Is he ... yours, Fetinba?"

"*She* ... is *mine*," said the man as they flipped their cards. "Or perhaps I'm hers."

"She's called Štít!" Jitka spoke as if she, herself, had chosen the name. Štít was old Kovalunth for *Shield*—a fine name for a war hound.

Vlk had to fight the urge not to shout his relief. He wasn't the villain in Fetinba's story, nor was he an afterthought in his own. He could continue to think of her as a rival to be bested.

"Štít proti Vzteku, if we're making formal introductions." The man's voice was hard to read as he made this correction. He didn't sound unhappy, but mild enough to make reading him difficult. "Štít will do, though."

Štít proti Vzteku. Vlk felt a smile sneaking its way onto his face... *Rage Shield.* At once, his mind filled with images of the battles the hound would have seen to earn such a name. *To have a varhound like you stood beside me. Vhat glory ve vould find!* He began stroking the dog, who gave his face a single lick before dipping down to drink from the bucket.

He heard a collective drawing of breaths, presumably at whatever the cards had shown, then the man spoke again through a grin.

"And *you*, Fetinba, are *mine*. Off the field, at least for this round."

Fetinba sucked her teeth. "So be-yit, Ruční Kopí. That means..." She gave a brief bark of satisfied laughter.

Pavel threw up his hands. "Hells. Vhy didn't you play that sooner, Andrej?" He sounded more confused than frustrated, though not by much.

Vlk lifted himself to see the table, careful to position himself so that he could continue petting Štít. Pavel and Fetinba held no cards. Andrej and the man—Ruční Kopí, apparently—held a pair and a single card, respectively. All four of them had a card turned skyward in front of them, with two piles in the middle. One of these was face-up, the other face-down. Andrej's card bore seven of what looked to be red spearheads. Fetinba's showed an armored man holding a black banner with a white diamond in its center. Pavel's card displayed seven red castles, and Ruční Kopí's was a figure in a red cloak and hood.

Andrej shrugged.

"True Trefning, boys," said the man. "A real skirmish. Pavel? Do you want to draw first or second?"

Pavel blinked. "I ... don't know. Vhich is best?"

The man offered a smile, reaching his dim hand over to grip Pavel's shoulder. "Fortunes of war. Your castles are higher in the order of precedence than Andrej's spears. You can make him choose the top card, or you can choose it. It's all down to chance now."

"Then vhy does it matter?"

Fetinba spoke up. "Right now, you're lear-ning. In bat-tle, though, if you can scare your foe, you may force them to make a mistake lay-tah."

The Count's man nodded, making a *there you have it* gesture.

Pavel reached for the cards, then stopped himself. "I'm too happy to eat vhatever's in reach. I think this time I vait for Andrej to eat first."

The man gave Pavel's shoulder a squeeze, nodding.

Andrej reached for the top card on the face-down pile, then flipped it over. It was another armored man with a banner—this one bearing a white knight's spur on it.

Pavel shook his head, sighing. He reached for the next card on the pile, flipping it over with surprising dexterity. It bore ten red spearheads and carried with it Pavel's sigh of frustration. He had no more cards in his hand.

"I vant to see vhy Andrej held onto that seven."

I vould have thought Pavel vould be angry. He sounds more interested in seeing who vins than angry at losing.

Andrej's face was calm and thoughtful, though it showed no sign of particularly deep concentration. He drew the banner-bearing card into his hand, placing the seven of spyd *(spears)* onto the face-up pile at table's center. After a moment, he began sliding the three cards he held in his hand, reordering them in an absent sort of way. Finally, he looked up as Ruční Kopí placed his only card on the table, face down.

"At your pleasure, Andrej." The man's voice was calm and cheerful.

Andrej nodded, selected a card, and placed it down.

The pair nodded at one another, then flipped their cards. Andrej had played the same banner-bearing man he'd just claimed. Ruční Kopí played a card bearing a man with a small crown on his head. Its six spires were topped with tiny round orbs.

Ruční Kopí knocked on the tabletop, eliciting a grin from Pavel. "Baron beats banner," said he.

Andrej nodded, saying nothing. He moved his *banner* card onto the face-up pile and waited.

Ruční Kopí leaned back, leaving his baron card face-up. "Not gonna re-draw till I have to."

Andrej took one of his remaining two cards and laid it on the table face-up. It showed six white spurs on a black field.

"*That* vas vhat I thought you vould play vhen I played the seven." Pavel squinted as if he were still trying to work out why Andrej had beaten him.

Ruční Kopí took his baron and tossed it on the discard pile. Andrej's six joined it. The man drew a fresh card, glancing at it before he grinned and placed it face-down on the table. The boy's remaining card followed a moment later.

Andrej's vaited. He couldn't beat the baron, and now Ruční Kopí doesn't have it anymore.

Both reached as if to flip their own card, then paused, seeking one another's eyes. Satisfied that each was ready, they flipped.

Thwip.

"Hells haul me home! *Damn* you, Andrej!" Rather than angry, Ruční Kopí sounded as if he were on the verge of real laughter. "*That* was well played."

Before Ruční Kopí sat another of what they were calling a *banner*. The armored figure held a white banner bearing a red spearhead in its center. In front of Andrej sat another baron card—this one with a red castle on two of its corners.

Štít lifted her head from the bucket to look around, then turned back to resume drinking.

"How did he know?" Pavel was still a few paces back, looking first to Andrej, then the Count's man with undisguised confusion.

"A banner can beat most cards," Andrej said. "Can't beat a baron, though, can it?"

Pavel shook his head. "But you *had* a baron. Vhy didn't you play that sooner?"

"Be-cause it wasn't worth the risk," Fetinba put in.

Ruční Kopí had taken up the cards and begun to shuffle them afresh. "Trefning means skirmish in Havalunth, Pavel. Yes?"

"Yes, you said this already."

"Well, skirmishes aren't the whole war, are they?"

Pavel sat back, considering. "No... they're a *part* of the var, though. You have to vin skirmishes to vin the var, just as you have to vin your rounds in a lyst to vin the whole tournament."

Ruční Kopí was nodding. "After a fashion, but it might be better to say you have to win the *right* skirmishes to win the war. You have to think about the whole war, not just a single skirmish."

Pavel nodded, then rolled his head from side to side, and seemed to chew on it.

"If you tire yourself out in the first round of the lyst, you've won that round, but at a cost. You have less energy for the rest of the rounds, yes?"

Pavel nodded, albeit slowly.

"You don't just need to be able to defeat your *first* foe. To win the tourney—to win the war—you have to have the strength and cunning to defeat your *last* foe, too. Do you see?"

Vlk could almost smell the smoke from Pavel's effort. The lesson seemed obvious to his thinking, but everyone was different, he supposed. Pavel had not been *cursed with an excess of opinion,* as his mother would say.

Andrej stiffened suddenly. Vlk saw his nostrils flare, chin pointed skyward.

He looks like an animal scenting something.

As if she'd heard his thoughts, the great red hound beside Vlk lifted her head from the bucket, growling softly and *also* scenting the air.

"That's smoke."

"So? There are fires all over camp, Honeybrow."

"Yes, but this is coming from *that* way." Andrej gestured to the northwest with his chin. "The wind's blowing toward us from that direction, and there are no fires between here and the gate for it to carry this way."

Ruční Kopí stood up, looking down at his hound. The man was opening his mouth to speak, even as he turned away from the table, when Vlk heard a woman call his name.

"Vlk! Stay there and don't let anyone leave!"

He knew the voice. It was one of Lady Kastan's folk, though he couldn't recall her name.

"Vlasta?" Fetinba, apparently, could.

Turning, he saw the old woman trotting toward them on a horse he remembered. It had been one of the only Flekket Vinds he'd ever seen, and he'd been utterly taken by its dappled beauty. Something in the horse's gait seemed off, though—as if she wanted to run, but was being held back.

The woman rode over, swinging out of the saddle with surprising grace. "Hajvarr, I need you to get me in to see Edmund right away." She handed her reins to Vlk with barely a nod of acknowledgement. "Fetinba, there's trouble on the come. Rally the rest of our number. Andrej? Go with her."

Vlk blinked, then shook his head as if to clear it. "Ne, I vant to go vith Andrej."

"I need you to take care of my horse and saddle all of those you can while there's time, Vlk." The woman's voice made it clear she *expected* his obedience.

Vell, she'll be disappointed. "I go vith Andrej. If there's trouble, I vant to fi—"

"*Villlk!*" Andrej made his voice sharp, extending the word until Vlk—and everyone else—had quieted. When they'd all turned to look at him, including the hound, he spoke again. His voice returned to its normal timbre. "See to Vlasta's tasks. Rally the other stable boys to help, if you can. I'll find you before... before whatever this is comes to pass."

Vlk looked at him for what seemed like a long moment. "... Opravdu?" *(Really?)*

Andrej nodded, grinning. "Jo. Pravdivý jako zítřek." (*Yeah. True as tomorrow.)*

Vlk gave a single, solemn nod, turned, and headed off. He hadn't gone far when he heard Pavel's heavy steps jogging up behind him.

"Ruční Kopí says I'm to help you vith vhatever I can."

Vlk turned, walking backward as he watched the boy's approach. He saw the Count's man level a finger at his hero's hound. She, in turn, sat back down beside Jitka, who instantly began to pet the massive beast.

"Vhy did the voman call him Hajvarr?"

Pavel shrugged. "They know each other vell, I think. Ruční Kopí isn't his *name.*"

"Vell, not his given name at least. I thought maybe it vas his varrior's name, the vay Count Edmund is Edmund the Tall." Ruční Kopí meant Hand Spear in the old tongue—an odd epithet, but a memorable one.

"Ne. Ruční Kopí's his rank—his job. He's the leader of the Count's personal guard. I'm to join vith him. Ruční Kopí asked my father, and he says I may."

Vlk fought back the urge to sigh. *Honeybrow gets service and training from a noble house. Lakkrid gets to train and fight vith his father and his father's men, as does Maksu. Pavel gets knocked out for being an unlucky oaf of a varrior, then gets revarded for it by being selected for the Count's personal guard. And I...*

"...Have vork to do," he murmured aloud.

"Vhat?"

"I said ve have vork to do. Take this horse into that stall over there. Get her some vater. I'll be back in a blink."

Pavel nodded, but Vlk barely noticed. He moved to the center of the stable complex, lifted his face toward the ceiling, and shouted. "Ke mě! Ke mě! Ve have vork, and ve need to be quick!"

Several stall doors squeaked open, then banged shut again. This arhythmic thumping heralded roughly a dozen sets of footfalls moving toward him in varying states of speed. Once he could see faces, he told them what was to be done. Horses saddled—as many as possible, as swiftly as may be. They listened, nodded, and raced off to see to it. Vlk wasn't in charge in any official sense, but orders were often delivered from the master to the nearest stable boy to hand, along with instructions to pass the word. Orders like this usually meant the count or his men would be on the move double-sharp due to some nearby threat—a caravan in trouble, or a large-scale bandit party spotted in the area. The idea that it might have something to do with trouble on its way to *them* never really occurred to any of them.

As Vlk walked back toward where he'd left Pavel, the idea finally occurred to *him*.

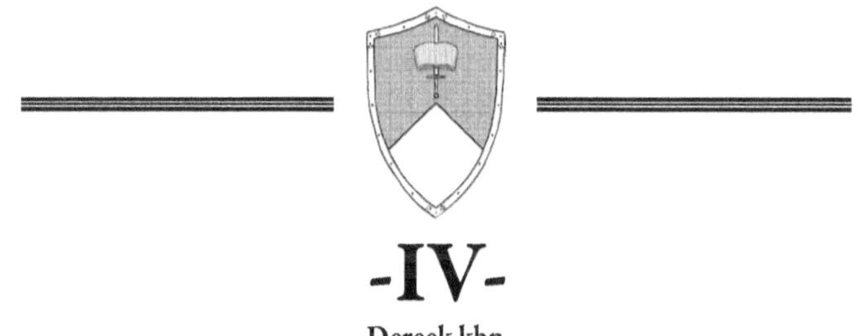

-IV-

Dereek khn
Yrxa Castle
5 Korunasykli: 22 Days after the Red Storm at Westsong

Methias paused at the bottom of the spiral staircase, just outside of The Cage's entrance. He avoided touching the strangely aware wood of the door itself but placed one hand on its metal pull ring as he waited. He'd have to cancel his own weave work, and power spent was power that couldn't be reclaimed.

So be it. I'll sleep early and easy tonight, at least.

With a conscious effort, he refocused his mind on the task ahead of him. It might've been wiser to wait—to recover his strength and steady his heart ... but no.

If I'm correct... if I can resolve this here and now...

He heard Daephone trundling down behind him. She said nothing, but he could hear the mild labor in her breath.

She's made the trek twice over in less than a quarter-hour ... in full harness, no less. Of course her breath's labored. My armor is lighter. Hers offers more protection, but then, she's more likely to see armed conflict than I. Still, perhaps it would be worth considering an augmentation to... No! Enough of that. Distractions will only add to the danger.

Speaking of... Given there's actual danger, best I use her title. Hopefully, it'll focus her mind on the matter at hand.

"I'm going to wake it up again. Be as ready for that as you can, Lankaajh." He kept his voice as light as the situation allowed.

Strictly speaking, The Cage and its faces aren't asleep. I've merely countered vibration with vibration. Explaining that—the concept that sound is what we call vibration loud enough to hear, that vibrations are measured as waves on the sea, and that a thing readily measured is a thing that can more readily be altered—would only serve my own ego. It'd be satisfying, but not very helpful.

"My lord?"

"Hmm?"

"Are you... Are you certain we shouldn't wait until you've rested?"

Until I've rested, Daephone, or until you have?

"I won't be long. Either this will work, or it won't. If it does, you'll know almost as quickly as I do."

"How?"

"You'll hear voices that aren't mine. I can't say how many, but far fewer than the entire choir. They'll be speaking the Trade Tongue, as well."

He waited to see if she would speak again. In the dim glow of the torchlight, he saw her shadow nod slowly along the wall to his left.

Despite his best efforts, Methias had been unable to definitively put an end to The Cage's shrieking madness thus far. As a stopgap measure, he'd created a series of temporary runes on the room's floor and high up on its walls. In the ordinary course, such runes made it possible for casters to converse over long distances. When active, the sound heard by one rune would issue from any other rune linked to it, up to half a league distant. The closer one got to that full mile and a half, the thinner and more distorted sound became, especially if the caster weren't well-versed in the subtler side of weave-waking.

The runes were also useful when planning to address a large number of people. By setting several such runes to project one way—from the person addressing the masses to the runes placed around an amphitheater, for instance—they would act to amplify the speaker's voice. All those present would be able to hear him or her with relative ease.

Settling on this latter use as a starting point, Methias had drawn several pairs of runes in proximity to one another. One of each pair listened, passing what it heard along to its mate. The other was set exclusively to receive that sound but to reverse it before reissuing it. It had been a reasonably clever solution, if an impermanent one.

It's a place to begin, at least. I admit it's inelegant. Inversion works to cancel out the screaming, gibbering din of The Cage itself, but... it's like stopping a child from screaming by shutting it in a soundproof room. It stops the noise, but it does nothing to sort out why he or she was screaming in the first place.

For a moment, he was struck by how unintentionally apt that analogy was. He forced the urge to explore that notion away. *Time enough for that later this evening. For now...*

"Are you ready, Lankaajh?"

He heard her draw a sharp breath in before speaking. A moment later, her voice came out quiet and sure.

"I am."

Without so much as a nod, Methias hauled on the pull ring and opened the great round-topped door. It crawled its sluggish way open, requiring his muscles to actively engage to compensate. Had his runes not been in play, the hinges would be screaming their protest at the treatment.

That's assuming I'd be able to hear their complaint over The Cage's chorus, but never mind.

As the door opened wide enough to admit him, he took a moment to drink in his new surroundings while he and Daephone could still hear one another. He began hunting for any sign of change since his last attempt.

Still, the spiced smell of old cinnamon and crypt dust. Still, the same pale starlight twinkled from the walls. There's no weave work here, which makes that light a riddle worth solving... but not just now.

The octagonal—*chamber? Can such a small place be called a chamber?*—room was modest insofar as depth and breadth, but it rose nearly fifteen feet from floor to vaulted ceiling. At a glance, the stone of the walls seemed to be stained a dim, somehow wet-looking green. As the eye roamed upward, the semblance of serpents skin gave way to darker hues. In uneven waves, they shifted into deep, star-shot blue, finally thickening between the buttressed arches into a shade Methias could only classify as *midnight*.

The room's color seemed to shift in subtle ways that were hard to identify. *It's as before—as if they somehow managed to cover the entire room with the kind of movement only glimpsed from the corner of the eye.*

Weave Author rites had been his first thought, but again, no. The room was utterly bereft of magic, save his own runes. There were traces of the weave held within the *door*, but they'd remain dormant until it was closed again.

Then The Cage will reappear, and the screaming will start once more... Well, as soon as I cancel the power I placed in the runes, at least.

His mind wanted to examine the walls, themselves—to try to solve that tiny mystery. With a small pang of regret, he resisted.

Sconces on the wall, sconces down the hall, he reminded himself. There was comfort in recalling the old catechism. If this failed, he would reactivate the runes and try to rest while the silence lasted. If it succeeded, he would have all the time he needed to examine the mundane miracle that was the shift and shudder of the room's walls.

The weave work he had in mind was straightforward enough. An abjuration—a promulgation rote that forced all but the very strongest of wills into a single, benign action or inaction. The key was that to attain the best chance of success, the command needed to be a single word that could be understood by the target or targets. *Duck, stop, silence*—these were all valid and fairly common uses of the rite. One could add more words to clarify the specific outcome, such as *speak your name,* but the cost for such clarity was substantial. Every additional word halved the potency of the rite, making it easier to resist.

Two abjurations prepared today. The question is, how best to use them? He smiled to himself. *If this works...*

"And if beef were blue," he began.

"Ssssstew would mirror sky?" Daephone sounded amused, hesitant, and more at ease all at a go.

"You don't need to be a caster to be wise. Fyken Presh is all the proof you could ask for on that... score." He blinked, a smile curving the corners of his mouth.

Hells, that's the second time you've helped me shake something loose, Daephone!

He was thinking of how the Old Man drilled breath control into the soldiery. He had them sing a marching cadence while they walked, marched, or jogged along. Focus on singing both improved their rhythm and cohesion and prevented them from thinking about their own breathing. Breath came easiest when it was controlled by the body, not the mind.

Song... it's perfect.

With hope in his heart utterly overshadowed by the need to test his theory, he slipped into the room at last. He reached back and, with an effort, pulled the door toward him.

As soon as it clicked closed, pale pilasters—the bones of some massive creature put to the architect's purpose—materialized, inch by inch, rising at close intervals along the walls. Somewhere near the eight-foot mark, their upward growth began to curve inward, toward the room's center. At the ceiling's apex, the bleached beams met at last, leaving a hole in the shape of a massive eye between them.

Behold The Cage.

As if his thought had summoned it, the negative space within the empty eye abruptly shimmered black. The effect was akin to a stone tossed into a pond on a moonless night. The dim starlight seemed to vibrate as that same rippling shadow spilled downward between the pilasters. When the gloom, at last, touched the floor, there was a moment of stillness that seemed to go on for an age.

Methias *willed* himself to be still—to be patient and unmoving in heart, body, and mind. He didn't fear, exactly, but there was a dreadful sense of anticipation. Would it work? Had he found the answer, albeit with Daephone's unintentional aid? Would something about The Cage change before he had the chance to test his theory?

Shapes began to emerge from the shadowed places along the walls. Once again, Methias thought of a dark pond on a moonless night. The slow pace with which they moved, coupled with the utter silence maintained by his own runes, worked in eerie concert. They transformed an already stressful situation into something nightmarish—the monsters in the mirk crawling ever closer, while the dreamer's limbs refuse to obey.

A fleeting flash of memory—a children's rope rhyme came floating back to him from across the years.

They come clawing, crawling, dragging, gnawing, and you can only cry. A scream, a song—the moment long, and silence as you—

Methias felt something brush against his booted calf and for a moment was lost to terror. Had something reached for him? Was he not alone, after all?

He leapt forward, screaming, though nothing came out. His eyes were hot, prickling things as fear tried to override all higher thought. Reaching for his sword with one hand, he raised the other, ready to ward off the hellish thing that had grabbed at...

The couch... I'd forgotten about the couch.

Directly beneath the massive black eye above, a tall and spectral-looking couch had materialized. It looked to be carved from ebony or some similarly hued wood, with plump, somehow bloated padding that mirrored the white of the pilasters. The couch's legs were each covered in identical friezes depicting nude men and women holding short blades or spears. These blank-faced folk were stood or knelt around an enclosed carriage drawn by glistening black horses. Both the bone-colored carriage and its shadowy steeds had been cunningly covered in fitted glass, or perhaps clear quartz. The overall detail was stunning, if off-putting.

I think it's the vapidity on their faces. It's clearly a deliberate thing. The solid blackness of their eyes is just a product of leaving eye-shaped holes, allowing the dark wood of the couch itself to be glimpsed through them. gives them a ... a haunted quality.

He forced himself to close his eyes, drew in a deep breath, and held it for a ten count. He needed to get himself back under control. Wielding the Weave demanded focus. Fear was an enemy to that focus—perhaps its greatest enemy.

As he opened his eyes, his gaze fell on the couch once more. The figures depicted on the friezes drew his attention almost immediately. There was something about them that tugged at his memory, but he couldn't place why.

They look as if they dream, he thought, and not for the first time. *They dream, yet they know it, and cannot escape.*

This grim thought was blessedly interrupted when he saw that the process had at last ended. Relaxing his arms, forcing his heart to slow once more, he turned in place to cast about.

He was surrounded. Between the bleached shores of the bone uprights, tossed on the black between, two dozen small skulls floated in dark suspension. Each was screaming, shouting, cackling—or would be, were they not silenced by his runes. They *had* to be the bones of children. The cruelty of that was almost too vast to give voice to. A dead child was a misery, though hardly uncommon. A dead child trapped to serve beyond their death, corrupted by the rites used to bind them...

One horror at a time, Lamlith. Jannon's voice came back to him, as it so often did when he was near his emotional limit. *You can't fix anything if you're trying to solve everything. One horror at a time.*

"One horror at a time."

The runes prevented him from hearing his own voice, but he repeated the refrain, nonetheless. Nodding to himself, he moved throughout The Cage, touching each rune in turn, discontinuing the slow decay of the power he'd imbued them with. As he did so, whole sections of the room erupted in sound. He recognized none of the languages assaulting his ears, if indeed the wretches weren't simply braying whatever random noise their state called for.

When the last runes had been deactivated, he moved to stand near the couch, closed his eyes, and tried to listen to the din as a whole. He'd hoped to be able to pick out *something* intelligible, but that proved a head-ache-inducing waste of time.

He drew in a breath and bowed his head. A moment later, he lifted it again, pointing his nose toward the rippling black eye above. Spreading his arms wide to either side, he loosed his abjuration at last.

"Puav ka zet ahg siiiiiiiiing!" He held this last word out in as high a note as he thought his baritone could maintain.

(I will you to sing!)

Most of the voices remained maddeningly incoherent in the chamber, but he heard at least two that matched him as he sang. Holding the note, he turned, walking toward the sound of these singers—trying to pick them out from the rest.

He got close but ran out of breath before he could truly find them. A wave of dizziness forced him to lower himself to his knees. Before he'd regained his equilibrium, the other singers had ceased.

He reached for his haversack. The action was met with high-pitched cackling, louder than ever, from the two sections before him.

Well, it's a start, at least. I have to thin out the rest of the noise, though.

Drawing out a piece of charcoal, he drew a thick triangle around him, pointing toward where he *hoped* he'd heard the voices singing. They, at least, might understand his speech and might respond in kind.

Then again, they might simply have been mimicking me, not under-standing the command at all.

He wouldn't have to wait long to find out, one way or the other. Once the triangle was drawn to his satisfaction, he stood and began to reactivate his runes. He had one more abjuration before he slept. Still, if it failed, at least he knew what to prepare for tomorrow. An idea—any idea—was better than groping in the dark.

As you said, Jannon. One horror at a time.

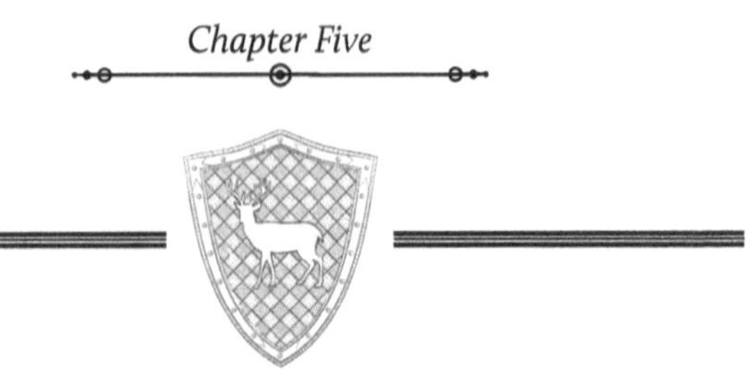

-V-

Venzene Duchy of Kovalun
County Jižní Pochod
Barony of Hartscross–The Ash March
5 Korunasykli: 22 Days after the Red Storm at Westsong

Kastan found frustration an unwelcome companion. Her blood was up... her senses keen for any hint of useful information about the ever-growing number of horsemen to the west. She needed to find her hunting party, and... and...

And what? They don't need me to tell them about the horsemen. This close to where the ash trees end, a body would have to be blind, deaf, and dead not to notice a herd that size.

No, her *hunting party* was composed of Rákos and her allotment of the Percoy household guard. They surely wouldn't need her to help or guide them. The truth was that she wanted to fight. The *problem* was that she was dressed for a leisurely ride in what—this close to Edmund's encampment—were considered safe lands. She wasn't unarmed, of course, but she had no sword... only an exceptionally long dagger. A good enough weapon for close combat with a fool of a highwayman, but less than ideal to do battle with an armed and armored soldier.

And they are indeed soldiers. She hadn't had more than a glimpse of them through the trees. It would have been too great a risk to get closer. Still, she'd seen both leather scale and chain hauberks on more than a few of the folk she'd spied. She thought she'd even seen a pair of men wearing thick wooden breastplates beneath their hide cloaks. These were called Béamwer Treyja—literally *wooden shirt*—in Eodenth and were reputed to stop arrows in much the way a wooden shield did.

This? This is Duke Harn's army? What she'd seen certainly *looked* Eodenth. But then, that was part of the deception they suspected, wasn't it? Eodenth, who'd had enough of raiding, or Harn and his hirelings trying to use the old laws to his advantage—the danger, at least in the short-term, was much the same.

Bjegota knows his way around these trees, and Rákos is a hunter. They'll be fine, surely. I'll likely be of more use back with Edmund at Jižní Lov.

Jafyl's ears were suddenly flat against his head. More than that, his nostrils had begun to flare. Clearly, *something* had made him uneasy. Kastan could feel his body coiling, preparing to bolt.

She tightened her grip on the reins, listening. Nothing—not even birdsong. Then the scent struck her.

Linseed oil ... and wax. Someone had recently unsheathed a sword. That scent was too telling to be anything else. Its relative strength sent two facts racing one another in her mind.

It's fresh, and it's close! Hells!

She loosened her grip on the reins, slid her feet so that they sat more firmly in the stirrups, and prepared herself for Jafyl to—

"Nekt, tu nekt, Kovalunsh dotter." A man's voice, low-toned and delighted, came from the trees just to the east. "Tu ge štille, ti ferd..." He rolled his Rs less severely than the Eoden Zhprek she'd learned, but she had no trouble understanding him.

(No, you don't, daughter of Kovalun. You stay quiet, my pretty...)

Kastan froze, letting the genuine sense of fear—of anticipation— flower in her chest. She rode them like a wave, tightening her grip on Jafyl's reins to hold him fast. The horse gave a little squeal, pawing at the ground in obvious anxiety, but otherwise held his ground.

He's alone. No sniggering, no other foot... No, there's a second and a third, or I'm a fool.

"Ti vánum ge rath, verek. Ge hem v r. Ge ti vani, nekt ti yarbrand." She didn't need to *make* her voice sound uncertain. She *knew* the Eodenth tongue but rarely had much chance to practice it. Much like her knowledge of Gnoerkish, it was easier to translate what one heard than what one wished to say.

(My father will be angry, war captain. Be his servant. Be my protector, not my enemy.)

"Shpeak th'trader'sh tongue. Hearing Eoden Zhprek pour out of your traitor'sh mouth makesh me shick."

Traitor's mouth? She was about to offer a reply when he spoke anew.

"Get `town from yor horse."

She complied, marking the other two figures from the corner of her eye.

"Shtep to me. Do it shmartly, before I get bored." Again, he rolled his Rs.

She took two steps toward him, Jafyl's reins in her dim hand.

"Shtop! I didn't tell you to bring your shteed. My kinshmen vill take care of hem."

"If I let the reins go, he'll bolt, Verek." Again Kastan used the honorific, though she doubted anyone else this man knew would consider it fitting. She'd kept her voice small and uncertain. It was still too soon to be certain of much. She'd heard two more but hadn't marked them visually yet.

Growling, the man stood up at last. Kastan looked him up, then down again. He had a hunter's build—lithe of limb and likely able to walk or run for long periods without tiring. She marked his dark, sun-baked skin, no hair atop his head, but a long fringe of thick and dirty blond started just above his ears. It hung in a scattering of small braids, as did his greying beard. He wore fetid furs and half-cured hides with a baldric stretching from his right shoulder to his left hip. An ancient-looking sword hung awkwardly in both hands near his waist, blade pointed down beside his left boot.

"Adsh? Ond eosh vim." *(Adsh? Hold her horse.)*

To her right, a youth close to Fetem's age walked toward her, glaring.

These two are related, surely. His hair is long and full, but he has an unbroken version of the swordsman's nose. If this one's seen sixteen springs, I'm the Emperor's heir.

Behind the youth, in the bushes from whence he'd come, she saw a girl much closer to Maksu's age watching this tableau with wide, dark eyes.

The youth—Adsh, apparently—stalked toward her wearing a look of uniquely male insolence. Were he alone, he would have had far less confidence. Hells, he might even have worn a nervous, hopeful smile. She kept her grip tight on the reins as he neared, lifting the hand that held them to her breast as if keeping them close to her heart. His eyes followed the hand, lingering upon it for a beat. As if waking from a daydream, he reached to snatch the reins away.

Kastan fought for a moment, as if too frightened to give up her horse. He yanked, meaning to *take* the reins with a sudden burst of strength. As her arm was pulled to near full extension, she stopped resisting. She released her grip, causing Adsh to momentarily stumble, and Jafyl to squeal and paw at the ground. The youth moved to adjust his footing, but it was too late.

Barely a blink and it was over. Her dim hand free of the reins, she brought that same arm up to wrap around his throat even as she slipped behind him. With her bright hand, she drew the knife from the small of her back, pressing its point against the tender flesh below the hinge of his jaw. Taking a half step to center her balance, she forced Adsh to lean back awkwardly against her left thigh.

His hands came up instantly, trying to peel her forearm away from his neck. "Vánum! Vánum!"

"Tu vánum nekt van tu, Adsh. Nekt zhu… nekt hem brand!" *(Your father can't protect you, Adsh. Not in time… not with his sword.)* She then shaped her voice toward the man. "Or do your children speak the Trade Tongue?"

He shook his head. She was dismayed to see he looked more angry than afraid for her prisoner's life.

"Coward… Douyar aliswen! You vould take the life of a boy? You vould revenge yourself in sucha vay? Douyar aliswen!" He delivered this in a strangled, R-rolling roar.

"If *I* am a wicked serpent, verek, then *tu* edh se doull brandemand. Se doull brandemand, en nekt vánum. *(You are a false warrior. A false warrior, and no father.)* Who was it that sent him to me—risking his life—heedless of what might happen? You have made war on me and lost. Now! Make the peace. Pay the price in pride, not in blood." She searched out his eyes. "Lay … down … your … sword."

It should have been over, but no. With a near-feral growl, he charged. He brought the sword up high over his head in both hands and simply ran at her. It was clumsy, but the look on his face was nothing short of savage.

She waited for as long as she could, had an instant of indecision, then shoved the unfortunate Adsh at his father. The man brought his sword down, hammering at the boy's shoulder out of unfocussed rage. Blessedly, he only managed to hit him with the blunt sverdets bein. The blow caused Adsh to fall at his feet, tangling them for a beat. *That* part was what Kastan had hoped for. The swordsman struck Adsh a second time, then kicked him for good measure, cursing. The sickening crack meant at least one bone hadn't survived unbroken. That *hadn't* been her intent.

Still kicking the boy—as if turning away was an act of deepest concentration—the swordsman tore his face up toward Kastan. His eyes were wide, and a somehow malevolent green.

She drew a quick draught of cold air, gauging his gait. A single thought flashed before her.

You didn't have to die, Eodenth.

Without so much as a grunt, she pushed forward out of her stance, shoving the dagger up under the shelf of the man's chin even as he drove toward her. She held it there, supporting his weight as the strength went out of him. She could smell the meat on his breath—a sweet, pork-like stench mingled with the fresh blood filling his mouth. No sooner had this registered than she saw the shocked look of clarity in his sage-colored eyes grow glassy and still.

She heard the unmistakable sound of first one, then two more arrows rend the air from somewhere behind the newly made corpse.

"My... my Lady! Kastan!" Rákos's voice, sounding pained but mightily relieved.

"There may be more," said she and said no more for the moment. Her voice was calm, though there was a clipped sharpness to it that she rarely showed others. Certainly, in the short time he and Andrej had been in her service, she'd never had call to use it.

She didn't waste time looking for Rákos in the treeline. Instead, she dropped the dead swordsman, eschewing her dagger for his sword. To her right, she saw the boy Adsh on his belly with an arrow in his back. He wouldn't survive. The arrow was buried deep where the heart rested. His fingers were twitching, as were his feet.

Rákos was coming toward her. Nodding at him, she held up her dim hand and walked to the unfortunate Adsh's side. She called his name once... twice. No reaction. Standing, she did the merciful thing, finishing him with her newly acquired sword.

"Are... are you vell? Did they—no, you don't look vounded. I vas afraid for your life, Lady. I know you know something of how to fight, but..." Rákos shook his head. "Ve must hurry. Vhile no more are *here*, there are unnumbered others like these, and close."

She ignored this.

"There was a girl."

"There vas. She vas quick and small. I missed her vith both arrows."

Kastan forced herself not to react. The idea of killing a child—even an enemy child who would surely report what she'd seen to the rest of her people—was abhorrent. It was pragmatic, but there were limits... weren't there?

"Lady?" His voice was both ragged and anxious.

"Where are the others?"

"Ve vere ambushed. I'm an archer, not a svordsman. Bjegota commanded me to run and warn the encampment. The voods are full of their scouts."

Perhaps they were captured? Hells, let them have been captured.

She moved over and pulled the baldric off of the man's corpse. As she'd thought, it held a back scabbard. She sheathed the blade, slung the baldric into position over her right shoulder, then saw to her dagger. There wasn't time to do more than wipe the bulk of the blood from both blade and bright hand, so she contented herself with that.

"I fear we're doomed to walk." She'd stood, turning as she spoke... only to find Jafyl still standing by, utterly nonplussed, idly cropping grass. "Or Jafyl can bear us... if he consents."

She shook her head, mounted up, then held a hand down for Rákos.

Edmund had been wrong. Those two, at least, had been Eodenth. The rest of the army *might* be mercenaries dressed to look the part. She supposed it was possible, but those two had unquestionably been Eodenth.

Rákos grunted as he got into place behind her.

"You're alright? Ready?"

His breath sounded a bit labored, but his response was steady and sure. "I'm as ready as may be, Lady."

With that, she turned Jafyl, making for Jižní Lov as swiftly as she dared.

THE ONES LEFT BEHIND

-I-

Barony of Hartscross–Jižní Lov
5 Korunasykli: 22 Days after the Red Storm at Westsong

Vlk exited the stables. The other boys were finishing the work of saddling the last of the horses, and Andrej still hadn't come for him.

He vill, though... if he can. Meanwhile, it was best he busied himself with other chores. To that end, he'd grabbed one of the tall buckets the master kept on hand. These were used to either carry apples, carrots, or the like from stall to stall or fresh water from the nearby force pump to refill the stone troughs. He'd been about this latter task when he saw Otta's waifish form heading into the stable complex.

That was strange. Otta was the dyer's daughter. She should have no business in the stables, nor had he ever seen her there before. Still, it wasn't as if the area were out of bounds. So long as someone was on hand and the work was still getting done at a pace, Milan Němá-noha was content.

Vlk liked Otta well enough, but he'd never considered her a friend, exactly. Of course they *knew* each other, but only peripherally. They'd spent plenty of time in one another's company when the camp's children were gathered for some game or other. There had been a good deal more of that—time—back before they'd each taken on apprenticeships, but that had been three years a'gone and more. Now, as far as he could tell, Otta's time was spent helping to sell wares at her family's stall on Maker's Row.

Either that or reigning over everyone vhenever ve're at play. He scowled, thinking of the last time they'd run a game of Zvonění. *The course she made vould have been hard enough if I vere allowed to be slow and careful. Then she set her monsters to chase me, and she'd chosen her hunters vell.* In the end, it hadn't been enough. He'd beaten her and her Dragon Bats that night.

Jitka shouted běh for me. And she vas my good luck charm. The memory made him smile, albeit briefly. Then his mind returned to the oddity of Otta's presence.

"Vhatever she vants, I'll find out soon enough."

Shrugging to himself, he went back about his business... until he'd actually entered the wide way that served as the complex's central hall. At that point, he could only gape. Pavel had apparently finished the few tasks Vlk had assigned him and was sitting on a mounting block. That was fair enough. He was a baker's boy, after all, unfamiliar with tack and tangled manes. He wore a dull, dreamer's smile, and held a half-eaten pastie in his bright hand. Behind him, stood on the mounting block's lowest step so she could easily reach, Otta stood with her hands kneading his shoulders. She wore an equally doe-eyed expression.

But on her face, it looks far less foolish. Pavel looks either drunken or as if he vere newly avakened from an afternoon sleep. Otta looks... like Jitka looked vith the hero's hound.

Otta was somewhere near Vlk's own age. He couldn't recall if she were older or younger, but in either case, it wasn't by more than a sykli or two. He saw her comb her long fingers through Pavel's dark hair. For some reason, her cheeks seemed to have caught fire.

I'd have svorn Otta hadn't given Pavel so much as a smile before now.

Vlk picked his jaw up, tried to make his face as expressionless as he could, and stepped over to the left and out of sight. As he reached the western paddock's heavy wooden gate, he allowed his face to wear his wonder once more.

Standing on the lowest rung, he lifted his full bucket up and over the ash-timber fence to fill the trough below. His eyes fell on the heavy wooden gate to his right. Some ravenous wretch had taken a mare-sized mouthful from its top. The sight drew a rueful smile onto his face.

How hungry vould you have to be to think a mouthful of Ashvood sounded good? Horses were strange creatures.

As the last of the water spilled down into the trough, he heard Otta's voice.

"I have to go. If I'm gone for too long, Father will be wroth with me."

Vhat's wrong vith her? She sounds... He couldn't place exactly *how* she sounded. Softer? Sleepy? Different from the merchant's mask she used at the dyer's stall. It was a far cry from her usual tones while trying to control their collective play, as well.

"Vell, thank you for the pastie, moje drahá."

Moje... drahá? My dear? Vhen in hells did Otta become his drahá?

"Of course... můj drahý." He heard a giggle escape her. "When you join Count Edmund's guard and earn a wage, you'll be eating my cooking all the time. Best get used to it."

"That's fair, but..."

"But what?" Now Otta added yet another new tone of voice. She sounded afraid and a touch angry.

"Vell, best you don't cook for anyone else... other than your parents, I mean."

"Why ... not?"

"I don't vant to get into trouble." This was followed by a long moment wherein only the horses and flies made any noise. It took a bit, but eventually, Pavel clarified. "If you cook like this for all of the other boys—even the men—I'll have to fight them off of you. I'll do it of course, but... Ruční Kopí vill be vroth vith me. The Count's guard can't just valk around hitting people... I asked."

"I see." She sounded as if she were fighting not to giggle.

"Pahoda. Ve *protect*. Ve don't *provoke*."

"Alright, then. I swear to you that I won't cook for anyone other than my parents and you." A pause as she walked away, "And our children, of course." This was followed by the sounds of light but rapid footfalls.

She's running ... avay He rolled his eyes. *And giggling?* Vlk shook his head and stepped off of the fence's bottom rung. He moved to put the now empty bucket back with the others, sighing. *Pavel has someone? Pavel? Artem is sparking for Daryna, if Jitka's right, and now Pavel and Otta? Pavel's an oaf. He's fine enough, but foolish. And children? Otta vants children ... vith Pavel?*

Vlk tried to make his face expressionless as he turned. He walked back to where the oaf in question sat but stopped short after only a few strides. He was reeling—struck by something he should have long since seen.

Honeybrow is, I think, chasing Fetinba! Hells, how had he missed that?

Pavel was brushing crumbs from his hands and smiling, but Vlk hardly noticed. He was still trying to process the realization and what it meant.

A moment later, the older boy's voice managed to punch most of the way through his fugue.

"Vhat else can I do, Vlk?"

He opened his mouth to respond, though he had no idea what he meant to say, when Andrej came bolting into the stables. Vlk was relieved, for the most part. He was still unsure how he felt about Andrej and Fetinba, but that was for later. Andrej's arrival should mean ... *something* was going to happen. He'd kept his word, at least. There was that. Besides, he didn't want to have to make polite conversation or create work for Pavel to be about if he didn't have to.

Then he actually *saw* Andrej. He seemed both paler and taller than he had earlier. Paler? Fair enough, but taller? That didn't make much sense, but then, a thing didn't have to make sense to be true.

Pavel must have seen something off, too. He'd stood up and stepped closer as the blond boy skidded to a stop. Andrej met Pavel's eye for a beat as if to tell him to be still. Then he turned to Vlk and began to speak.

"Fetch the eldest boy here—whoever's supposed to be in charge when the master's away."

Vlk felt his face growing hot as his anger rose. "You svore—"

"Vlk! Do as I say or I'm leaving you here. There's no time for this!"

He blinked as if slapped. His face was hot, and his scalp and the corners of his eyes were tingling. Without a word, he turned and headed off to do as Andrej had asked.

As he moved, he found himself vacillating between being embarrassed at his own childish behavior—his mistrust of Andrej, who was his friend—and his confusion as to who in all the hells the taller boy thought he was. *He's a hunter's son. He's only been part of Lady Kastan's camp for, vhat, a fortnight?* Still, there was something in his voice when he raised it—something that made it hard to ignore or turn away from.

It didn't take long to do as he'd been asked... *Told. I vas Told, not asked.* By the time he'd rounded the last corner, Vlk had himself under control once more. He grabbed Milan's senior apprentice, Ignác, and led him toward the stable entrance at a jog.

As they arrived, he caught a glimpse of Pavel's back as the older boy ran off. He had a moment to think, *I didn't know he could run that sviftly,* before Andrej spoke up.

"Ignác... that's your name, isn't it?"

Both Vlk and the senior apprentice nodded. An instant later, so did Andrej.

"You're to keep two horses ready to bolt. Riders will be coming like they just heard Havoc's Horn if riders are needed."

Vlk cut in before he'd strictly meant to. "Vait, vhat about the rest of—"

Andrej stilled him with a look, then turned back to Ignác.

"You're to keep the rest as if the Count's overdue to leave... All of them, mind. If anyone—anyone at all comes through here looking for a mount, get them mounted. Doesn't matter if it's an old woman or a young boy. So long as they look like they're fit to ride, get them mounted and send them to the east gate. *East Gate,* jo?"

Ignác nodded, then turned to Vlk, thumping him on the shoulder in a familiar way. He'd opened his mouth to speak when Andrej cut him off. His tone wasn't aggressive, but it held a confidence that was hard to dismiss.

"Ne. Vlk's with me. He has other duties."

Ignác ran a hand through his thick, red hair. "Who vants Vlk? Ve'll need every hand ve can get if ve're to do as you ask."

"I tell you this once... and quietly. So keep your teeth together about it unless you can say it soft." He stepped right up to Ignác—close enough that the toes of their boots were touching.

For his part, Ignác lifted his sleek eyebrows, looking down into Andrej's upturned face. Andrej had offered no hostility, which was good. Ignác was fully a head taller than Pavel, and Pavel, Vlk reckoned, was half a Jitka taller than *Andrej*. Still, something in Andrej's tone added a weight to his words that was nearly physical.

"We are under attack—likely a siege, and very soon. Everyone will know shortly, but the count wants to avoid a panic."

Ignác took the news in but shook his head almost at once. "Ne, ne. Nobody vould attack us directly. If the count vas vorried about an attack, he'd ride out to meet it."

Vlk looked between the two, unsure how he felt about having been left out of the conversation.

Andrej shook his head. "It'd be the smartest thing he could do—let the panic set in while he and his men raced away. But it doesn't matter. There isn't time for us to argue. I was told to come get Pavel and Vlk and deliver those orders to the man in charge of the stables. I've done that. Vlk?"

He stepped back, making a *let's go* gesture with his dim hand. It was then that Vlk noticed the long hunting knife that hung from Andrej's belt and the leather archery gauntlet he wore on his right hand and forearm. The knife was long enough that it looked like a short sword on Andrej's slim frame.

Vlk hurried after him before Ignác could argue. *He vas true. He kept his vord and came for me. He came, and now I'm to stand vith him instead of hiding vith the horses or behind my mother's skirts.*

"Andrej…" His heart was full of such joy and gratitude in that moment. But he found it hard to articulate any of that, even in his own mind.

Andrej gave a curt shake of his head.

"We're bound for the north wall. You'll more than likely be running fresh arrows, replacement bows, and empty quivers to and fro."

Vlk nodded, keeping pace even as Andrej sped his steps. Had he thought it would be otherwise? They *were* children after all. Not for much longer, perhaps, but at thirteen? Though it pained him to admit it, yes. They *were* reckoned to be children. A year Vlk's senior, Pavel was close to the age where he'd be accounted full-grown, and even he was considered a boy. Of course they wouldn't be fighting. They would be…

"Vait, you said *I* vill likely be doing this. Vhat vill *you* be doing?"

Andrej tried a grim grin but couldn't hold it. He started to sigh through his nose, but his mouth opened before he'd finished. He stopped as they neared the first set of stairs onto the wall walk, licking his lips.

Vlk thought he suddenly looked very young.

"I'll be shooting," he said in a small voice. "I'll be shooting, and you and Pavel will be running arrows and supplies to us."

That made a certain amount of sense. Andrej was a hunter. Admittedly, at thirteen, he was only an apprentice, but if his apprenticeship was like most others, Vlk reckoned his friend had been training with the bow and bringing down game for several years now.

He gave Andrej a respectful nod, but he felt strange. A moment ago, he'd been so happy—proud of being called out to help in the defense. Proud of being called out of the stables to stand as a warrior. Now, looking at Andrej and seeing his naked fear…

But he'll fight anyvay. He vill, and I have to do vhat I can to help him.

"Vhere vill you stand, so I can be ready?"

Andrej managed a smile. The expression didn't reach his eyes, but it *was* a smile. He swallowed hard, then spoke in a voice that started out halting and ended with a species of his earlier authority behind it.

"Foll… Follow me."

-II-

Dereek khn
Yrxa Castle
5 Korunasykli: 22 Days after the Red Storm at Westsong

Methias looked at the couch with a species of longing but resisted the urge to collapse upon it. Most of the runes had been reactivated, leaving an eerie quiet in their wake. Still, the newly silenced chorus of shrieks, shouts, lamentations, and laughter had taken its toll.

Working the rites took only minutes, but... stone in sky. I could sleep for a week. My head feels fit to split, and every muscle is either sore or tingling. He resisted the urge to rub his temples. *Not being able to understand them— and it is a Them, I'm almost certain—makes it all worse, somehow. I keep searching... keep hoping to find something familiar... some way to under- stand what has them all so agitated. Meanwhile, their voices echo from both the weave work that animates them and the shape of the room. It makes a near-physical shroud of their... madness? Is it truly madness, or just a simple language barrier with the long shadow of a death rite to darken it?*

It wouldn't be long before he had his answer.

He'd deliberately left two of The Cage's panels un-silenced for the nonce. Of the six skulls held between them, only a pair appeared to have understood the Trade Tongue. The rest were so much buzzing noise he'd have to try and ignore.

Still, a scant handful of screaming skulls should be easier to blot out than two dozen. It could've been worse. At least the panels in question were side by side.

He took a breath, then stepped fully into that soundless field, allowing himself ... *a moment*. Next he knew, he was kneeling as if he'd intended to center himself. Had he meant to do that?

Perhaps my body knows what I need better than my waking mind. Hells—but he was tired.

He let a long and long-since pent-up sigh escape. It flew out of his open mouth like a flock of freed doves into a perfect wedding-day sky.

When it was done, he allowed his eyes to drift closed. A small, contented smile tried to stumble its way onto his face, to no avail.

He still felt as if he were treading water. Had he really thought it would be enough to release his many masks in that blissful, soundless place? It had helped, certainly, but not as much as he'd hoped.

Methias became aware that he'd loosed a bemused snort, but he couldn't hear it. The essential weirdness of magically enforced silence meant that at least *one* of his senses had finally calmed. His closed eyes soothed another. It wasn't *all too much,* per se.

But I can see too much *from here. I need to carve out a place in space and time—a waking moment to breathe and be, somehow.*

But stone in sky, there were so, so many other important matters pressing in on him. It wasn't *just* the impending war with the King of the Dead, but that occupied a sizable part of his worry. And why not?

I alone seem interested in, or willing to do, any form of research on, the topics of Jannon's jailer or his master's plans. The rest of the company's content to blithely assume that if it isn't a matter of simply hitting the old monster, his lieutenants, or his legions hard enough, some other solution will, as in all good cradle tales, simply present itself.

And so it fell to him to find that inevitably necessary solution.

And if I don't choose the right way to couch what needs to be done, Hamad will ignore or outright refuse my council. Not Hamad. No, it must be Lord... Lord Hamad. If I want to avoid waking his ire, he must be revered. Hells, I had to all but bribe him before he would consent to take the company north to Shesh.

The Diplomat—just one of the myriad faces Methias was forced to wear in pursuit of his duties. When others saw him, they saw someone upon whom they could and should rely. They saw someone who might know the answer to the all-important question of *what to do,* and that was about all. Most would never know, which was well enough. Even if they knew, most weren't likely to ever truly understand.

The social philosophers of Shesh professed that *a man truly was whatever raiment he wore at any particular hour.* If a man was dressed as a warrior, he was a warrior. How *good* a warrior he was... was an altogether different matter.

Methias was a caster. All else aside, casters were seen as either folk to be feared or people to be petitioned. Sage, strategist, diplomat, leader, or law-giver—a caster was dressed in the raiment needed in that moment by virtue of being, well, a caster. Outside of the Venzene Empire, those who worked the Weave were presumed to simply *know*. Often they *did* know, but more often they merely made their best guess and tried to put out the resultant fires as swiftly as they could. It was expected. It was necessary. It was exhausting.

There was such noise, mentally speaking. Outside of the King of the Dead, there was the threat of Thorion... the tragedy of Traead... the development of Dereek khn... The world wasn't *on fire*—at least not yet. But there were so many potential pitfalls. Havoc's Horn, it was an act of will just to turn away from the easy distraction of the alliterative phrase. *Potential pitfalls, Jannon's jailer, screaming skulls*—they all danced around in his head, echoing along his mind's ear, trying to bully their way onto his tongue.

He bowed his head, trying to slow the thunder of his pulse by will-power alone.

Quite unexpectedly, he found himself smiling again. That smile wasted no time before broadening into a grin—a child's grin, full of hope and mischief. An idea had struck him with such force that his eyes veritably flew open.

Why, in this moment, do I need to swim against the current?

All semblance of propriety melted away. It was a thing he doubted most would believe him capable of, but never mind. Kneeling there on the pale stone floor, he slouched, arms dangling at his sides. An instant later, he allowed his head to roll back, looking up past all skulls great and small until he was staring at the birdcage-like bends of the pilasters above. He drew in a deep, satisfying breath, and held it for a few heartbeats.

When he released it, it came out as an all-encompassing scream. The runes did their work, stopping the noise before it could reach any ear. He shook from the effort, loosing all fear and woe in a single, silent breath. When it ended, he refilled his lungs to repeat the exercise. All of his frustrations began to fall away, at least for the moment.

After a few of those undeniably cathartic screams, he genuinely felt better... lighter, somehow. Nothing had *actually* changed. The rational part of his mind knew that well enough. The weight he'd been bearing—at least with regards to the war with the King of the Dead—would reassert itself all too soon. *Too much* would eventually come into view once more. For now, he felt as ready as may be to contend with The Cage.

Lowering his head, Methias let his gaze drift over the unaffected panels. Their six bleached occupants appeared to be speaking or, perhaps, laughing. As he was still within the radius of the runes, he could hear nothing. Even so, each jaw pistoned open and closed, which he supposed was sign enough.

He stood, albeit slowly, and once more retrieved the piece of charcoal he'd used on the floor. Drawing a deep breath down past his navel, he exited the influence of the runes.

The noise struck him with a near physical force. Six voices swelled in what seemed to be a chaotic competition to prove which of them was the loudest. They varied in tone and range. Some were a middling growl, others a high and womanish weeping, but all were the voices of children or very young men.

He stepped to the very edge of the triangle he'd drawn earlier. Fixing his eyes upon the panel with the fewest occupants, he loosed his day's final abjuration.

"Puav ka zet ahg siiiiiing!" Once more, he held the not—eyes and ears focused forward.

(I will you to sing!)

One of the two skulls before him sang almost instantly, jaw wide. He stepped toward it, raising his empty dim hand, then looked to the other panel. He saw a second skull obeying his command. Both held their notes in high registers, though one of them had a scratched quality to it. That second skull was, almost predictably, at the farthest point away from the first panel. He would have to stretch. He had no wish to touch these poor, death-blighted things, but the safest course was clear.

I've seen them shift as if floating, as well as the movement of their jaws. Eyes on one, hand on the other—that should prevent me from losing track by either my idiocy or their guile.

He laid the fingers of his dim hand atop the singer nearest him, then reached to mark the other with his charcoal. All sounds stopped, save one. The skull beneath his left hand sang still—a high, clear, powerful note that hurt his heart to hear. *Yet there's no vibration in my hand. The sound is a projection, like a performer throwing his voice...*

None of the other skulls moved. They hadn't been silenced. They had *gone* silent.

He lifted his hand away. All five of the un-runed skulls began chattering and cackling once more. The lone remaining singer still held that note, matching Methias's own sustained song. He replaced his hand atop the small bone once more. Again, all other skulls ceased their chatter and their mad animation.

Methias felt himself running out of breath. He fixed his eyes upon the skull beneath his hand and allowed the note he'd been holding to fall away.

At first, there was silence. It stretched out for several heartbeats. Then he felt the skull twitch beneath his fingertips, followed by the soft sound of a sobbing child.

Fear, loneliness, hopelessness... but no fever-mad sense of disconnected rage. Of all that I'd prepared myself for, this... This had never crossed his mind.

Death rites dealt in malevolence. A soul so called, made to reawaken as its former self, was twisted. It no longer had breath to bind it to Skolf, yet it remained to torment the living, leaving misery in its wake. It was like a fish forced from the water, but unable to die and move on to whatever came next.

A fish hauled from the water, or a bird in a ... cage. Is ... that what you did here, Singer? Is this place nothing more than your prison?

He was thinking of the once-elf who had occupied these lands before he came. The folk of the region had named her *the Shivering Song.* His hand had put an end to her and all that she'd known. And now there was this curs-ed cage, and the invisible tears of a dead child held in deathless bondage.

The sobs had grown louder; the skull shaking beneath his hand from their force.

How can I...

How could he help the poor creature? That was absurd. Wasn't it?

Why is it absurd?

Because he or she—hard to tell which by the pitch of the voice—is dead? That was reason enough, surely. After all, what of his oath... his robe and office?

Pity the deathless dead but end them just the same. Spare them their misery and spare the world their torment. He was meant to excise them, not offer them succor... or comfort.

All once-men or once-women are a threat, no matter their stature. Surely that's even true of a once-child...

The sobs continued, albeit softly. He could feel the skull shudder and move beneath his dim hand.

No. He shook his head. *Living or dead, he or she is still a child, as near as I can tell, and has already been robbed of whatever was meant to be ... next.*

Alright, fair, but even if it were right for him to lend his aid, what could he do? *Beyond finding a way to destroy this vile thing—this damnable cage—what other help is there for me to give?*

He slid his dim hand along the skull to rest along its right side, caressing its cheekbone with his thumb. He expected to have to check his revulsion, but no such sensation came.

The skull seemed to tip its face up toward him, floating there in the liquid shadow.

"Do you hear me?" He kept his voice low and soft.

It bobbed up and down. *Was that a nod?*

"Do you ... understand my speech?"

Again, it seemed to nod. Still, there was the sound of sobbing, but it was softening.

"Can you say something to me?"

"I..." More sobs. The misery driving them seemed to be growing. "I..."

It was no good. Whoever was tethered in this small skull was overwhelmed... was a breath away from drowning.

"Shhh." Methias groped for something more to say—something that might be of at least *some* use to the sadful creature. What came to him was that early memory of his own overwhelmed misery and Emil's visit to his bedside. He smiled, spent a moment to make a few minor changes for context, and spoke anew.

"You've spent too long amidst the noise and rage of this dark-some cage. I'll teach you a thing to help you find a moment to rest."

The sobs softened once more. Methias could almost *see* the hopeful look on the child's face... or at least he fancied he could.

"Hear me, now. You're drifting... drifting... drifting... drift. Drift 'neath all skies as wind through the grass sighs, and the pines sing songs of twi-light-ing. Where shadows shape dreams from waking mind's schemes, and we ... call the foes we are fighting. Clem-ent, this trip from a humble boat slip, where the dreaming waves wash clean the day. Cradle and bower hid from star showers, where no endless eye's ire can yet stay."

He repeated the words twice more. By the time he'd started his third recitation, the soft, tired voice of a child joined with his own. He thought the final words had been delivered through a relieved smile, based on tone. With no flesh to commend to it, however, the face could betray no such sight.

Still, there's hope. For now, that's a start.

-III-

Venzene Duchy of Kovalun
County Jižní Pochod
Barony of Hartscross–The Ash March

"Rákos, can you shoot from horseback?"

Kastan had taken them to within sight of the open space that marked the edge of the Ash March. She'd seen no new enemies, but could hear the occasional murmur of voices or whicker of horses greeting one another nearby. There would be a fast flight across low, rolling fields before they could get to the northern gate. *This* would be the dangerous part.

The? This will be the first dangerous part, but hardly the last. That army doesn't mean to pass on by, nor stop for a moot and a feast.

"Ne, Lady. I can fire fast enough from a still mount, but I von't be much good vhile ve ride, I fear. I *stride* far better than I ride." He tried to add a laugh to the end of this, but it came out strained, ending in a cough. Rákos stifled that cough as quickly as he could, burying his face in Kastan's back. "Forgive me, Lady."

Once his coughing fit had subsided, Kastan nodded to herself. "It's fine. Hold tight to me, and never mind propriety. I don't want to have to explain to Andrej why you fell and were left somewhere outside the walls."

"Y-yes Lady."

She thought she could almost *hear* the blush in his voice.

With a quick glance around, she made to move Jafyl forward but checked him almost immediately. She heard voices. They were close, but she couldn't determine exactly where their owners were. One voice rose above the rest—a woman—singing staves that rang high and altogether too clear.

And darksome, in some way I can't quite qualify. It sounded as if she were performing in an amphitheater. Whoever she was, something about her song made Kastan's flesh crawl.

"Sdraliana kr ka. Rhexrryn xro, rhexrryn xro, rhexrryn xro. Inagro dak. Grir, cor, grir xro. Taul misda ka rryl lluil. Taul misda ka thoriash xro."

Jafyl's ears were flat back against his head. She could feel him shaking—see the sweat breaking out along his neck.

"Ve must go!" Rákos voice was full of a tight-throated terror. "Ve must go now! If the lady's eye falls upon us, ve vill belong to her!"

Kastan resisted the fear that tried to infect her as well. It took its toll, turning her own heartbeat into a throbbing war drum at her temples, but she forced herself to be still.

"Tell me what you know. Do it now and do it swiftly. Who is she?"

"Lady, I—" His breath hitched. She saw his shadow shake its head on the ground beside them.

"*Now,* Rákos."

He started at the coldness in her voice. For a moment, he seemed incapable of answering. Finally, however, he let his breath out in a ragged sigh full of fear.

"I only know vhat I saw, Lady—vhat I heard. Every one of them— from the lowest lad to the lords of var in their mail—they looked to her. Her vill is their vill. She vas their mistress... their empress. She vielded a svord, and seemed alvays to be caught in a vind, even vhen the trees vere still."

Kastan ignored this last. It was clear that the hunter meant every word, but she knew how easily fear could make a miracle of the mundane.

"What did she look like?"

"She vore a fine gown. Her hair vas long, dark blonde or brown, and whipped about her like a virlvind."

Kastan stiffened. "The Fox Queen... The Fox Queen comes *north*?"

"If... if that ess her name, Lady."

Turning in the saddle so she could look over her shoulder, Kastan sought his eyes. "You said she wore a fine gown? Was it red, Rákos? Was it red, trimmed in crimson fur?"

"Ne, Lady. She vore a shade of blue."

"And her cloak or cape?"

"She vore none, Lady."

A sigh of obvious relief escaped her in a rush.

"Not her, then. It's said that the Fox Queen is only ever seen in red... in crimson."

"She must be a southern tale." Rákos sounded distant, speaking as if he were half-dreaming.

"True enough. Her word fame comes from Havalun—Zuzana Revedronningen, the Fox Queen." Kastan laid a hand on Jafyl's neck to keep him calm. She needn't have bothered—his ears were perked forward, and he stomped his foot for good measure. He wasn't nervous, she realized. He was excited. "It's said she commands a legion of displaced commoners, offering them aid and succor in her forest halls as she counts up the misdeeds of the landed gentry. If a noble house should ever grow too cruel, she will loose her legion to scourge that noble's line from Skolf, itself. She supposedly steals taxes, tribute, and even children if the family's offenses are great enough."

"Ess she a fae creature, then?"

Kastan shrugged. "She may be. I've heard at least a few tales that claim she rides either a ghostly steed or in a coach like the one in the tale of the Dead Singer."

"But she only vears red?"

"Aye." Kastan slipped into the old byword without even realizing it.

They listened as a chorus of voices chanted in time with the singer's refrain. After a moment where both of them shuddered, Rákos spoke again.

"Then this ess some other voman. Blue, as I say. I don't know the vords she sings, but they make my hair stand on end."

Kastan felt the same fear, but refused to give voice to it. Instead, she stroked Jafyl's silky neck and made ready to ride.

"Hold tight. I mean to fly as fast as Jafyl can carry us."

She waited just long enough to feel his arms tighten about her midriff, then spurred forward. A moment later and they were beyond the cover of the ash trees, Jafyl's hooves thundering toward the palisade's northern gate.

"Riders!" Rákos's voice was high and thin.

"How many?"

She felt him move behind her—presumably trying to look back without losing his balance.

"Six? Eight! Hells, eight!"

"Do I have to tell you not to foul me as I fight?"

In answer, she felt him lay his head against her back.

Good enough.

Praying that Jafyl wouldn't spook at a critical moment, Kastan reached back and drew her newly acquired sword.

-IV-

Dereek khn
Yrxa Castle
5 Korunasykli: 22 Days after the Red Storm at Westsong

Methias seated himself on the cool stone floor, the small skull drifting down with him. Its base still touched the pool of standing shadow from which it had first emerged. The rest of it lay on its side atop his left thigh. His sense was that the child bound up in the skull was still fearful—still attempting to find his or her equilibrium.

Well, I've plenty of time for that. No fear. If the proverbial hourglass empties, we'll just turn it over.

Apparently, contact with his thigh was enough to keep the other skulls at bay, at least for the moment. The room had remained silent for perhaps ten minutes.

He'd kept his hand resting along the skull's ancient crown and its left cheek. Quite suddenly he realized that at some point he'd begun stroking its surface... *In much the same way one might soothe any child, I suppose.* When had he started doing that?

"Where are..." the skull paused, as if reconsidering whether to ask or not.

The sound almost made Methias jump. In truth, he, himself, had been trying to work out how, or even *when,* to start the conversation they needed to have.

Patience paves the path once more. It had been a favorite phrase of his master, Emil's. *It'd become one of Jannon's favorites, too, once he'd heard me say it.* He pushed that memory gently aside.

"Where are...?" he prompted, trying not to push. He was rewarded with a tired chuckle—brief and half-hearted.

"Where ... did you come from?"

Methias looked down, meaning to smile. The sight of the small skull threatened to change that smile into a glower born of sadness and rage. That wouldn't do. The reaction might have been *caused* by the sight of the small skull, but it was *directed* at the thrice curs-ed Shimmering Song. *This child won't know that, though. So... masks on.* He closed his eyes and worked to collect his thoughts before answering.

"Where was I born, do you mean? Where was I raised?"

"Mmhmm."

"My youth was in Traead. It's a strange place but full of good people with generous hearts."

"Strange how?"

"They're very pious. Do you know that word?"

"Yes, Lord."

"Methias." He saw no need to force formality on the ... girl? Boy? He still couldn't be sure.

"Meth-*eye*-ussssss..." It sounded like the word had something of an alien taste to it, though apparently not a sour one.

"So they call me. Either it's my name, or it's an old word that means something foolish or slow. Everyone's been shouting it at me since I was small."

This elicited a more genuine giggle.

"What do I call you?"

A long period of silence met this question.

"Haven't fallen asleep on me, have you?"

"No..."

Methias waited a bit longer, but when nothing further seemed forthcoming, he spoke again.

"It wasn't a trick question, but I suppose you don't have to answer it honestly. You can make something up... if it pleases you. Either that or *I* shall have to. I suppose I can call you radish girl or horse boy if you like."

Another giggle. "I like horse boy, but if you use it too much, it'll make me sad."

"Oh?"

"I can't ride anymore. I *love* riding horses."

He, apparently. He seemed more frustrated than sad, which Methias took for a good enough sign for now.

"Do you have a better suggestion?"

"I don't know."

"Well," Methias made his voice playful, "you can't be Meth-*eye*-usss. That'll just be confusing."

Another giggle.

"My sister Nían used to call me Sleara."

"Well, Sleara," he risked being wrong, "*brother* of Nían, we're as well met as may be."

"We are, I think." Sleara's voice sounded unsure, but hopeful.

"So, you know—"

"...The word pious? Yes. It's a human word. It means worshipful or devoted... something like that."

Methias arched his brows. *A human word?*

"That's as good a definition as I could've offered." He kept his voice light. "I confess I've never heard the name Sleara, nor Nían."

"I've never heard the name Methias, either." Was that cheek ... or honesty?

"Well, the folk of Traead are pious, as I say. They spend a good deal of time each week in prayer, and pay honor and homage to Dannus, Hyrro, and Zarec—their three patrons."

"That isn't strange. Foolish, maybe, but not strange."

What an absurdly dismissive tone. "...Foolish?"

"Never mind. It doesn't matter."

"As you say."

After a long pause, Sleara spoke up again. He sounded genuine enough, but there was a strangely knowing tone underpinning his words.

"I *am* sorry, Methias. I didn't—I don't mean to insult you."

"And so you haven't."

"I don't mean to insult your *people,* either." And still, there was that underpinning of ... awareness? No, though it was close to that.

Well, there'll be time enough to solve that particular mystery.

Methias allowed a small chuckle to pass his lips. "And again, you haven't. I said I spent my *youth* in Traead."

"You ... were born elsewhere?"

"I was. My first memories are on an island far from here."

Sleara brightened. "I was born on an island, too. Rímhril."

Methias frowned, thinking. He knew that word, but he'd no idea why.

"What was *yours* like?" Sleara pressed him. His voice was bright and engaged ... and quick. "Was it warm? Cold? Green? Were there many people?" A pause. "Were there many horses?"

Methias laughed. "It was, and still is, both green and grey." He felt a soft smile settle onto his face as he pictured his long home. "The weather is almost always mild—the winds warmed and welcoming by the time they reach the great city. And the city? Ohhh Sleara... *that* place is a waking dream. Towers climb high into the sky, connected by broad bridges near their crowns. Those bridges cross over, under, and through one another, so that from the ground they form intricate patterns against the firmament. The air is sweet and clean, the rains gentle, and the song of the streets by sun or star is full of vigor and wonder..." He could almost see it—almost touch it. "In that place, the mind matters so, so much more than the miser's muse."

He trailed off, uncertain how to finish or even how best to contend with his suddenly roiling emotions. Thoughts of home meant thoughts of *her*... of Nybrynci. And Brynci? Her name... the memory of her face? Her voice? They were bright brands of pain that never truly faded.

"That sounds like Now... Nowwwwsh..."

"Nausha." Methias's voice was raw, suddenly. "Nausha is its name." He swallowed, leaning his head back—willing his eyes not to overspill. The attempt failed, predictably, and he drew his free bright hand up to drive his tears away. He wasn't sobbing, but even a year later, the ache was still fresh.

"You miss it." This wasn't a question, but was spoken with a gentleness that was hard to hear.

"I'm fortunate to have known it for as long as I did. Nothing's meant to last forever, of course. So we take our joy where we can find it."

Sleara seemed to dwell on that idea for a moment. His voice was soft when he next spoke—almost hesitant.

"I've been there... to your island. It was hard to walk *any*-where."

Methias laughed in spite of himself. "Kept looking up, did you?"

"Yes! Up, around, down—anywhere and everywhere. My mother threatened to tether me to her wrist if I didn't mind my surroundings."

"You'd have been in good company, Sleara. Even apprentices have to be tethered for the first week or so, unless they were born on the island."

"So you're a caster from Now Shou."

"Nausha. Now-*shah*."

Sleara repeated the pronunciation twice more before getting it right.

"But you *are*, yes? A caster from Nausha?"

"I am." Methias was grinning. The boy's enthusiasm was making it difficult to hold on to misery. "Why?"

"Can... can you free me?"

"Do you want pudding or porridge?"

"I ... can't eat, Methias." Sleara's voice wasn't pitiful. It was almost *pitying*. He sounded as if he were speaking to a much younger and clearly slow-witted child.

Methias laughed, though the laughter was kindly.

"Well? I *can't!*" This was carried on an almost reluctant giggle.

"Porridge isn't something most folk look forward to eating, is it?"

"No. No it is *not.*" Sleara paused, then spoke more slowly. "But it keeps you for the morning's chores. Pudding, though, makes even angry folk smile. I see. May I ... have both?"

Methias nodded. "Exactly. So? First?"

"*Pudding* of course."

"Naturally." He sniggered. "I *expect* so. There's almost always a way."

Sleara's next words came out on what sounded like a smiling sigh.

"Alright. Is it the porridge that you don't know how, or how long it'll take, then?"

"It is. I can't tell you more than that, sadly. There's still so much about The Cage I don't know. Hells, I didn't know how to stop the lot of you from screaming as if the place were on fire."

"Oh! Is that why you were singing?"

Methias smiled. "It was why *you* were singing. I had to find at least some way to interact."

"So you chose singing?"

"The rite only works on people who understand the caster. Most of the others trapped here don't speak the Trader's Tongue. Just you and one other. All anyone could hear was a mass of laughing, screaming, shouting voices. We had no idea what any of you were saying or why you were saying it so loudly. Come to that, I *still* don't know."

Sleara made a soft sound of understanding. "Most of us are just mad, I think. When one starts shouting, others do too. Some of us have been here since before I was born."

"How do you know *that*?"

Again he made a considering sound. "If I try, I can hear them. It's hard to single one voice out, though. But Lósgífel? She rarely spoke to more than one of us at a time. I wonder if that's why she sang so often..."

"Who is Lósgífel?"

"She called herself my *nimtrémna.*"

"I don't know that word."

"Mother's sister. I know the Trader's Tongue has a word for that, but—"

Methias made a soft *ahh* sound and smiled. "Aunt. She was your aunt?"

"She called herself that, but my ñimá had no sisters."

Ñimá... Ahhh! So, you're an elf-child. Well, that solves that particular riddle.

"Was it she who trapped you here?"

"I don't know. I *think* so." Sleara's voice became distant, tinged with regret. "She was the first outline I saw when I woke up here."

"Outline?"

"It's like looking up at someone with the sun directly behind them."

"As if I needed another reason to set you free." He sighed. "Well, at least I know the old singer's name now."

"Is she … coming back?"

"No."

"Did *you* kill her?"

"She was already dead, Sleara. She just hadn't stopped walking or singing yet. But yes. I put an end to her. She left me little choice." His voice had become bleak, but it was steady enough.

After a moment, Sleara spoke up again.

"I can tell you what I remember, if that'll help." His voice was cautious but hopeful. "I *know* that I can help you understand what the others are saying. I just … don't want you to grow too used to us here. I know we can be of use, but…"

"But you don't want to be here any longer than you must."

"I want to join the rest of me. It feels like I'm wearing a thick blanket against the cold—one that's too tight for me to move in. It doesn't hurt, but I need to either move or finally sleep." He paused, considering, then spoke a final word on the matter. "I'll help you, Methias, but … I know I can't hold you to any oath, but…"

"Peace, Sleara, Nían's brother. I give you my word that I'll do everything in my power to free you and the others. I'd be glad of your help, but one way or the other, I intend to free you from this damnable cage."

A moment of silence stretched out before Sleara spoke again. "Stand up, Methias. I'll tell you what I remember."

-V-

Barony of Hartscross–Jižní Lov
5 Korunasykli: 22 Days after the Red Storm at Westsong

Vlk let Andrej lead him to the western side of the gate, then up onto the wall walk. Spare gear had already been placed on the camp's side of the barbican. He stepped over to it and took visual stock, and made a mental note of where everything had been laid out. The strange shape of Andrej's horned bow was hard to miss. It seemed to be strung in a way that made it shorter than necessary. The yew wood, horn, and sinew beyond the string's attachment points curved forward as if pointing toward the enemy. Other than the bow, there were a trio of full quivers and a literal bucket full of additional arrows.

Andrej spoke from beside him.

"I'll take one quiver on my back. A second will sit on the ground against the wall on my bright side."

"Vhat about the third?"

"I'll pull from the quiver on the ground first. When it empties, I'll call you. You'll swap it for a full one, then refill the empty from the bucket. While you're doing that, I'll pull arrows from my back. Do you see?"

"Jo. You'll never be out vhile I refill for you."

Andrej was nodding. "To jo." He might have said more, but something caught his breath.

Vlk picked up a quiver and walked the few feet to his friend's side. The wall of the palisade came up to his breastbone here, giving him a fine view of the northern pasture. What he saw made him smile at first. Horses were running toward the gate, pursued by a dark stain of movement along the early winter's grass.

"Scouts...? Coming ahead of a larger group?"

Andrej stared out at them, saying nothing.

"Of a sort. They're outriders. They just aren't *ours*." This was a new voice—older, but light-hearted.

Vlk turned to see a slender man wearing the black kontusz of the

Bluemark guard. The newcomer was only slightly taller than Andrej and looked to be just this side of old. Aged or not, he was certainly arrayed for battle. He bore two quivers—one on his back, the other on his right hip—and a hunting sword like the ones Lakkrid's father and uncles wore.

The man pulled a crossbow from his dim side—the side furthest from Vlk—and pointed it at the floor between his feet. Vlk could see what looked like a steel stirrup attached to the weapon's front. He had just enough time to wonder what in all the hells *that* was for when the answer became self-evident. The new arrival bowed forward and slid his bright-foot into the stirrup, pressing it to the floor. He then used that new leverage to pull the string into the ready position. All the while, the archer's face was turned northward, looking over the wall in the direction of the enemy.

"Shift right." His voice was too conversational to make his words a strict command. When Andrej had dutifully obliged, the man set his feet, took barely a breath to aim, and...

Twang!

Vlk hadn't seen any movement on the man's part. He hadn't even seen him draw or fit a bolt into position. One had certainly flown free, though it hit nothing but the grass some distance away.

"Kara? Tobias? Pass the range along."

Looking past the man, Vlk saw perhaps two score or more Bluemark archers off to the west. There seemed to be a mix of long and short bows, and a surprising number of crossbows.

"Eyes, sergeant," said a woman. "Eyes." Then she turned and began speaking to her fellows, pointing to where the man's bolt stuck out of the grass.

"Who're you, then?"

"Andrej. I'm a hunter. This is Vlk. He'll be keeping my bow fed."

"Waltyr Wachfeld. It's good to know who I'll be shooting with." He paused as he re-readied his weapon. "Tell me, Andrej the hunter, have you ever seen a man die?" His voice was still easy. It made the question seem more avuncular than patronizing.

Vlk cut in. "Ve both have." He knew he sounded angry, which suited him fine. He *was* angry. It was fine for the Bluemark to die in service to the Count and his people. They were sellswords, after all. Sellswords were paid to die so that a land's people didn't have to, or so he'd been taught. Vlk had first thought that idea noble—perhaps even romantic. Now, however, when he thought of mercenaries, he thought only about that day in the play yard... of terrified Maksu... of his certainty that Lakkrid—who had been his friend for as long as he could recall—was about to die at the hands of several grown men dressed in black kontusze. "Ve've seen *your* men die."

Andrej stiffened but nodded his head.

The Bluemark sergeant—Waltyr, apparently—nodded slowly. He never cut his eyes away from the oncoming enemy, though they were still far off. "You were with the other children that day. Well, I suppose that makes sense."

"Ve vere the *men* who stood between *your* men and a small gnoerk child." Vlk's anger was hot and sour in his belly. It was pushing him to act, or at least to try to get this Waltyr fellow to *re*-act. He looked for some sign of the crossbowman heating up in turn, but his face remained calm and guileless.

"That's good. They weren't strictly *my* men, but they were Bluemark at the time." There was that same, easy, matter-of-fact tone.

Good? Vhat's good? That ve saw men die? Afraid ve vould shit ourselves at the first sight of blood?

"I'd heard it was only an orc boy and orc man against them," Waltyr continued. "I'm pleased to learn they weren't alone."

Vlk blinked. He was about to say something else, though he didn't know precisely what. He only knew that he wanted to force this man to show his true face. Before he could, however, the man addressed Andrej.

"That's a fine-looking bow. You'll be anxious to use it, but I'd like you to hold off for a bit."

Vlk drew in a breath to argue on Andrej's behalf, but the blond boy gainsaid him with a look.

Andrej pointed his bright hand toward the horsemen. That same group were converging as they picked up speed, pulling even further ahead of their fellows. "I could *almost* hit them from here. In another few moments, they'll all be in range."

Waltyr nodded. "I know. But a bow (even a northern Sheshik bow like that) is more tiring—more demanding on the archer's body. That means the longer and more swiftly you have to shoot, the tougher it is to hit as cleanly or with as much power. We need every shot to be as strong and on-target as the first. So, I want you to wait until the enemy crosses past the bolt I shot. That's about five hundred strides from the gate. Will you do that?"

Vlk was *certain* there had been some sort of insult wrapped in *Sergeant*

Waltyr's words. He was equally certain that the man had tried to give orders to Andrej, and Andrej didn't answer to sellswords. Frustratingly, he could *find* no insult, nor could he think of any actual orders Waltyr had given.

Come to that, who *did* Andrej count as his captain? *As our captain, not just Andrej's. I'm vith him, stood ready for the battle.*

His face fell. *...Vithout a veapon. I have no bow, vich is fine. I'm no archer. But I have no svord and no shield.*

"I can do that," said Andrej. "It'll make everything easier. I can aim for riders at that range."

"Vhat else vould you be aiming at?" There was no sarcasm in Vlk's voice, only confusion. *It's like saying "I'll put the food in my mouth." How else vould you eat it?*

Andrej delivered his answer in a calm but very small voice.

"Their horses, Vlk. If you want to stop a rider, you aim for his mount."

Waltyr actually turned his head to regard Andrej, though only for a beat. "Where did you learn that?"

To jo. Vhere? Vlk did his best to keep his thoughts from storming their way onto his face.

"*Learned* it at Rafe's Rest and from the men of Rosefort's garrison. *Saw* it during a raid at Měsíční Prst."

Waltyr nodded—two slow dips of his chin. "Well, you're certainly right. That's it exactly. Bigger target, easier to hit, no way for the horse to block the arrow. The rider either sees and turns his mount to dodge— maybe catches the arrow with a shield—or the horse goes down in a tangle of limbs."

Vlk looked at his friend with a newfound combination of awe, respect, and jealousy. He thought he *might* know Měsíční Prst, but *every* boy knew Rafe's Rest and Rosefort. Each had been the site of a pivotal victory for Count Edmund in the last war. While Andrej was certainly too young to remember those battles firsthand, the fact that he'd been to both places and, apparently, learned from the soldiers stationed there...

Vell, that explains vhy he's so hard to vin against. The Count's men here vant little enough to do vith us most days. If the fighting men of those places really spent time vith him, it's probably vhere he learned to fight ... and even vhere he learned to play cards.

"What in hells?"

Waltyr's voice snapped Vlk back to the moment at hand. Looking up, he marked the progress of the riders.

The bulk of the enemy force looked like the creeping shadow of a summer storm front on the pale grass. Perhaps a dozen harriers had ridden ahead of that force when last he'd looked. Now that number had swelled to nearly a score. Moments ago, Vlk had thought these latter were Count Edmund's scouts returning to the encampment. He'd been mistaken, according to Waltyr, though how he could've determined that, Vlk had no idea. Whoever they were, they were coming on like hell's own harbingers *...but they're almost half a league avay. Vhat is he—*

Then he saw it. Not only had the number of outriders grown larger, but there was another oddity. The foremost rider was moving in tight angles—first west, then sharply back to the east. As he watched, the rider stopped, and Vlk caught a flash as the sun reflected on some distant steel the rider either wore or held. An instant later, that same rider broke east, pulling away from the rest of his fellows, looped back south until he'd ridden past their last drogue rider, and finally cut back to the west. A lone lump lay atop the ground in his wake—surely a rider who'd been unhorsed.

"To jo," Vlk managed. "Vhat in hells..."

-VI-

"Rákos?" Kastan leaned forward over Jafyl's neck as they turned westward. "Hold tight! One death isn't likely to slow them down. Not unless it's mine. Things are going to get jouncy!"

He didn't respond verbally, but she felt his arms tighten about her midriff. That would have to do, at least for the moment. Time was short.

A few stragglers had joined in their pursuit. They were almost surely scouts. *That, or a picket force on patrol that thinks it smells blood, if the woman leading them was savvy enough to set pickets at all. As for smelling blood...*

She dismissed that thought as forcefully as she could. That kind of thinking led to fear, which, in turn, led to panic. She would *not* give into panic. Not this close to the relative safety of Jižní Lov, and not with Rákos's life in the balance.

She allowed Jafyl to set his own pace, so long as it was swift enough

to keep them moving. All battle was about movement, be it a combatant's own movement, or her ability to arrest her foe's. That was about four times as important when one was on horseback in an open field.

The stallion's nerve had held up better than she'd expected. At first, she thought he'd been reacting out of pure terror, but after that engagement, she wasn't so sure.

As they rode westward, Kastan's eye fell upon their combined shadow. She saw Rákos's slight form huddled against her back and had a moment to be grateful. If Rákos weren't so slight of frame, Jafyl wouldn't be able to maintain his speed and agility. *And we'd be dead.*

She caught the silhouette of his bow and half-empty quiver bouncing against his back, and came to a miserable realization... one she banished as swiftly as she could.

His gear is far more useful to me than he is.

True, if she had a bow—if she had enough arrows—she'd make quick work of their pursuers. She did not, and Rákos had no experience firing from a moving horse. He'd said as much. No, speed and swordcraft were the only play that offered any hope of success.

And hope doesn't hunt for you.

She'd nearly reached the halfway point along the jagged scar that was the enemy's line. It would have to be more wolf-pack tactics, unless and until she saw an opening.

Kastan held the reins as loose as she could and drew them back toward her belly. She had chosen this saddle for a comfortable afternoon ride, not a proper fight. Its stirrups were too wide and clunky for combat, and its meager horn was barely more than a decorative bone ridge.

Well, here's hoping it'll do for an improper fight. It's held up well enough so far. While she hadn't gotten them to safety yet, she could see the palisade's northern gate clearly, which was something.

There just happens to be a band of foemen in the way.

She jammed the end of the reins between Rákos's hands and her body. "Don't steer, just don't let them fall."

He didn't respond. The reins held fast. It would have to do.

She guided Jafyl with her legs, angling him at a diagonal toward the vague direction of northwest. Most of their harriers had tried to follow her, turning left in a wide circle. Their blood was up. Two of them, however, had begun turning to the right—westward, trying to cut her off.

Perfect...

She maneuvered straight toward them, keeping her sword down

along her bright side and out of their direct line of sight for the moment. They seemed surprised but delighted, spurring toward her with shouts that made an eerie harmony. She grinned, first adding a bit more pressure with her right leg, then pressing in with her heels.

Jafyl's ears perked so far forward that his shadow appeared to have sprouted a horn. He sped up and altered his angle as she'd directed, aiming just to the left of the closest rider—a man holding an ancient-looking morning star in one hand.

Just before her charge reached the point of no return, she altered her leg pressure. In response, Jafyl turned, bringing himself directly alongside the other horse.

The morning star rose high over the foeman's shoulder. At that instant, Kastan brought her sword up in both hands, throwing an angled hammer shot. The blow arced under his raised arms, down into his ribcage. His horse kept running, but the force of her blow sent its rider flying backward out of the saddle, trailing a thin wave of scarlet. The horseman gave a shocked scream, but the sound cut off as he struck the ground.

Another... Hells haul me home, but I want another!

She didn't have long to wait. The second rider—a woman wearing what looked like a buck's head leather helmet, horns and all—had ridden past her and was now racing back toward her on her right. She marked the harrier's progress, letting Jafyl set his own pace once more.

Her attacker was gaining, starting to howl, raising what looked like a woodcutter's axe as she hurtled on. Kastan reached her bright hand down and hauled back on the reins. Jafyl trumpeted his displeasure, but skidded to a stop amidst a cloud of the year's last grass and clods of dry soil.

The woman gave a high, ragged cry of victory. She began slamming her heels into her horse's flanks as if they were on fire and she was desperate to put them out.

Kastan drew in a breath, tightening both hands on the sword's hilt even as she inverted her grip. Once more, she gauged her foe's momentum, waiting until the rider could no longer turn aside. Pivoting her upper body, she slammed the blade backward—point first—along her right side.

Momentum did the rest. The harrier's own speed impaled her with nearly enough force to drive both women from their mounts. Kastan straightened her legs as if attempting to stand in the saddle. She had a moment to be grateful for the oversized stirrups she'd lamented moments back up the hourglass. Then she registered the searing pain rippling along the muscles of her arms and upper body.

Newly riderless, the harrier's horse screamed and snapped, but raced away in obvious terror. The weight of the corpse dragged her sword Skolfward with such force that she nearly lost it. She managed to keep hold, but the effort did nothing to silence the dull throbbing along her arms.

The body hit the grass with a sickening crack, the buck's-head helmet coming partially free. It revealed the sun-kissed face of a girl no older than sixteen.

Definitely Eodenth. Three isn't proof, but if they're all Eodenth, this cannot be Harn's doing.

She drew in a sharp breath, licked her lips, and spurred Jafyl into action once more. There would be time enough to process this discovery when there were fewer folk trying to kill her. For now, she forced herself to focus on the matter at hand.

The rest of the outriders, or scouts, or whatever they called themselves, had completed their wide wheel and were now sweeping toward her, screaming. Kastan glanced southward. She *might* make the palisade if there were archers at the ready along the wall walk.

And if any of them recognize me and open the gate, rather than trying to fill me with pins. I have to stay ahead of the riders if there's any hope of the guards letting us through. They might well deny us. Letting foemen inside the walls just to save we two, after all...

She pulled the reins free from the hunter's death grip. Turning Jafyl south toward Jižní Lov, she urged him onward, beginning to pick up speed.

Grinning a bitter grin, she called back over her shoulder.

"Hold tight, Rákos. *If* is a long word."

OF WRAITHS AND LIVING SWORDS

-I-

Venzene Duchy of Kovalun
County Jižní Pochod
Barony of Hartscross–Jižní Lov
5 Korunasykli: 22 Days after the Red Storm at Westsong

Vlk found it hard to turn his eyes away from the battlefield below. That lone horseman had, by the looks of things, taken out some three or four of the riders harrying him. While Vlk knew enough of swordplay to respect the man's prowess, what *really* impressed him was the horsemanship the rider had so clearly displayed.

Svords take enough practice to vield vell on foot, nevermind from horse-back. A rider has to learn to control his mount vith his legs if he means to fight from the saddle. Whoever that man is, vith skill like that, he must've been called to the line. If not, and if he lives to make it through the gate, someone vill tell the count vhat he's done, von't they? He grinned, feeling a mixture of hope and fleeting triumph. *I may finally get to vitness a knighting ceremony!*

A voice called out from somewhere behind and below him, putting an end to his wool-gathering. He couldn't place a name or face to it, but it scratched at the door of his memory.

"Excellency?"

Vlk turned, trying to find the owner of that somehow familiar voice. Instead—as if his thought had summoned the man—his eyes fell upon the Count.

The mountain that was Edmund had, for some reason, stopped a few strides away on the stair to Vlk's left. This put him several steps shy of the wall walk. He looked as if he'd been standing there for some time.

The choice of perch made for a surreal situation. Vlk and the Count stood at eye level with one another... and Edmund was looking his way. For a moment, he thought the count was staring at, or perhaps through, him specifically. The man's eyes were red, dry things, the knuckles of his dim hand white upon the pommel of his sword. He was murmuring something, but Vlk couldn't quite make it out.

For a few heartbeats, he could only meet the tall man's stare. Gradually, though, he reconsidered his earlier assessment. The count wasn't looking directly at him. The realization did little to ease his nerves.

Vhy is he looking at Andrej? Vhy is he looking at Andrej, and vy does he seem either vrathful or voeful?

The wind rose, whistling across the palisade's pointed top. As the gust died away, Vlk caught the tag end of the Count's soft speech. It sounded low, bitter, and yes—full of woe.

"...Where sweetness ceased at ashes' end ... to feed the greed of honored men. The place where peace was shattered first. They raze-ed fair Měsíční Prst..."

"Excellency?" After the sound of hardened boot soles tromping up nearby stairs, the voice had grown closer. "Excellency, I have everything set, at least until the order comes."

A hand came up to rest on Edmund's shoulder. The touch seemed to banish whatever was clouding his face, for he turned away to look out over the palisade wall some feet beyond him.

"We shall see who blinks first, Captain. Has Ruční Kopí returned?"

"He sent a runner with an order I don't much care for, but my men followed it."

Ahh. He could finally see who that voice belonged to. *Jastrab, the captain of the Bluemark.*

"What order?"

The sudden sound of rapid hoofbeats yanked Vlk's head around. He saw half a dozen horsemen in Percoy livery charging from beneath the shadow of the palisade, toward the enemy. They each bore drawn weapons—slender-looking swords or light maces of bright steel, fair enough weapons for the task at hand. They also wore a strangeness he'd never seen strapped to their dim arms. Each one had a round shield, sized for a child Jitka's age.

"*That* order," said Jastrab. For all his talk of dislike, his tone sounded more amused than displeased. "Your Ruční Kopí said we were to let them out, and *they* were to hope they could get back in through the northern gate."

Vlk had little enough time to wonder at either Jastrab's tone or that strange gear of war. The sound of raised voices further down the line of archers drew his attention away. The battle had shifted once more.

A blur of white raced from east to west across the field, hurtling toward the enemy line's flank. It took a moment for Vlk to realize what he was seeing. Even once he'd managed it, he found himself excited, but no less confused.

A pale horse... a pale horse veering a white caparison... a long one! Hells, look how it flies out in his wake! He thought he'd seen the quilted thing being cleaned in one of the back paddocks, but he'd no idea what horse or rider it belonged, too. The warrior atop it may as well have been wearing one, too. His kontusz and armor were white, as were his boots, helm, and bevor. *His var gear's stiffer than clothing, but it moves and shifts in the vind as they run... leather? Cloth?*

Whatever his raiment was made of, he was an eerie, but welcome, sight. His steed didn't charge across the hilly landscape. He *flew* over it, sweeping down upon the line like hell's own harbinger.

A longish weapon seemed to materialize in his hands as he neared the easternmost enemy. He stabbed forward as he rode, then brought the weapon's other end around like a quarterstaff, knocking the harrier from his steed. With barely a skip in his horse's stride, he slung his weapon high above his head and threw a vicious two-handed flat snap across what looked like either the foeman's neck or face. The impact of the horizontal slash drove the second harrier from his saddle with the speed of a falling stone.

Vlk could hear shouts of unrestrained delight along the wall walk, but he paid them little mind. There was simply too much else to concentrate on. Two more riders, both far more mundane-looking, were now racing up the white warrior's backtrail. One of them looked to be the other's squire. He was so short by comparison. He wore a full harness of mail, however, and the Bluemark Guard's black kontusz.

Vhat is he vielding? I see a veapon, but I can't make it out.

The other rider was easier to identify. He hadn't changed since Vlk had last seen him.

"That's Ruční Kopí!" he said, or at least thought he did. His voice was drowned out by the fresh rumble of the Percoy horses picking up speed—spurring into the fray. More shouts of excitement came from the far left of the wall walk, past the last of the Bluemark archery corps. Next he knew, he heard someone calling his name from somewhere off to the right.

Jitka?

The final blow to his distracted mind was a leather-clad forearm slamming into his chest.

"At the ready! Move!"

Andrej's archery gauntlet appeared to have small plates of hardened leather riveted onto its back. He doubted the taller boy had meant to strike him so hard, but *hells* that had hurt! Too surprised to be angry, Vlk stumbled backward and almost lost his footing. A massive hand gripped his left arm, dragging him upright before he could properly fall the twenty-odd feet to the uneven ground.

"A bad time to practice flying, dragon bat."

It took Vlk a blink to register who'd spoken. By the time he'd realized the kindly voice had belonged to Count Edmund, the man had stepped back to his former position on the stairs, looking out over the battlefield once more.

It was then that the first smell of rain struck his nose. *But the sky's nearly cloudless... Vhy do I smell rain?*

"Vlllllk!"

Jitka again, and closer this time. Battle might be joined by the archers at any moment, and little Jitka was desperate to get his attention. What in hells did she want? She didn't sound afraid.

She sounds ... excited?

-II-

Kastan's arms had given up their protests. Distantly, she could still feel their occasional throbbing complaint, but that didn't much matter—she had other things to focus on just now.

Havoc's Horn, where do they keep coming from? There had been fewer than a dozen when she'd started her run, back where the ash march ended. Their ranks had swelled to nearly a score by the time she'd drawn first blood. Now the enemy seemed to be everywhere—coming at her from all sides, one after the other.

She wasn't overwhelmed, exactly. But she kept catching herself looking this way and that in an effort to track the entire killing field at once. Her blood was pounding through her veins. Her body was covered in what felt like a rainstorm of sweat. She ached... *ached* for just a moment's respite.

It would come, eventually. Soon enough, the Inner Winter would fall upon her, and she would welcome it like a long-lost love.

Hells, let it be soon, while there's still time...

Since the first harriers had appeared to haunt Jafyl's steps, she'd been fighting to ignore her mounting sense of anxiety. There was always a distracting measure of doubt and confusion during conflict's first footfalls—a terror that gnawed at the edge of the mind.

What if I miss something crucial? What if I fail those in my charge? What if I'm too weak, too slow, too uncertain? What if today... What if today's the day that I die?

She caught a glimpse of Edmund's Ruční Kopí, Hajvarr. His enormous bay roared toward the enemy's disordered line in what could best be described as a speedy galumph. Its hooves seemed to bounce into one another each time they left Skolf.

Raising her blade to parry a wild strike from her latest foe, she saw Edmund's man throw a tight back-cut into the neck of the rider on his left. As Hajvarr finished his strike, his giant of a mount reared up and boxed the harrier on his right, driving the wretch out of the saddle. He fell screaming, trying too late to protect his now blood-soaked face.

Hajvarr's horse drummed his forelegs on the ground—perhaps on the rider he'd felled, Kastan couldn't tell from this angle—before returning them to Skolf. As he made ready to ride off toward a new target, Kastan saw the man's face. The Count's Ruční Kopí wore an enormous grin below bright eyes that were visible even at this distance.

Quite suddenly, she laughed aloud. She sounded mad to her own ears, but that meant nothing at all. The relief that washed over her drove any such self-consciousness far afield.

The Inner Winter wasn't a thing to be called forth in a warrior. She'd known better, and still she'd tried to *summon* it. Calling on a thing was, at bottom, an attempt to *control* that thing. The Inner Winter, as she'd been taught to call it, was an *absence* of control. A warrior trained over and over until that training became rote—until the body knew what to do, even if the mind was otherwise occupied.

And yet here am I. I've been waiting for that sense that I can... that I should let go and allow my body to do what it's been honed for. And all this while, I've been holding it hostage. Holding myself hostage.

She reached her dim hand down to squeeze Rákos's own. His hands were deathly cold, but no matter—they were still clasped tightly together around her midriff. That would do.

The cold clarity had, at last, descended upon her. With it came a kind of joy only known to those who wield the sword. Everything began to amuse her. Everything evoked a dull sort of delight that bordered on intoxication. It was as if she dreamed, merely watching her body react to the world around it. It was the magic of war... the perfectly distilled sense of *danger*—of *rightness*. It was the certainty that she was where and who she needed to be at that moment, and *that* was enough.

It was the song of the battlefield... the sword-song as it split first air, then armor, until her foe at last fled flesh. It wasn't the first time she'd felt this way in battle, and she doubted it would be the last—assuming she lived to fight on. When the song was at its end, she would either feel a desperate need to sleep, or a sense of soul-sickness that made food and cheer into a kind of poison. There was a price for dealing death, and that price must eventually come due. For now, though...

For now, there's only the sword-song. And while there's still breath in me, I mean to sing it.

She turned her attention back to her own fight, beaming.

Before her was a round-faced man with a merchant's belly. His arms bore genuine muscle, his eyes a familiar shade of malevolent green. He charged towards her, swinging his axe in powerful arcs just above his horse's ears. He fought with a ferocity she thought she might have approved of in other circumstances.

Yet for all that fire, you've little enough skill.

She parried the first two strikes, but had no interest in playing that game any longer than necessary. Riding double meant she had to defend them both, which limited her options.

He delivered another low back-cut. He'd meant to strike where Rákos's arms wrapped around her, just below her breasts. Kastan had other plans. She caught the blow on the blunted sverdets bein at the base of the blade, hooking her quillons up under the beard of his axe. Then she gave a terrific shove upward.

He drew his axe high over his dim shoulder to untangle their weapons, making his forthcoming back-cut, or perhaps angled hammer, obvious. She allowed her grin to broaden, seeking out his eyes. His smile seemed to soften, though his body betrayed no such slackening.

Their horses circled, snapping at one another as they came close. She saw him draw in a tight breath, then begin to drop his arm. *A hammer shot, then.* As his forearm crossed between his face and hers, she drove her pommel into the meat below his elbow, forcing the limb to collide with its owner's nose.

He cursed, then laughed, dropping his guard to display a delighted grin and a face painted freshly scarlet from his bleeding nose.

She laughed as well, nodding, but gestured for him to raise his weapon again.

Rubbing the point where she'd struck him as if trying to force a cramp to release, he re-readied his axe, grinning. His delight seemed to be too fierce a thing to keep in. Indeed, he drew breath as if to speak—but whatever he'd meant to say never made it past his lips.

Kastan drew herself up straight in the saddle, as if she meant to gain a higher vantage. At the same time, she dropped her bright hand, rolling her wrist. Her sword completed its spin by slamming into the place where the man's neck met his bright-shoulder. It'd been a mühlchen strike—a mill-wheel in miniature. It was the sort of strike that would make any swordsman smile. She drew back hard, ripping the flesh around the point of impact.

The harrier was still smiling as he fell from his saddle. She watched his horse bend down to sniff at its fallen master's boot. Finding nothing of any merit there, the riderless steed began cropping grass as if the world weren't full of the scents of blood, fire, and rain on the come.

Wait, rain? Fire?

She cast about, urging Jafyl into a trot. There was no fire, save perhaps the fires within the palisade. Looking up, there were only a few pale clouds high in the mid-afternoon sky.

Then why do I smell both burning pitch and imminent rain?

She saw her own warriors deep in the enemy ranks, slaughtering as they rode. *And where did all these harriers come from?*

As she watched, she saw two horsemen appear. They materialized as if landing after they'd jumped a felled tree.

Sorcery? Then aloud, her words clear, though her voice was shrill—"Sluneční ruka! Čarodějnictví! Sorcery! Čarodějnictví!"

(Sun's Hand! Sorcery!)

-III-

Vlk hovered a few feet behind Andrej. The taller boy was holding his bow at rest, left foot forward as he watched the battlefield below.

Left is his dim side. He vields a shield in his left hand, too, just like his bow.

He'd been trying to distract himself from his growing sense of frustration. Unfortunately, this particular non-discovery hadn't been much help on that score. Instead of witnessing the glory being won below, Vlk had to content himself with standing back by the supplies, watching a quiver on the grit and grass-strewn barbican floor. Meanwhile, Andrej could watch the battle—had to watch it, in fact, in order to pick his targets once the shooting began.

He heard the sounds of war... hoofbeats, the clang of metal parrying metal, the braying of horses wild with either terror or excitement. Overtopping this grim music were the shouts and screams of men and either warrior-women or boys his own age.

At some point, Jitka had stopped shouting for him, which was something. Still, he found himself wondering if the little girl had been sent away or had simply been disheartened about being ignored.

She's probably found Daryna. She'll be safer there. Ve'll make certain of it.

A noise from the soldiers to the east along the wall drew his attention that way, but he could see nothing.

"Vlllllk!" Jitka was somehow both whispering and shouting simultaneously. The effect was like hearing the whispering sound of sudden rain on a wooden roof. He looked back to the west and found her swaying—almost dancing toward him along the wall walk. Her pretty green eyes were huge and delighted above a star-bright smile. She was preceded by Štít—Ruční Kopí's Crimson Heart. The massive red hound moved with an eerie grace, tail held low, wagging in a hopeful sort of way.

Vlk felt Jitka's small hand slip into his as she slid up next to him. She half pulled him down as she stood on her toes to reach his ear.

"Štít's here to protect him, Vlk. The *stínový muž* said she had to find him and guard him. That's vhy ve're here."

He leaned away, looking down at Štít, who'd sat near the top of the stairs. A smile began to draw itself across his face, accompanied by an almost physical need to reach out and run his fingers through her thick, red fur. With an effort, he turned back to Jitka. Her face was full of a delighted pride that managed to avoid looking self-important.

"Ruční Kopí, you mean? Did Ruční Kopí order her to protect the Count?"

She looked at him as if he were deliberately misunderstanding her. That, or as if he were a fool. Either way, she made no effort to hide her annoyance. At least her voice was still something of a stage whisper. "Noooo, Vlllk. Not Ruční Kopí . The *stínový muž* told her!"

The Shadow Man? Who in all the hells is the Shadow Man?

He shook his head, then snapped it forward as the sounds beyond the wall briefly swelled. Andrej was perfectly still. Vlk barely saw the rise and fall of his chest as he looked out over the battlefield below.

"Štít? What are you doing here, ay? The alure's no place for you, is it? Is it?" Count Edmund was petting the hound's head with rough affection.

The Count's voice had drawn Vlk's attention that way. Štít was happy for the attention. She clearly *liked* Edmund, but she only seemed to have eyes for...

Andrej?

-IV-

It happened almost too quickly to follow, let alone react to. At first, it was only a single voice. All too soon—like fire in dry grass—the call spread from foe to foe, turning it into a battle cry... a *rallying* cry.

"Zcúr Kargást! Yaberd zcúr kargást! Yarberd douyar Kovalunsh sannys en dottarys!"

(The white wraith! Kill the white wraith! Kill the wicked sons and daughters of Kovalun!)

Kastan spurred Jafyl toward the press, sword held high.

"Sluneční ruka! To me! To me! Sluneční ruka! Ke mě!"

(Sun's Hand! To me!)

Kastan saw her folk fighting in pairs, just as she'd taught them... just as *she'd* been taught. She had a moment to register her own bitter wish that she was alone in the saddle—that she had the freedom to fight without having to compensate for... but no. That was monstrously unfair. Rákos was hers—was *her charge*.

He's no warrior, by his own admission. I can't hold that against him.

True enough, but as Jafyl flew toward the rest of the Sluneční ruka— the rest of *her* people—she still had to force herself to contend with just how badly she wanted to fight beside them. Oh, she would fight, but her role now was to command the rest of her warriors—her Sun's Hand. To get them back to Jižní Lov alive.

Hajvarr and that Bluemark guardsman are forming up with some of mine. Good.

She scanned the faces of the nearest Percoy warriors. *I see Tyesca, which should make her sword-sister... yes, that's Johanka at her right hand.*

As she watched, the pair dispatched the trio of horsemen nearest them. The final blow came from Johanka. With a kind of sick clarity, she saw the woman's flanged mace deliver a vicious wrap to the back of her foe's un-helmeted head. The blow resulted in a tiny cloud of rose color that hung in the air for a moment before fading into the general dust.

The pair turned, beginning to spur toward the palisade along Kastan's projected path, but two more horsemen leapt into reality beside them. The field was clear one instant, and full of blood and sudden thunder the next.

When Tyesca's foe burst into being, he'd leveled his spear and rammed it toward her left flank. She turned the thrust with her buckler, then grabbed the spear by its haft, yanking. The spearman *should* have let go of his weapon, drawing a secondary—a dagger, mace, or hunting sword. Instead, he tried to hold on and was hauled toward Tyesca for his trouble. She swept her slender sword out from under the spear's shadow in a rising back-cut to the man's neck. The resultant gout of blood—a brief, bright fountain—was almost too spectacular to be grotesque.

The harrier that appeared on Johanka's right was less reckless. He rammed his spear toward her belly, just as his counterpart had done with Tyesca. And Johanka's buckler was on the wrong hand to be of any use to counter the thrust. Instead, she used her mace.

Time chose that moment to slow. It crawled along at the perfect speed so that Kastan missed not so much as a mote of what came after. She had a moment of pride as Johanka threw a hard flat snap to the inside of the spear's haft, causing the thrust to go wide.

The harrier rode the force of Johanka's strike, rolling with it even as he allowed his mount to fall in beside hers. His hands slid toward the weapon's base, bringing it around his horse's head, then his own. He used the spear's haft like a quarterstaff at full extension, slamming it into the side of Johanka's helmeted head. She raised her mace to parry, but it was already too late. Johanka of Vesnice Percoy flew from the saddle and was immediately trampled by first her own, then her executioner's horse.

Kastan shrieked as she rode the man down. There was no fighting— no vengeance-soaked battle, hammer and tongs. She simply rode him down and put an end to him. She wasn't even certain how—that is, *with what manner of strike*—she'd felled him. Next she knew, she'd ridden up beside Tyesca, who nodded to her. *Nodded* to her. There were no words, no tears, no burning look of either rage or gratitude on the woman's round face. There was only a nod, which Kastan numbly returned as they rode toward their fellows.

-V-

"Captain!" Waltyr's voice was short, sharp, and just loud enough to cut through the noise of cheering and jeering men.

"Sergeant?"

Vlk heard the archer's next word as *majee.* Before he could do more than register it as a word he didn't know, movement drew his eye to the east again.

Jastrab hauled himself up onto the barbican by hand, eschewing the stairs on Edmund's other side. He came up on Waltyr's left, looking out beyond the pointed tops of the wall.

This time Vlk heard it more clearly.

"Makee? You're certain you saw sorcery, Sergeant?"

Waltyr said nothing for a long moment. After weighing his answer, he finally nodded. "I've watched horsemen jump into being from a blank patch of grass, Captain. I'd been wondering where they all came from. The area below us is one massive open field. There's nowhere for a horse to hide. There have to be almost thirty of them down there now. More than half of those are dead on the ground, but—"

He cut himself off. "There! By the wraith-rider! Do you see? Did you mark them?"

"I don't—" But that was as far as Jastrab got before chaos overtook their part of the palisade.

Everything seemed to change, and all at once. A tense and nightmarish jumble of events started, spun Vlk around, and left him bruised, confused, and terrified. It began with Andrej shouting the utterly useless negation everyone always shouts in times of fear or anger.

"No!"

He began loosing arrows one after another out over the wall. His draw was almost too fast to follow. The blond boy's eyes were wide and somehow vacant above his set jaw.

Waltyr shouted, but his well-chosen word wasn't much better.

"Andrej!"

The taller boy said nothing. He just kept shooting. He'd nearly exhausted the score of arrows in the quiver beside him by the time Vlk had chanced to look down again.

As Andrej reached for one of the few that remained, Jastrab stepped back, moved around the Sergeant, and reached a hand out to grab the boy's bow arm.

Andrej ducked away, firing once more, then pulled an arrow from the quiver on his back. His mouth, Vlk noticed, had curled into a snarl. While he wasn't ignoring the captain, he only looked away from the battlefield with quick, darting glances.

Štít growled and snapped, stepping toward the Bluemark's captain. Edmund called the hound's name, but she appeared willing to have none of it. She placed herself between Andrej and Jastrab, her crimson fur bristling.

Vlk knew people who were afraid of large dogs. He'd never understood why, but he'd accepted their fears as honest and genuine. Štít's low growl didn't make *him* afraid, exactly. Her wordless warning wasn't directed at him, and he knew it. Still, the sound crystalized, becoming one of those perfect moments where life's lesson arrives dressed and ready for the day.

Edmund tried to get a hand in Štít's fur, but again, she was having none of it. She raised her head with a suddenness that seemed to surprise all of them. She knocked Edmund's arm aside, took a further step back, and issued a rolling bark that sounded eerily like speech.

Roh-oo-arr!

As both the count and captain took a step toward Andrej, trying to bypass the massive hound, Jitka began to shout.

"Stop! No, stop! Ve have to *protect* him. The stínový muž told her to!"

Jitka stepped toward the hound, meaning to grab Edmund's right hand. At the same time, Jastrab stepped wide to the animal's left. Štít half jumped, half slid back and toward her own left... where she knocked into Jitka... who stumbled into Vlk. He had the presence of mind to grab onto Jitka, trying to stop her from falling.

But who vill stop ... me!

Over they went—Jitka screaming in his ear, nearly strangling him as she held on.

-VI-

He was fairly certain he'd hit the ground. The only proof of that was the fact that he was no longer falling, but under the circumstances, that seemed like proof enough. The world was full of a queer un-light—greys and blues, purples and bruised blacks.

But at least I live. A fall like that vould have been a miserable vay to die.

He sat up, looking around for Jitka. He saw what *looked* like her a few feet away. She was sitting on her knees, her face in her hands as she cried. He heard her, or at least he thought he did. Both the sight and sound of her were distorted into hazy echoes. He heard a woman's voice, however, fierce and clear.

"Back, both of you! Leave him be, or so help me…"

"I know that cub. S'one of Lakkrid's pack, and no mistake."

That was a familiar voice. A man's voice, both close and clear. It was behind him somewhere. Why was he moving so slowly?

"No matter. If he's crossed… no. Not crossed *yet*." This was another man from somewhere near the first.

"Help him! Vake him up! Stínový muž, vake him up!" Jitka, sounded as if she were shouting from somewhere inside a cave.

"Štít! Štít!" This was that second man. His voice seemed to be aimed upward.

"I hear you, Muž Přísahy, and I am about your work!" The woman shouted from on high somewhere in front of him.

Muž Přísahy? Oath man?

The same man replied, voice amused but full of authority.

"Are there enemies on the alure, Štít?"

"They're trying to stop him from shooting his bow!"

"Are they newcomers? Have they only just arrived from outside of the palisade?"

Vlk tried to shake his head. Hells it was hard to concentrate. He was so cold. His flesh seemed as if it were waking up from the numbness of too much pressure. A multitude of tiny ants felt as if they were crawling beneath his skin.

A face swam into a half-hazy focus in front of him. *Vhat's vrong vith my eyes?* It was familiar, but at first, he couldn't place it.

And then, suddenly, he could. *Red hair, oak-eyes, and yes. He vears the same leather armor the rest of them vear.*

"You're one of... one of Lakkrid's people. One of his father's men. Has he come..." His head was so numb, it was hard to think. "Has he come back, then?"

The man grinned, though Vlk noted the smile didn't reach his brown dreamer's lamps. They bore a pitying look of sad confusion Vlk didn't much care for.

"Nye, nye. They're still far afield. 'S yer name, pup? I know I've caught you runnin' with our cub a'fore, but I can't 'member what name brings you runnin' for supper."

"Vlk... I'm Vlk. Vhere..." He tried to shake his head, and the world started spinning. "Vhere is everyone? Vhy's it so..." He could hear the sounds of horses, of men and women speaking in a tongue he didn't know, but they were all distant. It reminded him of the sounds of the city when he'd traveled to Hartscross. Everything inside the walls had been loud and exciting. *This makes me think of how the city sounded vhen ve vere still outside at the gate. It vas loud, but... also soft.* Thinking about it now, he could almost see it. But that was nonsense.

"Quiet? Aye, well, you've had a tumble. One way or 'nother, we'll get you on yer feet, though, Vlk. Lakkrid'd not forgive me if I left you lying about after a fall like that, now would he?"

Vlk knew it wasn't *really* a question, but that was alright. The man's voice was something to concentrate on, other than Jitka's shouts and sobs. They were getting quieter, at any rate, so that was something.

Footsteps from near his head. When had he laid back down?

"Štít, you need to be..." This was that second man again, though his voice was both closer, and much quieter now.

"More careful. I know. But you gave me a task, Muž Přísahy. I was about your work, keeping the boy safe."

"I know. Believe me when I tell you I know, Štít. You did very well on that score. Still, you can't defend the boy if you're driven off for killing another child... even unintentionally."

The woman sighed. Why was there a woman called... called? Havoc's... Havoc's...

Havoc's vhat? Vhy can't I remember?

A shadow fell across him. A massive hound with red fur and eyes... eyes that were... golden? Glowing? Human? He couldn't concentrate. It was so hard to *think*.

Vlk felt a warm tongue caress his face. He tried to smile, but his muscles wouldn't obey.

"He'll waken in a moment, Muž Přísahy."

"Thank you. You've done well. Vlk, is it? Remember what I tell you now. Tell Edmund—say to the Count, this. Ebis..."

It was too late. Vlk saw a warm-looking yellow light, felt the heat of a hot hand on his chest and the soft touch of fingers through his untidy hair.

Jitka gasped, then laughed somewhere to his left.

"Can you hear me? Can you hear my voice, boy?"

It was Edmund. Vlk opened his eyes to see the count's mustachioed face smiling down at him. His entire body moved with the force of his sigh. He was so clearly relieved. "Don't try to talk. You've had a bad fall. I've called for my—"

Vlk sat up. He found that he'd apparently been laying in Edmund's lap, which was somewhat surreal. Using the bigger man's shoulder for leverage, he pulled himself up to his feet. He had to find her... had to—*there!*

Vlk took two steps to his right, ignoring Edmund's admonishment to be easy with his steps. He dropped to his knees before a seated red hound and threw his arms around her neck, burying his face in her luxuriant fur.

"I forgive you, Štít," he whispered. "I svear that I do. *I* am a Muž Přísahy, too."

-VII-

Kastan finished cutting Jafyl to the southwest, Tyesca right beside her. She could see six riders just ahead—four of her own, Hajvarr, and the lone member of the Bluemark Guard. She and Tyesca fell into step to Hajvarr's right.

Nearly there. We simply have to race through the final two-hundred or so strides to the northern gate.

Another few heartbeats and she came up with the sellsword's name.

That almost has to be Blevelsket. Hajvarr's spoken of her often enough.

Speaking of—Hajvarr looked past her, asking Tyesca the bitter, but necessary question. "Johanka?"

Eyes red either from grit or grief, Tyesca shook her head a single time.

Edmund's Ruční Kopí bowed his own in understanding. Looking back over his shoulder, he tried on a dour smile. "Well, so long as—"

Whatever he'd meant to say, Kastan never heard it. The air was suddenly thick with dust, shouts, and the storm-sounds of hoofbeats. Arrows began whistling overhead, coming from Jižní Lov's palisade.

But only from one spot. Strange.

She chanced a look back and felt her stomach drop. Three riders were in mid-career, charging toward the ghostly drogue member of their party, swords and axes held high. Behind them, she saw what might be as many as half-a-dozen more, leveling spears and holding their horses back until their way was clear.

"Yaberd hem! Yaberd hem! Yaberd zcúr kargást!"

(Kill him! Kill him! Kill the white wraith!)

"With me!" Kastan began to turn Jafyl, but Hajvarr grabbed her reins.

"No, Lady! We've lost one already trying to get you back to Edmund. *I'll* go."

"No, Hajvarr. I can't leave her out here. I *won't* leave her to die alone! Let go of—"

"Kastan!"

This was a voice she hadn't heard before. Looking, she saw the Bluemark woman smiling at her. "It's lovely to finally meet you, Lady. I hope we can speak again."

Hajvarr snapped his head around to look at the small soldier. "Blev— What are you—"

Blevelsket nodded back toward the harriers. "That man talks too much," said she and said no more. Instead, she reined up, turning her horse toward the enemy, and bolted off.

Kastan turned in her saddle, looking back past Rákos's hunched left shoulder. She saw Blevelsket racing toward the press, a long knife held by its blade in her bright hand. Beyond her, the rider in white was a blur with her boar spear. Her horse was trying to stomp and bite, but there were simply too many.

"Fetem... *Please....*"

Again, a stream of arrows raced over Kastan's head, aiming directly toward Fetinba's attackers. One struck an enemy horse square in its rump.

It reared, throwing its rider, then bolted away.

Blevelsket drew her arm back and threw both it and her blade forward in one exaggerated motion. The blade glinted in the late-day light, striking another of Fetem's foemen.

"Open the damned gate! Open it, or rain death down on these bastards!" Hajvarr's shout forced her to turn her eyes front, if only for a moment. The gate was so very near now...

"Nekt! Nekt! Yaberd hem! Yaberd zcúr Kargást!" The harrier shouted his imperative in an ecstasy of rage. His voice—already high and shrill—seemed now to be choked with dust and dragonfire in what sounded like equal measure.

Kastan turned back and saw Fetem and Blevelsket riding side by side. *Yes! Run! Hells be hid, don't let them catch you!*

Blevelsket suddenly peeled off, racing back toward the enemy. She drew a long and wicked-looking sword from a scabbard on her saddle as she rode.

"What is she—?!" Kastan shouted in genuine alarm. She didn't *know* the woman, but her willingness—her *insistence* that she go back to rescue a complete stranger...

Hajvarr laughed... and with obvious delight.

"Lady, she already told you. She thinks that man talks too much."

Kastan blinked, looking first at Hajvarr, then back to the killing field. Fetinba was now close enough—they all were, save Blevelsket. The air was suddenly full of archery fire from on high, covering Fetem as she neared them.

Blevelsket was hurtling toward the man who'd been calling for Fetinba's death. He rode unarmored, with a wild yellow beard on his face and a gleaming bald pate. He'd now been reduced to wordless screaming. He pointed what looked like a morning star at her as she rode to meet him.

Kastan watched as she rode through his guards, swerving to avoid them rather than slowing down to fight them. As for their still-shouting captain—he raised his morning star and charged to meet her. His battle cry was too garbled to hear at this distance, but it didn't much matter. Kastan thought it would be the last word he would utter on this or any other battlefield. As Blevelsket rode past him, he fell from his saddle in two pieces.

Hajvarr shook his head, face split in a wide grin. "Behold Blevelsket—Jastrab's Living Sword."

Kastan simply nodded, too emotionally drained to speak.

Their party came to a stop just beyond the northern gate. She turned Jafyl to get a better look at the carnage they'd escaped. There were easily two score or more dead on the ground and perhaps another two dozen riding toward them… and then there weren't. Between blinks, she saw the riders giving chase simply wink out of existence. A moment later, most of the dead on the field had disappeared as well. Perhaps a dozen such corpses remained. They looked like ugly, mottled boulders strewn haphazardly amongst the grass. She thought she saw a figure wearing green and gold among the dead—Johanka's broken body. Perhaps she should…

The gate opened. The call for the archers to put their bows down rang out in the sudden quiet.

"Come, Lady," said Hajvarr. "Edmund awaits."

-VIII-

As the gate closed behind them, she heard distant thunder, the music of many horses, and the deep rumble of unnumbered voices singing blasphemous staves.

"Sdraliana kr ka. Rhexrryn xro, rhexrryn xro, rhexrryn xro…"

CHAPTER EIGHT

LOST, AND IN THE WIND SAVED

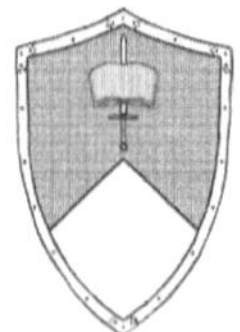

-I-

Dereek khn
Yrxa Castle
5 Korunasykli: 22 Days after the Red Storm at Westsong

A sea of stars...

That had been Methias's first, and for some time *only* thought. Those stars hung in all directions and in such bright profusion... they seemed to hover so close. He felt he could almost reach out a hand and touch their warmth. And there was he, standing *within* it—the apotheosis of all night skies. A deep blue-black that was too expressive and nuanced to be accounted stygian. And yes. Standing, not floating, for he could still feel the stones beneath him.

The night wind sang. The sound was lonely, but then, windsong had always sounded lonely to him... and somehow cold. It rose and fell all around, almost as if it were trapped. He heard it. But he felt none of its biting breath. The Cage had set his eyes and ears to fly, and now he was *here*, after a fashion. There just weren't any accompanying physical sensations.

He wasn't seeing a projection, or hearing sound carried from rune to rune. His eyes and ears told him without question that he was *here*. The rest of him was just as certain he hadn't gone anywhere at all. He marked the stone beneath his feet, the cool and motionless air on his exposed skin, and the gentle rise and fall of his own chest as he breathed. His other senses remained in Yrxa Castle. He was quite certain he still stood near the couch at The Cage's center.

Recognizing that fact did little to help him reclaim his ability to think clearly. He'd had no trouble *accepting* his situation. He'd just found the scope and power required to *create* such a situation nearly impossible to fathom. Weave Author rites could certainly craft convincing illusions. Such things were their meat and wine, after all, but this... Comparing this to Author rites was like comparing a crude tent to a newly finished castle.

Later, when he could process all of it, he would think on these things—examine them with a scholar's careful eye. But that was later. Now the sheer scope of it had all but obliterated his ability to think clearly.

Methias drew in a deep, shuddering breath and bowed his head in a species of wordless awe. At the same time, he managed to force his eyes to close. He needed to blot out the wonderment that was that endless sky... to regain perspective... to find a moment to breathe and be.

After a span that might have been heartbeats, or whole sykli, Sleara's voice came from somewhere just above him. The boy sounded as if he were trying to put on a brave face, but his sadness was a perfect melody against the music of the sobbing wind.

"This ... is my home."

"H..." Methias shook his head and tried again. "How? How did you..." He opened his eyes, lifted his chin, and answered his own question. Sleara and his people had *not* lived in the sky. Methias could see rolling foothills far below him, and the ocean beyond. It lapped at the pale greens and deep ochers of the shoreline with clean, dark fingers. Looking between his booted feet, he saw he stood on a wide shelf high up on a shadowy mountain.

Sleara gave a mirthless little chuckle—two notes that sounded as if they'd issued from a nose, rather than an open mouth.

"Look left."

Methias turned his head and drew in a sharp breath. A small skeleton lay in a few tatters of what must once have been clothing. Its head was missing, as was its right arm below the elbow. It lay intact otherwise.

"*That's* how I brought you here. That's the rest of me... most of it, anyway."

Not what I'd meant to ask you, but never mind. That... that'd been my...

my next question.

"Do you..." Methias forced himself to stare down at the weathered bones. It cost him, and quite a bit more than he'd expected. In an effort to refocus, he recalled a mnemonic from his early days of study. It was a thing designed both to motivate a wayward attention span, and to help recapture fleeting thoughts.

Sconces on the wall. Sconces down the... the hall. One pool of torchlight shows... shows the path ahead. And as the light... And as the light... stone in sky but it's hard to concentrate. What had I meant to ask him? Did he... did he remember... Ah!

"Do you remember much of your last days here?"

Sleara laughed. The sound wasn't altogether comforting. "What a gentle way to ask that." There was the sense of him shaking his head, though that might have been pure imagination. "You want to know if I remember my death—how and why it happened. *That's* what you're really asking. And yes. I remember all of it."

Methias felt his cheeks burning. "Sleara, I—"

"It's fine." The boy had again adopted that detached, dismissive tone.

"It isn't. I'm just trying to understand as much as I can about you, this place—*Rímhril*, did you call it(?)—and how it applies to The Cage."

Now came the sense of Sleara nodding. "The island is Rímhril. The *place*—the city, I suppose you might call it—is Arrétaln Drén."

"Ah-ree-*taln* Drenn." Methias looked around for some sign of a settlement but saw nothing.

"You won't see it. Not from here. You might be able to if you were really there, but not using my body this way."

Methias made a nod of acceptance. His mind was growing accustomed to his situation, but thinking was still maddeningly slow work. "The city is hidden, then? Fair enough, but why haven't they come to perform the necessary rites on your—"

"They can't." The interruption carried with it a terrible patience—cold and watchful.

Methias reached up to rub thumb and forefinger against the place above his nostrils. "The rite that binds you to The Cage won't... won't let them? Does it protect the site, somehow?" Images began to play out across the stage of his mind's eye. With maddening clarity, his treacherous imagination conjured scenes in which the small and ruined body stood—one-armed and headless—to attack physical intruders.

"No. Nothing like that." The boy's voice became small and

expressionless.

"Do they ... not know where to *find* you, then?"

"I... it's not important." That icy patience had begun to fracture.

"It is if I'm to try and put things to rights. I know next to nothing about Elven culture, least of all your funerary rites. If there's an Elven settlement near at hand, there should be *someone* I can ask for guidance, no?"

"They aren't going to help you."

"Won't they? Why wouldn't they want to ensure—"

"Because they're *gone*, Methias! They're all gone, don't you understand?" His voice was equal parts rage and grief, but there was something more beneath it. Something deeper.

Please let me be wrong... Methias was fairly and miserably certain he knew what that underlying something meant. He didn't see how it could be possible, but then...

But then what do I really know about Sleara, this place—this Arrétaln Drén, or elves as a whole?

"Sleara..." He made his voice soft, careful to remove any hint of frustration or codling patronization from it. "How can I understand what you haven't told me?" A pause. "How can I help if I don't understand?"

Sleara's voice sounded choked, as if he were fighting back a wave of fresh tears. "You can't. No one can."

"Sleara, I—"

"No!" The stars faded into shadow. Likewise the land and the sea, revealing The Cage's stark misery once more. "I've shown you what The Cage lets you do. I did as I promised. Leave me now."

Methias took a moment to get his bearings. As he did, he saw Sleara's small skull sliding back down the shadow of his imprisoning panel.

"Sleara," he began again, but the boy cut him off.

"I said leave me! I don't want to talk anymore!" His voice softened. "Not now."

Methias bowed his head. The exchange had forcibly reminded him of Jannon ... of a conversation they'd had. It had only been a few days after he'd found Methias beneath that blessed banyan tree. His mind tried to fix on it, though he had no desire to reopen that particular scar. That memory was painful, but always within easy reach.

He shook his head, sliding his foot backward even as he turned to leave. The leg bounced against something unyielding. That, in turn, caused his feet to tangle with one another. He stumbled backward, landing in an awkward-looking seated position on that twice-forgotten,

thrice-cursed couch.

The room was full of a sudden half-light, and Methias was…
Methias was…

…was…

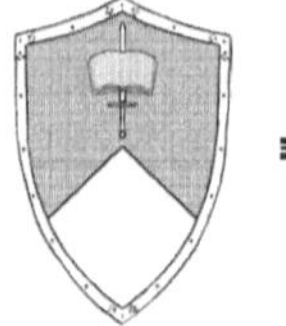

-II-

Kingdom of Traead
Ad Eniddia
14 Kamieńsykli: 10 years prior to the Red Storm at Westsong

Methias stands at one corner of Ad Eniddia's massive central belfry. He's looking out over the large, rather clean streets of this walled border town, *willing* himself not to cry. He has a belly full of mixed misery to contend with. The misery is justified, given recent events. And it's flavored with— though he doesn't himself realize it—a dash of quite typical adolescent angst. He will, after all, be thirteen in less than a fortnight.

The wind is good up here. It sings and strains… whispers and moans. It provides a surfeit of perfect, melancholy underscores and counterpoints to his moiling emotions.

That same wind now tugs at the heavy cloak he wears, ruffling his unruly auburn curls as if it were trying to comfort him … or coax him. For now, he pays it little mind. The constant weight of his haversack holds only a touch more of his attention… just enough to ensure it's still hung over his shoulders, and no more.

It'll be tonight. It has to be. Otherwise I'll just keep finding excuses to stay.

The sun is setting. He can't see it behind the iron-colored clouds, but he can hear it. It's in the subtle changes to the birdsong below.

Not that any of the others would mark it. His thoughts are sour. Before long, they'll boil over into anger… he hopes. He'll *need* anger if he means to leave the comforts of the last few days. That, or the weight of all that's happened will finally be too much.

I'll just wait here. Then, when the sun's down and everyone's headed to the hall for supper, I'll make for the postern gate. If I'm quick and quiet, I can get out of the city before I'm missed. If not… If not, I'll climb back up here and... and I'll—

His mind freezes, as does his blood. Voices on the stair below cause his breath to hitch, then halt as their speech becomes clear. With a collapsing sensation, he realizes there's nowhere to hide up here.

Maybe I... If I crawl up into the bell and wrap myself around the clapper...

His mind conjures an image of someone pulling the rope to ring the bell. The vibration alone might kill him. Certainly, he'd be hard pressed to cover his ears without falling the few dozen feet to the base of the tower.

"...stairs, my lord. He's been up there for oh, 'bout half a bell, I think." The man sounds aged, with a queerly high, almost reedy timbre.

"That's fine, Alwyn. Thank you." That's the velvet voice of Lord Jannon. It occasionally squeaks, but only on certain sounds. Laughter is a common culprit. At fifteen or sixteen, young Lord Jannon Saysh laughs easily and often. He's two, perhaps as many as three years older than Methias, but he carries himself in a way that makes him seem much older. "If you'd be good enough to keep—"

"Aye, young master. No fear. I sh'll see that no one disturbs your talk with the boy."

Methias vacillates between rage, relief, and shame. He doesn't want Jannon here, because Jannon will try to stop his plans. He desperately wants Jannon here to do exactly that—to *make* him stay. Then there's the shame. Shame of spurning the gifts and good fortune that Jannon has lavished upon him these past few days. Shame that he didn't leave sooner, one way or another. Shame that he's been too much a coward to do what he knows he ought to have done from the first—either go back to Nausha and turn himself in, or... or...

The wind whispers once more, adding to his sense of panic. It isn't the soft sound of voices carried up from the walled town below. It's at once more urgent and more ethereal than that. He knows he isn't hearing whispers from some unseen entity, but there's a sort of cathartic attraction to the idea. It isn't impossible, of course. The world is full of what fools call the *super*natural. And it would be such a relief if something—if *someone* was calling him. He knows it's only wishful, childish thinking. He deserves every drop of fear and pain the world sees fit to throw at him. But oh, how blessed a thing it would be if someone would step in to tell him what to do—tell him how to properly pay for his part in... in Emil's...

Footsteps on the stairs behind him. They pause before they reach the top. He can hear their muted echo bounce against the stairwell's near-claustrophobic walls. Perhaps Jannon is looking around. Perhaps he's collecting his thoughts?

It doesn't matter. Methias draws a breath and forces his spine to straighten, not turning to look at the handsome youth.

"You look as if you're *ready for it*." The voice is easy—cautious, but playful.

"For what, Lord?" Methias doesn't mean to speak. Hells, why *had* he spoken?

Jannon's voice takes on a slightly exaggerated formality. "Let this be the *last* blow you ever receive unanswered..." He pauses for a beat before continuing in his earlier timbre. "The final moment of a knighting ceremony—the last moment you stand unbelted."

"Un..."

"...Belted. It's what we call those who haven't been recognized as knights. They're fighting men, of course... or fighting *women*, though they're rare enough. In either case, being able to fight isn't the same as being called to serve as a knight. Such aspiring folk are *unbelted fighters*."

Methias feels his mind opening, as if trying to eat the young lord's words like a meal. New knowledge has always been an easy lure for him. He resists the impulse to begin asking questions.

No more excuses. No more ... distractions.

"I'm neither of those." His voice comes out flat—almost monotone.

Jannon laughs at this. The sound is gentle, and while it *is* at Methias's less-than-astounding observation, it isn't at his expense.

Still chuckling, Jannon takes the final steps up onto the belfry's alure and begins walking toward him. Methias stiffens.

"What is it?" The older boy sounds as if he's stopped mid step. His easy laugh's been replaced by a note of clear concern that's hard to hear.

"Nothing. I just want to..."

"Want toooo...?"

"Be alone, my lord. I wish to be left alone."

"You've been left alone for half a bell—ever since you and Caden had your little tussle. Surely that's enough time to brood."

Still stood with his back to the new arrival, Methias runs his tongue out over his lower lip. It's swollen from where the shorter boy—Caden— punched him nearly a full bell back up the hourglass. He tastes the metallic flavor of blood and feels a bitter little smile crawling into position. He'd let his mask slip and mocked Caden for not knowing how to read. *Most* children his age are illiterate, unless their apprenticeship requires the skill, but Methias's derision had been relentless. He'd courted this pain—bought and paid for it. Even now he finds himself pleased in a dour way he doesn't himself fully understand.

"I'll be down soon, my lord. Please. Just leave me be."

"No... No, I think you'd best come down with me. We'll go to the hall together." His voice is closer now—just behind. How Jannon's moved so silently is a mystery Methias refuses to focus on. He shakes his head in equal parts confusion and negation.

Jannon lets the silence spin out for a moment—or at least what he no doubt thinks of as silence. Methias hears the ghostly, breathy sound of a piper, a bird he's always loved. The song is mixed with that of other birds and the shrill, somehow plaintive sound of the wind over the angles of tiled roofs, stone walls, wooden fences. He even hears the massive rope that holds the great bell begin to creak and sway behind him.

A hand falls on his shoulder, causing him to jolt as he recoils. He teeters, falling forward. Feeling every nerve scream against Skolf's pull as it rushes up to meet him, he has a single, shining thought.

Good. Good, it's over.

As Methias's fall forward reaches the point of no return, he can feel Jannon's hand slide from his shoulder. The young lord *does* manage to grab a fist full of both his cloak and the haversack beneath it, though. An instant later, Methias feels himself yanked backward. The motion isn't physically painful, though it does force his feet back onto the heavy wooden floorboards. The sense of loss, of yet one more failure to add to his seemingly endless list, is another matter entirely.

"No! No, let me go! Let me! Let..." Is he weeping? It doesn't matter. "It was over! Let it be over! Jannon please! I just want it to be over!"

The space of a single step separates him from his prize—an end to the empty feeling of loss to his shame at having fled his master's house when he should've stayed to fight, to his rage at his powerlessness... his own cowardice.

He's disoriented as Jannon spins him around, crushing him to his chest. Jannon makes no noise—offers no words. For a moment of frozen time, Methias is simply *held*. The embrace has a somehow implacable gentility to it that he knows... he *knows* he's unworthy of.

He moves to shove himself free. When that fails, he stomps on the young lord's booted feet, kicks him, tries to punch his ribs—anything to make him let go. He screams, but the sound is muffled against Jannon's chest. Finally, he has no fight left in him. Sobbing, his body shaking with days of pent-up guilt, grief, and—he will later reflect—gratitude for the kindness he's been shown, Methias breaks. He throws his arms around his silent savior, and at last begins to grieve for Emil's death.

When he quiets, no longer clinging to Jannon quite so desperately, he becomes aware of fingers combing through his hair. He has no words for it, but he's more grateful for the kindness—for the contact—than any words could convey.

"Will you tell me your tale now, Lamlith?"

Unwilling to let go, Methias turns his face up to regard him. His eyes are wide with both fear and incomprehension. He's terrified at having to relive it—at the thought of how Jannon will react when he learns the truth. The incomprehension is simpler. He doesn't know the word Jannon used to address him.

He must be wearing his confusion, for Jannon smiles down, leaning back in order to look him in the face. "It means *little fire*."

"Oh." That's all Methias can say.

"Would it help if I told you I already know some of it? That nobody will find you here... well, nobody with any authority, at any rate?"

"I... My..." Methias starts to struggle again, trying to free himself, but stops almost instantly. He shakes his head, then bows it. "What will you do to me?"

"*To* you?" Jannon laughs in that easy way he has—the way that makes it hard not to laugh along. "I'm going to torture you with food and a safe place to sleep, warm clothes and a warm bed, and time."

"Time?"

"Time, Lamlith." He nods, looking for and finally meeting Methias's eyes. "I can't unmake whatever's really happened to you, but I can give you time to make peace with it... to learn whatever you can from it. There's a price, mind you, but I can give you that".

"What... what price?" He can feel his heartbeat. He's exhausted physically, mentally, and emotionally, but he hasn't lost his ability to feel fear.

Jannon's laugh is brief, soft, and gentle. "Honesty, Lamlith. You have to be honest with me and with yourself. That doesn't mean you have to tell me all of it. It just means you mustn't *lie* about anything." He smooths Methias's hair back. "Can you? Will you pay that price?"

Methias doesn't answer. He can't. He's too overwhelmed. Instead, he swallows hard, eyes brimming over. Laying his head against Jannon's chest once more, he shudders in the wake of a new sensation... relief.

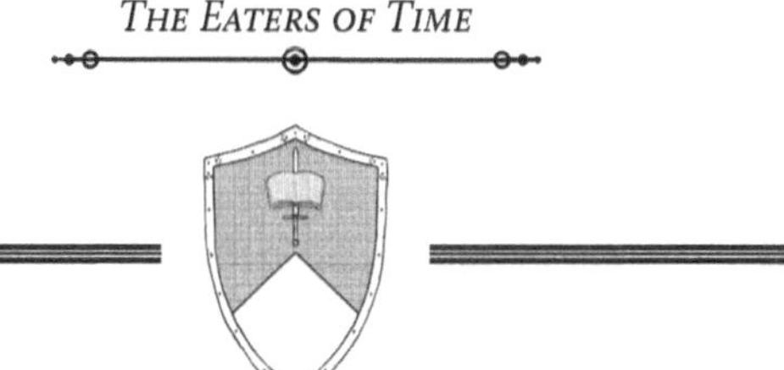

-III-

Dereek khn
Yrxa Castle
5 Korunasykli: 22 Days after the Red Storm at Westsong

Methias sat in mute absorption as the scene faded. He looked straight ahead from his perch on the couch, but saw none of what lay before him.

His face was wet, and he tasted iron as his heart began to slow. He needed no mirror to show him how pale he was. He could feel the color slowly creeping back up his shoulders and neck as he forced a swallow.

Gradually, he became aware of their eyes. Every skull caught in The Cage's confines was staring. They had no expressions, of course, but he had the sense that more than a few of them looked upon him with some degree of pity, or at least empathy.

It was Sleara who broke the silence at last. His voice had that uneven, almost smiling tone that was usually associated with slow, steady tears.

"How long ago was that?"

"Ten years?" Methias's own voice had come out breathy, and a bit shaky.

"And ... did you tell him?"

Methias offered a chuffing little laugh. "I did. That very night I told him all of it."

"And did he... How did he take the... the all-of-it?"

Methias was still smiling, though his head was now lowered so that he gazed at the stony floor. He rubbed his eyes, looking—he had no doubt—like a child who'd just woken from a nap. *Or one who's finally stopped crying. No reason to be embarrassed by it, is there?*

No, he supposed there wasn't. But it'd been strange. *We talk of reliving the past, but we usually mean either recreating it, or facing a vivid memory of it. This was more like actually returning to it.*

"Methias?"

"You saw it all, did you?"

"Mmhmm."

"So The Cage doesn't just let *you* show *me,* then."

Sleara took a long time to answer. When he finally did, his tone was sheepish and halting—still through a throat full of tears, though they sounded different somehow. "I... yes. I should've told you. Lósgífel used it to truly *see* what her prisoners or her subjects saw." He paused for a few beats. When Methias made no reply, he spoke again. This time, he sounded fearful as well as apologetic. "Methias, I didn't *not tell you* on purpose! I... I..."

His voice faded, becoming resigned. "No, that's a lie. I *did* keep it from you. I didn't want you to find out about the power! I was afraid that if you saw how useful we could be... how keeping us here would help you..." He fell silent again, but only for a moment. "Methias, please—say... *something.*" His voice was a terrified whisper now.

"Forgive me. Still trying to find my... my feet." He looked up and picked Sleara's skull out of the overall gloom, flashing a sad little smile at him. "I understand why you kept your own counsel on this *specific* use of The Cage. Mind you, I don't think you *needed* to."

"I... I trust you, Methias. I do, but—"

Methias shrugged his brows, then shook his head. "It isn't a matter of trust. You were right to be guarded. We've only just met today, after all."

"I don't understand, then. What did you mean I *didn't need to?*"

"I saw everything. I was in the memory as if it were happening *now.* It wasn't me remembering that day in Ad Eniddia." He paused, as if gathering his thoughts. "It was me *reliving* it, moment by moment."

"I don't... What do you mean?"

"When you took me to Rímhril, I saw and heard the world as it was at that time, *on* Rímhril. I *felt* the world *here*, in The Cage. I felt my feet on the stony floor, wasn't affected by Rímhril's wind or temperature, nor could I smell the sea."

"Alright?"

"When I was back at Ad Eniddia—at the Last Bell, I was *back at the Last Bell.* I was nearly thirteen, full of guilt and fear, loss and shame, and at the same time completely empty. I didn't want to *die.* I just didn't want to be *alive* anymore. This wasn't a memory of something a decade ago. It was in the now, for me—real, and miserably *present*. Do you see? I'll need to test the theory, but I think it would work irrespective of you and the others being imprisoned here."

"Oh," said Sleara, and said no more.

Methias sighed through a smile. "I mean to free the lot of you, Sleara ... one way or another. This discovery changes nothing as far as that goes."

"Oh!" Now he sounded hopeful. "This doesn't mean..."

"It does not." Methias's smile softened. "I'm sorry I didn't make that clearer sooner. As I say—I'm still trying to recover my wits."

"It's fine." Sleara paused, but only for the briefest of beats. "How did..."

He trailed off, apparently unsure how to return to the earlier subject.

"Jannon, you mean? He took it far better than I could've hoped. He took me in, helped me heal, and kept me in his counsels for..." He felt the warmth of new tears racing one another down his face. "For many years."

"But you told him all of it? You told him what you did, and he didn't... he didn't care?"

Methias shook his head, still smiling. "I told him all of it, yes. I'd hardly say he didn't care, though. He helped me unknot it all—helped me find my way back."

"But... but you killed your master! That didn't matter to Lord Jannon?"

Methias winced at the accusation. He felt a strong desire to glare at Sleara's skull—perhaps to spit some verbal venom at him in base retaliation. He resisted this knee-jerk reaction. Instead, he tried to force himself out of the quagmire that'd been holding his mind. To his relief, he found it no more difficult than crawling out of a comfortable bed. It took *effort*, but was nowhere near the inner-battle he'd expected.

"What... What's wrong? Why do you look like that?" Sleara ... afraid now. "What did I say?"

Methias shook his head. "I blamed myself for a very long time. I carried that with me like a sickness wherever I went—whatever I did. I can't absolve myself of *all* of it. Certainly, there are things I might've done differently, but that can always be said, can't it?" His tone made the question rhetorical. He became aware of a watchful stillness in the air—in The Cage. Still, he resisted the urge to shift his gaze away from Sleara.

"I don't... What do you..." Sleara's voice strove to maintain some sort of calm cohesion. Predictably, this only resulted in it jagging up and down, in and out as he tried to master his emotions.

"Jannon helped me see the truth, eventually. When I was ready for it."

"What... What truth?" Sleara's voice became small, now. It was the sort of sound it was easy to ignore or overlook, if one had a mind to do either.

"I was convinced, as I say, that I'd killed Emil, or at least caused his death. I was sure that I should've stood at his side when they came, or stayed to fight once he'd fallen. I'd proven an apt pupil, taken easily to the Weave, after all. Failing that, I should've stayed to make report on the men who'd snuck into my master's small tower. If I'd needed to run, I should've run to one of the Astunomía—our constabulary on Nausha. I should've let them sort the matter."

"Why *didn't* you? Why were you so scared too?"

"Instinct?" Methias chuckled, but there was little mirth in it. "I knew the man I'd found standing over Emil's body. I also hadn't *seen* him deliver the killing blow, and he was well known, and well respected." Methias shook his head. "I was a boy—just an apprentice who'd seen the aftermath, not the act itself. What could I possibly do? Who would listen to my word over his, and that of the men with him? The night Emil died, I only knew that I had to run. I nearly got caught, too, but luck was with me." He laughed a bitter, bemused little laugh. "Mind you, I wasn't able to put any of that into words until days later when I was alone... when I was hungry, cold, and half-mad in the wilds of Thorion County." He shook his head again. "In any event, Jannon helped me to heal—helped me work through all of it until I was finally clear-headed enough to see."

The room fell quiet for a longish moment. When Sleara finally broke the silence, his voice was thoughtful—perhaps even hopeful.

"See ... what?"

Methias had been allowing his mind to wander as it pleased. It took him a beat to reconnect to the conversation at hand. When he did, his smile shone out jewel-bright. "That I was more than capable of a great many things. I wasn't some useless, foolish lump just because I was young. I *also* wasn't a match for the situation I'd found myself in. I was a boy of twelve. A boy with a good grasp of the Weave, but a boy, nonetheless. I couldn't have defeated the men in our tower, as at least one of them was a much more experienced caster than I. And *he* was surrounded by at least one apprentice and several fighting men."

"So none of it was your—"

"I *chose*." Methias's interjection was gentle, but insistent. "I *chose* to mistrust the Astunomía. That may or may not have been a wise decision, but it was not a necessary one."

"I don't understand."

"How to explain it..." Methias adjusted his seated posture, causing his back to emit several satisfying pops. "Barring luck and a good many mistakes on the part of my master's killers, I wouldn't have been able to defeat them." He shook his head, then amended, "Best I speak plainly. I wouldn't have been able to *kill* them. To the contrary, staying to fight would've likely meant my death—which would've been useless. Fleeing the tower as they were slowly searching it was the correct, and really only, choice. There's no blame to be had for me there. Would you agree?"

"...Yes?" Sleara sounded dubious, as if he thought he were being tricked somehow.

"I didn't *personally* harm Emil. I wasn't somewhere I shouldn't be, nor doing something I wasn't meant to do. It was early morning, and I was still asleep when he was killed. There's no blame to be had for me there, either. Would you agree?"

"Yes." More certain this time—almost hopeful.

"So—I was right to run, and I'm not to blame for my master's death. Those things are fairly simple and straightforward, yes?"

"Mmhmm. I see. You were afraid that the... the... asstoo-nomm-ee-ah wouldn't listen to you. That's not as sure a thing to judge."

Methias made a "there you have it" gesture. "There are some things that you can't control. There are *always* things that you can, or could have. Do you see?"

Silence met this, but it was brief. When Sleara spoke again, his voice was soft, but steady.

"I'm not ready to talk about it yet."

Methias nodded, the curling ends of his auburn waves bouncing slightly. "Fair enough. You don't *have* to talk about it yet. Hells, you don't have to talk about it at all, truth be told. You just have to be honest."

"Will you... will you give me time?"

Methias smiled again. "I will, at least on this subject."

"On this... Oh!" The boy laughed. It made the chamber seem lighter, somehow. "You still need to know what everyone was screaming and shouting about when you first arrived!"

"Forgot in all the rest, did you?" Methias kept his voice gentle.

"I did." Sleara paused, seeming to collect his thoughts. "I know some of it now. I can... It isn't quite like *hearing* it. It's more like... like remembering it? Does that make any sense?"

"It does, actually. Also, you've been the only one speaking since our return from Rímhril, and I'm still seated on the couch. I'm not touching you at all."

"You're *right*! I think... I think the others are letting me translate for them? I'm not doing it on purpose, but I think that's right."

Methias nodded once more. "Do you need a few moments before we begin?"

Sleara paused, as if considering. When he spoke, it was slow and uncertain. "No? But begin what?"

"Begin trying to sort out who your fellows are, and what they've been set to watch for."

"Set to watch for... Yes, I think that's right. How did you—never mind. You're a caster. Of *course* you figured it out." Sleara paused long enough to chuckle at himself. "There isn't much to it, Methias. They keep saying the same thing. They—whoever *they* are—are moving from the River." The once-elf sounded off. His voice was slow, and low, and somehow guarded.

Guarded is close to it, but doesn't quite hit the mark. He sounds... sheepish?

"But we don't know who *they* are. Is that it?"

Sleara remained silent for a short span. When he answered at last, his voice remained in that same, low tone. "I'm afraid not. Just ... *them.* That's all."

He's embarrassed. That's what I'm hearing. That was reasonable, he supposed. The boy wanted to help, but wasn't seeing how he could.

Reasonable, yes, but things aren't as bad as all that, I think. Well... let's not get ahead of ourselves.

"Sleara, *you* can speak with the others, regardless of language, yes?"

"I... after a fashion?" Sleara fell silent, appearing to collect his thoughts. "We understand ideas... images. I can picture a thing, and the others can see that thing. Does that make ... sense?"

Methias gave a wobbled *after a fashion* sort of nod. Scratching his chin with his thumb, he spoke anew.

"Can you identify which of your fellows actually saw whatever they were set to watch for?"

Sleara paused, considering. "Yes?"

"You don't sound sure of that."

"No, that part I'm certain of. I'm just not certain I understand *why.*"

Methias smiled, looking up to find Sleara's skull amidst the dark curtain's other occupants. "I would like them, each in turn, to show me what they saw."

"How did you... I never told you The Cage could do that."

"Sleara..." He paused, forcing himself to choose his words carefully. Explaining too much of his thought process—of how he arrived at a given conclusion—tended to make others uncomfortable even at the best of times. He'd long since accepted this, but he'd never really understood it. To Methias, it was important to be able to trace back the road one traveled when solving a problem. To most others, mapping that road, so to speak, was tedious... sometimes even disturbing. He made an effort to soften his voice. "You showed me *now,* the present on Rímhril. Then *I* showed you a perfect memory from my past. You said Lósgífel used this chamber to interrogate prisoners. That, and to gain information from her subjects— which is essentially interrogation without the shackles or torture. Putting those two things together made it almost a certainty that you and the others trapped here could do the same thing... could *show* or *share* what you, yourselves, saw and heard."

Sleara appeared to drink that in. "Alright," he said after a brief span of silence. His tone seemed to suggest acceptance rather than understanding. "We can show you."

Methias nodded and stood up, placing the couch between himself and Sleara's floating skull. "Well then..." He drew a deep breath in through his nose, closing his eyes as he held it. A ten count later, he spoke through his exhalation and opened his dreamer's lamps anew. "Let's begin."

CHAPTER NINE

A SIEGE OF MISTS

-I-

Venzene Duchy of Kovalun
County Jižní Pochod
Barony of Hartscross–Jižní Lov
5 Korunasykli: 22 Days after the Red Storm at Westsong

Vlk sat back, watching the red hound withdraw. She padded up the wooden stairs, tail giving what seemed to him like a hopeful sort of wag as she returned to the alure.

"The stínový muž told Štít to come vake you up, Vlk." Jitka's voice was small and solemn as she crossed the short distance between them. She knelt beside him and reached to take his hand. For a moment, she appeared to content herself with that, but only for a moment. With a voice that was both serious and shy, she spoke again. "I vas afraid you *vouldn't* vake... that you vere dead."

He felt dazed. His thoughts were slow to clarify, as if glimpsed through a fog. Keeping his eyes on Štít, he nodded but slowly. His voice was scratched and low, as if he were still half asleep. "I heard. She vas afraid to leave Andrej, though."

Jitka made an *mmhmm* sound. A moment later, she'd dropped his hand as if it had suddenly caught fire. Still kneeling, she raised herself up. A bright blush suffused her small face as she scooted around to meet his eyes. She slid her arms around his neck. The hug was tight and nearly full-body. Her voice was a sweet, almost mewing sound.

"I'm glad you didn't die. I vould have been sad."

He laughed, returning the embrace, albeit with a bit less fervor. "Me too."

For a moment, she moved as if about to try climbing into his lap. He forced her back with gentle hands on her shoulders, squeezing them with a warmth that showed he was in no way annoyed. His mind was starting to clear. A moment later, something clicked in his memory.

"Did you know there vere two of them? Stínových *mužů*?"

"Two? Oh! I only heard the one!" Her voice was conversational in volume as she subsided. It was as if hearing the voices of folk one couldn't see was a matter of everyday course.

"Vhich one did you hear? Vait... you said you heard him telling Štít to come vaken me. You heard the older man, then." He grinned, releasing her shoulders and scooting back slightly. "The other vas one of Lakkrid's folk. A scout. The one vith red hair. Do you remember him?"

Jitka screwed up her face in concentration. Her expression was absurd, but so obviously genuine that he had to stifle another laugh.

"I don't know. The scouts all look the same."

Vlk had been opening his mouth to disagree when he heard a cheer go up from the barbican. Perhaps a dozen strides away, he saw the circle of fighting men widen as the northern gate opened inward. Nine horses came into view, two by two until the last—Ruční Kopí on his massive bay. Edmund stood by to greet their riders. His head was too tall to miss, even at this distance.

The opened gate let a gust of wind through. Vlk felt it playing with his dark brown curls, blowing thin grit up into his face. He sneezed, then ran his sleeve beneath his nose.

"Come." He stood, reaching a hand down to Jitka. When she'd made it to her feet, he led the way over to the stairs nearest the gate, moving to stand on them for a better vantage. He watched Lady Kastan turn her Sheshik stallion to face the rest of the riders. She held a sword aloft. He thought he saw darker spots along the blade's naked surface, but he couldn't be sure. Nor, indeed, did he know how he felt about the idea. He'd been told darker spots like that usually meant either rust or fresh droplets of blood.

"Poslouchej mě!" Her voice was fair, full of a natural authority. A moment later, she reverted to the Trade Tongue. "Hear me..." She bowed her head for a moment. Her horse began to rear beneath her, but it was a half-hearted thing. In any event, she paid it no mind. "Which of you made the decision to ride out onto that killing field?"

The assembled riders made no reply.

"Go on, then." Kastan's voice wasn't cold, per se, but it carried with it an absence of warmth. "Someone say *something*. Which of you gave the order? Who rallied you to ride out and risk your lives in an unnecessary fight?"

"Any man among us vould've done the same, Lady. At least any man who had the means—a horse, gear of var."

Other voices joined in almost at once, echoing the sentiment. Vlk couldn't see the man who'd first spoken, nor did he recognize the voice. Not that it much mattered. It might've been a Bluemark. It might just as easily have been some resident of the encampment he didn't personally know. All he *did* know was that it had come from one of the men that stood surrounding the riders.

Kastan didn't look for the speaker. She just continued looking at the others in her vanguard. It was a look Vlk wouldn't have wanted aimed at him. He'd done nothing one way or the other, yet *he* felt uncomfortable seeing that expression darken her face.

"Lady Kastan," Ruční Kopí spoke up. "If you would look on us for someone to blame, then look on me."

Vlk heard a veil-muffled voice from the white-armored wraith rider, but he wasn't close enough to make it out. Whatever he said, the Percoy men all nodded in their saddles.

Kastan shook her head, then bowed it briefly as if to collect her thoughts. "It was foolish. Brave, but foolish."

Finally, the black-clad boy at Ruční Kopí's side urged his horse forward. As he did, Vlk saw a long and singular warbraid along the little Bluemark's back.

"Lady Kastan, we," the boy gestured around, "...all of us made the decision. Even your brave Johanka. We rode out, and we would do it again." The bold page, or squire, or whatever he was, turned to look at the assembled faces of his fellow riders. They all nodded. "Most folk here would've done the same."

"There was no reason to put yourselves in—"

"*You* would have done the same." This was an older voice that Vlk knew. It had come from one of the Percoy riders—one whose face he recognized. His mind was still too sluggish to come up with the relevant name, but never mind. It would come back to him, eventually. "You would have done the same for any one of us—for the very *least* of us. Ctít strážce ohně, Lady! *(Honor the fire keeper).* You've only to look at the fellow behind you in the saddle for proof of that!" The speaker wasn't loud, but rather insistent.

"And in trade, Johanka's life—"

That same familiar voice cut across her once more, albeit gently. "Was willingly, if not gladly given, Lady. Her sacrifice should be honored, not diminished, surely."

"It couldn't be helped, Lady," another voice from the crowd. "*Most* women aren't cut out for war. She should be lauded for making the attempt, of course, but as I say: most women aren't—"

Kastan didn't turn, but her sword moved with a speed that was difficult to follow. The crowd grew utterly silent as the blade came to a stop, pointed at what Vlk presumed was the speaker's face or throat. No blood flew, so the man clearly wasn't dead.

"Reeeeeeally, Rolf Breckendorf?" A woman's voice came hurtling down from the barbican like a spear. Vlk could see a Bluemark archer with a longbow in hand and a sword on her back. Its ringed pommel peaked out over her right shoulder. "Women aren't cut out for war? Well, I'll just hand the captain my gear then, shall I?" Her tone made the question rhetorical—almost a statement.

"Erika, I *said* most... I obviously wasn't speakin' 'bout *you*!" The man's voice now sounded both defensive and ... afraid? Yes, Vlk would almost swear to it.

Each rider's face turned withering looks down toward the man who'd spoken. Even Hajvarr—Count Edmund's Ruční Kopí—looked down toward the speaker with dull disgust. One by one, those in Percoy livery slid their helmets off.

Vomen! Havoc's horn, they're all vomen?

Vlk tried not to gape. He managed it fairly well... right up until the face and voice he'd found so familiar was revealed to be Vlasta.

But she's so old! How... vhy does she vear armor and vield a svord? She's old enough to have been Lady Kastan's vet nurse!

Then the wraith rider lifted a spearless hand. Vlk knew who it would be as soon as the white glove began to move, and his heart sank. A moment later, Fetinba lowered her armored veil for all to see. She, too, was gazing at the speaker, but her face didn't bear any anger or disgust. Rather, she bore a look of detachment, as if looking at some stranger's unruly child. The assembled crowd must have been just as shocked as Vlk, for they remained in a state of stunned silence for a few beats.

Edmund broke the spell at last.

"Lady Kastan, it was *I* who ordered the gates open to let them hie after you. They came to me and explained what had happened. That you'd thought swiftly and sent Vlasta back to warn us all, while you remained to search for both information on our soon-to-be attackers and your own lost hunting party. Your decisive action gave us time to prepare. I wasn't about to reward your selfless decisions with abandonment."

She turned to look down at Edmund, though given his height, this amounted to little more than a dipping of her chin.

Vlk's voice caused all heads to turn his way. "Lady Kastan! You vere the lone rider? You... you vere..." He could barely breathe. He hadn't meant to speak, but his mouth or mind appeared to have other ideas. "Lady, you rode like hells's own harbinger!"

The crowd murmured and rumbled, making a sound somewhere between awed disconcert and surprised pride.

Edmund spoke up before Kastan could make any reply. His voice was rich and smooth and carried well. "They asked—Vlasta, my Ruční Kopí, and Sergeant Blevelsket. They asked leave to ride out to find and escort you back, should you be harried in sight of the encampment. I presume, Vlasta, that these others had the same freedom of choice?"

As Edmund drew the crowd's attention, Vlk was flooded with an almost abject sense of relief. Until recently, their lord had been a distant, intimidating figure. Now Vlk found himself feeling nothing but gratitude for the man's presence. Lakkrid had always spoken of the count with clear affection, as if they knew one another well. He'd believed him, though many of the other boys hadn't. Still, that didn't make Count Edmund any less intimidating. The man was called Edmund the Tall for a reason. He towered over... *everybody*. But never mind. If he was speaking, that meant all eyes were on *him*. And if they were on Edmund, they were no longer on Vlk.

Vlasta gave a single nod. "You are as perceptive as ever, Excellency. Each of them raced to their armor and made ready for battle. It's a thing none of us are strangers to, thanks to the training Lady Kastan's given us."

The count nodded, making a *there you have it* gesture.

Kastan looked at Edmund for a long moment. Vlk couldn't be sure, but he got the impression that she was coming to terms with the count's words.

"I would not have been parted from you, my lady. Not for the wide world. We *both* find ourselves fortunate that you inspire such loyalty, and train those who follow you with such fervor." Edmund's voice had taken on a queer note. It was full of emotion, yet both steady and sure. "*I have long seen your worth.*" He turned to gaze around the assemblage. "Has anyone here seen reason to doubt or question it?"

No one spoke. Vlk thought he heard chanting in some foreign tongue on the wind, but he couldn't be sure.

"My Lady?" Edmund reached a hand up, as if meaning to help her dismount. She murmured something to the man who rode double behind her. A moment later, she said something else to him. He leaned back, releasing her from his embrace. She slid from the saddle with easy grace. As she did, the man leaned heavily over, planting his hands in the place she'd just vacated.

That's Andrej's father... Vell, that should please him. Still, he doesn't look vell. His face is very pale, and his shirt is soaked through.

Vlk was yanked away from his assessment of Rákos by what came next. As soon as Kastan was on her feet before him, Edmund laid his massive hand to the side of her face—a gesture of relief and deep affection. Then he pulled her into a tight embrace, much to the collective gasps and surprised murmurs of the crowd.

Vlk had a moment of absolute rage that he didn't immediately understand. His mind had drawn down to a single, searing phrase.

How dare he!

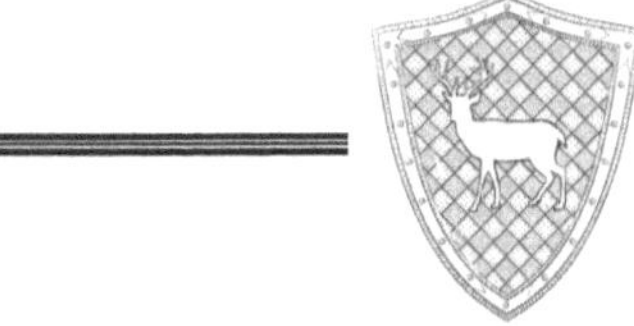

-II-

Kastan froze as Edmund's arms enfolded her. He leaned down, lowering his head toward her left shoulder as if he meant to kiss her neck. She could feel his mustache against her skin. Gooseflesh had all but *leapt* into being. Her face felt hot with a mixture of confusion and shame. Then she heard Edmund's whisper.

"Kastan, I beg you. Say nothing. Make no reply, but play along in all other respects. Embrace me now, and trust that I know your heart."

What in hells was he playing at? She *did* trust him, and so she obeyed.

That trust did precisely nothing to counter the essential weirdness of his touch. No sooner had she committed to the embrace than another unexpected emotional storm crashed over her. She felt herself *yielding* to it. She hadn't realized how much she'd needed warm, human contact after her race had been run. And Edmund was a man she both loved and respected. Still, to be publicly embraced like this was... Well, there was no chance of it being kept quiet amongst the populace first here, then county-wide... assuming they all survived.

He released her, taking her free dim-hand in his, then turning to the shocked assemblage.

"I ask you again," he boomed, "can any of you speak a word against her worth? Her worth as a Lady... as a leader?" He paused, taking pains to cast about in all directions before continuing. "Lady, leader, scout, swordsman... or perhaps it would be best to say swords-*woman*. Will any of you speak against her? *Fault* her?"

Silence. All eyes flitted between Edmund and Kastan, then back again.

"Can even *one* of you deny her love for this county, its people, its prosperity?"

Edmund, what in all the hells are you...

She knew he spoke the truth as he saw it—perhaps even the *objective* truth. It didn't make it any easier to hear. Her eyes had begun to mist over. To hear a man for whom she had such respect... to hear him speaking so openly as he sang her praises was an unexpected joy. She had barely enough time to register this feeling of gratitude before his next words forced her to gape, eyes wide.

"And yet none of you know the *sacrifices* she has made for the realm's benefit." He shook his head, then found and held her gaze for a beat. "Kastan, you have waited long enough. *We* have waited long enough."

"Ed... Excellency?"

He laced their fingers together, giving her hand a brief squeeze. "When first we met, my heart was too full of grief for my lost Noemi. I had no thought, save for battle. I lived only to be revenged for her death and the burning of Měsíční Prst." He paused, looking down. His next words came out in a softer tone—awed and full of gratitude. "You waited. Other suitors came, and you found gentle ways to rebuff their advances."

Kastan could only stare.

"Then your brother Caros's skill and goodly heart began their walk toward the Line. And you feared coloring his reputation with county favor. And *then* your father sought to marry the Baroness Kengar. Again and again, for propriety's sake, and for the good of the county, you waited. *We* waited. You learned to rule, to fight, to govern, and to guard. With gentility and grace, you spurned *all* suitors who came to call. All this time you've waited." He shook his head, a broad and hopeful smile on his boyish face. "I would have you wait no more."

Kastan's heart had sped up to such a pace that either she could no longer feel it, or it had stopped altogether. She couldn't tell which, nor did it much matter. Edmund had spoken her truths—truths she'd never guessed he'd been privy to—and dressed them in such mendacity... and *still,* she could only stare.

Then he dropped to one knee.

"I've grown tired of waiting, Lady, and past tired of making you keep this secret and your silence." Edmund looked up, meeting her black dreamer's lamps with his misted blue ones. He blinked very slowly, allowing those eyes to overspill. "I would have you stand with me—my lady-wife, knit soul to soul." He kissed the hand he held, squeezing it tightly—almost painfully. "My heart is in your hands now, and its drum beats fierce and sure. I would forever hold the gentle hand that lifts the sword."

Gasps, shrieks of either shock, joy, or a mixture of both, and an absurd crescendo of shushing sounds as everyone told everyone else to be quiet.

No! I'm caught, and there's nothing I can do! Her knees had begun to weaken, along with every muscle in her face. She could feel the color draining from it, even as it rushed to congregate in the two burning brands that were her cheeks. *He's asked me, and he's done it in such a public place that I've no recourse! Damn you, Edmund, how could... how...*

Edmund looked up at her with that broad, uncertain grin that made him look like a mustachioed boy. He squeezed her hand again, adding the tiniest pull toward him—too minor a movement for anyone to see.

Say nothing. Make no reply but play along in all other respects. Embrace me now, and trust that I know your heart. Those had been Edmund's whispered words. Suddenly she understood. All of it? No. She didn't understand *any* of what Edmund was doing, but he'd been clear enough in his request.

Say nothing. Make no reply but play along in all other respects. She could do that. Hells, what choice had he left her?

She didn't have to summon tears. Her fear and misery were more than enough to call them forth. The smile, on the other hand, she needed to will herself to maintain. She stepped back and made as if to haul him to his feet. His smile went from hopeful to relieved. He let himself be drawn up, then toward her. They embraced once more, both in tears for very different reasons.

"Thank you for your trust, Kastan. This part is almost over." His murmured words were nearly drowned out by the roar of the crowd's approval, despite his mouth being directly beside her ear.

She laughed as they broke apart, nodding through her tears.

"Olga?" Edmund turned toward a woman so aged she made Vlasta look like a young maiden. "Please take my Lady Kastan to your good husband. Hajvarr will accompany you both." He turned toward Ruční Kopí with a grin. "You'll protect the Lady Kastan again, Ruční Kopí, won't you?"

"I... I will, Excellency. As you say." Ruční Kopí seemed numb and wore a smile that stopped well below his eyes.

"Go with them, if you please. After all, we no longer need to hope for tomorrow!" He lifted his chin and spoke so that all and sundry heard his triumphant shout. "Přišel zítřek!" *(Tomorrow has come!)*

The assemblage cheered. Many congratulatory shouts rained down on Kastan, though she heard none from her own folk. They would know how odd—how *miserable* this situation was for her. *But they didn't hear Edmund's whispered words.* She would have to hold onto hope that he did, indeed, know her heart. That he knew how little she would've wanted this. With a bitter resolve hid firmly behind a mask of shocked joy, she reminded herself of that old axiom of Eobum's once again. Hope doesn't hunt *for* you.

No indeed. Nothing for it but to play this out. Play it out and look for a means of escape, if it comes to that.

After dismounting, Ruční Kopí walked to her side wearing a look of—she would've sworn to it—barely hidden terror. The old woman, Olga, fell into step beside her as the gate at last swung closed.

-III-

Vlk's mind was racing. In one breath, he was enraged. In the next, he was simply miserable. Then came the realization that he should be happy for the lady. This was surely a day long in coming. Her patience had been rewarded, as had her loyalty. But...

For a moment, he fell into a waking dream, wherein he was standing before her in the gloaming. She looked down at him, running her fingers through his brown curls as she spoke.

"I've told him no. Of course I have."

He felt himself smile as he lifted his chin to meet her eyes.

"I've paid your fool of a father and your silver-seeking mother. They've never seen you as I do. They see the boy they think you are, but it doesn't matter. They don't matter anymore. They won't dare bother us again, my brave knight. You're free... we're free." Her smile was everything—the antidote to all of life's little meannesses.

He beamed at her. He was afraid to speak, knowing somehow that it would break the spell.

"I'm yours now, if you'll have me." She looked vulnerable, suddenly—uncertain and afraid. *"Hells, I've given up the whole of the county for you. You won't abandon me, will you, Vlk?"*

"Vlk?"

"No..."

"No? *Vhat* do you say to me?"

Vlk felt an iron grip on his left forearm. Next he knew, he'd been all but yanked off of his feet for the second time in less than half a bell. He managed to haul his arm free just in the nick. He overbalanced, slamming into the palisade's wall on his right, and the dream broke apart. The mist over his mind cleared. He looked toward his attacker and saw...

"Father! I vas vool-gathering. I'm sorry!"

Liška glared at him for a long moment. At length he nodded, puffing air out through his nose. "You shouldn't be out here. Your mother ess vorried. Get home. *Now,* unless you'd not sit easy." He looked to the side, up at Jitka. She was half-cowering against the palisade wall, eyes enormous. "Go find Daryna... *now.*"

Jitka turned to Vlk as if for confirmation, but his father was having none of it.

"Don't look to Vlk. Do ess I say... *now.*" Liška's voice never raised in volume, but its intensity and authority were an almost physical force.

Vlk saw Jitka break into silent tears, then bolt down the stairs, heading deeper into the encampment.

"I von't be going home, father. I have *vork* here."

"Ruční Kopí! Hajvarr!" Jastrab's voice pulled Vlk's attention away from his father. The Bluemark's captain had come halfway down the stairs behind Vlk and was shouting past him toward the gate.

"Can it wait?" Ruční Kopí slowed his step as he and Lady Kastan walked past them.

"Can you call your damned hound?" Jastrab sounded more amused than annoyed.

Ruční Kopí laughed, calling to Štít. She barked a reply, but stayed where she was.

"Don't lie to me, boy," Vlk's father hissed, reasserting his claim on his attention. "I know vhat vork you have, and none off et ess here!" Liška leaned forward, brows knitting together as he glared.

"We can't get her to leave, either!" Jastrab's shout turned into a chuckle. "She's taken a shine to the boy!"

"Which one?"

"Andrej!"

Ruční Kopí stopped short. Vlk could see the look of surprise on his face. He shrugged. "Andrej! Come stand a watch with me?"

"I don't vork for *you,* Father." The look of anger and disbelief on Liška's face gave Vlk an *extreme* sense of satisfaction. "I'm here to help one of the count's archers."

"I'm meant to stay at my post..." Andrej sounded dubious.

"Your spot will be here when you get back, Andrej." This was Sergeant Waltyr. Vlk was almost sure of it. "No fear. There'll be plenty of time for you to stand up here and shoot his Excellency's enemies." The topic was grim, but at least the man sounded kindly. That was something.

"I'll be just behind you, Ruční Kopí," Andrej called. "We both will." A moment later, hunter and hound slid past Jastrab and down the stairs. The hero's hound slid by with a single lick to the back of Vlk's hand, but Andrej stopped to touch his friend's shoulder. "Keep an eye on the gear. I doubt I'll be long."

"My boy doesn't vork for you..."

Andrej stopped a single step further down the stair, bow in hand. He turned slowly to meet Liška's hostile gaze, speaking in a calm, matter-of-fact tone. "No. He works for the Count, as do we all. I was told to get someone my age to keep my quivers full on the wall. If not Vlk, who am I to use?" Andrej paused for a beat. "Uděláš to, strýčku??" *(Will you do it, uncle?)*

Liška was too stunned to fume. He met Andrej's calm, steady gaze with confusion. He'd clearly expected to be obeyed and was prepared for nothing else.

Vlk wasn't sure whether to be happy or angry. His father's reaction was priceless. And Andrej calling him *uncle* had burnished the entire exchange with a sheen of respect that Vlk doubted he could've managed. It had been cleverly done, but it had also served to turn Vlk's frustration at the man into a form of disgust.

A gasp from the crowd near the gate drew everyone's attention. Andrej looked, stiffened, then ran as if his life depended on it.

"Andrej! It's your father!" That was Pavel's voice from within the crowd. "Ruční Kopí! He's bleeding!"

"Bring him to my command tent. My scholar is there already." Edmund's voice was full of calm authority. He paused as the crowd began to part. "Easy now!"

"Liška, isn't it?" Jastrab's voice from just behind Vlk. "If you need to take him, we'll try and find someone to replace him. If not..." A heavy hand fell on Vlk's shoulder. "I'll keep an eye on him."

Liška looked shocked and gratified that the Bluemark captain knew him by name. He wasn't half as shocked as Vlk was. Why was this man offering to *help*? The Bluemark were all... were all...

Men. They're all men. Vell, men and vomen. Valtyr has been good enough, and the voman vith the bow... Erika? She took Lady Kastan's side... It wasn't very convenient—each Bluemark being his or her own person. It had been much easier and more satisfying when he could hate them on sight after what'd happened in the play yard.

But it's true. They did drive those men out of their group for vhat they did. Pravdivý jako zítřek.

(True as tomorrow.)

His father gave a slow nod, and what Vlk took as an uncomfortable smile before withdrawing. "Do vhat the captain tells you, Vlk. He ess a vise man who hess seen many bettles."

Vlk looked up at Jastrab, whose hand was still on his shoulder. He was met with a face, wearing what seemed like a very genuine smile.

"Help Waltyr while you wait for your friend. Andrej doesn't follow orders very well, but he's got good aim and no fear. We can work with that."

Vlk nodded, turned his back on his father without so much as a nod, and walked up to the alure with the captain.

-IV-

Kastan strove to turn back toward the gate, but Hajvarr gainsaid her.

"You must leave it to *them*, Lady. You've other duties."

"What duties do you suppose I have?" She kept her voice at a low hiss, though she did nothing to hide her frustration from him. "Other than my duty to my own, that is. I did *not* ride through all of that with Rákos just to let him die the moment we're back within our walls!"

He turned back and gave the elderly woman, Olga, a nod. Kastan felt the matron's arm snake around her own, turning her bodily with surprising strength.

Well, you've kept at least that much wit, Ruční Kopí. The thought was distant, yet it carried with it a strange sort of comfort. It would've been wholly inappropriate for *him* to have laid hands on her, save for moments when her safety was in question. No matter.

"No. Do not turn me as if I were lost and in need of guidance, Mistress. I will *not* leave him to an uncertain fate." She followed this pronouncement with an attempt to free her fettered arm.

"And the county, Excellency?" Olga's dry voice was smooth and unaffected.

Kastan prised her arm loose at last, turning and moving back toward the gate. She could see Andrej's father being placed on what appeared to be Fetinba's white kontusze. Taking a single step, she stopped short, as if an invisible barrier had barred her way. She had no memory of turning, but found herself meeting Olga's gaze. Trying to read it. What she saw in the elderly scholar's eyes filled her with dawning comprehension ... and dread.

"You are no healer, Lady, but you *do* have other duties." Hajvarr, too, kept his voice low while hiding none of his frustration from those around him. "Beyond that, he's being taken to the very place we mean to escort *you*. So Havoc's horn, sheath your damned sword and stop fighting *us* when there are enemies enough to go around!"

Kastan looked at her bright hand and registered the sword's weight for the first time in what felt like hours. Nodding, she sheathed the weapon across her back and allowed herself to be led toward Edmund's command tent.

When they arrived, there was a single guard stood outside of the tent. He was one of Ruční Kopí's, she was quite certain, though she hadn't the faintest idea what his name might've been. After Hajvarr passed a quick word that Pavel and some others were coming with both a wounded man and his own red hound in tow, the three of them passed into the large marquee.

Olga led them to the back of the tent, reaching behind a heavy, grey pelt to grab the canvas wall beneath it. She stepped back, pulling a section of canvas with her. The opening revealed a shallow landing. At its end, five heavily carpeted stairs led down into the count's private chambers.

Most of the encampment's permanent residence had their homes built in a similar fashion. Each tent hid the entryway to at least one underground room. Most were lined with stone and wood and housed both the resident's family and their worldly goods in relative comfort and safety. No storm could destroy the encampment as a whole, nor its reserves of food, fresh water, and dry goods. Each building was attached to a labyrinthine catacomb system that served both to honor the dead and interconnect the living. This meant that no household was entirely on its own in times of strife, no matter what storms might befall.

Kastan had never been in the count's residence—at least not here, at Jižní Lov. She'd attended several formal functions at his residence in the County Seat, along with the rest of the county's well-heeled and haughty, but that was hardly the same thing. She had no time to truly drink in her surroundings, however. She'd marked the thick rugs, wood paneling, and stone brazier at the front room's center before a familiar voice drew her attention.

"Lady Kastan? It *is*! My lay-dee, honor the fire keeper but it is such a joy to see you again!" The old man's delight made his quavering tones sound more like an expression of emotion than one of age. "Do forgive me, my lady. Had I known you were to bright-t-ten this cham-ber I would have made both it and its old owl prez-*ent*-able!" He enunciated each syllable of that last word—making it somehow rhythmic and warm.

"Master Radek!" She beamed as she turned to find him—frail-framed, thin-maned, and wide-eyed—gliding toward her with an ivory-toothed smile. The teeth were carved things, a rare and undoubtedly expensive gift from the count after the rebellion. It had been a much younger Radek who had tended to Caros's wounds after the bandit's arrow had struck his dim arm. Hells, had it been that many years a'gone?

She embraced the old fellow—a wholly inappropriate breach of station she was only too happy to flout. "How are you, Master Radek? I'd heard you were feeling poorly."

The old man melted into the embrace, though he withdrew himself before it could be mistaken for anything untoward. Chuckling, he patted her hand as she slid her arm through his. "Nothing to worry about, my lady. Though, I do thank you for your concern. I'm simply getting too old to take the stairs any more often than is strict-ly necessary." Again, he broke this last word into its component syllables. "But what's brought you down here, Lady? Happy though I am to see you, your presence here might be seen as..." He trailed off as his wife and Hajvarr walked down the stairs.

"Ah! Olga, my sweet, look who's come to see us!"

"I've brought her, Radek." Olga's voice was as dry and business-like as ever. "You've no need to keep up your deception."

"I've no idea what you mean, my sweeting." He sounded affronted, though the quaver in his voice made even that sound endearing.

"Radek, we don't have time for this," said Hajvarr. His voice at last matched the sense of fear she'd caught from him earlier. He was firmly in control of himself, but his fear was impossible to miss.

"Oh, now see here... You and your men *all-all-always* think there's no time. You've no time to read or talk—think or question. No, you're all far too busy standing around near the tour-na-ment field, looking windswept and in-ter-est-ing to... to..."

"Radek!" Olga's voice was a whipcrack. "Přišel zítřek!"

(Tomorrow has come.)

The old man froze. Kastan could feel his entire body shake, then tense. He squeezed her hand, bowed his head, then stood up straight. When he spoke again, the quaver in his voice was gone. It was replaced with a full, sad tone that made it clear that the man of a moment before—the man she'd known for almost a decade—had been a lie.

"Oh, my lady... I'm so sorry it's come to this."

She yanked her arm away, stepping back to face all three of them.

"You haven't told her, then." Radek's voice made this a statement, not a question. "No, I suppose you haven't had the time. I suppose I—"

"Need to toddle up those stairs," Olga cut in. "A wounded man will arrive shortly. Hajvarr? Be certain we aren't disturbed. Husband? Return as swiftly as the situation allows. I will explain everything to Her

Excellency. Go now."

Both men nodded their heads and made their way out.

Kastan was amazed to see Radek moving around nearly as smoothly as Hajvarr. She waited until they'd left, then turned her gaze on Olga.

"Count Edmund knows you don't have any interest in him, lady. You'll almost certainly avoid the marriage bed."

She fought the urge to glare... to raise her voice... to do *something* that would serve to vent her confused and impotent rage. "Then why did he... Why did *we* play that little comedy out?"

"Because the County needs continuity. Edmund has no heir, and if he named one without proper pomp and circumstance—without that heir having gained renown and reputation on his or her own? It would lead to bedlam, Lady. There would be squabbles over this man's right and that man's due. Without Edmund, those squabbles would turn to skirmishes, and the county would suffer. A living bride, on the other hand..."

Kastan sighed her understanding. "...Neatly sidesteps questions of succession. Very well." She shook her head in obvious frustration. "But surely there were other, more suitable—"

The derision in Olga's snort was almost a slap. "Hardly. He'd hoped to, perhaps, finally find someone to give him a child, but he's had no taste for that since Cyril and Georgi's rebellion. He recognizes the need for an heir of *some* kind, but..." She gave a soft sigh.

"But ... what?"

Olga bowed her head and shook it a single time. "If I'm being honest, I think he's afraid."

"Of children? That's *nonsense*. Edmund *adores* children. I've seen him often enough, doting on Lakkrid. And Fetinba had him wrapped around her little finger from the first."

"He fears dishonoring her memory.... *their* memory." She paused for a beat, looking not at, but through Kastan. "Noemi—his lost love? She was carrying his child when..."

She couldn't finish. She met Kastan's eyes with a look of such profound sadness that it seemed almost blasphemous to even bear witness to it.

Finally, Olga spoke again. "Hajvarr was Noemi's younger brother. He'd been squired to Edmund for some time when Syr Georgi razed Měsíční Prs. The Red Hound had been for the baby. He'd been traveling to present it to Noemi when..." She looked away, speaking the rest in an old but still anguished whisper. "It was Hajvarr who found the village's smoking ruin. After searching for survivors that didn't exist, it was he who rode to give Edmund the grim news. He bore a cloven shield painted in Georgi's arms."

Kastan simply stared, numb. Everyone had known about Noemi, though mainly it was the county's women who dwelt upon that aspect of the war. Songs and poems that spoke of the rebellion *all* told of Edmund's love for the Orchardist's daughter. That she'd been with child? That had somehow been left out of the tales and tragic tellings—by design, no doubt.

It felt as if she'd been riding in a thick fog. Now that the sun was burning through the gloom, she'd looked around to find the landscape utterly unfamiliar.

"So." Olga's voice had taken on a forced crispness. "Edmund has sired no heirs. He's simply found no woman that matches his memory of Noemi, nor makes him forget her for more than a moment. He's kept the idea alive, of course. Failing that, he'd hoped to pass the throne on to one of three people—Aetanis Haluzfeld, your brother Caros, or you."

"If he was of a mind to do that, why hasn't he done so already?" Kastan sighed, lifting a hand, then dropping it to her thigh. "Ah, because he'd hoped to name Aetanis, and wanted him to grow into the position. That, or fail to do so." She laughed. It was a bitter thing. "And *that* was why Aetanis was tasked with leading Edmund's men at the War of Counties. And here am I, thinking it was a mere concession of curtesy toward the ass's brilliant father."

"But none of that matters now. Edmund is out of time."

Kastan's head snapped up. "What? Why? This is just precautionary, surely."

"Edmund has named you as his intended, and publicly. Havoc's Horn, the words he spoke to you were from his proposal to *her*. He had a song written to mark the occasion, but after Noemi's death he forbade its performance in any hall." Olga shook her head. "I suspect those were all of the words he could recall. Whether it was a prayer to her shadow or a signal to me, I couldn't say, but I recall the song well enough."

Kastan would gladly have wept, if she could've. Her eyes were hot, dry things just now. She felt guilty in a vague, subsurface manner. As if she somehow should have known—should have been more of a comfort to Edmund. She did love him. Not in an amorous or romantic way, perhaps, but she did love him.

But what could I possibly have done? Even knowing... what could I... Her mind seemed to seize up. *Caros... he must've known, surely. He fought at Edmund's side—was among his personal guard during almost the entirety of the rebellion!*

Olga's voice cut this realization short.

"So yes, Lady Kastan. He *could* back out, or allow *you* to back out, but that won't come to pass. You *are* the publicly recognized Consort, and will thus be named Baroness of Hartscross—Countess of Jižní Pochod." The older woman moved to a door Kastan hadn't noticed before. Upon reaching it, Olga turned back to regard her. "All that remains is for us to complete some administrative tasks, and for you to be given some necessary knowledge."

Kastan shook her head. "No. No, Edmund would never give up, in, or over so lightly. Someone has pressed him into this."

"*There,* you are correct."

"Then the entire *matter* is precautionary. If he is coerced by witch or wiles, it falls to us to set him free. If we *fail,* then, and *only* then, would I assume the county throne." Low and muffled voices floated down from beyond the canvas. They'd finally arrived with poor Rákos. She spared a thought for his speedy recovery, then turned back to gaze at Olga's affectless face. "Well?"

"May I speak plainly, Lady?"

"Without me having to tease your drift out of you? That would be a welcome change, yes."

Olga ignored this jibe and stepped closer. "I need you to stop acting like a child. You *are* the Baroness of Hartscross—the Countess of Jižní Pochod. Only a conversation and a few scratches of a quill stand between you and that reality. *And...*" She held up a hand to gainsay Kastan, who was indeed drawing breath to protest. "If you continue to waste time, you are only serving to make your future, and the future of the *entire county,* more difficult after Edmund's death."

Kastan... stared. For a moment, it was all she could do. Finally, she shook her head. "Edmund has survived countless battles in far less fortified locations, Olga. And Jastrab's men are here, bolstering the county's own... I know the enemy is monstrous, but..."

"Kastan, no. Edmund has made his will known. He knows battle, as you say. He knows it better than anyone save, perhaps Baron Vagiaedelt. And in his estimation, he will die, and soon. Possibly even this very day. It may be assassins he fears. It may be this new attacker you so recently outpaced to return to us. In either case, the outcome is the same. Edmund expects to be killed. He has publicly named you as his long-silent, long-suffering love, and in doing so, all but assured your smooth ascension. Now, will you *accept* what I've told you? Or must we waste time and—lest we forget—*lives?*"

Kastan found the woman's eyes. She held their gaze for a long moment, searching for a lie that wasn't there.

"Lady, I have known Edmund since he was a boy. He has always sought to better the world around him and the lives of those within his reach, to aid. I've no desire to stand here as you search for ways to thwart Edmund's final act of benevolence, but I will. Your decision to outwit *your* duty does nothing to change my own."

It was enough. Kastan bowed her head in acceptance. She spoke in a humble, resigned tone.

"What must I learn, and what must I do?"

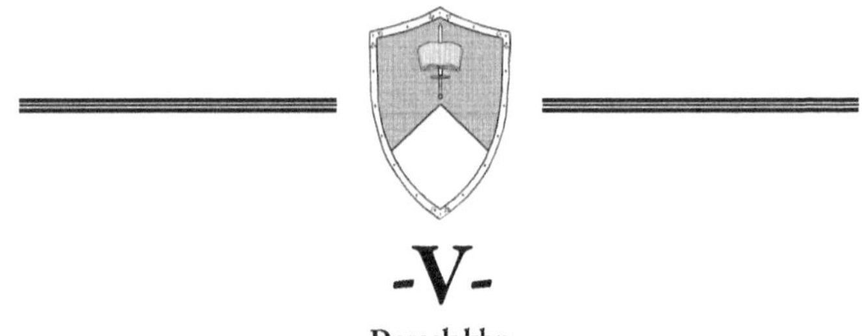

-V-

Dereek khn
Yrxa Castle
5 Korunasykli: 22 Days after the Red Storm at Westsong

"Lankaajh? I need you to step in here for a moment, please. All's well. No fear on that score." Methias paused for a beat, considering. "If you feel the need to call someone else to stand guard first, I'll understand. It's you, specifically, that I need in here, though... your particular expertise." He did his best to keep his voice neutral and calm. The truth was, his mind was racing and dragging his pulse along for the ride.

"My lord? Have you solved it, then?"

You sound hopeful. I fear I'm going to disappoint you, Daephone.

"I've made progress, certainly. I understand a good deal more about The Cage now than I did. But there's still work to be done. We won't hear uncontrollable screaming, though. Not for a while, at least."

She nodded, then leaned her head back, rolling the stiffness out of her neck. "Will you wait out here while I go fetch Tharus, Lord?"

He grunted, then nodded. *Never fight a battle you can't win.* That was another of Fyken Presh's axioms. The battle, in this case, was about whether to push Daephone to enter the chamber now, as opposed to summoning

Tharus. Methias didn't *need* to hurry her. He simply *wanted* to. He was certain she could help him to identify what he couldn't quite place.

Leaning back into the room for a moment, he spoke aloud. "I won't be long. I need to fetch someone."

Sleara's head nodded and bobbed along the shadowy surface between the pilasters. "I don't think we mean to go anywhere, Methias." He made his voice playful, if a bit dry.

Methias stepped fully out of the chamber, smiling as he closed the door behind him. "Shall we go together? Or shall I seek him out myself?"

An instant later, he noticed Daephone's thin-lipped stare. She gave a cautious blink, a slow nod, and made an *after-you* gesture.

An interval approaching ten minutes came and went. Things were as well as may be—well enough to be going on with, anyway. Tharus had been stationed beyond the door, and Daephone now stood beside him within The Cage. She'd seen the chamber in its active state on more than one occasion. And Methias had thought an end to the screaming madness would put her more at ease. To the contrary, its watchful silence seemed to increase her anxiety.

Well, as you always said, Emil... Wait. You taught me, but who's taught Daephone?

Methias's grin was brief but bright. "My master, Emil Draksh, made us memorize many axioms—many statements of truth that were self-evident."

"If... never mind, my lord. Forgive me. Go on."

Methias frowned, albeit briefly. "No, please. Say what you were meant to say."

She chewed on her lower lip for a beat, then gave a brisk nod. "Yes, my lord. You said they were self-evident things."

"I did."

"If they were self-evident, why did he make you memorize them by rote?"

Methias made an *ah* sound. "For the same reason Fyken Presh does when teaching and training. Short phrases help secure the ideas *behind* those phrases in the mind of the student. They're expressions of simple truths that we often lose sight of, day by day. Memorizing the axiom and being able to recite it by rote means it's harder to forget. Not impossible, of course."

"But harder. *I* see." She paused as if to file that answer away, then returned her attention to both Methias and the room at large. "Thank you."

Methias gave a nod, then went back to his earlier point.

"One of his first axioms was that *ignorance* is fear's favorite food."

Daephone seemed to chew on that, mouthing it in a slow, deliberate rhythm. Finally, she gave another crisp nod. "It's easier to be afraid of a thing you don't know, can't name, or can't see. That's what you mean."

"Exactly. Children are afraid of the dark because they don't know what's in it. Folk fear change because it's unknown—it's new."

Her eyes made it clear that she understood and needed no further examples. At least, that was how Methias translated the look.

"I mean to explain what I know of The Cage and its function to you. Then use it—along with your experience and knowledge—to gather information." He paused to make certain she had no questions or comments. Satisfied, he continued. "The chamber grants each skull the ability to create sight and sound, but no physical sensation. They can recall memory, or they can show what is happening in a place where some part of them rests." Methias saw her confusion and clarified. "Where their other bones are buried, for instance."

Daephone winced, but nodded. Methias saw her gripping the hilt of her war hammer, but she'd otherwise grown utterly, almost disturbingly calm.

"I'll lay a hand upon your shoulder, so as not to interfere with your shield or striking arm. You'll need neither, as I say. The Cage will be altering sight and sound, but nothing physical. We'll still be stood here, regardless of what we see. Still, always safe..."

"Never sorry. Aye, my lord."

"My hand on your shoulder should ensure that we don't lose sight of one another. Also... focus on what you see and hear. Don't let yourself dwell on any memories that crop up." He paused to find her eyes. It was important that he underscore this point. And that he do so *without* turning the warning into a self-fulfilling prophecy. "This is neither the time nor the place to let yourself gather wool. If your discipline fails you on that score, we may both find ourselves watching whatever memory you've unintentionally conjured up."

Her lips had narrowed to a thin line. "I don't care for this, Lord."

"I know, but you've seen more of the River than I. You've seen more of *Thorion* than I, too. I need to know where at least *one* of these places can be found."

She nodded. "Snow will fall, my lord. My not caring for it doesn't make it any less likely to happen. Nor does it make it any less necessary."

Methias grinned. "It does not."

"If it's necessary," she shrugged. "So be it. Snow will fall."

He gave a nod, setting his bright hand upon her dim side shoulder. For a moment, he was tempted to summon a shield of his own. They were in step as if they stood in a shield wall, after all. He resisted the urge.

"Sleara?"

As when Sleara had shown him Rímhril, the room's sights and sounds transformed between blinks of the eye. The pair found themselves standing a dozen or so feet back from the river that marked Dereek khn's southern border. He knew they stood near its northern bank based on the direction of the current—westward out of the swamp surrounding Yrxa Castle. Other than what side of the River they appeared on, he'd been unable to ascribe any special significance about this, or any other place The Cage's prisoners had shown him.

All things concerned, Daephone Ironbane took the sudden shift with surprising ease. She stiffened, but adapted readily to the new sights and sounds. She *was* from Nausha, of course, just as Methias was. And she'd seen her share of the Weave worked both there and here in Dereek khn. Still, he was genuinely impressed by the calm with which she comported herself.

"I don't think I've been here before, Lord. The *clarity* is ... staggering!" Her voice was a harsh whisper—a distant crow's caw in autumn rain.

"It is, indeed." He let her look around for a moment longer. When it was clear there had been no sudden realization, he spoke again. "There are two more sites—one on either side of the River. Are you ready?"

She nodded.

He heard the familiar creak of leather as her demi-gauntlet's strap flexed. *She's tightening her grip on the heater shield. That's the only outward sign that she's on edge, and even that might signify nothing. It could be exactly what it sounds like—an adjustment of how her shield's bar sits in her dim-side fist.*

He lifted his chin and called Sleara's name again. This time, the world shifted to an area south of the River. Based on the current, he was almost certain they'd moved farther east, back toward the swamp that surrounded Yrxa Castle. The water's movement was slow and sweet here. They were in the shadow of a small, bluish banyan. It was likely a relatively young thing, given its overall size. He'd seen some in Thorion and further south that were the size of farmhouses.

Daephone saw nothing here that struck her as familiar, other than a vague recollection of seeing the tree before.

"In truth, though, I may be thinking of another tree entirely. There *are* a few of the blue ones on the Thorion side of the River. Only a few, though." She shook her head as if to ward off an insect—sudden and sharp movements that caused Methias to wince and lean away. "Forgive me, Lord. I know that isn't much help. I'm no scout, as you know."

"True, but you *were* among those looking for additional fords when we were preparing for the Long Moon."

She nodded. "We need more scouts and striders." Her voice was only a murmur, but she'd clearly meant for him to hear it.

"Well, with luck, we'll soon have some. The Lansel *was* hoping to recruit other Eodenth on the way to or from Shesh. Beyond that, he hoped to find some among the desert tribes, or within one of the cities. In the meantime, we bide with what we have."

She brightened. "*That's* Farin's plan? I hadn't heard that. Good. I've been thinking more than a bit about how he wanted the army structured." She blanched, then amended, "How the *throne* wants it structured."

Methias chuckled. "Peace, Ironbane. I knew you meant nothing by it. Shall we move on to the final location?"

Her ears pinked a touch, but she nodded just the same. Sleara brought the final site to life without Methias having to ask.

Daephone fetched a sigh of frustration. "No, Lord. There are familiar pines here, but..."

"But they're pines. We have them all over the realm."

"Exactly. This *might* be near Kowmor, but it might just as easily be to the far west for all we know."

"NlorNo, it's closer to Enroff Alifehv than that. The River's slower here. Kor Kowmor might be right, actually. Well spotted, Lankaajh." Enroff Alifehv—Future Dawning—was the name given to the ford nearest the swamp's edge; the place where the River exited its muddy mirk, meandering westward. The place where the final battle of the Long Moon had begun. "The first site was further west. The second was closer, and this one is closer still. The current moves more slowly at each place, in turn. "

She blinked, giving an accepting nod. "I... hadn't noticed that, Lord."

"Perhaps not, but you *did* notice familiar pines. That may be enough. There *is* something more, though."

"Lord?" The question was perfunctory. It only seemed to signify acknowledgement of his shifting topics.

The ghost of a grin crept across Methias's face. "I wanted this part sorted first, so as not to cloud the matter any further. This entire situation is shrouded in quite enough mental mist already, I think."

She quirked a wry smile at that.

Wry, yes, but genuine. Good. That's something.

"I will have each one speak in turn. Speak, mind. Not gibber. I have a rough translation, but cannot quite place the languages. They sound... well, no. Let me not poison the well. Best you draw your own conclusions. Are you ready?"

She gave a dip of her chin that served as a nod.

"In order, then... Sleara?"

The image shifted to the first location. As it did, a voice spoke in either fear or excitement. As with all of the imprisoned folk, the voice sounded young. Its vowels were somewhat rounded, with an undercurrent of upward inflection. In the same manner in which Sleara had spoken on Rímhril, this voice seemed as if it were coming from behind, and just overhead.

"De kommer! De marsjerer! De kommer fra elven—de kommer fra elvens bunn!"

It repeated twice more before Methias raised his left hand in token of peace. Sleara must've silenced the poor speaker. *That, or the speaker had seen what is as common a gesture as you could hope to find.* He rolled his eyes, dipping his chin in self-recrimination.

"Is it familiar to you?"

"It's Venzene, Lord. I'm almost sure of that much. I couldn't say more than that, though."

He waited a few beats to ensure she had no more to offer, then made a beckoning gesture with that same hand. The scene shifted to the second location—the one with the banyan. Another voice spoke up. This one gave the warning in a lilting, musical tone. The speaker shortened his or her tongue on certain letters and flattened the pronunciation of certain vowels.

"Wo aaye! kia! Wo darya se aaye, wo pani k neeche se aaye!"

Again, he let the voice repeat its message of warning several times before signaling for silence.

"*That* comes from Thorion. I know that much for certain. I've heard it in the market among some of the darker-skinned folk. Not those of Sheshik stock. Their skin is more... golden brown? Light brown? Come to that, I've seen some that are light-skinned enough to call them *pale*, and others dark skinned enough to simply call them *brown*." She paused, shaking her head. "It's hard to separate *people* by skin color when it gets down to it. A single person is one thing. Easy enough to compare one to another. An entire culture? An artist could do it, I expect, but..." She sighed. "I've seen folk who sound like this. And I've seen them in Thorionden. That much I can say."

Methias let her run out of words before speaking. "That will do, Lankaajh." He offered a warm smile, stepping forward to face her more directly. "It's a start. We've one more. Are you ready?"

She nodded.

The voice that accompanied this third site was crisp and precise. It made a trill of its Rs, and gave the impression of a young scout reporting danger, rather than a frantic flood of warning words.

"Graf! Graf—bitte! Sie kommen! Sie kommen—Nebelblut, Herr! Sie marschieren! Sie kommen aus dem Fluss—sie kommen von unter dem Wasser!"

She didn't wait for the phrase to repeat. "Gerstealunth, lord. I'm sure of it. I recognize the word *Graf*."

Methias beamed. "I agree with all three assessments, but once more, you've proven invaluable. I only know Kovalunth and some Eodenth. And the heraldic words to blazon arms—all of which are in Havalunth. I'd hoped you might recognize at least one of them. Thank you largely."

"I can do better than that, Lord." She flashed a thin little smile. "I'd wager there's at least one or two folk with Fyken Presh that are from Venzene."

"Oh? That's excellent, Lankaajh." He flashed a grateful grin at her, then lifted his brows in sudden realization. "And Fyken has one, at least, from Thorion—the bachelor knight Morakogunn is grooming for service in the Yebu ke."

Daephone blinked, then bowed her head. "As you say."

"Well, that will do, then. We've seen what we need to." He lifted his chin. "Sleara?"

The image faded, replaced with the grim sight of staring skulls. Daephone's fists tightened, producing that creaking leather sound again. "We're done here, then, my lord?"

"We are." He turned to escort her from the chamber. "And I need to ride for Fyken's fortress."

"Now, my lord?"

"Now," he agreed. "I need the translation more directly rendered if I'm to address its warning."

They exited, but not before Methias turned to the room and said,

"My thanks. I'll return once I've sorted this. You've my promise."

When the door was closed at last, Methias turned to find Tharus had already started up the stairs. He fought back the mild disappointment and started up with the Lankaajh just behind.

Daephone finally decided to ask the question she'd clearly been holding back. "My lord, you said you had a rough translation?"

"I did, and I do." He lifted his chin, then spoke in the voice of someone reading aloud. "They come. They're coming from the River."

Daephone stopped just before they'd reached the small chamber at ground level. "They?"

He grinned, though there was no mirth in it. "Ah, you see the problem. I've seen the memory of the moments tied to that warning. I've seen water move, vegetation move... all as if something were walking through it. I've seen no *thing* doing the walking, however. I need a better translation. That means I need a native speaker of at least *one* of the languages we've heard."

She nodded. "So you're bound for Kor Kowmor."

"I am."

He opened the door and entered the smallish sitting room. A lanky youth of Sheshik stock was just sitting down. He wore raiment that marked him as a member of Daephone's order, the Ban'ze Ruun. His hair had been pulled back in innumerable braids. Each was small and tightly woven so that his locks appeared to have been combed by something with impossibly thick teeth. His beard was close and neatly trimmed. A brindled mastiff sat at his feet, looking up and appearing to smile at the newcomers.

Methias resisted the urge to focus on the dog. Instead, he offered the man a warm smile and a nod to indicate him. "And *Tharus* will accompany me."

Tharus nodded, reaching down to stroke the massive dog's great head. His voice left the auditory impression of beard stubble. "Dannus deliver me... *Finally.*" He twitched a smile. "When do we leave?"

-VI-

Venzene Duchy of Kovalun
County Jižní Pochod
Barony of Hartscross–Jižní Lov
5 Korunasykli: 22 Days after the Red Storm at Westsong

Vlk leaned his bright arm along the top of the barbican's wooden wall. This part of the barrier had been flattened, though he could see poniards of sharpened wood and pitted, perhaps even serrated iron sticking out just below the alure.

"You're saying *those* vill keep men from climbing the valls?"

Waltyr grinned sidelong at him from his left, but it was Jastrab who answered.

"Well, no. *We* will keep them from climbing the walls. But if things go poorly, those will slow them down, at the very least. They've been here since the count first ordered the palisade stood up. You *live* here and I'd bet you've never noticed them before, have you?"

Vlk shook his head.

"See? If you were to climb the outside, you'd have to contend with them. They stick out too far to just ignore or hope to miss. They're left out in the rain and snow, sure, but they're also kept sharp enough to draw blood. They'll cut through a rope as that rope is jostled, slice a hand trying to grip them without knowing where or exactly *how* to grip them, and they'll make a ladder sit uneven against the wall. It's not perfect, of course. No defense ever is. They have their uses, though."

Vlk gave a slow, sage nod. What the captain said made a certain amount of sense.

"Then there's the matter of the magic." This was a new voice— rolling and full.

Vlk turned to find a tall man with thick ginger hair and a well-groomed beard to match. A sword rested over his right shoulder. It was held in place by a leather baldric as black as his kontusz. As the man cleared the stairs, Vlk could see a gleaming steel helm dangling from his right hand.

Jastrab looked back at the younger man, grinning. "There *is* that."

"Magic?" Vlk tried not to show how much of his awe was born out of fear. Like most, however, the very thought of magic called up images of... well, of monsters like those who were massing outside... somewhere. He knew they were there. He could hear their stomach-churning chants. He simply couldn't *see* them anywhere.

But vhere are they hiding?

The land all around was full of grasses that the animals found good to eat, and little else. There *were* trees within sight, but they formed a sort of natural border around the great field. Vlk could find nothing that would protect an enemy from an archer's eye. *And the voices seem somehow closer than the trees.*

"Jastrab, didn't you tell the boy about the magic?" The bearded man quirked a smile, then shot his brows up in sudden realization. "Oh! Hells, I'm sorry, Captain. I didn't realize you meant to use him to *fuel* our magics!"

Vlk blanched, then stepped back, scanning his surroundings. He felt his bright fist clenching, and had just drawn breath preparatory to doing ... *something,* when the redhead laughed.

"Look at his *fist!*" More laughter, this time joined in on by both Waltyr and Jastrab. "This one's ready for a fight! Are we keeping him?"

Jastrab reached down to squeeze Vlk's shoulder. "Not up to us. He's alright, though." As Jastrab finally found Vlk's eyes, he spoke again. "No magic here. Other than the magic of knowing what to do in a fight like this. Training and trust, Vlk. That's the magic that matters. I'd take it against sorcery any day."

"And you'll take it today," said Waltyr. "We all will. Still, we've fought worse."

"You have?" Vlk shivered. Why was it so cold? He resisted the urge to rub his own upper arms to warm them. He didn't want to show the nerves bubbling inside his belly.

"We have." This was the ginger again. "Hells, at least the walls here are in good repair."

Jastrab and Waltyr both grinned.

"Thinking of Eoalun?" Jastrab sounded wistful. "Now *that* was a battle."

"Ekburg, aye captain. That ruin was nearly *our* ruin." The ginger man grinned over to Waltyr. "You'd shot your stores completely dry, da. And when they'd started coming through the breach where the wood had rotted away..."

Vlk blinked, and hard. He wanted to hear about the battle, of course. What boy wouldn't? But he was struggling with the realization that this man was Waltyr's *son!*

"Oh, I remember it all too well." Waltyr turned to Vlk, grinning. "Ulrek," he indicated the other man, "earned his name that day. Three men came through the wall—a Eoalunth warlord and two men who may as well have been giants. Havoc's Horn, they were as tall as you seated on the captain's shoulders."

Vlk's eyes were huge. He leaned in toward Waltyr, but not out of being caught up in the tale. No, it was just becoming harder to hear his voice clearly over the chanting. Thus far there had been nobody along the grasses... nobody still living and moving, at any rate. Still, the voices sounded as if they were getting closer. Added to that, he was growing colder.

"We're stood on the grand building's weather-chewed parapet—up perhaps twice the height of a man? And Ulrek sees them breaking through. He shouts *Odvážna krv*! Then he leaps down and lands with his knee on the warlord's shield."

"My knee cop was padded. That, and the battle blessing was on me by that point."

"Battle blessing?" Vlk turned to Ulrek, but his body language made it clear that he was asking all three of them.

It was Jastrab who answered. "Battle fever, battle blessing, the red curtain, the war fire—it's all the same thing. When the fight's happening here and now? When you're *in* the fight, instead of the fear *before* the fight?"

Vlk nodded as if he understood. He *thought* he did, but...

Jastrab must've seen his uncertainty. "The idea of pain, or fear, or anything outside of whatever thoughts keep you alive? Those things drop away. Training gives your body the tools to—hopefully, at least—get you through. You don't think about women, wine, or where your next meal is coming from. You fight until the fight is over... one way or another." He grinned. "There's always time for pain after."

Walter's voice came rolling out past a wide smile as he took up the tale. "So, Ulrek knocks the warlord back into his absurdly large men, pushes off of the shield, then *shik-shik-shik!* He stabs all three of them somewhere above their shoulders, then steps back through the breach, calling for a wagon, or something else to block the hole."

"And so he earned his name," said Jastrab. "Ulrek Redeagle."

"Well, I had to do *something*, Captain. Waltyr the Lion's reputation was a tall tree to climb."

"The Lion?" Vlk gaped at Waltyr.

"Stop."

Jastrab's entire aspect had undergone a shift so abrupt, Vlk found himself taking an involuntary step back. The man's voice had become icy. "Sergeant? Back downstairs. Now. Make ready."

Ulrek blinked, then jogged back down the stairs without another word.

"Waltyr? Do you—"

"I see it, Captain. Do I shoot, or no?"

Vlk turned to follow the men's collective gaze. He saw some sort of mist—grey and actively rolling—had all but covered the field below. The sky, too, was full of low, moiling grey clouds.

A lone figure walked through the mist. Whoever it was, they were small of stature. A weapon of some sort hung along the walker's back.

"Stay the line, Sergeant." Jastrab's voice still held that note of frosty calm.

The figure finally grew close enough to see. Vlk jumped forward, giving a laugh of joy and triumph.

"Lakkrid! Laaaaaakkrid!"

Jastrab grabbed him by the shoulder, hauling Vlk back toward him and placing a hand over the boy's mouth. "Never give the enemy any more information than you have to. Names, plans, number of people—hells, number of times you've sneezed today." The captain's voice remained frosty. His grip was firm, but stopped well short of painful. "Do you understand?"

Vlk nodded.

"Good. Now," Jastrab released him, then turned him so their eyes could meet. "That's Eobum's boy's name you shouted, yes?" When Vlk nodded his agreement, Jastrab continued. "Are you *certain* that is the same boy?"

Vlk blinked, then turned to look back. His heart *wanted* it to be Lakkrid, but no. The boy had moved closer, but stopped far enough out that no thrown spear would reach him... arrows, certainly, but nothing thrown.

The boy *was* of gnoerkish blood, and about the same build as his old friend. That was all Vlk was prepared to say for certain, though. The fellow's skin was paler than Lakkrid's. The chancy light made it hard to tell the exact color, but he looked almost... golden. His hair was dark like Lakkrid's, but much shorter.

"No, Captain. It *isn't* Lakkrid. I don't know vhy I thought it vas, but he isn't Lakkrid."

Jastrab stepped up beside him, nodding. "Then we wait."

The boy below lifted his hands toward his face, cupping them to shape his voice. It came out scratched, and far deeper than Lakkrid's.

"Hail!" He paused for a beat, as if to let the word ring out. "I bear a message!"

Jastrab shouted back, cupping his own hands around his mouth. "On whose behalf? Whose message do you bear?"

Vlk looked back to see Count Edmund standing a few steps below the barbican. He seemed intent, but not unhappy that Jastrab had spoken for the encampment.

"I am Laagi Gakzaksh, Thadzpreklg. I bear a message for Edmund the Tall from Jarl Gar Thadzprek! Will you hear my message?"

Jastrab spoke quietly, though loud enough for Edmund to hear him. "*Yar*-ull... That's a Eodenth lord, isn't it?"

"It is," Edmund said. "And much of the rest of that is Eodenth, though I don't speak it beyond a few words. That's... actually surprising."

"A bit far to go for his Grace's purposes, I agree. Still..."

"He said... He said *ullg* at the end of his name." Vlk was murmuring to himself, but apparently Jastrab hadn't missed the sound.

"What does *ullllg* mean? And what in hells language is it from?"

"It means *son of*. Lakkrid told me that vhen ve first met. *I'm Lackkrid Yo-boom-ullg*." He looked back to first Jastrab, then Edmund. "It means son of."

Edmund gave a nod of acceptance, if not shared knowledge. Jastrab looked between them, then nodded. "Then he's delivering a message for his father—this Eoalunth Lord." He grinned a *what-the-hells* grin. Lifting his chin and cupping his hands around his mouth again, he made his reply.

"What is your father's message, boy?"

"The Jarl Gar Thadzprek wishes to treat with Edmund the Tall, who alone has kept his sword and banner out of our lands. His nobles have not, and they have paid the price. Yet Edmund the Tall is not our enemy ... yet. Will he come and treat with us? He may do so with any guard he sees fit to require, or, if he wishes, we will come to him within the safety of his walls."

Edmund grunted. "I would know what he wishes to treat with me *about* before agreeing to meet with this Jarl."

Jastrab nodded. "Of what does your father wish to treat? Already you have confessed to breaking Vévoda Harn's peace, and making Count Edmund's nobles what was it? *Pay the price?* Why should his Excellency Edmund treat with someone who has made such a confession?"

Vlk could see the boy doing something with his hands to the right of his own head, then bowing it as if in deep thought. A tense moment passed, the mist swirling all around the boy's lower body. Finally, he lifted his head and raised his hands toward his mouth. Then he stopped.

Thunder cracked the stillness with such force that a large portion of the Bluemark archers could be seen wincing, raising hands to ears, or stepping back a pace.

"Sdraliana kr ka. Rhexrryn xro, rhexrryn xro, rhexrryn xro. Inagro dak, grir, cor, grir xro. Taul misda ka rryl lluil. Taul misda ka thoriash xro."

The sound came from a multitude that was nowhere to be seen. The boy appeared to take on a posture of surprise, but no fear. The voices swelled, the wind rose, and the mist parted.

Vlk knew his horses. The largest one he'd ever seen stood at nineteen hands from *Skolf to shoulders*, as they say. His master said he'd never seen or heard of one taller than twenty hands, which was nearly seven feet tall. That, he'd said, had been in his youth—a Mądra Ręka he'd taken care of for some knight or other.

The unnatural creature that now moved forward seemingly from nothing was horse-*shaped*, but that was where the similarities died. The thing looked like a storm cloud given equine form and flesh. Vlk reckoned it stood at *least* twenty-three hands from Skolf to shoulder. It looked angry and over-muscled, even for its own massive frame. Its mane, tail, and the feathering around its lower legs seemed to be made of red and silver lightning.

Upon this nightmare steed rode a man of fire-tanned flesh. There was no saddle between him and his mount. The rider carried a massive, bearded axe in one hand. His hair was long, but very thin. From this distance, it appeared to be interrupted by either dark adornments of cord or braid, or large scars that had healed poorly along his scalp.

The man reached a hand down to his left and hauled the gnoerk boy into position before him. Once the boy had settled, the horse reared up, pawed at the sky, and gave a shriek of such force that Vlk found himself with his arms wrapped tightly around the nearest adult—Jastrab. Thunder seemed to answer the steed's spine-scraping cry. When the sound faded, Vlk released Jastrab and ventured to cast about. A substantial number of archers appeared to be in similar states of recovery.

Vlk heard the boy speaking again and turned to face him. He found it hard to look at the steed, so he focused on its riders. *Hells, they look different, but they do call to mind Lakkrid and his father...*

Indeed, the man had one arm around the boy's belly. The boy, on the other hand, leaned his head back against the man's broad chest, moving his hands out before him as he spoke.

"Behold... Jarl Gar Thadzprek!" Vlk saw the man nod. "You have asked what he wishes to treat with Edmund about?"

"I have." Jastrab made his voice cold, but Vlk heard the shudder in the man's next intake of breath. "In answer, you have brought him. That is no answer at all."

The man moved his arm from around the boy's middle and tapped him on the forearm. He then began dancing his fingers in a rapid, nonsensical series of movements.

"We would see our clans—our people joined together. Great glory and earned endings are on the come. We would have Edmund the Tall stand beside us as they arrive." The boy's face never left the movement of the man's hand, but his voice remained audible even over the wind.

Jastrab bowed his head, speaking only to those around him. "Excellency?"

Edmund didn't remain silent for long. "Say to him this."

Jastrab nodded, relaying Edmund's words as quickly as the count spoke them. "Edmund the Tall cannot stand idly by while men ride to war within or through lands he is sworn to protect. If you wish to gain aid or succor here, first we must—"

Vlk saw the man moving his hand again. The boy kept his face turned toward that hand, but shaped his voice up toward the parapet once more.

"No. You misunderstand. We do not *seek* aid or succor. We come to *offer* it. Stand and fight for what is just. Stand beside us as we make those who have raided and raped, reaped and ruined in the name of greed, and over... over grudges that are *centuries* gone! Ride with us. Treat with me, and the very Empire will see justice. You are a man whose sword and shield are always said to be pointed in the... in the correct... direction! Show us that there is worth in your name... in the things you are said to stand for!"

The man put his arm around the boy's middle again, smiling through an emphatic nod.

Edmund shook his head. "Enough."

"Excellency?" Jastrab sounded doubtful. "Edmund? What are you thinking about doing?"

In answer, Edmund lifted his chin and raised his voice.

"And if I say that I cannot help you—will not stand with you as you burn your way across Kovalun? Across the rest of the Empire?"

Vlk saw the rider bow his head. He didn't raise it again as his hand began to dance into the boy's line of sight.

"Is that what you say? Is it what Edmund the Tall—Edmund the Just—Edmund the champion of story, song, and the wrongly slain now say to me?" The boy's voice carried well. The wind itself seemed to aid in bringing it to them. He sounded sad, bitter, but unsurprised.

"It is what I *must* say. I *am* Edmund the Tall, yes, but I am more. I am *Count* Edmund—a Knight of his Grace Vévoda Harn of Visoka Kovalun. Yet I say to you this, Jarl. Take your men back to Eoden. Take them home, and you have my word that I will not pursue you, nor will any who owe their allegiance to me. I will account the matter ended. More. I will appoint new houses to rule over those newly emptied lands. I shall replace the houses you have taken your vengeance on with those who share my own wish to leave Eoden lands and Eoden folk in peace."

Vlk was outraged, but he didn't himself know how to articulate why. To let those who raided and killed folk in the county live to ride home again with their confessed crimes unanswered? It simply felt *wrong* to him.

He snapped his head up as the boy spoke again.

"Then you have made your decision. There is a price to be paid—a price for commanding men and passing judgement. You say you cannot stand idly by and allow us to continue on? *We* cannot allow you to remain here, stood against us while we continue on."

With that, the man lifted his axe high. Lightning rent the clouds, but instead of thunder, a wall of sound—hundreds of voices at once—delivered the final rendition of their endless chanting.

"Sdraliana kr ka. Rhexrryn xro, rhexrryn xro, rhexrryn xro. Inagro dak, grir, cor, grir xro. Taul misda ka rryl lluil. Taul misda ka thoriash xro."

The noise made Vlk scream and fall to his knees. His hands went to cover his ears. When the initial barrage had passed and he pulled them away again, he realized they were wet. Looking at his palms, he saw several smeared drops of blood.

Getting to his feet, wiping at his streaming eyes and trying not to wet himself, he looked out over the wall again. The world was a sea of men and war machines. Some were mounted, some stood hard by their siege engines, others stood in wide walls bristling with spears.

He drew in breath, meaning to shout something, though he'd no idea what. It was at that moment that the sky opened, and a torrent of stinging rain began to fall.

The siege had begun.

CHAPTER TEN

OBSCURING THE HOURGLASS

-I-

Venzene Duchy of Kovalun
County Jižní Pochod
Barony of Hartscross–Jižní Lov
5 Korunasykli: 22 Days after the Red Storm at Westsong

"Vild yellow beard! Off your right shoulder! Vith the big svord!" Vlk pointed, moving his finger as the man he'd indicated turned this way and that. *He looks as if he's barking orders to the men around him.* "Do you see him?" *Hells, I can barely hear myself! Surely Valtyr can't hear me, can he?*

Vlk got an answer to his question almost before his mind had fully formed it. Waltyr's crossbow sang to his left. The string made a queerly truncated, muffled *thoop*, made especially soft by the rain. The resultant death it dealt, on the other hand, had an impossible, almost sorcerous power to it.

Vlk watched as the man he'd described twitched. The wretch stumbled back against his fellows with a quarrel hanging from his open stew hole. He looked for all the world like he was smoking a pipe... or would have, had his mouth not spewed something dark all over his rain-soaked beard. Arms flailing, sword cutting into at least one of his comrades, he collapsed backward in a heap of knees, elbows, and steel.

Waltyr had told him to watch for those in command—those shouting orders or pointing. Having the sergeant aim and fire where he directed was a sickening sort of power.

My finger kills them. Valtyr is my... my Doom Finger.

"Well spotted. Next?" The sergeant's voice was warm but focused. As far as Vlk could tell, the man's every action seemed that way. It didn't matter whether he was speaking, reloading, shooting, or calling out targets to the archers he commanded. Waltyr was just one of those men who always seemed sure of who he was and of what he needed to do next.

Vlk tilted his head to cast about, shivering as the cold rain ran into his ear. It was uncomfortable. Hells, it was a damned misery, but he was grateful for the rain. It had washed away both the vomit the first few deaths had elicited and the proof that he'd pissed himself. That had happened early on, when arrows had flown past his ear and into the upright that stood between him and Waltyr.

How long had the battle gone on? It felt like hours. Strangely, it also felt like it had been only moments. He thought the sun might give him an idea of how much time had truly passed, but there *was* no sun. The sky was a rolling, roiling grey that was too dark, somehow. It was painted a purplish cast in some places, and a poisonous, dusky red in others. That *might* mean it was near sunset, but he couldn't be sure.

He shook his head, though he doubted the archer had seen it. Coughing, he watched his breath smoke in the chill.

Time doesn't matter anymore. He was coming to terms with that. What had he thought? That they would cancel the war on account of rain? Dark?

"Nobody vill call us in for fear ve'll catch colds." He shook his head again—this time at his own foolishness, then set about looking for more targets.

To je pravda. (It's true.) Valtyr is my doom finger. He laughed, uncertain why in hells he'd done so. Turning, he thought he might share the phrase with the man, himself. That thought winked out as his eye fell on something that, for a moment, stopped his heart.

"Valtyr! Right of the engine vith the metal bowl! The metal ladle! I see fire! Do you see the torch bearer?" He marked the one giving orders and pointed, stabbing his finger at the empty air. "There! Red beard, no hair—he's holding a... he's *aiming* the spear! Over his shoul—"

Vlk felt something hook the back of his left leg and *yank*. He had just enough time to register the sudden rush of cold, wet air as he fell through it. Then *crack!* His right arm and the entire right side of his head were somewhere between stinging, throbbing, and numb. Sound became queerly muffled. Beyond, or perhaps *beneath* all of that, he felt dizzy and disoriented.

He didn't hear but rather felt himself moan. As he rolled onto his back, he saw a burning ball of pitch roughly the size of the damned sun fly directly overhead... *into* Jižní Lov. Was it low enough to have spat fire on the place he'd been standing as it passed? He didn't know. In a daze, he watched the fiery mass arc down into the center of the group of men Waltyr and Jastrab had called *the northern reserves.* The screams of women, or men whose screams *sounded* like women, filled the air, even as men rushed to contain the rolling, spreading mass.

He saw a figure in white come charging up the stairs. Backlit by the greasy fire, she looked unnatural.

Am I dead? Has a haunt come to claim me...? No. No, that's Fetinba... Vhy is she up here? Andrej is avay, so vhy is she here?

She knelt down beside him, looking him over. He felt like he should be embarrassed, if not outright angry that she, of all people, was trying to tend to him. He wasn't any more a child than she was...

"Vlk, do you he-ah me?"

He nodded, then winced. His head was no longer merely throbbing. It was *screaming.*

She helped him to sit up, which further infuriated him, albeit distantly.

"What are you still doing out he-ah? You should be home, gar-ding the smalla chil—"

"He's spotting for me." Waltyr's voice. "Is he alright?"

Fetinba nodded, her veil moving in a dull ripple as she did. She continued addressing herself to Vlk, for now at least. "All right. Good ee-nuff. What happened? Are you woon-ded?"

Again, it was Waltyr who made reply as he reloaded. "I swept his dim side to get him clear. It was faster than explaining or trying to grab him." His voice was sharpened by a clear note of concern. He enunciated each syllable as he asked again. *"Is he all right?"*

Vlk was touched. The sergeant's regard... the thought of proving unworthy of that regard... With an effort, he fought through the fog in his head.

Then there was Fetinba. He had the chance to study her strange raiment as she checked him over. It looked like it was some sort of tightly woven cloth gambeson. It, and the rest of her armor, appeared quilted with many small diamond shapes. Only her gloves, boots, and bonnet appeared to be made of leather. *Probably doe skin. They're vhite, anyvay.*

She made his eyes follow her finger as she moved it this way and that. Then she spoke over her shoulder. "Good ee-nuff." She stood, then moved off to Waltyr's left. "He'll hurt for a bit, but..." She shrugged as if to say, *what of that?*

A moment later and Vlk saw her lift one of the fallen Bluemark's bows, beginning to shoot. *Of course, she can shoot a bow. Vhy not? She can probably smith a svord, heal a horse, and fly as vell. Anděl Fetinba. (Fetinba the angel)* He shook his head, then stood up beside the sergeant.

"Vlk, if you need to step away..." Waltyr sounded concerned, but that was all.

"No. I'm here, and I'm alright. My head hurts, but I'm alright." As if to underscore this, he turned toward the battlefield ... and jumped back almost to the edge of the barbican. "Down! Down, Valtyr! Three of them! They're at the valls! Axes and a ram!"

Waltyr looked, cursed, and stepped up onto the wall itself. "Wraith? Don't let them shoot me." He didn't wait for a reply. Instead, he leaned forward at an impossible angle, dim hand raised to grab the lip of the wooden canapé above. Aiming down the wall, he fired his crossbow one-handed.

Thoop!

Vlk heard what might have been a scream. It was difficult to be sure amidst the rest of the battle din.

Waltyr stepped back off the waist-high wall, then leaned so he could look down the line. Shaking his head, he turned to Vlk even as his hands and feet did the business of reloading and re-readying his weapon. "Can you run?"

Vlk nodded. He had to clench his fist against the pain the motion caused, but he nodded nonetheless. Waltyr *mustn't* send him away to hide with the other children.

"Good. I need you to run down the line. When you see someone reloading, get their attention and tell them *watch for sappers in close.* Repeat what you're to say."

Vlk repeated the message.

"Good. Who are you to tell?"

"The ... archers? Oh!" he slapped his own forehead with the heel of his hand and *instantly* regretted it. He saw stars, and his headache roared as if in triumph. "I... mmm." He sucked his teeth, then made his answer. "Anyone who's just loosed their arrow. Jo."

Waltyr nodded. "Good. Go." And with that, the archer turned back to the battle below.

Vlk spared a glance into the courtyard. Most of the fire's spread had been put out. A handful of the encampment's men were holding the remaining ball of pitch on the end of—what else?—several long pitchforks. He saw a smaller siege engine being pushed into position nearby, and another with what looked like some sort of sling attached to its armature being set up off to the west of the gate.

Vhat am I doing? He shook his head, felt a double lance of pain behind his eyes, then tore off down the line of archers to pass the word.

-II-

Kastan shook her head, trying to absorb the scope of Edmund's plans. *With Hengrek Blacktower's death, his heir assumes power. And that heir rode to fight at Edmund's side during the rebellion.* She re-read a second scroll. *With the consolidation of Eastern Kovalun, Edmund holds enough territory to challenge Harn's authority. And Eoden is sealed from external threat.*

None of it much mattered, at least for the moment. The force outside was most assuredly not a group of sellswords hired by the duke to *look* like Eodenth raiders. She had no idea who they were, or why they'd come to wage war, but they weren't Harn's hidden hand.

She studied a note Edmund had struck through with several deep lines. *Lines? They look more like gouges. One's sliced most of the way through the parchment.* She leaned down to squint over the scroll, trying to make it out amidst the visual noise. *His hand is normally so fair. This note looks as if it were written in either haste ... or anger.* An instant later she began to snort, then giggle as she held back outright laughter.

"Excellency." Olga chopped the word into its component syllables. "Time is *short.*"

Kastan nodded, wiping her eyes. "Eobum would *never* have accepted that kind of power. A *Count of Eoden?* Even under Edmund, whom he loves, he would see that for the trap it is." She was fast becoming an expert on that very trap, after all.

Olga sighed, stepping over to the small writing table where Kastan was sitting. She gave the briefest of glances at the scroll in question, then shook her head. "And do you not see Edmund's *multiple* efforts to cross out the notion? He knows it well. That doesn't change his own desire to see it *done*... but he knows the Eoalunth's heart well enough."

Kastan snapped her head up, all amusement gone. "The *Eodenth's* heart, I'm certain you meant to say." She made her tone flat and more than a bit chilly. "Or if you've trouble with that, perhaps you would find it easier to use his actual *rank* when speaking of him. In which case, Mistress, you would say that Edmund knows the *Commander's* heart."

"The *Commander* is Eoalunth, and if you believe you've time to chastise me for my choice of words, then it is *clear* to me that I deserve such. It means I have failed to impress upon you precisely how—short—time— is." She planted the backs of her fists on her hips, but otherwise kept herself in check.

Kastan was just drawing breath to make a retort of some kind when movement caught her attention. The heavy canvas flap opened at the top of the short stair, revealing the grave face of Ruční Kopí.

"Hajvarr?" Kastan stood at once, ignoring Olga's attempts to urge her back to her seat. She watched as his throat worked to swallow the bitterest part of whatever he was thinking or feeling.

"I *know* him," said he. "I'd swear I do." He shook his head. "Radek says... it won't be long."

Kastan went to him, mounting the stairs with swift, sure strides. "He has a son... Andrej. We—"

"Peace." Hajvarr met her eyes. "He's with him now."

She nodded, bowed her head to collect herself, then moved past him into the tent's main room.

Her nose twitched as the mingled perfumes of burned wax, vomit, open wounds, and raw egg assaulted her. The last of these, she knew, was smeared over a wound to slow bleeding. But one look at Rákos made it plain he was beyond such measures. Still, Radek had done his best, she had no doubt.

The hunter rested on a pallet of uncured hides that had been covered in cotton batting. His long shirt lay open. Someone—Radek, most likely— had sliced the garment down the middle and pulled it apart. Rákos's bare chest seemed sunken as he labored to breathe, head gleaming with sweat in the lantern's circle of light.

Kastan saw his eyes rolling beneath their greyish lids, as if he were in the throes of a vivid dream. She willed herself not to shudder.

Andrej stood at his father's feet, gazing at the dying man's troubled face. His own face was wet, though his breathing was slow and even. Štít sat to the boy's left, leaning into his side. He stroked her sleek head, but the motion was a slow, automatic thing.

She marked the tools of both father and son—Sheshik bows and half-full quivers—laying across the singular table. Radek stood beside that same table, stirring something in a wooden mug. His apothecar's instruments were close at hand.

As she stepped over to Andrej, she saw the wounds at last. Rákos had what looked to be three holes on his left side, very near, if not directly over, his kidney. Something in one of his wounds caught the light as she moved.

Hells hall me home. Arrows? When was he hit by arrows? None of our pursuers...

She realized with a sick shock that she'd never checked him over before they'd mounted up. *He sounded short of breath... His hands were like ice. I should've... should've...*

Should've what, exactly? She knew some rough leechcraft, but she couldn't have stopped their mad run for the gate in order to tend to him. And he'd not told her anything about his wounds, even when he had explained how he'd gotten separated from the rest of his hunting party.

Some ownness must fall to him, surely.

Even so, I might have done ... something, had I known.

She walked to stand behind Andrej, placing her hands on his shoulders. She felt him stiffen, but only for an instant.

"I have you, Andrej." She gave his shoulders a warm, brief squeeze. "I have you. Pravdivý jako zítřek." *(True as tomorrow.)*

There was an audible click as he swallowed. Nodding, he reached a hand up to squeeze her own.

Radek came to stand beside her. He kept his voice soft so as not to disturb his patient, but made no attempt to honey his words. She did note that he'd returned to his old man's quaver—a disguise that made her flesh crawl, now that she knew it for what it was.

"He was pierced by fully four of them... jagged, broad-head-ded hunting arrows, Lady. Beastly things that do almost as much harm on their way out as they do up-on impact." His face softened as he read her expression. "You look surprised. Well, Ruční Kopí was just as surprised. He tells me there were no archers among your harriers." He sighed through his nose. "He must have snapped off the shafts at some point. I was able to re-move two of them, but I fear they did their work on his kidney. Another had already been ripped out, causing con-sid-er-able damage. It would have ended him almost instant-ly had it not first pierced his quiver. Removing the final one would cause him un-necessary pain and would only serve to short-ten his re-main-ning time with us."

Kastan made a nod of acceptance. She knew her role in this. She also knew the answer to the question she must now ask, but she asked it anyway. "Is there anything to be done for him? Is there no way to save him?"

She felt Andrej stiffen. An instant later, she realized he was quite lit-erally holding his breath.

"We can make him comfortable, Excellency. In truth, it is a mark of his strength and force of will that he has sur-vived as long as he has. I've seen war-riors of *great* stature and renown fall to less-ser wounds than this."

She squeezed the boy's shoulders again, resisting the urge to turn him—to embrace him. He began to breathe once more. He bowed his blond head for a moment, then returned to his vigil.

"Shall I give him to drink, Excellency?"

"Will it drive him deeper into sleep? If there's a chance he might—"

Rákos chose that moment to take the matter out of their hands. He coughed his way into a sitting position, eyes snapping open and staring about with a wild, desperate intensity.

"Bjegota, dolů! Pozor!" *(Bjegota, down! Watch out!)* He coughed again, then vomited a nearly silent gout of blood. He tried to turn, as if wanting to avoid fouling his own chest. In the end, it made little difference.

"One of the arrows must have nicked the lung." Radek pulled several cotton cloths from his apothecar's effects and set about cleaning the dying man. He kept his voice modulated and calm, but addressed his speech to the room as a whole. "The wounds to his kidney are bad enough. That causes the body to poison itself—confusion, delirium, perhaps a final few moments of clarity before the end. If the lungs are damaged as well..."

In a voice that came out as a wet whisper, Rákos spoke anew.

"Kde je? Kde je můj chlapec?? *(Where is? Where is my boy?)*

Andrej tried to speak, but at first no sound came. He swallowed, cleared his throat, and tried again. This time, his voice came out calm—full of a warmth and strength that somehow overshadowed the war raging just outside.

"I'm here, Father. Jsem tady." *(I'm right here.)*

"Obchodní jazyk, Andrej... Obchodní jazyk." *(The Trade Tongue.)* Rákos seemed caught between sly chiding and fevered frustration. "Poslouchej minulost. Mluv s budoucností, ano?" *(Listen to the past. Speak with the future, yes?)* He gave another cough—this one blessedly dry, but very weak.

Andrej gave a breathy laugh, bowing his head for a moment. "To jo. I know. I'm... I'm sorry."

Rákos grinned with pink teeth. His entire aspect appeared to deflate as he exhaled.

Hajvarr spoke in surprise from the entrance to the residence. "*Pamatuji* si tě, Rákos! Kdysi jsi mě káral stejným způsobem... Jsem Hajvarr, syn Vojtěch. Pamatuješ si mě?" *(I remember you, Rákos! You used to scold me the same way... I'm Hajvarr, son of Vojtech. Do you remember me?)*

Rákos nodded, pointed to Hajvarr and tried to speak. Kastan couldn't decide if he looked sad or uncertain. His voice was gone. He didn't seem to have enough breath for even a whisper. Still pointing to Hajvarr, he mouthed something that looked like *know* and *me*. Making a sour face of either pain or frustration, he shook his head, then pointed to himself.

Hajvarr put up both hands in a placating gesture. "It's fine. I promise you I take no offense. *Rest* now."

The hunter shook his head and lay back, eyes streaming.

"Excellency, he's in ter-rible pain... May I give him..."

Kastan gave a nod, then watched as Radek poured a final powder into the mug before bringing it to Rákos and helping him to drink.

When it was over, and Radek had wiped the man's lips clean, he returned to place the empty mug back on the table. "Say what you mean to say, boy. You may not have another chance."

Andrej gulped, nodded, and drew a deep breath. He let it out in a shudder but forced himself to walk the few feet, then kneel at his father's side. He kissed the man's brow, took his bright hand between both of his own, and whispered into the hunter's ear.

Rákos reached up with his dim hand and pulled the boy down so their foreheads touched. The contact was brief but felt even to Kastan like the only *true* thing in the tent. All else seemed thin and unimportant.

The dying man then turned toward Hajvarr, reaching his newly freed dim hand out toward him. Ruční Kopí came close and dropped to his knees beside him, clasping the outstretched hand in both of his just as Andrej had. Rákos accepted the contact, but only briefly, pulling his hand away.

Kastan found his eyes almost too bright to look at. They seemed to be seeing nothing and everything at once. He pointed to himself, then back to Hajvarr, smiling a sad smile. Nodding, he pointed to Hajvarr again, then to Andrej, and finally to his own head.

Hajvarr grinned. "Yes—exactly. I was about your boy's age. You brought us a boar..."

Rákos gave a nod, then made his first and second fingers walk a shaking circle in mid-air.

Again, Hajvarr nodded. It was clear that he was concentrating on keeping both his voice and face under control. "You wandered all over the area. You hunted all the wide lands in the north of the county."

Rákos grabbed Hajvarr's ear as if to haul himself up. Kastan could see he was shuddering. He drew in a rattling breath, then spoke in a painful rasp.

"Je mi líto. Nemohl... Že jsem ji nemohl zachránit." *(I'm sorry. I couldn't... I couldn't save her.)*

"You *did* save her. You brought Lady Kastan home safely. She's right here... Look." Andrej squeezed his father's hand between both of his, then pointed to where Kastan stood. The boy's eyes searched for hers, pleading without words for her to approach—to say ... *something* that would comfort his father.

Kastan forced a courtly smile onto her face and came to kneel beside Andrej. "I cannot thank you enough, brave Rákos. You raced back to warn me—to warn the entire encampment—and gave no thought to your own safety. Many, *many* lives were saved by your good heart."

With great effort, he lifted the hand that Andrej held. He moved it toward Kastan, eyes desperate.

Kastan placed her hands over Andrej's, which were, in turn, placed over Rákos's own. "I have him. I won't abandon Andrej. Never think it. He belongs to m-my household for as long as he wishes to. You have my oath on it."

Rákos looked suddenly alarmed. He tried to draw breath, eyes wide. His face grew pale as he fought for consciousness.

"Otče? *Otče?* Breathe... breeeeeeathe..." Andrej sat forward, pulling his hand free... moving his arm around his father's shoulders. The man turned his head to face him, mouthing something. Then he slipped out of consciousness and knew no more.

Andrej lowered his father's head back down, with Hajvarr's help.

He's slipped consciousness, but he hasn't yet slipped sideways. It won't be long, though. I should go back to Olga, but...

But no. One look at Andrej drove all doubt from her heart. Even now, he was wetting a cloth in the water Radek had used moments before. As she watched, he rang it out, and with gentle hands began to clean his father's stained beard. The scene upended the hourglass, bringing her back to a time when she wasn't much older than the grieving boy beside her. She was, for a moment, cast back to her mother Klara's last days under the lash of the wasting sickness... days in which Kastan alone had been charged with that awful, final vigil. No, she was *precisely* where she needed to be.

As if reading her mind, Andrej glanced over at her and nodded. "You'll be just in there?"

Hajvarr's red hound had come over and curled up behind the boy. Kastan ran a gentle finger along the animal's black muzzle, then along the thick crimson of her brow. Turning to Andrej, she leaned over and kissed the top of his head.

He smiled at her. It was a grateful smile, if both weak and distracted. "You're *sure*?"

He nodded again.

She hesitated. "I won't be long. If you need *anything...*"

"I'll call. Thank you, Lady."

She stood, looking down at him for a long moment, then headed back to hasten matters with Olga along.

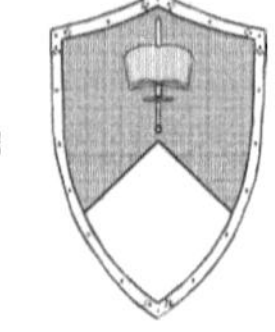

-III-

Dereek khn
Kor Kowmor
5 Korunasykli: 22 Days after the Red Storm at Westsong

The day's colors had all been strange... sharpened to a distracting, other-worldly edge. The eye-watering brightness of sun and sky, leaf and long stem, left the impression one was viewing them through slow-melting ice. What was more, the very *sun* appeared complicit in whatever ordinary magic was at play. It seemed to lumber its way to its customary noontime place, then become too tired to continue at any real speed.

Jastar observed all of this, but he had enough to distract himself. The Old Man had made them run in full kit, and over hilly terrain, for half a bell before breakfast. Then Gurin had shown him several new principles of unarmed combat before forcing him to spar with a variable number of opponents. They attacked as a group, then one at a time, and finally two at once, with the third man rushing in on the flank without warning. Then Jastar was allowed a brief respite for the midday meal.

His mind tried to wander back to the dream he'd been pulled from, but he found the effort both difficult and somehow painful. He recalled a snatch of song, or perhaps it had been a lay of some antiquity. He couldn't recall where he'd heard it before, but it came back to him like an old, forgotten friend.

"What do you court when the catapults quiet? What do you ask when the arrows aren't aimed? What do you seek when your sword's set aside? Why do you fight? Out of fear or for fame?"

Pallith's voice took up the melody from somewhere behind and to Jastar's right. His voice grew closer with each word.

"Where is the wind when the wings are all withered? Where lives the song when the strings cease to sing? Where rests your rage when foes are forgiven? Why do you weep? For your loss, or your gain?" He gave a warm little laugh, then hunkered down at Jast's side. "I didn't expect to ever hear *that* again… Certainly never in Dereek khn."

Jastar noted that Pallith's emphasis was slightly off with the rest of the men and women he'd heard saying the realm's name. He put focus on the *Der* and truncated the E sound that came after. *Dair*eek-han.

"D'you know, I couldn't think where I knew it from. I'd have guessed Rahn—now *Sir* Rahn."

Pallith grinned, eyes mostly closing. "It was something my mother used to sing. She passed before I met you, but my father and I would sing it in memory of her. When I began fighting in tournaments, he would sing it softly as I armored up. He'd be holding my helm for me, or perhaps my shield as I slid my gauntlets on, and begin softly singing it. It became a ritual for us."

Jastar tilted his head back and sighed in recognition. "Aye, *that's* it. I knew *I* hadn't crafted it, so I must've heard it … somewhere. Yessss, I remember your father singing it now. A pretty thing, that song."

"Old." Pallith nodded. "Old when my mother was born, but, aye. A pretty thing."

"How goes your training, then? Has *the Mattock* shown you how to break the wall?"

Pallith bowed his head, looking away. "Nooo. Not as of yet, at least. She'll try again shortly, I have no doubt."

She? There are a good deal more warrior-women here than I first thought.

"You've been breaking through walls since... Well, for years now." He'd been about to say *since our first tournament together.* That would've been at Greenfork. Greenfork which had been Pallith's home. Greenfork... where his father had been sentenced to swing. He'd thought it best to change tack.

"She's not teaching me how to break *other* walls, my friend. She's trying to break through *my* shield wall. She's come close, but as of this moment? I remain melmu." Pallith offered a flash of mostly white teeth.

Jast had been about to ask what that word actually meant when Gurin had called his name. Bidding Pallith goodbye, at least for the nonce, he'd stood up and jogged over to begin the afternoon's training.

The day continued sleepwalking toward its end. There were more bouts of running, then his first training—at least here in Dereek khn—with what they called the ralbrend. Valad had referred to the weapon as a *great-sword*, but that was the only difference. The training itself was the same, at least thus far. Finally, there had been a strange hour in which Jastar had to interview three men and one woman in order to determine which one was lying to him.

"I think I see. Two of them are lying, Lanbachsel."

"Very good, indeed. You're *almost* right, but you've missed someone."

"No, Lanbachsel, I'm certain that—of the four—only two of them tried to play me false."

Gurin nodded. "What was the order I gave you to execute, Jastar? What were my instructions?"

Jastar held his frustrated sigh in abeyance, repeating the Lanbachsel's words. "Your role is to determine truth from fiction in this affair, and name the person playing you false."

Gurin nodded. "How many people were involved in this exercise?"

Jast arched his brow. "Five."

"Counting yourself?"

He nodded. "Five, counting myself."

Gurin met his eyes, waiting.

Jastar looked at the sun once more. It hung low in the sky at long last. *Perhaps an hour before sunset? Certainly less than two, presuming this interminable day finally ends.* It came into his mind that the world was in a state of anticipation… unless that was the Lanbachsel's gaze boring into him.

He was saved from further frustration when a younger man in the livery of the Ban'ze Ruun—the Smoldering Hammers—arrived. He looked Sheshik in origin, though his skin was a lighter tone than many Jastar had seen. A war hound trotted beside him, which was odd. Hunters had hounds. Had this man been a member of the order of the bow—a thing he'd heard the army had, but had yet to see—that would be one thing. A line soldier? In uniform, no less?

"Lanbachsel?" The man's voice scratched at the ear. "This is Sir Jastar, is it?"

Gurin lifted his chin in recognition. "Tharus. Ire."

He'd no idea what the fellow wanted, but he apparently knew who Jastar was, which was interesting. A moment later, interesting curdled into something sour.

"The Old Man sent me for him. We've ridden hard from Yrxa."

Gurin lifted his brows. "The Ironbane need him for something?"

The Sheshik man shook his bearded head. "Methias wants anyone from Thorion."

Jastar fought the falling frost of panic.

"I *should* say, he wants anyone from Thorion, or from anywhere in the Empire." He paused. "You only know the *one* Imperial tongue, aye, Lanbachsel?"

Gurin sighed. "Aye and aye. That and Calyari."

"No need to trouble yourself, then. First of the two-two has that covered."

Gurin nodded, offering a thin smile. "Well? Best go with the bachsel, Jastar. Tharus? Will you be here for the evening mess?"

Jastar's helmet lay beside him on the grass, his gloves and gauntlets stored within it. He now made rather a business of crouching down to recover them, then slip them on. He felt Gurin's eyes on him as he picked his helm up off the grass. When he'd burned up all the time he felt he could justify, he rose, gauntleted, with steel hat in hand.

The newcomer—Tharus, apparently—shrugged. "That's up to Methias. Nrcarnhecn jhoaz aqan, ruunth hecn."

When Jastar righted himself again, he saw the giant of a man was grinning.

"Aye. Tears come later, with smiles or sobs. Fair enough. It'll likely come down to what the folk of Thorion and Venzene can tell him." He sighed. "Well, *if* you stay, and your duties permit, come find me. If not—"

Tharus stood at attention for a beat, returned the nod that Gurin gave him, and glanced at Jastar to ensure he was ready.

Jast followed suit—standing at rough attention, helm under his arm. When the Lanbachsel had dismissed him, he let Tharus lead him off to, apparently, meet this Lord Methias.

-IV-

The center ring of Kor Kowmor was empty, save Fyken and Methias. Several archers stood a nominal watch on the walls, and a few non-fighting folk could be heard inside the hall that served as Kowmor's main mess, but otherwise, they had the open area to themselves.

Methias took a bumper of brandy from Fyken, saluted him with it, and smiled. Bringing the wooden goblet to his lips, he stopped long enough to take a rather indelicate sniff of its contents.

Ahhh, just about my favorite drink in the wide world. The realization gave birth to a small suspicion. Rather than dwell on it...

"Katxsel, have you been saving this?"

The aged soldier snorted. "Aye, but not for you, Lord. As to why you find it here? You've *yourself* to blame for introducing me to it." The man sketched laughter over the crisp autumn air. "Did you suppose you were the *only* person in Dereek khn to appreciate the taste of pear and cinnamon brandy?"

Methias blushed, shaking his head. *How very self-important of me. You're quite right, Fyken. How to reply without proving myself any more the fool... Ah!*

Grinning, he took a small sip of the sweet fire before speaking. "Well, of all crimes to be guilty of, improving your taste isn't one I expect to lose much sleep over."

Fyken arched his brows, then chuckled. "Aye, well... fair enough." He cocked his head to one side, then nodded. "Sounds as if some of them are almost here. Likely the Ban'ze Ruun's third of the two-two with the necessary others in tow, if I were a betting man."

Methias nodded, taking a longer sip before speaking. "You'd win that wager. I hear Apiné's voice—I'm all but certain." He'd been standing in front of Fyken. Now he moved to stand beside him. "Tell me, before they arrive."

"If you're asking about Apiné, she's proving me right, Lord. Her men are well-trained and shouldn't lose a step while she's learning from you." He scratched at his chin in an absent sort of manner. "As for *Sir* Jastar, he's got skill and to spare. Honestly, he's taken to the training far more readily than most. He may be exactly what he says he is, or something more. He's not boasting about his skill, though. I'd trust his sword arm. As for his motives ... that's for you and the Fellhammer to judge."

"Thank you for that, truly. It wasn't what I'd meant to *ask*, but it's good to hear."

"Oh...? What then?"

"While it's just we two, I'd ask how you *really* are, Fyken Presh?" Methias did his best to scrub any sense of placation or patronization from his tone. Still, Fyken was called *the Old Man* for good reason. At seventy-five, the soldier was one of the realm's secret treasures, as far as Methias saw it. "Outside of that limp, you present yourself as being in better physical condition than almost anyone I've ever met. But if there's anything you need..."

Fyken eyed him, then bowed his head. "I bide, Lord. And with fewer than my share of age's aches and pains. Willows willing, time won't drown my bones for a goodly while yet." A pointed draught from his wooden goblet made it clear that he wished that particular avenue of conversation to be left at that.

Methias gave a nod, then finished his brandy with a mixture of delight and disappointment. *Such a drink should be savored, not swallowed as if it were a dipper of water, but never mind.* He placed the empty vessel on a nearby bench with as little fanfare as possible. Best the others not see him lording his privileged position over them.

He saw a quintet of the Ban'ze Ruun walking in his direction from the innermost gate. They were chatting in an amiable sort of way... right up until they first caught sight of him and Fyken. All obvious chatter ceased, and—he'd swear to it—several of them seemed to make a conscious effort to measure their strides so that they moved in step with one another.

Apiné led them with untroubled strides. Her short, red-gold waves were plastered to the sides of her head—a product of the day's training. She cut an unremarkable figure in her hauberk and pauldrons. Such gear of war hid the curves of her body, as proper armor should. Still, she projected a calm confidence that'd helped her rise both within the ranks of the Dereek khnderath *and* to Methias's personal attention.

"My lord," she began as they crossed the final ten feet, "may I present Bachsel Morric and Mosel Kujin—both of my lance," She gestured toward the two men to her left. "Mosel Yarison, and Gilsel Edani—first of the two-two." She indicated the man and woman on her right. Turning to Fyken, she bowed her head before adding, "Katxsel, reporting as ordered."

As they came to a stop, Apiné stomped her right boot once, then came to attention. The other Hammers reacted to the stomp, standing at attention as well.

Fyken sipped his brandy as if he had all the time in the world.

Methias began mentally counting. He reached twenty-six before Fyken nodded and let them off the proverbial hook.

"At your ease," said he. Turning to Methias, he arched a brow as if to ask if he wanted any sort of introduction.

He gave a minute shake of his head by way of reply, then turned his attention to Apiné. "Thank you." He then addressed himself to the group at large. "I've asked Lanbachsel Apiné to bring you here to aid me—and indeed the realm as a whole—in translating something. Actually, several somethings. May I ask where you're each originally from?"

"I'm from Koruna Všech, Lord." The speaker had perhaps a decade on Methias. He was shorter than the other men around him, with a mouse-brown beard and bright amber eyes.

"You're Morric, yes? Morric Bone Shroud?" Methias saw the man's color rise at being recognized.

"I... I am, Lord. Though Morric will do if rank isn't necessary."

Methias resisted the urge to shake his head at the deflection. *Yet there's no hint of churlishness in your voice, nor does your humility feel ... false. So this is not a backhanded cry for attention, then. Fair enough, but Havoc's Horn! How you thought to remain anonymous after felling so many of the restless dead that night is beyond me.*

"As you like, Morric. As I say, it isn't your hammer or shield-arm I need just now. You're from the Venzene capital. Good enough. Thank you."

He turned to the others expectantly. The Sheshik man spoke up next. He was of average height, but his limbs were long. His skin was a deep reddish-brown—a color that seemed mirrored by his eyes when he stood still. His accent was somehow luxuriant. He rolled many of his Rs and made a meal of most of his vowel sounds. The sum total made him not only easy to understand, but an utter joy to listen to. Methias felt sure the fellow dabbled in storytelling or poetry on nights round the fire.

"I ... have never lived *in* the Empire, Lord... I *did,* however, spend much time guarding the caravans that came south from the Last Grass. I would never pass for a native of Thorion, Traead, or the Empire, but I speak *some* of many tongues."

Methias considered for a moment before speaking. "You are ... Kujin the Viper, surely."

Kujin beamed, displaying impossibly white teeth. "The same, Lord. You honor me."

"You honor *yourself,* Kujin ... and the realm. Fast hands make for fine hearth tales." Methias waited a moment, then nodded. He turned to the other two with an air of polite expectance. They looked awkward and uncertain as to who should speak next. He thought they were from either Kovalun or Kamienalun, but time would tell. Apiné was drawing breath to speak when the sound of a single, deep bark warmed the air.

"Hello, Ire." Methias reached a hand out to receive the hound, who readily trotted over. Forcing his eyes away, he tried to banish the grin that had flowered on his face, with minimal success. He saw Tharus approaching with a man in mail of a different style than that issued by the realm's military. It was more a chain shirt than a hauberk, and Methias noted a steel mantle rather than pauldrons. As they crossed the last few strides, he marked the man's warbraid and the telltale silver star adorning its end.

So this is Sir Jastar, is it?

"My lord?" Tharus ended his walk, standing to the woman—Edani's— right. As Jastar came to a stop beside him, Tharus spoke on. "Sir Jastar."

Jastar offered a brief bow. "Lord." Then he gave a deferential nod to Fyken. "Katxsel."

"You're from Thorion, then. Have you traveled much outside of the county?"

Jastar blinked as if needing to process the question. "No, my lord. To a tournament at Schwalbenwald, once—in Gerstealun. And to Traead and the unclaimed hills in the south, but that's all."

Methias nodded. "No fear. You may yet be able to help." He gathered his thoughts, then spoke anew. "First for those of you who've spent time in Venzene lands..." He reached into his haversack and, after a moment of concentration, pulled out a thin volume bound in slate and leather. Flipping toward the middle where he'd left a corner folded double, he glanced over his notes and read aloud. "De kommer. De marsjerer." He then sought the eyes of each person in turn.

"Who, Lord?" Morric, sounding confused.

Well, that's a good start. Methias addressed himself to Morric. "Bachsel, de kommer fra elven—de kommer fra elvens bunn."

"Elven?" This was the woman—Edani.

Morric shook his head. "Not what you think, Gilsel. Elven is *river* in Havalunth."

"Hold your translation for the moment, Morric," said Methias. "For now, it's enough that you *can* translate it. That, and the fact that you recognize it as Havalunth."

Morric gave a nod of confused acceptance.

Returning his eye to the page, Methias turned to face Jastar. "Wo aaye. Kia. Wo…" he paused, then tried again. "Wo darya se aaye, wo pani…" He sighed through his nose. "Wo pani k neeche se aaye." Looking up to find the man's eyes, Methias saw a look of such perfect vacuity that he almost laughed. "Not a tongue you know, then."

Jastar cocked his head to one side as if in thought. "Not one I *speak*… but it's familiar to me." He paused, then shook his head. "If we may, Lord, I'd like to circle back to it in a moment. Let me try and unknot the memory."

Methias nodded. "Fair. I can do that."

"Lord?" Tharus's beard stubble voice lilted upward at the word's end. Once Methias had turned his attention that way, he continued. "I've heard it. At the Last Bell, actually. It's from the *other* folk of Thorion—the *first* people of Thorion."

All eyes turned to regard Tharus, who shrugged a pauldron-covered shoulder.

Sir Jastar snapped his fingers, face brightening. "That's it!" His eyes danced, "And we've someone in this very fortress who speaks at least some of the tongue."

Methias waited for a name that appeared not to be coming. Finally, Fyken drew breath in obvious preparation to force the matter. Whether deliberate or unconscious, Jastar chose that moment to speak once more.

"I don't know whose lance he's in. Katxsel? I'm speaking of Pallith."

Apiné turned to Kujin. "If you would?"

The Viper nodded, bowed to Methias and Fyken, and waited for permission to depart. Fyken gave it, and Methias turned back to Tharus and Jastar.

"You've my thanks." He then turned back to the book he was still holding and read the final warning. "Sie kommen—Nebelblut, Herr! Sie marschieren! Sie kommen aus dem Fluss—sie kommen von unter dem Wasser!"

"It's ... Gerstealunth, Lord. I can tell you that much, but not much more." This was Yarisan. He shook his shaggy head of black hair and pooched out his lower lip. "I'm sorry I can't be of more help."

Methias offered a grin. "Yarisan, you remind me of someone I recently met on the road. A boy who made his home near the Obserwatorzy Zmierzchu."

Yarisan brightened visibly. "I was born in sight of those mountains, Lord. You've a keen ear. Though Lanbachsel Gurin grew up far closer to them than I—Auburg, if memory serves."

"I'm surprised he isn't here with you, then."

"I know for a fact that Lanbachsel Gurin only speaks the Trade Tongue, Calyari, and Kamienalunth, Lord. When Katxsel Fyken asked for Yarisan..." Tharus trailed off.

Methias made a gesture of acceptance. After a moment of thoughtful silence, Fyken spoke up from his left.

"Lord? My Gerstealunth is still serviceable. Do you still want the translations kept in abeyance?

"If you please..." Methias did his best to hide his surprise. It was common enough for folk to know two—sometimes three languages. But most stopped after learning the Trade Tongue and whatever other language was in common use where they lived. Fyken hadn't come from the duchy of Gerstealun, but rather that of Lesalun. He'd also learned a good deal of Calyari over the last year. His familiarity with yet another tongue wasn't astonishing, but it *was* worthy of note.

Kujin appeared with Pallith in tow. A few moments later, the new arrival confirmed that he did, indeed, understand the words of the second warning.

"My father insisted on it, Lord. It was important that the old ways weren't lost."

When the entirety of all three warnings had been read aloud, and translated into the trade tongue, they made a grim proclamation, indeed.

"They come. They are marching—the mist-bloods. They come from the River. They come from *beneath* the River."

Methias turned to Fyken and ... froze. Ramud Ayumbra was seated in mid-air, floating just over Fyken's shoulder.

"Ask," said he. His voice was as frustratingly neutral as ever.

"And what, or who, are the mist-bloods? Do any of you know?"

One by one, they all shook their heads. When Methias looked at Ramud Ayumbra, the meoli gave a solemn nod. "In this anguish-ed age, Meth-hyoos Ar-thod, the empty-eyed world of man uses the word *goblin* ... to name them."

"Goblins," said Methias. "Mist-bloods are goblins."

Pallith and Jastar exchanged a look with one another, then turned back to Methias.

"Lord, they come from the mountains to trouble the unwary or unguarded at night. They live in the deep places, not the River."

Thorion has lived with these Nebelblut on one side of the River and the Shivering Song on the other? I don't know whether to pity them or parade them about as heroes.

"The warnings say otherwise." Apiné shook her head. "If they're wrong, so be it. Can we afford to take that risk?"

"A good question," said Methias. "Another might be—*do they have anything to do with the coming war?*"

"We could send messengers." This was Edani. "That, and send out mounted patrols along the north side of the River... With the two-two here on a training rotation, surely we can afford to send a lance or two of Foakhuleek, no?"

Fyken gave a slow, considering nod at that idea.

Methias hadn't seen it happen, but the meoli had winked out of existence at some point in the last few heartbeats. *Well, the goblins almost have to be related to the larger war. Their proximity to Yrxa castle, their apparent change in action, if Pallith and Jastar are correct... And the largest proof of all is the appearance of the old meoli himself. He came without warning or preamble and volunteered the translation. No, this has to play some part in the larger conflict.*

He shook his head, then turned to Jastar and Pallith. "What's the nearest settlement," he looked up, found the sun, and pointed to the southeast, "along *that* path?"

The sons of Thorion looked at one another again, though this particular silent conference was mercifully brief.

Pallith delivered their conclusion. "Wick, Lord."

Jastar then took up the tale. "It's a good place, Lord. Well-fortified and well-peopled."

Methias nodded. "Good." He adjusted his stance to include Fyken in his regard. "Katxsel, I mean to take some of your charges."

Fyken nodded. "How many?"

Methias saw Jastar looking confused, and perhaps unhappy, but paid it little mind. "I shall take Apiné's lance, and the sons of Thorion, here."

"Pallith is *in* my lance, Lord." Apiné was grinning—clearly delighted with the situation.

"Good. That makes this simpler. Is... Who else is here from the Yebu Ke?"

"Cr ke Ibhroth." Fyken's voice had a comfortable, *this is all just business to me, Lord,* tone.

Methias sighed, grinning in spite of himself. He liked Ibhroth, though he had no idea why. *Everyone seems to like him. And everyone seems to find him irksome.*

"Well, no help for it. He'll have to do. Sir Jastar? If you'd be good enough to fetch him?" Turning to Apiné, he spoke again. "Full kits. Gather your lance, help Sir Jastar and Cr ke Ibhroth, should they need it. I want everyone ready for field duty in half a bell." Turning, at last, to Yarisan and Edani, he offered a brief but genuine smile. "Thank your commander for me. It's... Denythis, now, isn't it?" When they nodded, clearly surprised and gratified at the recognition, he continued, "Thank him for your loan, and thank you for the help."

"The Gilsel made a fair point. I'm going to send out a mounted patrol, Lord. Best we not be blindsided."

Methias nodded, then stepped back. As he did, he saw Fyken step forward, dismissing the assembled men and women. Tharus remained. He was, after all, at Kor Kowmor *with* Methias.

"May I speak my mind, Lord?" Fyken turned to face him.

"I think you'd better."

"Is it wise to walk into Thorion with armed men—even if it's only an oversized lance? Nobody who lays eyes on you will think you're sellswords."

Methias nodded. "Necessary. Jastar has the credibility to get a message through to whoever rules that town, but I can't risk sending him alone. Not against a foe that can hide from even the weave." He gave another nod in response to Fyken's look of surprise. "I saw the places associated with the warnings. I saw the River part, as if many creatures moved through it toward the southern shore. I saw foliage part in much the same way. I neither saw nor heard *them*, though. If I cannot detect them at range, even when I know and am looking at where they are affecting the land around them..."

Fyken cocked his head to one side, then nodded. "Then you can't

leave it up to hope and faith that a lone rider can get a message through."

"Exactly."

He paused to look down at Ire, who had begun snoring. As he looked up again, he caught Tharus's thin grin. He turned back to Fyken Presh, smiling.

"I'll need one more thing from you, Katxsel. Find me a place in the courtyard that can be guarded, but won't be in a place folk are likely to walk."

Fyken arched his brows, grinning. "I know just the place. What are you planning?"

"Luck is a garden, Fyken. You have to select the right location, sow the right seeds, and protect them while they grow. Otherwise, you'll be left with nothing to harvest."

-V-

Venzene Duchy of Kovalun
County Jižní Pochod
Barony of Hartscross–Jižní Lov
5 Korunasykli: 22 Days after the Red Storm at Westsong

Vlk had spent what seemed like an age on his feet. He'd passed news, called targets, fetched more ammunition, and contorted himself into nearly every position he could think of. This last was more than an effort to make himself a less obvious target. It was also the need to react to the allied archers as they slipped sideways, struck by enemy fire. They might fall forward or backward off the alure or to either side as they were struck. Then there were those on the walls who'd simply panicked, fleeing deeper into Jižní Lov and paying as little attention as possible to anyone or anything they knocked down along the way.

He'd watched a young Bluemark archer fall, and the man next to him simply go mad. His eyes had grown huge and glassy, his mouth dripping spittle. The madman dropped his bow, drew his sword, hacked at his dead friend's body twice, kicked it, then turned, making a sound somewhere between laughter and tears. He bounced off the other archers, slicing into the arm of one before slipping in the rain and crashing down the nearby stairs.

They're like untrained horses smelling blood for the first time. Vlk had been too awed to do much more than stare. *They're vild, angry, and terri-fied—as much a danger to themselves as anyone else.*

For all of that, he thought the battle was going well. The enemy kept sending men to the walls in an effort to make what Waltyr called *a breach.* Even to his unpracticed eye the idea seemed pointless. The walls were stout, after all. Even if that weren't the case, Waltyr and his men felled foes until they either faded away into nothing or lay stacked against the wall like cordwood for a bloody winter to come.

Then came a thing that froze his heart. He saw the war leader on his stormcloud steed, his boy seated before him. The nightmare mount reared, then leapt forward ... and *upward.* As Vlk stared, the beast ran on the very air, racing toward the roof of the barbican.

Horrified, Vlk began to run toward Waltyr at the far end of the plat-form, shouting his name. Before he'd made it under the wooden canopy's near end, he saw the storm rider's boy leap down to the peaked roof.

As he ran, Vlk saw Waltyr turn to him, follow his gaze, then step back to aim his crossbow upward. Most adults seemed to willfully ignore or outwardly disdain boys his age. They certainly didn't *listen* to them. Not so with Waltyr Wachfeld. One grown man in *thrice a thousand* was Waltyr.

The sergeant loosed a bolt which passed *right through* the damned horse. The quarrel nearly struck Laagi—the gnoerkish boy—as he stalked toward Vlk's side of the barbican.

At that point, Vlk's run carried him beneath the canopy. He'd made it five feet further before it happened. The storm rider floated down. He no longer rode his monster steed. Instead, it was as if his entire lower body were surrounded by its own storm cloud.

Vlk found himself in an ecstasy of indecision... and panic. Should he race to help Waltyr? Should he focus on the gnoerk boy he knew was moving toward where he himself had just been?

He was spared the pressure of decision. The storm rider fell on Waltyr like a living tine of lightning. As Vlk watched, the monster brought his axe down with both hands, striking the left side of Waltyr's skull with a canted hammer shot that was audible even at that distance. He heard him-self scream. Waltyr fell, and all he could do was scream.

The storm rider's arm rose high, as if in triumph. Lightning split the clouds, thunder cracking just behind. Then he hurled his axe over the wall, deep within the fortress's courtyard. The storm began to swirl, wind spinning faster and faster, swallowing his screams. Then... the rain was gone. The sun was setting, but the sky was full of ordinary golds and pinks.

Vlk's screams caught in his throat when he saw Fetinba. She turned to the enemy chieftain and loosed what looked like a perfect shot toward his neck. The storm cloud that was his lower half seemed to rise all around him before the arrow struck home. He turned to face her, but she was already in motion.

As the other Bluemarks moved westward—away from Waltyr's killer—Fetinba dropped her borrowed bow and ran at the scarred storm rider. Just before she reached him, she jumped out, off the barbican, grabbed the nearest upright, and swung herself feet-first toward the monster.

He caught her in mid-career with a massive backhand, striking her out of the air and over the edge, toward the courtyard.

Again Vlk screamed, but this time it was a roar of rage as much as it was a cry of horror. Still making that strange, guttural noise, he reached down and pulled one of the Bluemark dead's short swords free from its scabbard. The thought that this particular Bluemark was more useful in death than the score or so that were still retreating westward along the alure was brief, but powerful.

"Odvážna krv!" Jastrab's clarion voice preceded him as he stalked up the stairs. He bore an oval shield and a gleaming sword. A helm of bright steel crowned his head above his wind-ruffled black kontusz.

A figure moved down the stairs in Jastrab's wake—something swathed in white. The realization that Fetinba was alive, that the captain had likely caught her as she fell, was enough to keep Vlk's horror at bay, at least for the moment. He watched as Jastrab squared off with the storm rider, *willing* the man to do what he could not... willing him to avenge Waltyr's death.

Movement to his right, down in the courtyard, caught his eye. He saw a figure in a red kontusz knock a Bluemark aside, then bolt into a tent.

Coward, he thought, but that was all he had time for. He heard an *oof* a few paces behind him. Spinning, he saw the gnoerkish boy walking with purpose toward him. He unslung the weapon from his back—a battle axe inlaid with a reddish-gold metal. As he walked, he pulled the leather caps off the weapon's edges.

The gnoerk boy—Laagi—met his eyes and shook his head. He gestured with his right hand, indicating that Vlk should run.

Probably a wise idea. This was no tournament—no babe's lyst. Yet here was an opponent he had a chance of defeating. The gnoerk was about Andrej's size, after all.

Vhy else have I been training, if not to do my part vhen the time comes? Vlk hefted his borrowed blade, shaking his head as he readied himself.

-VI-

Kastan stood behind Andrej with her arms around his chest. His head was bowed, his hands wrapped tightly around her forearms. His breath held a tiny shake buried within it, and she felt a few stray drops hit her wrist where his silent tears had fallen. Still, he was holding up far better than she'd feared he might. Grief was natural, especially in a situation like this. *Debilitating* grief was apt to get all involved hurt, if not outright killed for their trouble, at least until the battle was ended.

Rákos had slipped sideways minutes earlier. Andrej had been with him, as had Kastan, much to Olga's obvious, if silent, consternation. Now, far earlier than was the custom, Rákos would be brought down to the crypts and laid to a hasty rest. He would be left there until the battle's end. When the hourglass had been righted again, and there was time, Kastan had assured the boy that they would give him a proper ceremony. For now, this would have to do. Leaving the dead man in Edmund's command tent was both unkind and unwise. The dead left out in the open ran the risk of making the living ill or calling Skolf's vermin out from their hidden holes. Questions of health be damned, leaving him out in the open like a sack of old meal would have been a sign of utter disrespect. It would also have been monstrously cruel to Andrej.

She watched as Hajvarr moved the body onto a bier. When Radek had done his best to arrange Rákos's limbs in as natural a semblance of sleep as he could, Hajvarr looked to Andrej.

"It's time," he said, and said no more.

Andrej gave Kastan's arms a brief, tight squeeze, then released her, nodding.

Hajvarr gestured to Pavel, the baker's son and his new... page? Protégé? *Armsman. We'll call him Hajvarr's armsman until something else presents itself.* The big lad drew in a breath to steady himself, and both he and Hajvarr took the ends of the bier in hand, lifting it and beginning to move toward the back of the tent.

As Rákos's sad form disappeared through the canvas, she and Andrej had a moment alone. She stepped back, turning him to face her. He was pliable, offering no resistance. She leaned forward and planted a gentle kiss on his brow, then smoothed back his blond waves.

He gave a weak, little laugh, then looked up at her through glassy eyes. "I don't..." He blinked, causing a few tears to carve their way down his face. "I don't know what to do now."

She drew him in, trying to comfort him—to reassure him. "I told you. I have you. You'll have a place with I and mine for as long as you want. You belong—"

He gently withdrew, smiling and blushing as he met her eyes. "I know, Lady. I know, and..." he shook his head. "I'm grateful, truly. There's nowhere I'd rather be. My father wanted us to join the scouts, but I'd rather stay with..." He bowed his head. "I'd rather stay where I am."

He was thinking of Fetinba; she knew. The idea made her smile. "If not that, then what?"

Andrej cast an eye toward the entrance to the residence. "I've never been to a funerary rite, lady. And Rákos never talked about death, save that if he told me to, I should either run or hide. That if he was felled, I shouldn't go after whoever felled him. I don't know ... what I'm meant to do now."

She nodded, making an *ah* sound. "We'll walk down together. Radek will say a few words from the old rites... Normally we'd all speak a word about his life and wish his shadow well. But..."

"But there isn't time with a battle raging outside." He cocked his head toward the door, listening to the sounds of men dying, people screaming, and the omnipresent storm. "*They* aren't being carried down to be given the old rites. *They're* fighting and dying—some of them, anyway. We should be out there doing what we can... So, no. No words."

She nodded, smiling as she again smoothed back his hair. "You remind me of Caros at your age. He was far too serious and would see far too much horror far too soon."

He blushed again. "Your brother is a great man. If I'm anything like him, then ... I'll count..." His voice cut off. He burst into tears so rapidly and with such power that he collapsed to his knees, shaking. Kastan dropped down and embraced him once more, rocking him back and forth as he wept.

When the worst of it had passed, she helped him to his feet. The pair of them turned toward the back wall. Hajvarr's red hound sat there staring at them. As they approached, she whimpered far back in her throat, standing up to meet them.

Andrej grinned, stroking her head and scratching behind her ears. She licked his face, then tried to put her head beneath his chin, causing him to laugh.

Kastan walked on, leaving him in Štít's red hands. *Or paws, I suppose.* Stepping down into the residence, she saw Olga standing there with her arms folded. In her hands were two items—a metal scroll case and Edmund's žezlo. This latter was the rod of county rulership. They were present for official ceremonies, whenever possible. This one was made of steel, by the looks of it, with the reddish-gold seal of the county's ruling house atop its head.

Olga met her eyes and stepped forward. Her voice was the same implacable iron as ever. If the woman knew how to laugh, Kastan had certainly never heard it.

"This *never* leaves you, Excellency. Not in the bath. Not in the jakes. It joins you in bed, should we be lucky enough to see beds again. Am I understood?"

"You are, Mistress." *Understood and awfully haughty,* she thought but did not say. "I know how important the žezlo is. No fear."

"You do not, but we shall remedy that. Among other things, the seal on its crown is the master seal of the county. With it, all official writs may be marked with the legal and registered chop of the county throne. With it, other seals and signet rings may be made."

Kastan arched her brows and nodded. Olga was correct. She had *not* known that.

"Also, it was *this* I was speaking of." She proffered the scroll case. It looked like it might be made of actual silver. "This contains the proof of your claim to the throne, as well as Edmund's own signet ring. Paper is never fireproof, as they say, but within these papers lay the indelible legal proof of your claim to the county throne. Until your investiture, this must never leave you. Once that happy day comes to pass, you can have it interred in a vault as you see fit."

Kastan's eyes went wide, then narrowed in thought. An instant later she'd grown pale. Andrej's boots and Štít's clicking claws brought her back to the moment at hand. "To that end, Mistress…"

Olga nodded. "Yes, Excellency. Sad that your first act will be a funerary rite, albeit a short one. Still—there's a thing I need to show you at the place of honor ... where Hajvarr, I have no doubt, is taking your hunter."

Kastan saw Andrej stiffen at that choice of words, but that was all. She also saw that he'd taken back his archery gear, as well as his father's bow, which he held in his bare left hand.

The three of them—four if they counted Hajvarr's Karmínové Srdce—moved to the small entry hall at the back of the residence. A moment later, they'd passed through the broad wooden door, and entered the catacombs. Štít led them, presumably following her master's scent.

I must remember to thank Hajvarr. Leaving her behind was a subtle kindness most folk wouldn't have thought of, let alone bothered with.

At that moment, the hound stopped, bushed out her fur, and began to growl in a tone that froze Kastan's blood.

Andrej stepped in front of the women. His father's bow in hand, he drew an arrow from his quiver and nocked it into place against the bowstring. She saw his own bow had been artfully placed against his back, looping around his quiver. Grinning, she plucked it free and selected one of his arrows. "I'll just borrow yours," said she.

Whether Andrej had heard her or not was left in doubt. A vast, bruise-colored fog came ripping into the hall. The sound was ear-shattering, as if a hundred horses were screaming beneath the vaulted ceilings of an enclosed stone stable, and she was stood in its center.

The crimson heart howled. The sound was full, haunting, and bright amidst the monstrous engine of noise the impossible storm was making... And Kastan felt suddenly calm. Inexplicably, unmistakably unafraid.

The silver and purple storm winked out, taking the hellish sound with it, and all light save one. The lantern nearest them was somehow still burning bright. Her ears were ringing, though she knew she hadn't gone deaf. The tag end of the red hound's howl was proof enough on that score.

She'd drawn breath, meaning to ask if everyone was alright, but the sound caught in her throat.

Thud... thud... thud...

The sickly pale violet of an unnatural dawn began somewhere down the hall. It summoned, unbidden, a memory of late nights around low fires. A memory of Sigdemane at Haluz Věže—a time where only the oldest stories had been told by the very drunk or the very mad.

It's familiar, but... Hells why do I know this? No... no, not the hells. No, something about Havoc's Horn, I think. Something about swords and... and a dying man's tears

She shuddered at the memory, though she'd no idea why.

Nothing moved up ahead, save that creeping stain of witchlight.

Thump... thump... thump... Crack!

The sound of a hammer breaking through stone rolled toward them. Rising slowly behind that fearful knell, there were growls... whispers... voices...

CHAPTER ELEVEN

SHADOWS SHOWN

-I-

Venzene Duchy of Kovalun
County Jižní Pochod
Barony of Hartscross–Jižní Lov
5 Korunasykli: 22 Days after the Red Storm at Westsong

Vlk balked the circle with Laagi. Their slow, steady stalking was more a counterclockwise ellipse than a circle, but that could hardly be helped. It was due as much to the scattering of Bluemark dead as it was the narrowness of the alure. No matter. He maneuvered without crossing his feet, blade pointed at his foe. He was as ready as he could make himself to contend with the half-gnoerk boy.

The koftgar's inlay on the invader's axe was stunning. It almost had to be an heirloom weapon. He'd only ever seen such work on the ceremonial swords of the older nobles who'd visited the camp. Beautifying an axe in such a way was something he'd never even *considered*.

Best I not look at it for too long. There was danger in being distracted, and he knew it. Even now, the thought that began with the phrase *if I beat him* tried to arrest his mind. *But no. This is no sparring match.* The axe wasn't a prize to add greedy hope to the excitement of a lyst. Beating the boy before him almost surely meant killing him—a thing Vlk *thought* he could do, but...

"You *can* withdraw. You may not believe me, but I swear to you I won't stop you or stand in your way."

Laagi's scratched voice made him seem *far* more confident than Vlk felt. That realization was followed immediately by another.

"I believe you, Laagi. I just von't go."

If he was surprised that Vlk had marked his name, it didn't show. He nodded, face growing sad. "Alright. What name do they call you? I'll tell the tale 'round the fire."

"Vlk. Vlk Liškalg." He made a point of enunciating the gno-erkish suffix.

Laagi stopped for a beat, glared death down toward Vlk, and made as if to continue balking the circle ... then lunged, slamming the axe down toward the shorter boy's shoulder. Vlk stepped forward into the strike, bringing his own weapon to bear. He caught the battleaxe on its metal bone—the long steel barrel that attached the axe's head to its wooden haft—but it was a near thing.

The pair struggled in a contest of strength, axe grinding against shortsword.

"You mock me. Now I'm *glad* you decided to stay, Villlk." Laagi's voice was a growl of righteous disgust.

Vlk let the taller boy slowly gain ground in much the way Andrej had with Fetinba. As he did, he adjusted his back leg, redistributing his weight. When his center of balance was as low as he thought he could recover from, he moved. Roaring, he pistoned upward, delivering a punishing headbutt to the place just over his foe's left eye.

Laagi fell back, snarling. He felt at his brow, checking to be sure there was no real blood. The blow hadn't managed to split the skin, but there would certainly be a bruise for several days.

As Laagi recovered, Vlk adjusted his balance and glanced back over his shoulder. Jastrab was punching his shield into the Stormrider's face, then his belly. He was using the center boss of metal like a gauntleted fist.

Vhy? Vhy isn't he using his...

Suddenly he understood. Jastrab's bright side was his *left*. That put his sword-arm up against the wall. While that wall was only about waist high, such an obstacle would make it harder to recover after throwing a sword strike. Best the captain wait for the right strike.

He's using his shield to create an opening.

He'd spared all the time he could watching that bout. Turning back, he found Laagi's eyes and spoke.

"I'm not mocking you! I'm *fighting* you."

Laagi sneered. "Aye, well. Any chance to fight a filthy savage, I suppose. If you live, you can pat yourself on the back and tell the tale of how you bested the mindless brute."

Vlk actually lowered his sword for a moment. His surprise must have shown, for Laagi paused to gauge him. He met his foe's eyes, trying to make the older boy understand that he was speaking the truth.

"If you're a savage, I'm the lost son of the Vévoda! No, I'm only fighting you because you and your father are attacking us!" He took a step forward, glaring.

They had the same impulse at nearly the same moment. Both boys leapt into the fray—slashing, dodging, trying to wound without being wounded. Their weapons clashed again, though this time there was no contest of strength. Laagi blocked, tried without success to strike with his counterweighted metal pommel, then drove his knee up into Vlk's belly.

Vlk doubled over, more out of shock and a lack of breath than any pain. He waited for a beat. As Laagi moved to bring the axe's pommel down again, no doubt hoping to finish the fight once and for all, he drove forward.

His foe clearly hadn't been expecting that, for he flailed as he was driven backward. Vlk slammed him against one of the uprights. At the moment of impact, he raised his head at speed. The ploy worked, after a fashion. His head was screaming again, but his skull had connected with the shelf under Laagi's chin with a satisfying *thump*.

Vlk had the advantage. Laagi knew it, too. The look in his eye made that plain. The impact against the upright beam appeared to have knocked the wind out of the taller boy. His dim arm pressed against his foe's chest, Vlk drew back to deliver the killing blow … and froze.

The sound of drums rent the air with sudden force. It was as if his mind didn't know how to absorb the noise… the alien unity of unnumbered heartbeats. His eyes were wide, his muscles tensed as if he were seizing, and his mouth had gone bone dry. He couldn't *think*. His pulse skipped and thudded until it, too, matched that hellish avalanche of sound.

Laagi offered a thin smile, bringing his tiny lower tusks into alignment with his wide button of a nose. He shoved Vlk backwards a pace, then slipped out of melee range.

The touch seemed to waken him, forcing muscles that had no interest in moving to react, if only to keep him upright. Everything hurt all at once. He remembered an old man's jibe—*Vant for your arm to stop hurting? I could stomp on your foot for you. You'd forget alllll about your arm!*—and shook his head in dark bemusement. Even *that* sent a fresh shudder of pain through him.

The battle din was all around. He marked it, but only in a distant, automatic way. Siege engines hurled fire, stones, and spears to and fro across both sides of the outer wall. Men screamed. *Women* screamed, or perhaps they were boys his own age. It was all real—all true, full of death, and danger. The world seemed to be waiting for Havoc's Horn to sound, declaring this battle among the very last conflicts it would ever know.

But no. Surely not. This was *his* first, and quite possibly last, battlefield. It was *not* among the Last Battles—the final days at the world's ending. That was foolishness.

Turning … *straining* toward the outer wall, he found Laagi a few feet away. He was facing outward, but kept Vlk in his periphery.

"Be patient, Vlk," the older boy said. "I'll help you slip sideways when I've finished. That, or I'll knock you into the Twilight Sea for a time and claim you as a slave." He kicked a languid arm out of his way—one of the Bluemark archers dead at his feet. The haft of an azhkast jutted from her chest. It looked like a stripped sapling... something harvested too soon. "Either way, you'll know defeat at a gnoerkish hand soon enough."

Vlk stepped away from the inner edge of the alure, moving on sore, angry legs. "I already know what that's like, Laagi."

The gnoerk snorted. "If you did, you'd be dead already … or a slave." He stepped back, hauling his axe over his right shoulder, then bringing it down *hard*. The sound of metal striking metal was sharp against the drums and the battle din.

As the axe came up for another strike, Vlk finally saw what Laagi was doing. The barbican where they stood commanded the northern gate. That gate was heavy and well-crafted in its own right, but it was secured by an enormous door bar. The beam stretched almost half-again the width of the gate itself. The damned thing required a system of heavy chains to raise or lower it. From his vantage point, Vlk could see a counterweight of some sort, a spoked wheel, and a length of what looked like iron chain with a hook holding it in place. He hadn't a clue how it worked. What he *did* know was that Laagi was standing over it—axe in hand—trying to destroy the mechanism, freeing the bar!

"Lakkrid vouldn't do *either* of those things..."

Laagi stopped, but only for a moment. "Lakkrid?" He shook his head. "And who owns Lakkrid?"

Vlk gaped, then sneered. "Don't vorry, Laagi. It'll be Korunní Spánek soon. I'll remember you to Lakkrid vhen I gift him your axe." He stalked toward him, readying himself to put an end to this ... and froze for the second time in as many minutes, first out of confusion, then out of fresh terror.

He saw a line of what should, based on their armor, be allied men on horseback *appear* on the far west of the battlefield. No sooner had he registered this than a massive wooden traveling carriage faded—*faded* into existence on the far side of the new arrivals. Then came movement at Laagi's feet.

She lives? Did the spear only pierce her breast, not her heart?

This happy—if grim—thought was drowned in an icy lake of horror as he saw the woman's pale skin shift to a moon-kissed blue. She pulled herself to her feet, then turned toward Vlk. Her mouth was full of uneven fangs, and her nails had gone ragged, turning the color of dried blood.

Vlk felt scalding warmth on his inner thighs as his bladder let go for the second time that day. From somewhere behind him , a breathy, wordless scream rent the air. This was followed by something knocking against a shield over and over again until the thin *dwang* came as it was forced off center. Finally, he heard the wet *chump* of a blade splitting flesh and a high tenor scream of pain.

The Stormrider sped past him, though he heard nothing of the man's footfalls. Above the roiling cloud that seemed to make up his lower half, the Eodenth Jarl's body was covered in deep slashes, blackening bruises, and one shallow stab wound in his left bicep.

Monster met nightmare. The Eodenth's axe—when had he gone down into the courtyard to retrieve that(?)—hacked off the Bluemark woman's head. Vlk watched it fly out over the wall through dreamer's eyes.

The Stormrider was already moving on to attack... *There are more of them. Vhy are there more of them?*

Vlk couldn't make sense of it. How could *anyone* make sense of it? They would die up here fighting their own dead once-hirelings. The enemy had won without having ever had to breach the walls.

He looked around, finally glancing back over his shoulder. Captain Jastrab was half moaning, half growling in obvious pain. His face had broken out in a sickly sheen of sweat, and his eyes screamed louder than *he* did. He'd managed to get himself into a sitting position, back braced against the waist-high wall. Vlk could see where the Stormrider's axe had cut into the uppermost part of the captain's right hip, just above his leg cuisse. The split flesh showed the raw red meat below, and a lighter colored thing that almost *had* to be exposed bone. Just *looking* at it made Vlk's gorge rise.

Jastrab was hacking over and over again at one of his former folk. It had already been slashed to pale, blue-skinned ribbons, yet it still tried to crawl toward him. The captain's eyes were wide not only with pain, but with an inarticulate horror. Still, he looked to be fully aware of his surroundings. His eyes were impossibly wide and shot with blood, but they showed no sign of madness. His oval shield had been knocked out of his grasp. It now rested between him and Vlk—away from all hands, living or dead.

Vlk drunk-walked over to it, hefted it, and made as if to sit down against the wall. *If I cover myself vith the shield, and nobody marks me...*

Arrows began whistling. A roar went up from somewhere further to the west along the alure.

"Odvážna krv!"

Vlk *knew* that voice, didn't he? That was the Bluemark's battle cry— *brave* something. Maybe blood? It *sounded* like Lesalunth. That tongue was similar to old Kovalunth, but... It didn't matter. What *did* matter was that he'd swear he knew that voice...

"Jižní meče! Jižní meče! Yish-nee *meh-cheh!*" Edmund's well-worn battle cry... a phrase known since the days of the rebellion. *Southern Swords.*

Now Vlk was sure of it. He felt his heart fighting against the implacable, pulse-consuming rhythm of the hellish drums.

The Stormrider was fighting toward Laagi. He laid about himself with his axe, still gleaming despite the blood and gore dripping off it. From over the man's shoulder, a score or more living Bluemark soldiers and county guardsmen raced toward them. The black kontusze of the sellswords mingled with the white ones of Jižní Pochod—a dark, fuming river roaring toward the once-men.

Then Vlk saw him: Edmund the Tall in his war glory, broad-bladed sword in one hand, a heater shield bearing his arms—the *county's* arms— in the other. His helm was of bright steel that caught the sun, burnishing it in the gold of utter, perfect hope. If his helm shone brightly, then his *eyes* glowed like the sun off fresh-fallen snow.

Seeing the silver hart on the count's shield, hearing that battle cry, Vlk felt his spine straighten. He heard his own voice added to Edmund's.

"Jižní meče!" Fear had fled, taking with it the shame of feeling over-matched. He forgot even the shame of having wet himself a moment ago. With a surge of utter *rightness*, he lowered his shield into position and charged.

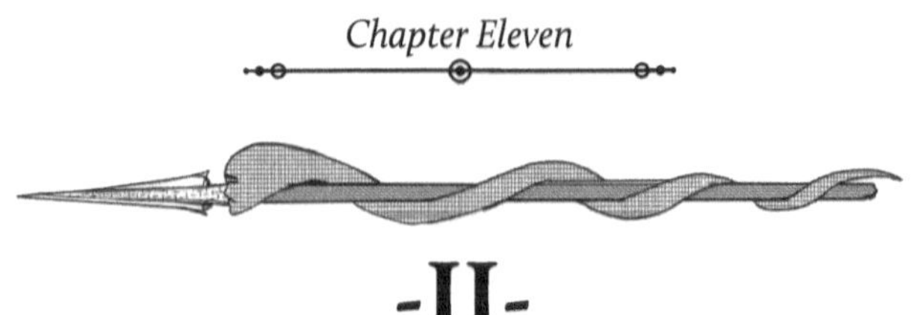

-II-

Venzene Duchy of Kovalun
County Jižní Pochod
Barony of Hartscross–Jižní Lov

…Lashjuk's eyes were watering. She somehow managed to reach up and grasp one part of the keel pole that ran the coach's length, hooking her ankles over another. If she was patient for just a moment longer, she would be able to…

Ebistian laughed, high and somewhat madly. "You took Haluzfeld to nearly no purpose! You failed utterly! You weren't able to gain Vagiaedelt. Your position is tenuous at best—another incompetent, small-minded devil serving nothing but its own designs."

A woman's voice came in answer, clearly of Kovalunth high birth. "Do you not recognize the flesh I wear, Shepherd?" She sounded indignant now—affronted, and somehow petty. "I am become Eliška of Haluzfeld! I am enough, for now, until Edmund has been brought to heel! Now be gone! You are of no use to our plans. I demand that you depart this place at once, in the name of Nawen of Vápntagh!"

"Yesss, I'm certain you *do*! Well, T'lendak, fortunately, I answer to only one creature by need and due. Any others must earn my respect them-selves, and the Storm Queen hasn't managed to do so in *centuries*. Now… I suggest you tend to your men before they're overrun."

Eliška met this derision with a throat full of disdainful laughter. "Shepherd, my men have this matter well in hand. We've nothing to fear from Count Edmund's meager defenders, I assure you."

Ebistian sounded as if he were absolutely delighted as he made his reply.

"No, you're *quite* right. You've nothing to fear from Edmund's men … alone. Rikten? Order the attack, please?"

"Yes, Shepherd," came the reply.

"What?! No!" The woman's horrified tones were almost comical to hear.

The man, apparently called Rikten, overrode her, a smug and alto-gether satisfied note in his voice. "Cut the heathens down! Charge! Charge! Charge!"

Ebistian simply laughed as the horses and most of the footmen charged away toward the encampment.

There won't be a better time... Lashjuk made ready to move.

"I know you are there..." Ebistian's voice was silken, even over the sound of the noblewoman's curses as she raced toward the battlefield. Lashjuk felt her skin crawl. She stayed as still as she could, though her arms and legs were both stinging from holding herself aloft.

Slow, deliberate footsteps drew closer. They made whispering sounds as they moved over the grasses.

"I can almost... *almost* hear you."

His voice was like sweet, numbing poison dripping into her ear... quickening her pulse... making her mouth run dry. She bit down on the sides of her tongue and was rewarded with a brightening clarity of mind.

Ebistian uttered a melodic rill of laughter. "I suppose I expected you to follow, eventually. I confess, I'd have been disappointed if you hadn't." He paused, tsking his tongue against the roof of his mouth. To her right, she saw several inches of his blue kontusz above his feet. They were clad in soft leather things embroidered with golden thread.

"And you *cannot* simply *show* yourself here and now, can you. No... No, of *course* not. Where would be the pleasure in *that*?" His voice came bouncing under the carriage as if he'd pointed his face Skolfward. "This sort of game *does* grow tiresome, though ... even for me. Not knowing when, or where... Ah well. I shall make it easier for you then, shall I..."

Lashjuk saw the pretensions that were his boots turn away, then shuddered as he called out. "Július! Július, to me!"

"Yes, Shepherd." The voice was that of a young man. He sounded as if he hadn't yet reached his twentieth year, though she couldn't be sure. He jogged toward the coach. She could see hard leather boots of black with yellow trousers tucked into them. They came to rest near Ebistian's soft shoes.

"I have need of you, Július. I need you to help me drag someone out of hiding." He sounded as if he were smiling.

"Of course, Father. Thank you for this trust. Where? How can I serve?" Young Július sounded like a two-legged puppy. His voice and manner were nearly shaking with delight.

Ebistian's voice grew warm now. "Clear your mind and listen, Július. If you listen *closely* ... you'll hear our guest..."

Lashjuk held her breath, making ready to drop from the carriage's keel and roll to its far side. Then she would plunge into the nearby tree line and look for a place to hide ... or to craft an ambush.

"Father?"

"Hush..."

The wind rose, shaking the trees. As it did, Lashjuk lowered herself from the keel and axle, laying her back on the soft grasses with maddening slowness. She hoped the wind would cover the sound of her movements, but thought it best to rely on care rather than hope.

"Now, my brave boy..." He began to whisper something. It was impossible to make out over the sounds of swords, horses, and screams. An instant later, Július spoke in a fair, rhythmic voice.

"Claim now the gifts that the Grey would deny you. Wander no more through the places of pain. Come find the light that first sharpened shadow. Stand beneath unwatchful sky once again."

"I shall always love the sound of your voice, my boy. Very well spoken. Again, if you please." Ebistian's voice had grown soft, misted with either sorrow or longing.

Július repeated the chant twice more. As he finished the final recitation, he drew in a deep breath, as if he were gasping with surprise.

"Sau? Oth mepresh?" Ebistian's voice was somehow hopeful, almost shy.

That's Sheshik, she thought. *I'd swear to it.*

When Július spoke his reply, it was the same voice, but very clearly *not* the same person. That or the youth was among the most gifted actors in all the world. His accent had changed from manor-born Kovalunth into something rich and rolling.

He sounds cultured. An educated man of high Sheshik birth, surely.

"Hai, Ebistian Osir." His smile was evident through tone alone.

"Oth mepresh! Oth ush neph mepresh..." Ebistian sounded as if he were on the verge of tears.

She saw the two men's feet move together, was startled to hear the soft sounds of what could only be a kiss. There was no sense of passion in it, but rather one of relief after a long sundering.

Was... was he... Not trying to lure me out of hiding? Lashjuk couldn't be certain, but...

"My Sau." Ebistian spoke with a warmth that far outstripped the tone he'd used when speaking with Lord Alojz. "I *have* missed you..."

She saw their feet turn toward the battle.

"Hai, Osir. To lose time is painful. To *find* it... a gift."

Ebistian laughed. "And to *make* time?"

"...Is the truest sorcery in all the world. I have not forgotten your teachings, Osir." Sau—if that was his name—delivered this airy nonsense with a strange combination of warm sincerity and haughty derision. After a pause, he spoke again.

"I watched the T'lendak's army pass. Her mistress haunts the sky above this place within the Grey. She'll not thank you for interfering with her designs."

Ebistian sighed as he spoke. His words sounded untroubled, descending through a short series of notes as he went on. "Well, let her darkle there for as long as she likes." He was smiling again, by the sound of it. "Her servant brought an army into direct conflict with my *own* plans, and into a territory I've been grooming for more than two centuries now." He paused, then spoke in a tone of dismissal, but no rancor. "Yes, yes, my Prince. I'm quite certain that her T'lendak servant is to blame. I admit there's little love between the Storm Queen and I, but the pact still holds."

He gave another soft sigh. "It won't matter for much longer, I suppose. He'll be here before long."

"Sooner than you think, Seeker. This very battle will likely be enough to let him make the journey. Haunek is culling the lands of the Barghad k Qabaile as we speak."

"Ah, Loegrem's lost land. Well, that should please the griffin-tamer once he learns of it. Cleansing the blight of Byt's legacy from his once-home."

"Loegrem rides at his right hand even now, Seeker. As you say, it will—not—be—long."

Ebistian's voice grew silken once more. "Then come join me while there's still time to be easy. I've a gnoerkish boy to show you. Young, beautiful, and full of promise."

Sau gave a smooth, simple laugh. "Ohhhh, Osir... is he for me, or for you?"

Lashjuk bit her tongue again, if only to keep herself from screaming. She thought she could probably manage to kill one of them, but not both. And certainly not the score or more of footmen guarding the perimeter some ten strides away.

Ebistian turned his feet back toward the carriage, but paused. His hand made audible contact with the door's pull ring. "I haven't decided, honestly. I'd thought to add him to the flock—to raise him in our ways, if only for the sake of irony. But now ... there just isn't time." He sighed. "He's too small for you, mepresh. At least while we're about our work. He's about the age you were when first we met."

"Well then, if you don't mean to teach him as you did me, why not teach him to sing? Recall your own youth once more. The gift of your Július will suit me well enough. If this body is wounded too badly, or if you get tired of seeing it, I shall find another. But you... You *do* look..."

"Age-ed?" Ebistian sounded amused.

"Tired, Osir. It is no thing that cannot be amended."

Ebistian made a noncommittal *mmm* sound, then addressed himself to the carriage. "Dar fendoly." His voice became rich, and somehow flat as he delivered this. The carriage gave a subtle shudder. "Perhaps you're right. For now? Come." The carriage door opened, and the two men stepped up and out of sight.

Lashjuk's limbs still throbbed and burned from the prolonged effort of holding herself in suspension. But those sensations were little more than buzzing flies. She breathed heavily, as if she'd run a race. After several seconds wherein she tried to digest all she'd heard, she drew her dim hand to her mouth and bit down. She grabbed handfuls of grass and earth with the other. It was all she could think to do in order to suppress the shriek of impotent rage that threatened to burst from her.

When she'd choked enough of her frustration down, she forced herself to do as she'd been taught. Luck had been both with and against her of late. She would need to do something about that.

A cheat at chance, she thought, and felt a predator's grin forming. That was what Eobum had called Adric before sending her to spend the day walking at his side. She'd resented the idea of being told where to go and who to spend time with on their journey north, but the lesson had been enlightening, to say the least.

"Sift the timely from the tedious, Lady. That's chance's first chain, and no mistake. Tries t' distract you with birdsong, ale, insults, an' injury. Truth? They tend to be more drizzle 'n downpour. Best learn to put by what 'y' can. Keep yer eye on what 'y' have to."

She could do that—would have to do it if she meant to save her Maksu.

So, what parts are timely then? She considered, careful not to completely ignore her surroundings. It wouldn't do for someone to find her, or for Ebistian to drive his carriage away with her underneath it.

This Sau creature suggested Ebistian teach my Maksu to sing. That cannot possibly be as innocent as it sounds. They care nothing for the battle at hand, either of them. That, or Ebistian assumes his forces will turn the tide in Edmund's favor.

She looked to her right, trying to gauge the flow of the battlefield. She knew nothing of sieges or armies, but it looked to her as if Ebistian's forces were slicing through the enemy's back ranks and sowing chaos.

Edmund will undoubtedly want to thank his savior for arriving in the nick. I can do nothing about that. I'd never get past the Count's guard to speak to him in private, even if I...

She snarled far back in her throat. Why was she even *thinking* about Edmund? What did she care? He was nothing to her, after all. It was Eobum's influence, she was sure.

That thought drove a shard of fresh pain into her already battered heart. Glowering, she pushed it down as best she could.

Time to be soft later. If I see the Lady Kastan, perhaps I can tell her. She, at least, would hear me. The amusing thought that she could likely even tell the Lady everything in Grimdash zaksh—the gnoerkish tongue—walked her glower part way toward a smile.

Another thought bullied its way to the fore before that smile had fully flowered. *Ebistian said something before opening the carriage door. He used that same flat tone when he used his sorcery on us, before.* She tried to recall his words. She didn't dare say them aloud, in case they actually *worked*, but she thought she had them.

The carriage is taller than a standing man, and long. Not large enough to get lost in, but ... Maksu has to be in there, though he won't be alone. Sau—who or whatever he is—is in the body of one of Ebistian's soldiers, which means he's both armed and armored. She stiffened, remembering that Ebistian, himself, wore a sword. *And it's on his right hip, so his bright's his left hand.*

She resisted the urge to sigh. *I have to wait.* It would do Maksu no good if she were to race in to rescue him, only to die in the attempt. She knew something of how to fight, now—knew something of the way of the spear. She knew enough to know that she wasn't a match for both Sau and Ebistian in an enclosed space... not even with the element of surprise on her side.

"I have to wait." She mouthed the words, feeling the sobs rising in her... forcing herself to remain silent as she wept. "I have ... to ... wait."

-III-

Screams...

Kastan heard screams, as if they were coming from deep within a mountain cave. There were no words, but there was a *sense* to what she was hearing. The unnumbered voices managed to convey fear, pain, rage, sadness...

But it's all the same, somehow. It's desperation—all of it. And it's drawing near.

Within seconds, those disparate screams had faded. They were replaced by a faraway dissonance... a choral moan. The witchy, un-dawn light up ahead was growing closer, too. It bobbed as if it were a lantern light being carried toward them.

Štít widened her stance, lowering her front half as the light drew closer. Her howl at an end, she began growling once more. The sound was at once terrifying and comforting.

Kastan spoke to Olga over her shoulder. "Grab that lantern when we move. We have to assume *all* the others have gone out. And I want that light to move with us."

"Yes, Excellency," she said and said no more. Olga's voice was more clipped than it had been, but that was the only change. There was unease, of course, but no panic. The light shifted as the matron did as she'd been bidden.

"Andrej? Make ready to—"

"No fear. I'll shoot until you give the word or my arrows run dry, Lady. Štít and I'll be the rear guard." His voice was cold. More, it carried within it an eerie sense of acceptance.

Kastan blinked as she processed that. *You really are like Caros. Your first instinct is to stand in trouble's way in order to buy me time.* The realization called up a confused tumble of touched pride and hurt disapproval.

"We protect *each other*, Andrej."

He nodded, drew breath to make reply, then loosed that breath in utter, wordless horror.

The source of the bruised light didn't come around the corner. It dimmed for a beat, then came floating *through* the corner... through the very wall itself. The shrouded, vaguely human-shaped *something* glided across the stone passage little more than a dozen strides ahead. Stopping at the leftmost wall's edge, it turned to regard them.

Its hooded head was a dusky suggestion, but its eyes... They were bright outlines of pale purple. While the face they were set in was vague and undefined, those eyes were somehow *too* defined. She could see the creature's irises, its lashes, and even a delicate tracery of veins. These glowed visible over transparent shadows where its whites would other-wise have been.

The malevolent curiosity with which it regarded them was unutter-ably familiar. It left Kastan with the ineffable sense that it knew her, knew what she had done, and would be the instrument of her inescapable pen-ance. What she had done to *earn* such a scourging, she didn't know, but while the creature floated in its bruise-colored shroud—looking through her in wordless judgement—she knew it was true.

Haunted Forest, she thought, and her blood turned to ice. *We dress as you... haunt the place in which we feign to have fallen, pretending to hunt the living—the other children as they hide, or run from candle to candle. We play at... Cti strážce ohně! (Honor the fire keeper.)*

Her body suffused with a rush of heat as understanding broke. *Zvonění v Jeskyni has its roots in mining. It's a game we play to teach the children what to do in the dark when... when...*

"Stand fast!" Her voice was a harsh whisper. "If we run, it'll give chase. Stand fast and stay—in—the light. Do you hear me?"

"*Yes*, Excellency," Olga managed.

Andrej said nothing, but nodded. She saw the boy was shaking. The creature hadn't turned its gaze from them, but it had moved no closer, either. His fear and the realization about the children's game combined to steady her. A moment later, she felt the inner winter enfold her. *That* was a welcome feeling, indeed.

The haunt made a burbling, murmuring noise like an old man's grumble. Beneath it, she heard a guttural drone. Again, it was as if the sound came from a deep cavern, but that eerie choral dissonance had clearly issued from the creature. It then floated through the wall it had stopped at before, taking its terrible light and the sharpest edge of its spine-scraping fear with it.

The red hound's growl ceased, and Kastan felt the equilibrium of her companions returning to something approaching normal.

"How did you...?" Andrej's voice was a ragged squeak. He cleared his throat. While he didn't turn to face her, Kastan saw color rising to darken his ears. "How did you *know*? How did you know it wouldn't attack?"

"Haunted Forest," said she.

"The game?"

"Ah," Olga's sigh was shaky as her fear ebbed away. Still, she sounded as if she were smiling. "They aren't *all* just play. Many of the old games served an important purpose. I didn't know that Haunted Forest was one of those, but—"

A woman's scream cut her off, then was itself cut off. Then—distant, but clear—a man's laughter echoed. It underpinned the brief, bright song of a child's terror before that, too, fell silent.

Kastan looked toward the sound, then to Andrej, who faced away from her. "I'm returning your bow, Andrej. Hold still." She slid the weapon into position on his back, threading his quiver through it. She replaced her borrowed arrow as well. "You'll need to shoot around me."

She heard Olga draw a breath as if she meant to say something. Before she'd finished, Kastan had drawn her newly acquired sword. It had served her well enough in the saddle. Hopefully, it would do the same on foot.

Olga flapped her free hand, pawing at Kastan's dim arm. "Excellency, we must—"

"*No*, Olga. The dead aren't haunting a forest we can simply pass by. They're among our living folk down here."

"We can go back up and around—"

"I'll not abandon those here in the undertown without so much as a word of warning or a chance to escape. If I see there's nothing to be done, so be it. Until then..."

A familiar ringing came from somewhere deeper within the undertown—a sword scraping fast against a whetstone as it cleared its sheath. Then came the sounds of combat... of shouts... of Hajvarr.

"We go," said Kastan. "Mark the turns in your mind as we make them. I don't want to guess at the road back out once we've won through. And listen for that hum. It might warn us faster than our eyes." She had an idea that the haunts might follow the movement of their lantern. If so...

Andrej nodded, walking forward with Štít at his side.

"How can you be sure we *will* win through?" Olga sounded more harassed than angry or frightened, though she moved along in Kastan's wake.

"Training, Mistress." She heard a sound that suggested Olga was about to express her dissatisfaction with that answer and preempted her. "Assess the situation honestly, then make a decision. Fight or fade."

"Then *fade,* Lady. Why not fade?"

"If it looks like you'll lose, and you don't *have* to keep fighting, then fade. If you can't fade, fight as if lives are on the line, because they are."

Andrej stopped long enough to look back over his shoulder at the pair of them. At first, she thought he was silently asking her to clarify—perhaps even to justify what she'd said. Then she realized the truth. They'd come to a place where a choice needed to be made. Forward or to the left.

The echoes in this place made it hard to tell exactly where the sounds of combat were coming from. The constant presence of that darksome droning—punctuated by the occasional unfinished scream—went a fair bit toward driving *hard* all the way to *impossible.*

She grinned. "You're asking the wrong lady, Andrej." When he blinked at her, she directed her gaze to the boy's immediate left ... and to Štít.

A moment later and they'd followed the red hound down the left corridor. They had to stop several times as they caught sight of purple lights fading into walls or heard the first hint of drones drawing near. Some of these were higher pitched, she noted. Perhaps they were women in life?

The deeper into the undertown they ventured, the more harrying their race became. The haunts would stop, turning to glare at their little circle of light and freezing for several tense moments. As if unwilling to wait for Kastan's band to be driven into action by fear or need, the creatures would turn and continue on the way they'd been going.

This will be a strange tale, should we survive it. We defeat the haunts by doing what they cannot—by being still.

Eventually, the sounds of battle drew closer. She heard Hajvarr's voice amidst the laughing, growling sounds of things that might once have been human. She could understand none of it, but there was nothing to be done about that now. At least she could be sure that Hajvarr was close.

Skidding to a halt just before what must certainly be the final turn, she put a hand on Andrej's shoulder to stop him. When he looked up at her, she pointed ahead, then to herself, then to him, miming pulling on a bowstring. He nodded. She would go first, and he would be just behind, ready to shoot. To Olga, then, she patted her free hand toward the ground.

Stay here, she mouthed. When Olga nodded, she added, *wait for my,* she pointed to herself, *call.* She put her hand beside her mouth and made as if to shout. Again, Olga nodded.

There wasn't time for more of a battle plan than that. Hopefully Štít would stay quiet until the battle was joined, but if not...

Kastan slid forward, put her back to the near side of the corner, and chanced a glance around its edge.

The massive statue of an anděl—a wide-winged angel dominated what she *thought* was the southern wall. They were the messengers and guardians of the Hallowed Halls, and thus crypts and cemeteries across Kovalun had versions of that same statue. Her right hand should've held a spear pointed skyward. This angel's hand was empty. The rest of the chamber's walls housed hundreds of urns, and empty places where urns had not yet been interred. Perhaps a dozen stone burial vessels lay in rows along the floor. Several of these sarcophagi had been forced open. Their stone lids lay cracked beside them.

Her ears had not deceived her. Hajvarr stood with his sword at the ready, face touched with a bitter smile as he faced what he likely expected to be his final fight.

Pavel was just behind him, to his right. He wielded the statue's ceremonial longspear, held across his body, point toward the foemen. His eyes were wide, his face wet with tears of obvious fright.

Yet he's standing fast. Brave as sin in the dark.

Six once-men stood in a semi-circle around Edmund's Ruční Kopí and his armsman. Two of them held spears at the ready. The others bore swords, laughing as they feigned slashes and thrusts at both man and boy. None of them were armored, which was a blessing. Instead, they were clad in the courtly raiment of rank among Edmund's personal guard.

She felt a moment of profound sadness as her eyes fell on a familiar form. *Radek...*

He lay a few strides away from the monstrous game the dead played with the living. She marked a wound on his neck—a horrid gash where something had tried to rip his throat out. She forced herself not to react to the sight of the old man's body. Keeping herself in check seemed to redouble the clarity of the inner winter—a gift she refused to waste.

I don't see Rákos. His body isn't here—not on a stone slab, not on the ground, not even among the—

She looked again at the assembled once-men and felt a shock of recognition. She knew one of them—a man called Arnost. He'd been one of Caros's friends, or as close to friends as their respective stations would allow. They had met at Edmund's side during the rebellion. He'd been a guest at her table a year agone, and she'd heard of his passing not long after. His heart had given out. As with the monsters beside him, his flesh shone a preternatural combination of star-shot blue and liquid shadow, but it *was* Arnost.

Kastan understood where the haunts had come from now, but that would have to wait.

She turned, laying her dim hand on Olga's shoulder and shaking her head. "Radek" she mouthed. "I'm sorry, Olga."

If Kastan hadn't warned her, she might fumble the lantern out of shock. Olga gaped, swallowed, and nodded. Her nostrils flared several times, and she nodded again. Tears sprang to her eyes, but her breathing was quite steady. She gestured to the lantern she held, then on toward the crypt chamber.

Good enough. Later, there would be time for empathy... for the woman's loss. Later, Kastan would grieve and would help Olga grieve for the man's death. For now, though, there was the gift of the inner winter. For now, there was a sword to swing and foes to be felled. And that was enough.

She drew in a breath, held it for a moment, then charged. "Jižní meče! Andrej! Spearmen! Jižní meče!"

-IV-

Slam!

Vlk's shoulder made an audible pop as he rammed his borrowed shield into Laagi. His mind screamed at him. Yes, of *course* that hurt! Didn't you hear the *pop*?

But that was nonsense. There had been more pain in his forearm from having to *brace* the damned thing than from ramming it with his shoulder. Jastrab's shield—which was really far too large and heavy for him—was a center-gripped oval. That meant there was neither strap nor bar to hold it flush against his arm. Instead, the shield bore a surprisingly lightweight boss in its center. Within that was a well-worn wooden bar. *More maneuverable than Lakkrid's kite, but...* but this took more strength to keep between him and his foe.

Laagi stumbled backward, dim arm flailing for balance. One of the once-men caught him quite by accident as it rose, but its grip was tenuous. The Stormrider gave another breathy howl, this one as wordless as the other. He grabbed Laagi's shoulder and thrust him free of the former Bluemark archer. Then he rammed his own shoulder into the creature, knocking it out and over the wall with its black kontusz fluttering.

Laagi cast a look back up at his father, but the man had already turned to meet Edmund's onslaught.

Vlk saw the two racing the last few strides toward one another and grumbled. He wanted to *see* that bout!

And you'll let me, von't you Laagi? If I vatch Edmund fight, you'll just go on trying to break that chain, or vhataever it is you're trying to break. He allowed a sour little grin to bloom on his face. As Laagi stepped toward him, he pounced, trying to do as Jastrab had. He used the shield's boss as a gauntlet, punching—driving him back from the chain device.

"Urk! Ed delrgan, Vlk!"

Vlk—who had no idea what the boy had just said—allowed his smile to stretch toward a grin. *He sounds angry. Good!*

"Really? Are you sure?"

Laagi slammed his axe into the bottom of Vlk's borrowed shield. *That should have stuck into the vood. Is the axe blunted?*

The blow forced the oval's bottom in toward his thigh, which, in turn, forced its top to table out and away from his upper body. He realized what that meant an instant before it happened. With agonizing slowness, he looked over just in time to see Laagi's sallow-looking fist crash into his temple.

"I'm sure."

Laagi sounded winded, but he was still on his feet. Vlk, on the other hand, went down like a sack of milled grain. His head was shrieking, sharp spears of pain trying to push their way out of his skull. He was weeping. He could feel his sinuses stuffing, causing his nose to run, and could feel the shuddering sensation of silent sobs.

Through tear-bleary eyes, he saw the Stormrider hurl blow after blow down on Edmund's shield. He tried to will himself to stop sobbing and was rewarded with a slow numbing of his pain. He had the sense to mistrust that particular form of relief, but couldn't work out what to *do* with that mistrust.

More than a few of the once-men still threatened the alure. The Bluemark and the men of the county were doing their best to send them over the wall, but it was slow going. Edmund and the Jarl were still locked in battle—hammer and tongs, as the old soldiers say. Even so, they each had to divert from one another to dispatch the monsters as they came near.

The invader fought with an eerie rage that seemed bottomless. He was the living echo of a cradle tale—hell's own harbinger, an angry storm cloud churning where his lower half should be. Edmund, on the other hand, seemed content to weather the onslaught, moving his heater this way and that, or simply leaning away from whatever shot his opponent threw.

The Stormrider finally grew tired of the stalemate. He floated upward, battleaxe cocked back over one shoulder. Then he fell on Edmund. He descended with the speed of a catapult's stone, and as he dropped out of the air, he brought the axe down in a canted hammer shot.

Vlk screamed. He felt his throat tearing with the force of it, though the sound was far away. Edmund fell under the weight of that inhuman blow. Even now he was...

was...

...Was erupting upward from a crouch that had started long *before* the Stormrider finished his fall. Edmund rose, batting the axe aside with his heater, and sliced up and into the Jarl's bright arm below the elbow. Axe, arm, and blood fell out over the wall, and the man to whom they'd all belonged threw his head back, screaming.

"Ng!" Laagi's scream was full of shocked horror, which made perfect sense. What made far *less* sense was his continued assault on the chain assembly. Even as he wept, he slammed the axe's blade down on the chain over and over again.

Vlk almost shook his head but stopped himself. The last few moments had taught him well. That motion would send a fresh hammer of pain into his head, and he didn't know how much more of that he could take.

If Edmund the Tall can face down the once-men, and the Stormrider, then I can face down the monster's son. The count shouldn't have to vin the battle all on his own...

He left his sword on the alure where he'd collapsed, found his borrowed shield, and turned to do his duty to count and county. He drew in a breath, then another, then growled in his largely unbroken voice, charging. Laagi saw him coming, aimed his battleaxe, and brought it down a final time on the hook that held the chain in place.

Vlk found his foe utterly unbraced against his charge. He crashed into the gnoerkish boy and sent him flailing... stumbling... falling out over the wall to the invading army below.

The Stormrider's roar of pain changed to one of horror. He shot upward, then raced down after his fallen son.

Laagi's final blow hacked the hook from its mounting place. That, in turn, caused the counterweight to plummet. As its chain unwound into the hole below, the spoked wheel spun at an impossible rate. The massive bar—which had until now kept the gate braced—arced upward with an unearthly speed. It crashed into the bottom of the barbican, snapping many of its boards.

Vlk saw Edmund and many of his men hurled from the alure by the force of the beam. He thought he saw the count fly *outside* the walls, but he couldn't be sure. He stumbled back from where he'd sent Laagi to his death, but the rising boards and the crash of stumbling soldiers knocked him back off of the platform. He had a moment of fiery pain along his back, then knew no more.

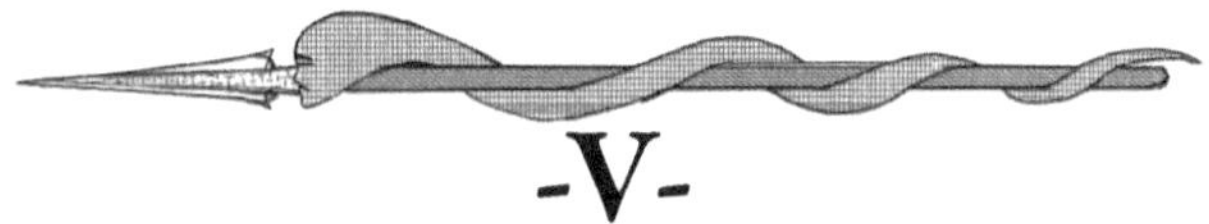

-V-

Time never moves at the speed we want it to, does it?

Lashjuk lay beneath Ebistian's carriage and tried not to let her anxiety—her rage—get the best of her. She knew the treachery of time far too well. Dread of something always slowed that something's arrival. Delight always seemed to speed its departure.

Black flowers of fear did their best to bloom before her mind's eye. She fought to ignore them, but several made determined attempts to return to her mental stage. She beat back a tumble of images wherein the two men did everything from undressing and deflowering her Maksu to *field*-dressing, roasting, and devouring him like highland beef at a Korunní Spánek feast. She felt *useless* lying beneath the carriage and waiting for an opportunity. Yet she knew it was the only play.

Ebistian still holds too many cards.

That was true, especially now that he had this Sau fellow with him. She'd been forced into a game of Trefning she hadn't wanted to play. But what choice? Maksu's life, maybe even his shadow, was on the line.

What she wanted to do—*all* she wanted to do at that moment was to roll out from beneath the carriage, rip open the door, kill Ebistian and whoever Sau was, and find her boy. If she could do that...

If she could do that, what came next? Use the power of *motherhood* to fight her way through the hordes of enemies? Fend off the foemen with her knife and three azhkasts?

And do it one-armed. Best not to forget that. Ebistian may still have Maksu under his sway. I'll have to hold him with one hand and a weapon with the other. She almost laughed, but managed to stop herself before it was too late. It wouldn't do if she summoned more enemies in a fit of derisive, self-directed laughter. *No. I have to wait. There's nothing else for it.* She didn't have any interest in being patient, but she could practice that maddening art if she had to. *And for now ... I do.*

She watched the battlefield as best she could. Ebistian's mounted men had begun by surprising the enemy's back ranks, but it hadn't lasted. The woman—Eliška, she'd called herself—had ridden into the midst of her own forces, splitting them so that their ranks stood back to back. One half continued the assault on the encampment, while the other sought to contend with Rikten and the rest of Ebistian's horsemen.

Wait... Urk! Did I actually drop into the Twilight Sea? She could have sworn there had been an entire group of attackers there. She was *sure* she hadn't looked away, yet they were gone.

As she watched, another group winked out of existence. *How in hells?*

Ebistian's remaining guards—all footmen—were cheering from a few strides away.

"Oh look! There! Holič! He's *got* one!"

Lashjuk saw a single rider bearing not a spear, but a lance. Its point lowered as he raced toward the enemy—a man who was plainly trying to exhort others into action. The rider—Holič, apparently—must have braced his weapon, for it leveled off and held there for a beat before slamming the foeman right out of his saddle. A blink later and better than a score of enemies simply ceased to be there.

"Ha!" The men were cheering louder than ever.

Their joy was cut short when a rumbling *crack* split the air. She tried to look in that direction but couldn't see anything through the feathered feat of the carriage's driving team. Then she did a double-take.

Bone! They were walking beasts of bone when I last saw them! She gaped. Now they looked like plow horses. When, and more importantly *how* had that happened? She didn't have long to ponder the question.

A great cheer went up from the attacking force nearest the walls. As she couldn't see much in that direction, she looked back at Rikten and his riders. They were massing a goodly way behind the enemy line. Another joyful eruption of sound came from the battle's front ranks, but she paid it no mind. She saw Ebistian's horsemen rally around their captain, Rikten, form a broad line with their mounts, and charge.

They rode into the enemy's back rank just as a new roar rose from the direction of the walls. This was far louder than the first, as if someone had opened a tavern door and let the mirth out into the streets.

Then she realized what was missing. At some point, Rikten's men had silenced all the drummers. No wonder she found herself thinking more clearly. Her temples weren't throbbing in time with that hellish rhythm any longer. *And the ramming of things against the walls... it's stopped as well.*

Suddenly the swell in volume made perfect sense to her. *They must have battered open the gate...*

She had a moment to wonder how Edmund and his defenders were faring, but no more. As if her thought had forced it into being, a rider approached at speed, reined up, and pounded on the carriage door.

"Shepherd! Shepherd, open to me!"

Ebistian pushed the door outward, sounding less than pleased. "Holič? Explain yourself ... *now.*"

"Father, it's Edmund. The Count's fallen from the barbican ... *outside* the walls. Rikten says he lives, but..."

"But not for long without aid. You were right to disturb me so." Ebistian's voice was calm, clear, and all business. He sounded completely affectless—a creature of quick efficiency. "Guard him. We shall arrive shortly and see what's to be done." He paused, and when he next spoke, he sounded pleased. "It looks as if Rikten and the Count's men have the ethnarch of Eodenth rage well in hand. When we have Edmund—alive, preferably—and the way is clear, you and the others will provide an escort into the encampment."

Holič acknowledged his master's orders, then rode away to execute them.

Lashjuk took a moment to drink in the enormity of her own feelings. She was pleased that Edmund lived, saddened by the news of him being near death, and fearful for Eobum and the unit, for Lakkrid, for her Sulok ... Hells, for the county as a whole.

Still—my Maksu is the first and only matter. Should I... She corrected herself. *When I rescue him, and if there's something I can do for Edmund...*

She shook her head, trying to untangle her own mind. Nobles were to be mistrusted and for unnumbered, well-worn reasons. But Edmund was...

A noise pulled her from these long thoughts. Ebistian's men were moving at a pace, positioning themselves either upon or beside the carriage. A moment later, Lashjuk had wedged herself as best she could, riding beneath the carriage once more as it trundled over the broken bat-tlefield. She had a brief respite for her stinging arms and legs as Ebistian's men loaded Edmund aboard, but all too soon they were moving again.

And once we're inside Jižní Lov... Well, that was to be seen. She would have more options within, surely.

Do you know that? she asked herself. *...Or are you just hoping?*

An answer came, swift and sure. She could almost hear Eobum say it. *"Hope doesn't hunt for you, Lashjuk."* No indeed. She would have to do her *own* hunting.

I can do that. A brave sentiment, yet for all the terror — all the hatred and fear moiling just under the surface of her waking mind, there was a sense of *rightness* to the notion. Oh, there was a desperate part of her screaming to be heard while there was still time. She was a mason's wife ... a mother. Her domain was hearth and home, not the hunt. And she'd *failed* at that ...hadn't she?

As if in answer, her mind conjured up another memory. And while it was both sweet and painful, Lashjuk wouldn't have traded it for the wide world. She and Eobum had been out atop the terrace. It'd been a beautiful night, once the storm had passed.

"You can play-act if you like, Ordinary Woman, but your huntress's heart will always catch you out."

Lashjuk smiled, feeling tears prick the corners of her eyes. She still had to find a way to rescue her boy. But the memory had centered her, somehow. That sense of inner cold filled her ... *surrounded* her. True, she still *felt* the twin suns of rage and desperation that'd been sapping her will, but that was all right. The carriage trundled on toward the open gate of Jižní Lov, and Lashjuk felt as if a stone had rolled off of her heart.

-VI-

Kastan ran, pouring on as much speed as she dared. It was faster to go over the room's obstacles than to go around them. She vaulted atop an unopened sarcophagus and ignored the heart-stopping *panic* that tried to seize her as its occupant *thumped* from within, seeking to free itself.

She managed to cover about two-thirds of the gap between her and the once-men before they reacted.

As she'd expected, it was a spearman who first spun toward her. What she had *not* expected was the speed with which it moved. Its motion was impossibly quick, almost too fast to follow. It took a skittering step, shifted the spear back to generate power for its thrust … and fell with an arrow in its head. Fell? No, it collapsed, like a puppet whose strings had been cut.

Bless your eye, Andrej.

She didn't pause, slicing at its neck as she ran past its motionless form. She shouted again—"Jižní meče!"—and cocked her sword over her right shoulder. The swordsman she'd targeted spun with that same inhuman grace, smiling as it threw a back cut exactly where Kastan *should* have been.

The weapon of choice among most of Edmund's guard was the Černý mráz *(black frost)* sword. These were short, thick, and broad—a perfect weapon for fighting in caverns or castle halls. Kastan's battlefield acquisition was an arming sword, giving her nearly a foot of range on most of the once-men… including this one.

Kastan stepped wide, rolling to her right well before her foe's outermost range. Letting her momentum carry her forward, she allowed her hips to rotate, delivering a flat snap to the once-man's neck. She felt the shriveled meat beneath her blade resist the force she'd generated, but only for an instant. Then the head lolled to one side, held by a dry strip of old muscle. The body stumbled for a beat, then collapsed the way its fellow had.

Two! If we can take down one more, swiftly, then we've won. We'll be able to overwhelm the last three.

She saw Pavel staving off the remaining spearman, Hajvarr beside him. Edmund's Ruční Kopí was holding off two dead guardsmen at once, but only just. He'd removed one of the swordsmen's arms, yet the creature fought on, undeterred. She saw three arrows jutting from the remaining spearman, like spines on a morning star.

Andrej felled one. I felled one. Why…

"Take their heads!" she cried. "Only their heads!"

Hajvarr stepped in front of Pavel and drove a hammer shot down onto the enemy spearman's outstretched arms, causing its spear to clatter to the floor. No sooner had that shot landed than Hajvarr rolled his wrist in a mühlchen. As he finished the wheel, he leaned away to give his swing ample space, finishing the motion in a back cut that took the creature's head.

Pavel stepped back, not uttering a sound, but with enormous dark eyes. He tried to bring his spear in line to engage the once-men Ruční Kopí had left unattended, to no avail. His weapon was too long for such quick repositioning, especially with Hajvarr stood so close. Instead, Pavel dropped the angel's gift, diving forward to grab at an enemy's forearm, trying to keep it from hitting his master's turned back.

The once-man didn't try to dislodge his hands. It *laughed*, leaning in as if it meant to *kiss* him...

Kastan was already in motion, running toward him. But the one-armed swordsman lunged at her, forcing her to parry and dodge backward.

"No!"

Hajvarr's shout of fear was punctuated by the sudden *thunk* of an arrow and the clattering of a sword against the ground. Whether he'd been reacting to Pavel's plight or hers was anyone's guess.

Kastan moved to make use of her greater range. Like the others, this once-man wielded a Černý mráz sword, but the damnable thing kept in close. That horrific speed kept him near enough that she could smell the strange scents of the grave—cinnamon and dry, rotting pork. Her gorge rose, but she forced it back down.

A spear pierced its belly from behind, causing it to stop and look down in rather comedic surprise. Kastan wasted no time. She took a single step back, then threw a flat snap, taking its head.

Hajvarr stood, spear in hand, smiling that bitter smile of his. They nodded to one another and turned, looking for other enemies.

"Andrej!"

Pavel's voice was such an unknown to her that at first she couldn't identify it. Then she saw him. He had picked up one of the Černý mráz blades and run toward the hall from which she'd attacked. Her eyes flitted that way...

"Arnost! Arnost, leave him! Arnost, no!"

She saw it all through the inner winter's dilated eye. And though she ran across the chamber as swiftly as her legs would carry her, the truth was clear. Both she and Hajvarr would arrive too late. Štít stood between Arnost and Andrej, issuing fearsome, thunderous challenges to the once-man. He moved to lunge past her, but she leapt to meet him, closing her jaws on his forearm.

"Beast! Xro gri thoriash!" Arnost delivered this through a throat full of gravel he hadn't possessed in life. His words drove a spear of pain into Kastan's head, staggering her and, likely, everyone else for several seconds.

At the same instant, a gout of utterly red fire burst into being amidst the hound's crimson fur. Štít flew into the nearby wall with the force of the hellish power. She struggled to her feet, growling, as if under a weight rather than set ablaze.

The once kindly, grizzled old armsman turned malevolent eyes back to Andrej. The boy loosed his bow against the monster, but Arnost simply laughed, slicing the arrow out of the air with a lazy flick of his rotting wrist. Stepping forward, he reared back with a hammer shot just at the outermost range of his weapon.

Andrej's muscles were coiled, eyes wide and serious. He was prepared to move, but he clearly wasn't sure where to move *to.* If he rolled to one side, Olga would take the blow meant for him. He could rush forward, but that might end the same way. He was frozen in indecision.

"Down." The voice was flat and darksome—sure and implacable.

What came next was the sound of shattering glass and an explosion of eye-watering light as Olga's lantern slammed against the incoming sword strike. Arnost screamed, but only for a few heartbeats. Then he collapsed in a foul-smelling heap.

Pavel didn't slow. He leapt the burning body in a move that seemed surprisingly agile. Kastan saw him throw an arm around Andrej—who looked stunned, but otherwise unharmed—then turn to face what was left of Arnost.

The red fire that had surrounded Štít fell away, leaving her looking tired. *Bowed but unbroken,* Kastan thought as she skidded to a halt near the boys.

Hajvarr, who still wore his chain shirt, arrived a moment later. He looked down at his hound, then crouched so he could meet her at eye level. "My brave girl..." He began stroking her sleek fur. "My brave girl." He turned back to Kastan. "She's ... unharmed."

Kastan nodded, fighting the urge to fuss over both Andrej and Pavel, who were clearly unharmed as well, physically. She locked eyes with Olga, who nodded at her.

"No point holding onto light just to see us *die* by it, Excellency."

She offered the matron a half-smirk, but for an instant that was all she could manage. As she drew in breath to say ... *something* in reply, Hajvarr spoke up again.

"No, Excellency. I mean, she's *unharmed.* Not a lick of fur burned..." He sounded as if he were struggling between fear and astonished relief. True, the Karmínové Srdce was an exception. It was a creature of the oldest magic. But every citizen of the Venzene Empire thought of magic as a source of fear—as the weapon of the great enemy, those cannibal demons who dwelt on Nausha.

Andrej looked to Pavel, smiling in silent gratitude. Then he looked to Olga, walked to her, and embraced her. The woman's mouth worked, but no sound came out. She bowed her head and returned the embrace, albeit briefly.

Kastan turned, walking towards Hajvarr, and stopped mid stride, cocking her head to listen. *Drones... I hear them, but they're muffled. And there are too many.* The sound was swelling—building on itself as new tones joined it. And it was growing...

"Hajvarr! Bring her to Arnost's body! Bring her to the fire! Everyone to the fire! Now!" She didn't wait to see if they obeyed. Instead, she moved over to grab another of the loathsome once-men they'd felled, dragging it over to Arnost's immolated form. "Be ready to light it, but—hear me— wait for my word." She swept their faces with a glance, saw nothing to make her feel the need to repeat herself, and moved off to drag another body over. The drone was impossibly loud now. She *might* have time to drag this second corpse over before...

An ocean of pale, bruise-colored light flooded into the chamber through both the east and western walls. Unnumbered haunts came hurtling on, roaring their endless, dissonant song.

Kastan screamed, but the sound was swallowed by the unholy choir. She saw them—most of them, anyway—falling on her brave little band, and all she could do was scream. She thought she heard Štít's howl through the din, but couldn't be certain. What did it matter? Even with whatever magic made crimson hearts what they were, Štít couldn't survive such an overwhelming attack.

Even If that weren't so, that power didn't flow through the others. And once Hajvarr was dead, she couldn't survive either. They're bound to one another. When one falls, the other follows.

The light was growing closer. The darksome drone grew louder still as a pack of the haunts split off and raced toward her. It was over. She raised her sword, though her arms seemed disinterested in the task, and tried to make peace with her life.

The haunts shuddered, seeming to slow in midair. It was as if they were caught in a sudden, strong wind. She heard a low, loud buzzing sound from somewhere behind her, drawing ever closer.

"Nasze cienie są *długie!*" A man's voice heralded his charge into the chamber. He wore a red kontusz with both sword and shield strapped to his back. He was tall, crowned with a sallet helmet of polished steel, a short-hafted spear in one hand and something *spinning* in the other. It was this something which was issuing the braying *burrr* sound. He slowed from a run to a steady walk, turning the roaring, spinning thing this way and that. And wherever he pointed the circle the spin made, the haunts fell back.

More—they become ragged, as if their shrouds were being frayed.

He thrust his roaring weapon toward the nearest pack of haunts, and they simply vanished, screaming with voices that came from somewhere deep and lightless.

"To my spear-hand, lady! Stay near, but away from my hurre!" The word had come out like hoo-ra—the R rolling a single time. She thought it sounded Havalunth, but it might just as easily have been something else.

I don't care if it's from the moon or made up special for the occasion. It—and he—just saved my life!

She moved to flank him as he'd directed, nodding to him as they walked his hurre deeper into the chamber. The haunts seemed powerless against whatever might lay within the item. They fell back, tried to flee, tried to attack *her.* Each time they faced the width of the spinning circle of sound, they shrieked and, as far as she could tell, ceased to be.

Finally, enough of them had cleared that she could see what was left of Hajvarr and the others... of Andrej. They were all on the stony ground, faces frozen in fear and horror... and wonder?

"You live? You live!" Tears burst from her eyes. She was laughing and weeping, and—

"Lady!" Her rescuer's voice brought her up sharp. "I'll make a path for you. Be ready to run."

"But..."

But he was already in motion. He drove through them, holding his hurre out before him like a spinning round-shield.

"Raz, dva, ted'!" At the last moment, he rotated the roarer upward, spinning it above his head, parallel with the floor.

She ran. Andrej stood to meet her, and she threw her arms around him. He shook as they embraced... or perhaps she did.

Looking up at the red-clad figure, she saw his face for the first time. She'd seen him before, she was certain, but couldn't place where. Nor did she have much chance to study it, for he turned and stalked back into the fray.

"What will you—"

"Stay with the red hound, Lady. Let me know if any more come behind me as I work!"

Kastan didn't understand his purpose, but she did as she'd been bidden. After checking to ensure everyone was unharmed—how that could possibly be, she had no idea, yet it was so—they each watched for new threats. Blessedly, none came. The man strode the length and breadth of the chamber, spinning his hurre at every wisp of violet light. He laid his spear down against a wall at one point, then transferred the roarer to his other hand without really losing the spin. Sweat poured off his face, but he didn't stop until the last light of damnation had finally fled.

Once the spinning stopped, he took several shuddering breaths, then walked over to Kastan's band.

"I *never* ... expected," he paused for breath, "to find *you,* of all people, down here." He bowed, then all but collapsed to one knee before Kastan. "Is your brother here as... as well, lady?"

Kastan passed Andrej her sword, then reached down to remove the man's sallet. That revealed a tumble of black hair, most of it in sweat-soaked clumps. She knew the face, but not the name. The black hair atop the red, however...

"Skar? Is it Skar?" Hajvarr, sounding delighted. "Hells be hid, man! I'd have thought you'd be on the road to Zlaté Pole by now."

"Skar... Ah! Lord Azherd's man! I *knew* I knew you!" Kastan was also delighted. She'd hosted Azhferd and his armsman for a month at the end of the rebellion. This had been in her father's house, before he'd remarried, and before she'd been granted the lands of Sunŭv Dar. At first she'd feared the lord was there to seek her hand. When it was clear that wasn't so, she'd found him among the most genuine conversation partners she'd ever had.

Skar gave a strained but gratified smile. "Aye, lady. The lord's chief sergeant. I'm surprised you remember me."

She felt her smile broaden. "You barely spoke, sergeant. But sometimes that can make a more powerful impression than endless quacking." Hells, that had been something like ten years agone.

He bowed his head to acknowledge the compliment, then grinned up at Hajvarr. "I had other duties. They led me here ... an hour before the attack." Kastan reached down to help him up. Nodding his thanks, he spoke again. "We don't have much time, Lady. Gather who you like, but if we don't leave soon, we won't leave at all. Havoc's Horn is about to sound again."

At first, she thought he was only trying to underscore the strange horror they'd just survived—perhaps even the horrors above where the battle no doubt still raged on. Something in his eyes made her pause. Made her think that this was a man *not* prone to exaggeration. With regret, she turned away from her profound relief and focused on the matter at hand.

"Tell me what you know and what you suspect, sergeant."

"Lady, there isn't time for talking…"

"If time is short, then speak quickly and to the point. You needn't tell us all of it, but you *must* be able to give me more than *follow me,* surely."

He bowed his head, but only for a moment. "Very well. Send the others to gather who you will. While they work, we will speak. Will that serve?"

She nodded. "It will, at that."

CHAPTER TWELVE

THE EARLIEST HARVEST

-I-

Dereek khn
Ali Oacn March
5 Korunasykli: 22 Days after the Red Storm at Westsong

Jastar was a study in suppressed frustration. He'd been *worried* a bell and a bit back up the hourglass. Now he understood the trap he might've gotten himself into. And if he was right, there weren't many good options left to him.

Oh, he was glad to be riding to Wick's aid, given the strange warnings. It was more than just his duty to the Thorion Throne. When trouble came to call, he wanted to ensure that Ricgerd of Wick did not stand alone. After Westsong, he felt he owed Sirs Reginald and Robis. Riding to Wick meant the chance to make good on that debt. The difficulty was, he feared, rendering that help would put his current position at risk. If anyone who knew him happened to be there...

He'd mustered with the others at speed, ready to race off to save, or at least warn, the folk of that long-loyal fastness. Jast had been impressed by how the Dereek khnii force—essentially a double lance's worth of men and horses—had gotten themselves sorted and on the road in such haste. Now the ten of them had been mounted and moving for nearly an hour ... at a *walk*. It was as if there were nothing more dramatic ahead of them than a ride to the local watering hole. And *that* had given him time to contemplate just how precarious his situation really was. How strange

Dereek khn had turned out to be.

This nobleman... this *Methias*... had ridden into Kor Kowmor and interrupted their training. Why? Well, to ask for help in translating a trio of cryptic warnings, of course! That sort of thing *was*, after all, every soldier's stock in trade!

As absurd a notion as it'd seemed, he had to admit it had been a wise decision in the end. Methias *had* gotten his translations. Then he'd told the Old Man (*told* him!) he was going to take men from the fortress. And had Fyken objected? No, of course not! He'd blithely gone along with it. After all, a *nobleman* had spoken.

Jast wasn't surprised, merely disappointed. He'd started to hope—to *believe*—that sense would overrule self-import in Dereek khn. A standing, uniformly-trained army was a potent weapon for a realm's ruler to wield. Now it seemed as if any nobleman had the right to saunter in and simply *take* a lance and a personal guard with him into the field—even if that meant interrupting what Fyken called a *sword cycle.*

"Long thoughts, Sir Jast?" Ibhroth slowed his horse's pace, dropping back to fall in beside him.

Jastar tried to scowl at the young Eodenth Yebu Ke. The man's insistence on using the shortened version of his name felt disrespectful—like a verbal backhand.

He couldn't hold it. The scowl fell from his face almost as soon as it had taken up residence. Ibhroth was one of those folks it was hard to stay angry *around*, let alone *at*.

"You could hardly blame me."

The Cr ke gave a sage little nod at that. "Aye, fair. Battle sweats are common enough. No fear. Still..." He shrugged one plated shoulder. "Just had to check."

If he thinks it's only battle sweats—just fear of the fight ahead—then so be it. Perhaps I can use that to my advantage. Maybe I can get him to talk under the guise of helping me calm those battle sweats.

"I just... Why are we moving so damned slow? Surely we should be racing for the River, no? It'll be slow enough going once we cross. It's upsy south of the bank, and it'll be a patchwork of forests and glens until we reach Wick's fields."

Ibhroth gave a slow nod, looking as if he were either thinking or suppressing wind. When he finally gave his answer, it was clear he'd been giving the matter actual thought. "I 'spect Lord Methias is prob'ly looking to save the horse's strength for the crossing."

"The crossing? You'll not tell me we mean to *swim* the horses across. There's a ford or a causeway, surely."

Ibhroth shrugged. It was Apiné who made reply, however.

"Not where we mean to cross. Not yet, at least."

"So we *do* mean to swim the horses. That'll be slow work, but I expect it can't be helped."

In response, Apiné gave a little laugh. It was a light sound directed at his comment, not at his expense. Jastar was just drawing breath to ask to be let in on the joke—whatever it was—when Methias reined up and called a halt. They'd broken through the tree line, breasting the last hill north of the River.

It's like we've left the wonder behind. I know what I'm seeing is what passed for normal before arriving in Dereek khn, but it all seems so… dim here.

The hillside had a sad shag of late autumn grass sleeping along its surface. The color left an odd sense that the green world was somehow ailing, at least when compared to the lush lands around Kowmor. The green gave way to a thin strand of drying mud before the River's ribbon.

If it had ever *had* a proper name, Jastar had never heard it. It had simply been called *the River,* unless the speaker or singer were trying to sound portentous. Then it was *the shivering foam* or *the shivering flood.*

"There we are," said Methias. He sounded cheerful. "Lanbachsel? If you'd be good enough to find me the most shallow spot in sight, please?"

Apiné nodded, waved the rest of her lance forward, and jogged them down the hill.

"Sir Jastar?" Methias pointed just to the west, diagonally from where they stood. "Wick is *that* way, is it? I don't want us to go too far astray once we've crossed."

Jast looked, shrugged, and gave a noncommittal nod. "Roughly, yes, Lord."

Methias gave a brief squint, his nose wrinkling. The expression suggested he didn't much care for that answer, but what of that? It was all Jast could offer. He was a knight, not a scout or hunter.

Perhaps five minutes passed in relative silence. Jastar tried several approaches in his mind, but could think of no innocuous way of probing for more information. He had an abundance of questions, but the only one he could justify asking in this situation was apt to bear no real fruit.

Well, I can at least prove myself right on that score.

He lifted his chin, speaking to no one in particular. "Pretty as this place is, you'd think someone would've found a better name for it than *the River.*"

Ibhroth blinked at him. Methias actually turned in his saddle to regard him. Jastar noted for the first time that the lord's horse had saddle and halter, but no bit or bridle—no reins of any kind.

"I agree," said Methias. "Yet all maps I've run across—both in Thorion and abroad—have the River *noted...* but nameless. I thought that might be due to the presence of the old singer, but I've seen maps that predate her coming. No name for it there, either."

"Here! I think this is as shallow as we will find, Lanbachsel." This was one of the final two members of the two-two's third lance—a red-maned and bearded man called Ghenys. The other turned out to be that fellow whose name meant *the Bear.* He had a Traedish given name, but Jastar couldn't recall it. Something *the Kieran.*

Jast watched as Apiné trotted over, looked at the point Ghenys indicated, and nodded. He caught other movement out of the corner of his eye as Ibhroth scratched his head.

"Thought the river were called—"

But what Ibhroth *thought* would have to wait. Apiné called up the embankment toward them. "Aye. Lord? This is the best we're likely to find. Good job the Ali Oacn's slow and sweet here."

At first Jastar thought she'd said *ah, the ocean,* but as Methias spoke up he realized he'd misheard. That second word was, apparently, oh-sen— yet more Calyari he'd have to learn.

"Fair," the lord said. "Let's hope the Ali Oacn is slow and sweet *enough* not to flood too badly. On me, then..."

Methias rode down the hill at a modest walk, stopping just before his horse's hooves found the mud. Apiné directed them into a double-column stretching behind the lord and to either side. She took up a drogue position. This placed her opposite Methias, straddling the back of their formation.

"At your word, Lord."

Jastar did his best to take this all in. The formation seemed like a lot of unnecessary faffing about, but nothing the Dereek khnderath had shown him so far suggested they were prone to such things. *So... I wait.*

No sooner had he finished that thought than Methias spoke, raising his right hand—palm toward the sky.

"Nuth puav iyth throth nuq. Puehv ka odar cza thros vahd kon..." His voice shook on this last word, lengthening the N as first his hand, then the very *ground* shook.

The water *rose*. It was as if the hunched shoulder of some massive creature were emerging from its hiding place. The flood fell to either side. When it cleared, a ramp of river stone stood, spanning half the width of the waterway.

Jastar gaped. A host of birds darkened the sky as they fled the trees, but he hardly noticed. His horse danced beneath him, screaming. He managed to get the mare under control before he was thrown. Getting *himself* under control was another matter entirely. He could hear Apiné begin to speak, but...

He was so overawed at the display that Ibhroth had to physically elbow him back into focus.

"Onto the stone, now! To the middle, mind! Do *not* ride all the way to the far edge! Leave the horses enough room to build to a canter before they reach the other platform!" As they all moved—all save Methias, that is—Jast noticed that only his *own* horse seemed agitated over what'd just happened. The other mounts seemed either calm or outright excited by the sudden shift in the landscape.

Storms be swift... even their horses are mad!

Apiné spoke on, shouting to be heard clearly over the rumble and the River's roar. No longer slow and sweet, it now crashed into the new-risen stone. "It's kept aloft by his will! When he releases that will to raise the next one, you'll feel this half begin to lower back to the River's bed! We need to be ready to move from this to the next as soon as we can. On my mark..."

Lord Methias exhaled as if he'd been holding his breath. Perhaps he had. Jastar couldn't be sure. Speak the truth and spurn the treasure—at this moment, he was barely certain of his own damned name.

The lord's horse walked forward, returning the nobleman to his former position at the front of the formation. He dropped his hand, bowed his head, and drew a breath that visibly expanded his chest. He repeated both the gesture and the words he'd spoken to call the causeway into being. An instant later, Jastar felt the ground beneath his horse's feet shudder. First, the platform he was on began sinking, then the new stone parted the water ahead.

"Now!"

Apiné's shout could barely be heard over the din. The horses in the lead cantered from one platform to the next, giving a light hop to account for the height difference. Jast's horse tried to balk at the jump, but he got her through it. The rest of the horses looked as if they'd damn near *trained* for this sort of maneuver.

Perhaps they have... Falxes fall, perhaps they have. The idea of a disciplined force trained for fighting amidst magic is... Hells!

It was early to think about harvesting what information he could and hieing back home, but if he reported nothing else back to the countess, he had to send word about *this*. Dereek khn has an army, has sorcery to spare, and looks as if they train them to work directly *with* one another.

When all were across save him and Apiné, Methias dropped his hand, then bowed his head. His mount seemed to know what to do, for the beast dashed forward, Apiné close behind. Once they were all across, they watched the stone sink below the waterline. When it was over and the River again flowed within its channel, Apiné spoke again.

"By my gifted display of power... I will..." She ran her tongue out over her lips, "I will..." Her head shook. "I've lost it. Something-something *stone way?*"

Methias grinned. "Close, Lanbachsel. That's nearly all of it. 'By my *gift* of power.' Or perhaps 'by my *offering* of power' would be a better translation to the Trade Tongue. Also... O-dar cza thros." He made the last word rhyme with *close*. "Odar—open, as in cause to open. Cza—A, and thros, which means an impermanent thing."

She smacked the heel of her hand against her forehead, smiling. "I knew *dar*, but not o-dar. The rest just fell away in my confusion."

"Time, Lanbachsel. It'll come in time."

She nodded. "Do you need a moment, Lord?" She sounded more courteous than concerned.

"Before we go on? No. I'll rest on the road. No fear. Two wide, if you please? On me. Sir Jastar? You know the territory far better than I. You'll ride just behind me, at Tharus's left hand."

Jastar looked first to Apiné, then to Ibhroth. Neither of them seemed to understand or acknowledge his silent question.

"Yes, Lord," said he, and rode into position.

-II-

Thorion County
The Shivering March
5 Korunasykli: 22 Days after the Red Storm at Westsong

They'd ridden for perhaps three quarters of an hour. The sky had covered itself in a hazy twilight that turned every shadow soft and downy. Their path had taken them through thickets of pine and poplar, oak and willow, and—within the last few minutes—hawthorn. These thickets and groves had been separated by gorgeous glens of lady's mantle, sedge, and heather grass.

Methias had ridden in relative silence. He'd been content to let Mezofel run and natter in his head. Such conversation—if indeed that was the right word for it—always amused and delighted him. It wasn't quite *speech,* according to the more traditional definition of the word. No familiar ever quite *spoke* to the caster whose cloth they'd been cut from. Yet after so many miles and so many years together, Methias had learned a trick or two.

I'll need to find a way to explain the how of it to her, I think. If she hasn't changed her mind by the time we return home, she'll need as much understanding as I can give her. He paused for a moment, allowing Mezofel's message to filter through his mind's eye and ear. He let out an audible chuckle. *No, I don't mean to teach her how to talk to you. Just how I've learned to listen.*

"Lord?" Jastar sounded as if Methias's chuckle had set him on edge.

Given his reaction to everything else thus far, I'm just pleased he hasn't turned tail and fled back to Thorion. In all honesty, if he hadn't been knighted by the County Throne, I'd have left him at the kor. His rank and station here should make gaining an audience much easier when we arrive—should even lend weight to my words, which may well save lives.

"Nothing, Sir Jastar. A conversation came to mind and made me smile. Nothing more."

He resisted the urge to chuckle again when Mezofel chastised him for that reply.

I only spoke the truth, thank you. The fact that your side of our conversations always involves "coming to mind" is quite beside the point.

His face fell. *How bad?* He nodded.

"There's been trouble over this next hill. We'll see it for ourselves once we clear the hawthorns."

Tharus's beard-stubble voice made a grunt of agreement. He sighed through his speech a moment later. "Aye, Me—" He cleared his throat. "Aye, my lord. There's death not far ahead, though it's from a bit back up the hourglass."

He saw Jastar do battle with and ultimately defeat the urge to both gawk and ask questions. "As you say," was all he allowed into the air.

Impressive. He's a man of excellent self-control.

"Weapons, Lord?" Apiné's tone made it clear her question was little more than a formality.

"No, Lanbachsel. In easy reach, mind, but no." He paused to absorb Mezofel's message, nodded, then turned to speak over his right shoulder. "You're right, Tharus. Before the sun sank behind the hills, at a guess."

A moment later and they'd broken through the hawthorns. They found themselves at the edge of a hilltop—the tallest within view, and by several feet. The early moonlight shone down on the open heath across from them. In the gloaming, they could see the wreckage of what looked to be a merchant's wagon. It lay there like an overturned beetle. One of its wheels was missing, presumably buried in the wild sedge that surrounded it.

Methias stiffened for a beat, processing what Mezofel relayed to him. He stood up in his stirrups, looking down along the gentle slope of their own hill.

"There." At the place where the dip between the hills bottomed out, a horse's broken body lay blanketed in shadow.

Methias sighed, calling back over his shoulder. "Lanbachsel? Secure the next hilltop. Touch nothing you don't need to touch. Tharus, Jastar? Stand a watch up here. Ibhroth? With me." He didn't wait for a reply. With the slightest pressure from his knees, Mezofel trotted down the near side of the hill.

He came up beside the sadful body, wincing. The animal had been piebald—either deep brown or black—but had a strangeness to the white patches that he couldn't at first place. It was too dark to tell the difference, nor did he think it much mattered, save that the dark patches made him think of Mezofel. His own charger's sable skin and coal-colored coat had always brought to mind a warm blanket on a windy winter's night. Now, looking down—seeing what'd been visited upon the beast below—he felt a shiver that had nothing to do with the wind.

Ibhroth came down after him. "Lord? Do you ... see it?"

Methias wrestled himself away from the miserable thought of *what if this had been Mezofel.* Further, he forced himself to reject the urge to say what he'd been thinking—how painful it was to contemplate what had been done to this creature. How much seeing it hurt his heart.

He swallowed, then glanced at Ibhroth's eyes. *No, he's looking at the body. He didn't see me swallow, so couldn't have misread it. Good. I... I should answer him, though. Before he asks again.*

"Tell me what you see, Cr ke."

The Yebu Ke nodded, giving a thorough once-over to the poor thing before answering. This was why Methias had chosen his company for this grim chore. It was absurd to think all Eodenth were trackers, just as it was absurd to think all Naushaii were casters. Yet a goodly portion of each realm's respective populace *did* fall into those groups, he and Ibhroth among them.

"Didn't fall, Lord." He shook his head. "Attacked, else I'm the Emperor of Ashes." He stood in the saddle for a moment. "...Sweat lines in its fur from where its harness hung." He paused to point. "D'you see the strap of leather pinned beneath its front? Poor bastard's legs were broke after the fall, not 'cause of it."

I must hear his conclusions, not interrupt by stating my own. He may see a thing I don't. And if I speak first, he may decide his thoughts aren't wanted, or worth sharing.

Methias nodded. "Anything more, Cr ke?"

Ibhroth considered. "Been chewed on. Odd that an animal'd start a meal then flee, though..."

Methias followed the man's eyes. He understood exactly what had struck him as being so strange now. He waited to see if the young Eodenth would see it as well. It would be better if he himself weren't the only one to mark the truth, but the hourglass was emptying. He couldn't afford to give the man too much more time.

"Ah..." The Yebu Ke didn't sound *pleased,* but he sounded satisfied. "Missed it 'neath the mane, but there's a hole in its neck. An arrow—a broad-headed one, or I'm blind."

Fighting the urge to sigh, Methias forced himself to speak. He didn't want to, but there wasn't much choice. "Cr ke... do you see the legs?"

Ibhroth nodded, following Methias's gaze to the nearest one. It was clearly broken, bone showing through the too-ragged flesh. "Aye lord. I see. As I say, they've been... Gah!" He actually jumped a little, unintentionally forcing his horse to rear. When he had his steed under control again, he turned to Methias with a look of horror on his beardless face.

"Why is... why is the blood *white?*" His tannish dreamer's lamps raked over the body. They seemed to stop at all of the places showing what, at first glance, had looked to be piebald coloration. His face grew pale. "Bear's breath... It's white everywhere that's been gnawed!" This last had come out in a strangled croak.

Methias closed his eyes for a moment, then gave a nod toward where the third of the two-two held the lower hillock. He lifted his chin toward the men on watch. "Tharus? Sir Jastar? If you'd join the others?"

Shuddering, Ibhroth followed Methias's gaze, then followed his horse as they rejoined Apiné and her folk.

Other than the broken wagon, the hill was empty. Methias could see a road to the south. He raised his head to lock eyes, first with Pallith, then Jastar. "Does that road run all the way to Wick?"

They looked at it, then at one another for a beat. It was Pallith who answered.

"Yes, Lord. From Eastshadow to Wick. There is a fork that will run directly to Thorionden's gate to the south as well."

Methias nodded. "The blood from the horse's wounds ... was white."

Tharus and the folk of the third all grew grim, nodding. Ibhroth and Jastar looked to Methias, then the others. Finally, it was Jastar who asked the obvious question.

"What ... does that mean, Lord?"

"There are creatures whose death blow can damage if not outright devour a man's *force.*"

"Falx's fall... Things that can eat a man's spirit?"

"No. The spirit is something different. It's altogether *real,* but it's something else." He shook his head. "Language often fails us. *Force* is so regularly borrowed to mean other things—from weight and pressure to raw strength, demand to destructive power. You might have heard force called by a different term—the shadow." His instinct was to both explore the reasons why Jastar had leapt to link *force* to *spirit,* and to explain the differences in detail here and now. *But no. The hourglass is emptying. And nothing eats at time quite like self-indulgence.*

Pallith bowed his head, kissing his fingertips in a plea for spiritual protection that needed no explanation.

Methias saw varying degrees of understanding on the assembled faces. He had to summarize. What did they *need* to know?

"The shadow is what binds the spirit to the flesh. It holds all that you see and do—all that you learn and experience throughout your life. There's more, much of it bound up with the Weave... what you might have grown up hearing called magic or sorcery, Sir Jastar." After a pause to gauge his audience, he shook his head. "It doesn't matter. What does is this. Creatures who can do this gain real power—genuine strength, in one form or another, by taking a dying man's shadow. It not only makes the eater more potent a foe, but it can stop a spirit from continuing on to whatever might be next for them. It can even turn, or help to turn, such an unfortunate into a haunt."

Jastar blanched, clearly shaken. "Storms be swift... What manner of monster could do *that*?"

It was the Kieran who answered. His voice was low and grim—leagues from the bright music of his usual easy laugh. "Once-men... some of them, anyway. I know there are other creatures with that power, but I couldn't name them. Some of the unquiet dead, though? Aye, they've been known to have access to such arts."

Tharus spoke up from atop his brindled stallion. His voice was quiet, his face grave. He looked as if he were trying to suppress a shudder. "The isbryd drayag come to mind. The wraith dragons. This isn't their work, though. They don't eat animal shadows. Also, they're beaked, not fanged."

Tharus's words struck Methias like a fist. Pangs of pain, sadness, regret, and inadequacy did battle for dominance within him. He looked away from Tharus's haunted face.

Self-indulgence, he reminded himself. *Nothing eats at time like self-indulgence.*

Sweeping them all with his eyes, Methias offered them a thin grin. "At bottom, we've been lucky. We've learned this bit of news *before* we face the foe... a foe that likely doesn't know we're coming." He turned Mezofel toward the moon-washed way that led to Wick. "Ibhroth? Jastar? When the fighting starts, you stay with me, or you stand with the Ban'ze Ruun. Apiné's folk know what they're about, as does Tharus. It won't matter if the foe's living or dead."

Mezofel carried him forward at a walk. "Now, come. We're for the red, ruined road."

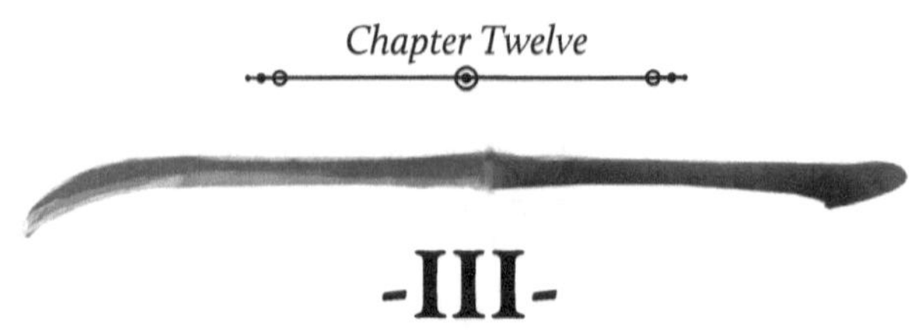

-III-

County Thorion
Wick
5 Korunasykli: 22 Days after the Red Storm at Westsong

Gordan paced the wide alure that crowned Wick's wall. The sunless chill scraped at his mood as much as it did his flesh, and he was agitated.

Agitated? No. That's underselling it. I'm... I'm...

He didn't know *what* he was. Angry, fearful, embarrassed, confused? He was all of these things and more. No word or phrase felt weighty enough to accurately describe it. *Hells, is there even a word for it? If I could name it, I could probably stomach it!*

Well, if he couldn't name the stew of emotions churning within him, he could at least name its cause. It was the goblins—the Nebelblut.

Goblin... He spat over the side to the grasses below. *Falx's fall, but goblin is such a soft name for them. Such a fanciful, cradle-tale term.*

Only after that thought had fully formed did he realize how accurate a sentiment it was. Of course, it sounded like a cradle-tale term. It *was* a cradle-tale term. Likely it had been chosen because of how readily it rolled off the tongue, regardless of what languages a body spoke.

He tried to laugh at himself, but his heart wasn't in it. He was too intent on looking for—*smelling* for sign that the alien things were near. No hint of their scent came to him. As for seeing...

True twilight's all but claimed the sky. This is the dangerous time—the uncertain time. The fading daylight turned everything vague, while the torches and lanterns did their best to help the eye wander. *A watch at dusk is bad enough when bandits are about. With the Nebelblut...*

The wind shook the trees. The movement made him think of narrowed eyes looking out past the foliage. Foliage that had been pushed aside by fingers with far too many joints...

Gordan shook his head, trying to banish the black flowers now thriving in the fertile ground of his imagination. *How much time do we still have? How long before they're upon us?*

He turned to look at the village below, then lifted his gaze to the broad lands beyond it. He could just make out the sun's final flirtation with the day—a pale, purple light lowering in the west.

Unbidden, a song floated into his head. He couldn't think of its name, but it had started infecting his mind back before he'd left Eastshadow. Lyrically it was a dove-caller—something sweet, meant to make women smile and sigh. But the way its melody bounced from word to word, it wasn't far off from a drinking song. It just wasn't quite bombastic enough for such a label. Drinking song or dove-caller, his mind seized on it as if it were a last ledge before the fall. And he'd no idea why.

He heard someone nearby singing it in a soft baritone. Gradually, he realized the voice was his own.

...The snows draw close upon winter winds,
A strange and silver sweetness while my love, she is away.

Each eddy's dance where the rivers bend,
Every waterfall and forest glen,
A perfect, purple passing while my love, she is away.

What storms may come? What horrors hum,
In darkest... coldest...

He stopped singing, trying and failing to fight the shudder that strode up his spine. *Things are bleak enough without me calling down worse.* Havoc's Horn, were *all* songs hiding secret horror within their staves?

Well, at least there's no movement among the outer grasses, save a few sheep and cattle in their wooden pens. If they aren't smelling them, maybe...

No. No, he knew what he'd seen. The... whatever it was, now. The *former goblin,* he supposed, had mouthed words to him... words in the Trade Tongue. He'd swear to it.

Gordan turned back to the east, resuming his vigil. When the monsters came—*if* they came—it would almost certainly be from that direction.

He registered the sound of rapid footfalls mounting the nearby stairs *just* before an unfamiliar voice called out.

"Sir Gordan is it?" The man sounded as if he were from the southwest of the county—probably somewhere between Southwall and Oakwind. Gordan felt his spine stiffen at the use of his honorific. He puffed out a shaky stream of air. It was still too warm for his breath to show, and he was glad. It would be better if no one saw the shameful proof of his fear.

Forcing his voice to steady, he gestured for the speaker to join him up on the wall without turning away from his vigil. "I answer to that name."

Not one, but two men joined him on the alure—one with short blond hair cut in a meticulous style, the other with a shag of light brown on both head and face. They were armed and armored in leather breastplates and bracers of deep blue. Only the blond wore a cloak, also of blue.

"We're sent by—"

"The Lord Ricgerd. I know."

"By Sir Kaith, actually, though the Lord Ricgerd is with him." The man's voice was as mild as milk. Still, Gordan had to fight not to do a double-take.

"Kaith is here?"

The blond gave a single nod, looking out over the parapet. "Aye, Sir. He's sent us on ahead to see what's to see. We were *told* we were besieged..." His tone implied the addition of *all evidence to the contrary*. That was reasonable. Clearly, Wick was *not*, at this precise moment, under siege. Yet it wouldn't be much longer.

"We are—or soon will be. We need every hand at the ready. Arrows and archers, swords and boards, and those who can wield them." Gordan felt a flare of anger rise and welcomed it like an old friend. "Are you *questioning* me...?" He trailed off in a way that invited the blond man to fill in the missing name.

"Terrek, Sir. Sergeant Terrek." The man's voice was still mild, yet it had shifted to something slightly colder, almost clipped. "Your assessment."

Gordan blinked, turning to look at the man's hawkish profile. Terrek might have been Gordan's own age. *Then again, you could just as easily have as much as a decade on me. Your bearing makes it hard to do more than guess.*

Both the sergeant and his heretofore silent companion were scanning the landscape beyond the wall with real scrutiny. Valad would've said they weren't just looking, but actually *seeing* their surroundings.

After a beat or two, Terrek elaborated. "You asked if I were questioning you, Sir. I'm questioning your *assessment*. You have knowledge we d'not. As I say, we were told we *were*—at this moment—besieged. That's plainly not so, which means the messenger made a mis-take." He separated that last word into two distinct syllables. "So yes, Sir. I'm questioning you, so I know how best to help."

This man is ... Kaith's? Not Greggor's? He had to fight back a spate of jealous disbelief. Kaith was clever enough in his way. But if Ylspeth's former steward wished upon an early summer star... This Terrek fellow comported himself as a man both war-wise and court-clever. *Greggor wouldn't let such a man fall into that pup's service. He'd recruit him into his own, surely.*

"Vilmocz? I see Sir Gordan's brother knight watching from near the gatehouse."

Terrek said nothing more. His companion gave a brief bow of his head in Gordan's direction, then turned and jogged toward Raegus. When he'd gone far enough to be out of earshot, Terrek spoke again.

"Sir? What am I looking for? What, exactly, is the threat we face?"

Gordan considered, pleased that his mind was working once more. "If I told you, it would only serve to confuse you, sergeant. We live in strange times. For now, attend the east and leave it at that." He didn't want to waste time trying to justify fear based on goblins... on goblin *sorcery*. And this Terrek fellow was from the county's southern marches. Goblins never really ranged that far south, outside of the occasional tavern tale. Likely as not, the sergeant thought of goblins as little more than thieves and mischief-makers, if he thought of them at all.

No need to give him reasons to dismiss me as a liar or a coward. He'll see the truth soon enough once they attack.

"Surely you can give me *some* idea, Sir Gordan. Are we sniffing out scouts? Siege camps? Archers?" A pause. "Once-men?"

Gordan curled the left side of his mouth into something between a smirk and a sneer. His mental fog really was clearing now. He'd managed to shake off some of his earlier panic, too. He'd no idea how, let alone why, but he welcomed it. So Kaith had bragged to his sergeant about Westsong, had he? No surprise, really. He'd done well enough to *survive* that red ruin. Likely as not, the legend of that hellish place was how the youth had cozened a man like this into his service.

He's probing for weakness. It's deftly done, but he's testing the waters to see what he can get away with. I have to regain control over this conversation. Either I'm a knight of Thorion, or I'm not. If I let this man dictate what I do and don't say, I give up command and respect. I cannot do that.

"If anything strange—anything different than what's down there *right now*—comes to your attention, Sergeant, it's worth reporting. You'll smell trouble coming, I've no doubt."

He was just about to mentally pat himself on the back for sowing the seeds of future fireside tales—*Sir Gordan told me I'd smell trouble, and he spoke no lie!*—when he heard a familiar voice.

"Terrek? Gordan?" Kaith spoke without alarm, but with a decided lack of certainty. He was somewhere below, within Wick's wooden walls.

"Here, Lord!" The sergeant raised his voice only a touch—just enough to carry.

A moment later, a broad, well-muscled man thundered up the stairs. His face was dominated by a black mustache. His hair hung down along either side of his face, looking more defeated than tamed. It was like looking at a younger version of Sir Reginald stretched out by a lifetime of physical labor.

That'll be Ricgerd, surely. A lord, but no knight. I never did get to cross swords with him. According to Barnic, he's brutal in a fight, but Barnic bested him in tournament play not long up the hour—

"Report." The man's voice sounded much the way his footfalls had—unintentionally booming.

Terrek bowed his head to the man, then gave Gordan an expectant look. This was proper—the armsman deferring to the knight. Recognizing that did nothing to loosen Gordan's tongue. He was just *staring* at the Lord of Wick, and he'd no idea why.

Another figure walked rather more sedately up the stairs in Ricgerd's wake. He wore a knight's white belt and gold chain. While Gordan couldn't at once place him, he thought he looked familiar.

I'm sure I must've seen him at tournament at some point. Wick has no knights now that Sir Reginald's slipped sideways. Perhaps he's come to pay his respects to the fallen. Another thought roared to the fore, bringing with it a new flare of anger. *That, or he's a bachelor knight looking to puppet the unbelted Lord Ricgerd. Perhaps that's why Kaith is here—to give the Countess eyes and ears in what passes for Wick's court? But he's no match for a seasoned knight's ambitions!*

The fellow was armored in a chain hauberk, steel cuisses, knee and elbow cops, and a blue patterned steel mantle. Common among Thorion's knights for the past twenty years or so, the steel mantle served to protect a man's shoulders and neck. All told, it was a fortune in armor—easily several hundred gold shires' worth of work and weight.

The knight smiled, gesturing to him as he spoke. "My lord, may I present Sir Gordan. Gordan? Lord Ricgerd Wick."

With a start, Gordan realized the man's identity. This *was* Kaith. How had he *not* recognized Greggor's little guardsman?

He bowed to the lord, but his mind was racing. *When... How did he transform himself so completely? That mantle alone would've...*

Black bile rose in the back of his throat. He choked it down while he still could. Here he was—a knight of Thorion, yes, but without the manorial lands and incomes which were his due. Neither he, Raegus, Aethan, nor Jastar had been given manors of their own. Yet *Kaith* clearly had.

Aye. Kaith's been reborn to the manor and raided its coffers the first chance he had.

"Sir Gordan was among those who fought at Westsong, Lord."

*And now you sing my praises? No, Kaith. I didn't stand with **you** at Westsong. You can spin the tale out that way if you...*

Wait. Wait, no. He hadn't spoken as if Gordan had stood beside him at Westsong. Kaith hadn't even said that he'd *been* at Westsong, though Ricgerd surely knew it.

"Then we'll be glad of his sword," said Ricgerd. His face had split into a wide smile that seemed altogether genuine.

Gordan found himself bowing his head once again, though he still hadn't spoken since the pair's arrival on the alure.

"Terrek?" Kaith's voice was easy, just to the right of conversational.

"I believe I know what we face, Lord. Your brother knight can correct me if I'm wrong, but I believe that we're to expect a sizable force of Nebelblut."

Gordan blinked, and hard. He'd drawn breath to either confirm the sergeant's suspicion or ask him how in all the hells he'd known. Nothing came out save a sighed, "Ah."

"I've not heard that word. Who or what are they?" Kaith's voice indicated little more than polite interest.

How? How can he just... just state his ignorance so boldly? Showing that sort of uncertainty to one of his men... Gordan marked Terrek as someone who would likely soon be in need of a new lord to serve. *Men follow strength and decisiveness, not weakness and ignorance!*

"Goblins, Lord. Such are called goblins by most folk."

Kaith and Ricgerd both nodded, then turned to Gordan as if for confirmation.

"I... yes. That's it exactly, Sergeant. You surprise me. As you say, most don't know that word." Gordan flashed a brief smile Terrek's way, then turned to address Ricgerd. "Sir Raegus and I were dispatched to deliver word to you, and ensure it's delivered to Rockvale as well."

Ricgerd arched his brows. "Dispatched? Who is it that thought goblins were enough of a threat to dispatch not one, but two knights to my gate?"

Kaith brightened. "Rae's here? Excellent." Then, to Ricgerd: "He was at Westsong, as well. *All* of Sir Valad's squires and armsmen were." Turning back to Gordan, he added, "Barnic sent you, did he?"

Gordan tried not to bristle. He thought he succeeded marginally well, but it was a near thing. "A man staggered into Eastshadow's great hall. He and his sword sister came to warn Sir Barnic about the Nebelblut. That they were massing. That they were, in fact, on a war footing. And that the northern marches needed warning. The Lord Eastshadow *asked* Sir Raegus and I to make the journey, and we were happy to accept." He turned back to Ricgerd fully. "I've fought them, Lord. We can kill them, but they're far more dangerous than the tales suggest."

"Sir? Who was the man? The woman? What were their names?" Terrek's voice was clipped again.

"That's unimportant, Sergeant." If Gordan were to court this man in advance of the day that Kaith inevitably chased him away, he needed to demonstrate his leadership at every opportunity.

"Nye. Might be that it's just the opposite. His name, if you please, Sir."

Gordan's anger rose again. Who did this fellow think—

"Sergeant?" said Kaith. "I'm certain Sir Gordan knows what he's about." He still used that same conversational tone. "Brother? Finish your tale. If by its end we have questions, we can ask them then."

It was as if Gordan had been doused in cold water. The heat of a moment ago had been replaced by a sudden spike of genuine shame. Why had he behaved so? And worse, what would Valad have said if he'd witnessed the last few minutes?

He met Kaith's eye, then looked away. "The man was called Padrutt, Sergeant. The woman, Doanne. They were—"

"Wardens," Terrek finished. "I know them well." He turned to Kaith and Ricgerd, though it was to Kaith he spoke. "My lord, they're both in the group currently patrolling the Shivering March. Their commander is a good man—Gorman of Birchorg."

Kaith nodded. "Sir Valgar's lands. Fair enough."

Gordan had the presence of mind not to gape or glare. Kaith wasn't *deliberately* trying to anger him. But still... Valgar had an estate? *Valgar?*

Then he finally registered what Terrek had said. "How..." He sighed. "So you *know* Padrutt, then, Sergeant."

"Terrek comes to my service after his own with the Wardens, as does Vilmocz." Kaith nodded over Gordan's shoulder to where Raegus was passing a word with the man.

"Ah." For a moment, that was all he could say.

"Sir Gordan." Ricgerd sounded as if he were growing annoyed. "I've left my table with the promise of swords under the stars. Yet plainly there *is* no enemy here—goblin or otherwise. Now either tell us your drift or let me find you and your brother a seat by my fire."

Gordan sighed and nodded. "As you say, Lord. It began just over a week agone. I chanced to be on the wall when they attacked Eastshadow."

-IV-

County Thorion
Wick
5 Korunasykli: 22 Days after the Red Storm at Westsong

Kaith tried to read Gordan as the man eked out his tale. Valad's former squire was putting on a *hells haul them home* demeanor, but he wasn't fooling anyone.

Fear? And shame at feeling that fear? That made little enough sense, given what had happened. *Perhaps I'm missing something?*

Ricgerd growled as he spoke. "So not one, but *two* knights of Thorion—two of what I'm given to understand are called the *Valadin...*" After breaking the order's name into syllables for emphasis, Ricgerd stopped for several beats, holding Gordan's gaze. "*Two* of you—both mounted—couldn't best a pair of goblin lances. Goblins bearing no shields. No weapons to speak of. Goblins who were afoot and were spread out before you on an *open field*. In the face of such a force, you made the decision to race back to *warn* us. Have I got that right ... *Sir?*"

Gordan's right fist clenched and unclenched. "You *have*, Lord, though you speak as a man who's never had to fight the devils."

"And *you* speak as a man who—"

"Lord Ricgerd..." Kaith overrode the man in as gentle a manner as he could. "If I may?"

Ricgerd—who'd been drawing himself up for the moment the conversation would turn physical—subsided. His nod looked disappointed rather than contrite, but that would do.

Kaith addressed himself to Gordan. "You said you felled one at

Eastshadow. That they *can* be killed, but it takes some doing. Can you explain any further?"

Gordan managed to unclench his bright fist, nodding. "They don't bleed the way a man does. Their skin *is* skin, but it..." He shook his head. "I don't know how to explain it."

Ricgerd growled, then drew in an audible breath through his nose. *Your derision will have to wait. We need information, not infighting.*

Kaith spoke up before Wick's master could open his mouth. "My lord, there are no heralds among us on this particular patch of wall. And only Terrek is a scout. We wield weapons, not words, is what I mean to say. Given a chance to think, Sir Gordan will find the right ones in a moment, I'm sure."

Gordan relaxed at that. He offered a grateful nod to Kaith before turning to address all three of them at once. He seemed to be trying to order his thoughts—perhaps looking for a simile that might make things clearer.

"It's like... like their entire body is covered in layers of hide... like hides wrapped about a pell, actually." Gordan brightened, nodding. "Aye, that's about as near the mark as no matter. Hides that need to be a bit tighter 'round the pell."

"...So they're in that sloppy, *slow-your-blow-down* state?" Ricgerd's anger had been replaced by a thoughtfulness of both face and voice.

Gordan nodded. "That's it exactly, my lord. And..." He trailed off, turning his head to look out over the wall. The language of his body spoke nothing of fear now. He just seemed to need something external to focus on as he collected his thoughts.

After a moment, Ricgerd grew impatient again. "Sir Gordan?"

Kaith saw his brother knight stiffen, straighten, and nod. His back still to them, and with the air of a man who's come to a difficult decision, Gordan spoke anew.

"What I tell you now won't go down easy. Yet you must hear it. I told you that they were holding down a bandit."

"Aye," said Ricgerd. "One less bandit in the world isn't something to lose sleep ov—"

"They held him down until another of them appeared." Gordan broke in, though his voice was flat and affectless. "A Nebelblut as tall as a man. He wielded an arming sword in his bright hand and one of their arrows in his dim. He was broad and well-muscled and sent an unnatural fear before him. It can be resisted, but the body, or perhaps the mind, *wants* to flee."

Ricgerd's mouth had begun a twitch that would likely end in yet another sneer. Before it could, Terrek spoke up.

"Nebelbrecher."

"Sergeant?" Kaith fought the urge to smile. This was why he hadn't sent Terrek off to watch from a different vantage. He'd served as a Warden of the shivering march for years. If anyone could help identify what Gordan had seen...

Terrek repeated himself, enunciating the word slowly. He made Nebel rhyme with *people*, and 'brecher rhyme with *taker*, save that the K sound came out more like an H.

"And does it render into the Trade Tongue?" Ricgerd sounded annoyed, though not specifically at Terrek.

"Mist-breakers, Lord Wick." Terrek shook his head a single time, then spoke on. "They're Nebelblut champions—maybe Nebelblut elders. They're tall, as Sir Gordan says, and bold. A Nebelblut attacks from stealth as often as it can, and usually in groups of three. The breakers care nothing for stealth. They're more than a match for any two men, unless those men work well together." He turned from Kaith and Ricgerd, nodding to Gordan. "And you're not wrong 'bout the fear, Sir Gordan. Yes, it *can* be cast aside. And *yes,* man's instinct is to turn and fly ... as fast and as far away as may be."

Gordan nodded but still didn't turn. "That's what he was—If indeed it was a he." He paused for a beat, then went on in that same flat tone. "He walked up the little heath they had the bandit stretched out on, parried my stroke as I rode by... parried it with lazy ease, mind you. When I'd wheeled about for another pass, he'd driven his arrow like a dagger—by hand, I mean. When it struck the man, there was a brief dazzle of light. Don't ask me the color, for I can't name it. Nor does it much matter. The important bit is what came after."

Kaith studied him, trying to understand what was going on beneath Gordan's words. The words were important enough. Yet the more Gordan spoke—especially in this empty, flat tone—the more certain Kaith became that there was something else at play here.

"The tall one..." He glanced briefly at Terrek for confirmation. "The Nebelbrecher?" When the sergeant nodded, Gordan returned his gaze to the landscape outside of Wick's walls. "Aye, fine. The Nebelbrecher withdrew his arrow and staggered backward... changing. He seemed to stretch in all directions at once, as if being filled by something. I know that sounds like a Eodenth in silks, but hear me. Have you ever filled an empty wine or water skin? You've seen the way it stretches and swells as it gets fuller? *That's* what it reminded me of."

Kaith tried both to picture it and to push the idea as far from his mind's eye as possible. As he'd never seen a goblin before, he was stuck visualizing a man whose arms and legs, cheeks and belly were filling up with water.

The silence held for a time. The only lights now were of torch and lantern, moon and star. The world seemed lost in long thoughts.

It was Ricgerd who finally broke the spell. "But filling with *what,* exactly?"

Gordan shook his head. "It happened fast. So fast the Nebelbrecher staggered under the weight of it all. When it..." He paused, drew in a deep breath, and spoke again. This time his voice came out in a higher register, as if he were speaking to someone at the back of a large room.

...Or fighting to ride herd on his emotions, Kaith thought, but did not say.

"When it was over, the creature was taller than any horse's withers. Not *twice* as tall as a man, but..." He shrugged. "Half-again? It had grown muscle to match its new size, and its skin had gone from sickly green to a blue not much lighter than Kaith's mantle. A slateish blue that reminded me of..."

"Of Westsong," Kaith finished. His voice was soft. He was trying to process how the goblins were connected to the damnable dead. It made no sense, given how long goblins had plagued the northeast of the county. Why would they be dealing in the dead now?

"No." Gordan shook his head, bringing Kaith out of his reverie. "The flesh of the once-men was a swirling thing—shadow mixed with moonlight. That's how Rahn describes it, at least. The Nebelbrecher wore flesh that was as close to one color as yours or mine. It was darker, too. Darker than the once-men."

"You... You saw this with your own eyes, Sir Gordan?" Terrek sounded nothing short of stunned. It was a tone that came out thin and breathy. Strange, coming from the former Warden.

"Aye. He turned when it was over, leveled a finger at me—*directly* at me, and..." He swallowed. After drawing in a ragged breath, he tried again. "He mouthed words to me ... in the Trade Tongue. He said... he said, '*The ending walks,*' or perhaps '*wakes.*' I've never tried to read lips in my life, but he spoke slowly. He *wanted* me to understand him."

"And so you ran here." Ricgerd nodded. His voice was thoughtful, and with no trace of its former derision.

Gordan bowed his head. "I know how mad it sounds, but—"

As his balding brother knight trailed off, Kaith finally thought he understood. Gordan assumed he would be seen as a coward. He feared that the glaring truth would be taken for a lie. That his *tales of glory* were a cloak used to hide something inglorious.

But if Barnic gave him the commission to ride here—a commission to deliver a warning about this very threat, no less... Hells, why would Gordan expect to be called a coward or a liar?

Maybe... you should ask him? Greggor's voice spoke up in his mind— snuck up, truth be told. *Unless, Kaith, you know the answer already or have turned wizard since last we had occasion to speak.* He bowed his head, fighting the urge to smile.

"You've not become a liar since last we met, have you?" He made his voice gentle, wanting Gordan to understand that the question was perfunctory.

The man shook his head, keeping his back to the alure's other occupants.

Kaith reached a hand out to touch Gordan's shoulder. He managed to turn him, but he wouldn't meet Kaith's eyes. "Gordan... *Sir* Gordan, did you really think that, after Westsong, we would think your story was false? That you'd invent such a tale to make yourself look tall?" A pause, during which the man's chin rose to reveal his haunted eyes. "After the Red Storm, did you really think *I* would doubt you?"

Gordan smiled, bowing his mostly bald head. "I did, actually. It sounds mad to *my* ears, Kaith. And I lived it." He chuckled. Some of his color had returned, leaving him looking as if he'd just walked off the lyst field. "But thank you. Truly... thank you."

Kaith nodded, stepping back to Ricgerd's side. Before he'd finished the movement, Terrek spoke up.

"If... Lord Ricgerd, Sir Kaith... I need a—"

At that moment, many things happened at once.

A crash shattered the watchful calm of the new-fallen night. Snapping his head in that direction, Kaith saw what had happened at once. A team of oxen had hauled a massive cart of stacked stones into position athwart Wick's main gate. Now those same oxen mooed their baleful displeasure.

Bracing a settlement's gate with heavily laden wagons was a normal enough practice. In places where that gate was designed to keep out raiders, but not a proper siege, it was all but a *necessity.* The crash had come from an issue with the cart's rear axle, by the looks of things. It appeared to have snapped just before the wagon settled in its proper place. Forcing the main gate open would still be a difficult task, but not an impossible one.

No sooner had the situation at the gate clarified itself than Olshnak came charging up the nearby stair.

"Sir Kaith! Sir Kaith!" The orc's voice tore at Kaith's ears.

And a body *slammed* into him from the left. It didn't knock him asprawl, merely to one side.

"Down!" Terrek's voice—short and sharp. An arrow screamed just behind the sergeant's back.

He crouched. He saw Gordan had done the same. Ricgerd was drawing his sword, glaring about.

"More courage than sense, Lord!" Olshnak shouldered Ricgerd toward Kaith and Terrek. He unslung Kaith's own heater shield, moving it between Ricgerd and the low alure wall. The Lord of Wick roared, rounding on the orc, then realized what had happened and gave him a nod by way of thanks.

"Sir Kaith, they're—" Olshnak was cut off by another three arrows impacting the shield he held.

Kaith felt his nose wrinkle. A scent had struck him nearly as hard as Terrek's body check had. It was a low, noisome thing, full of rot and rue. They had spent so much time on the wall—so many eyes and ears watching along the alure—and yet they had noticed *nothing!*

Gordan growled, looking about—presumably for something to hurl back out at their attackers.

"Sir Kaith!" Olshnak once more, insistent now. "I think I know what they're planning. We *must* get the gate open!"

"Open? Are you mad?" Ricgerd had moved to crouch down beside Terrek and Kaith. "Hells, shall I order a feast in their honor as well? Would *that* serve?"

"They won't come in through the gate, Lord. They'll take the easier road..."

The night was rent by screams from within the village—far too many screams. Olshnak bowed his head.

"We're too late. They're already inside."

Kaith stared at him, trying to understand. Then another scent struck him—the fetid stench of Wick's open...

"Sewers! Hells! They've come in through the sewers! Ricgerd, gather all of your men—all the men you can see or call for. Get them off the walls and onto the ground! We have to protect your people!"

He didn't wait for a response, turning instead to Terrek. "Get Vilmocz and Huron. I need you to secure a stone building—a grain silo, a stable, *something*. Preferably near one of the smaller gates."

"Where, Lord?" Terrek had understood him. That much showed plainly in his eyes. He was looking for clarification—a specific direction.

"Pick an inn yard! It doesn't matter. Just send Huron to find me when you've secured it. And make *damned* sure it doesn't have a sewer entrance we can't secure. Go!"

Terrek went, as did Ricgerd. Olshnak and Gordan looked at him, waiting.

"Gordan—find bows for yourself and Rae. We need to shoot as many arrows as we can. If we can thin the herd, good, but that isn't what really matters."

Gordan grinned. "You want to know what they're doing."

Kaith nodded, offering a thin smile of his own for good measure. "You said they can climb wooden walls. I want us to know when they start. My hope is that the more we shoot at them, the slower they'll be to attempt the climb. Be ready for my call and mark your nearest way to the streets below."

Gordan nodded, heading off as fast as he could while crouching.

"And me?" Olshnak's voice sounded surprised, fearful, and hopeful all at a go.

"Take your two guards and see what, if anything, you can do about that damned wagon blocking the gate. If the answer's nothing, then fall back to Terrek and help where you can."

"I can do that. But what'll you be doing?"

Kaith took his shield from Olshnak. "Gathering torches and lamp oil."

"For?"

"For later. Now move. You've your own work to be about."

Olshnak hesitated, then nodded. "Yes, Sir Kaith. Be careful."

You don't think I know what I'm doing, he thought. Rather than making him angry, the realization made Kaith smile. *Well, you're probably right, but I won't be doing it at all, until and unless enough of us fail our individual tasks.* He *hoped* it wouldn't be necessary to strike so much as a single spark, but if it was...

He was thinking of Westsong—of Countess Ylspeth's plan, and how well it had worked. Combat was, at bottom, about control. Seeing her Excellency use *fire* to control Westsong's battlefield had made a profound impact on him. It had changed the way he thought about battles and

killing fields alike. She'd tasked him with mixing an oily combination of substances, most of which he hadn't recognized. He'd painted several buildings with the foul stuff. As promised, it had burned for hours, ignoring the rainstorm that dominated his memory of that night. Using the terrain was one thing. Even altering it by felling trees or moving stones to reshape that battlefield hadn't been an unknown concept. Greggor and Valgar had seen to his training on that score.

But using fire? Altering the field by harnessing a destructive force like that? He shook his head.

Careful to keep his shield between him and the archers outside, Kaith made his way down the stairs and set about gathering supplies he hoped he wouldn't need.

CHAPTER THIRTEEN

SHADOWS SHRIVEN

-I-

Venzene Duchy of Kovalun
County Jižní Pochod
Barony of Hartscross–Jižní Lov
5 Korunasykli: 22 Days after the Red Storm at Westsong

Kastan was more than a touch reluctant to send the boys off alone. Skar had made it clear the haunts wouldn't return for at least a day, barring some new sorcery. The problem was, while it was *likely* the lot of the horrors had all been here for the attack a few moments ago, there was no way to be sure. There might well be others lurking about, and the idea of sending Andrej and Pavel out to gather who they could without so much as a *candle* to guide them...

They'd all exchanged uncertain looks with one another for a few silent beats. Then Pavel broke the spell.

"Vhy don't ve light the lanterns?"

"They all went out." Olga sounded harassed, but managed to keep the bite of frustration in her voice under control. She was looking up, down, at each of their faces—anywhere but at Radek's sadful form.

"But... did the lanterns *break*? I don't think I heard any glass shattering." He looked over to Hajvarr for confirmation.

Kastan turned to him with a look of dawning comprehension. "No... no shattered glass. The lights went out as that smoke rolled through. I thought it was some kind of monstrous sorcery, but…"

"It was, Lady," said Skar. "It's what woke the dead. But if it didn't *destroy* the lanterns, then they should be able to re-light. I have a flint and steel in my haversack. We could—"

"There's no need," said Olga. "Take the lantern down, then pull the hook that held it *outward*. You'll find a small chest behind it, unlocked. There should be a vial of oil, some flax wicks, one or two tallow candles, and flint and steel for striking."

"A Fire Keeper's reliquary?" Andrej grinned. "Which one has it?"

"All of them *should*." Olga allowed a thin smile as Andrej's look of surprise lit his face.

Kastan quirked a smile of her own. "Cti strážce ohně, Mistress."

"Honor her indeed." Olga looked around the small group, sounding sour, but smiling with genuine amusement. "Did you lot think the fire-keepers carried everything with them *all the time?*"

A few moments later found Kastan, Olga, and Skar watching as Pavel and Andrej were swallowed by the darkness. Ruční Kopí had taken his red hound back the way she, Olga, and Andrej had come to find yet another lantern, and—she suspected—to make certain that direction was as safe as may be.

Pavel had gone to the left. She heard a sound like a millstone in miniature from that quarter. The scraping was brief, stopping almost as suddenly as it had begun. She saw Olga turn her head to face her, nodding. A moment later, she heard that same sound twice over. Then came the tap-*click*, tap-*click*, tap-*click* of flint on steel.

"That'll be Andrej."

"How can you possibly know that?" Olga didn't seem particularly interested in the answer, though she still managed to sound dubious.

Skar spoke up from her left. "Is he the blond boy? The archer?"

Light as bright as new hope flared in the gloom. It came from the right, beginning to move closer. An instant later and a similar light flared to the left.

"The same." Kastan offered a nod. She then turned to Olga. "The lighter tapping sound? That's a woodsman's trick to line up the edges before the actual strike." She saw the woman nod in a distracted sort of way. "A trick taught me by Edmund's scouts."

"*Your* scouts, Excellency." Olga's voice was once more that implacable, *Deny the truth all you like—it'll change nothing* tone.

Kastan resisted the urge to roll her eyes. Casting about, she noted

Skar's expression. He wore the look of a man carrying a heavy burden, and not knowing where, or even if, he *ought* to lay that burden down.

A final flood of light came from where Hajvarr had gone. He returned with Štít at his heel, a lit lantern in hand. This he placed on the ground beneath the anděl statue. Without a word, Kastan relocated to the new source of light. Olga and Skar joined her a moment later. Once they were seated within the stone lady's regard, Kastan found Hajvarr's face.

"With your permission, Excellency, I think it'd be best if we not send the boys alone." He shook his head as if to forestall her. "I can go with Pavel. Štít can follow Andrej—she's taken a shine to him. She'll fight to protect him if it comes to that."

Kastan had drawn breath to make reply, but Olga cut in before she could.

"We *cannot* leave her Excellency unguarded." *As you well know, boy,* was left unspoken, but the implication was loud enough to wake the...

"And so, I won't. Skar didn't save us just so he could kill the Lady *himself,* Olga. I know he serves a lord from beyond our borders, but I also know that lord. More importantly, I know *Skar.* I've not seen him in two years, as Edmund hasn't gone back to tournament in all that time, but I know him and trust him. Will you tell me that *my* word isn't enough? Or must we sit and debate the matter?"

Kastan had never seen this side of Hajvarr, He was controlled, cold, and a hair's breadth away from outright fury.

"And will *you* tell *me* that an unrenewed friendship is enough to risk the future of the county on? Is a decades-old conflict and time at tourney enough to wager her Excellency's life on?" At last, it was Olga's turn to show a bit of pique.

"Even if my word *isn't* good enough for your comfort, Kastan is a more capable sword than half the lordlings that claim to be on the hunt for their spurs! Hells, Olga, I'd take her at my back over any *four* of the men in Edmund's service! Were you resting your eyes while the once-men still stood?"

That was a flattering thing to hear. Kastan bowed her head, willing herself not to blush at such high praise.

Olga's breath as she prepared her retort was enough to pull Kastan's attention back to the matter at hand. She was interested to see that Skar himself seemed to be paying no mind to the discussion, but that was neither here nor there. *She* had decided she'd had enough. As entertaining as it might be to watch the pair of them verbally spar with one another, there simply wasn't time.

"*If* you would be kind enough to let me speak…"

Both Olga and Hajvarr snapped their heads toward her. She saw Andrej and Pavel walking up behind Štít, though they prudently stopped there. "Hajvarr? Go with Pavel. Gather all of those you can. Tell them to take food and water, clothing, and whatever else they can carry, so long as they're not too burdened to run. If they argue, leave them. If there's trouble, settle it. Clear?"

Hajvarr nodded.

"Andrej? Take Štít. Go back to the command tent. Let Hajvarr's men know that when you return, they're to come with you into the catacombs to find me."

"Return? Where am I going?"

"To find Vlasta, Tyesca, Fetinba… any of our people. Get them to the horses. I'll want them saddled and ready to ride for Zlaté Pole as soon as we can arrange it." Andrej nodded, not bothering to hide his relief at being sent to find Fetem.

She waited for a four-count. Nobody moved.

"Well? To it!" She made her voice sharp rather than loud. They got the message, heading off to do as she'd commanded.

"I'm … sorry, Lady." Skar bowed his head.

"For?"

"You were to be married. The Count's proposal was…" He shook his head. "There should be no dark clouds on such a day. I'm sorry your joy's been overshadowed by all … of this." He gestured around.

Kastan bowed her head, nodding. "Thank you." It was all that she dared to say. She didn't want to marry Edmund. Of course she didn't. She *also* didn't want him to fall in battle, on this or any other day… which was plainly what he'd feared would come to pass.

She drew a breath that was far more ragged than she'd expected, then turned her dark dreamer's lamps back to Azhferd's armsman.

"Tell me what I need to know, Skar. Tell me what we face, how you knew how to best the haunts… all of it that time will allow."

He nodded. "As you say, Lady."

-II-

Laagi stood on a storm cloud, laughing. It was a short, spikey sound, every jagged swell of which sent a spear of pain through Vlk's head.

"That isn't *fair,* Laagi!" He was standing on a section of the alure west of the barbican. The sun shone dim and almost orange above him, though the rain fell all around. It was a red rain—a blood rain, full of tears and anger. Each drop screamed as it fell, so that all around him the sound was a physical force. "If you vant me to fight, you have to let me have a cloud too! Give me my cloud! Either give me my cloud back or you can find someone else to fight with in the tournament!"

"What 'n hells *is* it?" This was a different voice—a familiar one, though Vlk couldn't quite place the man it belonged to. It reminded him of dogs and horses, and he had no idea why.

Laagi laughed again, pulling someone from behind him. Vlk saw what looked like a Sheshik version of Kastan. She had the same black silk for hair, the same jet-colored dreamer's lamps, but her skin was dark and somehow lustrous.

She looks as if she's been carved out of forest shadows, he thought, and again, had no idea why. Nor did it matter. He heard himself scream in rage and fear, though he had no idea what words he'd shouted.

"It's outside, so for now, it doesn't matter. We have other matters to focus on just now." Another man's voice, but this one was full of authority.

"Laagi! There's something outside! You have to come down! Come down, or give me my cloud so ve can fight it together! You have to let her go so ve can fight to save her!"

Vlk looked around for the voices, but the sobbing, screaming rain made it hard to focus on them. Laagi shouted down to him, pulling his eyes back upward.

"I can't fight, Vlk!" Laagi laughed. "If I fight, I have to give her up!" He turned his prisoner toward Vlk, bodily... only she *wasn't* a prisoner. She slowly snaked her arms around his neck and mouthed two words that Vlk couldn't hear, but had no trouble understanding.

"My love…"

Their lips met. Their kiss was long, frozen in time as they breathed for one another.

Vlk screamed again, though he experienced a queer doubling of sound. He was sure he could hear himself speaking to Laagi in that same raised voice. Yet he could *also* hear himself screaming.

"She isn't yours, Laagi! You can't have my voman *and* my cloud! And if you take her, then Lakkrid and I vill kill Andrej! Then he'll become my cloud, and I'll fly up and take her back from you!"

"If you kill Andrej, then you'll have made your father…"

Whatever Laagi thought Vlk's father would be, it was never quite made clear. He heard footsteps coming closer, thumping along wooden boards. They slowed, then stopped as they drew near.

"Vlk? Vlk, I know I'm a lark to be 'round, but hells be hid, boy… Ya can't keep doin' this." He called over his shoulder. "Aedelt?"

"What is it? What do you see?"

Vlk tried to open his eyes. He couldn't do it, then came to the horrid realization that his eyes *were* open.

"D'you 'member the cub your red hound helped? Vlk?"

"I do. He left before I could tell him about Ebistian. I'd hoped to get word to Edmund while there was still time, but…"

"He's here, Excellency. He's here, and *not* here. I can't explain it."

The man—Aedelt, apparently—sighed, then jogged over the same wooden boards.

"Ah…"

"Ah? What in hells does *ah* mean?"

"Hroth… Your name is… is Hroth." Vlk thought he'd only… well, *thought* that realization. Hroth's reaction suggested otherwise.

"Aye, Vlk. S'me, and no mistake. Must've missed me and the Baron. You've tried to slip sideways again."

Vlk blinked, or thought he did. He could still see Laagi on his cloud—still saw him with his mouth on the Sheshik beauty that was both Kastan and not Kastan.

"I vant… Laagi has my vom… voman. He has my voman and my cloud. Hroth? Vhy is the rain screaming? Vhy am… Vhy…" But it was no good. He couldn't form words.

"He'll linger, then join us if he doesn't get help soon."

"Well, where's your damned dog?"

Aedelt remained silent for a long moment. So long, in fact, that Vlk saw Laagi come back into focus. He was still kissing the woman, but he pulled an arm away from her to bring Lakkrid up on his other side. Laagi's dim arm was around Lakkrid's shoulders, while his bright still crushed the not-Kastan to him. Lakkrid was laughing and waving, even as the two beside him continued what must be the longest kiss in history.

Vlk moaned. He was ready to cry. Even now, he felt the corners of his eyes begin to prickle. Laagi had everything! He'd *taken* everything! He had Vlk's cloud, his woman, his best friend…

"If he has Lakkrid, he von't… He von't need me … for the tournament!" Vlk tried to shout this, but he couldn't. He stood there, looking up and shouting at Laagi, yet only air came out.

"Who has Lakkrid, Vlk? Who?"

Vlk tried to pull away, running along the alure. His legs were so, so heavy. He made himself jump, but well-muscled forearms came up out of the poplar boards below him—the Ashwood wall beside him. They were made *of* the wall… the wood itself.

And vood is all around me!

They grabbed at him, though he dodged. He kicked one, stomped another, then felt himself jump. He used the reaching arms as points to run along—to leap from one to the next, ever higher.

He was impossibly high, now. He saw Laagi remove his arm from around Lakkrid, reaching down for Vlk to grab his hand…

"Aedelt! Aedelllllt!" Hroth's voice, shouting directly into his ear. Into his head. Into…

-III-

The carriage had stopped. They were still outside, and a goodly way back from the encampment's main gate. The sound of folk fighting and dying was a tumult that set Lashjuk's very tusks on edge. She didn't dare lower herself to the ground. In this noise, she'd never hear the call that they were readying themselves to move again.

As she tried to grasp the ebb and flow of the battle—no easy task, given she had almost no view of what had become the killing field— Lashjuk began to sense something else. It was a persistent tugging at her attention, like a daydream that refused to be dismissed.

The sense grew more and more insistent until she finally acknowledged it and fell into the daydream. Her mind offered up a glimpse of the strange creature that had brought her here. She seized upon it, hating the feeling of weakness, but the relief at no longer being alone was too potent to ignore.

She wondered if it would hear her if she spoke in all of this damnable noise. No sooner had this thought occurred to her than an answer came.

She began *physically* whispering. Mentally, she was trying to shout over the cacophony. The thought struck her that she was—quite literally—struggling to hear herself think.

"Is this enough? Can you... You can? Gi awka glem! *That's* a blessing!" She marveled at her sudden depth of feeling. Far beyond mere relief, she was genuinely glad to feel the creature's touch in her mind, if indeed that was where the contact point was.

She listened, or perhaps simply registered whatever the creature was sending to her. It was odd. It wasn't speech, exactly. It was nearer akin to a tumble of images and a sense of what it was trying to convey. She found it easier to repeat what she understood it to be saying or asking, at least when the ideas being communicated were complex ones.

"I'm stuck waiting," she whispered. "He has guards, and now he has this Sau fellow... Sau, yes." An image flashed across her mind's eye. She caught a glimpse of a slender Sheshik man. He was young, pale brown, with dark, wide eyes. "His voice certainly *sounded* Sheshik, but I think he's a ghost of some kind. Perhaps a devil-thing. A spirit, or a thing from the hells. He took one of Ebistian's men, and now wears him like a kontusz."

The carriage lurched forward, stopping almost at once. She winced.

"I'm wrapped around the underside of a massive carriage, holding on for dear damned *life* lest I fall off and get discovered. Or worse, I get left behind, unable to catch them. Do I want help? I thought you'd run out of strength!"

Screams assaulted her ears, followed by a jubilant wall of sound. "Jižní meče! Jižní meče! Edmund! Edmund! Jižní meče!"

"You've been doing *what* to the enemy as they die?" She shook her head, unable to grasp the meaning. "It doesn't matter. I'm pleased you're more yourself again. If you *can* help me, then..." She paused, trying to make sense of the images. "How ... can you help? Hells, I've no idea what you can *do!* How am *I* meant to know how you can help?"

She gritted her teeth, glaring at the underside of the carriage. It should have carried at least *some* dust or dirt, surely. But no, it was damned near pristine—a fact that did nothing to improve her mood. Absurd that such a thing should bother her, but it did.

"Unpleasant? You think I'm being *unpleasant?* I'm a barely trained scout in the midst of a war with no allies who can swing a sword or hold a shield, my son is in the hands of that demon—or perhaps I should say, *those demons*—and my arms and legs are on *fire!* How pleasant would *you* be to speak with?"

In answer, she felt a frozen numbness radiate down her limbs, then fade. In its wake she felt... it wasn't a numbness, but the fatigue was a distant memory.

"How?" She shook her head. "Never mind. Just ... thank you. This is excellent." The lack of pain made concentrating on what she could hear a *far* more manageable task.

She heard the sounds of metal stabbing into flesh, of men slipping on the blood-muddy ground, of death in all of its forms. She also heard a growling woman riding in her direction. Then the coach door opened above, and Ebistian's voice sliced through the rest of the din.

"T'lendak? Speak the words, or sacrifice the flesh you wear. I care not, but the pact still holds. I make you the offer as courtesy demands, and I await your decision."

Eliška reined up and remained silent for some time. When she spoke, it was in a tone of cold resignation. "Your path has proven superior this day. The field of battle and all of its prizes are yours, Shadow Eater. Name your terms. Once agreed upon, the Storm Queen and the court at the Red Rim of Ruin will abide."

Ebistian's voice slid out past a frigid-sounding smile. It made Lashjuk's skin crawl.

"I accept your words in accordance with the pact. You will speak in gratitude for I and mine slaying the monster who controlled your actions. You will ride in at my left hand and support my claims within the Empire as a whole. I care nothing for Eoalun, which is the Storm Queen's by ancient right."

"And those taken prisoner by your *allies?*" She sounded as if she'd all but spat that last word.

"*I* will not seek your surviving folk as prisoner or example. Still, you and your folk did attack this place without direct provocation. I will not stop the ruler of this encampment, or indeed the County as a whole, from having their respective ways with those who drew swords against them. But as I say, *I* will not order any retribution to be carried out against them. And I will intervene on your direct behalf, should it come to that. Are we agreed?"

In a voice of disgust, Eliška spoke. "We are agreed, Shepherd. The pact holds."

"Of course it does. Now... take your place at my side. The goodly folk of the county wish to laud our timely arrival."

With that, the carriage rolled forward, passing into the encampment amidst deafening cheers.

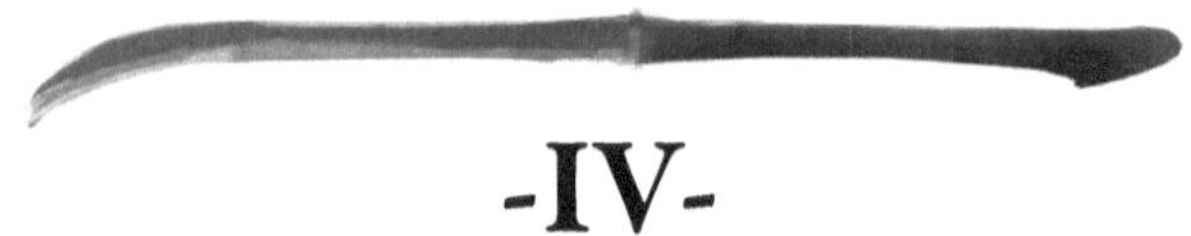

-IV-

County Thorion
Eastshadow
5 Korunasykli: 22 Days after the Red Storm at Westsong

...Barnic turned back to Aethan. "Archers need to focus along the corners—northeast and northwest more than anywhere else. At least for the first volley. Be prepared to spread out along the walls as needed. Send word to the other district captains. Where's your banner-bearer?"

"He's just there." Aethan waved a pimple-faced youth over. The boy held a banner pole in one hand, its flag still tightly furled, and a massive horn in the other. As he approached, Aethan continued speaking. "You want to make them look north while your man runs south." He grinned, looking a touch more like himself. "Won't work, but it's better than sitting and waiting."

"You're so sure?"

"Not at all, brother." His grin widened as he pointed to nearby archers to get into position. "Remember Valad's talk of how to view the world? Is the mug half full or half empty?"

Barnic nodded, snorting. "Yes, and aye, and I do."

"Well, I always find it easier to be sad I'm through half a measure than happy I've half a measure left." He placed a hand on Barnic's shoulder and spoke a final word before stepping forward to their archery line. "I'd rather think fondly on what I've lost than try and cheer myself with what I've got left. Makes me savor every drop in the mug, rather than pretend everything's just fine."

Barnic turned to regard his runner, but the man was already down the stairs, waiting by the gate. "Fair," said he.

Aethan drew his sword, making ready to give the orders as necessary. "At your word, Lord Eastshadow..."

Barnic looked out over the force that surrounded him. No change. They just… *stood* there, looking up at him with their shining maws on display. So be it. He saw the banner-bearer had unfurled his flag—the black sword pointing to the right upon a silver field. He saw there were several other banners still wrapped and bound along the crossbar of the pole.

With a final look down at the gate, confirming men were prepared to open and close it again swiftly. All was in readiness, for good or ill.

"Eastshadow? Make ready!"

And so comes my first true test, he thought. *I confess, Valad, I don't know if this is the right play. And I fear how many will die following my orders. But I know exactly what you'd say at a time like this.*

He heard the sound of many bows being bent … and smiled. "Aethan? The dancing point of…"

They shouted the word together. "Now!"

Men growled, murmuring curses or prayers to whatever god, saint, or ancestor they gave their grace. Bowstrings twanged over and over again. Arrows rent the evening air as they flew toward their targets. These were the first notes of a battle hymn that was old before time was first tallied.

Aethan was shouting as he moved along the wall. "Eastshadow! Eastshadow! This isn't about Thorion! Not about gold or good will! These hungry things mean to take much more than your lives! They'll take your *ale!*" Men laughed, bleeding off some of their tension. "Bring them down before they bring *you* down! Stand or fall, they mean to show your wives what kind of men you are! Any creature you spy with a bow in its paw, fill it with pins until it forgets how to move! East … shadow!"

"Eastshadow!" their shouted reply was bright and bold beneath the moon. It went a goodly way toward driving back the early evening's chill.

As men shouted, raining down what death they could deal, the grand palisade's gate slid open just long enough to let Barnic's runner out. It was pushed closed and barred almost at once.

Barnic saw the man in motion before the door bar settled back into its cradle. His runner wasted no time—a glance at his surroundings, and no more. He sprinted down the wide way between the walled districts. And he most certainly did *not* disappoint. The guardsman, whose name he hadn't taken the time to learn, ran as if hell's harbinger was but a black breath away. And he was *agile,* as if he wore nothing heavier than a summer-weight tunic.

*Second skin, just as you said. I'll need to do better at learning names, though. Actually—h*e glanced away from his runner for a beat to wave over a nearby archer. Then returned his attention to the man of the moment.

"Havoc's Horn!" The guardsman was now squaring off with a goblin. Where in hells had he come from, and how had he gotten in front of the man? ...The *unarmed* man!

Barnic watched in helpless horror as the Nebelblut produced a sword out of thin air. *It looks like a talwar*, his pitiless mind whispered. These were curved, single-edged blades which widened at their tip. They'd been the preferred blade of the Barghad people—the first folk of the region, from back before there *was* a Thorion. Kaith had told him something about their making once, before a tournament in the south. How their craft had been the father of modern Thorion steel. He'd only been half listening.

The guardsman paused, dropped his center of balance, then leapt forward. He meant to grapple with the Nebelblut, reaching for its sword arm in an effort to gain control of the weapon. The creature was either too swift or too skilled. It lifted its sword higher as the guard made his move. Barnic could see what looked like a monstrous *fang* descending from the blade's pommel. As the nameless guard crossed into range, the goblin hammered that fang down into his dim-side shoulder in three blurs of motion.

"Ar-*cherrr!*" Barnic's heart was in his throat, trying to hammer its way out into the fetid evening air. The man he'd beckoned finally made it to his side.

"Lord?"

Barnic wanted to scream at the fellow. *Hells be hid! Use your damned eyes!* But he knew that wouldn't serve.

"Do *not* let that man die! Now bend your bow!"

The archer did as he was bidden, but seemed to take an age to aim. Barnic's runner had fallen back, stumbling and covered in blood along his left side. The man tripped either over his own feet or due to the terrain—Barnic couldn't tell which in the dim. He crashed to the early winter's grass, landing on his rump with his bright arm to brace him. The Nebelblut stepped forward, raising his talwar high to deliver the deathblow.

I remember the lyst prize that day... a gorgeous talwar with silver koftgari. I still have it. It'll be buried among the rest of my possessions inside somewhere. If you live, it's yours. If you fall, I'll yield it up for your death rite.

The archer loosed his arrow and had a second pin nocked before the first one had finished its flight. It struck the goblin on the back of his bright hand, somewhere near the wrist. The impact forced the beast to drop the weapon before reaching to pull the arrow free.

The guardsman wasted no time. He snatched up the fallen sword. Then, rising to one knee, he *slammed* the talwar forward, stabbing it upward and into the creature's chest.

When Barnic spoke, his voice sounded as if the outcome were exactly what he'd expected, and no more. "What's ... your name, archer?" In truth, he was *elated,* but his joy had been stolen—Interrupted by what he saw upon the Nebelblut's death.

The guardsman was engulfed in a surge of white light, albeit for only an eye blink. When it passed, he stood, lifting and looking at first one hand, then the other with no apparent pain. He lifted the talwar in his bright hand, turning to wave his thanks up to Barnic and the archer. As he did, the sword crumbled, showering the man with what looked like snow or dust.

"Hob, Lord Eastshadow. I'm Hob of Third Well."

Barnic nodded to Hob, though he kept his eyes on the guardsman below. The snow, or whatever it was, had ceased. The runner shook his head, waved once more, then turned. He passed the goblin's body, returning to his mission—finding Captain Cadwyd and organizing the defense of the individual districts.

"That'ne's Ossie... er, Oswald, Lord. Mi'cousin."

Barnic nodded. "Also of Third Well?"

"Second, mi'lord. Mi'mum and his were twinses."

"When this is over, I'll want a word with you both. You're to be commended for that." He gestured out toward the goblin's corpse. He saw the guardsman—Oswald, apparently—slip past the gate into First Well. The wide wooden door slid closed behind him.

Good. A start, at least.

He turned to the archer. "Keep watch, Hob. I want no surprises from that direction. Speak before shooting, or at least *while* you're shooting. I mean to rely on you to report what you see in time for me to do something about it. Am I understood?"

Hob was grinning. "Aye, mi'lord. Every word. No fear."

Nodding, Barnic turned to see how Aethan was doing with the rest of the battle.

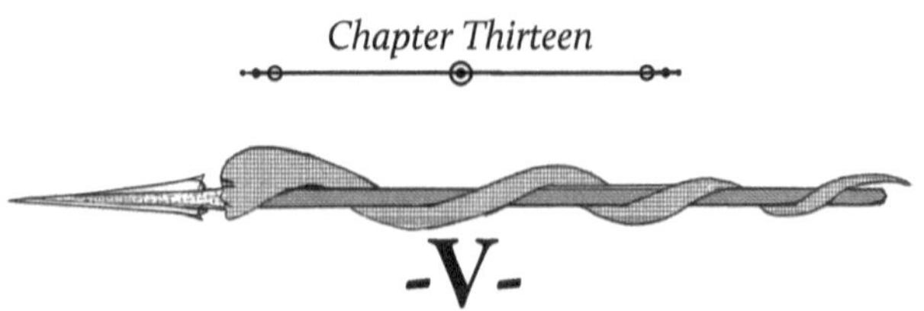

-V-

Lashjuk felt the carriage roll to a stop. Despite the roar of the victorious men—and presumably women—who had defended Jižní Lov, she caught the sound of the door opening above.

"Poslouchej mě! Poslouchej mě jižní meče!" Ebistian's voice cut through the cacophony like a knife in the dark. The gasps as the crowd hushed were astonished and fearful.

They expect him to tell them of a new threat on the come. Little do they know he is that threat. Lashjuk resisted the desire to roll out of her hiding place. It would be so simple to reach up and throttle the man ... and make that her dying act. No, there were too many hands holding too many weapons within striking distance. And they were all far more skilled than she.

"Count Edmund ... has been wounded."

Voices growled. Shouted negations. Some even wept openly.

"He *lives*—for now, at least—but he may not last long. He *cannot* last long if we do not get him care! Is the Lord Alojz still alive?"

You cozening shit. You know full well he isn't here, she thought, but did not say.

As if he'd heard her, the unfamiliar voice of a young man delivered this news that was not news. "He's not here, Lord!"

"Lord, he's been gone for *days* now!" An older man this time. She knew this one, didn't she? One of the men who... one of the men who'd come to camp the morning before they'd left? She thought so, but couldn't be sure. It hadn't been she who'd spoken with the boys' fathers, after all. They'd come on Eobum's request, to be roundly thanked for raising their sons to stand up and defend those weaker than they. She'd been torn as to whether or not she'd wanted to involve herself, even though it had been Maksu they'd stood by. In the end, she'd opted to leave the matter to Eobum.

Hells, had I begun to think of him as my partner, even back then? She realized she had, on some level. The realization was painful. The idea that they'd—that *she'd* wasted so much time...

Ebistian's voice snapped her mind back to the matter at hand.

"It is the Lord Alojz whom I serve. I am chief scholar to the house of Černook. I will do all that I can for Edmund, but I *must* get him to safety before some other calamity befalls this goodly place."

That called up a rumble of wary anger from the crowd.

"We must inform Lady Kastan!" said someone.

"Aye! She must be told!" said another.

"Hard as it is to hear on such a day, she'll want to be by her lord's side, yet we *need* her!"

After this third voice had offered up its wisdom, Ebistian spoke again.

"As my Lord Alojz Černook is the custodian of these lands, until he returns, or the count recovers, I shall assume command." This was met with a churning mixture of confusion and muted anger. With no clear voice to unite the crowd, Ebistian overrode their prattle with relative ease. "I go to His Excellency's command tent. There I shall render what help I may to Edmund the Tall. If *you* would help him?" He allowed a pregnant pause to hang in the air before speaking again. "Tend to your wounded, tend to the gate, and tend to the prisoners you've captured."

"What of Lady Kastan? Has she been wounded as well?"

"We will hope not," Ebistian's voice was starting to show a touch of pique, but it was unlikely to be noticed by the masses. "Make way now. Count Edmund needs rest and what healing arts can be brought to bear. Make way!"

Well, Kastan lives, or so they think. That's something. Kastan lives and Ebistian seemed to grow more annoyed with each mention of her name. Anything or anyone who annoyed that silver-tongued serpent was worth smiling about.

She felt the carriage moving once more. It veered left once it passed beyond the gate itself. She could see wooden stairs along the vehicle's left side. These led to the walkways that topped the wall. She'd been weighing out the idea of using those pathways as a means of moving around the encampment when she heard shouts of alarm.

The carriage came to an abrupt halt. With the sounds of crunched gravel, creaking wood, and armored horsemen no longer making her strain to hear, the shouts became audible, if not intelligible.

"Stormrider! Stormrider! The cloud! The Jarl! He's come back!" On and on, the crowd continued its fearful rant. She knew better than to simply dismiss such obvious fear, yet she had no way to make sense of it ... until she saw him.

Gi awka glem! Eobum! Eobum! How?

She nearly leapt out from her hiding place, ready to run to him. An instant later, her merciless eyes showed her the truth, and out went her new fire. Her sudden flare of hope and joy were gone.

Not Eobum. Of course, it's not Eobum. They could be kin, but no. Whoever this man is, he isn't my Eobum. Looking at him, she saw that his chest was broader. His hair was darker, too, and it sprouted from a scalp with a forest of scars on it. Questions of his heritage notwithstanding, the idea that Eobum would arrive either upon or within his own personal storm cloud was ... absurd.

Yet I speak with a size-changing serpent creature and traveled asleep upon its back.

Ebistian opened the door. His voice suggested that he was looking up at the new arrival. Lashjuk found that while this *Stormrider* had moved to a point where she could no longer see him directly, she could make out a vague shadow on the grey ground.

"You have lost," said Ebistian. "You may withdraw, or you... Can you not hear me?"

"The Jarl can hear you, Shepherd. What he *cannot* do is speak."

Ebistian's shadow held up a hand toward the Stormrider. It then turned toward where she judged Eliška to be. This was born out when the woman spoke up again, as if in response to a questioning look.

"He offended his Venzene masters when they raided Eoalun this year. They cut out his tongue, then bound him and rode their horses over his legs. All, of course, in an effort to teach him ... *a lesson.*" Eliška's voice was cold, making no attempt to hide her disgust.

"And they left his ears intact—the better to hear a world he could barely be a part of any more. Does he speak the Trade Tongue?" Ebistian's tone was one of unaffected surprise. Moreover, it displayed what sounded like genuine sadness.

She saw the Stormrider's shadow move in hand gestures, much of which blended into his overall form.

Ebistian shook his head. "Do you read?"

The Stormrider shook his own. He clenched his fist, then shook it at something below.

"T'lendak?"

"He speaks in the gnoerkish hand-tongue," said she. "I've never learned it."

"No... No, of course not, nor have I." His shadow shook its head. "Surely there's someone who can translate."

"His child." She drew in a sharp breath. "Ah... his child is dead."

Lashjuk saw the Stormrider's shadow lift a body not much larger than her Sulok's. *Why in all the hells did you bring a boy that age to a place you meant to turn into a killing field?* Life was hard, and the world dangerous. Bringing a child to a place where there *might* be danger was very different from bringing that same child to a place that was, by design, dangerous.

"Is the boy among your court now?"

"He is not," said Eliška. "He and his boy have been with us for too short a time for such. Yet the Jarl *is* chosen by the Storm Queen, Shepherd. If you would do her this service, she would consider it a boon to be repaid..."

Ebistian snorted. "This man has not been chosen by the *Storm Queen*, T'lendak. What manner of fool do you take me for? He and his boy were chosen by *you*. Your mistress had no part in it at all."

Eliška huffed, but said nothing.

The Stormrider shifted the limp body he held onto one arm, then pointed down. Then he drew his free hand along his own throat as if he meant to cut himself.

"*That* is who felled your child, Jarl?" Ebistian seemed to have forgotten the supposedly dire situation Edmund was in. His tone still held that sense of honest sympathy, which was difficult to listen to.

The Stormrider's shadow nodded.

"You would take your revenge?"

Again, the Stormrider nodded.

"And if I can give you more? If I can give you *justice* instead?"

The Stormrider appeared to draw back, his shadow growing smaller for a beat or two.

"Give them both to me, Jarl. I will restore your boy to you in full and in earnest. At your word, and within the hour, you will have him at your side again."

The Jarl's shadow turned to its right. Eliška spoke up. "He has this power, my brave Jarl. On *this* matter, I trust that he means what he says, and will bring your herald back to you."

"His *son*, T'lendak." Ebistian's voice was a snarl of disgust. "The boy may have duties to do for his father, just as any child does. But do not mistake duty for purpose." He returned to his earlier tone of sympathy as he addressed the man who could be Eobum's kin once more. "Will you allow me to do this for you?"

The Jarl nodded.

"And in return, you will do ... what you think best to repay me. I trust to your good will on that score."

"Wait, what? No! Shepherd, he is chosen, I say! Chosen by—"

"A small-minded T'lendak who thought to bring bloodshed into my land. Yes, I know."

"Yes, but the pact!"

"Is of either no consequence, or utter consequence—both of which serve my point far better than yours. Either the Jarl elects to stand with me or do me some small service in token of his gratitude for what I now do, or I am generous with what is rightfully mine as a part of the spoils of the battlefield. Terms to which *you agreed* not half a bell ago. Now, be silent."

Ebistian stepped from the coach, walking over to where the Jarl floated. He took first the dead child from his father, passing him gently up to the driver. He then took another child, one Lashjuk had seen before. As Ebistian carried him toward the waiting carriage, he woke. His voice was groggy, as if he still slept.

"Vhere... vhere are ve going, Lord?"

"To a place where your pain can best be seen to, child."

"I... I think I can valk, Lord. My head doesn't hurt quite so badly anymore."

"We will get you to the Count's command tent and see to your injuries." He entered the carriage. "For now, rest in comfort while you've the opportunity."

The door closed, the Stormrider floated upward on his cloud, and the carriage resumed what was left of its journey.

The crowd cheered as he withdrew, though there was a good deal of confusion within that cheer. It was confusion that Lashjuk shared, but that did nothing to improve her mood. Nothing was ever simple.

It wasn't enough that she had to rescue Maksu—potentially against his own will, no less. *No. Now I must rescue Andrej as well. Andrej or Vlk... whichever one that was. He stood between my Maksu and the Bluemark. I cannot repay that by abandoning him.*

Shaking her head, she waited. *But not for much longer.* She grinned, eyes slitted. *Not for much longer.*

-VI-

Vlk fell into a fitful doze as he was carried into the carriage. The next he knew, he felt warm sun on his bruised face, a perfect breeze ruffling his dark brown hair, and the urge to sneeze. This last had come from the altogether comforting scent of freshly cut oats. As he wrinkled his nose in an attempt to hold back the fit, he thought he'd caught the scents of apples and pears as well.

"You're not as subtle as you think you are, my young friend."

It was the voice of the man who was carrying him—a grandfather, if ever he'd seen one. Yet the fellow was strong, at least. Vlk tried not to smile, but found he couldn't help himself.

"Therrrrre we are. Just a little farther now."

Vlk turned his head away to sneeze at last. He managed it, despite the lurch his stomach took, but that wasn't the worst of it. When the sneeze was done, he cried out in a pain so profound that for a moment he couldn't get any air. When he tried to inhale, the stabbing pulse all across his skull seemed to rise a notch.

"Shhhh, shh-shh-shhhhh." His rescuer, surely, though the voice seemed far away.

"Vlk? Villk!" He heard a high-pitched growl calling his name in utter delight.

The man chuckled. "I take it you know the boy, Maksu."

Vlk felt himself lowered gently to a bed that was softer than spring grass. A small hand slipped into his, followed by a nervous squeeze. He returned it, tentatively at first, for fear that it or *any* motion might add to the *pum-pum-pum* of the wardrum that was his skull.

"He saved me, Father. When before? When I was still weak? Some of the Bluemark tried to hurt... and all of the other children backed away. They were afraid and scared that they'd get into trouble, or yelled at, or worse..." He squeezed Vlk's hand again. "Vlk and Andrej, though, they stepped in front of me, ready to fight the Bluemarks. Father??"

"Mmm?" The man sounded more amused than annoyed.

"Why do they wear black if they're the Bluemark? Shouldn't they be the Blackmark?"

This elicited a short, surprised laugh of what sounded like genuine amusement. "Some might think so, Maksu. But they call themselves that because they're each the children of some noble either past or present somewhere in the Empire."

"But then... then why aren't they living in castles with their fathers?" His voice grew small. "Or do their fathers not want them?"

The man—Maksu's father, apparently, though how that could possibly be was too great a task to tackle just now—answered through what sounded like a sad smile. "My clever boy. That's it exactly. They come from fathers who are either dead now, disgraced because they've done something wrong, or as you say, are foolish enough that they don't want their children around."

"Were they bad?"

"The fathers?"

"Noooo, Father." Maksu laughed. "The Bluemarks when they were small. Is *that* why their fathers don't want them?"

"Some of them, perhaps. But mostly I think that it's something else. Tell me, my clever boy, have you ever wanted more food than your belly could hold?"

"...Yes?"

"Have you ever wanted to stay up late, or have a late lay in even though you *know* you shouldn't? That if you don't get enough sleep you'll be tired all day, or if you lay in bed too long, you won't get all of your chores done and still have time to play?"

"Yes, Father..." Maksu sounded embarrassed, as if he'd been caught doing those very things just now.

"I think the fathers of the Bluemark are like that, but instead of being made to do what's *right*, they're privileged enough to simply do what they *want*."

"What...? I don't understand."

"The act of trying to make a baby is a joyful one, Maksu. It leaves a man breathless... leaves him feeling both proud and tired. If a man doesn't *want* a baby, he has another choice. He can simply perform that same act, and—should a baby come into the world—ignore it. He can choose to abandon it... pretend it doesn't exist. He can leave it and its mother to fend for themselves."

"That's... I don't like that, Father."

The man laughed. "No, I shouldn't think so. You're too wise and too loving a boy to *like* such a thing. Most of the time, the girl's family feels the same as you. They do their best to force the man to do right by the girl he's kindled. If that man is a *nobleman*... if he's someone very wealthy, the world has different rules for him. He *should* look after his child, if not the girl he made that child with. But if she's a commoner—if she has no wealth or power, as is so often the case..."

"She can't make him do... *anything*. Not if he's got more gold than she does. Father, I don't like that. Why do people let that... Why do people let the gold..." He growled, though it came out more of a chirrup. "I just don't like it."

"I don't like it either, Maksu..." Vlk was smiling in spite of himself. He still didn't trust opening his eyes, but the conversation and the fresh, clean feel of this place seemed to be calming the ache in his head.

Maksu made a strange noise that was somewhere between a squeal and a shout of *yay!* When it was over, Vlk felt a smallish body press into his, trying to hug him.

He laughed. He didn't know what else to do. "Vait, Maksu... Vait. Let me try and sit up."

"Careful, Vlk." Maksu's father sounded as if he were honestly concerned. "You've taken quite a beating."

He felt a hand that was far too large to be Maksu's slide beneath his back, helping to ease him into a sitting position. He drew in several deep breaths, then opened his eyes as gingerly as he could.

It was as his other senses had told him. He *was* sitting on a soft, wood-framed bed. That bed, however, was out under a hazy blue sky, and, yes, in the middle of a field of oats. He saw the old man smiling down at him with such a look of relief that Vlk could only smile back. To his right, Maksu bounced from foot to foot as if he needed to make water. His face was a mask of such excited joy that Vlk found himself laughing. Maksu joined in at once, then, unable to wait any longer, fell on Vlk. The embrace was powerful—almost too much so, despite the boy being a few years younger. When he'd finally had enough, pulling back to flash a toothy grin Vlk's way, he found his voice.

"I didn't think I'd see you again, Vlk. Not you, not Andrej, not..." He trailed off, bowing his head.

"Vell, you finally came home. I knew you vould at some point."

At that instant, he saw three things over Maksu's bowed head. One of them made him smile, one made him afraid, and the third made him think he was dreaming.

A castle loomed up in the middle distance, looking old and stately. The *stone* looked old, but the structure looked almost new, which was—as far as he knew—impossible. Stone tended to take ages to build, and while that construction was going on, the existing stonework was being beaten by wind and rain, snow and ice. Between where they sat on the strange, out-of-doors bed and the equally strange castle lay an orchard. He could see now what his nose had been literally itching to tell him—pears and apples a-plenty. His mouth began to water. When had he last eaten?

Directly behind Maksu was another bed. Upon it lay the prostrate form of Edmund the Tall—bloody, bandaged, and breathing as if in a deep and troubled sleep.

He'd drawn breath to cry out at the sight. True, Edmund was breathing, but not even Maksu's squealed shout had caused him to stir. A memory charged onto the stage of his mind's eye... a memory of the count flying out over the wall. It had happened moments after Laagi broke the counterweight device. Then came the image of Edmund's face after his own fall. That'd been ages ago...

No. It had been earlier *today!* Hells, had it only been a few hours? He shuddered at the realization.

I vas in Count Edmund's lap as I voke up. I'd been speaking vith... Vith Hroth and... and Baron Ay-something. He vanted to varn me, I think.

He froze, a chill skidding up his spine. At that moment, his eyes fell upon the door. It stood open against the backdrop of the fields and fruit trees, supported by... *nothing*. It was wide enough for even Edmund's broad shoulders to fit through. And while the room it revealed was dark and difficult to make out from here, that paled in comparison to its essential weirdness.

Maksu's *father* followed his gaze, then turned back with a somewhat less genuine smile on his thin lips.

"And *that* young Vlk, must remain our secret. We should arrive shor—"

A knocking sound issued from within the darkness of that un-door.

"Ah, we've arrived. Sau?" He raised his voice, calling to someone Vlk hadn't seen.

"Yes. I heard the knock, Seeker." An armored man walked over from somewhere behind Vlk. He gave Maksu's shoulder a little squeeze, then walked to where the count lay. As slender as the warrior was by comparison, he lifted Edmund with no more difficulty than Maksu's father had lifted Vlk. He then walked over to the un-door and stepped through it, disappearing into the dark.

"Come, Vlk. Maksu? Stay here, please."

"Father, please... I want to go with Vlk. I've hardly gotten to see him! Besides, I want to be there when the count wakes up! I *know* him. I met him in my camp place, and again when he came to stop the Bluemarks from doing more... um, bad things... Pleeeeease?"

The man bowed his head, smiling. "Alllllright. You may come with us, but you must remain *in the command tent* until you're told otherwise. Are we agreed?"

Maksu bounced with excitement. "Yes, Father! I promise!" He pulled Vlk's arm around his shoulders, helping him to stand.

Vlk didn't resist. He was glad of the help. "Vill the count be alright, Lord?" He and Maksu began walking with the old man toward the un-door.

"We shall hope so, young Vlk. We shall hope so. It would be sad to see him sacrificed unnecessarily. Count Edmund is a great man, loved by many."

Vlk stopped himself from nodding at that, but it was a near thing. The pain, he was quite sure, would've been enough to bring him to his knees. He settled for a grunt of agreement, instead.

A few beats later found him drawing in a deep breath, trying to calm his fear as he stepped through the un-door. He found himself in a large chamber with padded benches along one wall and a large stack of cushions sticking out of an open trunk along the other. Edmund was stretched across two of the benches.

Maksu's father opened and stepped through a door that, at first, Vlk hadn't seen. As the light from outside poured in, the gnoerk boy helped him toward the door.

Rather than letting him step down from the carriage on his own, the old man lifted Vlk, then lowered him to his feet. He looked back at Maksu, who jumped down on his own. Vlk saw no un-door—no sign of the land of oats and apple trees he'd just left.

"Come, children, inside. Quickly, now."

Maksu moved to prop Vlk up again, and the two of them led the way into Edmund's large marquee.

-VII-

The three of them sat in the small circle of lantern light. The others had been gone for long enough that their footfalls were now a distant echo.

Kastan drew a breath. She supposed she'd have to nudge Skar into speaking. Taking a moment to meet his eyes, she was surprised to find his sharp, almost accusatory gaze aimed toward Olga.

"How much have you explained to her? Not much, I would imagine, given her position was only announced what, an hour agone? Two?"

Olga shrugged one languid shoulder in reply, but said nothing.

"It's past time, wouldn't you agree?"

"I..."

Kastan broke in. "If you insist on speaking about me as if I weren't sat beside you..."

"Lady, forgive me. It helps to know where to begin. What you've already been told. Little to nothing, apparently. That means you'll have no context to frame things if I speak too swiftly."

Kastan looked first to Olga, then back to Skar. The former was scowling down at her lap, while the latter appeared to be collecting his thoughts.

"I'll skip ahead where I can. Let me come at this from the side."

She offered him a cautious nod.

"How old is the Empire, Lady?"

Olga snorted, which made a certain amount of sense. Skar was indeed coming at the issue from the side. It was rather like answering the question, *where is so and so from* by asking, *do you know how children come into the world?*

"Are we speaking of the First Alliance, the Unification, or the Dawn of the All Crown?" Kastan tried to make her voice confer neutrality, but wasn't certain she'd succeeded.

"Let's go as far back as you can recall from your lessons."

Kastan sighed, but let her frustration with the line of discussion pass... for the moment. She reminded herself that this man hadn't struck her as someone to waste time or mince words. Looking up at nothing in particular, she spoke as if reciting the words to a half-remembered song or poem.

"The founding of the First Alliance came from a fertile mind. A sword-seeker once a sea slayer. First father of Havalun—*Ogmundr Runesmoen*—fleet and fierce. He sailed the sea of heroes for to seek true steel. Elven train-ed, Elven trade—Dirden taught and temper-ed all." She paused, gauging Skar's reaction. "That was... eight hundred years agone? Nine?"

Skar made a gesture of acceptance. "And before that?" He bore her look of confusion for a few beats, then tried again. "What was there—*who* was there on these lands before Ogmundr sailed west?"

She looked at Olga, then back, shrugging. "Tribesmen, I expect."

"Until Ogmundr brought the first alliance to these *tribes* and ushered them out of the dark. Until he, and later his son Knud helped forge them into what would become Kovalun."

She made a *there you have it* gesture. "Aye, with the help of what they'd learned from the elves of Are Dirden—metal shaping, swordcraft, and so on." She resisted the urge to add, *can we get on with this, please?*

"I see your impatience. We're nearly to it, Lady. How much do you know of stonework?"

Olga lifted her hands, then dropped them to her thighs with an audible slap. She accompanied this with a long-suffering sigh, and an exaggerated look to the high ceiling. Skar ignored her, focusing on Kastan's face as she spoke.

"Let's say... nothing. I know where to purchase it, what questions to ask before hiring someone to tend or repair it, and so on. Not much beyond that."

"How old is this chamber? These catacombs?"

She laughed. "Perhaps ten years? Perhaps as many as twelve? Edmund had it built after his border war, and before the rebellion. This is common knowledge, Skar."

"But you've hired men to work for your estate, and your fathers, yes?"

She nodded. "Of course, but—"

"And what is the largest thing you've had built from first stone to full structure?"

She was getting annoyed now. "A defensive wall around my brother's manor. It replaced the wooden palisade that had fallen into disrepair. Now what does this have—"

"How long did it take you?"

"That's quite enough, Sergeant," Olga cut in. "We're grateful for your aid, but you've no call to be rude to her Excellency. She isn't your ever-more-tattling sister. She is—"

"In need of haste and answers. Answers which neither you nor your fellows have as yet provided, *scholar.*" He all but spat the word, then turned his attention back to Kastan. "Lady?"

Kastan was too taken aback by the exchange to do more than look between them for a few beats. *What is it you've yet to tell me, Olga?* This was all in relation to the dead—the once-men, and the danger they represented. The idea that Olga knew or had known something about them was difficult to fathom. At length, she turned fully back to Skar and gave him his answer.

"Once the necessary people had arrived? Not quite three years. Percoy is too far away to haul stone from Bialy Klif. We could've managed the distance, but there are no roads that run the route. We wound up having to pull from the Červenávýška quarry. Expensive, but faster than crossing rough country and ducal borders."

"So call it three years. Three years to build a *stone wall,* mind you." He cast about, then looked back with his brows arched.

She took his point at once. "So then... hells, he couldn't have built the catacombs in *twenty* years. Jižní Lov is home to ... what?" She looked to Olga. "Nearly five hundred souls? All of whom have housing in the undertown? And some of *that* is grand enough to be two, sometimes three levels below ground?"

Olga nodded, though she looked as if she'd done so against her better judgement.

"This place, Lady... This very place predates the All Crown. It predates the *Unification.*"

She wanted to scoff. In fact, she'd drawn breath to do that very thing when the look in his eyes drew her up short. "How? You're telling me that the undertown is older than Venzene itself? How?"

"*That...* is the correct question, Lady. The peoples who ruled here before had grown far wiser than we. Yet for all that they built—all that they achieved and understood—they were undone. They were unable to hold back the tide. And so their great works were cast down, destroyed, or buried beneath the cold ground."

"I... I don't understand you, Skar."

"What do you know about Havoc's Horn?"

She sighed, trying to collect her thoughts. Her pulse was racing. She had no idea why that should be, but that changed nothing. "We say it in a fit of surprise or pique. It's an expression used for everything from barking your shin to losing at trefning—no different from *hells*. And *that's* just a shortened version of *hells be hid* or *hells haul them home*."

"That's all you recall?"

She nodded, then cocked her head to one side. "I think so?"

"*Scholar?* Will *you?*"

When Olga made no reply, he shook his head and spoke on.

"Long lay the land, dozing in the darkless day. Leave the last dream. Loose the last dawn." He held Kastan's gaze for several beats as if looking for recognition. At length, he spoke on.

"Woe wounds the world. Time's taste, a dying man's tears. Weep now. Waste time. War now wastes truth."

Kastan felt her eyes grow wide. She *did* know this. The memory had been gathering dust, forgotten in a corner of her mind, but yes. She knew it. It had been from a slim volume of old alliterative poetry her mother had possessed. As Skar now voyaged on the next quatrain, she found herself joining her voice to his.

"While well still waits, Herald, wind now Havoc's horn. Wake the world's halls. Warn the world's hands."

She'd read every book she could when she'd been small. After Klara had passed, it had been down to her to select something fitting to read aloud at the farewell service. Though a more appropriate piece had been selected in the end, she'd all but wallowed in the words of that final quatrain for several days.

"The folk who built this place... who ruled these lands before us..."

"Truly sergeant? *That* is what you've been stumbling toward? *That* is your grand and vital context? That is what her Excellency so desperately needed to understand?" Olga laughed. The sound was full not just of mockery, but relief. "I commend you that you have learned to read despite your station. I only wish you had used that learning for something more useful—something that actually *mattered*."

Skar's expression was nonplussed.

"Mistress?" Kastan felt her own dark cloud lifted by the sound of Olga's laughter. Still, something in Skar's eyes held her own relief in abeyance.

Olga stood, shaking her head as her laughter died away. "Excellency..." She loosed an involuntary chuckle. "The rise of groups of the unquiet dead is a rare, but well-documented thing. It comes from blights, or from curses. Yet the Sergeant sees the very *End Times* upon us!"

"There isn't a good deal of room for doubt, *scholar*. No fear if you elect not to believe me. Your belief isn't a requirement for the Storm Queen to sweep across the land."

More laughter. "The Storm Queen, is it?"

"Who is—"

"Oh, Excellency," Olga continued, already mid-answer. "The dreaded Storm Queen was a figure that comes to us out of antiquity. She was, according to Eoalunth oral tradition, a... Now let me see if I have this... a Norok Veretis? Something like that. She attacked with her rabble and caused no end of trouble for the scattered tribes of what is now central and northern Venzene."

"Norokh Verekys." Kastan made Norokh rhyme with *lock,* and Verekys with *miss.* To her mind, *Miss* was exactly what she felt Olga's example had done. "It means great gathering of captains or war chieftains."

Olga sighed, shaking her head.. "What matters is that, while *yes,* there is mention of her in the archives, that mention only speaks of her in passages which read more like cradle tales than chronicles of history."

"You admit that you know exactly who and what I'm speaking of. Yet you continue to waste time deriding my every word?" Skar's voice was calm—a fact which leant him an air of danger. He still sat, as did Kastan. And the language of his body showed more confusion than frustration, but still...

He's coiled, somehow. His body tells no such tale, yet he feels—there's no better word for it—coiled.

"Of *course* I do!" Olga paced, shaking her head as she chuckled. "Every region has its monsters and shadow shakers, my young friend. Shesh has the Sharpened Shadow. The dwarves, if you can find any willing to blather about it, have the Golden One—a man who supposedly stopped the sun's heart, whatever that is. Hells, the first folk of Thorion supposedly have a legend about a being called the God Eater. Are *they* awakening and riding to destroy Jižní Lov as well?"

Skar's face went blank by degrees as she ranted on. When it was over, he allowed the silence to hang in the air until the echo of Olga's voice had well and truly faded. When he spoke at last, his voice had taken on the implacable tone which Olga had abandoned not long back up the hourglass.

"Listen to me, scholar. I will say this, and then I will say no more. I have seen the Storm Queen's champion. He is above, leading the attack even now. He rides—physically rides—on a storm cloud. I saw him with my own two eyes. Saw him draw the storm from the sky and hurl it down to call the dead. Knowing what that ragged cloud meant… knowing what it would *do,* I ran in after it. And I was *right* to run after it, as you see."

He turned back to Kastan, addressing himself to her alone, though his voice remained at the same volume.

"I have trained to do battle with these things since I first picked up a sword, Lady. My Lord Azhferd has no part of it and knows nothing of it. Had there been need—an encounter of some sort, perhaps… But there has never been such. Not in all of my time in his service. And we who serve in love? We do all that we can to spare those *whom* we serve. We intercept pain and trouble so that they never need know of it. When trouble confronts those same folk, as it has here…" He shook his head.

Kastan considered. The man was clearly in earnest, regardless of whether he were friend or fool. *And can I truly ignore any explanation at this point? Given all that I've seen?* She didn't think so, Olga's derision be damned.

"Tell me the plainest part of your drift. What is it you mean to suggest we do, Sergeant?"

"Aye, Lady. I tell you as it was told to me. When we have grown too bold, and too learn-ed for his liking, the Storm Queen's master will wake. His court—the Storm Queen among them—will take the field and wage war against the world itself. Then Havoc's Horn will sound. The sky will *race to red,* the *rain will fall on friend and foe alike,* and he will *know the world once more.* Then, Lady, all things end."

She stared through him for a long moment, considering. At length, she nodded. "Is there more? Or is your tale told?" She did her best to use the voice she'd developed for matters of court and formal occasions. It was a tone of open neutrality, with as little implication hidden behind it as she could manage.

"That's the meat of it, Lady. I'm no scholar, blessedly. But that's as much as I understand, and as plain as I can put it." He held her gaze for a moment longer, then made as if to stand. "For my part, I'm leaving this place while I can. I would see you and those you lead escape with me. If you wish to go your own way, I cannot and will not stop you. I've my own duties, after all."

Kastan didn't know how to respond. She was left with so many questions, yet none of them mattered just now. What *did* matter was whether she believed Skar or Olga.

Skar saved my life and Andrej's. He saved them all. He speaks what sounds to me like paranoid madness, or at least it would have, had I not already fought the once-men... had I not already seen his knowledge in action. Yet Olga hasn't led me astray thus far. She knows more than I in most, if not all, matters save warfare. And Olga is loyal to Edmund—and, by extension, to me. Skar saved our lives physically, yet Olga is trying to save the entire county.

She'd all but made up her mind. Standing, she walked to the center of the room, facing them both. She took a breath, held it for a beat, then released it.

"You *did* try, my love. That's surely worth ... something."

Radek lumbered to his feet. His voice was jagged and raw as if he were suffering from a sore throat. Turning from Olga with that same unnatural speed, he addressed himself to Kastan.

"Excellency? You'll have to forgive me. I fear I've failed to prepare you for all of this. But you see, everything has been accelerated. There simply wasn't enough time." His skin was growing paler by the beat, beginning to swirl in that familiar moon-kissed blue and liquid shadow cast. His eyes were full of an unnatural darkness above his predator's grin. "And now, of course... I have other duties..."

CHAPTER FOURTEEN

A PROCESSION OF LAST GASPS

-I-

County Thorion
Eastshadow
5 Korunasykli: 22 Days after the Red Storm at Westsong

Barnic's breath smoked as he stalked along the alure of his grand palisade. He was doing his best to both understand the battle-field and give encouragement to his men. In truth, though, it seemed as if they were far calmer than he.

Most of them have lived here their entire lives, he reminded himself. *Their fathers and their father's fathers have faced these creatures and the Shivering Song since time was first tallied.*

Still, this attack was larger in scale than any in living memory, and by a goodly amount, based on what he'd been given to understand. The fact that his men's courage was *holding* spoke well of them.

It says a great deal about Sir Cedric's legacy as well, rest him. He'd be proud, I've no doubt.

More than a few of Eastshadow's archers had taken wounds from goblin arrows, but they'd been shoulder and leg strikes. The bulk of those wounded men were now in the courtyard below, bracing the gate. Others were acting as a second set of eyes on the walls.

The enemy surrounded them on three sides. They were focused on bow work, which itself was no great surprise. Their particular *tactic* was another matter. Goblin archers would disappear into the grasses as if they'd plunged beneath dark water. Then they'd pop up and fire from some other part of the battlefield. That grass was only knee-high in most places. How they hid at all was a damned mystery. What was more, even their footmen played this deadly game. They would leap out of concealment once a Nebelblut archer began shooting. Then they'd act as living bulwarks to absorb most incoming arrows. The monstrous things were *sacrificing* themselves to protect their bowmen.

At least that's a tactic they can't use along Seven Gate itself. The road's little more than beaten earth... barely a patch of grass taller than my ankle. So that's all to the good.

He'd actually begun to smile when it clicked at last. *Only why haven't they pressed a proper attack yet? They have enough bodies to assault at least one other well, but...*

He glanced at where Hob maintained his vigil over the south. The man swung his leather-clad head from left to right, keeping watch over the rest of Eastshadow's districts. His bow was nocked, but otherwise unbent. *So all's still as well as may be on that side. Then what are they—*

"Down!" Aethan slammed his pauldron-clad shoulder into Barnic's unarmored chest. He fell backward, staggering and winded. The impact forced the sword from his hand. It clattered on the boards a few steps away. Arrows split the air not far from where he'd just stood. He could hear other volleys ripping their way up over the walls.

An arrow *thumped* just behind him. He heard it strike Aethan's heater shield. This was followed instantly by a second, then a third.

Barnic managed to recover his balance. He kept himself in something of a crouch as he turned around to face his brother knight. Aethan was bent at the waist and seemed to loom over him in a half-crouch of his own. His outsized heater shield covered them both from above. Its edge was braced atop the wall—an old trick that let its wielder conserve some of his strength and endurance.

Barnic met Aethan's eyes, shot a meaningful glance to the shield, and grinned up at him. "If a foe won't fall quickly, ration your fatigue..."

Aethan joined in, finishing Valad's proverb with him. "...And settle in for a siege."

They both laughed. The sound was bright and brave against the dark. That laughter died long before it could peter out, for there were shouts of alarm, rage, and fear from all directions.

Aethan cursed. "They're on the walls! Swords! Swords!"

Barnic echoed the call, scrambling backward and trying to get to his feet, to no avail. A hand gripped his bright shoulder and *squeezed*. The sensation was a mixture of raw heat and bitter cold. It reminded him of frosty autumn mornings when he'd been out splitting wood. His hands would scream and throb as the impact of the maul shot through the wooden handle. Now *he* was about to scream as the creature's many-jointed fingers dug into his shoulder.

The Nebelblut pressed him forward onto his knees. It was a short, squat creature, even by goblin standards. Yet with him knee-bound, it seemed to tower over him from behind. The stench was enough to make him dizzy, but the pain blazed through the sensation like midday sun through a winter's haze. A serrated dagger, long and wicked looking, was clenched in its other hand. As it redoubled its efforts to keep him on his knees, the goblin flipped the weapon, inverting its blade.

Barnic struggled, reaching for the sword he'd dropped. No good. He saw Aethan contending with another of the damnable things some feet away. Hob wasn't far beyond him. His bow was bent, aimed directly at...

Barnic reached up and punched the goblin in his open, drooling maw. The wave of disgust was instant, but he was able to choke it down. The *pain* on the other hand... For a moment, he thought he'd broken his hand—possibly his wrist. It had been like punching a mossy, wet tree.

The Nebelblut reeled back, too stunned by the unexpected blow to bite down. Hob's arrow screamed through the air. His shot missed his lord by inches, taking the goblin in its shoulder. The dagger fell from its many-jointed fingers as it tried to recover from both punch and pin. The Lord of Eastshadow caught the oversized poniard in his dim hand. He had a moment to register that the weapon's wooden hilt was both uneven and tacky to the touch before he rammed it home, punching it through the beast's chest. It stiffened, shook, then fell at his feet.

Standing, he rushed over to Aethan, now engaged with two of the monsters. The goblin had the right idea as far as the weapon was concerned. He transferred the dagger to his other hand and held it inverted. Again he registered that light stickiness, but never mind. As he ran, he gave a curt nod to Hob.

The nearest Nebelblut had heard his hurried footsteps and was turning. It was markedly taller than his last foe, despite its strange, almost servile hunch forward. The thing held an axe in its hand—an unexpected weapon for such a creature, somehow.

No good, my friend, he thought as he took the final steps into range. The axe was cocked back as its wielder readied a hammer shot. Dangerous if it landed, but Barnic beat the strike with ease. He lifted his dim hand, ramming his forearm into the goblin's in order to foul the blow. As he did, he growled, "East-*shadow!*" and slammed his stolen blade directly into the thing's right eye.

It opened its horror-show mouth as if to scream, but nothing came out. It twitched, then went limp, collapsing at his feet. He felt a brief chill pass through him and resisted the urge to shudder. There was *work* here. The goblins weren't likely to stop so he could fetch a cloak or some mulled ale.

Aethan dispatched his own sparring partner, forcing him to fall out beyond the parapet. He made no sound as he fell, but the muted *thud* as he impacted was something, at least.

As his brother knight turned to face him, Barnic grinned and held up his borrowed dagger. He'd meant to offer a brief salute with it, but the weapon puffed out of existence. His hand was full of a flaking substance, like ash and wood shavings.

He looked at his hand, then up at Aethan—and fell back. Aethan's amber eyes had gone wide and wild. He'd begun to shout an inarticulate mixture of fear and force as he first stepped back, then charged past Barnic. They collided for a second time as Aethan raced by. This time, the impact nearly knocked the Lord of Eastshadow over his own damned walls.

Reclaiming his balance, Barnic turned and saw a Nebelblut as tall as he was. It stood far straighter than the other goblins and held a posture of delighted calm. As Aethan came within range, the creature dropped down, kicking a leg out to sweep Aethan's own. The maneuver took the knight's feet right out from under him. He fell first onto the alure, then Skolf's pull dragged him onto the wooden stairs that led into the courtyard.

The goblin produced a short spear between blinks and brought it up over his head as he prepared to end Aethan's life. Barnic saw his sword still on the boards where it had fallen.

If I waste time bending to grab it...

A weathered face appeared over the tall goblin's shoulder. It was the loutish sergeant Jastar'd needed to lay low back up the hourglass. The fellow opened his mouth in a mostly toothless snarl as he reached up to grab the spear haft.

Eastshadow's lord had a single, burning thought. *That'll do!*

He snatched up his fallen sword and raced toward the goblin. The creature leaned its chin forward, then cracked the back of its grotesque head into the sergeant's face. The man roared, instinctively releasing the spear haft and grabbing for his pulped nose.

Barnic screamed a wordless battle cry as he drew near. He cocked back his sword, readying a hard flat snap, but he knew he'd be too late. And he was right. The goblin *did* bring the spear down. He arced it past the right side of his own body, stabbing behind him and impaling the sergeant.

Barnic's heart swelled. *I can save Aethan! I can save him!*

Later, assuming he lived, he would reexamine how quickly he'd been willing to ignore the ugly truth—that one of his men had all but sacrificed himself so that Aethan could be saved. But that was for later. Now, he would make the Nebelblut...

All of his power went into that flat snap, lunging his body past the beast to drive the strike. He connected and was blinded for a beat by an eye-searing white light. It was like the sun reflecting on ice. He felt the impact of the blade's collision, but there was something wrong. When his eyes adjusted, he finally realized what that something was.

His sword *had* connected. It was now held by its blade in a massive blue fist. The goblin was gone. In its place was a creature of impossible size. Its skin had taken on a dark, slate-blue cast. Every muscle was on display. It must have been more than eight feet from toe to top, with a chest like a shield wall. It looked at Barnic with a face that showed far too much intelligence for such a brutish body and smiled.

Barnic *gaped.* He didn't know what else to do. He felt himself stepping backward, though he'd made—*could* make no conscious decision to move. He knew he should do something. This devil-thing had to be stopped, but the creature's presence was a thing of utter awe.

The hellish thing began forcing the weapon down with slow, deliberate pressure. Another of Barnic's men shouted, "Deee-monnn!" as he charged, sword held high.

That man is dead, he thought, though that thought was little more than a distant whisper.

The blue giant raised his left hand—the one that *wasn't* putting pressure on Barnic's sword—and made a fist. As his fingers clenched, a dagger appeared at the end of that fist.

A katar... a punch dagger. Once more, his mind cared nothing for his emotional state. Anger, fear, sadness, joy—it made no difference. It would define and categorize whatever he encountered, and that was that.

He tried to pull his sword away, but his muscles didn't want to obey. They compromised in a half-hearted tugging motion that accomplished nothing. Still meeting his dark eyes with its yellow ones, the monster twisted at the waist. It threw a left cross to strike the shouting, charging man as he came into range over its right shoulder.

I could strike now... Its body's out of position. The monster wouldn't be able to defend itself. I should...I should do that. I—

But it was too late. Barnic's mind had been too slow—too sluggish to get his own body to react.

The creature was once more suffused with that snowy glare, and when it had passed, the horror had changed again. Gone was the slate blue alien flesh. In its place stood a creature with skin of deepest gold. It had lost some of its height and much of its breadth, though it cut a formidable enough figure just the same. It still managed to tower over him by more than a foot. Its face had changed into something nearer to human, as well. Where once there had been two thin slits between its eyes and oversized mouth, it now bore a smallish, straight nose with wide nostrils. The creature looked almost *regal,* as if it had been created for the sole purpose of sitting in judgement.

"Therrrrrre." It didn't speak... it *purred.* Its baritone voice was melodious, sounding as if it had come from a place of deep satisfaction. "Nowww, Parindoon ki gandagi... *Now* we have a chance..."

It talks! It doesn't have some childish, half-animal mind. It speaks! It speaks ... in the Trade Tongue!

He'd heard that phrase before, he realized. But why did he associate it with children, or inn rooms full of smoke and spice?

The golden creature gave him no more time to think. A sense of cold so deep and sudden it burned raced up his bright hand. He dropped the sword he'd held with loose fingers, yelping. The unnatural thing before him reached its left hand out, splaying its fingers as if about to wave at someone a goodly distance away.

"This is a gift, Parindoon ki gandagi." His hand glowed... *glowed!* A warm, golden light grew, then leapt from his open palm, striking the roof of Eastshadow's great hall. Flames erupted from the building. They bathed the world in an awful orange light.

Then came the screams.

Barnic wanted to shout as well, but he had no voice. He simply stared at the fire, thinking of the women and children of the grand palisade who'd fled into that hall for protection. All at once, he realized that he was likely hearing those same women and children as they added their screams to the music of the battlefield.

Movement caught his eye. He turned back toward the golden devil.

It now held a talwar in its bright hand, much like the one Oswald wound up wielding. This weapon, however, had a faint golden glow rippling off its edge.

The ... whatever it now was ... gave him a craving look that vacillated between lust and hunger. It placed the curved sword's single edge up under Barnic's chin, yellow eyes dancing. "Better you serve a useful purpose before the Face of Endings casts—"

The inhuman *thing* let loose a cry of enormous pain. Barnic felt a frigid line drawn across his senses as the blade scraped the skin beneath his jaw. He stepped back—stumbled back, in fact. He all but slipped over the edge and down into his courtyard.

Wait... why *hadn't* he?

Looking down, he saw that his foot had slipped onto an outsized heater shield balanced atop one of the deep-set stairs—Aethan's! He saw droplets of blood falling onto its surface, looking like red rain. With a start, he realized it was *his* blood.

So the talwar broke the skin after all.

Aethan had eschewed his shield, leaving it on the stair behind him. He now knelt with his sword at not-quite-full extension, rammed up and into the golden thing's groin. For an instant, Barnic could only stare. Then he snapped out of his torpor and reached for the thing's slackening bright hand. It turned to him, eyes wide with wounded betrayal, of all things. It fought not to lose its weapon, but the effort only added to the agony of Aethan's fatal strike.

Barnic prised the talwar loose, stepped back, and...

The sky, cloudless a moment ago, flashed red. Thunder roared overhead, heralding a sudden downpour. Barnic had a moment of heart-stopping horror. Three words took up residence in his mind, trying to force their way onto his lips.

The red storm... The red storm... The red storm! The red—

With an effort, he forced his mouth to remain closed. Forced his mind to clear. He had no time to panic. There were enemies on his walls, his hall was burning, and there was a sword in his hand. The monster before him was responsible for the killing of his men and for setting his hall ablaze.

He tightened his grip on the weapon's warm wooden hilt. There was a brief sensation of pain along his palm, followed by a feeling of utter *rightness* as he prepared to mete out punishment. It conjured a small and satisfied smile onto his face, sharpening his features in the mingle of star and firelight.

The creature met his eyes. It drew a ragged, blood-choked breath as if it meant to speak, but he gave it no time.

"This ... is a gift," he growled and sliced at the thing's golden throat. To his surprise, his back cut bit deep enough that it almost took the monster's head.

The Lord of Eastshadow drew his sword arm back, moved as if to help his brother knight up ... and froze. Pale strength flowed into him with such force that he cried aloud. He felt himself shudder, his senses sharpening. He thought, for a moment, that he was *floating*, for the alure seemed to be retreating from him.

Aethan was calling his name from somewhere, but the sound of ripping and stretching in his ears made it difficult to focus. He *anticipated* pain, but none came.

When it was over, he looked around, then down at his bright hand. As expected, the sword disappeared, leaving only ash and wood shavings in its place.

"Barni? Barni what in all the hells?"

He looked at Aethan, feeling every drop of the rain strike him. Why was the man kneeling? *No wait... He's not kneeling. He looks... smaller, somehow.*

He shook his head, trying to bring his focus back. He inhaled, held it for a beat, then spoke. "We have to see to the fire, brother. We cannot rely on the rain, though it'll help." He stopped, cocking his head to one side. Was his voice different?

"They're fleeing!" someone shouted. "We've won! We *beat* the bastards!"

Barnic looked out over the wall and saw it was so. Goblin bodies lie around the palisade, both on the walls and out before them.

"Barni, I..."

Barnic turned back to regard his former squire brother. The man still looked overawed. *So—a task he can be set upon then.*

"Aethan, the fire—get it put out. Get the women and children out! The rest can wait. Now *to it!*"

Aethan shuddered, then bowed formally. "Yes, my ord!" And with that, he turned to his task.

Nothing about this makes sense. None of it. Least of all the fact that I'm calm again. Lives are still at stake, and the Nebelblut might well come back for their dead, if nothing else.

There was always more—always another problem, another battle, another horror.

He shook his head, feeling a grin curl its way onto his face. "You were right, Excellency. Westsong *was* only the beginning."

-II-

County Thorion
Wick

Olshnak had known the truth fully a dozen strides away from the cursed cart. Given time and labor enough, he could empty it, and—with the right tools—remove and replace the snapped axle. There was just one problem.

I do not have the time, the labor, or the tools.

"Olshnak?"

He grunted acknowledgement, then held up a hand to silence Tomet. He needed to do what his guards could not—think.

Can we move it at all? Possibly? If Tomet and Jek worked one end, and the ox hauled on the other...

An arrow fell to the ground a few strides to his left. It skidded along the cobblestones, making a scraping sound that didn't seem quite right to his ear. Turning, he walked toward it.

As he moved, he glanced at Wick's lord. Ricgerd was engaged north-ward along the town's main road. His booming voice seemed like an endless repetition of *come on!* and *follow me!* He was neither inspiring, nor much of a tactical leader.

And now I'm an expert tactician, am I? Surely there are times where the correct decision is to just attack...

He shook his head, bending to retrieve the arrow. *Bone? No. Wood, I'm almost sure. It's been made well—wood scraped and sanded until it has a texture Like animal bone. Odd, but impressive.* He noted a tacky, dark stain on the outside of the arrow's notch. *Blood? That or something like it.*

Cutting through both his musings and the battle blather Lord Ricgerd was spewing, he heard a sound like a dagger being scraped along a whetstone. At first, he ignored it, trying to solve the riddle of the false bone arrow. Then he became aware of a darker, lower stench assailing his nose.

That's either the-sickest-dog-that-ever-was shitting on the cobbles out of pure panic, or we need to move. More of them are coming up from the sewers, and nearby.

"Olshnak?" Jek this time. Something in his voice sounded off.

The silver-haired gnoerk turned, meaning to ask what was wrong, but there was no need. What looked to be little more than a goblin child stood beyond Jek and Tomet.

Well, that explains the reek. Where he'd come from was a question Olshnak didn't have time to contemplate just now. The creature held a spear every inch of nine feet in length, with a haft as thick as the gnoerk's wrist. The juxtaposition—small goblin and long spear—would've been comical, were it not for Tomet standing skewered at the spear's end.

In the ordinary course, this wouldn't have bothered Olshnak any more than it would Tomet. His guards found most weapons about as effective against them as a child swinging a half-full sack of dry washing around. It was an annoyance and could irritate if it struck. Hells, it might even force a body to move a step or two. But it would do no lasting harm.

Yet something *was* wrong. The look on both of their faces made that plain.

"Don't stand there like a pair of lemons. Kill the damned thing!"

Neither of them moved. An instant later, Olshnak saw why.

A shudder of autumn-colored light flowed from Tomet, up the spear's haft, and into the goblin. It didn't last long—no more than the time it took to register both color and movement. Then came a brief, blinding flare of starlight. When it was gone, so was the horrid goblin-creature. In its place, a vast, blue monster stood wearing an expression of greedy awe. It looked as if it had been carved out of stone.

Ahnsiblundeek gi! (Moon warden's blood.) Olshnak fought the desire to cry out, more out of shock than terror. He looked the alien devil up, then down, assessing.

Well, if I make it indoors, at least that thing can't follow. Its head's too tall, and its chest too broad to clear damn near any entrance in Wick!

The spear was gone. The beast looked at one massive hand, then the other, then leered ... at Jek.

It was then Olshnak saw Tomet. He stood as stone in the shifting light. His stance was unchanged—knees bent to absorb the impact of a heavy spear thrust that would never come.

"Olshnak? Where did Tomet go?" Jek's tone came out hollow and haunted. His voice remained in that same limited scale of notes, yet he sounded almost as if he were on the edge of tears.

If only he knew how to summon them. That was absurd. Nor did it much matter.

"Kill the damned thing, Jek! Kill it now!"

But Jek didn't move to attack. He reached out a hand to touch Tomet and watched as he turned to dust. His mail coat, helm, and other gear clattered to the floor. The sound of arrows roared over Wick, men, women, and children screaming in fear or battle lust, and the slate-skinned demon laughed. No sound came out, but his head was thrown back in unmistakable laughter.

Olshnak stepped to Jek's back, reaching to pull the guard's sword from its sheath. Jek did not object. He merely stared at the pile of ash where Tomet had lately stood.

Once he'd managed to get the weapon clear, Olshnak turned to face the creature. It was still laughing. Apparently, it either hadn't heard him draw the arming sword or considered neither he nor it a threat.

He saw movement off to his left, behind the blue bastard's shoulder. *Wrong coloration for a goblin. I saw blue, but it was too short to be another of these damned things.* Making up his mind, Olshnak stepped to his right, spreading his feet apart and making himself a target.

A brown-skinned figure leapt up behind the monstrous thing's right shoulder, a short blade cocked back over his own. As Skolf began to assert its pull again, the newcomer delivered a near-perfect flat snap to the cackling creature's throat. Its eyes flew wide as it crashed to its knees. Yet it clearly still lived.

Hells haul me home, Olshnak thought, and stepped forward as he brought a hammer shot down onto the demon's face. The blow drew a strange sort of dark amber blood, but the thing clearly still lived. Its yellow eyes looked up at him with wide incomprehension and—he'd have sworn to it—betrayal.

He threw two more hammers at the beast's head, linked by a mühlchen for added power. After that, the massive thing collapsed into a lumpy, blue hillock and moved no more.

Huron rose from his crouch behind the fallen beast. He looked down at it, then turned his honey-haired head to look up at Olshnak.

"Young, brave, and eager for the grave, boy." Olshnak offered a thin grin. "Sir Kaith teach you that?" He shook his head. "Never mind. Tell me later. You've my thanks. Now, where are we bound?"

Huron's brown skin had gone ashy, but his gaze was steady. He nodded. "Sign of the Boar and Bottle. Two lanes north, on the left. I'm for Sir's Kaith, Gordan, and ... the other one."

"Raegus," Olshnak said, nodding. "Here." He reached down to pluck up Tomet's sword belt. "Best to have a spare. If we fight in the open, you'll want a proper arming sword." He could say more, but this wasn't the time.

Huron nodded, taking the belt and throwing it over one shoulder like a baldric. "Boar and Bottle."

"Boar and Bottle. Aye."

With that, Huron ran off to the east. Olshnak took a moment to remove his belt, then slip Tomet's mail shirt over his head. It fit well enough. Certainly, it was better than the cloth gambeson he wore. That garment sufficed as padding, now, which was something.

He fastened his belt, then recovered Jek's sword and a small pendant on a leather cord that he'd sifted from the ashes.

"Come on. We need to go."

Jek didn't respond. Olshnak realized he hadn't moved since Tomet's ... death? End? How did one describe what'd happened to him?

"Jek... *now*."

"Where is Tomet? Olshnak, he's gone. There's no sign or sense of him. I can't... I can't *find* him."

Olshnak tried again with the same result. Then he stepped over to stand so that he blocked Jek's view of the fallen guard's remains.

"Jek, we have work. We have to make report. The goblin managed to somehow *take* Tomet, and right now, you and I are the only ones who know that. We *have* to make report. And we can't do that if we don't escape. Now come with me ... while there's time."

But it was no good. Jek merely stood there, looking lost and alone. It was as if Olshnak hadn't said a word.

Shaking his head, he reached up under the guardsman's chin and beneath his mail. As expected, he found another small pendant there—an uncut stone of greenish blue, hung from a leather cord. He slid it off, over Jek's head. He'd been half-hoping to get a reaction, but the silent figure paid him no mind.

After holding the stone up to the moon, he nodded and slipped it around his own neck with Tomet's. He still heard screams and the sounds of battle—still heard arrows whistling overhead.

Last time. He comes to his senses, or I leave him.

"Jek? I'm going. Will you follow?"

The guardsman spoke in a soft voice, as if from far away. "Where is Tomet? Why can't I find him?"

Shaking his head, Olshnak headed off to find the Boar and Bottle, and perhaps a way out of this deathtrap.

-III-

Kaith had found a handcart, the kind most often used to haul firewood. It was now nearly half-full with torches and leather flasks of oil. He met Huron near the eastern wall. Looking down at the supplies he'd collected, Kaith turned a questioning gaze up to his friend's anxious face.

"I'm guessing this'll have to do?"

Huron arched his brows and quirked a smile. The expression made the spearhead of hair on his chin look either uneven or askew. "How are things upon the wall? If there's time, I can help you gather." This last word came out in two distinct syllables.

"One task at a turn, Huron." He grinned. "Where are we set?"

"Sign of the Boar and Bottle. Two lanes north, to the left."

Kaith nodded. "Ricgerd?"

"Figh-ting his way back south."

"*Back* south?"

"He charged up to the gate of the Braided Tower, figh-ting wherever he found foes, I think. He's spun back and is pressing to-ward us." He paused. "Vilmocz should be where the lane meets the road, marking the turn."

Kaith considered, then nodded. "Olshnak?" He looked toward the gate as he spoke, then shook his head. "Never mind." He paused, doing a double take. "Why is one of his men just *standing* there?"

Huron shrugged. "One of his is dead. A goblin. When I left Olshnak, the goblin-thing that had done the killing was dead, and he and his remaining guard were bound for the inn."

Kaith grunted, then pressed on. "I'll call Gordan and Raegus. Take the supplies to Terrek's inn. When you arrive, if there's no fighting to be done, pull the oil flasks to the top of the cart. We'll need them first, if we need them at all. If there's nothing else to be done while everyone gathers, grab what horses you can. Questions?"

Huron blinked, cocked his head to one side, then shook it. "The cart to Sergeant Terrek. If there's time, pull the flasks to the top. If there's *still* time, gather horses."

Kaith grinned. "One last thing."

Huron waited.

"We don't want a mob crowding the west wall's postern gate. If it comes to that—and I fear it will—we'll set up archers to cover the people as they flee."

Huron considered, then nodded again. "Where will we go if it comes to that?"

"If it's west? Rockvale. It's the only choice." Sir Trallot wouldn't much care for the sudden influx of refugees, but where else could they go?

He gave Huron a nod that served as a dismissal. The younger man nodded back, grabbed the pushcart, and jogged off.

Kaith mounted the stairs, unslinging his shield as he went. He kept it in position as he crossed the alure to the nearest person in sight.

"Sir Raegus..." He saw Rae stiffen, then shoot a grin toward him from over his shoulder. "It's time."

Rae nodded, loosed two arrows in quick succession, then withdrew behind Kaith's shield. They moved together toward Gordan until they came across the next set of stairs down. Kaith held them up, turning to pass a final word.

"Boar and Bottle. Two lanes north on the west side. We'll want eyes and arrows to protect the people if and when we head west. Clear?"

"Boar and Bottle. Aye. And Kaith?" He paused long enough to elicit a questioning look. "I was surprised when your man told me you were already within Wick's walls. I'm *still* surprised, but..." He shook his head. "I'm glad... Glad you're here with us."

Kaith flashed him a grin. "That makes one of us, but we can laugh about that later."

Raegus nodded, chuckling as he headed down the stair.

Kaith watched him go and allowed himself a moment to breathe. The Countess wanted Wick secure. That made sense for a few reasons. Wick was wealthy, defensible, and a place from which they could supply and support military efforts against an assault from the north, should one be forthcoming. Yet with the goblin attack, he was almost certain they were going to have to abandon this place, at least for a time.

They'd discovered a weakness that, if he were honest, should have been obvious. Sewer outflows *should* have a steel grate over them—one that was difficult to breach. That meant a strong, small lock, heavy bars sunk deep into Skolf and reinforced, and...

Storms be swift. Am I describing a sewer's grate or a castle's 'cullis?

He shook his head. "That's enough of that. Come on, *Sir* Kaith." But that was where his self-admonishment ended. He felt a surge of resolve that had no source to credit it. He cast about for some explanation—some sight or sound his undermind had caught, but there was nothing.

His blue dreamer's lamps fell on Gordan as he loosed an arrow, then dropped below the wall's line. He crouch-walked in Kaith's direction for a few feet, then stopped. Kaith noted with satisfaction that Gordan had an arrow nocked and his bowstring stretched—partially pulled back, ready for a full, fast draw and quick release.

Several arrows came arcing low over the wall right where his brother had been standing. Marking the pins' paths, Valad's former armsman rose at speed, already aiming over the wall, and loosed. Before his draw arm had relaxed, Gordan was already crouched and moving back the way he'd come.

Kaith admired the tactic, filing it away for later use. For now, the hourglass was emptying. He hefted his shield and dashed to Gordan's side.

"Time to go, brother."

Gordan looked at him, balding pate gleaming in the early moonlight. "Where?"

Kaith told him. After a moment's consideration, Gordan made a dismissive gesture.

"Go. I'll be along."

Kaith blinked, shook his head, and winced out of reflex as an arrow struck his shield. "You've done what you can here, Gordan. We need to move while we're able."

Gordan ignored him, taking an exaggerated sliding step to his right—still crouching. "Just go. I'll... I'll meet you there. Make sure Raegus gets out."

Kaith's jaw dropped as he tried to process what the man was saying. Again, he saw Gordan erupt to his full height, finishing his draw and aiming as he stood. Then he loosed. He was back in his crouch an instant later.

"Gordan... we need you *with* us."

Gordan looked pointedly away, down toward his knocked arrow. "I'll do more good from here. Now go." His voice was empty somehow, save for the tiniest tremor.

"Gordan, no. You—"

"You aren't someone I *answer* to, Kaith!" He didn't shout so much as snarl. "Now, if you want to stay on the wall instead of whatever you have planned, find a bow... or don't. Just..." His voice became quiet, almost desperate. "Just let me hold the line. The things out there? You can call them goblins or *Nebelblut*. Hells, call them Sheshik shite for all it matters. None of it speaks to—none of you *understand* what they really are."

"Then *tell* me! If you know things we don't, I've no call to doubt you! Stand with us and *explain!*"

"Death," said he. "Death's very hands are down there, Kaith."

Kaith neither glared nor rolled his eyes at this dramatic pronouncement—but that act of resistance cost him some of his hard-won self-possession. "Aye, *fine!* But they're also *in here*! We're wasting time!"

"Then you'd best be about your work ... *Sir.*" Once more, Gordan popped up, loosed a pin, then dropped back down.

Kaith did his best to ignore the stinging derision in the knight's voice. He didn't altogether succeed. When he spoke again, it came out in a tone of mounting anger.

"*We'd* best be about it, you mean! If you stay here, you'll only—"

"It's *fine*, Kaith. When the Falx finally comes for you..." He shrugged.

Kaith's face darkened as he rose. He stalked the few strides that separated them, shield held above the wall to block most of the enemy archers. As he moved, the heater took one arrow, then another, then a third. A fourth struck somewhere along the back of his neck, but his steel mantle turned it.

"Burn the Falx, *Sir* Gordan." His voice was black and bitter.

Gordan winced as if Kaith had physically slapped him. "Burn the—?"

"Falx, Sir Gordan. Yes! Burn it, hang it, throw it from the damned walls!" He spat on the boards between them for emphasis. "I lost Sirs Robis and Lamwreigh at Westsong. *Hells,* I lost *Samik*! I had time to call his name and add *one* word of warning—*one* line command! And what did I do?" His voice became a growl. "I chose the wrong one. I chose the wrong word, and Samik *died*. Lamwreigh *died*. And Robis—"

But it was too much. He bowed his head. His eyes were red and dry, but he feared blinking. Blinking meant closing his eyes, and Robis would be waiting for him there in the dark... or Lamwreigh. He might even be *blessed* with a return visit from Lanian, shouting *catch me*, or trying to drag him under dark water.

Gordan looked up at him with wide eyes. Those eyes showed disbelief, but no confusion. He winced as the moon cleared the thin clouds above, and Kaith's shadow loomed over him.

"I will *not* lose another due to pride, or weakness, or self-doubt." He leaned down, dominating the space Gordan occupied. When he spoke, his voice was dark and strained, as if an unseen hand gripped his throat. "Now, *Sir* Gordan... Get on your damned feet and get down those stairs before I *throw* you down them."

Gordan blanched, then flushed. His eyes grew clear, full of shame and new resolve. He nodded. "Boar and Bottle."

Kaith returned the nod, then crouched beside him. He shadowed Gordan in silence as they moved, covering them both with his shield.

As his brother knight began heading down the stairs, Kaith paused as something occurred to him.

"How many pins do you still have?"

He paused to check his quiver. "Seven."

Kaith nodded. "Go. I'll grab another quiver and be right behind you."

"Right." And with that, he jogged off toward the gate and the main road.

-IV-

County Thorion
Wick

The battle music seemed omnipresent, but Gordan's eyes told him a different tale. Most of the blood and thunder was to the north along Wick's main thoroughfare. The rest of the noise was coming from outside of the village. He could hear things scraping along the wooden gate and the timbers that made up three of Wick's four walls. It wouldn't be long before the goblins *owned* those walls, which would tighten the noose even further.

Ah! That must be why Kaith's man chose a place along the western wall. Stone should make it harder for the devils to climb. Heartened by the realization, Gordan picked up his pace.

He saw a man just *standing* there between a blueish boulder and the broken cart that blocked the main gate. He was dressed in a well-worn chain shirt and a sword belt with an empty scabbard. Gordan headed toward him, then stopped short. His eyes had fallen on the blue boulder, marking its ruined face. It had ended its days wearing a strange look of embarrassed surprise. He shuddered, but forced himself to turn to the man.

"Time for us to go."

He thought he heard the armsman speaking in a half-whisper, but couldn't be sure. He stepped over, putting a hand on his shoulder. "Come. We'll find you a new sword."

"I can't f-fi..."

Gordan nodded. "That's fine. The foe doesn't know that. Stand in the back ranks. Make them think we have more fight in us than we do." He tried to make his voice reasonable, but wound up sounding patronizing even to his *own* ears.

"Where'ss... ss..."

"The Boar and Bottle. Come with me."

"Jek, is it? Or is that Tomet? I can't tell you two apart unless you're side by side." Kaith jogged up, moving to stand beside Gordan.

"*Another* of yours, Kaith?" He tried on a grin that felt false and awkward on his face.

"Came with Olshnak. I think it's Jek. Come on. We've no time for this."

Kaith snapped his fingers in front of Jek's eyes. Gordan hadn't noticed until then, but the fellow's dreamer's lamps looked as if they weren't lit. They were brownish, if his own weren't lying to him. They just weren't aware of what was going on around them. There was no reaction whatsoever to Kaith's snapping fingers.

"I don't want to leave you here, Jek, but you're not giving me much choice."

Gordan stepped back, blinking. "We cannot just ... *leave* him!"

He made an *oof* sound as his brother knight tossed a full quiver at his chest. Kaith shook his head. He grabbed the still man's arm and tried to lead him north along the road, but Jek didn't budge. Kaith's expression grew strained, then detached.

"I'm not trading his life for everyone else's. We'll have to hope for the best—that we win the day and don't have to flee. If not..." He shook his head and started off down the road.

A few beats later, Gordan fell into step beside him. "What in all the hells happened to him, d'ya think?"

Kaith shrugged. "Battle barrel burst, I'd guess."

"What?"

He drew his sword, gesturing for Gordan to take the far side of the street as they jogged. "The battle barrel—Greggor calls it that. *A man can only take so much pouring through his eyes, he says. If too much happens too quickly, some folk find their battle barrel's burst. They cannot hold it all in and remain on this side of madness. That's how he framed it, anyroad.*

They might freeze, become fearful of their own shadow..." He shrugged. "Draw in on themselves."

Gordan saw the back of Wick's guardsmen fighting some thirty or forty strides up ahead. They stood in an untidy clump, Ricgerd at their head. He was shouting to be heard and swinging a sword that was far too long for combat in close quarters.

Nocking an arrow, he stretched his bow to the ready position. "What can be done about it? How do you... what, *mend* the battle barrel, I suppose?"

Kaith stopped with a dozen strides between them and the back of the line, assessing. Finally, he shook his head. "If you find an answer to that, you'll be a wealthy man. There's no shame in running out of road— In finding you're no longer able to weather war. No shame at finding you can't weather *anything*, so long as you've made your best effort."

"But if an armsman can't weather war, as you put it, what good are they?"

Kaith snorted. "You're *absolutely* right, Gordan. What good is someone who can't fight? We surely don't need smiths or bakers, farmers or makers, aye?"

He took Kaith's point at once and was drawing breath to rephrase— perhaps even to apologize—when Kaith spoke again. He made his voice short and sharp, cutting through the battle din and Gordan's own thoughts.

"Three arrows. No more. We can't afford to waste them. I'm going to drive the line forward. We *have* to get them off of that corner. The Boar's just down that very lane. Do you remember how fire limited the front at Westsong?"

Gordan blinked. "A... aye?"

"Good. That, Sir Gordan, is what I mean to do near the postern gate. Tell Rae and Olshnak, and anyone else who's not too scared to stand. We've oil and torches. Save me some of each, but get the buildings on either side ready for burning at my word. Clear?"

Gordan blinked, then smiled. His heart had calmed as he took in Kaith's words. "Aye. Clear. Speak the truth and spurn the treasure. I'm just glad there's a damned *plan*."

Kaith nodded, readying his shield, and stalked forward.

"Shield wall! Shielllllllllld wallllllll! Lock it up! Lock it up! Dress that line... Now! Thorion—Thorion—Thorion!"

Gordan shook his head, grinning in spite of himself.

At first, nothing came of it, but as Kaith neared, continuing to shout those same commands, others took up the call. Before long, they'd managed to brace one another, coalescing into an uneven but serviceable formation.

"*Ricgerrrrd?* Those damned things are *in my way!* I need you to move them! Make readyyy!"

Now he's commanding the local lord? The realization that Kaith had commanded *Gordan* a few minutes back up the hourglass became a brief source of sheepish frustration, but he pushed it aside for later.

"Aye, Sir Kaith! Wick! Wick! Wick!"

The armsmen took up the call, shouting *Wick* over and over again as they made ready to move.

"Back rank! On my signal, fall back! Move toward me, aye?"

"Aye!"

The sound of terrified people to the west hung in the air, punctuated by the armsmen shouting, *Wick! Wick! Wick!*

Gordan saw Kaith draw a breath, give one last cast about, then nod before raising his voice again.

"Ricgerrrrd! Advance by step! Step! Step! Step! Dress that line! Step! Step! Step!"

The men had taken up the call to *step* by the third time Kaith shouted it. As for Gordan, he looked for targets, but only saw one worth wasting an arrow on. A single goblin was physically climbing up onto one of the shields along Wick's right flank. Gordan waited, drew in a breath as he drew back his bowstring, and...

If he'd heard the *twang*, he hadn't registered it. The battle music was deafening amidst the cobbled streets and stone buildings. Still, he saw his target fly back with an arrow sticking from his head. That was enough to be going on with.

He *knew* they could be felled. He'd killed one with several blows of his sword that night at Eastshadow, but it had left him feeling empty and useless. Their hides were too damned thick. He'd learned *this* night that they were far simpler to kill at range. Arrows had an easier time of it than sword strokes. He didn't know why that should be, but it clearly was. And that knowledge filled him with a deep sense of satisfaction—one that flared every time he managed to take one off of the field.

Ricgerd's line—although he supposed it was Kaith's line, now—was pushing the enemy back foot by blood-soaked foot. Wick's warriors had gained enough ground to open up about half of the lane. That meant there was room for a single horse to slip through, if they'd had any.

"Kaith! I've got the room. I'm moving!"

Kaith turned, first eyeing Gordan, then the westward lane, before nodding. "Go!" He held his sword aloft once more, then shouted to Ricgerd's guardsmen, "Rear guard! Rear Guard! On me! On me!"

Gordan raced to the corner, then stopped to have a shifty down the lane. No point in running blind if he didn't need to. He saw a massive crowd pushed most of the way back against the stone wall. They were near the narrow postern gate, but *near* and *blocking* were two very different things. Well over a hundred men, women, and children were massed there in varying states of panic.

He saw Kaith's orc. The tusk was standing near a sandblood who wore the same blue leather as that Terrek fellow. They were discussing something, the orc pointing at nearby buildings as the sandblood nodded his brown-skinned head. He thought he'd caught a glimpse of two more blue-clad men, but they were in the press of other bodies, which made identification difficult.

Nodding to himself, Gordan took a last look around Wick's main road. To his left, all was as it had been. Kaith's rear guard had fallen back to him, and he was giving them instructions. What those orders *were* was another matter. His fellow Valadin was speaking, not shouting. The rest of Ricgerd's men—perhaps a score or so—were holding their position, trying to keep the silent goblins where they were for the nonce.

They'd be far less fearsome if they had voices, I think. Even when they're swinging their weapons or being struck by ours, they make no sound of rage or pain. As for your plan, Kaith... I don't see it. As long as you understand it, that'll have to do.

He took a glance to his right, back south toward the gate ... and froze.

He saw a goblin that might have stood as tall as his midriff. It was *mounting* the corpse of the blue boulder. The sad form of Jek remained standing a few feet behind this grotesquery, unmoving. Gordan didn't have time to be revolted, for no sooner had the creature crawled atop the dead thing than it made a short spear materialize from nothing. It lined up its shot and rammed the weapon down into the body. It did this several more times in rapid succession, then made as if to smear the blood along the weapon's haft.

Gordan was so busy watching this unsettling rite that he came within a hair's breadth of missing what was going on around it. Goblins were coming up onto, then scaling down the southern wall and onto Wick's streets. As they dropped to the cobbles below, they began racing toward

Kaith's rear.

He bent his bow and took the lead goblin runner in the chest. Again he felt that surge of satisfaction, but there wasn't time to revel in it.

"Kaith! Circle up!"

Kaith echoed Gordan's order, as did the back rank. He hoped that meant they saw what he was now seeing.

He'd drawn another arrow and was about to loose it when his eyes found the tiny ritualist again. He'd—or perhaps she'd, who could tell?—rolled onto his back atop the boulder-like blue body. This left the spear in a lewd-looking position, its haft pointing skyward. The creature slid his hands up to the weapon's middle and *pulled.*

Havoc's—

The goblin's spear glowed a blinding white, then winked out of existence. The large blue corpse it had impaled itself on sat up, tossing the ritualist aside with casual disregard.

More and more goblins found their feet on the road, sprinting toward the battle line. Gordan felled one more of the charging Nebelblut, but he missed another with room to spare. His eyes kept drifting back to the revived blue devil. Its back was to him. Yet he felt a mounting sense of fear that went far beyond simple dread. Unable to force his gaze away, he watched as it pulled a curved sword out of empty air, then swung it in a wide back cut. He couldn't see the demon's target, but he didn't need to. Unless he was very much mistaken, Kaith's man Jek wouldn't have to worry about repairing his battle barrel after all.

The Nebelblut were close now—too close to ignore. He cursed, but the sound died on his tongue. The massive slate-skinned thing was now suffused with that eye-watering winter light.

Gordan didn't wait. He bent his bow, releasing arrow after arrow, aiming *past* the nearer threats to stop the... the... He didn't know what to call it.

But it has to be... I have to...

It was no good. He hit his mark at least three times, but nothing seemed to happen... until the light was gone. When it winked out, he saw the creature had been replaced by a dusky, golden-brown *thing* of impossible size.

Memory forced its way onto the stage of his mind. He was a boy again, perhaps ten or eleven. He'd been little more than a fresh-faced page in Valad's household. He recalled riding with his new lord to Thorionden for some tournament or other. He was to watch and learn, which was all well and good, but when the fighting was ended...

The great grey monsters had processed through the streets. They'd been described as the Ivory Heralds of the Divine—enormous, four-legged creatures with long noses and massive, curved ivory tusks.

They stomped and trumpeted as they went. Hathi. That's what the Barghad pages and servants called them.

The burnished beast looked at its own massive hands in delighted surprise, then turned and sent forth a roar of deep, spine-shaking laughter.

"It's as big as a hathi," Gordan murmured. "As big as a hathi, but it walks on two legs. It walks upright and wields weapons of war... *laughing*. Westsong was nothing. Westsong was..."

"Gordan! Sir Gor-dan!"

He snapped back to the moment at hand. The fear wasn't so much gone as it was pushed aside for later examination. "Kaith?"

"Command the rear guard—the shield wall. Stay that damned line for as long as you can!"

"Done! Lock it up!" Gordan stepped out behind the men in question. The task focused him—helped him to stave off his sense of fear and awe. *This* he could do. Eight men, perhaps nine, stood shoulder to shoulder. Their shields drawn tight, left edge over neighbor's right as they waited to die. He watched one man literally wet himself as the goblins drew near. The terrified guardsman was shaking, but he stood his ground.

Hells, he might not even realize he's done it. Gordan had to fight back the urge to snort laughter. He was picturing the man shouting in anger, demanding to know who'd done it—who'd pissed in his pants.

Biting his own tongue, Gordan addressed his men once more. "Stand fast! Stand fast! We only need to hold them for a little while!" He saw a stone water trough off to his left opposite their exit lane and moved toward it. "Brace! Brace! Stay that line!" He stepped up onto its corner, aimed, and loosed.

"Ricgerd! Time to leave! Retreat by step! Step! Step! Step!" As they moved, the men repeated that word along with Kaith, until he gave new orders. "Line stop! Refuse right. Refuse the right! Refuse! Refuse! Refuse! Line stop!" This command was a wheel walked backwards. It was as if the man on the far left of the line was the axle upon which the other men turned. When Kaith stopped them, their backs were to the Boar and Bottle's street. They'd be able to perform a fighting withdrawal, defending the townsfolk as they escaped west.

For his part, Gordan continued shooting, shouting at his men to dress their line. The hathi-sized monster was rubbing his enormous palms together, watching all of this with a delighted grin on his face... His far too intelligent face.

"We're out of time! Ricgerd? Fall back and get as many people as you can through that gate!" He pointed to the west. "Sons of Wick? Back ranks first. Stay with as many of your neighbors as you can. *They* can't fight. Get them to Rockvale as fast as their tired legs can carry them. Ricgerd?"

"You heard Sir Kaith! Retreat by ranks!"

No sooner had this process begun—individual lines of armsmen retreating toward the gate—then it happened. The dusky gold demon roared in a familiar tongue, though not one he could place. It walked with deliberate slowness toward them. Halfway along the road, it held its right hand out to the side—and it was, indeed, a hand, no paw or claw in sight—and closed its fingers on a massive morning star.

"Kaith...?" Gordan tried to keep the rising panic out of his voice. He *thought* he'd managed it, but couldn't be sure. It was hard to tell over the sudden swell of all the *other* terrified voices.

"I see it!"

How in hells are you so calm? For his part, Gordan was a breath away from following the example of the guard who'd pissed himself.

"Sons of Wick? Where are your wives and children?" Kaith asked this question with volume and force, but no panic.

Cries of "Back there, Lord!" and "Tryin' tae'scape, If'ee can!" came in response.

"Our role, then, is to *stay this line* and buy them as much time as we can! They'll need fighting men to keep them 'live 'long the road, and we'll oblige rank by rank. But—"

The monster's morning star knocked a wooden upright out from under a shop's covered walkway. It bellowed, shaping its voice toward the place where he and Kaith stood with the men, then gave another of those laughing roars.

As the sound died away, Gordan first heard, then glanced over to *see* fully six men in the middle ranks shouting and shoving their way toward the rear. The rest of their men would've succumbed to full-bore hysteria in another moment, and he could hardly have blamed them. He was surprised, therefore, to hear his *own* voice bark at them over the din.

"Dress that line! Lock it up! Lock it up, right now!"

Kaith took up the call right away, moving to stand on the far side of the line from Gordan.

It worked. Those who'd already panicked made it through to the rear, but the rest clung to the orders they'd been given, and the voices that had issued them.

The goblins had withdrawn from their northern front, though where they'd gone was anyone's guess. Now they withdrew from the southern one. Gordan could still see them. They'd gathered to either side of the street as if making way for the lumbering fiend with the morning star.

Which is exactly what they're doing. They're lining the streets... getting out of his way. Why?

The answer came to him an instant before it came to everyone else.

"Kaith! They're making room for him! He's going to—"

A deep, muscular sound that was more groan than roar split the air. The dark golden-skinned demon lowered his head, splayed the massive fingers of his free hand along the cobbles, then threw on a terrific burst of speed. He crashed into their line like a river bursting through its dam.

Three men flew back as if they'd been quarrels shot from a crossbow. Everyone was shouting, screaming, falling, fighting, fleeing. Gordan's breath came in rapid gasps, as if he'd run a great distance. It was the fear, of course. And who could blame him now?

Only a fool wouldn't be terrified at this point!

He ran backward, stepping off the trough and looking for either a way out or a clear shot. He had emptied one quiver, and as he fumbled to reposition the full one Kaith had given him, he saw Raegus running up on the beast's left flank.

His mind was blank. He had no higher thought. His fingers closed on an arrow's shaft, pulled it over his shoulder, fitted, drew, and released it before Rae had taken his second step. The arrow sank into the beast's bright arm, eliciting a sound that was too deep to qualify as a yelp. The monster turned to him, then back to the terrified mass of Wick's armsmen. Gordan loosed another, then another, both aimed at that same arm.

It was enough. Well, no. It was *more* than enough. The beast turned on Gordan with yellow-eyed fury. He put both hands on the haft of his weapon, shook the very buildings with the sound of his rage, and swept a low flat snap which knocked the remaining men into one another, then crushed them into the side of the corner building ... and into Raegus.

"Rrrrrrah!"

Kaith gave a rising shout as he charged. Lowering his shoulder, he canted his heater, so the shield covered both his head and most of his upper body as he ran. He held his sword in a dump block—hilt flat against the back of his head, blade flat against his spine. As the monster recovered from its impossible, cradle-tale flat snap, Kaith rammed into its left thigh. The impact served to slide the beast's leg back a bit, lowering its stance in the process, but it didn't manage much more than that. Then Kaith pivoted to his right, delivering a hammer shot on the beast's exposed *other* leg.

It gave another of those deep, Skolf-shaking roars, then raised its morning star to deliver a hammer of its own. In that moment, Gordan's entire world narrowed to a single point of focus. He took aim at the beast's exposed armpit, neither drawing breath nor expelling it. He could see the ripple of muscle as it began to bring its weapon down toward Kaith's un-helmeted head.

He loosed.

The arrow sunk in almost to the fletching. The creature issued a great, guttural *howl* of fury, backhanding Kaith aside as it flailed to reach the exposed part of the arrow. Gordan had a moment of shining pride. He'd saved Kaith, for now at least, and bought the others some additional time to flee.

He pulled another arrow, hoping to find another exposed target on the golden giant. It finally reached down to snatch up one of the goblins. Then it thrust that goblin toward its wounded armpit. The smaller creature managed to wrench the pin free just before Gordan's arrow took it in the side of its head.

The giant threw the corpse at him. Gordan ducked, turning and hunting for either cover or an open road to run down, but it was no good. He'd taken a single step toward the postern gate when the body barreled into him and brought him to the ground.

The goblin was of average size and build, but storms be swift, it was *heavy!* For a terrible instant, he couldn't get air. Black flowers bloomed before his eyes. With an almighty effort, he managed to shove the body off and rip noisome air back into his lungs. He was just pushing himself to his feet when he realized that something was hurtling toward him. He looked up and glimpsed the spiked ball of the morning star rushing down from overhead.

-V-

Kaith heard someone shouting his name, but it was too far away to mean anything. The great golden-brown beast had broken their line—had, in fact, laid *waste* to that line—and spelled the end for them despite his best efforts.

He tried to move, though he wasn't sure what had prompted the action. It was over, after all. Wasn't it?

His legs seemed as if they'd fallen asleep. He felt his muscles move, felt his feet scrabbling for purchase, but they kept sliding on various pieces of debris.

He had done all he could. He'd made a plan that had been tested in the crucible of Westsong. Had organized Ricgerd's defense. He'd even snapped Gordan out of his spiraling, death-seeking state in time for the man to make a real and true difference. And in the end? What had it all come to?

There was no time to set fire to cover our flight. The best part of Ricgerd's defenders lay dead or dying at the hands of that... that thing. Raegus crushed. Huron, Terrek, Ricgerd, Gordan, and the rest... He realized he had no idea where any of them were. *Falxes fall... Let them have made it to safety. Let all of this death and misery have accomplished ... something.*

And still, someone was calling his name. He knew the voice, didn't he? It was growing closer, but it sounded ever more desperate.

He tried again to move his legs, to find his feet, but it was no good. He couldn't see much—just a pale portion of sky spread above him. It looked like a tear in the surrounding, formless black.

I'm under something, I think. He turned his head, hearing the world as if through a distant, opened window. His vision swam. He caught a nose full of what almost had to be a fresh application of oil.

"Sir Kaith! Kaith! Where in all the hells *is* he?" Was that ... Ricgerd's voice?

His head was beginning to clear ... and throb. He tried to move his bright arm, but it was pinned by something. His dim-side shoulder was trapped as well, though he could feel the familiar presence of his heater still strapped to that arm.

"Sir Kaith!" Huron's voice. He was quite sure of it.

"Ea' have no time, Lord. Ee've got folk—*loyal* folk waitin' for ee in th' braided tower!"

That's Alec-Aleks, I think.

Ricgerd did his best to ignore him. It worked for a few beats, but it wasn't long before Alec-Aleks tried again.

"Ricgerd, ee're wastin' time. Leave the worthless wandought to 'is fate! Tavin an' the lads're waitin' tae give ee proper council! "

Kaith felt his face twist into a smirk at the venom in the man's voice. A *wandought* was a drunkard's insult. In his father's day, it had meant a useless or weak man. In inns and taverns all over Thorion, it had changed its meaning to a man unable to *make iron for the forge.* A man either too old or too young to make love ... or at least to father children.

"*Sir* Kaith put his life on the very line, Aleks Silverson. The goblins won't stare up at that light-leaching thing for long. Now *help* me! That, or leave me! Just... Havoc's Horn, shut *up*!"

But Aleks wasn't finished. He sounded both angry and sulky. "*I* was in the press as well! He weren't the only one. N'all he did was flutter his stewhole and try 'n steal eer glory!"

They were getting closer. Better still, his throbbing head was beginning to fade.

Bright-arm's pinned. He tried to suck in air, but coughed it out at once. The oil fumes and the stench of the goblins were too much. Out of reflex, he tried to bring his dim arm to his face as he coughed. When the world stopped spinning, he realized something else. *My bright arm's pinned, but my dim's only pinned at the shoulder. Shield's still strapped to my arm. Well then? Let's see if...*

He curled the shield in toward his body, then slammed it against the cobbles. *Thwack!*

Then again. *Thwack!*

"Kaith! Kaith!" Huron's voice, and with such obvious relief that Kaith felt his eyes overspill in gratitude. "I have heem! Here! He's just here!"

Kaith felt the pressure he hadn't fully registered lift from his body. It had come from a combination of the overturned handcart he'd used to gather fire supplies and an armored body flung atop it.

Ricgerd embraced him, nearly breaking his ribs. "I *knew* you lived!"

Kaith grinned, then shook his head ... and wished he hadn't. The pain was instant.

"Sir Kaith?" Huron's voice, full of concern.

"It's nothing." He looked around, trying to gauge the battlefield. He'd been thrown almost to the postern gate. At first he saw only the dead laying broken all around. Then he saw the press of the living as they screamed at and trampled one another in an effort to get through.

Kaith pushed himself away from Ricgerd and the others. He walked toward them, hoping he had the endurance to shout without falling over.

"Sir Kaith? What are you—"

"Wiiiiiiiick!" He was surprised at how long he was able to keep the word hung in the air. For a wonder, his head seemed to clear rather than darken with pain.

The thirty or so folk trying to injure their neighbors stopped to look at him. They'd been shocked by the noise. Their faces screamed the truth. They'd only turned out of fear of what *else* might be about to happen to them.

"*We* will keep them off you while you head outside. If we have to—"

But it was no good. They turned at once, ignoring him and returning to their panicked exodus.

Ricgerd put a hand on his shoulder, smirking. "Brave, sensible, and useless. They're dead, just as we are." His face made it clear he believed that, but it didn't seem to worry him much.

As Kaith met his eyes, Ricgerd nodded over his shoulder. Kaith looked ... and *gaped*. Where the devil with the morning star had last stood, there now appeared to be a yawning rip in the very air. It seemed to devour the light around it, save at its edges. These were painted in that same blinding white that had surrounded the creature when it had undergone its change. As he watched, the light from the edges began to stretch in toward the rift's center.

Then his eyes fell on Gordan, or at least what was left of him. He'd been driven into the cobbles. So much of him had been rendered into blood and gore, but there could be no doubt.

"Gordan..."

Kaith could still feel Ricgerd's hand on one of his shoulders. Huron moved to stand at the other. Both men kept their silence for as long as they dared.

When he found his voice again, Kaith asked what he felt to be the obvious, but far more pressing question. "And what in all the hells that ever were is ... that?"

He realized how useless and unanswerable that question was. He was, therefore, taken aback when someone did, in fact, provide an answer.

"The beginning," said Huron. "The beginning of the end ... of all endings."

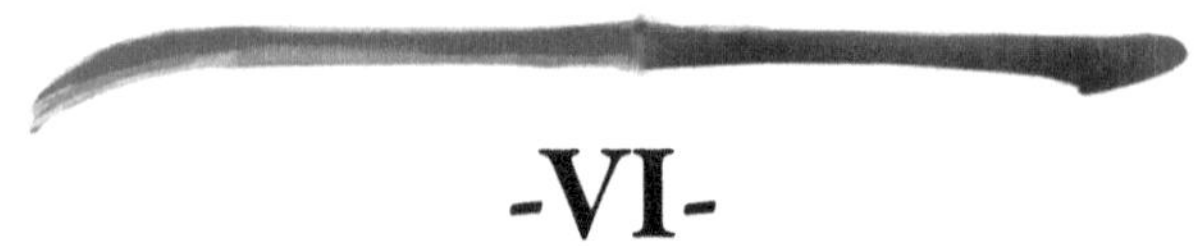

-VI-

The Grey Between

At the end of his life, Gordan felt pain, but that pain was brief. He found himself standing before a pulsing, shuddering emptiness that drew in a massive burst of living shadow. Other men, women, and children were huddled together near this emptiness, staring up at it in horror and dismay.

"Will you come, Gordan, son of Rheinallt?"

A woman's voice. Full of warmth, and spoken through a sad smile, he was sure of it.

"Where?"

"Turn and see me, Knight of the Valadin. Turn and see me or turn and go your way."

There was no malice in her voice, yet there was steel. She would welcome him, or she would wish him well. She would *not* try to wheedle or waste time.

Gordan turned to her—turned away from the shuddering mass of the empty looming above him—and caught his breath.

She was perfection. She stood in battle dress—a well-used and well-cared-for suit of mail overtopped by an armored riding skirt. She held a wicked-looking halberd at her ease in one hand. The other dangled empty at her side. One long war braid of pale honey lay against her left shoulder. Her eyes danced as her lips parted in a small smile.

"I know you... I'm *certain* I know you, Lady."

She nodded, her smile growing a touch wider. Her skin had the glow of dream-women, yet he knew this was no dream.

"You do know me. But can you *name* me? I think it's only fair to ask. You've not spoken to me or sought out my aid or succor in a goodly while... save once." She grinned. "I don't want just *anyone* drinking in my hall, sleeping in my hall... passing out and breaking wind in my hall, Sir Gordan." Her eyes danced.

He shook his head, but only to clear it. "You're ... Traeadish."

"Mmm. I am."

His eyes grew wide, then filled with tears. "I'm... I'm dead, aren't I." It wasn't a question. "This isn't some goblin or *Nebelblut* sorcery, is it?" He all but spat that foreign word.

"If you want to see Nebelblut sorcery, turn around."

He did. The great emptiness that had been lingering above him was coalescing into ... something.

"What is it?"

"My great enemy. Well, *one* of my great enemies. One can never have too many of those, I think. Not while well still waits."

He looked back at her, but she was walking up beside him.

"I *do* know you. I just... I'm not sure how to address you." He paused, then said aloud the thing he'd been afraid to admit even to himself. "I fear that saying your name will make it all true. That saying it aloud will make it... I don't know, final?"

She nodded. Her look left the impression that she understood his fear and thought no less of him for admitting it.

"That makes sense. It isn't *true,* but it makes sense."

"There's nothing to be done?"

"We can stay and watch as he finishes absorbing your shadow."

"My shadow... But I'm right here. I'm *only* shadow now."

She laughed, a musical thing full of a joy that could not—*would not*—be extinguished.

"You're a spirit now, Sir Gordan. You've been removed from the Cycle of Seas. You'll never be reborn, never be a whisper in some later-born son or daughter's dreams. They eat your shadow, the Nebelblut. When they kill, at least with one of their own weapons, they eat all that you've learned and experienced. They devour your past and any future you might have been a part of. Now you're timeless. You'll know all that you know at this moment and learn nothing more of substance, no matter how much time passes. You'll find you have trouble even drawing conclusions. No solving of new riddles, no betterment on past performances. No progress."

He turned to regard her profile. "Unless I go with you?"

She allowed that beatific smile to brush her lips once more. "If you remain here in the Grey Between, you'll fade to nothing or become a haunt—the expression of a lone thought driven by a hunger you cannot imagine. Or? You can speak my name, take my hand, and come with me to my hall. There, at least, my power will grant you a touch of shadow. A tether to the pull and indeed the *pool* of the faithful."

He bowed his head. "I followed less than half of that." He grinned. "But it's enough. If I can't return to them, then..." He shuddered, both weeping and smiling. "I accept your invitation ... Saint Hyrro."

"Mmm." She smiled through the sound and nodded, turning so he could take her left arm. "Well, unless I'm much mistaken, the Red Storm is coming. The *true* Red Storm—not that drizzle you fought beneath at Westsong." She sighed and shook her head. "I expect I'm about to become very busy. But *first*... your time on Skolf has come to an end. Let me welcome you home, Sir Gordan. If you'd do me the honor, I would like to hear you sing at tonight's feast."

He laughed as he inclined his head to her. Taking the proffered arm, he put his back to the shuddering emptiness that was even now completing its transformation.

"My Lady, it would be my decided pleasure," said he. Gordan—*Sir* Gordan of Knell's Stone, knight of the Valadin smiled through his tears and walked, leaving Skolf and all its woes behind.

SHADOW, SHEPHERD, FATHER, FIEND

-I-

Venzene Duchy of Kovalun
County Jižní Pochod
Barony of Hartscross–Jižní Lov
5 Korunasykli: 22 Days after the Red Storm at Westsong

Vlk and Maksu rounded toward the front of Edmund's command tent. They were stopped for a beat at the entrance by two of the Count's guardsmen. Tall and well-muscled, the men wore the sleeves of their white kontusze unbuttoned and thrown back over their shoulders. The green and gold diamonds on the cuffs of their bolero jackets marked them as men of Count Edmund's personal guard. They held their short-bladed spears upright, but the warriors looked either anxious or terrified. Given the day's events, who could blame them? They'd no doubt spent their time standing on that same patch of ground, unable to do more than witness the battle going on all round them.

The man on Vlk's left stroked his mustache with his free hand. The guardsman on the right had just drawn breath to send the boys away when Maksu's *father* came up behind them.

"The count is wounded. My carriage is just there." There was a pause, wherein Vlk saw the guard's eyes flit to their right. "My men will carry him in. You must hold the tent open for them. I can attend him, but ... is his scholar within?"

The guardsmen both grew pale, but they looked more angry than fearful to Vlk's unpracticed eye.

"No, Lord. He's gone to attend Lady Kastan's huntsman."

Vlk heard footsteps crunching on the grass and dirt, then felt the old man's hand on his back. "Very well. I am Ebistian Konecléta, Lord Alojz's chief scholar. I shall see to Edmund's care as best I can. Now move aside."

The guards hesitated for a moment, then obeyed as four men came up carrying Edmund between them.

Maksu helped Vlk into the tent. That was good. Not only was he still suffering from a constant low throb in his head, but he'd grown ... not woozy, but *angry*. It had happened as the old man spoke to the count's guards. When he'd said his name. Alarm bells were ringing somewhere far and wee in the back of his mind, and he'd no clear idea why. His senses appeared to have *sharpened*. As so often happened when he was afraid, his first instinct was to fight, not to flee. But who was he meant to fight? This old man? Why? He'd been nothing but kind to him, and to Maksu. Why the blue boy was calling this Ebistian *father* was a riddle he hadn't solved, but what of that? At bottom, it wasn't Vlk's business.

But Ebistian... Vhy does that name fill me with ... anger?

Perhaps it was anger at the potential death of the Count? He respected the man. Hells, *everyone* respected him. He was Edmund the Tall! Vlk had dreamt about the Count of Hartscross calling him to the line for as long as he could remember. They'd only just met face to face, though he'd *seen* the mountain that was Edmund often enough. Vlk had, after all, lived in Jižní Lov all his life. The thought of him dying was just ... unthinkable.

The smells of blood and waste were dim but difficult to ignore as they passed under the tent's open flap. The younger man—Sau, apparently, spoke in a firm but kindly voice.

"Maksu? Stand behind the table."

They moved to obey. The table's lone lantern made their shadows dance along the tent's ceiling. Vlk did a minor double-take at the lantern itself. It was of the sort that hung along the paths of the undertown—an old thing of iron and glass. He saw a second lantern made of wood and animal bladders casting its diffused glow from the tent's back corner. *That* was the common-craft lantern found all over the encampment.

They saw Edmund carried in. After a moment's indecision, the old man pointed to an area near the common-craft lantern. Before they put him down, another two guards came quickly inside and spread a quartet of large pillows where Edmund was to be placed. Vlk had seen the cushions along one wall within the carriage. He nodded his approval to no one in particular.

As those guards left, two more came in—one holding another pair of cushions, the other the familiar form of Laagi.

"Lord?"

"Yes Vlk?"

"Vill he live?"

"As I say, we'll hope—"

"Laagi, Lord." Vlk indicated the place where the boy now lay with a nod of his head.

"Is *that* his name... How is it you come to know it?"

Vlk pinked, bowing his head before answering. "I vas the one who... I fought him. I *thought* I'd killed him. He and his father vere the ones who attacked us."

Maksu turned awed eyes up to regard Vlk. "You fought?"

Vlk gave a shallow nod, taking his arm from around Maksu's shoulders to lean both hands on the tall tabletop.

"Yes, Maksu," the old man said. "I admit I was impressed when I heard that tale. By all accounts, our Vlk was very brave indeed. But, Vlk... that you took the time to learn the *name* of your foe... that shows the mark of not just a brave boy, but of a keen-minded one. Fine qualities in a warrior."

Vlk felt a strange mixture of pride and discomfiture at the praise. *Or at the man giving it. He seems varmhearted and honest, and he's treated Maksu vell, vhich is good, but... there's something off about him, I think.*

"Well, your foe will live to fight again, Vlk. His body is broken, but he isn't beyond recall."

He gave a slow nod at that. He didn't understand how it could be— how *anyone* could have survived a fall from the top of the wall, but...

But I survived. Vell, I did, but I had help. I had...

But that took his mind back to the conversations he'd had while in the between-place. He felt a wave of disorientation wash over him. Gripping the tabletop, he felt Maksu's hand against his back to steady him.

"No, you *must* let me in. My *son* is vithin this tent! Vlk? Vlk!"

Vlk shuddered. He knew that voice all too well, even muffled by the furs that lined the inner walls.

"Let her in," Ebistian called. He didn't sound any more pleased about the interruption than Vlk was.

She shoved her way through the tent flap, performing several stagger-steps as if being buffeted by gusts of strong wind. She first stopped short as her eyes fell on Vlk, then again as she glared at the boy beside him. She'd inhaled preparatory to a rant—a rant which would include venom if she were wroth with him, or a snarling overprotectiveness if she'd only been afraid. He actually hoped for the former. The latter meant she'd be weeping and kissing him even as she scolded.

Before she could take either path, Ebistian spoke up in his melodious voice.

"You are our Vlk's mother, I take it?"

Vlk saw her face before she spun on the speaker. She was delighted to have a target to vent her frustration at. Looking at the old man, however, she physically stepped back as if he'd burst into flames.

"I... Yes, Lord. Vlk ess mi boy. I vas afraid vhen my hushbandt said he'd seen him carried into your vagon." She paused, then blurted out, "He'll be here shoon—my hushband."

"My *carriage*. Yes." Ebistian looked at her with an expression that suggested he'd smelled something unpleasant. "And what do they call you?"

"Duša, lord."

Ebistian offered a slight inclination of his head at that. "Well Duša, as you see, he's well enough to stand ... with help."

She looked at Vlk, seeming to alternate her weight from one foot to the other as if she might need to make water. "I... Yes, Lord. Vlk? Come avay from that tushk. I vish to take him home, Lord."

Ebistian wrinkled his nose for an instant, then shook his head. "It would be best if he remained here, I think."

Duša didn't answer for a long moment, though she clearly wanted to. At length, her voice came out in a strange mixture of halting insistence. "Nnn... nnn... No, Lord. I... I vish to ... to take him—"

Ebistian rolled his eyes. "Sejh ahg puehv ang, Duša. No... you do *not*." Whatever tongue Ebistian had begun in came out in a murmured, angry rush. By contrast, the words he'd spoken in the Trade Tongue had been warm and engaging.

Duša blinked, stepping back. "I ... do not." Her voice was almost flat as she said this. It wasn't a question so much as it was an uncertain statement.

Ebistian nodded. "Quite correct. His injuries were great."

"Injuries..."

Vlk didn't have the faintest idea what this was, but he was hard-pressed not to begin laughing at his mother's obvious fear and confusion. This Ebistian was proving to be a far better fellow than he'd expected. Especially if the man could arrange it so Vlk wouldn't have to be dragged home like some lost child.

"Yes... yes, he was very brave. You should be proud of what your boy accomplished before his injuries took him from you. He was a hero upon the walls."

Duša began to choke back sobs. "Vas... Vas there no-thing that could be done for him?"

Ebistian bowed his head, shaking it. "Resign yourself, Duša. Resign yourself and be comforted that all that could be done has been done. It is out of your hands now. You must wait outside and hope for a gift from the Hallowed Halls."

She bowed her head, then turned and headed out without a backward glance. Vlk stared after her. His face bore a frozen grin that promised laughter to come.

After a moment, Ebistian chuckled. "Well, Vlk. I think it's safe to say that your poor mother will be sad to lose you. But..." He strode over to the boys, reaching a hand down to cup Vlk's chin. "*We* will be glad to call you our own. Won't we, Maksu?"

Maksu's grin was impossibly large. He bounced in place. "Yes! He's really ours now, Father?"

Ebistian nodded, searching for Vlk's eyes. For his part, Vlk's grin had begun to fade, but he forced it back into position. All at once it was of utmost importance that he not let anyone see what he was really thinking. He didn't understand any of this—including the urge to keep himself to himself—but he felt sure that something was wrong.

"Vlk! We're brothers now! And Father will make us strong—strong enough so that no one will *ever* hurt our family! You'll see!"

He tried to turn his face to look at the blue-skinned gnoerk. Ebistian allowed this, running a finger behind Vlk's dim-side ear as he stepped back. The old man's touch caused a shudder to run up his spine, but in a way that made it hard to tell if he felt delighted or disturbed by it.

Ebistian was now smiling down at the pair. He'd drawn breath to say something more when an odd expression graced his features.

"Ah? Ahhhh." The old man sounded as if he'd been surprised into resignation. "Mepresh?"

"I feel it, Seeker."

"The God Eater and the Griffin Tamer..." Ebistian sighed, shaking his head. "Ah well. I make... half a bell? Well, within the hour, at any rate."

Vlk saw Sau turn toward the tent's exit, head cocked to one side as if lost in calculation. Finally, he nodded. "There is no question, Seeker. It will be soon."

Ebistian smiled through a theatrical sigh. "Ah, me... I'd hoped, but we never quite have long enough, do we?" He turned, walking over to kneel beside the count. "Excellency, we simply ran out of time. I wish you peace at the end of your life and look forward to seeing you again when all roads end."

Vlk watched as the silver-haired scholar leaned down to plant a gentle kiss on Edmund's brow. Tears prickled the corners of his eyes. He didn't know what had changed, but he understood that Edmund was about to die. He might have held his own swirling emotions in check were it not for Maksu. The younger boy did nothing to hide his sobs. They were small things—soft and contained but they still hurt to hear. Vlk turned to him and put a hand on his shoulder. He'd meant to pull him in for an embrace they likely both needed, so he was surprised and a touch confused when Maksu simply looked at him, then back to Edmund's makeshift pallet. The boy was clenching his fists.

He's trying to hold back his sadness. I thought he vould need comfort. Hells... I do. But if he can be strong, then so can I.

Ebistian was murmuring what sounded like a prayer in some forgotten tongue. "Puav zul zeteek lehm, civ puav ka zul zet kol, Edmund fi Hartscross." He took a moment to wipe tears away, though his voice had remained steady. Stroking the dying man's hair, he took a shuddering breath before speaking again. "Ayom, Hecnkenid... puav ka zeteek wolth ahg iyth uund."

Sau walked over and laid a hand on Ebistian's shoulder, squeezing. With a brief look up at the younger man, he placed his hand over Sau's and looked back down at Edmund. Finally, Ebistian stood.

"You both bore that very well, boys. I'm very proud of you for that."

Maksu gave a deep nod, still issuing soft sobs.

Vlk wiped at his eyes, then looked up at the old man.

"Vlk, the boy's name is Longee?"

Vlk sniffled, then spoke his reply. "Laagi, Fa— ...Lord. Laahg-ee. Do you vant his father's name?"

Ebistian shook his head. "No need, my brave boy. His given name is enough for me to speak the ancient words."

Vlk nodded.

"Sau? Tell the T'lendak, take the others, and begin. There's no point waiting now." He turned toward Laagi's prostrate form, then turned back before Sau could take his second step. "And send me Rikten. Have him wait beside the carriage. I will instruct him there. No need to trouble the boys with such boring blather."

Sau nodded. "Of course, Seeker." With that, he exited the tent.

Ebistian knelt by the gnoerkish boy's body and took his hand. "Laagi... Puav del zet hol lehm puav maks ozul. Muunts kan zyn."

A moment later, Ebistian stood and smiled at the boys. "Stay here. Laagi will be disoriented when he wakes. And there's still a good deal of danger outside. Go with no one. Not unless they're a part of our family. Am I understood?"

They both nodded, saying nothing. A moment later, Ebistian left the marquee.

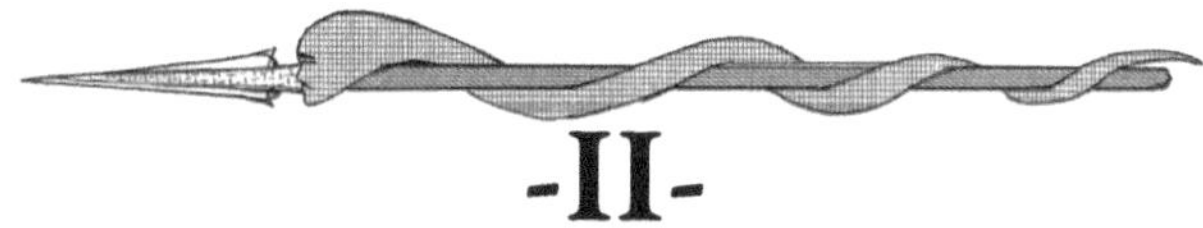

-II-

Stone seeks to see itself in the stonerite. Its craft calls for time, not temper. No eager eye or hurried hand will help you see a stone's true shape any faster.

Lashjuk found herself mentally repeating this old stonemason's proverb as she lay in wait. It was hard advice to accept, but wasn't good advice often that way?

She recalled her Guuvra trying to teach it, and the earliest lessons of his trade, to their children. The boys hadn't seemed interested, but their daughter Maklo had taken to it all right away. Guuvra had been as calm as ever, but she thought he'd been delighted the girl had shown not only interest but aptitude for the work. He'd taken her on as an apprentice two years agone and expected her to join the Kamieniarz lodge before long.

All over now... She bit down on her lower lip, welcoming the tiny stab of pain. *All over for him and her, but not for our Maksu. Not for Sulok, and not for me.*

That was true, but she kept feeling as if she might miss her chance to act. She knew there was no such thing as a *perfect moment*—not in any way one could, or even should, look for. She hadn't needed anyone from the unit to teach her *that*. She'd spent the latter half of her life raising children, after all.

No, it wasn't a *perfect moment* she was waiting for. It was a *good enough* one. She wanted to have at least some chance of success when she, at last, moved. And while there were far fewer guards than there had been, there were still too many for her to take on alone. She had the... whatever it was that had been helping her, but it wasn't a physical thing. She had no idea how, or even *if*, it could be of any use to her when it came to a fight. She wasn't sure if her fear of being too late was a matter of anxiety or instinct, though she thought it was the former.

But how long can I bide?

A good question. Another good question was, what other useful choice did she have at present?

The command tent is set apart, so there's no stealthy approach. It's been thoroughly staked down, so there's no easy way to roll beneath its sides. I could run for the entrance, but the count's men would stop me. And even if they didn't, there are at least three of Ebistian's guards and his driver to give chase. If I were alone, I might outrun them. They're armored, after all. But with Maksu in one hand? Likely fighting me every step of the way... if he's still under the old goat's thrall?

And so, she resigned herself to waiting ... *still.*

"I've word from the Shepherd. Time has caught us. The King returns... Where is the woman?"

Or perhaps my waiting is nearly done.

"Július? What's happened to your voice?" This was one of the nearby guards. He sounded as if he were making good-natured sport of the youth, which made a certain amount of sense. The guard in question was one of Ebistian's horsemen. That meant he hadn't been present when Sau was first summoned.

"Your Július is gone, child. Now where is—"

"*Child*, is it?" The guardsman gave a dangerous little chuckle. "Mind your tongue, boy. Lest I take you over my knee before all and sundry."

Sau sighed. "I will explain *once*. Then it will be your task to tell your fellows—the *rest* of Ebistian's children. Július is gone. His shadow has returned to the Dark Sea. He has offered up his body, that I might walk with the King on Skolf once more. I am Sau Ra Nemsetak."

There was a collective gasp of awed disbelief. The guard who'd spoken with such derision a moment ago now did so with obvious fear.

"I... The Sharpened Shadow... Yes, Lord. W-welcome back, Lord."

Sau remained silent until the man had stopped his blathering. It didn't take long. When the Sheshik specter spoke again, his voice was both dismissive and unaffected.

"I thank you, child. Now to the matter at hand. Your Shepherd has asked me to set things in motion. Havoc's Horn has been sounded in the southeast. Lord Haunak and Lord Loegrem have opened the way. We no longer need concern ourselves with this place. Now... Where is the T'lendak? Ah. I see her."

"Yes, Lord. Shall we bring them *all* into the fold?"

This question was met with a noise of consideration before Sau answered. "The warriors, and anyone you believe, would be of particular use to us. We aren't massing our full might just yet. The Zwołanie will be some time in coming. Still, I see no harm in creating a useful force if there is an opportunity to do so."

The Zwołanie? The... convocation? What in hells is that?

Apparently Ebistian's guardsman was just as confused, at least at first. "The... Oh! The *Svolání!* Yes, Lord."

Sau made an *ah* sound. "So you are sons of Čeněk. I must ask your Shepherd what prompted him to abandon the sons of Cibor."

"As ... you say, Lord."

"A matter for another time, child. Go. And send Rikten here. Your Shepherd wishes to instruct him on other matters."

"Yes, Lord."

They've left! There should only be Sau, the driver, and Edmund's guard. If I—but the sound of hoofbeats drew her up short.

"T'lendak," Sau began. "He rises. Havoc's Horn has sounded. Our time in this place is both short and inconsequential."

Eliška's voice came out sounding at once delighted and disbelieving. "A brave proclamation, boy. Yet you deliver such news in this ill-fitting tongue?"

Sau sighed. "Rhex misda rryl, T'lendak."

Lashjuk cocked her head to one side, trying to make sense of that. *Rez miss-da rill?* It was at once like no language she'd ever heard, and in part like *every* language she'd ever heard. What was more, the words lingered in her head. They reminded her of children—or, indeed, full-grown children, as so many adults turned out to be—trying to convince one another to commit some mischief.

That's near enough the mark. That, or to convince them that something really isn't so dangerous ... that they surely won't get into any trouble...

Eliška grunted as if she'd been slapped. "How do you..."

"Oth Sau Ra Nemsetak. Now, Vassal of Storms... do you have any among your remaining rabble that are *actually* of the faithful? Of the King's army?"

"They are *all* of the—"

"Spare me such men-da-city, devil." Sau broke the word into its component syllables. "Most within your current retinue are folk to which you have sung songs of fury and outrage, or else have bribed with power. *They* are not the King's faithful. They are the *Storm Queen's* faithful." He sighed once more, then tried again. "Summon those you account worthy. The rest will be dressed and made ready for the Keening."

"...How long do we have?"

"Not long."

The woman issued something between a growl and a squeal of girlish delight. Then came the sound of her horse spurring away. It was now or nev—

"Lord? Ess... ess there vord on my Vlk?"

Lashjuk had to stop herself from cursing aloud. Sau's booted feet turned toward the newcomer. "It will take time. If he returns to you at all, it will take—"

There came the sound of something ripping through the air, then a meaty *thump*. Sau grunted, lumbering forward and knocking the woman asprawl before collapsing atop her. There was a pair of sickening, wet, popping noises as they struck the ground, then a muffled cry of pain before she fell silent. Dust puffed up beneath them in a roiling grey haze. The fletched end of a small arrow was buried deep in Sau's borrowed back.

Lashjuk turned her head away and drew in a sharp breath just in time to avoid coughing or sneezing. The pale cloud may not have given her away, but it did force her mind back to thoughts of the Stormrider.

"Lord!"

The carriage shook. The driver's voice came hurtling down from above right before its owner did. Lashjuk saw the man take a cautious step toward the vehicle's rear. He cursed, then dropped down to one knee to examine Sau. She heard the wounded man's quiet moan.

She felt the carriage as it rocked. Someone was climbing on its right side. A muted *twang* came from somewhere overhead. Then the carriage shifted as the climber moved above.

The driver heard it, too. He stood, stepping back and drawing a knife. "Wait. I... I *know* you. You're..."

The carriage shook again. Then his words were cut off as something whipped through the air and struck him. An instant later, he fell on top of both Sau and the woman with a throwing knife in his throat.

Then came Ebistian's voice, crawling into her ear like an unwelcome song. Its music was untroubled—almost amused.

"Alright... That will do."

She dropped down from the carriage's keel, careful to make as little noise as she could. She still needed to remain hid from sight, but not for much longer.

As he spoke again, it was clear Ebistian was coming closer. She thought she heard two sets of footfalls in the grass and scree, but she couldn't be certain.

"Lord, please stand behind me..."

No, I was right. There are two. Ebistian has another guard with him. Lashjuk could see the hem of a white kontusz just ahead of Ebistian's blue one.

"There's no need. He means me no harm. Though he *does* owe me an explanation as to what it is he's doing here."

"A question I should ask you, Shepherd. You are no varrior. A battlefield vhere all can see your coach? Vhere the survivors can see your face? Survivors *alvays* tell the tale of vhat they saw. Of *who* they saw. You know that better than anyone. You vould never risk such a thing. So, you can't have come seeking var. I thought you may have followed us, but..." The voice from atop the carriage trailed off for a beat. "Did Alojz send for you? Ess *that* vhy you've come?"

Ebistian gave a sour little laugh at this. "I can see that you've had your share of... oh, let us call them *difficulties*. And so I shall forgive you your overreach." Here his voice grew stony. "And remind you of your station. Now why are you *here*, Rákos?"

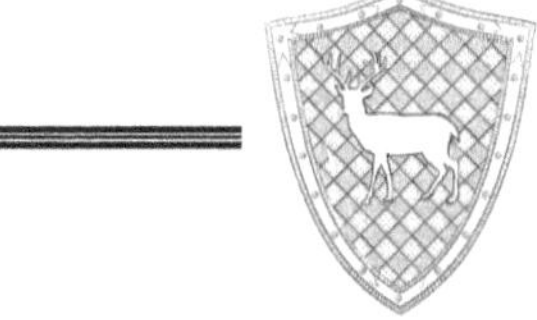

-III-

"Radek?" Olga's voice was thin and foggy, as if she dreamed.

"Yes indeed, my heart's root!" Radek sounded nothing short of delighted, save for the gurgling growl in his voice.

"Radek, what... what's become of you?"

While Olga talked, Kastan stepped back toward the urns and drew her sword anew. *We've become fast friends, you and I, haven't we?* When she'd first wielded the weapon, it had felt clumsy and ill-weighted for her arm. Now it felt as if it had been made to fit her hand.

Radek's eyes followed her as she moved. His voice, however, remained directed at his wife's fearful form.

"Ohhhh, come now, my heart's gleam. There's no need to look so surprised. I've done it! I've earned the King's favor! This is the start of my second life! Of *our* second life!" He laughed, a wet gibber that scraped at the mind. As he did so, he extended his right hand, wrapping its blue madness around a thin strand of rippling red that hadn't been there a moment ago. That shimmering cord spilled down to rest some of its length on the floor at his feet. The air suddenly smelled of spring rain—clean, crisp, and strong enough to make the head swim. "Let me quiet the boy, then we can make our case to her Excellency."

Skar's hurre hung from a hook on his belt. As Kastan watched, he moved his hand toward it, even as he hefted his short spear.

"Radek... Radek, no. Lay down, now. You're dead and gone. This... this is..."

"My second life, culver. No feeeeeear! I shall share it with you! Of *course* I will! The King *always* rewards his faithful *pet*!" The once-man sounded as if he were speaking to a weeping child. He punctuated his words with a flick of his wrist. The motion made the red line dance and snap. It looked like a whip, though it wasn't of any *mortal* design. As it moved, it forked in tines and tongues, sizzling the air. "A kiss, a kiss from finest fire... Heh-ha! I never would have expected the Storm Queen's court to be the one that welcomed us, but..." He shrugged as if to say, *any roof in a rainstorm.*

It's made of ... red lightning? Hells be hid... His whip is made of red lightning! Kastan felt her knees begin to weaken. She forced the feeling of fear aside and tried to ready herself. *I need to watch his movements. I've already been surprised by these things and their impossible quickness once, and it nearly cost us our lives.*

Radek turned his somehow ruined face toward Skar. It hadn't been ruined a moment agone—his death had been from a *throat* wound. Now his face was a swirling mass of darksome damage that seemed to writhe beneath the skin.

"A parting gift to recall your time in Hartscross, boy." He began to swirl the red whip in front of him, moving so the spiral faced Skar directly.

"Ayom ahg puehv gos, gryleyn! Del puehv sakkr!"

Out of the blur of the spiraling red whip came a livid red light. It coalesced into the form of a mature hart with massive antlers. Its hooves sparked and smoked, as did its breath. Small arcs of red and orange darted between the points jutting from its brow. The creature was breathtaking as it pawed at the stone floor, then lowered its head to charge Skar.

As the hellish hart leapt forward, Skar brought his hurre around in mid-roar. He aimed its spin just as he had with the haunts, the circle of its motion held like a shield. The red thing moved as if caught in a sudden wind, then blinked out of existence.

Radek laughed. "Well *well*, child... Let us see if your roaring arm can outlast the power I wield! If you tire before my might wears out, your parting gift will return in allll its splendor!"

Kastan wanted to charge, but something held her back. Instinct? The Inner Winter? Perhaps both. She only knew the feeling was strong.

Olga stepped toward her husband, face set. "Ra-dek... Don't force me to use—"

Whatever she'd meant to threaten never had the chance to sway him. His whip snaked out and wrapped around her, dragging her toward him.

"A kiss, a kiss, my dear..." He opened a mouth full of darksome fangs as she drew near.

Kastan drove forward, doing the only thing she could think to do. She threw a hammer shot. She meant to sever the whip, hoping it would both free Olga and diminish Radek's newfound power.

It worked ... after a fashion. Olga was freed, falling back onto what passed for her posterior. But the red storm light leapt up Kastan's blade, causing her to seize. It was as if her every nerve had been touched with a heated bit of steel. She smelled the sweet scent of meat over a fresh fire, mixed with the acrid scent of burning hair. Then she knew no more.

-IV-

"Maksu, ve... ve really should go."

Maksu stood up from where he knelt by Laagi. Vlk was surprised to see... not a look of anger or disagreement, but one of concern.

"Vlk... you protected me." He wrapped his arms around Vlk, laying his head against the taller boy's chest. "Let me protect *you* now. I'm stronger than I was. I know you're hurt from your fighting, but I'm not. Father will be back soon, and I won't let *anything* happen to you while we wait." He leaned his head back to look up and meet Vlk's eyes. "Alright?"

He hadn't realized how much he'd needed that embrace. The day's horror—Waltyr, Laagi, the dead rising, his *two* visits to the between-place—it was all still trapped inside his head and heart. He returned the gesture, offering a smile he hadn't planned to wear.

"I'm not afraid, Maksu. Vell, not of being alone vithout any grown people. I'm just..."

Edmund gave a rattling gasp, then stopped breathing altogether. Several beats passed with both boys unable to do more than stare. Without warning, the man drew in a great and whooping breath.

"*That* frightens me."

"Father told us he won't survive. I'm sad to hear it. I *like* the Count. He's tall and strong and kind. Did you see how angry he was when the Bluemarks were standing there with swords out?"

Vlk nodded, but his heart was torn. *He'd* been angry, too. But that had been before toda—before he'd met *other* Bluemark guardsmen. Ulrek and Waltyr had been better men than any he'd met. Hells, even the captain had been better than he'd thought possible.

Another of those wheezing exhalations rocked Edmund's body, followed by no breath at all. Maksu pulled himself away from Vlk to watch. His face was studious, somehow. Again, Edmund drew breath in a great whoop, but this time he wasn't alone. Laagi, too, had drawn a deep lungful of air.

Vlk's heart stopped for a moment. Ebistian had been right! Laagi *was* alive!

Maksu walked over to the gnoerk boy and knelt beside him once more. He took Laagi's sallow hand between both of his blue ones.

Vlk could only stare for a long moment. Then a realization struck him like a punch to the stomach. Screwing up his courage, he crossed over to Edmund's makeshift pallet and knelt. He took the count's massive hand between both of his, just as Maksu had.

"He shouldn't take his last breath vith no one beside him. Lakkrid vould be here if he could, and he and his father vill vant to know someone vas vith him in the end."

Maksu said nothing, but that was alright.

A tense few moments passed in silence. Then—a miracle that nearly caused Vlk to cry out—Edmund squeezed his hand and opened his eyes.

"I... Do you see me?"

Edmund gave a shallow nod, smiling as best he could.

"I should go find—"

But Edmund squeezed down on his hand, shaking his head. His eyes were glassy and bloodshot ... and far too bright.

"Vlk," he mouthed. "You b-b-brave..." No voice carried his words. He didn't have enough breath for proper speech.

Vlk swallowed hard, then made himself smile down at the count as he spoke. "You vere a varlord. Your voice chased avay fear and... and..." And what? He didn't know. He thought he should say ... *something*. But...

Edmund's smile grew. With an almighty effort, he reached his other hand up and ruffled Vlk's hair. As the man's hand fell away, it slid behind the boy's dim-side ear. The touch made him feel clean again, somehow. It seemed to cancel out the oddity of Ebistian's touch on his bright side.

"Vlk... You... Kas-ss-tan'sss kniiight." He drew in another of those too-deep breaths. "Ss-strong and b-bray-brave. C-h-hall to the line. Prom-misss..."

Vlk heard another of those rattling exhalations. Somehow, he knew there would be no more. The great man's eyes were still open—still held Vlk's own. But the light was leaving them even now.

"I... I..."

But it was no good. Vlk couldn't speak. He tried to nod, but once his head had lowered, he couldn't lift it again. He felt Edmund's hand go slack, and all he could do was hang his head and weep.

He felt a hand on his shoulder, and was surprised to hear a voice other than Maksu's.

"I'm sorry, Vlk. For your loss, yes, though not for the man's death. Edmund the Tall should never have chosen to be our enemy. My father never wanted that."

Vlk accepted the touch, though he didn't move or speak.

"Aehe, Laagi?" Maksu's words were so much useless gibbering—right up until Laagi answered him in the Trade Tongue.

"Because I thought he was just another Venzene Fenlok... another Fennk bragging about the black blood he claimed to know. And I... You're proof that I was wrong, Lakkrid."

"Elf's reach? Elf's brother? I don't... I don't understand, Laagi. What do elves have to do with ... anything? And also, I'm not Lakkrid. I'm Maksu. Lakkrid's my... He's my... um."

"Kin? Your palrym?"

Maksu sounded as if he'd brightened. "Uhuh. We're palrym."

Laggi removed his hand from Vlk's shoulder after a squeeze. "Maksu, you're young, but you should ask your mother and father about the elves. The damned fen *made* the Empire... or at least helped the humans make it." He paused. "It doesn't matter. I need to find my father. I'm glad you lived, Vlk. Now that we've won, I'll want you fighting beside me. If... if you won't do that, I'll do what I can to make certain you aren't killed out of hand. You deserve better than that."

"No! Laagi, Father says we must stay *here* until he gets back!"

"Maksu, *my* father's waiting for me outside somewhere. And without me, there aren't many who can act as his voice. Ed wrin ragzak."

"Ohhhhh."

Vlk lifted Edmund's hand to his lips, placing a kiss on his knuckles, then drew in a deep breath and did the thing he feared doing the most. He reached down and closed the man's empty eyes.

When it was done, he turned and stood. "Maksu," he sniffled. "If he vants to go, let him go. Ve don't need to hold him. Ebistian didn't say ve had to keep *him* here. Only that ve had to stay till someone ve knew came to find us."

Maksu considered, then nodded. "Ok, Vlk. Zgoda. Um, I mean, um... Souhlas!"

Laagi offered a good-natured smirk over Maksu's head—two older boys sharing a knowing and universal sentiment. *Smalls. What can you do?*

Vlk gave a nod that served for both boys at once. Laagi turned and made it a single step before he grabbed him by the shoulder.

"Vait!" he hissed. He heard a sound outside the tent—voices, yes, but another sound he'd come to know very well. The *twang* of a crossbow.

-V-

"And vhere *should* I have taken him, Shepherd? Vhere else vould ve have found safety? Ve vere hunting near Haluzfeld vhen the Red Court attacked. They vere unnumbered and vell-organized. They used sorcery to move themselves and their engines, much as you do. So vhere vould *you* have had us go?" Rákos sounded incredulous, full of disgust. "Ve hid, then ve ran southeast."

Lashjuk heard the county-clad guardsman draw breath several times as if he meant to speak, but no words came out. Everyone in the empire feared sorcery, but few feared it more than the armsmen who might be forced to *contend* with it.

Ebistian made a dismissive noise. "Sorcery. Well, Eoalunth sorcery be damned. That attack was *weeks* agone, Rákos. I applaud you for proving my faith in you well-founded. At the least, you did not stand frozen, waiting for the final blow to fall. Yet… why did you not make for Rosefort? You would have found allies there, and *I* would have had word perhaps a week sooner. Yet you elected to come *here?*"

"I vould *never* have risked taking him there. They came from the East! Given Rosefort ess so close to the Eodenth border? No, the risk vas too great."

Lashjuk was certain the man atop the carriage was holding something back. She'd no idea what, but there was *something*. Ebistian seemed to have reached the same conclusion, for when he spoke next, his voice had grown low and somehow dangerous.

"What aren't you telling me, Rákos? You are *far* too skilled in trail-craft to fear being caught by that rabble."

"The Storm Queen ess more clever than you think, Shepherd. If it vere only her outriders, ve could likely have remained hidden. But I vould not risk Andrej against your old ally's magic."

Ahh, so it is *the same Rákos!* She'd met both him and his boy briefly as they'd trooped out of the northern gate… hells, a week agone? A fortnight? Regardless, there might well be more than one Rákos in the encampment. More than one with a boy named Andrej? She thought not.

"Honestly, Shepherd… Vhat could ve do against such might? *You* have sorcery. I do not. You may have taught some of your other folk those secret skills, but of all that you've taught me, you've kept that to your—"

The guard was moving now. He stepped back, his boots turning to face Ebistian. Lashjuk could hear him reposition his spear.

"Lord? Does this man speak truth? *Are* you a… a kouzelník? You *cannot* be in league with the Eoalunth witch who sent those horse humpers to kill our wives and chil—"

"Drae ny dur, xu lal." Ebistian's voice was a dismissive slide, a sighed tone which sounded like a long-suffering parent yielding to a wheedling child. As Ebistian finished speaking in that strange tongue, the guard dropped his spear, shrieked like a ryś—what the highborn call a *lynx*—and ran off. Ebistian caught the weapon on the top of his foot, then bounced it up to his hands. It was a deft maneuver for a man his age.

Lashjuk's palms were pressed against the cold ground. She *had* been about to spring up and reveal herself, azhkast at the ready. She'd stopped herself in the very nick. Now, for what seemed like the hundredth time, she waited.

"Vell, I've made you act in anger, Shepherd. That's a small victory." Rákos sounded both pleased and disappointed all at a go.

"Not at all, Rákos. I simply grew tired of his useless company. *You* pose me no threat, despite your childish attempts to undo me." He sighed through this last, sounding more than a trifle bored. "I suppose I could've killed him or forced him into my thrall, but it would've been to no purpose. No, far simpler to frighten him off and have done."

"He vill come back to himself, though. And vhen he does, you'll have to answer to hess accusations. You *and* your closies."

Ebistian laughed. The sound was so unaffected that Lashjuk found *herself* beginning to grin.

"Rákos, it is *over.* None of our plans *matter* anymore. The way is open. The King returns. I sent that man off, yes, but even now, the culling has begun in preparation for the—"

"—The Keening. Opravdu? The King ess *truly* returning?" Rákos didn't sound hopeful. He sounded terrified.

"Ohhhh yes. I have given you truth. Now you must return the courtesy. Why did you bring the boy here?"

"I vanted to bring him before Alojz." At first, Rákos spoke in a small, embarrassed tone. Yet his voice seemed to gain a cold surety as he pressed on. "He, at least, vould hear me—vould hear *us.* Andrej ess mine, Shepherd. I *vill* not let your intrigues rob me of him. I'll not let you rob *him!* Not of hess life, and not of hess future! He deserves to make hess *own* choices, *vithout* you moving him around like a piece on a king's var board."

Ebistian listened to this in silence. After a pause, he asked a question in a quite ordinary tone. "And what did the Lord Alojz tell you?"

"He… he bade me seek a vay into the good graces of the Count's scouts. It vould serve all purposes. Their commander loves Edmund, Andrej vould gain both training and a better view of the land Edmund rules, and a chance to earn reputation. And *ve* vould have a force to keep him safe."

"All the while being close to the *true* seat of the county. A clever plan, in its way. But—and hear me now, Rákos—bauth puav zeteek gilk."

Silence met this odd string of words. Then Ebistian sighed.

"Why are you *dead*, Rákos? You're dead, yet you *look* very much alive..." The question of *how* may not have been spoken aloud, but its implication was impossible to miss.

"The Storm Queen's outriders took me. Then they voke me again. I saw your coach riding into camp and knew you vould be here. So I fed before I came to find you. I vanted to be at my clearest vhen ve spoke. Vanted to be able to enjoy that very look on your face vhen you tried to own my soul again."

"Ahh. And how many of your brothers did you kill in order to ready yourself, then?"

"Only one. A young footman of yours I'd not seen before. Two, if ve count that boy vith my quarrel in his back. The rest vere all of the Red Court. I have done you *that* service, at least."

"And so you've taken as much shadow as your new body needs. For now, at any rate. Well played, child. Puehv ka jhoaz zeteek ka, mavkan. Now, put that crossbow aside and come down here. I would have you stand before me ... ere the end."

The carriage shook above her. She heard a dull tap, then saw a pair of pale boots drop down to where the guard had stood a moment before.

Ebistian stepped back, turning to face the man. "You began your second life and thought yourself beyond my reach. Mavken—free of fear and the weakness of mortal flesh, just as we taught you. Brave, but foolish, Rákos. You've wasted your one advantage. I did indeed think you still lived. Had you attacked me rather than scratching the itch of self-indulgence... But no. No, you needed to—how did you put it?—*see that look on my face when I tried to own your soul?*"

He stabbed his scavenged spear into the grey ground behind him, then drew the sword that hung on his right hip.

"Ah well. Rákos of Měsíční Prst, you are a traitor. Given you entered my service by way of betrayal, I suppose I shouldn't be surprised." He widened his stance. "Neither you nor the boy much matter now, but rest assured, hunter... *I shall take excellent care of him.*" His voice dropped into a low and dangerous purr for this final, terrible stave.

It was enough. Lashjuk uncoiled from beneath the carriage. She came up behind Ebistian with an azhkast in her fists and *drove* it forward. At the same moment, the old man's blade hurtled toward the hunter's neck at an unnatural speed. She saw the look of blissful satisfaction cross Rákos's face as he marked her movement, but it was short-lived. Ebistian's sword took the man's head just as Lashjuk's short spear plunged through his back and out through his chest.

He exhaled a thin puff of air, then collapsed against her. His sword slipped from his hand, clanging against the carriage's dark wooden side. His hands wrapped around the weapon's haft below the spear's bloody head.

Lashjuk growled from over his shoulder, feeling a sense of satisfaction she hadn't anticipated. She shook, then drew in a breath, before *yanking* the weapon back. She sidestepped as Ebistian stumbled and tripped over the small stack of dead or unconscious bodies—the driver, Sau, and the woman. As he fell backward, she turned her body to follow his progress.

The next few beats were a blur. She was stabbing her azhkast into him again and again, growling as she worked. Her palms were hot, her back and arms sore. Before her rage could fly from her altogether, she leaned her face down over his. She was panting, mouth dry and stomach clenched, but her eyes were quite clear.

"Maksu is *my* son... *Shepherd.* You will never lay eye or hand on him again."

He was trying to say something. His eyes were enormous and quite beautiful...

She snapped her own closed, then turned away. "I know what your kind can do, zajh. You won't work your will on I or mine ever again." She was remembering Geatbern-Kuba that never was. *He* had been a zajh—a shaman whose power had come close to killing Eobum and his folk.

But this time, the battle is utterly mine. Eobum wasn't here to help me. Nobody was here to help me. She laughed to herself. *My huntress's heart, Eobum. Aye and aye. My huntress's heart and this monster is its first real prey. A kill to be proud of, if ever there was such a thing.*

She heard him gurgling behind her, still trying to say ... something. It was so much gibberish to her ear.

She opened her eyes, meaning to turn back—perhaps to find and pierce what passed for his blackened heart. Standing a few feet in front of her, just past the now headless body of the hunter, she saw Andrej. The blond boy stood with a massive red hound at his side. He surveyed the scene with a thin layer of self-control painted on his face. The hound looked at her, then wagged its tail in a hopeful sort of way.

"F-father," he managed, then sniffled. "You killed... killed him."

Lashjuk was starting to shake her head when she saw where he was looking. His eyes were fixed on the still form of Ebistian. She replaced her now-bloody azhkast in her brace and offered Andrej an unguarded smile. "I did," said she. And before she could offer more, he flung himself into her arms, weeping.

"Over... It's... He's..." But he had no words. He was shaking with such obvious relief that for a moment, all she could do was hold him, stroking his hair and making soft *shushing* noises.

"Andrej? Is... Štít?" A woman's voice from somewhere behind her. Andrej loosened the hoop of his arms from Lashjuk's waist, though he was unwilling to sever all contact. He looked at the red hound as it walked up beside him and barked a single time. The tone was warm, not quite *playful*... Satisfied? Well, no matter.

Lashjuk kept a protective arm around Andrej's shoulders as she turned to find the voice's owner. Nobody had come up behind her... A thing she realized she hadn't been prepared for. She mentally chastised herself to be more aware of her surroundings.

"Ha... We finally meet, little cousin. I'm... I'm pleased." The voice came from Vlk's mother. Came from it, yes, but it didn't *belong* to Vlk's mother. This voice sounded cultured—of highborn education. It sounded as if it had barely been kissed by old Kovalunth. The woman in question had a Kovalunth accent an inch thick when she'd first called to Sau.

"I... I don't..."

"Understand. I know, cousin. There won't be time for me to explain it to you. This woman's body is badly broken. I cannot borrow it for long."

Lashjuk expected Andrej to be at least as taken aback by this strange pronouncement as she was. On the contrary, the boy appeared untroubled, overall.

"Who are you, then? Do... do you work for Father?"

The woman spat. "He is *not* your father, boy. But nevermind. Sink down to Štít's level. Meet her eyes."

Lashjuk looked between woman, boy, and dog and found she had no idea what to think, or who to trust. Still, at least the woman didn't appear to think much of Ebistian. That was something.

Andrej disentangled himself the rest of the way. Before he could do more, Lashjuk's hand caught his shoulder.

"Are you *certain*?" Certain of what? She herself had no idea. She felt a strong urge to ask the question, and that was enough for her.

Andrej offered a grateful grin. He sniffled again, wiping the back of his hand beneath his nose. "Of whoever *she* is? No. Of *Štít*? Yes." With that, he dropped to one knee and met the great red beast's bright gaze. He raised his voice enough for it to carry. "Now what, cousin?"

"Hold her gaze, and h-h-hold your fingers deep into her fur."

"Alright..." Andrej's tone was one part acceptance and one part report that he'd done as bidden.

"F-f-fi-ine. Štít? Andrej nier ad, nier iddor... nier trae lam. N... nier seh?"

The hound gave a throaty bark in seeming reply.

The woman's breath was shallow, now. Her unaccented voice came out a dry, cracked thing as if she were fighting to stay awake. "An... Andrej. Štít nier trand, nier talp, nee... yer bweh... bweh... buedh. Nier s-s-she?"

"I don't..."

"Do you *accept*... do you agree?"

"To *what?*"

"To... to Štít. I called her f-for *you*, Andrej. She was brought here for... for..."

But Štít had begun to growl. Her eyes were flitting to the side, back over the boy's shoulder. Then came the sound of wood and metal scraping the stony ground.

Lashjuk turned her head away from Andrej and the great red creature before him. Her movements were slow, as if she were locked in some terrible dream. What she saw next filled her insides with sharpened shards of ice. Ebistian, bloody and gaunt, was leaning on the departed guard's spear with both hands. He was standing over the woman's pinned form, mouth moving in a sluggish, red-lipped mockery of speech.

After her initial feeling of horrified revulsion, Lashjuk came to a dark and lovely realization. Ebistian was a man she would gladly kill a second time.

She reached back to pull a fresh azhkast, took aim, and threw. The weapon sailed true, striking him in his chest and knocking him asprawl. The impact came just as he'd lowered the point of his makeshift prop down to the woman's throat. A red rush ran out across the grey ground from where spearpoint met skin.

The dying woman called Andrej's name through a sickening, blood-choked gurgle. Then she fell silent.

"I agree!" Andrej's voice was strangled and desperate. "I accept! N-nier seh! Nier seh!"

Lashjuk laid her hand on his shoulder, saying nothing. A beat went by in silence. Then she walked over to Ebistian's miserable body. She knelt down... felt for a pulse... smiled. She wrapped her bright hand around the haft of her weapon, placed a foot on the devil's bloody chest and belly, and stood. She kept that foot there, bracing her as she pulled the weapon free. When it was done, she spat in the fiend's sightless, open eye.

"What?"

Lashjuk snapped her head back toward Andrej, then took a final glance at Ebistian as she spoke. "I didn't speak."

Andrej laughed with surprised delight. Satisfied that the zajh was indeed dead, Lashjuk turned and walked back to the boy's side.

"No! I had no idea!"

He was speaking to the hound. At first, she thought this was strange—that perhaps he'd suffered a shock and grown addled. Then she realized how foolish she was being.

"Is she speaking to you, Andrej?"

"I... How did you... Oh. I was speaking back to her out loud, wasn't I." It was a sheepish non-question. She answered it anyway.

"You were. You were, and we need to move before his right hand returns. Rikten is a man I would rather not meet over the corpse of his master."

"It's strange," he said as he stood. "I can't *hear* her, exactly, but..."

"But you can *sense* her meaning. Images and flashes of color."

Andrej stopped in mid-stride, staring at Lashjuk in frank disbelief. "*How...*" His voice was too breathy from surprise to carry much volume, which was just as well. The last thing they needed just now was company.

She smiled, placing a hand on his shoulder as much to guide him as to offer encouragement. "You'll get used to it in time. I'd no idea a hound could meld with a person's shadow, mind you. But you'll get used to it in time."

"You're a..."

"Woman in haste. We can talk about this when we're actually safe."

He nodded, then began to walk. Coming to the sadful form of the headless hunter, he stopped and knelt down. She was surprised to see that there appeared to be little to no blood from his death—not on the ground, nor on either part of his body.

Strange.

"Thank you," said Andrej. "Thank you for all that you taught me and tried to give me. I'm free now. And so are you, Otec."

Lashjuk bowed her head as he spoke his final word to Rákos's departing shadow. Then she cocked it to one side, sensing her *own* invisible aid.

"Andrej, we need to move. Something's coming, and we need to be inside when it does."

"I have to warn—"

Andrej took a single step forward, as if he meant to sprint. His hound growled, bringing him up short.

"But if... What? The... sharpening stone? The... *sharpening*? I don't—"

"I do. The Keening. The devils mentioned it was coming. If it's coming, we're leaving. Come on."

He nodded, and they rounded to the front of the tent. They saw the fallen form of another of Edmund's guards, a bolt in his chest. Lashjuk hurried him along past the poor fellow. They entered the tent with the red hound leading the way.

-VI-

"We need weapons, Vlk. Something better than our eating daggers." Laagi's whisper came out calm, if a bit clipped. "Maksu? See if you can find something for us."

Vlk looked at Laagi, then at Maksu, nodding. He kept his voice low, but above Laagi's whisper. Loud whispers were often easier to hear and locate than soft speech—a truth taught him by years of playing Haunted Forest. "He's right. Ve need something better—something *longer* if you can find it. But be as soft as you can. Ve don't vant whoever's outside to know ve're here."

Maksu nodded, his expression serious. He moved toward the table, then toward the back of the tent. He hissed an odd little whispered *ooooh* that squeaked near its middle.

Vlk and Laagi had moved to opposite corners of the tent's front. Now they both looked back just in time to see Maksu slip through an opening. Vlk caught a glimpse of stairs down and relaxed. He glanced toward Laagi, who wore an expression of confused concern, offering him a nod. Laagi shrugged one shoulder as if to say *so be it,* and the pair went back to listening.

There were voices, then an odd scream that froze his blood. Given

Laagi's face, he'd been just as frightened by it. The sound came toward them... then kept going toward the southeast.

Both boys breathed a visible sigh of relief, then smiled at one another. *You see? Ve might've been friends if you and your father hadn't...*

His thoughts were cut off by more voices. A dog barked, making him think of Štít. He hoped she and her master... but that led him to thoughts of Pavel and Andrej. Hells, were any of them even alive? And hadn't they all come back to tend to Andrej's wounded father?

Maksu reappeared. He held two arming swords, one in each hand, the flats of their blades laid over his shoulders. His face was a comical mask of near-ceremonial seriousness and childish pride. He'd found exactly what the older boys had asked for, and he knew it.

Vlk beamed at him, nodding. He stepped to meet the smaller boy, taking one of the swords and marveling at its weight. Maksu *had* grown stronger. This weapon was manageable, but far too long and heavy for everyday use. He looked at the intricate work of the pommel—a metal heater in miniature, as thick as both of his thumbs, bearing an etching of the count's arms.

"These aren't real," Laagi whispered.

"Real enough." Vlk stepped back and swung his borrowed weapon around, testing its balance. It would do, at least for a short fight.

"No, I mean, it's not for fighting. It's to show, not to sharpen." Laagi slid his hand up the naked blade, gripping it tight. He pulled his hand away, showing Vlk his undamaged palm. "They're sword-shaped cudgels, not swords. Hit, don't slice."

Vlk looked at his own blade and saw Laagi was right. That was disappointing, but it was better than nothing.

It'll be like vielding practice svords. Heavy practice svords, but still. He nodded, then took up position again near the front corner.

Maksu walked back to stand behind the table. It was a good thought, putting the obstacle between him and whoever might charge into the tent. He'd made it about halfway when it happened.

Slender, golden fingers snaked into the tent at somewhere near Vlk's eye level. They wrapped around the lip of the canvas flap and pulled it outward. Then a second hand—this one pale and pink—reached forward and pushed aside the fur that kept the cold at bay, sliding it along on its hooks.

Vlk made ready, nodding at Laagi who was doing the same.

A bark preceded a furry black face and a broad mass of red fur.

"Štít?" Vlk couldn't help himself. He dropped his sword and

laughed. "Štít!"

Laagi looked at him uncertainly—doubly so when Andrej stepped in, calling Vlk's name in delighted surprise. If his expression at the sight of hound and human showed uncertainty, his reaction upon the gnoerkish woman's entry was nothing short of awe.

Vlk understood why. She was breathtaking. Tall, with a face of deepest gold and eyes of mid-day blue, she was at once fair and fell in equal measure. Her trousers were dun colored, and her beaked boots and long shirt were of a red so weathered as to be almost brown. At first glance, he thought she wore a hood of dark blue silk, which was strange and distracting to look upon. With a jolt, he realized he was seeing the ordinary magic of her hair.

Breathtaking? That was underselling it. He found himself *staring,* uncertain how to look at her. What he did know was that doing so made his face grow hot. He would have been wary, save that she'd come in with Andrej.

And that led his mind back to his friend. Vlk forced himself to turn away, stepping over to put a hand on Andrej's shoulder.

"You're alive! I vasn't sure vhere you and the others vent. Vhen you veren't *here,* I feared..."

But Andrej's happy smile had shattered as his eyes fell on Edmund's body. He stepped past Vlk, not noticing Laagi or Maksu at all. As if it were against his will, he dropped to his knees beside the count and simply *stared.*

"You're Vlk." The gnoerkish woman's voice was a scratched song of restrained emotion. She turned to Laagi for a beat and spoke in her own tongue. "Nqel, geklg. Erld sngsh. Erld nak, awka nqel."

He tried to reply, but no words came out. At length, he gave up and just nodded. Satisfied, the woman turned her luminous blue dreamer's lamps on Vlk once more.

"I am," said he. He knew he should offer some form of respect—Lady, Mistress, Teta, or the like. And he'd have gladly done so if he knew which one to use.

"I'm pleased. You seem none the worse for wear." She looked him up, then down, nodding. "I have hard news, but before I tell you my drift, you must answer me something. Where is—"

But Štít had begun to growl. She stepped forward with slow, measured movements. Her head was low, and her tail was slung high, bushed out behind her.

A blue blur caught Vlk's eye as Maksu ran toward the rear of the tent.

The red hound followed him, barking.

"No!" the woman shouted, racing after Štít. Vlk and Laagi joined her, crying for the beast to stop.

Boy and bolting hound plunged through the rear flap before any of them had crossed the room. Maksu was screaming. There was a loud *thud,* followed by the sound of something ceramic shattering, then more of the boy's inarticulate cries ... which were fading... fading...

They burst through the canvas, took only a beat to process the layout of their new surroundings, then bolted down the stairs as if their heads were on fire.

"Maksu! *Maksu!"*

But the boy was giggling now.

Vlk was the first to see him. He was on his back atop a rug, pinned between Štít's massive paws. She was licking his face, her tail moving at a speed that turned it into a blur.

The woman dashed over. As soon as she came within arm's reach, Štít sat back and looked at her as if to say, *I've caught him. He's all yours now.*

"Og? Og!" Maksu was on his feet and in his mother's arms before she'd finished the act of kneeling down beside him. He was shuddering—not with tears, but with utter, relieved delight.

Vlk grinned, thumping Laagi on his shoulder. The boy gave a sad smile, nodding as he turned to go. Štít stopped him with a bark, then nuzzled the top of her crimson head beneath his dim hand. The gnoerk boy didn't seem able to stop himself. He turned, knelt down, and began petting the beast as if they were old friends.

Vlk turned to regard Maksu and his mother again and couldn't help but smile. The pair were murmuring to one another in their own tongue. Each bore looks of as near to perfect contentment as he thought he'd ever seen.

Then Andrej was there, standing at the top of the stairs. He held a lit lantern—the one that looked as if it had come from the undertown.

"The rain's started."

Laagi—who was getting his face licked and resisting his every instinct to laugh, judging by the look of concentration on his face—asked Vlk's question for him. "So?"

"The Shar... er, Keening."

Vlk hadn't the slightest idea what in all the hells *that* was, but Laagi seemed to.

"Then it's time I go. My father will need me."

"It's too dangerous." Andrej shook his head. "There's something in the rain that's... that's bad."

Laagi smiled, showing two tiny, yellowing lower tusks. "For you, yes. My father is the Storm Queen's champion. I've nothing to fear from the King's Keening." He stood, walking to Lashjuk and Maksu. "Take care of your Og, nk. She's too pretty to lose, and you won't get another."

Maksu grinned. "I will." He paused, looked at his mother, then back to the gnoerk boy. "Laagi? You could stay with us... you and your Ng."

The woman met Laagi's eye and nodded. "I know you won't—that your father won't. *You* need to know that you can. Your Storm Queen and the devil *Shepherd* who stole my son are close kith if not kin. If you stay with them, you'll be on the wrong side of the battlefield."

Laagi's smile softened. "All I know now is that my father needs me. I was in the Shadow Lands, Og—the Grey Lands, and the Shepherd brought me back. I can't waste that gift."

She nodded, laying a hand to Laagi's cheek. He bore this—even bowed his head to lean into the touch. She passed a final word with him before sliding her hand away. "Laagi, erld lash Ng. Erld nak awka lak, de nak, lak, gush."

He nodded. "Bruu og. Bruu." He stopped at Vlk's side, unable to resist scratching behind Štít's ears as he did. "Vlk? I meant what I said. I'd gladly fight beside you. And if you won't fight for me, I'll do whatever I can to keep you as *safe* as I can. You're strong, loyal, and honest. You aren't like your father."

Vlk grinned. "I'm *nothing* like my father. Vhen ve vin, I'll do vhatever I can for you... vhich starts now. Štít has an itch I have to see to. If that gnoerk boy I vas fighting fled vhile I vas busy tending to the var hound..."

Laagi rolled his eyes, grinning as he headed off. Vlk *did* drop down to scratch at Štít's back. He thought he heard Andrej and Laagi pass a quiet word between them, but he couldn't be certain.

A moment later, and it didn't matter.

"Her Excellency's waiting. She'll need what news we have."

Maksu's mother turned, lifting her son bodily. "*Her* Excellency?"

Andrej nodded. "Kastan. I'll take you to her."

With that, they all trooped into the undertown.

-VII-

"Kastan? *Kastan*... Kastan... *look*. Open your eyes. Kastan, *please*... see me plain. And hear me plain. While the hammer's not yet fallen."

It's a man's voice—familiar, but strange to her ears. It makes her want to smile, for it sounds free and unweathered. It also makes her want to weep, but she doesn't understand why.

She tries to open her eyes but finds that they won't obey.

"Not like *that,* girl." This is another voice—another man, full of impatience and frustration that doesn't feel as if it's aimed at her alone. "Relax the muscles of your face. Now... when I tell you to—and *not* before—you must shrug your brows, as if you mean to express surprise or disbelief. Lift from the temples. Let your forehead follow."

She begins to do as she's been instructed, though the entire affair is one shade away from being laughable. Shrug her brows? How in all the hells is she supposed to...

"I did *not* tell you to be-gin!" The older voice breaks this last word into two distinct syllables.

She stops at once.

"Soft, soft. No need to take your anger out on *her*." This is the younger man again. He sounds as if he's speaking through a thin grin.

"Yes, yes. You're right, of course. It isn't as if she might come back to herself at any moment, is it? We're *certainly* not in need of haste."

The older fellow's derision makes her want to laugh, though she resists the urge.

"Kastan?" he continues. "When your eyes open, you will be tempted to rise. Tempted to look about. Do *neither.* Do not even sit up, let alone stand. We will come into your line of sight. *You* must remain as still as you can. Now ... begin."

She begins. And once she does, she finds that she understands the older man's meaning right away. There's a moment of pleasant dizziness focused in the center of her brow. It's a glimpse of what it feels like to be several swift cups of mulled cider into a cold winter's night—not bleary-eyed, but rather full of mellow goodwill toward the wide, wild world.

Her eyes open, which is strange, for they *feel* closed. She sees the chamber she's been... been... doing *something* in. Its high ceilings are bright with a grey light that makes her moan. She doesn't know why that should be. Light of any color has never made her moan before.

"*There...* No, no, don't turn your head. We're a breath away." This is the younger one again.

He leans over her. He's tall and well-built. His hair is a pale blond wave that would, if it grew much longer, fall down over each of his ears. His upper lip bears a thin mustache. His smile is ... warm. Yes, full of love and a familiar warmth. Yet she cannot find the name that goes with that face. It dances just out of memory's reach.

"I'm sorry, Kastan. I never wanted to lay this burden at your feet. I'd hoped you would find your own way—find your own joy in someone. There..." He shakes his head. "There simply wasn't time."

Another face looms over her vision, his forehead seeming to touch the mustachioed man's. His hair spills down over his shoulders, hanging shadows across much of his face. Yet his eyes... they're shrewd, hard things, difficult to look away from. As he speaks, it becomes clear this is the older voice she's been hearing.

"You'll need to wake soon, and there's much you need to hear. Do you know us?"

She tries to shake her head and nearly screams. Her body feels as if it's fallen asleep the way a foot sometimes will. Pins, needles, and fire from toe to top.

"Hells be hid, girl. Are you incapable of following such simple instructions?"

"Aedelt!" The younger man's voice cuts across the elder like a whip-crack. "Save your rage for those who've earned it." He looks back down into Kastan's face. "It's Edmund. I've... I've slipped sideways. You are the Countess of Jižní Pochod now... while Jižní Pochod lasts."

She tries to speak and finds, to her surprise, that she can. In fact, her voice sounds far more awake and aware than she feels. "Edmund, I... I'm so, so sorry. I—"

He cuts her off, albeit with as much gentleness as he can muster. "I know. But Aedelt's right. We *are* pressed for time. There is a man called Ebistian. He's Alojz's chief scholar. He's the one who undid me—took my shadow from me and gave it to another. He's a sorcerer."

Here Aedelt cuts in. "And while he's dead, I doubt very much that will slow him down for as long as it ought to. He and the force that attacked us are in league with one another. They serve someone they continue to call the King."

"But..."

"But Venzene has no king. It has an emperor. I know. Hush, now."

Kastan hushes. What more can she do? Let them talk. If she *is* the Countess, that makes Baron Vägiaedelt of Haluzfeld her vassal. So fair enough. She'll hold her tongue for now and save her questions for the end. And then, come hell's own harbinger, she *will* have her say, and all the way to the end.

Edmund takes up the tale. "Do you have my žezlo?"

Kastan resists the urge to nod. "I do. Olga gave it to me."

Edmund's young face becomes washed in obvious relief. "Good. In the grand chamber of the undertown—where you'll be when your eyes open—do you know the great statue? The woman with the spear?"

"Aye. The angel... the anděl."

"The very same. Remove her spear and place the žezlo in her grasp, then twist as the clock's arms twist. You'll hear a click, then something like the single chime of a small bell. Pull out toward yourself. Not up, mind. Outward. Then step back. She will open to you and show you the way. What's there is yours now. When you're ready, remove the žezlo. Do you understand?"

Aedelt cuts in. "It doesn't matter if you *believe,* mind you. Only that you understand."

"I ... do."

Edmund flushes at that particular choice of words, but presses on. "You, erm... You've a choice to make. We have ... Aedelt? You'd better explain."

"Mmmm. Kastan, there are forty-nine days. Forty-nine days of the soul, as I've no doubt your tutors explained to you. Much of what they say has some agenda behind it. Often it's little more than well-meaning blather, but there *are* truths."

Kastan makes an *mmm* sound. "I was taught that, when we slip sideways, the dead have forty-nine days to see and say from within the Grey Between. By the end of that time, the spirit has gone on to whatever comes next for it—the hells, the Hallowed Halls, and so on."

Aedelt nods, brightening. "Yes, indeed. Their shadow begins its journey back to the Sea, from whence we all come. That's the way of things—or *was* the way of things. Until Ebistian worked his will. By some foul art, he has taken Edmund's shadow and given it to another."

"But ... Aedelt, I don't understand. You said his spirit was taken. Yet here he is. Here you *both* are..."

Aedelt sighs. "There isn't time for this. Not for a full explanation." He pauses, wearing a look of consideration. "The spirit is a painting of all you are and all you know. The shadow is all that you have done and might yet do—all that you've created, or might create. It is your sense of force, your experiences, your talents... your *time* on Skolf. For now, let that be enough."

Kastan gapes. She can find no words. It's difficult enough to come to terms with the news Edmund has fallen. To hear now that he and all that he's seen and done will be... what, erased?

"No... not *erased*. You said this ... Ebistian—he *stole* your shadow and gave it to another." She looks from Edmund to Aedelt. "So that means this other now has all of Edmund's... has Edmund's..."

"Shadow. Yes. Edmund, I admit to being wrong. She *is* as keen minded as you said. Lady, Edmund's shadow is gone. His spirit *might* make it to the Hallowed Halls, but..."

"But you don't know that for certain."

Edmund allows his smile to soften, becoming resigned. "We do not."

"Then what can we—"

"Nothing, Lady," says Edmund. "We tell you this so you know the danger of this monster and his following. We tell you so that you at least have some warning. You have something else, as well... or will soon."

Kastan waits, knowing there must be more.

"You have my son."

"Your..."

"Andrej," says Aedelt. "My cousin—my cousin's son."

She reels. There's a vague sensation of tears prickling the corners of her eyes, but distantly, like the chill that runs up the spine at the first whistle of winter winds beyond the shuttered sill.

Andrej... Andrej is your heir... your son. Oh, Edmund... She tries to speak, to offer some word of consolation, but she can't find her voice. *Honor the fire keeper, it must be like losing him all over again. That he lived... that he was here within arm's reach and... and you never knew...*

"It was for him that I called Štít," Aedelt's voice grows low and resigned. "I performed that rite while he was still in the womb, though his time was nearing. I knew he still *lived,* as the hound still walked. But the bond must be consecrated once the child is born. Until then, the power of that bond is limited. Štít lived, so the boy lived. His name? His location? I didn't know them, and Štít couldn't do more than gaze in the boy's vague direction."

"When did you know?" Her voice finally comes to her. It's to Edmund she asks the question, though it's Aedelt who makes reply.

"He didn't. Had I been able to find him, or even *rumor* of him, I would have raced to Edmund's side to give him the happy news. To burden him with what may have been false hope?"

Edmund nods. "I hate you for being wise enough to see it, but it was likely the right decision. I'd have been hard pressed not to spend my every waking moment and each coin in my coffers to search for him. Now he's beyond my reach, unless..."

He seems to steady himself for a beat, then presses on. "Kastan... I have one final question—one final boon to beg. I ask you to take him and claim him as your heir. To guide him and teach him as best you can. If you feel it's too much, I'll understand. Aedelt knows a way that I might remain with him, but..."

Aedelt cuts in, as business-like as before. "It involves drawing Edmund's spirit into an item—a weapon or piece of well-made jewelry. That sort of thing. The risks? When Edmund reveals himself, or even acts in some way to aid the boy, Andrej may reject him out of fear or disgust. By that point, it will be too late. Edmund would be trapped within the item in question until that item is destroyed. And then? We've no idea what becomes of a shadow or its spirit once such a thing happens." He pauses for a moment, then adds one more log to the bonfire. "And even if Andrej accepts this item, the boy will die one day. When he does, Edmund will remain trapped within the item."

"I cannot abandon him further. I must ask someone to stand in my stead, or I must take the field, as it were."

"Stop." Kastan's mind flutters from point to point, trying to make sense of it all. "This is more than I need to hear. Edmund, I've already told Andrej he'll remain in and with my household for as long as he likes. I've already claimed him. To do as you ask is little more than a step beyond what I've already sworn to do. No fear."

Edmund's face begins to shimmer. "Kastan, I... I cannot begin to thank you." He's smiling through his tears, yes. But he's also fading. They're *both* fading.

"We'll do what we can, Kastan," says Aedelt. "We'll walk with you for as long as we can. Watch for the Shepherd. Watch for Ebistian and word of the Storm Queen..."

But his voice is dim. The grey light is dim. The world is... dim.

CHAPTER SIXTEEN

CANDLES ONE BY ONE

-I-

County Thorion
Wick
5 Korunasykli: 22 Days after the Red Storm at Westsong

Jastar did his best to keep his head clear. The screams and crashes they'd been hearing for the past few minutes of travel made that more than a little difficult. The battle din summoned horrific and miserable images to the stage of his mind's eye. And while he knew he needed to push such thoughts away, it was against his use to sit idle while Thorion or its people were threatened.

His nose caught wind of a far-too-familiar stench. It was distant, but distinct. He'd been about to say something—to let the column know the cunning little bastards were close—but at that moment, Methias held up a hand to halt their progress.

"Unless I'm very much mistaken, the bend ahead will clear the tree line and bring Wick into view. Sir Jastar?"

He looked at the back of Methias's head and bit down on his own frustration. *The pompous ass can't even be bothered to turn his damned head when asking a question.*

But it wasn't the discourtesy that was fraying his temper. In truth, it was the man's *calm.* And it wasn't limited to the Lord Methias, either. To Jast's frustration, most of the folk he rode with wore confirmed countenances that looked more disinterested in the nearby slaughter than disturbed by it.

This whole overstuffed lance appears content to just wait and see how the Falx falls. They all look ... bored! Only Pallith seems genuinely concerned about what the lot of us are riding toward.

He knew that wasn't the case—could not be the case. The sounds of suffering nearby meant obvious trouble, and they'd ridden out at the first rumor of this same trouble. Yet there was this *sense...*

"Jastar?"

He bowed his head. *I'm a fool, Valad. The dancing point of now, I know.*

He forced his tone to be easy as he answered the lord. "Aye. Should be the final bend. We'll catch glimpses through the thinning trees as we close the distance, but we won't see much until we clear round the corner."

Methias nodded. "Tharus? Dismount please."

The Sheshik man did as bidden. Methias wore his usual flat non-expression as he left his brindled mount behind—a mount that wore a halter, Jastar noted, but bore neither bit nor bridle. *That* was odd.

As Tharus finished walking the few feet forward to stand at Methias's left side, the lord spoke up again.

"My right hand, if you please."

Jastar fought and won the battle to avoid rolling his eyes or speaking his frustration aloud at this needless nonsense. That frustration rose another notch a moment later. No sooner had Tharus obliged than Methias spoke up with yet *another* additional instruction.

"And a few steps onto the grass?" Tharus moved in dutiful silence. When he'd made it a few feet beyond the road's shoulder, Methias at last gave a satisfied nod. "Good enough. Shield at the ready?"

The man unslung his heater, spread his stance as if to enter combat—though his bright hand was empty—and nodded.

Methias opened and closed his fingers several times as he spoke. "If you finish before I need you to finish, wave your bright arm. Lanbachsel?" He raised his voice at this last.

"Aye, eyes on, Lord." Apiné's voice was steady but held a note of anticipation.

"The rest of you, keep watch." With that, Methias pointed his right forefinger at Tharus's back. "Puav ang cza zan fi ka. Cza zan ahg hol gryl." His quiet voice carried with it the cold force of command. From Methias, that tone seemed far too dark somehow.

A brief shimmer showed at Tharus's feet. Then it was gone. Then *he* was gone—carried upward without anything between his boots and the pale brown of the moon-brushed soil.

Jastar gaped. He closed his mouth a moment later, but it took an effort. He saw the bearded man *scores* of feet in the air, stood on nothing but hope and madness, yet supported by whatever invisible force Methias commanded. The Sheshik man stood with his shield toward Wick, gazing in that direction.

All at once, the reality of what was going on struck him. *They're scouting from on high! No archer will find it easy to put a pin in him with that shield in the way, and from there he can see the entire battlefield! Falxes fall... How can Thorion counter ... that?*

Then another thought—a far more worrisome thought struck him. *If they can lift men up so high, can those men not be archers? No field commander would be safe! And if they could be made wide enough, or shaped? Storms be swift, it's an instant siege tower! One raised with no warning!*

Methias's face was locked in concentration. The muscles of his neck—those that could be seen over his raiment, at any rate—showed a purely physical tension as he bore down on his power. The group sat astride in relative silence for several minutes. Jastar tried in vain to ignore the sounds of screams and sobs in the near distance.

"Down, Lord." This was red-haired Ghenys.

Jast looked up and had just enough time to see Tharus's arm waving before the man began to lower.

Apiné spoke up almost before the man had made it to the ground. "Well? What are we facing?"

Tharus walked back to his horse, speaking in his beard-stubble voice as he moved. "Goblins... and something more. The goblins? There are ... more than I can count. They swarm like sweet-venoms over a sleeping faun."

Jast knew those troublesome insects. As a boy, he'd let Gordan and Raegus talk him into joining in with them as they *bit the bug*. That was what the act was called in the south of Thorion, and it was just as absurd and vile as it sounded. The insects looked like long-legged ants carrying tiny green leaves. Eating the damnable things caused a pleasurable sort of delirium and was said to grant prophetic visions. There were even tales of bug-eaters seeing and speaking with the dead, which was why Jastar had agreed to join in. The more recent the bug's death, the more vivid the world became. Eating one alive, therefore...

"And what *else* did you see? Goblins, and..."

"I don't... I don't really know, Morric. A strange... light? It's like someone's hung a black cloth near the middle of town, then set lanterns close enough to brush it with light? Strange, I admit. But as I say, I don't..." He shrugged. "I don't *know*."

"Dannus deliver me," the Kieran growled. "Are... are they still defending the walls, or have we missed that stage of the siege?"

"No, Xaithrin. The creatures have their run of the walls."

Zay-thrin? So That's the bear's given name. Xaithrin the Kieran, or Xaithrin the whole Kieran. If there'd been any doubt of the man's heritage, both his given name and his choice of religious interjection laid it to rest. They were as Traeadish as Traeadish could be.

"And your mason's eye?" Methias spoke in a comfortable voice, as if this were all happening far away, or in some story.

Tharus shook his head, grunting. "A knuckle. A bor knok. It's three defensible walls of wood attached to a restored stone one. Streets would be a perfect place for a trap, if there'd been time to lay one. Bor knok commands the only approach, and the hill looks steep 'nough to hold for *donkey's*."

Wait, he's Traeadish? He looks as if he's from Shesh! There can't be too many Sheshik folk in Traead. But donkey's? I've only ever heard that from the Traeadish traders, or their priests. The expression had something to do with how long it would take to load a ship, he thought, though he couldn't be sure. No matter its origin, its meaning was clear—a long, long time.

Speaking of—Methias sat in silence for what seemed like an age. It was surely no more than a few beats, but it *felt* like an inordinate amount of time for what should be a simple matter. Everyone else remained silent. Their faces once more wore those expressions of detachment.

Hells, someone say ... something. We're wasting time and paying for that waste in Wickish blood.

As if he'd read the run of Jastar's thoughts, Methias spoke at last. "Alright. Lanbachsel?"

"Lord?"

"We need... Wait. Tharus, does the township have only the one gate? Sir Jastar? Gilsel Pallith? You've both been to Wick. Do either of you know?"

"I'd bet there's one somewhere in that stone," said Tharus. "The western wall, I mean. I saw folk fleeing westward from the city, and there was what looked like a small mob near that strange banner-thing."

Jastar considered. "I've *been* to Wick more than a few times, but only fought there once. I think I recall a postern in the western wall, but I wouldn't wager lives on it."

Pallith's near sing-song voice sounded as if it were delivered through a surprised smile. "No, you're quite right. There is. All of Wick's fields are on its northern and western sides. There's no gate to the north anymore. They tore it down and walled it off once the tower was finished. This was when my father was still a boy. But there *is* a gate to the west. It's... what, a bit south of the halfway point Bachsel?" He looked at Tharus, who nodded.

"Thereabouts, aye."

Methias mulled that over. "Tharus? Did you see any goblins that *weren't* pouring into Wick?"

"*See,* no. There were some shooting at those who fled westward, but the walls or the grasses hid them from me."

"The rest were on or within the walls?"

Tharus nodded. "Near as I could tell. I would've expected fires, but there aren't many."

Again, Jastar had to bite back his own frustration at what seemed like overcomplicating matters.

"Lanbachsel? Leave me Gilsel Pallith. Cr ke? You and Sir Jastar will ride in his stead. I'll need larger melee shields to guard me. Jastar's jousting shield and your sword won't be of much use on that score."

All involved nodded, waiting.

Methias considered for a beat longer, then nodded to himself. "Stay out of sight, but go as swiftly as you can. Ride north."

"We're running away?"

As soon as the accusation left Jastar's lips, he regretted it. Other than Methias—who still hadn't bothered to turn 'round—every eye was on him. None of them seemed to echo his concerns. All of them wore looks of either annoyance or disgust at his outburst.

The lord went on as if Jast hadn't spoken at all. It might've been better had he shown at least *some* pique or frustration, but no. Not even a hint of chilly disdain.

"Tharus, I presume the trees are fairly light this close to the eastern walls?"

"They are."

Nodding, Methias went on. "Stay as deep as you can, Apiné. Best if they neither see nor hear you till you're north of the tower."

"Then we cut west?"

"Then you cut west, as close to the northern wall as you can. Keep one of your number with the horses. The rest? Dismount and move back south, swift and single-file."

Apiné grinned. "Shields lead the way right up to the postern gate? Then what?"

"Sweep the gate clear and set what defense you can. We'll give you a few minutes before we ride, but we'll head west of the walls and should be in position before you're at the gate."

Ghenys piped up. "Will we need so many at the gate, Lord?"

Jastar expected someone to glare at the red-haired man for speaking out of turn—to tell him to keep his head-hole buttoned. No one so much as blinked at his interjection. Quite the contrary, both Xaithrin the Kieran and Kujin the Viper were nodding their heads, looking between Methias and Apiné.

"I mean to save as many as we can, which means I'll be too busy to catch arrows, other than the traditional way—hence my borrowing of Pallith. Still, I expect you'll need the extra hands more than I will. You'll almost certainly have bodies to shift."

"Lord? Oh! Hells..." This was Morric. The proverbial torch had lit over his head, but Jastar still didn't understand. Neither did several of the others, based on their looks of confusion.

Methias gave Morric a brief look of commiseration. "I know. It's a grim prospect. I'd be happy to be wrong, but... *something* has to be keeping Wick's remaining folk from hieing west as a mass. Tharus mentioned no siege equipment, so my guess is that the goblins are piling up the dead arrow by arrow at the postern gate."

Apiné grunted in disgust but nodded. "Right. We ride north. Stay hidden as best we can. We cut west along the wall, dismount, leave a rear guard with the horses. Single-file to the postern. Clear the dead, or *whatever's* slowing down the escape for Wick's remaining folk. You should be in position to the west, and you'll draw their attention as best you can."

Methias nodded.

"Do we have a retreat plan?"

The lord appeared to think on that for a few beats. "Yes. You make your way to me. If that can't be done, you head east as fast as you can, then north to the ford at Oacn Alifehv."

You want us to race... toward you if we need to run away?

Jastar kept this thought to himself for fear of yet another collective glare. He bent forward as if to check his stirrup. The very last thing he wanted was for the others to mark his frustrated confusion—his *anger* at how absurd this plan seemed.

Apiné spoke up—all business now. "Right then. If you've any loose buckles or buttons, tie or fasten them down. We need to be swift and silent. Two-two-three? On me."

Methias at last turned to face them. His eyes were distant things—a hazel turned amber as it caught the moon. In less than a minute, they were on the move.

I hate every part of this. We should be racing to the gate—either gate— and carving through the beasts. If the tower's as defensible as Tharus says, why in hells aren't we just pushing through to that?

Still, Apiné's Third Lance was well-trained as a unit, based on all that he'd seen. And he'd do better to admit it. He knew *nothing* of magic or how to use it in the field. Time would tell the tale. He just hoped he'd still be around to pass that tale on to the Countess when all was said and done.

-II-

Olshnak saw his path now as a series of priorities.

I need to not just see but recall as much detail as I can. No stone's too small. But if I focus too much on any one thing, I risk missing others. I need to escape this place. If I don't make report on what's happened here, many more will die. And if I'm able, I need to try and save Sir Kaith—and, if possible, his armsmen.

It wasn't so much that the armsmen mattered as people... not to the greater war, at least. No, it was that those who'd survived this place would, to some extent, know what to expect when fighting them again. Failing that, their minds might have plucked another detail out of the forest of details they were now stood within.

He saw Aleks Silverson glance between the mob at the postern gate, the Braided Tower, and the silent, still goblins. The hellish mymmerkins were just standing there, watching them, on occasion looking up at the rift where the giant thing had felled Sir Gordan.

Silverson made a point of not looking at that strange rip in the air. Well, on that score, who could blame him? Looking at it hurt Olshnak's head, yet he had to see it. To study it as best he could. They weren't any of them going anywhere for a few beats... if they made it out at all. The goblins were between them and the main gate, and the press of screaming, sobbing folk were squeezing through the postern with an *aching* slowness.

"We need to clear a path, I think." Huron fell back beside him. "I can make it up onto the walls, but I've no way down the other side. No rope, nor steps. I could shoot, but I've no bow."

Silverson was still casting about, looking lost—and angry about it. Olshnak considered the idle youth, making no effort to hide his study. He made his voice sharp to gain the fellow's full attention.

"You've lived here all your life. Where is Wick's carpenter housed?"

"What? How sh' I know?"

Olshnak bowed his head so as not to let the man see him roll his eyes. When the urge had passed, he looked back up, searching for the dullard's mud-coloured dreamer's lamps.

"Given your hope to be elevated as one of Lord Ricgerd's vassals? You *must* know the other tradesmen in the village." Based on Aleks's shocked glare, he hadn't realized anyone else knew of his ambitions.

So you're twice the fool I took you for. Servants listen, and servants gossip. Your wealth's taught you to think of them as pets, not people … to your cost.

"You've *no* idea?"

"Mind eer tongue, *tusk*. Else when this is over, it'll be cut from ee…"

Olshnak was certain the man fancied himself threatening, but it was all worthless wind. The fool had no personal force to carry out his threats. He was a freeman, but that offered no protection if he killed the property of a knight of Thorion, let alone that of the damned Throne.

Huron was stepping over, trying to placate the fellow. "Olshnak only seeks to aid in our escape. He knows much of making and breaking, balance and breaching."

But Aleks Silverson spat at Huron's feet. The display was about as impressive as the lone silver braid in his otherwise dark hair—an affectation if ever there was one. "Mind eer own, sandblood. Ee'll meet the same end as the tusk if ee're n' respectful t' me." For emphasis, the youth put his hand to his sheathed sword.

Olshnak laid a hand on Huron's shoulder. The armsman was quite pliable, stepping back without much urging. His face showed confusion, but no concern.

How quickly we forget the power of folk like that. It was ironic, really. In truth, Huron—now a free man in service to a knight—was actually *more* vulnerable to this fellow's reprisals than Olshnak. Were Huron still a slave, Aleks would have to weigh out, and, in all likelihood, *pay out* for the anger of the slave's owner. Most owners were willing to take coin in recompense for damaged or dead slaves, but some demanded blood for the slight.

For the second time in two days, Olshnak chastised himself for finding the *good* in slavery. *Next, I'll be lauding fever for granting me a day without work, or the grave for letting me finally sleep.*

He snorted, eliciting looks from both Huron and the silversmith's son or grandson—however many generations removed Aleks Silverson was from the trade that gave him his name.

He looked from Huron to the screaming, weeping, and for some reason, stalling exodus of Wick's citizens. Huron had the right of it. There had to be a blockage of some sort. He could think of no other reason for the maddening slowness. The gate wasn't *massive,* but it was large enough for a narrow cart to drive through.

"Huron?" When the youth acknowledged him with a questioning look, he continued. "Your sergeant and *the tactician* are deep in the press, and Sir Kaith's trying to hold a defensive wall, else I'd ask them first." Huron grinned at the mocking description of Vilmocz—Kaith's other, more loutish armsman. "I think you've the right of it. There must be something on the other side of that gate. Can you mount the wall and have a shifty at it? At worst, you might find a bow, string, and a full quiver or two. We've no more archers left on this side of the wall."

Huron nodded. "Can, and will."

As the armsman jogged off, Aleks stepped over and tried to cow Olshnak with another of his glares. "Ee're a herald, *tusk.* Eer 'dvice ain't a thing 's needed, nor wan'ed."

Olshnak stepped to his left and dipped down to pick up a fallen armsman's shield, sliding it into place. Standing, he drew breath to make reply, but the words caught in his throat. He saw a row of goblins in the rear ranks drawing back their bows. *One* of them was aiming at the oblivious yapping pup that was Aleks Silverson.

That worthy grinned, blind to his danger, and delighted to see what he thought was fear on the gnoerk's face. His expression showed surprise, therefore, when Olshnak's sudden charge knocked him onto his self-important backside.

"Arrows! Shields up! Arrows!"

Olshnak's initial push let him get his newly claimed heater into position just in time. He blocked an arrow meant for a resigned-looking grand-dame at the back of the line. Once the pin thunked into his shield, he looked over his shoulder to be sure she was unscathed. She looked surprised, but only for a beat. She reached her leathery hand up to caress his green cheek, nodding, before withdrawing it.

Aleks struggled to his feet, growling, and hunted for a shield.

Kaith had given the order to dress the line. He and Ricgerd were doing their best to hold their last ragged defenders together. Terrek and Vilmocz were trying to push through toward the back of the mob, but it was like fighting a strong current. They'd been needed there a moment ago—had tried to keep something approaching order among the fleeing folk. And while that had been a fool's errand, they'd done their best. Now they were needed to help act as rear guard, but...

"Eat your fill, my brothers and sisters. Their fear and valor have seasoned them for long enough. The Face of Endings comes, and there is work to be done." It was a male voice, but not a mortal one. That didn't make much sense, yet it was an undeniable truth. It seemed to come from everywhere and nowhere at once. It was *full,* but not booming, though it rolled with a strange, almost mournful greed.

The nearest goblins reacted at once, racing forward toward Wick's last wall, even as goblin archers continued to loose arrows from their back ranks.

"Olshnak!" Huron's voice from somewhere above. "Riders! There are riders!"

-III-

Kaith anchored the left side of their line—the traditional place from where men expected orders to come. That voice had shaken him, but there wasn't time to contend with that just now.

"Dress the line! Remember, it's stabs, not cuts if you want them to stay down!"

He was pleased to hear them echo the command to dress the line—to feel the mild thumping as their shield wall tightened up. He was *less* pleased when Ricgerd appeared at his left shoulder.

"Back, Ricgerd! *Second* rank!"

"There *is* no second rank, Kaith!"

"You're it! That sword's too big for the wall!"

Kaith dropped his center of balance for a blink, then rammed upward to knock the first goblins back into their fellows. A quick glance to his right told him men all along their defensive line were doing the same. *Good. Good enough, at least... for now.*

"Fight in our shadows. If they get past our line, it'll be *you* who has to put them down! Now, to it!"

Ricgerd growled at that but did as bidden.

An instant later, Kaith felt a hand grip his shield shoulder, trying to pull him back just as he was about to drive forward into another few goblin chargers. He lost his balance for a beat but regained it in time to catch and kill one of the beasts. A second vaulted onto, then over Kaith's shield, landing in their back ranks.

Alec-Aleks's pup's snarl had managed to spit the words, "'Ow dare ee" at Kaith before he screamed in either panic or pain.

Kaith cursed. He glanced at the attackers, thought he *might* be able to risk it, then glanced over his shoulder. Ricgerd was engaged about halfway down the line. He was using his oversized sword to both knock great swathes of goblins off allied shields and shoulders and deliver the occasional vicious stab to end one of them. Nearer at hand, Alec-Aleks was on his back, trying to crawl away from the lone goblin that loomed over him. His own sword, Kaith noted, was still in its sheath at his waist. The goblin's was raised up over its shoulder, preparing to deliver the death blow.

He had a moment of indecision, but as so often happened in such situations, Greggor's voice spoke up in his mind.

Do what you can. The rest? Leave it where you found it. And learn from it. There're enough woes in life. Don't ever willingly add "If Only I'ds" to that already long list.

He took a breath and spun in place, keeping his shield where it was. He delivered a low back cut to the creature's back leg. The blow knocked it on its side, causing its curved—*talwar? Is that a damned talwar?*—sword to fly from its grotesque fingers.

"Stab the damned thing!"

He'd given Alec-Aleks all the time he dared. Already, more goblins were slamming into his shield, trying to pull it down. He turned his body back toward the attackers and left the silver-braided skelpie to his fate... for the moment, at any rate. He couldn't afford to just *hope* the foe in his backfield had been taken care of.

As he repelled the next pair of goblins—*they're getting more organized,* he thought—he nearly had his forehead split by a pair of incoming arrows. He managed to half-crouch behind his heater in just the nick. Before he stood again, he heard the unmistakable sound of a sword clearing leather behind him. Then came Alec-Aleks's voice. It was changed, somehow. It was as if the act of killing the goblin had restored—or perhaps outright *granted* him—a species of self-confidence.

"Lord Ricgerd! We need to make for the Braided Tower ... *now*." His voice wasn't an excitable shout. It was an attempt at an emphatic, if not downright threatening, *command*.

"Kaith?" Ricgerd's voice. He wasn't asking for permission, so much as a tactical read on the idea. Ricgerd had always been a tourney fighter, not a group tactician. It was fortunate the man both recognized and, indeed, reveled in that fact. For all his grumbling bluster, Wick's lord knew his own shortcomings, and was only too happy to lean on those he felt he could trust in those matters.

Kaith considered, opening his shield from the wall as if it were a door and stabbing the climber that was trying to kill his neighbor. He must've taken too long to answer for Alec-Aleks's liking. The man stepped forward, snarling a rebuke toward his lord.

"Sir Kaith isn't lord here, Ricgerd. *You* are! We've a better chance of holding them off from the tower's stones. Give the damned order and have done!"

Kaith snapped his shield closed, hearing the screams behind him as arrows struck the mass of fleeing folk. The enemy had finally opted to aim *past* Wick's last defenders. He cast an eye back toward the gate and saw, for a wonder, that the exodus had picked up its pace at long last. He reckoned there might be as many as two score left on this side of the wall. A final glance toward the north made the decision clear. There were too many to fight through. The only path would be single-file, and the goblins had already proven they were adept at scaling buildings bare-handed.

"Stay the line! We're nearly ready to withdraw, and we'll never make the tower. *Stay—this—line!*"

Ricgerd echoed Kaith's order, and the others took up the call. Most of them, he knew, had already resigned themselves to die here. They contented themselves, he reckoned, with the notion that by their efforts, their kith and kin might yet live. Kaith hoped for a bit more. In another few beats, he'd give the order to retreat by step. Ricgerd would argue about being sent out first, but he'd go. Once *he* was out, the rest would follow.

Casting about one last time, he saw three things. Alec-Aleks seemed to have indeed found his fire, for he walked with purpose and resignation toward the line. Enough of the Wickish refugees had cleared out that he could begin their withdrawal. And, as he turned back to refuse yet another disorganized goblin charge, his eyes fell on the black rift where Gordan had fallen.

Only it *wasn't* black anymore. The starlight had drawn in toward the center, making the thing look like a giant eye turned on its side.

No, not like an eye. That is an eye! The eye of some ancient thing adjusting to the light!

He had no idea how he knew that, or where the thought had come from, but he was as certain of that as he was that it was time to go.

He drew air down into his lungs. "Ricgerd? Shield wall? Retreat by step! Ret—"

"Ee've corrupted my lord... My *friend*. N'more, wandought..."

Kaith had just enough time to register the bastard's words before the blow came. Then his legs gave out. He felt burning, stinging pain along the back of his bright-leg, where thigh met torso. He'd have been happy to scream, but before he could get more than a shouted growl out, the world upended, the ground had come rushing up to meet him, and his head struck something hard. Light and pain became his whole world.

His body sent out bursts of white agony to all points north of his neck. Even the simple act of *inhaling* hurt his face. He thought he heard men screaming. Ricgerd? Yes, Ricgerd was shouting... *screaming,* actually. Where had Kaith heard that sound before?

It was... was when he'd lost his... his crimson heart.

Kaith thought he felt hands on him, then a moment of vertigo that ended with blissful, empty quiet.

-IV-

Venzene Duchy of Kovalun
County Jižní Pochod
Barony of Hartscross–Jižní Lov

Lashjuk moved along the stone corridor at speed, just behind Andrej, his hound, and his lantern. Maksu and Vlk jogged at her heels. She didn't relish the idea of running deeper underground, of limiting her escape options, but there was nothing for it.

They couldn't fight all the forces arrayed against them without help. There were too damned many. This Red Storm was coming, whatever that was. Both Eliška and the devil Ebistian's men were preparing for that event, and they'd ridden into the encampment as heroes. Who would listen to a gnoerkish woman speaking out against them? She'd have truth on her side, but what of that? The folk of the Empire had long since proven that truth only mattered if it came from a familiar face—most often one that reminded them of hearth and home.

She had to believe that Eobum was right. That Kastan was different. *"She's proof, Lashjuk,"* he'd said.

"Of?"

"The idea that gold doesn't always drown goodness."

Folk would listen to a noblewoman... she hoped. *I just need to get her to listen to me.*

It galled her to have to find someone socially acceptable to speak on her behalf, but there was nothing for it. If she and the boys joined up with Kastan, there was at least some hope the lot of them could make a plan to—

"Wait!" she hissed. She grabbed the lip of Andrej's quiver, holding him back. She'd heard something up ahead.

Laughter? Yes, a man's mad laughter, and a strange, whirring roar. This latter sounded as if it were winding down. As if it were growing tired.

She turned to Vlk and Maksu. Laying a hand on her son's shoulder, she addressed herself to the human boy. "Vlk? You were willing to defend Maksu once before without anyone asking you to."

He nodded, blushing through a lopsided grin.

"Now I *ask* you to. There's trouble ahead, and I'll have an easier time contending with it if I know you're standing beside my boy. Will you?"

Vlk put an arm around Maksu's shoulders, offering a solemn nod. "Ve'll protect each other."

Maksu beamed up at the older boy, then turned back to his mother, nodding. "I've gotten strong, Og. I don't know how to fight like Vlk and Andrej, but I'm strong now."

Lashjuk offered an approving smile to the pair of them. "Aye," said she and fought the urge to wince. Eobum's word again... Time for that later.

"Can you use a bow?" Vlk shook his head. "Alright. Here." She pulled one of her azhkasts and handed it to him.

The boy looked at the weapon with a delighted grin on his face. "A spear? I can use a spear. No fear." He was too focused on the weapon to notice his rhyme, but Maksu wasn't. He giggled, but had the sense to stifle the sound before it got out of hand.

Lashjuk turned to Andrej. What she saw brought a grim smile to her lips. He was on one knee with his lantern beside him. He'd nocked an arrow, and his bow was already stretched.

"We go," said she.

Soon after they'd begun to move, Štít began a low growl in the back of her red throat. She kept pace, but also kept looking around, as if trying to find the source of whatever she was smelling, to no avail.

Finally, they came to a large burial chamber lit by a single lantern. As their feet crossed the threshold from catacomb to crypt, the hound began to rend the air with great, snarling sounds that were almost speech. Once their new surroundings came into focus, Lashjuk began to growl as well. What she saw made her heart race with a potent mix of fear and confusion.

Kastan lay on the cold ground. She looked unharmed, but it was difficult to be sure. Another woman lay several feet away, whose state was in far less doubt.

"...Olga," Andrej whispered. Then he swallowed several times.

Her throat had been opened as if by some rabid animal. Despite that, her face lay in perfect repose, as if her savaging had come *after* her death. She looked as if she'd died wearing a soft smile. The juxtaposition of peace and misery were hard to look at. It was something of a blessing, therefore, that the chamber's *other* occupants made for such a jarring distraction.

Stood over Kastan was a man in a deep red kontusz—one she knew all too well. He was helmeted and wielded a spear not much longer than her azhkast in one hand and a spinning, roaring thing in the other.

This latter was aimed so that the circle it created faced the room's only other figure. A man in scholar's robes, with a face that was at once blue and swirling black. The fellow had a mouth full of jagged, dark fangs, and eyes that swam with an unearthly, indistinct glow. A rippling red cord descended from his right fist, seeming to move and shudder of its own accord.

"*Once*-man..." Vlk's voice shook. He hissed for Maksu to get behind him, exhaling through his nose in short, sharp bursts.

Huntress's heart be damned. How in hells do I protect us from... Wait.

She kept her voice low as she spoke to Andrej. "You know her. Do you know *him*? Either of them?"

For a moment, it didn't seem as if the boy could answer. Finally, he managed a jouncy nod. "R... Radek. The count's scholar, and Olga's hus... husband." His throat made an audible click as he choked down his quite visceral reaction.

She nodded, raising her voice just enough so that all three boys could hear. "Stay here. Nevermind hiding. Just stay together and come when I call."

She didn't wait for a reply. The man in red had dropped his spear, now trying to keep the... whatever it was... spinning in both hands and failing by degrees.

Lashjuk made her face flat and placid. She squared her shoulders, drew a breath, and walked from the light of Andrej's lantern toward the chamber's center.

"Radek? Master Radek? Why are you wasting time here?" Her voice was cold and full of an implacable certainty she didn't *begin* to feel.

The devil-thing turned a surprised and ruined face her way. Surprise on something so fearsome and unnatural was somehow almost comedic. At first, she resisted the urge to react to that fact, but only for a beat.

Better I look amused than afraid. Always negotiate from a place of superiority, whether you have one or not.

She snorted, allowing her face to relax into a bemused sneer. "Why do you wear *that* look, scholar? Did you think you could hide from your duties down here indefinitely?"

The creature stepped back, re-centering his aspect, so it focused on her. He looked indignant, which looked almost as absurd as his earlier expression. "What do you mean, woman? Who are you to speak to me of my—"

She made her interjecting sigh loud enough to override him. "Now you seek to waste yet *more* time? The King returns, and there is work to be done. Why do you linger here?"

His indignance had redoubled, adding obvious suspicion to the haze of his eyes. "And yet you would deliver such news in—"

Again, she overrode him with a sigh of *supreme* exasperation. As it neared its end, she rolled her eyes, placed her empty hands on her hips as if scolding her children, and hoped that she recalled what she'd heard correctly.

"Rez miss da rill, Radek... The Lord Sau walks, and is here. Lord Ebistian's coach is above, and the Keening is near enough that we *do not have time* for this nonsense. Now, why are you idling down here when there is *work* to be done?"

She forced her face to grow darker and more frustrated as she spoke, willing him to yield the conversational field. *I'm dead if he doesn't. I've no idea how to kill someone who's already... What? Fire? What use is that? I have no...*

Her not-quite-one-sided conversation with the serpent-thing that had brought her here was cut off midstream.

"The Shepherd is above? And the Sharpened Shadow? What of the Storm Queen? Is she..."

"She watched her army ride past in the Grey. She watches *all* of this, and you are still wasting time! The culling has begun already." Lashjuk groped for the woman's name, but couldn't lay mental hands on it. "Join ... her while there's time."

"Her? Her whom?"

But the woman was stirring—the *dead* woman. Radek turned toward her, his face splitting into a grotesque yet somehow endearing smile.

"Olllga!" He sounded as if a long-lost friend had surprised him with a visit.

"Eliška, scholar." Lashjuk's voice was sharp, trying to draw his attention back to her. "T'lendak."

Olga sat up, absently taking Radek's hand as she adjusted to the world of wakefulness. As she did, Lashjuk stepped over and reached down to pick up the lantern. This took her past the man in red. With a start, she realized she knew him. His face showed a man who sleepwalks, but his haunted eyes followed her every move.

"I welcome you to your second life, my heart's root," Radek said. "In a moment, you will feel the change—cold, needling, then numbness as if you've grown used to the day's chill."

Lashjuk steeled herself, then stepped back toward Radek. "She waits, scholar. Well, no. She works without you. A fact she won't thank you for."

"I shall be *a-long* woman. My lady-wife must finish her rebirth, then we shall deal with the traitor, and *then* we shall join the rest of the King's faithful for the Keening. Have no fear. Now... run along..."

He turned, raising his dim hand to make a dismissive gesture. As he did, she brought the lantern up, *slamming* it into his monstrous face. The glass shattered, and he became a shrieking pyre.

Kastan leapt to her feet, lifting her sword and taking Radek—the screaming candle—somewhere near his neck. She stepped back to stand at Lashjuk's side, turning to face Olga.

Azhferd's armsman got to his feet behind them, then shouted an inarticulate warning. A monstrous hart of fire and red lightning burst into being. Its arrival came with a wave of licking red light that slammed into all three warriors, knocking them asprawl.

Olga still stood, looking like the Queen of Red Places, tall and stoic beside the beast. As it reared and plunged, sending sparks in every direction, the woman lifted her hand as if to touch the hellish thing. Then she drew it back as if hauling on a snarling hound's leash. A tether of sickly violet light materialized in her hand. Its end lashed around the hart's fiery neck like a lead rope, but the creature began to rear again. For a beat, the struggle seemed to bathe Olga's face in rippling light. An instant later, the truth became clear—the light was moving of its own accord.

Štít snarled her way into the chamber, leaping for the flame creature. The two began fighting with the ferocious abandon that is the sole purview of wild things. The boys were next, racing over to Lashjuk and Kastan, trying to place themselves between them and the feral combat.

Lashjuk was the first to her feet. She moved to help the red guardsman to his feet. One look at his face and she knew he would be little to no help. He was out on his feet, though it was clear he was struggling to fight on.

"Protect the boys!" Her words were sharp, causing his dazed eyes to grow a touch more focused.

He nodded, picking up his spear.

"I'll..." But he could say no more. He settled for another nod. As he moved into position, it was obvious he was in a great deal of pain.

As she turned back to the fight, she sensed her unseen ally again. She saw a flashback to the moment they'd first met—the moment they'd first *truly* met.

Another can enter your body, with permission...

She knew she wasn't hearing the serpent creature directly, but rather hearing the memory of its voice. Then the image of Olga's violet tether replayed itself before her mind's eye. She looked around, saw another wave of red fire beginning to build beneath the hart's hooves, and nodded.

You can counter Olga's works, and there's no time to teach me how to do it. Take my body long enough to save my son... to save his friends... to save us all!

-V-

County Thorion
Wick

"Jast?"

He was all but knocked asprawl as an armored figure embraced him. "Jast—Jast—*Jast!*" Now he was being shaken by the shoulders. "What in hells are you *doing here?*"

"Rae? *Raegus*?" Jastar returned the embrace, delighted at the unexpected reunion. "Might ask you the same question. Who sent you? Barnic? Marcza?"

"Sir Jastar?" Apiné's voice was tight, managing to convey several things at once.

"Come, Sir Raegus. Tell me your drift as we work. We need to shift the rest of the bodies away from the gate. And these poor folk aren't going to get up of their own accord and kindly step aside."

Rae stiffened, then nodded. "Aye... Westsong notwithstanding." He turned to bark at the Wickish folk who'd followed him as he'd squeezed through the gap. "Help us move them or get 'ee gone west. I'll be along swift as summer storms, but make for Rockvale. And watch for goblin archers looking for an easy mark!"

They nodded—some of them, anyway—and bolted westward. Apiné had set up shields two to a side, held with their points extended. The canted angle would make it harder for arrows to get past. True, the shield-man's lower legs were vulnerable, but that didn't much matter... at least not yet. The defensive posture was necessary, but boring by design. It offered some protection for the unshielded folk as they escaped. It *also* meant that Jastar, Ibhroth, and now Raegus were left with the grizzlier task.

Methias had been right thus far. The goblins had stacked those they'd killed athwart the gate's mouth. There must have been more than a score of them. He and Ibhroth had thus far found sacks of grain, wool, carrots, and coin amidst the corpses. He supposed the strange mix amounted to whatever the fleeing folk were able to grab on their way out of doors.

Aye, he was right enough. For all that, I'd love to know what in hells he's doing over there.

Jastar glanced to the southwest, where their so-called distraction stood. The two men of the Hammers were standing with their shields locked, weapons at the ready. The horses were a shadow behind them. Tharus's hound was there, which was odd. Jastar couldn't remember having seen the beast on their run to Wick. As for the Lord Methias? His noble self was stood there looking around, as if unsure what he was supposed to be doing.

The dancing point. Aye and fine. Let the lord look after himself. Leastways 'til I've seen to my part here. Once that's done, then I can worry about someone else's.

Rae helped Jastar lift a heavyset fellow out of the way. "Barnic sent us—Gordan and I. He, Kaith and I have been through it. I tell you, Jast

I've about had my fill of Zarec's Charity."

"That bad?" This was the Bear, who sounded amused rather than afraid.

Jastar saw Ibhroth's look of confusion as he moved a pair of large sacks off the pile. "Ever fought a battle you were certain you'd lose?"

The man shook his head, reaching down for a woman's body. He had to jump aside to dodge a pair of tall children bolting out of the widening gap.

Morric spoke up. "We have, most of us. Why?"

"Zarec's Charity is to put you in what looks like an impossible situation. It teaches you humility, and to push your own endurance past its limits—mind and body," said Jastar. "It was one of the few things our knight embraced from the Traeadish faith."

Xaithrin the Bear laughed. "Pretty. It also means a thing is too damned hard. Enough is e-damned-nough!"

They all laughed at that. All save Raegus. When the laughter had died away and they'd gotten the large fellow shifted, he met Jastar's eyes. "Gordan's off to see Valad. Kaith too, I expect."

Jastar froze. For a moment, that was all he could do. Men died. Of course they did. And in a battle like this? It made sense, but it didn't feel right. Not after having survived Westsong.

"C'mon Sir Jastar," Ibhroth called. "Not but a few more to clear. Then we can be about our *real* work."

Jastar nodded, pushing the woe aside for now. He needed a strong stomach, a stiff spine, and a hard heart if he were to see this so-called rescue through.

I can mourn them later... will mourn them later. For now...

But there was no more time. They'd cleared enough that the dam had burst, so to speak. The world was full of screams, sobs, and—beneath it all—the arrhythmic sounds of weapons striking heavy shields.

-VI-

Olshnak leapt forward. He'd meant to bash Aleks Silverson with his shield in hopes of knocking him away from Kaith. He never had the chance. Ricgerd and several of the nearest shieldmen engaged the cozening bastard—a decision that turned their defensive wall into a snarling mass of limbs. Their left flank was curling in on itself. And the goblins were only too happy to roll it up like a piece of parchment.

He was just thinking, *we need to get them back in good order somehow,* when his gaze fell on Vilmocz. The armsman was just pushing through the rear of the fleeing folk. Kaith's man would've been free to act were it not for a tall goblin readying its attack.

The monster made an odd sort of javelin appear as if by some sorcerer's trick. The weapon looked long and thin, but its head appeared barbed. It brought the weapon up over its shoulder, aiming at Vilmocz's unsuspecting and un-helmeted head.

Olshnak growled his frustration. *We need every skilled shield we have if we've a hope in hells of surviving. So while he may not miss his head, I need him to keep it a while longer.*

"Vil-*mocz!*" He raced forward and shouldered the man down in time, but felt the spear drive his borrowed chain shirt into his back. It and the padded gambeson beneath managed to turn the blow, but *oh,* did it sting!

Vilmocz staggered, looked as if he might come up swinging, then wore an expression of wonder. It didn't stay on his face for long, but his utter shock at having been saved by someone he'd tried to have killed not long up the hourglass was hard to miss.

"We have to get that wall in order, or we're done! Kaith's been betrayed by that silver-braided bastard, but the goblins are—"

Vilmocz shoved past him, nodding. "Get the sandblood, tusk! Him and Terrek!"

Olshnak ignored the slurs. This wasn't the time. Vilmocz seemed too taciturn to teach, anyway. Shaking his head, he reached down and scooped up the short spear, adding it to his borrowed arsenal.

"Huron!" He backed up the nearby stairs, not wanting to turn away from the goblins. "Huron! To me!" He moved with as much speed as he dared. But Huron wasn't answering, which didn't seem much like him.

As he made it to the top of the wall, he spun and looked for the youth. Perhaps a dozen feet to the south, he saw a blueish blur running backward toward him. Huron was drawing and loosing arrows with a nearly supernatural speed. It would also have been an *impressive* speed had he hit his mark more than one in every four times. He aimed at the goblins that were climbing onto the stone alure from beyond Wick's walls. He managed to fell one of his quartet of pursuers. But the kill had cost him. He managed to skitter back to Olshnak's side, but he was down to his last arrow.

"With me!" Olshnak raised his borrowed shield, hefted the heavy javelin over his bright shoulder, and...

His aim had been true—true enough, at any rate. The weapon *should* have struck the goblin square in its belly. Given the angle and the opposing forces of hurled spear and hurtling goblin, there was every chance the blow could've knocked the sarding thing back over the wall where it had come from! But no. As absurd... as impossible as it was to contemplate, the goblin had snatched the spear out of mid-air, spun it with a motion too deft to follow, then drew it over his shoulder to hurl back toward its source. Toward Olshnak.

I'm dead... Half a lifetime in bondage of one sort or another, and this is where I...

The goblin staggered backward and dropped his weapon before he could throw it, knocking into both of his fellows. An arrow was buried in the beast's throat. One of the drogue goblins actually tumbled over the wall to the grasses a score or more feet below.

Olshnak was all but undone by the miracle. He'd *known* that goblin had carried his death. Could imagine no other outcome. And yet, here he was...

Aye, here I am standing around like a damned beef-wit, when there's...

He heard Terrek's voice barking orders to whatever warriors they still had, and growled. He seemed to be doing that a lot today.

"With me! We're going!"

The Sheshik youth fell in behind him without a word. They raced down the wooden stairs as fast as they dared. Ricgerd and Vilmocz were carrying Kaith's familiar form on an oversized shield. They were just disappearing through this side of the postern gate as Olshnak's feet struck the cobbles. Terrek was, indeed, holding together some half-dozen men in a thin line. They walked backwards, trying to curl their line to cover the entirety of the small gate.

He saw one *other* thing. Aleks Silverson was alone, surrounded by goblins. He was laughing as they brought him down, swarming over him, stabbing down with long, wicked-looking knives.

"Sergeant!" Olshnak shouted to be heard over the wind.

Wait, wind? There Is no wind. I hear it as if it were all around, but...

Then he caught sight of the rift. Of the *eye*. That was what it looked like now—the lone orb of some giant laying on its side. He couldn't make sense of it, save for the undercurrent of horror it called forth in him. And for the realization that the wind was somehow coming from *within* that dark dreamer's lamp.

"Sergeant, we have to go! Sir Kaith's through the gate! We have to move!" Olshnak wasn't trying to start a panicked rout, but after what he'd just seen?

But the horror was just beginning. The eye rolled. Not its black pupil, but the eye *itself* rolled like a wheel. When it concluded this silent shift, it rose up and cast about. It seemed to widen in surprise, then lower to the street to regard Terrek's thin iron line.

There could be no more doubt. This wasn't *like* an eye. It *was* an eye.

Olshnak heard a sudden scrape of something on stone. The sound snapped him out of his torpor, and he looked for its source. He found Huron scavenging a shield from one of the fallen. They were at the gate now, with Terrek's terrified men standing an unreal watch mere feet away. Olshnak felt Huron's hand on his arm, guiding him through.

"Go on, Olshnak. I'll be just behind you."

How in hells are you so...

But he could see the truth. Huron wasn't *calm*. He was resigned. He would try to escape, but even now he recognized the all-but-certain truth.

Time and again today you've poured fresh sand into my hourglass, Huron. And I...

A voice he didn't know was shouting Kaith's name from somewhere beyond the wall. The sound broke him from his long thoughts. He met Huron's eyes, hating that there was no time to repay his many kindnesses. Offering a nod he hoped would convey more than mere acceptance for this final gift, Olshnak bolted out of Wick and into uncertainty.

-VII-

Venzene Duchy of Kovalun
County Jižní Pochod
Barony of Hartscross–Jižní Lov

Lashjuk found herself outside of her body once more. It hadn't been a pleasant experience the first time, and it wasn't much better now. To be fair, that first time had been on the heels of Ebistian's sorcery, but still. Any wonder she might have felt was muted by the woe surrounding each event and a lifetime of Venzene fearmongering against magic in all of its forms.

She'd been terrified of the serpent-thing when it had first spoken to her. And when she'd realized she was out of her own body, that terror had redoubled. Things hadn't been much improved by the sight of what she thought of as *life lights* everywhere. But worst of all had been the threats to her sons, her man, and her new comrades.

So, she quirked a wry smile, *not much has changed, Štít notwithstanding.*

The red hound was suffused with a warm golden glow. The color served to highlight the deep hues of her fur, turning it into a thing of staggering beauty even as she leapt and snapped.

As for Štít's foe... that was another matter. Lashjuk saw it without her living eyes now. The fiery hart was, in actuality, a core of angry vermilion light. Through some sorcery or other, that light had been surrounded by a deer-shaped fire.

It seems... terrified, though not of the red hound. She didn't know how that could be, or indeed where she'd gotten the idea, but it was too strong a thing to just ignore. There was raw anger, yes. And that *was* directed at Štít. Still, she'd *swear* a suppressed terror hid within that light, informing its rage.

Beyond this savage contest, she saw Olga. Two Olgas, in fact. At first she thought the woman had two heads, but no. There was Olga, violet light spilling from her bright hand. And there was the brighter, truer Olga, standing behind her twin's dim-side shoulder.

"Most impressive, tusk." The woman's voice sounded genuine despite the ignorant slur. It had an odd echo to it, making the flat tone feel less unaffected than it otherwise might. It *had* to be Olga's, yet her mouth wasn't moving. "Most aren't skilled enough to *touch* such levels of Walking or Calling, let alone both at once."

I've no idea what she's on about. She stepped toward the woman... the *women,* she supposed.

"It doesn't matter. What *does* matter is stopping you and your pet from—"

Olga rolled her eyes. "It isn't *mine,* woman. Not yet, at any rate. My Radek summoned him, poor fool. Too drunk on his own power, I suppose... for all the good it did him. Now that his second life has ended, the creature's lost its tether. How can you not know that?"

The truer-looking Olga stared at Lashjuk with a frown of confused derision. It didn't stay stamped on her face for very long. Both sets of eyes went wide.

"You've left your body? How? You've given your stín *that much power?*"

"My ... stín ? Oh, my cień—my shadow."

"Og!" Maksu's voice was little more than breathy awe. Could he hear her? Even in this state?

Looking back at her body, Lashjuk realized the truth. The boy was reacting to the greenish cord of light that now ran from her physical hand to the neck of the conjured creature. That light was brighter and somehow more solid than Olga's violet tether. No sooner had she recognized that fact then her body spoke. As before, hearing a version of her own voice speaking independent of her own will was unnerving. Still, feeling unnerved was the least of her worries just now.

"Release the sunderkin, woman. I mean to send it back to—"

Olga cut in, but this time, the voice had a queer doubling. Both Olgas were speaking now. This secondary voice was a ruined, coarse growl.

"The creature is my burden to bear, not yours. If I do as you say, the lot of them will die here and now, duskling. That may not matter to *you,* but your mistress won't thank you for condemning—"

"Silence bloodforged. Do as I say and your end will be swift. Do it not, and..."

This is ridiculous. They're so busy trying to shut each other down, they don't even hear one another.

The old woman had grown silent, eyes first widening, then narrowing. When she spoke again, her twin voices carried with them a haunting note of real venom. "You aren't half as clever as you pretend, orský stín. If you were, you would see that I am, at this very moment, staving *off* my second life's full beginning."

"Oh, and *now* you think to distract me with lies?" Lashjuk's body gave a strange, hissing laugh of incredulity.

Orský stín? ...Ah, orc's shadow.

Lashjuk rolled her eyes. She'd had enough. Turning to her body, she made her voice hard and clear, just as she did when disciplining her children.

"Be silent." She turned back to Olga. "*Both* of you, until I ask you to speak."

They looked too surprised to argue. Lashjuk cast about for a few beats and saw the children stood surrounding Kastan. Azhferd's armsman, staggered but stalwart, had interposed himself between them and the beast's battle. Good enough.

"Now," said she, "Olga? How have you staved off the..." She tried to recall the last few moments of the conversation, to no avail. "How have you staved off your... your second life?"

Olga sighed. "Much as you, I've allowed my shadow into my body—*summoned* it there. But my shadow serves me. I've not empowered it as you have with your own. If I departed my body altogether, it would finish its rebirth. Thus I remain half in, half out, as you see. Whether that process would call me back to my flesh or trap my shadow there in my stead is a question I've no desire to have answered. In this state, at least for the nonce, I've kept the new red sand within my second hourglass from completing its descent. It cannot last, so whatever it is you mean to do, do it and have done. If you dawdle, her Excellency won't be around to thank you for tarrying over the task."

I have to admit, I'm surprised at how forthcoming she's being. Lashjuk nodded, processing Olga's words as best she could. *Magic is something I still know far too little about. Having power is one thing. Knowing how to use it is quite another. Having gold teaches you nothing of how to wield wealth.* For all that, Lashjuk didn't feel as if Olga was playing her false. *The question is, am I prepared to risk my life—our lives on that?*

Lashjuk turned back to her own body and spoke again. "Can you send the creature away on your own? Are you certain you have the power?"

Her body seemed to consider this for a longer time than she would've liked. Meanwhile, the beasts continued their frantic fray a few feet away. Neither seemed to have a clear upper hand, hoof, or paw.

"I cannot say for certain," she heard herself say at last.

"Fine. Do we need to flee? Send the others away?" She looked from her own face to Olga's, and back again. "Well?"

"There's no way of knowing. Your enemy, from what you told my husband, is already slaughtering those who wait above ground. I've no idea how long the sunderkin's summons will last, as I've no idea how potent my husband's will and power became. I could find out, but—"

"But that would mean embracing your second life—becoming a once-woman." Lashjuk nodded.

Another thought struck her. Having to fight against the beast's rage couldn't make holding it any easier. Perhaps that was a non-magical way of thinking, but...

She shook her head. She'd *had* a notion, but the snarling, squealing, barking noises of the warring animals had driven it from her head. The pair seemed locked in a stalemate, although how she knew that she couldn't have said. How did one determine the relative health of a creature made of fire and light?

"Štít? Stop!"

To her surprise, the animal did as bidden. She moved off out of range, pacing in a half-moon before the burning thing and growling deep within her throat.

Lashjuk turned to the creature of fire, considering. "Can *you* hear me?" It turned to face her, still clearly agitated, fighting against the twin restraints of Olga and her own body. "Can you understand me?"

It bowed its head, then leapt at her. She jumped aside just in the nick. The two tethers pulled taught, and Andrej's apparent birthright leapt back into the fray.

Olga laughed. "Woman, you *are* a fool. You're a child with her own siege engine..."

Lashjuk ignored her.

Olga and her physical form held the creature in relative restraint, but it was clear the effort cost them both. What was worse, the hart and the hound were still half-circling, stomping, biting—doing everything they could to end one another.

"Štít? Štít! To me!"

The Karmínové Srdce *wuffed* deep in her chest, but did as she'd been bidden. Lashjuk tried to turn her mind back to the problem at hand and was all but assaulted by a thought so absurd she almost screamed.

Wait... both? Am I... are we all just stubborn fools?

She faced both Olga and her own body and asked a question that should have been obvious from the first. "You both have some control over it with your tethers. Can you *both* send it back to where it came from? Can you *both* work to send it home?"

They looked at one another, then away. That was answer enough.

"Do it. No argument unless there's a risk to the boys. At my word, *both* of you work your wills and send this thing back to whatever pit it came from. Are you ready?" They both looked predisposed to argue, but she gave them no time. "Well?"

"Return home, sunderkin?" Her own voice asked this question in a grudging, sulky tone.

"Fine. I send you home?"

She saw her own head shake. "Clarity. I command you to return home now."

Olga sucked her teeth, shaking her head. Her pique seemed to be fueled by annoyance more than disagreement. "Archaic, overstuffed non-sense, but so be it. Return home sunderkin... I command you to return home now. Yes?"

"Insolent bondswoman..."

"*Answer* her. Is she correct?" Lashjuk couldn't help but be amused, though she tried not to show it. *The power of motherhood might win the day after all.*

"Yes. The... *woman* is correct." Her body's occupant caught her glare and pivoted away from whatever insult it had planned on using instead of the word *woman*, which was good enough.

"Good. Ready? And... *now!*"

"Cruden, aqanriv. Puav ang zet ahg cruden ruulth," Both Olga and her own body spoke in surprising unison. Their voices had melded into one before they'd begun the second syllable of their strange chant. The tethers they held—whatever their true nature was—widened and began to ripple down their length toward the blazing beast.

When those ripples reached the hart itself, it screamed in an odd, hollow tone, then reared up on its hind legs. Štít gave a brief, baleful howl, then leapt toward the rest of the room's occupants. The *sunderkin*—if that was what it was called—brought its front hooves down onto the stone floor with a sound like no other. It was as if thunder had somehow been trapped beneath a vaulted ceiling of stone and heavy wooden trusses. A whirlwind of fire burst into being where the hooves impacted, sweeping through the chamber a blink behind that unearthly sound.

Lashjuk screamed. Her *body* screamed. She thought she saw Štít knock the boys to the ground, but she couldn't be certain. The world was full of light and the muscular sound of the sunderkin's parting gift.

When her senses came back into enough focus to know where the damned floor was, she tried to cast about. She was back in her own body, for a start. And she had the searing pain to prove it. She felt as if she'd been struck full-force and head-on by a burning quarry stone.

Still, pain's proof of life. Life doesn't mean safety, though. Best see what there is to see, and nevermind my megrims.

As she struggled to sit up, several realizations came to her at once. The sunderkin was indeed gone, which was a good start. Štít lay on her side, unmoving, her body emitting tiny tendrils of either smoke or steam. She was relieved to see first Andrej, then Maksu and Vlk stirring behind the hound, looking as if they were waking from a miserable night's sleep. Both Kastan and Azhferd's man were trying to force themselves upright, and were rewarded with a double helping of frustration for their trouble. They moved as if they were drunkards at the end of a long night's professional drinking, then seemed to give up and lay back down. All of this came to her in two flaps of a wing, as Eranoric was so fond of saying.

It was at that point she first heard, then saw something across the chamber. A bearded man in laborer's clothing held the passage they themselves had come through. He stood there, pointing a familiar crossbow at her. His face hurt to look at. He was drowning in a frenzied stew of emotions she couldn't quite name. There was rage, of course. And with that rage came something wicked and greedy. It was the black joy of a person who's long fantasized about justifiable cruelty.

He licked his lips, then his mouth twitched. The motion made his dark-blond beard dance.

"You've *failed*, tusk." He leered at her, a sour smile darkening his face further as he caught her look of confusion. "Oh, you killed my vife... my Duša, but the Lord Ebistian? The Lord Sau? No, tusk. You've failed to put out their candles... but I von't fail to put out *yours*."

He shifted the crossbow the tiniest bit, aiming it at her head. His eyes were wide and shining, his face wet with either spittle or tears—she couldn't tell which.

I'm dead, she thought.

"Father! No! She saved us! She—"

"Vlk, she took your *mother* from us... took your friend Andrej's *father... orphaned* him!" The man was shaking now. "I have it from the Lord Ebistian. She attacked him as vell. She von't kill another. I von't suffer the ungrateful tusk bitch to live after vhat she's done."

"Mother's ... *dead?*"

"She ess. And that savage ess the one who took her from us."

"Father, no... she vouldn't do that. I tell you, she's *saved* us!"

"*She* didn't take Rákos. *Ebistian* did! I was *there!*" Andrej's voice broke with rage and terror. Small wonder, as the man's rant suggested that Ebistian had somehow survived.

"Be *silent!* Both of you! I know vhat I saw! The Lord Ebistian covered in vounds from a spear's point—a spear point like the one that took your mother from us! Lord Ebistian told me enough, and the *proof* ess right there! See! The orcish cunt shtill hess the blood on her veapon!" He spat on the ground, then glared at her.

She cursed herself for not bothering to clean Ebistian's blood from her azhkast. Aldhelm had told her how much damage blood could do to metal if left for too long. And she would've seen to it as soon as there had been actual time, but now...

Now the hourglass is teetering. Soon it'll fall, shattering on the floor.

Vlk's father looked as if he were trying to will his hands to stop shaking, albeit with limited success.

"I saw your magic—saw it force fire into the room as you tried to murder her Excellency. No fear, tusk. Ve can add *that* to your list of crimes." The man's voice had become strangely breathy, the way certain smokers' did when trying to recapture that long-ago first pull. "If I see it again, though, I'll start vith your pup instead."

"...Og?"

"It's alright, Maksu. Stay with Kastan and the boys." Her voice sounded far more controlled than she'd expected, given the combination of fear and pain she felt. Hopefully, it would be enough to keep Maksu from doing something foolish. If the boy tried to run toward her, the crossbowman might twitch out of pure reaction. He didn't look practiced. In fact, he looked as if he were trying to work up the courage needed to do what he came here to do. Still, if he were startled into reacting, his courage wouldn't much matter. *Anyone* could stumble into passable aim.

Her mind replayed a night around the fire early in their trek north. After Aderano had finished the tale of one of the unit's earliest exploits, Sulok had asked if it was hard to kill a person. Eobum's response had surprised her.

"Every man thinks they could take a life when the time comes. Most will never find out. It's easier in the heat of the moment. Harder if you've time to consider what you're doing. A good man kills when he has to and no more. If you can keep a foe talking, you've a better chance of reasoning with, outwitting, or outfighting them."

There had been more, but it wasn't relevant to her current situation. *The man's a talker. He could've put a pin in me many times over by now if he weren't.*

"Vise to keep your cub vhere he is. Ve'll take care of him. He'll grow to know hess place and be heppier for it... so long as you take vhat you've earned."

"Father, *stop* this!" Vlk was getting to his feet somewhere off to the left. "You're wrong! I tell you she saved us all! It vas she who stopped that mons—"

"Keep your teeth together, boy! You speak of monsters? Look at her! *Look!*" He thrust his crossbow towards her. "You think they look like that for no reason? The vorld paints them and gives them fengs to varn good folk *avay*! They're savages! Half-vild things that vill turn on their betters and... and..." He choked out a sob, drew in a sharp, wet-sounding breath through his nose, and exhaled through a wide-open maw.

Lashjuk listened to all of this in silence. She shook her head but saw no point in offering any verbal defense. To what end? He *wanted* to kill her.

Somehow Ebistian still lives. And that demon's given the man Rákos's crossbow, feeding on his fears—telling him he's in the right. That he's always been in the right. She closed her eyes, trying to think past the pain. *If Kastan were awake, or if Eobum were here, then...*

She winced. *Hells, everything is throbbing, but my right side is screaming!* She'd managed to get to her knees, but that was as far as she'd made it before the pain demanded she stop. *If I can force my legs to work, maybe I...*

He was working up his resolve at last. His eyes grew wide. A strange and somehow mad light danced in their depths. The man's shaking had moved the weapon's aim out of true. Bringing it to bear once more, he purred out a final word to send her off with.

"Now ve'll be revenged for what you've done."

"Father... *Liška*! Put the damned thing *down!*" Vlk's voice was underpinned by the swift scraping of boots on old stone. But Liška was no longer listening. There was an echoing *thoop* sound, and the bolt flew true.

Lashjuk tried to push herself away, meant to throw herself to the left, but her arm refused to engage. Her vision filled with a dun-colored darkness. Half a beat later there came the sound of a muffled, somehow wet impact, then a gasp. It took her a beat to understand what had happened. And by then, it was far too late.

A deep, boiling rage raced to fill her every vein—her every thought. But that must wait. There would be time to abandon herself to that rage soon enough. For now...

Vlk staggered, then fell back against her. The quarrel was buried deep within the flesh beneath his breastbone. She caught him with her one good arm, lowering him to her lap. His eyes rolled, mouth spilling blood as he tried to speak.

Liška screamed. Maksu screamed. Lashjuk *could not* scream. She choked down her grief and rage, but the effort cost her. She could only stare down, holding Vlk's bloody body. Holding Vlk's desperate gaze as he strove for breath, shuddered, and slipped sideways.

CHAPTER SEVENTEEN

ENDLESS EYE'S IRE

-I-

County Thorion
Wick
5 Korunasykli: 22 Days after the Red Storm at Westsong

The trio's trek to Wick's west side had demanded substantial con-centration. Methias's weave work served to keep them hidden from most eyes, but only so long as he did the mental equivalent of clenching his fist. He led them to a small hillock behind which they could hide their remaining horses from most sightlines, then relaxed his control.

A single clever weave author can hide traps, treasure, or any number of other troubles for the unsuspecting traveler, Galganus. Those who are night blind are at such a caster's mercy. Those who are voluntarily night blind... So you see, the simplest act of casting has uses. Even as the hourglass empties.

It was a lesson Emil had only needed to teach him once. It had also dovetailed with what his master called *foundational axioms*—pithy truths upon which casting, and indeed scores of mundane tasks, could be based. *Build shelter before the rain, light fire 'fore it's too dark to find flint, study before you're to be tested.* Years later, to his everlasting delight, Jannon added a proverb of his own to this litany late one night. *Take your sleep 'fore sleep takes you.* It all came down to preparation, which, in turn, came down to knowledge.

And so, as a matter of course, he'd employed his Eye of Night once they'd dismounted. The weave *was* present here in small pockets, though none of it was in active use. Through the Eye of Night, the patterns made by the intertwining strands revealed two important facts.

The work's stable, and it's … insular. So, some sort of alterative permanent enchantment on a physical item. Yet with an utter lack of even base attempts at seeing or listening? Odd. I'd first thought that they might be traps to ensnare anyone fleeing west, but no. Traps—at least magical ones—needed a means to trigger. They needed to be able to use at least one sense to recognize when they were meant to activate. *Yet if they aren't traps, why are they just lying about?*

He kept low against the hill as he walked toward the nearest source. What he found was a young woman's corpse flat on its face with an arrow in its back. He let his eyes linger, looking to confirm what he suspected.

Aye, it's the arrow. As there were no traces of Sagacite threads to sense or detect him, he wrested it free. It was like no pin he'd seen before, shape notwithstanding. It *looked* like wood, but he had his doubts. The shaft was the no-color of winter rain, which didn't match any tree he'd ever seen. And there was something else off about it he couldn't quite place.

He turned and crouch-walked back to Tharus and Pallith. As he moved beneath the moonlight, he realized what the other oddity was. The arrow wasn't fletched with any feathers he'd come into contact with. They were leathery things of a glossy green hue—beautiful, but strange.

Strange or not, they'll need to keep for the moment. With an effort, he managed to pull his mind back to the matter at hand.

After rejoining the others, he spent a quiet few minutes trying to read the field. Now his mind raced to combine the varying bits of information he'd gleaned thus far. He was certain he'd missed things, but he knew better than to dwell on that. He was a caster, making him many things to many people. *Today* he was a scout, lack of training be damned. He would learn, or they would all burn, and that was that.

What he saw didn't much please him, but it didn't surprise him, either. He'd known the bitter truth from the moment they'd arrived. He couldn't take on the entire attacking force with what he had in man or magical power. Trying to *retake* Wick was an altogether different matter from holding it. While he was ready to hurl power into the fray, his resources were limited. There was no point in spending their lives on a battle they couldn't win. Their best hope was to create a corridor of escape and save who they could. Meanwhile, he would search for a way to do more.

The Nebelblut didn't seem to much care about what was going on outside Wick's walls. They tried to shoot at the folk who fled westward, but the attempt seemed somehow half-hearted. Even when Apiné's force showed itself, there was barely any reaction from the goblins. A few arrows flew toward the western gate off and on, but nothing alert, disciplined shieldmen had to fear.

He'd seen a few groups of men fleeing along the wall walk. How they'd hoped to escape that way, he had no idea, nor did it much matter. They found—or perhaps it would be more accurate to say that they'd been found *by*—fresh foes before they'd made it a dozen yards. The goblins were as near as no matter to... everywhere.

The Nebelblut were disorganized, but only to a point. At first glance they appeared to be a fractious mob, but he'd seen smaller units of three or six moving in tidy order along Wick's wide alure. They weren't mindless, either. They were willing to sacrifice one another in pursuit of a kill, but again, those smaller units covered one another well. Often, they would set one or two archers in a rearguard position. These would either scatter a group of men before they could pose an organized threat or prevent an ally from getting overwhelmed by too many foes.

And that brings me back to the pin I recovered.

The arrow held a sufficiency of weave work within it, which would've been fine under ordinary circumstances. War weavers—those Weave fabricants who specialized in ensorcelled gear of war—often crafted empowered arrows and the like. Such things were a goodly portion of their stock in trade. They allowed for what, in the grand scheme of things, were minor enchantments to be delivered at far greater range.

But that enchantment is expelled upon impact. They're no more reusable than a mug of mead. Once they've been emptied, they've ... been emptied. Yet here was this goblin pin still holding its power, even after it had struck and killed a fleeing woman.

I suppose I may as well try to collect as many of these as I can while there's time. We'll likely have to flee this place with our horse's tails on fire. He smirked. *No, Mezofel. Not literally. Leastways, I hope not. Just an expression, like when I say you must be made of apples.*

He wished he had the time to study the thing's patterns in depth, but he knew better. That would take at least half a bell, and only if he were fortunate enough to have encountered similar weave work before. Otherwise, it could take days, if it weren't beyond his current ability to understand in the first place.

And that's sidestepping the inherent dangers of... no. None of that matters just now. Not when there's a battle going on, he reminded himself. *If I get lost in thought, my men will wind up lost. Dead on the field because their lord was too busy gathering wool.*

Methias shook his head. "Idiot," he said to no one in particular.

"Lord?" Pallith stood a few feet away, facing Wick's walls. He and Tharus were shoulder to shoulder, their shields raised to block incoming arrows.

"Just keeping myself on task, Bachsel. There's a mystery here, but I've no time to solve it now." He turned his attention to Tharus. "May I borrow Ire for a few beats? Assuming he consents?"

Tharus grunted, a sound which served him as a chuckle. "I'll leave it to him to decide, Lord."

Methias turned to cast about for the hound and saw him trotting over from a few yards north. Grinning, he turned away from their two-shield wall and made as if to crouch down. As he did so, his hand slid against the grain of the goblin pin, and he winced. Giving the arrow an accusatory glare, he realized it had drawn blood. It was a minor matter, but he preferred his blood on the inside, as a rule.

A wave of fatigue struck him hard enough to make him dizzy. It passed before he was able to quantify its source, leaving him all but exhausted in its wake.

Hells be hid, I feel like the battle's already over. I ought to have plenty of force left. Even the wraith ride rote shouldn't have taken this much out of me.

That was true. The weave work he'd used to let them approach unseen had taken its toll, but no more so than he'd expected.

Movement drew his full attention. A patch of nearby grass shook. Then another, then a third. *The wind's all but nonexistent near this little hillock, and yet...*

"Make ready!" But that was all he had time to say before the goblins were upon them.

-II-

Jastar shouldered what looked to be a laborer to one side. "Mind your *footing,* ya fool!"

The fellow glared back as he ran on, but Jastar didn't think he'd registered the rebuke. His eyes were wide and panicky, which was more than reasonable given the circumstances.

Reaching down, he lifted a young girl out of harm's way. She might've been five or six... no older than eight, surely. When she'd stumbled, the laborer had nearly kicked her, then stomped on her for good measure. Jast doubted the man would've even noticed in his fright.

She clung to him for a moment, shaking. Then she jumped, racing to stand behind him once Raegus began shouting.

"Kaith? *Kaith!*"

"Out of the damned way!" This second voice was all but a force of nature—bold, demanding, and terrified all at a go.

As the current batch of escapees thinned, Jastar saw two men carrying a body between them. He'd heard Raegus's shout, yet the sight of Kaith being carried *upon his shield* from the battlefield still gave him a jolt of shock.

"Is he... Lord, is he...?" But Rae couldn't bring himself to finish the question.

The mustachioed man answered in a gruff baritone. "Alive, aye. But not for long if you don't get *out of my damned way!*" This was the same force of nature he'd heard a moment before.

Raegus obliged, but spoke on. "Glad, though, I am to know it. What about Sir Gordan?"

Kaith's other bearer—a man in blue leather—answered in a brusque, no-nonsense growl. "Dead."

Rae stopped his progress, letting them pull away. His eyes swam, and though his mouth worked, no sound escaped it.

So you really are gone, then, Jastar thought. *I never would've expected you to be the first of us, Gordan. My coin would've been on Alnik or maybe Jaran.*

As the shield bearers came near, Jastar drew a breath to ask another question, but it fled his mind long before it could reach his mouth. The world began to scream, and in an instant, he understood why. An enormous, disembodied *eye* rose over Wick's wall. It regarded them for a beat, looked westward toward where Methias and his protectors stood, and sank back behind the walls once more.

"Eyes on meee!" Apiné's voice snapped everyone out of their collective gawk. When most of them had obliged—they were too terrified to do much else, truth be told—she spoke on. "You two with the wounded man. Do you want him to live?" She barely gave them a chance to answer before she pressed on. "Get him over here. We'll protect him as best we can. You won't be able to carry him all the way to Rockvale between you, and as the goblins have archers. there's every chance one or both of you will fall to one of their pins within sight of Wick's walls."

The man Raegus had called *Lord* spoke up in a voice of softened terror. "Can you save him?"

"I don't know." Apiné did little to soften the blow. "What I *do* know is, if you try to carry him between you, all three of you are likely to die this day. I won't stop you from trying, but I won't step so much as a foot to help if you head west with him now. So, make your choice."

This grim proclamation was met with silence, but it didn't last long. The armsman in blue spoke up.

"Lord? Staying this close to the walls is foolish. Racing west with Sir Kaith between us without a distraction, though? That would be like giving ourselves to the bastards as a Koruni Spanek gift. I say we stay, 'least for now."

The lord swallowed, then gave a single sharp nod of his head. They carried Kaith over and set him down before the Lanbachsel. The lord remained on his knees beside the wounded warrior, then raised his head to meet Apiné's eyes. "I'm Ricgerd, Lady. Lord of this place, while such things hold. I thank you for your help." He paused to take a shuddering breath. His next words were spoken through a throat full of pain and thwarted rage. "You have to save him. He must... he has to..."

Apiné nodded. "I'm Apiné, Lanbachsel of the Ban'ze Ruun. These are my men—most of them, at any rate. We'll do all we can to help him and you, as will our lord, I've no doubt."

The next wave of folk rushed out of Wick, but they were silent as they ran. Their eyes were glazed, as if they'd seen more than they knew how to make sense of.

Jastar looked over his shoulder, down at the little girl still clinging to his belt from behind. He knelt, moving her around to face him.

"When I tell you, I want you to run over to stand near your lord. If I have to fight, you'll be safer there." He tried to make his voice soft and encouraging. He must've managed it, for she gave him a grave nod, her brown eyes wide and quite beautiful. A moment later found her standing next to Lord Ricgerd and Kaith. The blue-clad armsman unslung his shield and came to stand next to Raegus.

This cannot last. Whatever you're planning, Methias, I wish you'd get on with it.

-III-

Methias saw three of the creatures erupt from the grasses, one just beyond striking range. The other two emerged a few feet behind and to either side of the first. These latter leapt, snarling and silent, toward Pallith and Tharus. They let Ire be for now, though he marked several arrows striking the grasses near the war hound.

The grass moved, but none of it ripped free. What does that remind me of?

That thought rolled around beneath the surface of his waking mind. The rest of his attention was focused on keeping himself alive. The goblin nearest him made a curved sword appear out of nowhere. It lunged toward him with the weapon's oversized tip poised to stab.

I know that trick as well. The thought was full of amusement, despite his danger. He lifted his empty dim-hand, turning its back toward the creature.

"Duimtiq! Puehv ado!" *(Squire! My shield!)* As he closed the fingers of his hand, a rectangular tower shield bearing the realm's device materialized on his arm. Its arrival came in time to turn the thrust, but just barely.

If the creature was surprised by this turn of events, it wasted no time dwelling on it. Instead, it grabbed his shield, trying to pull it away with the many-jointed fingers of its dim hand. Meanwhile, it kept throwing strike after strike, trying to get either around or over the bulwark.

Not well-trained, are you? Flat snaps? Hammers? Really? Are you aiming to strike me or my shield?

He felt himself smiling at these thoughts, despite the danger. Many men fell prey to panic in such moments. They were terrified by the sight of a foe coming so close. Of that foe arresting their movements. Of the sight and sound of a weapon battering against their shield. Such a reaction was understandable, but it was often fatal.

Methias had spent far too many years under Jannon's gentle hand. He knew better.

I'm in no position to draw my sword, but... Still on one knee, Methias leaned back, using his weight to pull his shield with him. The goblin leaned back as well, trying to out-muscle him.

There we are … and… Now!

Methias stopped fighting the goblin's pull. Instead, he yielded to it. He pushed forward, adding the creature's strength to his own as he rose to strike. In his bright-fist he held the goblin arrow he'd been contemplating. He spun the thing inverted so its point stuck out below his fist. As he rose, he growled, driving the pin into the Nebelblut's right eye. It dropped its sword, shuddered, and went limp.

A torrent of power flooded into him. His every sense sharpened to a fidelity he'd never known. It wasn't that every light stung his eyes. It was that the *reflection* of light from every surface, each blade of grass, was damned near blinding. The sound of his fellows as they battled the other two Nebelblut was a succession of close thunderclaps *whamming* against his ear … yes. But the sound of their booted feet upon the grasses, the noise of their chainmail scraping against *everything,* all combined to make a nerve-scraping roar of discord. And all of it was underpinned by the cacophony of screams, grunts of effort, and the weeping of women, children, even grown men in the near distance. It was almost too much to bear. Yet he *could* bear it. It stretched his tolerances to their absolute limits, but yes. He *could* weather it.

As this new normal asserted itself, he became aware of other things. There was a strange, not-quite colorlessness wherever he let his gaze linger. And there were whispers. He could hear them, but they were little more than ambient noise. He tried to focus on the sounds. Doing so didn't make them any more intelligible, but it *did* have an effect. He began to giggle almost at once. He'd no idea what was so funny, but it took an actual effort to stop himself.

A fresh torrent of folk streamed from Wick, screaming in terror as they fled toward the west. Ire continued to advance toward him, snarling. Tharus snapped his hound's name as much out of confusion as fear.

Methias thought he heard someone shouting *wraith* in the distance, which forced his mind back to something… something he'd noticed about the goblins and the way they'd appeared from the grasses. It was then he marked the lone Nebelblut archer glowering at him from across the sedge and heather grass. Even at this distance, he could see the wrinkled creature had but one good eye—its left. Its regard was difficult to bear, yet he couldn't look away.

At first, he took the parade of images that sprinted across the stage of his mind's eye as a welcome thing. A message from Mezofel, his familiar—his friend. All too soon he realized that, while the touch of this other mind was familiar, it most assuredly was not from *his* familiar.

He caught the briefest glimpse of himself pulling a coin purse out of a Nebelblut's hand. Next, he was treated to the sight of this same one-eyed goblin leaning—*leering* over him, bringing a long, curved dagger down toward his face. This was followed by one of that same creature standing above him as if he were on his knees. The message seemed clear. The Nebelblut felt that Methias had stolen from it, and his life now belonged to the goblin.

You and yours began this. Not I or mine. But no sooner had he sent that thought toward the archer than it turned its head northward, pointing at where the rest of his folk were guarding the postern gate.

Looking at them made him shudder. He felt himself begin to giggle again and clamped down on the urge. As he turned back toward the one-eyed archer, he realized that Pallith and Tharus had dispatched their foes. He also realized that Ire was several feet away and growling… at *him*.

Looking at the men brought the mad laughter bubbling up again. His stomach clenched, and for some reason, his mouth began to water. Ire's growl grew more aggressive. As he turned in the hound's direction, he felt true fear for himself for the first time in ages. The mastiff's hackles were raised and his teeth were bared, but that was the very least of it. Ire's brindled coat glowed with a golden light that hurt to look at.

Yet why should it hurt? I know that light—know it better than most.

As if to refute this thought, Ire advanced toward him. With each step, that golden under-light seemed to grow brighter.

Methias finally managed to prise his hand free of the pin and began to rise. Two things stopped him in mid-motion. The first was the realization that the arrow he'd used to kill the Nebelblut was disintegrating before his eyes. It grew dark, turning to ash between blinks. The second was a collective scream from what seemed like every direction at once.

An enormous, free-floating eye rose above the walls. It appeared to mark him in specific, then set again, like some malevolent moon in a child's nightmare.

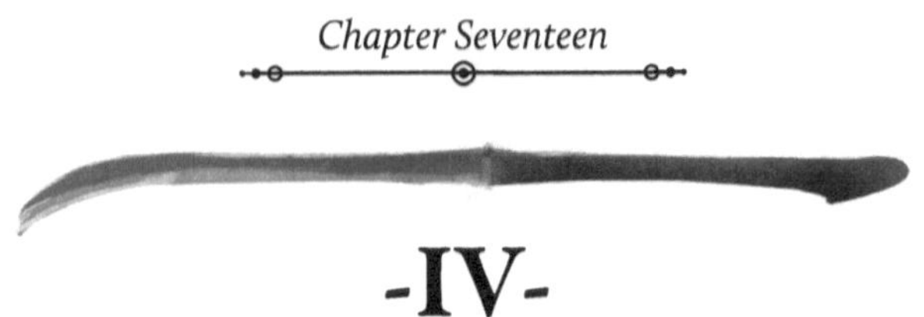

-IV-

Olshnak passed beneath the shadow of the postern's small murder hole—the area atop the wall from which defenders could rain arrows, boiling oil or water, or similar defenses down on enemies trying to breach the gate. His proximity to the gate itself meant there were more folk behind him than before him.

He was still trying to come to terms with all that had happened this night, and he'd allowed himself to be carried along at whatever speed the small mob dictated. Before long, he found himself outside amidst shieldmen wearing and bearing unfamiliar livery.

"Tusk!" Vilmocz made his voice sharp. Once Olshnak met the arms-man's eyes, his tone lost its keenest edge. "To me."

Olshnak made his way over, hefting his borrowed shield. "Will he live?"

"Dunno. We'll hope so. Terrek? The sandblood?"

"Holding the line. Huron told me to..."

But he couldn't finish. Huron had no power over him. He couldn't claim he'd been *ordered* to leave through the gate. He knew it was right—knew he needed to report what had happened here. But that didn't make him feel any less like a coward.

He saw a handful of men and horses to the west and a few goblin bodies on the ground before them. Two of the men held shields that looked like those standing here.

No army come to save us, but far better than nothing.

"Lord Ricgerd?" This was a voice Olshnak didn't know. "It looks as if there are no guards with this group." A pause. "Your remaining armsmen are holding back the tide. Best get you to safety with this lot."

Olshnak looked back and saw the lord on his knees beside Sir Kaith. The knight looked very pale. He wasn't awake, and given his appearance, Olshnak doubted he would ever wake again. As he watched, he saw Ricgerd take Kaith's hand, grimacing.

"Lord?"

"I'll be staying."

"Lord, no. We *must* get you to Rock—"

"I said no!" Ricgerd's voice was that same thunder Olshnak had heard in the great hall of the Braided Tower just before the man had leapt to strike Kaith. Hells, had that been all of two days agone?

The man was a knight. If his raiment weren't enough to make that clear, the way in which he spoke to Ricgerd next left no room for doubt. He was either a knight or a man courting his own punishment.

"Ricgerd *yes*. You're *going*, Lord. You've a responsibility to the County throne, as well as a duty to protect your own people." The knight gestured toward several of those people stood hard by, anxious to set off, yet afraid to go unprotected. "Now, on your feet."

"I've a responsibility to my people, right enough. And I've a responsibility to my kith and kin." Ricgerd looked up at the group of refugees, picking out a man seemingly at random. "You, there. You're Atfet, the Chandler's son, are you not?"

"I... I am, Lord." The Barghad man was as terrified as the rest, yet he'd been distracted from that terror by the realization that his lord knew him on sight.

"This group is yours to lead. Make your way west toward Rockvale. Sir Raegus will be just behind you, acting as your rearguard. Now go."

"Y-yes, Lord." And with that, the man led the score or more outside the gate off westward at a jog.

"Lord Ricgerd..."

Ricgerd cut the knight off. "I have *spoken!*"

"You have... and proved yourself toothless by it. Falxes fall, man, you cannot command a knight of the realm to—"

"Actually, sir, he can." Olshnak had spoken before he realized he'd meant to. His thoughts ran wry but resolute. *Nothing for it now. May as well say it.*

He sighed. "A lord may call upon any knight within or upon his lands to aid in their defense. That knight may only deny the request if it would result in certain death, or—where the knight himself is also a landed lord— if that act of succor ignores a threat to his own lands."

Folk continued to stream out of the postern gate. The sounds of combat were growing ever closer as Terrek's men withdrew.

"And who are you?" The knight's voice was controlled but held a clear ice chip of frustration in it.

Ricgerd answered the question before Olshnak could. "He's Sir Kaith's herald. Now, *Sir* Raegus, as you have no land of your own, I think you'd best get after those folk."

"No!" Raegus's voice was as full of grief as it was anger. "I'm more used to everyone here. You're their lord. Why in hells aren't *you* going?"

"Because *Kaith* can't go! My father's gone, Robis is gone, and I wasn't with either of them when... I'll not leave Kaith to face the end alone the same way. If he can be saved, I mean to see him saved. If not, then I'll take as many of them with me as I can before I see them lay so much as a gnarled *finger* on him. Now for the last time, *Sir* Raegus. *Go!*"

Moon and stars had been blanketed by thin mist and the rising smoke from Wick's few fires. It had otherwise been quite clear for most of the night. Now, as if to underscore Ricgerd's words, the night sky was shattered by an abrupt flash of crimson light. This was followed almost at once by cracking thunder as the sky *opened.* The sudden downpour went far beyond unexpected. It added an unreality to an already nightmarish situation. Warm summer rain in early winter? Red light in the sky? Goblins on the walls? The eye of some invisible giant casting them in its insane regard?

No, not insane. That was the real horror. The eye looked *entirely* sane. As far as insanity went, Olshnak didn't think it would take much more to send most of these folk over the edge. *One more wondrous thing just might do it. And then... we're all dead.*

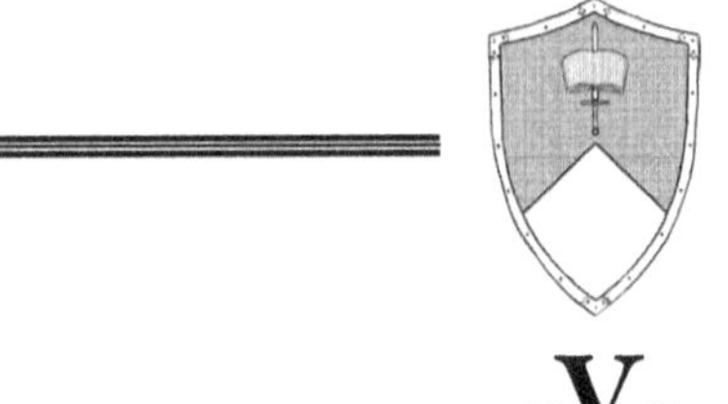

-V-

The night sky burst into carmine-colored light. With impossible suddenness, moon and stars alike were obscured by heavy clouds. Thunder rent the air, and the sky *opened,* drenching the world in frigid...

No. The rain should be cold, given the season. But it isn't. It's...warm.

Realization struck Methias like a mailed fist. He felt true fear for the second time this night—fear not only for himself but for the entire world.

The Keening. It's the Keening.

"It's the Keening," he repeated aloud. "The way is open. The King of the Dead... He's free."

He shook his head as if to clear it. "Tharus, Pallith? Keep your shields high. I won't hear or see you for a few moments. Duimtiq, puehv ado," he said again. Between blinks, his shield was gone once more. That accomplished, he stepped fully behind the pair and dropped to his knees.

Raising his hands to his ears, he gripped them so that his knuckles pointed over his shoulders. Squeezing his own head so that his hands muted as much sound as he could manage, he gazed toward Wick, drew as deep a breath as he could, and moved his mouth without expelling any air. "Puav ka puehv qua, puehv qleegek, xu puehv xejhfehv," he focused his eyes on a space above and between Apiné's men before finishing, "lakth." *(I will my mind, my whispers, and my hearing ... there.)*

The shift was disorienting, but that was nothing he hadn't expected. His vision went dark, tinged in red as if he gazed at the sun through closed eyelids. His ears were assaulted by sounds that had been distant a moment before and were now all around him. Jastar was shouting at someone over the rain, which *also* fit with his expectations. The man was a knight, after all. And one who'd struck him as level-headed enough to take charge if need be.

"Enough! I'm past tired of arguing. Raegus, go! Leave Kaith and Lord Ricgerd with us. Take as many of them west as you can, but hells be hid, *go!*"

"Jast, don't send me away. I..." This was another voice—presumably this Raegus person.

Apiné cut across him. "Sir Raegus, either stay or go, but stone in sky, get out of the damned way!"

Methias had been about to interject when he heard a bone-shattering *crack* from beyond the wall.

It's like hearing an egg break from the inside, he thought and shuddered. As similes went, that left a good deal to be desired, yet the imagery refused to leave his mind. He'd almost gasped, which would've meant he'd wasted the power he'd used. As it was, his temples were beginning to throb—a sure sign he was running out of time.

"Apiné! The hourglass is emptying, so make me repeat nothing. Find me the flattest ground you can and stand on its south-easternmost corner. Put your back to its edge, facing the walls. The rest of you, stand clear of her and *do not* let anyone further north than her right boot. Questions?"

He felt something brush against his left elbow, nearly forcing his hand to release that ear. He'd have to leave that to Tharus and Pallith, for now.

"Where... I don't see—"

Jastar's questions were overridden by Apiné's clipped tones. "How large a field, Lord?"

"As large as you can find. Enough to hold a wagon, at the least. If it's smaller than that, put a man on the northwest corner." His voice was getting raspy. That was no surprise, given the burning sensation in his lungs. "Good enough?"

"Aye, Lord. We'll see to it."

Methias nodded, though none of them could see it. "Sir... Raegus? Hold a mo—"

"He's gone, Lord. Racing westward to act as a rearguard."

"Hells. Well... we'll have to... to hope..." But it was no good. His head was swimming. He could hold his breath no longer.

"Ah-pin-nay? Go!" And with that, he felt himself falling. He struck the grassy ground and saw black flowers bloom across his closed eyes. He was breathing again, and his body made it clear he'd been a fool to stop that long-loved activity. His arms, his face, even his fingers were all tingling as his heart pounded.

"Methias? Methias are you... Ire, *stop* that! Meth—Er, Lord? Are you..."

Methias opened his eyes, pushing himself to a seated position. "Just out of breath, Tharus. Just out of ... breath."

Ire was still snarling at him. The hound's posture made him look as if he'd scented prey. He wasn't *quite* within arm's reach, but stood near enough to make his point.

Again, that sense of personal fear welled up, followed by the mad urge to giggle. He managed to push both sensations down, but it took even more of a concerted effort than it had before. He got to his feet and ducked out of reflex as an arrow struck Pallith's shield.

"No fear, Lord. My shield is stout enough. But what are we planning? What will we do? You cannot mean for us to just stand here while the mist bloods take the village."

Methias grinned, hoping his voice would carry that sound. "Not at all. But give me a moment."

He looked toward the rest of his men, choking down another gibbering fit. Apiné was perhaps a dozen yards from the stone wall, standing as he'd requested. He'd been about to act when he saw another figure. This one almost *had* to be Xaithrin. He moved at a lumbering jog, crossing behind Apiné.

"Xaithrin hol Kieran... where are you... ah! Good enough." The man came to a stop at what must be the northwestern corner, as he'd asked. It was longer than he'd needed, which was good, though it was narrow.

Not quite wide enough for a wagon. Well, it'll have to do.

"We run together. Pallith? Don't worry about your horse. Mezofel will bring her."

"Y-yes, Lord."

He moved his fingers so as to make a line between Xaithrin and

Apiné. Getting as close to each as he dared, he rounded his focus and tried to perceive the entire field at once.

"Ayach xu vahd, vloo puehv kegryleek itor!" *(Earth and stone, be my guardian against the sky's anger.)*

The ground shook. An instant later, the field his folk stood beside first humped up, then tore loose. The air was filled with fresh screams.

I don't know why I'm surprised, he thought. *To them, this must look like the final doom. Their village overrun, an enormous eye free-floating in the air, a storm out of a clear night's sky, and now the very ground is moving? Of course they're screaming.* He wasn't certain what else he could've done to prevent their panic, but he did regret being part of what had caused it.

When it finished, the ground formed a rough barn bay with openings that faced both north and south. It stood half as high as Wick's wall and looked as stable as he could've hoped, given it was made of stone and soil.

"That'll do. With me, now!"

With that, Methias raced toward the gate. He heard their booted feet crunching along the grass behind him a moment later. Ire's snarling self raced along in their wake. Mezofel understood the run of his thoughts well enough, so he wasn't surprised when he heard the rapid tattoo of hoofbeats running up his back trail as well.

"In! In!" he shouted as he ran toward the strange new structure. "Leave me room toward the north to work, but hurry! Everyone in!"

They got everyone moving with as much speed as they could, given the panic. Only Sir Jastar looked rebellious and looking was where that seemed to stop.

Methias ran around the outside of his makeshift shelter, coming to its northern opening. "Pallith, get whoever's with the horses to head this way. I think it has to be Morric. Go!" He heard the man shouting as he moved to obey. "Tharus? Make certain nobody gets past you while I work. When I'm done, it won't matter, but until then?"

"Done!" His grainy voice sounded nothing short of delighted.

As soon as Methias entered, he paced off a few strides south, drew his sword, and used it to draw in the fresh earth. He worked with a will, trying with all his might to ignore the hunger and hysteria warring within him. Whatever the Nebelblut had done to him, it would pass.

That, or I'll have to make it pass. Either way, it has to wait.

The people crowded in. They were terrified, and with just cause. After all, what safety was there to be had in an earthwork tunnel?

Methias's stomach seemed to make a fist. The cramp was a clawing, pulsing thing that held him fast. Yet his other senses appeared to sharpen further. He smelled the rich, fatty scents of well-fed people... people who had been seasoned by fear and wonder. He could ease his pain. He could drink their dread like the wine it was, and he would be sated... would be *strengthened*. He would be...

Damned! I'd be damned if I did that. That was true. And if he satisfied himself—If he fed until he was full? *There'll be a new realm added to the hells just for me...*

As if in response to that happy thought, Ire stepped toward him. The hound wasn't growling now. He was *howling*. Methias shrank away. The sound sent a shudder through him, but when it passed, he felt a measure of control return.

No time to think on that now. He turned back to his work. With palpable relief, he realized he was almost finished.

Then came a shout of such utter triumph that the *world itself* appeared to fall silent. Only the wind and rain served to underpin its unnatural intensity. It boomed across the land, roaring out its message with far more force than an unaltered voice could hope to muster. And it came from everywhere at once.

"Red the root. And red the stone. Red the rage for empty throne. Bear forever burnished bone. Bear your guilt. Bear it alone." His voice—and it *was* a man's voice, deep and dark—seemed to take an age to fade. When it had gone at last, there was a moment of uneasy calm—a vain hope that whatever that had been, it'd now passed.

Methias winced out of both shock and the briefest stab of pain. Even so, his undermind made the necessary connections with his own weave work.

It's like the runes I used in The Cage—projecting and carrying the sound, rather than forcing it to circle back on itself.

No sooner had this realization struck him then the voice came again, louder somehow—a righteous anger denied.

"Do you *hear me?* I walk! *We* walk! And we *will* find you! You cannot hide!"

Thunder was his only answer.

Methias forced his mind away from the mystery this presented. As he drew the last line in the soil, he stepped back.

"Vloo vahd, crayach. Zuam zeteek rin." *(Be stone, fresh earth. Hold your shape.)* Once he'd finished the rote's verbal component, the fertile soil at his feet turned grey, hardening into solid stone. The images he'd drawn in the dirt were now graven, as if created with a wide chisel. The work was inexpert, by artistic standards, but it would do for his needs.

He looked up, making his voice carry to address the thirty or so people that had crowded through the southern entrance.

"Hear me! In a moment, Sir Jastar of Thorionden will lead you onto this stone. It and he will take you to safety. You'll be given beds, food, and what healing we can offer. From there, we can sort what's next for you." This was met with confused murmurs, but no outright refusals. "Tharus, hold your shield high." When he'd done so, Methias continued. "This device—the sigil you see on this shield? Any who bear that symbol where you're going are *my* men. They will do all that they can to protect you. Sir Jastar? Step to Tharus, please."

Jastar did as he'd been asked, but wore a face that showed both awe and fear.

"Lord? Are you—"

Before he could get his question out, another man overrode him. "Who are you? And where will your sorcery take us? Will there be a leach there?" He sounded as if hope and fear were waging war within either his head or heart. Perhaps both.

"I am Methias Arthod... the Lantatt—or *High Lord* if that's easier to remember—of Dereek khn, your northern neighbor. Healers? Yes. There will be at least one healer waiting on the other side. Others will be sent for if need be. As for where you're going, it'll take you to one of my fastnesses. You'll be as safe there as I can make you. Bring the wounded through straight away. Morric?"

"Here, Lord." The man spoke up from behind him.

"Go through with the horses first. They'll slow things down a pace if we have to move them through a crowd on the other side." When the man had nodded, he turned back to Jastar. "What was your question?"

The knight shook his head. "Nothing, Lord. I'll see it... Oh, there *is* something, actually. What should I tell the Old Man?"

"Nothing. Tell the guards awaiting you on the other side how many we have, and to make ready just in case. They'll tell Fyken and get everything in order."

Jastar gave a slow nod. "You... prepared for this." His tone made it clear that this was a surprised observation, rather than a question.

Methias nodded. "Just a bit of gardening, Jastar. Now, on my mark." He centered his focus on the wayfaring conduit he'd made, pleased he still had full control of his faculties. Both his new hunger and the urge to gibber were, for the nonce, dull things gnawing at the back of his mind.

Looking at the stone, he crouched down, laying his hand atop its smooth surface. "Gil hol dojhah. Zul sev luukth." *(Complete the circle. Take us there.)*

There was a brief flash of twilight-colored light. Methias stood, satisfied.

"Go on Morric. Sir Jastar, move everyone off the spot you arrive on as swiftly as you can. Nobody else can follow if someone's still stood upon it. The others will be along."

"Kaith? Kaith! Breathe, Kaith! Help him! Help—"

But Methias was already moving, careful to step around the conduit he'd made. It would only last for so long, and he could do little to help anyone if he found himself back at Kor Kowmor. "Don't wait, Morric. Go."

The wounded man's face was the pale color of new parchment, and his lips had gone a dull grey. The former was a sure sign of blood loss. The latter meant death was stalking him close. Methias grimaced. When he spoke, he made his voice both short and sharp. If he was going to save this fellow...

"We're out of time. If there's any hope, do as I say and keep your teeth together unless you don't understand what I ask. Lay him down, grab his feet and his shoulders. You'll be moving him."

They did as bidden. The eye of every local was upon him, though he was pleased to see his Dereek khnderath keeping their focus outward.

"Put him here. Duimtiq, puehv ado." The tower shield appeared on his arm once more. He stripped it off and laid it on the ground as fast as he could. "Go on." They obeyed. As they did, Methias saw the grisly wound on the back of the man's right leg.

A leg you might not keep, my friend, though we'll do what we can.

He pulled a flat, oval stone from his haversack—a river-smoothed rock about the length of his middle finger. "Lanbachsel? I'll need to borrow two of yours, please."

Apiné nodded. "Kujin? Xaithrin?"

The two men hooked their hammers onto their belts, slinging their shields across their backs as they stepped over.

Methias looked at them both in turn. "You'll need to be on either side. You two?" He shifted his gaze to the man's bearers. "This will keep him alive, but you'll need the help. He's about to get very heavy. Tell the healer to remove the stone when he's ready to tend to him. And if you love this man, hells be hid, do *not* drop him."

With that, Methias placed the stone in the wounded man's mouth. "Muunts qluu zet aanq." *(Become what you hold.)*

A creeping stain of grey crawled across the warrior's face, then spread over his entire body. The process took less than a minute. A few folk managed a gasp, but it sounded more surprise than shocked or afraid. Most just stared in mute acceptance.

When it was done, Methias tapped the man's forehead and was satisfied. He'd turned to stone, and would remain that way until the exemplar was removed. He stood, nodding to the mustachioed man who'd seemed so concerned. "Walk with care. This hasn't healed him, only *held* him in state. Still, he's safe to move now."

The fellow's mouth moved, but no words came out of it. Finally, he nodded, looked to the three men standing around the shield with him, and bent to his task.

They carried him on Methias's tower shield, stepped onto the conduit, and were gone. And with that, their escape from Wick had begun in earnest.

-VI-

Venzene Duchy of Kovalun
County Jižní Pochod
Barony of Hartscross–Jižní Lov

Lashjuk couldn't weep.

Oh, she *recognized* her own grief. She was no more immune to the horror of the dead boy cradled in her lap than he'd been to the quarrel in his father's crossbow. That grief had simply been sacrificed as fuel—all but lost in the bright burn of her rage. Not that it was doing her much good. For all her blinding inner fire, her rage remained, for the moment, impotent. Her legs ached, the nerves in her bright arm alternated between numb and gnawed on, and the only thing that throbbed more than the muscles of her chest and back was her head. This latter had an unfair advantage in the contest of *what part hurts the worst.*

And then there was Maksu. She dreaded his misery, no matter how justified it was. He'd witnessed the murder of someone important to him for the third time in about as many weeks. His father, his sister, and now his friend.

Vlk's father Liška was still screaming, tearing at his beard in between bouts of trying to shove his entire fist into his own mouth.

I'd be glad to shut his stew hole with an azhkast, but my dim arm's too dim for the task. And my bright's broken, I think. She held out hope that her anger might burn its way through her pain. Such things were common enough when feelings were at their fiercest. If not, she may well die here beside brave Vlk.

She heard Maksu mewling and sniffling behind her. His scream as Vlk slipped sideways had been terrible to hear—a ragged, shrill song of shock and suffering. Yet she couldn't bring herself to lift her hands to her ears. Nevermind the physical pain it would've caused. Doing so would've meant letting Vlk slide to the floor like a burden she was eager to be rid of. And he deserved better.

Can you hear me? Are you... Are you there? She felt foolish. She was trying to think toward the serpent creature. For all she knew, it might be dead as well, just as Olga and Radek were. *Hells, and maybe Kastan and Lord Azhferd's man as well.*

That thought gave her pause. When had *Lady* Kastan become just *Kastan* to her?

She started, feeling the thing's tenuous presence at the fringe of a sense she couldn't quite name. *Are you...* She felt like an idiot for asking, yet her concern was genuine. *Are you wounded? Are you alright?*

Its familiar presence was a relief, but the warmth accompanying that relief began to fade in a hurry. She found it difficult to understand the serpent's odd means of communication at the best of times. The ache in her head did nothing to make it any easier. She had the sense that while it had indeed been wounded, it would recover in time.

I'm glad, she thought—and meant it.

Liška's scream rose a notch as he bit down on his fist. His eyes were red and streaming. As she bowed her head, her gaze seemed to snap to Vlk's lightless dreamer's lamps. Their weight drove any spark of sympathy she might've had for the man's grief far afield.

That man needs... deserves to die. I can't stand, and my bright arm is too wounded to use. I've no way to put an end to the low-bellied murderer without your—What do you mean, you can do nothing? You kept me from feeling pain when I hid beneath the carriage!

An image of a dark cloth being drawn over her eyes. *I don't understand. Blind... blindfold? Ah... you blinded me to the pain? Can you not do that again?*

She winced. This last image had been of an arm snapping over some-one's knee, bent at an unnatural angle.

It's too much for you to help me... An image of herself throwing her borrowed azhkast into the Vodnik rolled across her mind's eye. *Kill... Ah. My wounds are ... too much for you to ... defeat? Mmm. Well, what can be done? If he has any more bolts...*

As if her thoughts had somehow drawn his attention, Liška directed the full force of his misery at her. "You... you've killed... killed my boy! Called him to take the bolt meant for your whore heart! Ty čarodějko, zloděje duší! It's you! *Your* fault!"

Lashjuk's mind tried to translate the snarled Kovalunth curse. *Witch thief of souls? Something like that, anyway.*

His chest was heaving as he tried to use his pain. It was an old trick—covering fear and shame with the lustrous veneer of righteous rage. The act of self-deception was ever an easy sell. And this was no exception. Liška bellowed, filling the chamber with his terrible grief as he lumbered toward her. She could only watch as he came on.

He'd covered half the distance when a new sound rent the air. Andrej loosed a shriek that any gnoerk would be proud of. The force of it twisted his voice into a jagged growl that raised gooseflesh on the back of her neck. He rushed at Liška, a hunting knife clenched in his fist. On a boy his age, the weapon looked more like a hunting *sword.* He slashed hard as he came into range, catching the man on his forearm. Bright blood flew through the air—red raindrops caught in the lantern light.

Liška howled and delivered a closed-fist backhand to Andrej's head, knocking him asprawl and sending his weapon skittering along the stony floor.

"Stay *down,* boy! This tusk killed my vife and took Vlk from us both! For them and your own otec, she hess to pay!"

Liška turned back and resumed his trek toward her, but a blue blur ran at him from his other side. Maksu made no noise until he struck, shouting, "Erld raggrim erld lg! Erld!" *(You killed your son! You!)*

Maksu's fist connected with the outside of Liška's knee. The man *howled* in pain and rage, collapsing to his knees on the stone floor... *hard.*

"Awka erld *derag* ed Og!" *(And you won't do it to my mother!)*

Lashjuk was as proud and impressed as she was terrified. She'd drawn breath to shout for Maksu to back away, but the warning came out as a wordless snarl. Liška remained on his knees, his face a picture of ago-nized rage. Screaming, he delivered a right cross to Maksu's belly with what looked to be full force. The blow doubled the boy over, causing him to vomit.

Her muscles tensed as she tried to rise, to no avail. Her legs refused to un-bend, let alone support her weight. Steadying Vlk's sadful form, she readied herself. She would only have an eye blink to draw and plunge her eating dagger into the brutish bastard as he neared.

A shadow passed over her. When her eyes at last tracked the movement to its source, she saw Kastan standing before Liška with a sword to his throat. The sound of unnumbered footfalls echoed down some hall not far away, but that could wait.

"I ... saw you," Kastan began. Her words were halting, punctuated by pauses to catch her breath. "I saw you... heard your acc... accusation. Then... I saw you assault a woman who had ... just saved our lives. You tried to kill her."

Liška's face was wet with both tears and runners of snot. His voice was thick with pain but quite understandable for all that.

"Excellency... the tusk cun—the *tusk* killed my vife! She snared my Vlk... forced him to stand before—"

Kastan spat on the floor directly in front of him—an insult as old as time. "Liar. You refused to hear him. You refused to hear *anyone.*" She shook her head in disgust. "The man who sent you down here—this *Ebistian*? He took Edmund from us. He and his are the authors of most, if not all, of our woes, and on that man's word, you tried to kill Lashjuk. You *did* kill Vlk."

"Lady, no..."

Kastan overrode him, voice low and deliberate. "And for all of this... for all that you've wrought, I grant you what mercy I can render. You will not have to suffer under the weight of guilt for siding with Edmund's murderer, nor for your part in your own family's end. I, Kastan—Countess of Jižní Pochod —sentence you ... to die."

With that, she took him in the throat. Liška gurgled, then fell onto his side. His expression was more surprised than fearful—as if something had gone terribly wrong, and he had no idea how to set it to rights again.

Once he struck the ground, Kastan stepped back, drew her sword up high, and drove it through the man's heart. She stood there for a moment, looking down at him. Without warning, she yanked her sword free and began hacking at his corpse with great, two-handed, overhead strikes. Each was delivered with a growled burst of sound—a wordless torrent of frenzied grief. It was at once difficult to witness, and—in a primal, visceral way—quite satisfying to watch.

Andrej moved to help Maksu up, then stood with his arm around the younger boy's shoulders. Štít struggled to her feet and walked slowly over to sit in front of the pair, her back to them. All three looked battered and bruised. And though the boys held their composure, it was by the merest of threads. They had the same impulse at the same time. Each reached a hand out to begin petting the hound.

Kastan stopped at last. She stood, catching her breath.

"Lashjuk?" A man's voice—Lord Azhferd's man.

Lashjuk regarded him with tired eyes, letting her expression serve as her reply. He knelt beside her, looking as done up as she felt. It made her want to smile.

"I'm sorry for Guuvra and Maklo." He paused, reading her face, then went on. "I'm Skar. Lord Azhferd's—"

"I know who you are. I've known your face for as long as I've lived in Wieża Szymona." She was in too much pain—was too full of frustrated rage to make her voice cold, but no matter.

"Aye, Lady. When Lord Azhferd heard you were overdue, he sent me with another of his men to make certain—"

"That his investment hadn't been stolen?" Her anger was returning, and she was glad.

Skar's face wore an expression of genuine surprise. "No, Lady. Well, if it had, we'd have discovered that as well, but no. We were sent to make certain you and your family were alright. When we reached Bialy Klif and learned what'd happened..."

He bowed his head. "I set Iwo to accompany your kin back to Auburg. There was only one direction you could've gone, as you didn't meet us on the road. I'd been here before, so thought it worth the ride to see if anyone had seen or heard about you and your boys. I've come to take you home, Lady—or had, before the Storm Queen's attack."

He looked back over his shoulder. The source of the footfalls was almost upon them. "I fear now that I may not get the chance."

He stood, reaching down to help her up. She laid Vlk on the ground with as much gentleness as she could. After running her fingers through the brown mop of his hair, she closed his eyes and, at last, accepted Skar's help to stand. The pain was immediate, but once her knees were at last unbent, it began to fade.

"Excellency? Boys?" They'd begun moving before Skar had spoken. "I'll hold them off for as long as I can. The rest of you..."

"Will hold them off with you," said Kastan. "I'm not sure there's anywhere left to run, given what little time we have. They sound as if they're almost upon us."

They stood in a tight little knot beneath the angel's stony gaze, waiting for the end.

A moment later, the room was full of frightened men, women, and children. And there, at their head, stood Hajvarr and Pavel.

-VII-

County Thorion
Wick

Olshnak watched the new arrivals from the north take charge. He did his best to be surreptitious about it, but his time was limited. He had to get what information he could, then slip away before anyone noticed.

At least there's hope that Kaith might live. And hells, if he does, he'll become even more valuable to the cause. A foreign throne holding one of Thorion's knights? One of the storied survivors of Westsong? Aye... that'll be a hinge to turn things on. The Countess won't be pleased, but her pleasure's the least of my concerns just now.

He marked the arms their rescuers bore on shield and tabard, the quality of their gear, their obvious organization... The only difficult bit was trying to mark their way of speaking. He'd heard a stew of accents thus far. *Impressive, given there's barely a double handful of them. Traeadish, Sheshik, Eodenth, or I've gone deaf. And is that western Venzene I hear? As for the woman... both she and the lord himself are from somewhere else entirely. I've no idea where, though I know I've heard folk who sound similar.*

He'd seen enough, he reckoned, and withdrew toward the back of the small herd of refugees to make his escape. He'd made it to the rear when a voice pulled him up short.

"Nqel, Nk." *(Hold, brother.)*

Olshnak fought the urge to hunch his shoulders. He should run. He knew that. *But if I do, it might start a panic that would cost lives. Gi awka glem, it might cause them to send someone after me, fearing betrayal, or just that I've run mad and am in need of harsh help....*

He stopped, but remained facing away. "Jash?" *(What?)*

"Re ed. Erld gar, erld lak, awka erld zaksh." *(Come with me. Your shield, your eye, and your voice.)*

Olshnak still hadn't turned to face the speaker. He wanted to deny the man, whoever he was. And that would be easier if he could keep him a disembodied voice. *So how do I dismiss him without just racing away?*

There was a moment of uncomfortable silence while he groped for a solution. *Wait... He speaks Grimdash, but he isn't a gnoerk. There weren't any among either group. So...* He would lay a trap for this fellow—a question that would give Olshnak all the reason in the world to take offense and beat an angry retreat.

Slurs were common amongst most cultures. They usually served as a way to make the poorest among them feel a sense of solidarity with their own kind. After all, no matter how bad your lot in life was, at least you weren't one of *them.* The practice wasn't limited to pale-skinned people, of course. Most cultures had their own pejoratives for one group or another. They were less well-known in the wider world because they were often couched in local languages, rather than the Trade Tongue.

Folk from eastern and central Shesh were *sandbloods.* Those from that land's northern and western regions were labeled *scar sights* or *shifties* for their slanted eyes. The Barghad k Qabaile—Thorion's first people—were *sap skins.* Only elves and half-elves seemed immune, and even that wasn't without exception.

Making his voice a growled monotone, he spoke his reply. "Zaksh ed jash tusk enjh ... nk." *(Tell me what tusk really means ... brother.)*

It was bad enough the word *Gnoerk* had long-since been bastardized to *orc. That'd* been a relatively honest mistake, at least initially. *I am a Gnoerk* had been heard as *I am an* Orc, or so the story went. But *tusk* was a descriptive term gnoerks had been painted with since time was first tallied—an easy way to *other* them whenever it suited.

The escapees moved forward, murmuring to one another. As for the disembodied voice? There was a brief moment of silence. A few beats later, an answer came wrapped in confusion, but no hesitation.

"*Ed* gakdush majhejh hshek gnoerk. Gnoerkish rag? Ngnk Bokod Ognk ...Aehe?" *(My kind believe it means gnoerk. As for the gnoerkish use? Father's brother or mother's brother ...Why?)*

Olshnak froze. He turned to face his interlocutor as if he were helpless not to. The man who'd named himself lord—this *Methias*—looked back at him with an expectant, if impatient, expression. For a moment, he could only blink. He was certain there must be *some* humans who took the time to learn the historical truth, but he hadn't met any who'd bothered.

The lord had been right, of course. Over the last hundred years or so, gnoerks began to adopt it as a term of endearment toward one another. It was used in place of the Trade Tongue word *uncle*. At some point it had shifted further, becoming a compliment about a fellow gnoerk's intelligence or overall capability. While humans still used it as an insult, among gnoerks it was something of a badge of self-respect or honor.

Methias broke the silence. He spoke with urgency, but no panic. "Nk, halg ga... *Gek* ga demajhejh ed. Awka el delrgan. Re ed." *(Brother, those within... The captain within won't believe me. And we've no time. Come with me.)*

"What can *I* do, Lord?"

Methias flashed a grin. "You've just proven it. You're the only black blood here. They'll have marked you—what defenders are still left. They don't know I or mine from a Sheshik Calif, and if we're to save them too, we'll need to be swift. A familiar face, unless they hate you out of hand, should help convince them. Now—come with me, Nk... please."

This last word was so full of honest hope that Olshnak could only nod. Before he knew it, he was striding along at the lord's side.

"Olshnak, lord."

"Methias Arthod. This is Pallith." He indicated the armored Barghad man walking close behind him, then spoke over his shoulder. "Apiné? When everyone else has gone through, you and yours will do the same. If I'm not with you, station guards on the Kowmor side. Better you defend from there. The conduit will be dormant soon enough, and I don't want you lot trapped and having to fight your way back home." He paused as he caught sight of the bodies that had been set aside to clear the gate. "And before you go? Collect as many enemy arrows for me as you can. Don't throw lives away to do it, but gather all that you're able."

With that, they passed out into the warm summer rain, back beneath the gaze of the unmanned murder holes and toward Terrek's thin iron line.

-VIII-

There was no sign of the monstrous floating eye. Come to that, Methias found the memory of it slipping, as if it might've been some sort of daydream or delusion. He knew better, but...

He shook his head, forcing himself to refocus. That would have to be a mystery for later. There were more pressing matters right in front of him.

Wick's remaining defenders had done far better for themselves than they'd had any right to, given their numbers. Eight souls held back the tide of goblin flesh as the King's rain fell. They'd erected a thin shield wall, curving it back into a semi-circle with its edges touching the stone to either side of the gate. Two armsmen in blue leather stood at its center, acting as a focal point for enemy and ally alike.

Beyond them, unnumbered goblins stretched back to Wick's main thoroughfare. Their rear ranks included many archers, but their bows were pointed down as if at rest. The disparity of numbers would have been quite enough to call the skirmish terrifying. But the essential *alienness* of the goblins—voiceless and all but expressionless as they moved, fought, and died—cast a surreal, nightmarish pall over the entire affair.

Methias came to a stop a few strides from the battle line and considered the enemy in silence. *The goblins should have been able to put an end to this long since, but they're still disorganized. They might be forgiven for that, all things concerned. There must be a hundred or more of them, so their victory's all but assured. Still...*

He'd seen the same pattern earlier on the walls. The goblins moved and attacked in packs of two or three. Each member looked to be armed with a sword or morning star—a reasonable choice for frontline combat, though somewhat less effective if only one side wields shields. For some reason, each pack remained focused on a single defender at any one time.

The Nebelblut seem determined to fight in a way that erodes their own advantages. The shape of the street and its buildings already turns the battlefield into a limited front. And they've pushed the defenders against a literal wall. A choke point like that lessened the impact of their numbers. *They've no spears or glaives in their second or third ranks... Their archers are sitting idle. And their front line's more or less ignoring any defender other than their target. It makes them easy kills for the shieldmen to either side of their chosen foe.* It was absurd, but what of that? It *was*, and nevermind the rest.

He reached into his haversack, focusing on the item he needed. An instant later, he held a small, worn leather pouch. *Right now, the only thing keeping them from victory is their own foolishness. And that could end at any time. So...*

The teeming rain made conversation difficult, but not impossible. Methias made a beckoning gesture, keeping his voice low as he spoke to his companions.

"Olshnak? At my word, get them on side and moving, quick as you can. Pallith? Drive forward to help clear out the remaining goblins and make ready to withdraw. Are you both ready?"

When they'd each nodded, Methias opened the pouch's mouth and reached inside. After rooting around, he finally found what he'd been looking for—a small metal carpenter's tack. Drawing in a tight breath, he pierced his fingertip with it, exhaling when the deed was done. He waited a beat, then withdrew his hand, pulling the drawstring tight. With a final nod to each man, Methias stepped forward.

"Zul puehv hecn, xu ovye!" His voice was full and clear in the relative quiet. It carried well, causing a momentary pause in the goblin onslaught. As he spoke, he threw the pouch high over the Wickish line. Its height shortened the distance it flew, but at least it cleared the allied shields. The pouch came down somewhere between the enemy's second and third ranks. *(Take my blood and grow!)*

For a beat, nothing happened. Then a rumble rolled across the cobbled stone. A rush of red-tinged brown burst into being amidst the goblin ranks. A pale cloud of dust billowed and swirled beneath it before succumbing to the falling rain. The Nebelblut found themselves lifted from their feet. The silent things didn't scream. On the contrary, their faces showed an unnerving calm that best resembled mild surprise. When it was over, a wall of interwoven thorns—some large enough to be considered *spikes*—covered the full width of the gate's street and just under half its length. This wall of woe stood as tall as a man and was made even taller by virtue of the goblins it had impaled as it grew.

To their credit, the men of Wick were confused—perhaps even unnerved. They were *not*, however, panicked.

"Now," said Methias. His voice held a calm he didn't come close to feeling. The hunger was clawing its way back. The sight of the men before him and the goblins hung like meat to dry beyond... It was enough to make his mouth water.

"Sergeant! Huron! Kill who you have to, but hells be hid, hurry! There isn't much time!" As Olshnak shouted, he ran forward toward the line's middle.

Pallith raced toward its left. He began barking orders as soon as Olshnak's voice had died away. "Make the square! Make the square!" They reacted, moving as if their heads were on fire. The men of Wick drew their formation's curved sides into straight-ish lines while holding as much cohesion as they could. The two men who'd anchored their line against the stone wall slid their way along until they were in the gate's mouth.

Methias was impressed. The lot of them reacted as if they were in a daze, but they knew the formation, which was something he hadn't expected. Then there was the matter of those first two men through the gate. They hadn't taken the opportunity to flee, which showed courage. Whether that courage came from resolve or resignation, it was a candle he meant to keep alight.

One of the men in blue—the sergeant, like as not—got the idea and echoed Pallith's order. He looked back to confirm they'd obeyed, then gave the next command in the sequence.

"Right, lads, give me a column! Collapse into a column! Olshnak? Stay behind us. Huron? With me!" With that, the two men in blue shoved forward amidst the chaos of the few remaining goblins.

Methias stepped toward the wall to his right. The gate's corridor was only wide enough for a single cart to pass through. And unless he was very much mistaken...

Once the men had fallen into a column formation, Pallith assumed command again. "Retreat by step! Step! Step! Step! Step!"

The men echoed the command, stepping backward toward Methias as fast as they could. Once the last man was beneath the safety of the unoccupied murder holes, Pallith gave the order to turn and follow him out. He stopped on the far side of the outer gate and began directing them toward the rest of his unit and the conduit.

Methias looked toward Wick's streets once more. He saw the two armsmen in blue trying to put an end to the remaining Nebelblut. The armsmen's sudden aggression, coupled with the confusion his own weave work had wrought in the enemy ranks, had served the men well. Some half-dozen of the creatures lay dead around them. Now, as the armsmen made to withdraw, the goblins appeared to have remembered how to fight.

If they'd fought like this against Wick's shield wall, they'd have won before I arrived!

That thought was all he had time for. "Olshnak! Give me that shield and get to Pallith!"

The gnoerk fell back to meet him, handing the shield over with agonizing slowness. That done, Methias drew War Cry and raced into the fray.

He reached the Sheshik man's side just in time to take his place. A goblin morning star shattered the armsman's battered wooden shield. The strike had enough power behind it to keep going, cracking into the man's chest, and sending him crashing to the ground.

The goblin was having trouble freeing his weapon. One of its spikes was caught in either the fellow's armor or his flesh. Methias didn't so much as slow his step. He *rammed* forward, bashing the beast in its vacant face, forcing it to release the weapon and stagger back.

"Olshnak!" He let the word serve double duty as a summons and a battle cry. Slamming his borrowed shield into place beside the sergeant, he brought War Cry down onto that same goblin, driving the sword into the place where neck and shoulder met. The weapon bit, but it took far more force than he'd expected. Was it the rain? He didn't know. And it was a question worth answering if they were to fight these creatures again.

"No point in runnin'," the sergeant said through a bitter grin. "They'd just fill us with pins, and we'd die tired."

Methias punched his shield forward, interrupting a tall goblin's hammer shot before he could deliver it. He followed this with a wrap shot to the creature's head, then a hammer of his own for good measure. The goblin dropped out of sight without a sound.

"Is that what we're still doing here, sergeant?"

"Aye. No use in *all* of us dying. Figure we'll stay the line and waird as long' wi can. Have tae hope the others get enough of a lead while these beasties fecht wi us."

Methias was instantly charmed by the man's dialect. He had no real trouble understanding it. It was too similar to the mix of Traeadish and the Trade Tongue spoken in the Last Bell. *Waird* meant *guard, fecht* meant *fight,* and so on. Still, some part of his mind wanted to start picking the wealth of words and phrases apart to confirm their roots.

Things like that will have to wait, though. Ah well.

He smiled, taking real pleasure in what came next. "A good enough plan, but I'd guess Sir Kaith won't be pleased you're not there to greet him when he wakes." Olshnak was helping the other armsman limp away. The fact that he'd survived the goblin attack with enough strength to limp at all turned Methias's smile into a broad grin. "I've already sent the rest of your men on to meet him. When you're tired of fighting, we can join them."

The sergeant paused, pulled his shield back toward his body, and threw a hard back cut to knock the last goblin asprawl. That done, he brightened in a way that called Fyken Presh to mind. "You make the thorns, did you?"

Methias nodded. "I did. Made a way out, too."

"Right then. Let's hope *that* holds better than your thorns." With that, he began to withdraw toward the gate.

Methias stayed in lockstep with the sergeant, though the comment left him confused. He kept his eyes on the thorns, seeing movement somewhere deep within their mass. Meanwhile, the nearest goblins were stumbling to their feet and casting about, as if disoriented.

But we felled all the goblins on this side of the...

All at once, he realized what he should've seen already. The Nebelblut were moving *through* the thorns... gliding through them as if they were a body of water.

"Run!" he snapped. "Don't wait, just go! Now!"

The sergeant hesitated, then did as bidden. When he'd gone, Methias walked to stand athwart the center of the inner gate, facing the ever-growing mass of Nebelblut. They each held weapons, and they were ambling toward him, but that was all he could say for certain. They looked directly at him, faces painted with expressions of vague anger or disgust.

If I'm right... well, even if I'm not, this should buy me enough time.

He sheathed War Cry, dropped his shield to the ground beside him, and cupped his hands. He dipped his chin so that he faced his upturned palms, drew in a deep breath, and spoke aloud in a low and angry growl.

"Not even the wraith dragon's art will save you from me. You aren't isbryd drayag. You're Nebelblut. And you've taken your last lives today."

The air around his hands began to ripple and dance. His words echoed, the sound looping back over itself faster and faster until it became a droning, wordless roar. He kept his hands cupped, holding the sound within them as he watched the goblins mill toward him.

When enough of them had drawn near, he raised his dim hand with the care of a barmaid carrying a full pitcher of ale. "Xoaxeet ahg riv xu gal!" (*Thunder to break and shatter!*)

As he finished the incantation, he rotated his wrist and aimed his palm forward. A shockwave of sound slammed into the Nebelblut, knocking them backward as if they were dead leaves caught in an autumn wind. The thorns bore the force for a few beats, until they, too, were uprooted and sent flying east along the cobbles. The outer walls of the two closest buildings cracked under the assault. Shingled stones flew from the near side of their roofs to clatter to the ground like grey rain further along Wick's wet streets.

As the noise dissipated and sanity reasserted itself, he heard footsteps just behind him. He'd expected Pallith, or perhaps Olshnak. He was surprised, therefore, when Ibhroth's voice came drifting to his ears.

"Hors-es *run...*"

Then he heard Pallith speak up. "Are there more? Is... is it over, Lord?"

Methias had drawn breath to respond when a figure strode out onto the road before them. Where he'd come from was yet another in the long line of this evening's mysteries. The figure was tall and well-muscled, with long, flowing dark hair. He moved at an easy pace, giving a wide, expansive gesture with his hands as if to welcome them.

"You have drawn me out," he said with a laugh. "Forced me to take the field to treat with you. And so I have, and so I do. For you have earned such a bat—"

He stopped both his striding and his speech some ten feet away. His skin appeared golden, much like Pallith's, and his speech was accented in a similar fashion. He might've been mistaken for a warrior or nobleman of similar heritage, at a glance.

But his eyes are inverted—white pupils, and black where the whites should be. And did I see fangs when he smiled?

"Ahhhh. You are the one who has tasted of our gifts. You have eaten of our harvest—eaten of our time." He smiled again, removing any doubt about his fanged teeth. "And so I welcome you, cousin. You are *of us* now. Should you be willing to take your place beside me." He paused, looking up and running a black tongue out to taste the rain.

"Rakshasa... he's a Rakshasa!" Pallith's terror was sudden and bright. "Lord, we must go. We must go *now!*"

"*You* must go, bhanja. *Methias* must stay, at least for a time." The creature Pallith had called *Rakshasa* seemed to consider, then nodded as if making up his mind. "Yes, Pallith. *You* must go... and take Ibhroth with you. Methias and I have other matters to discuss."

Methias heard Ibhroth wrest his ralbrend clear of its back sheath. He doubted the sword would do him much good in this situation, but it might.

He turned to regard the man out of the corner of his eye and nearly doubled over with pain. His stomach felt as if it were trying to make a fist and drive it up into his chest. He tried to hold his posture, his pain, his mind, and the remaining charge of sound held in his bright hand. He failed. The spell rolled away with the destructive power of an echo in the dark—haunting and ephemeral, but otherwise harmless.

The pain redoubled, radiating throughout his limbs, forcing fingers and toes alike to curl. He did manage to maintain his posture and the focus of his mind, though the pain made it both an effort.

And... if I'm to save these two, I must seem ... in control.

"I agree. Better I face you alone. Pallith, Ibhroth? Go."

The growl in his voice might have sounded intimidating. *Or they hear the truth in every word... that I'm in pain and putting on a brave and angry face to get them to flee.*

"Lord, I beg you. You must not stay and fight this demon." Pallith sounded as if his courage hung by the merest thread.

"Aye, and if you insist, then don't face him *'lone!* I'd sooner take the Hammer's advice, but sending me away? What's the Yebu Ke for if not this?"

Ibhroth was right, of course, at least in principle. The Yebu Ke were a complicated subject, though. And this wasn't the time to *uncomplicate* them. Still, he needed to make some reply, and not one that seemed as if it were dreamt up just for the occasion. But what would satisfy... ahhh.

"Ibhroth? You and you alone among the Yebu Ke have seen what I'm about to face. Pallith knows something of him and his kin. You *two* must make report. Now... go on."

It worked. Ibhroth drew in a sharp breath through his nose, spoke his acceptance, and headed out with Pallith. And now Methias stood alone with the Rakshasa and his force of Nebelblut.

"Shall we begin?"

KING'S RAIN, KITH'S TEARS

-I-

Venzene Duchy of Kovalun
County Jižní Pochod
Barony of Hartscross–Jižní Lov
5 Korunasykli: 22 Days after the Red Storm at Westsong

For a moment, Kastan could only stare. She *understood* what she was seeing. She was just having a difficult time accepting it. The notion that Edmund's Ruční Kopí—*her* Ruční Kopí—stood before her with a small mob of survivors seemed like an impossibility.

Hajvarr and his armsman Pavel had cuts and bruises to spare. Pavel bore a long, jagged gash on his forehead. It was bleeding, but at a glance, it seemed clear it was a shallow thing.

…If bruise and boy were real.

…If *any* of the shadowed, shocked faces were real.

…If this wasn't some final fever dream before she slipped sideways.

After everything else that's happened today? After every truth revealed— every veil torn aside? Kastan shook her head, resisting the urge to close her eyes for anything longer than a blink.

"Kas—Excellency?" Hajvarr's voice drew her from her long thoughts. "It's been bad in the undertown, but it might be worse above. Our would-be saviors have turned on us. They're putting everyone they can lay hands on to the sword, then standing them up again. Some of the Bluemark are making it hard for them, but there just aren't enough. A good many fled once the dead started rising." His tone held more sympathy than blame. "We've managed to save some fifty souls, but..."

His eye fell on Vlk's still form. He bowed his head, then turned to Pavel with a look of shocked sympathy. The baker's boy was ashen-faced, but his eyes left no doubt that he was in control of his emotions.

"Jitka von't... it'll be hard for her."

As if he'd summoned her, a little girl came walking through the crowd. She looked dazed. Her vacant expression and the meandering way she moved were difficult things to look at. Were she older, one might be forgiven for thinking her drunk on daddy's abandoned ale pot. She held the hand of the dyer's daughter—Kastan couldn't recall her name. The pair moved to stand next to Pavel, who took the older girl's free hand at once.

"Vlk? Vlk, vhy are you..." The little girl took another unsteady step forward, releasing the hand she held. "Vhy are you... Vlk?"

Her eyes went wide, then closed in anguished disbelief. She staggered as if slapped. "Vhy? Vhy did someone let... Vhy is he..." But it was no good.

She spun around and threw herself at Pavel. He handed Hajvarr his spear and released the hand he still held. Bending down, he lifted Jitka, letting her screams and sobs crash against his big barrel chest. A beat later, he shifted her, so that she rode in one arm. He used the other to pull the dyer's daughter in to join the embrace. She, too, was weeping, albeit in silence.

And oh, was Kastan not jealous in that moment. To be able to give in and just ... let her guard down and weep for all they'd lost, as little Jitka was. She thought she'd have given almost anything to surrender like that. She wanted nothing more than for someone she trusted—Hajvarr, Caros, *someone*—to wrap her in a strong embrace and tell her that it would be... that it *was* alright.

But no. I... I am the Countess of Jižní Pochod now. Pravdivý jako zítřek.

The full weight of it struck her with a stark, sudden brutality. Yes, Hajvarr, Pavel... all of them were real, which meant all the *rest* of it was real.

She cast about. The sight of fifty-odd faces wearing haunted, lost expressions made everything doubly clear to her.

They're terrified, as well they should be. They're hungry for help—for hope—just as I am. But it's me they're looking to... me they're expecting to provide it. She marveled at her own foolishness. Of *course,* they were looking to her. She was their liege now. Who in hells else would they be looking to in this evil hour?

Very well. She couldn't embrace Hajvarr in hopes of being comforted, but there was something she *could* do.

To grieve alone takes ages. To grieve in groups takes burdens, so they say.

It was a lesson Caros had taught her after their mother had passed. As the heir to their father's land and title, he'd been expected to swallow his pain. Their father had been no comfort to either of them—he'd been too busy trying to drown his own grief. And so she alone had seen her brother's tears. She alone had felt the weight of his grief. And thereby had she discovered the miracle: the act of *giving* comfort was a balm to all wounded hearts at once.

Nodding more to herself than anyone else, Kastan turned and stepped to where the boys stood, stroking Štít. She met Andrej's misted blue eyes. They were grave, wounded things that turned her own grief to anger. That he should have to suffer so much in so short a time... it wasn't fair—any of it.

Not that it changes anything.

She sheathed her sword for the first time in what felt like an age. As soon as her hands were free, Andrej fell against her. She returned the embrace, stroking his hair and trying not to give in to her own pain.

Lashjuk moved to her left, embracing her own boy in much the same way. The four of them stood in silence for a time. It was far too brief, and far too public for anyone's liking, but it served its purpose. The ordinary magic—the simple knowledge that none of them had to face this misery alone—had robbed their grief of its sharpest edge. And that was no small matter.

Kastan pushed Andrej out to arm's length with as much gentleness as she could manage. Leaning toward him, she touched her forehead to his, which caused a sad smile to bloom on his face.

"You told me you would stay with me," she murmured to him, wearing a similar expression on her own face. "That there was no place you would rather be. Has that changed?"

"*Mm*-mm." He shook his head. "Where would I go, Lady?"

She kissed his brow, then met his eyes again. "I'll tell you now the same thing someone else I love told me. Will you hear it?"

He nodded, eyes beginning to mist over once more.

"Andrej, I beg you. Say nothing. Make no reply, but play along in all other respects."

His eyes widened, but he nodded, embracing her again.

She could feel him shake—could feel his fear. After a moment, she turned them both to face the milling members of this once-great community. She kept an arm around Andrej's shoulders, holding him tight to her side. Raising her voice, she addressed the milling mass of frightened folk.

"We'll be leaving this place. If you've provisions, keep close watch on them. It may be some time before we're able to find more. If any of you know anything of fighting, hunting, or trailcraft, come make it known to Ruční Kopí. Hajvarr? I leave the task of organization to you." Once Hajvarr nodded his acceptance, she turned to the dyer's daughter.

"Step forward, then turn to face the others." Once she'd done so— looking wide-eyed and panicky—Kastan continued. "If any of you know something of leechcraft, cooking, or scholarship, make it known to—"

The girl spun around, blushing deepest scarlet. "Excellency, I... I know *nothing* of healing or the scribal arts!" Her voice was a terrified, breathy peal of sound.

"Otta... You've a fair hand, you cook vell, and you remember *every-thing*," said Pavel. "If her Excellency vants your help..."

And now I know her name, Kastan mused. *Thank you, Pavel.*

"I..." Otta bounced from foot to foot for a moment, then sub-sided. "You're right, můj drahý." She gave Kastan a curtsey. "Forgive me, Excellency." And with that, she turned back to face the assemblage.

Kastan gave Pavel a grin and a nod, then thanked Otta. She let the silence play out for a moment while she collected her thoughts. She drew in a breath, held it, and spoke the words aloud for the first time.

"As most of you know, Edmund asked for my hand today." There were murmurs of condolence and acceptance of this, but she didn't allow them to linger. "He laid bare a good many truths that were wisely kept hid from common knowledge. He felt it best, and I ... never spoke a word of protest on the matter. After naming me his intended, he took steps to ensure that all was legal and proper. I *am* his lawful successor, holding all rights and responsibilities of his office."

She swallowed, laying her free hand on the county žezlo hung from her belt. "Yet there was more."

They nodded at this, offering a collective, inarticulate murmur in reply.

Well, she thought, *I've told all the truth I can. Now I must tell the lie. Tell the lie and hope to make it true.*

She steeled herself, drew a sharp breath in through her nose, and spoke the words.

"One such hidden truth was my Andrej. *Edmund's* Andrej, kept hidden for these many years."

The murmuring stopped for a beat, then erupted again. She thought most of the crowd seemed excited, rather than afraid, but she could not— *would not* yield the momentum she'd gained. Not even to such joy. She took a breath, then overrode them.

"Now Edmund is gone. The very devils who kill our kin, turning them into cradle tale monsters above, have taken him from us." They gasped and growled at this. Her own eyes were streaming, though her voice remained quite steady. "I am now the recognized Baroness of Hartscross ... the lawful Countess of Jižní Pochod. And as such, it falls to me to speak the words Edmund and I were meant to have spoken together."

The voices fell silent. Every eye was upon her. Yet no gaze wielded more weight than Hajvarr's. His eyes had always held a shrewdness and focus that was hard to endure for any length of time.

She did her best to ignore him for the nonce. She had other matters to contend with, her racing heart chiefest among them. Allowing her eyes to grow distant, she said the words that would both bind her to and fulfill her promise.

"I, Kastan Perc—" she silenced herself. "...No. No, that's no longer right." An odd little laugh escaped her lips, even as her eyes streamed. "I, Kastan *Hartscross*, hereby recognize Andrej as my lawful son and heir, granting him all rights and responsibilities, honors and obligations due his station."

They stared with wide, shocked eyes as they processed this declaration. None looked more surprised than Hajvarr. *And none look more angry. I'll speak with him as soon as time allows. For now...*

She raised her voice, injecting a note of joy into it that was a struggle to maintain. "For Lord Andrej Hartscross... for my Edmund's son! Jižní meče!"

They repeated the words with a surprising amount of zeal. The people were, indeed, hungry for hope. A ready-made heir might not have mattered to most folk in the ordinary course, but given the horrors above? Any sense of normality was a roof to seek shelter beneath until the storm passed.

She felt Andrej's arm tighten around her waist. He bowed his head, then looked up to meet the eyes of the surviving folk of this once proud place. He opened his mouth, closed it again, then stepped from her side.

"I... I thank you. My... My mother will lead us safely from this place, and for many years to come. But I thank you."

They nodded their approval, saying things like *aye,* and *well spoken, Lord,* and *now we know why Edmund never wedded.*

Andrej bore this for a few moments, then gave them another deep bow of his head before returning to Kastan. Meeting her eyes—*holding* her eyes—he gave her a weak smile and a look of such naked exhaustion she couldn't help but laugh. He laughed as well, though it came out thin, as if he were holding back tears.

"I have... questions... Mmm-*mother,* when there's time."

She nodded, laying her palms against his hairless face. "I expect you do. When we've stopped for the night... Will that serve?"

He nodded, still wearing that weak, wrung-out smile. She'd meant to say more, but was caught off guard when a low alto voice scratched its way into her ear.

"Excellency?"

She turned to find Lashjuk standing beside her. The gnoerkish woman's pale golden face wore an inscrutable expression. Kastan's pulse picked up speed once more, though whether this was the woman's unearthly beauty or her own fear of yet another crisis stalking close, she didn't know.

"Lady?"

Lashjuk met her eyes, then cut them to the left. "A word?"

-II-

**Dereek khn
Kor Kowmor**

The vast, distant ocean of storm clouds flickered with a wyrding crimson light. The whole of the southern sky was painted the color of ruin.

The rain was *leagues* to the south. Jastar knew that, but the distance wasn't what mattered.

No. What matters is that it looks far, far too much like Westsong.

Still, the activity at Kor Kowmor offered him some comfort. Fyken Presh had, it seemed, been ready for anything. Not long after the first Wickish feet had set foot on Kowmor's cobbles, he'd limped his way into First Ward and taken control.

"Bachsel Morric? Give the horses to Jasidor. Take *everyone* to Second Ward." Morric's acknowledgment was still exiting his mouth when the

Katxsel turned to address an orcish man. "Hangash? The other half of third lance may arrive with trouble nipping at their heels. If that happens, I want the rest of the two-two here and at the ready. Denythis and Sevasti Vah-een should both be in the barracks. Have them muster their lances and bring them here. *Now.* Once they're on the move, get you to higher ground. Questions?" He'd given them barely a beat to reply. "Go!"

They went, and Jastar couldn't help but smile.

That flared sense of well-being didn't last long. He'd found it difficult to watch the men bearing Kaith ... or what may as well have been Kaith's effigy.

A few of the non-marshal members of Kowmor's staff stepped in to help. While everyone seemed both concerned and even outright disturbed by the sight, nobody appeared confused by it. The idea that they'd seen such before produced a wave of outright horror in him. Turning a man to stone? And back again? If it saved Kaith's life, then Jastar could hardly complain. But it was one more example of how magic could shift the balance of power for good or ill.

Once they'd disappeared into Second Ward, and Kaith could no longer be a distraction, that sense of unreality began to fade. Jastar allowed his head to hang for a moment as he began trying to make sense of all he'd seen. The weight and import of his commission had never been clearer to him. He *needed* to either bring Dereek khn on side or find a way to defend against its wrath.

He'd no idea how he was meant to do either of those things, but that was another matter.

The exodus from Wick continued as best it could. The Old Man's training cadre kept the new arrivals moving northward. Food, water, blankets, and bandages were all being distributed in Second Ward. Everything had been organized in short order. Kor Kowmor's staff was, it seemed, a model of efficiency even in such a situation as this.

The rest of the two-two wasn't long in coming. They'd stayed out of the way, arraying themselves in a line beside the arrival point. They held their shields and their slender war hammers in readiness as the refugees came on, although they were careful not to project menace in their direction.

After a protracted period wherein no more of the Wickish arrived, Ibhroth appeared, followed by Apiné and red-maned Ghenys. The two hammers held a quiet conference with the Old Man and the leaders of the other lances.

Ibhroth came to stand next to Jastar. "S'rough, Sir Jast. Wish we could've saved more." He sighed, shaking his head. "Still, s'pose saving some's better than saving none, ain't it?" His tone made it clear this was more a statement than a question.

Jastar nodded, though he kept his eyes on the arrival spot. "The folk we *did* save—be it here with us now or racing toward Rockvale—aren't likely to complain. They expected to die. Instead, they live to tell the tale. Better not to have lived that tale, I grant you, but given the circumstances?" He shrugged.

"Aye, fair. S'pose it's just down to waiting, now."

Perhaps two minutes passed before Pallith appeared with an orcish man—Kaith's *herald,* if Jast had heard rightly. The orc cast about, doing an almost comical double take at his new surroundings, then growled something Jastar couldn't quite make out. Several hands raised to point northward, toward Second Ward. The orc headed that way with a shallow nod that served as thanks.

"Lanbachsel..." Pallith's skin had turned the color of old milk. "Rakshasa. There was a rakshasa. The lord commanded us to return."

Apiné offered a slow, considering nod. "Not just stories, then." She paused for a beat, then nodded again. "I take it he's just behind you?"

Pallith shook his head. "He said he'd face it alone." He sounded as if he were going to be ill—that, or as if he were on the brink of tears.

Apiné sucked her teeth, then nodded. "Then we must trust that he knows what he's about."

Jastar was astonished to see that everyone was either nodding at this or wearing a look of grim acceptance. He raised his chin to project his voice.

"Whom or what is a rakshasa?"

"Rak-*sha*-sa, Jast. A demon of the old world. They... they are flesh eaters... shapeshifters."

Jastar blanched, then bowed his head. *Well, Jast, you wanted a way to bring them on side.*

He made to step forward, but Ibhroth laid a hand on his shoulder to gainsay him.

"Sir Jastar, don't. They've got the right of it."

Jastar turned his head to shoot a withering glance first to Ibhroth's oak-colored eyes, then to the hand that gripped his pauldron. Ibhroth got the message and removed his hand, but he seemed more frustrated than cowed. No matter.

Jast stepped toward the line of Ban'ze Ruun, speaking as he went. "We cannot leave him there to face this thing alone."

"We can," said Apiné, "and we will. It's as I said, Sir Jastar. The Lord knows what he's about. If he's commanded us to leave him—if he intends to fight this battle alone, he has good reason."

Jastar forced his face to remain calm, his voice to remain reasonable. "And Tharus? Where is he?"

Apiné frowned, turning to Pallith.

"He ... refused to follow. He said... he said he arrived with Methias, and he would leave the same way. We're the same rank, he and I. I couldn't *order* him to return with me..." Pallith shrugged, clearly frustrated at his own impotence.

Apiné sighed, nodding. She opened her mouth to speak, but Jastar overrode her.

"You lot do as you like." He began to walk toward the arrival spot. "I'm going back."

"We have our orders, Jast," said Pallith.

"You must trust that Methias knows his business," Apiné said.

Jastar's next step would take him onto the... the... whatever its right name was—the thing that would take him back to Wick. He stopped, turning to face the assembled Dereek khnderathii soldiers.

"No, Apiné. I mustn't. I still haven't gotten the Old Man's approval to join the Yebu Ke. As of this moment, I don't answer to any of you. Even if I did... Tharus has the right of it." With that, he stepped backward.

Next he knew, he was assaulted by the sights, sounds, and smells of the Wickish battlefield. He heard a dull ringing noise as something metal impacted something much, much softer. Turning, he saw Tharus and his hound standing over a trio of felled goblins. The hound turned toward him and gave a brief bark of greeting.

Tharus glanced back over his shoulder and grinned. "Thal ter nier buedh, Sir Jastar. If I'd known you were coming back, I might've saved you some."

So he's Treaedish after all. Thal ter nier buedh. That's... I offer you peace, I think.

He gave the man a lopsided grin as he stepped over. "Can't offer you peace in return, Tharus. We've too much killing to do. Methias is facing a damned demon... alone. That hardly seems fair to me. Is he always this selfish?" He kept his voice light, but there was no hiding the sharp edge beneath the surface.

Tharus stiffened. "He is."

Did I misjudge you, Tharus? Are you going to stand idly by like the rest of them?

No sooner had these thoughts formed in Jast's head than the hammer and his hound stepped toward the postern gate they'd worked so hard to clear. Jastar grinned to himself, readied both sword and shield ... and followed.

-III-

The Grey Between

"Not how I'd have liked things to go, if I'm honest. Can't say it were much fun ridin' round on your back, Vlk."

Vlk resisted the urge to open his eyes. He was numb, which was a gift considering how the day had gone overall. He had no wish to swim upward toward the place where all the pain waited for him.

"C'monnnn. Quit shammin' sleep. 'Fraid those are gone days."

He let his eyes open *just* a sliver. The world once more seemed awash in that strange unlight. He'd seen it before, but that had been when he'd...

Vlk bolted upright, eyes wide as he looked this way and that in a panic. He heard soft laughter from that same voice and turned to see the scout he'd spoken with after his fall.

"You're... vell, you're laughing at me, for a start." Despite his fear, Vlk felt his mouth curl into a grin.

"Aye, well, if you could see the look on your face, you'd laugh, too."

Vlk shot him a playful glare. "You're one to talk about faces, Hroth. Vhen you laugh, your eyes try to run *avay* from yours."

He giggled at his own brave wit. To speak to a grown man in such a way was asking for trouble. Still, he thought the rangy fellow could be counted on to take the jibe in fun.

Hroth snorted, eyebrows rising to fade into his red mop of hair. "Aye, yer in a better mood this time, at least." He wore a lopsided grin that was about as far away from anger as summer was from winter.

Vlk's laughter stopped short as realization struck him. "Vait, you never told me your name. But... but you *are* Hroth, aren't you? Hrothgian?"

The scout nodded. "So they tell me. If I had to guess, it's 'cause of how close you and I got the past hour or so." He paused, reading Vlk's expression before going on. "Last time I seen you... well, let's just say you got a touch grabby."

He tried to think. "Vait, vhen I vas dreaming about Laagi? I thought I heard your voice before I voke up."

Hroth nodded. "Don't know nothin' 'bout your dream, but you were half-here again. You pulled me along with you when you stood back up in the real world. Rode 'round on your shoulder for a bit. Saw the old buzzard's secret garden and so on."

"Vait! I didn't vant to look him in the eye! *That* vas vhy! I... I didn't exactly *hear* you, but..."

"Aye, I was pullin' on yer ear, right enough. His dreamer's lamps may as well have been *real* lamps. They glowed when he was lookin' for your eyes."

Vlk shook his head, glowering. "Vell, vhatever you did, it vorked. Thank you."

"S'all over now." He laid a hand on Vlk's shoulder and squeezed. "S'not so bad, really. Bit sad, though. You'll miss yer mates, and no mistake."

"Miss my...?"

The realization hit him full force, and he deflated, beginning to cry.

Strong arms enfolded him. At almost any other time, he would have rejected the gesture outright. Such comfort from a friend his own age was one thing. An adult offering that same comfort was quite another. That sort of thing was for children, after all, and he *was not* a child. But this time... it was all too big for him to face alone. He thought he'd do just about anything for someone to tell him that it—that *he* was alright.

"I'm dead... I'm dead... I don't... I don't *vant* to be dead... I vant to be a knight! I vant to see my friends!" He shoved Hroth, then balled up his fists and struck the man in the chest. "Put me back! I vant to go back! I *need* to go back! I need to show them—show my fool of a father vhat... vhat I..."

But it was no good. The sheer weight of it all held him fast. For a moment, he had no words and could only kneel there, shuddering. All of this Hroth bore with a silence that was somehow neither cold nor detached. When Vlk had calmed enough to stop shaking, the man spoke at last.

"Aye, it's a hard thing, Vlk. Happened to me not long up the hourglass. We was ambushed by that same devil man whose coach we were in."

"Ebistian." Vlk hunched his shoulders. The memory of his brief time with the man brought an undefined sense of shame he couldn't put into words. "Maksu's... vell, he vanted us to call him father." He offered a weak snort. "He thought that vord vas a show of respect. Fathers are cowardly, deaf, *vasteful* things."

Vlk pushed himself to his feet, turning away from Hroth. He began to feel stronger. His shock and fear were ebbing away, his anger drawing down to a single, thin line. He stood, clenching and unclenching his fists.

"Father is the vorst insult I could've *given* the silver-haired snake eater. Fathers are so afraid of looking—of *being* veak that they *never hear you* even vhen you tell them the truth!" He would've given anything in that moment for Liška to be stood before him. "They're so afraid of you seeing how useless they've become that they'd sooner *kill* you than hear vhat you have to say!"

Light exploded across his vision. A burning blue brilliance surrounded him, filling him with a focused rage. It was all so *clear*. He could see to Liška, now. He could *make* him listen. And if he would not listen, then he would learn one final lesson at his son's hand.

"One final lesson for vhat he's done. One final lesson for his foolish, veak—"

But there were hands on his shoulders from behind. "Nye, cub. It's an itch you wanna scratch inna worst way, an no mistake. But nye. That way won't wake you up again."

"Let me go, Hroth."

"Nye. Won't 'til you've cried off." His voice was gentle but resolute. "Turn round now, Vlk. Show me your dreamer's lamps."

"I said—"

Hroth shook him. Hard. "I heard you. Was you who didn't hear *me*. Lakkrid won't thankee for givin' in like that. You're the best of the lot, to hear him tell it."

Vlk blinked. He knew that name, didn't he? But no. No, his father needed to...

"He needs to..."

"S'right, Vlk. That's it. Now turn 'round and see me."

He felt a shift behind him and knew Hroth had gotten knee-bound again. With a reluctance he, himself, didn't quite understand, Vlk turned to meet his gaze once more. After a moment, he felt his rage fade. It was *there,* but quiet for the moment.

"*There* he is." Hroth smiled. "Guess Eobum's cub was right 'bout you.

To hear his Excellency tell it, lots of folk ain't got the strength to turn away from that blue misery."

"Vhat... vhat vas it? I still feel angry, but... it vas so *strong*. I vanted blood. Not *somone's tripped me and I vant to punch them for it* anger, but—"

"Real blood, aye. Told you, I know all about it. Been nearly a week, and I *still* have to fight it off sometimes. Won't matter soon, I think, but, aye. It's a hard thing."

"Von't matter soon?"

Hroth grinned, though his expression was tinged with a sad resignation. "Aye. Time tae move on, soon. Cannae stay like this forever. To hear the Baron tell it, the longer we stay, the easier it is to give in to the blue. 'Sides, much as I wanna see my own mates, there's what comes next."

Vlk cocked his head to the side. He wanted to resist the urge to ask but found he couldn't. Nor, he realized, did he understand why he'd wanted to in the first place. Shaking his head, he allowed himself to smirk.

"Go on. Tell me vhat comes next."

Hroth's grin widened. "Aye, I s'pose I can do that, but only if it *really* matters to you."

Vlk shoved him, his smirk widening into a grin. "Don't make me beat it out of you. You're a scout, not a varrior, after all."

"Oh, no warrior, is it?"

Vlk nodded, fighting back laughter. "Just a man who goes and sees... then runs back to tell the varriors vhat trouble lies ahead. After that, you hide vhile men like me do our vork."

"Men like *you?*" Hroth mock-glared, then dove for him, knocking him to the ground and tickling his belly. "No *varrior*, eh? We scouts are no *varriors?* Eh? Is this *varrior* enough for you, Vlk?"

"Alright! Alright! You're a varrior! *You're a varrior!*" Vlk's laughter rolled an enormous weight off of his heart. When the assault ended and Hroth had helped him to his feet, he found he couldn't stop grinning.

Then came the voices.

"I don't know what more I can tell you... either of you. If you've a question, ask it. But I've told all I can think of that matters." A woman's voice—perhaps his mother's age?

Hroth put a hand on his shoulder. "C'mon. No point standin' 'round here. 'Sides, his Excellency's better at tellin' it than I am."

Vlk let himself be led down a hall that seemed familiar, but was too indistinct for anything more descriptive. Hroth ushered him into a chamber that might have been someone's home, once. Dim furnishings lined the walls, and the ghost of a central hearth burned with a white fire that gave off light, but no heat. He saw two men and a woman seated apart from one another.

"I suppose that'll have to do, Olga." The eldest of the three sat back, considering.

"I remember you…" Vlk looked at the older man—a muscular, slender fellow with curtains of blondish hair framing his face. "You vere the one who spoke vith me earlier, vhen I fell."

The man regarded him with a thin smile. "Indeed, I was. You're the boy I'd meant to deliver my message to the Count. Pity I took so long to gather my thoughts. We might have avoided a good deal of trouble." He shook his head, though his smile remained. "I am, or was, the Baron Vagiaedelt. This—"

"You're the count's var-vinner! His… his stratég!"

Aedelt smirked. "My reputation precedes me. Yes, I was Edmund's strategist… his *stratég*, as you say."

"You still are. Did you think a little thing like death would get you out of your oath, Aedelt?" The other man offered the baron a good-natured sneer as he spoke. It made his thin mustache twitch.

The baron shot the man a cool look, then offered what looked like an honest grin. "No, Excellency. If I did, I'd have moved on already. You still need me for a little while longer, and we both know it."

The mustachioed fellow sighed through his own grin. "My friend? I'd say that sounded arrogant if I didn't know how you'd reply." He took on a tone of gentle mockery. "*Oh, but Excellency… is it arrogance if it's accurate?*"

Aedelt snorted. "Well? Is it?"

"Yes. Yes, it is. It's also quite beside the point. I *do* need you, but even if I didn't, I'd still be glad you were with me. It shouldn't have taken another war, let alone our deaths, for us to hear one another's voice again. But never mind. Now's better than never."

Smiling, he shook his head, then turned his misted blue eyes on Vlk. "I fear you aren't free from your oath to me either."

Vlk blinked, then gaped. *Edmund! It's Count Edmund! He looks so … young!* Then he wondered why—in all the hells that ever were—he should be surprised. He'd been holding the man's hand as he died not long ago. If this was the between place, where *else* would Edmund be?

"Yes, Excellency," he managed.

Edmund nodded. "Aedelt will explain what you're to do. It won't be difficult, but it *is* important. You're to carry a message with you—a secret we hope one day will make a difference."

"I hope you're right, Excellency. The both of you." This was the woman. Her chestnut hair was bound in a bun atop her narrow head. Her face looked pinched, as if she'd bitten into something sour.

Aedelt rolled his eyes. "If you've a way to prove me wrong, Olga, I'm happy to hear you. If you're only going to sit and sulk, however..."

"I'm not sulking, *Excellency*. I'm frustrated that your plan is little more than burying treasure, then *hoping* your heirs find it once times are tight and taxes are due. We need a means to help the world *today*. Not centuries from now when the King returns. Your plan is sound enough for the future, but if he isn't stopped here and now, there will *be* no future. Surely you see that."

Vlk watched as the men looked at one another, then back to Olga.

It was the baron who broke the silence. "Our scope for affecting the here and now is ... limited. I have just over twenty-five days before the pull becomes inexorable. Hroth has perhaps a week more than that. We can guide some of them while we linger, but you know the risks that comes with."

Edmund arched his brows. "She may, but *I* do not. Nor, I suspect, does Hroth, unless you've already explained it to him."

Aedelt's voice became clipped. His expression made it clear he wanted to get past this part and back to the matter at hand. "If left undirected, it takes forty-nine days for the shadow to complete its journey back to the Dark Sea."

"Is that where things like the Hallowed Halls or the Endeløs Turnering are?"

"No, Excellency. You're speaking of the afterlife. Think of spirits as paintings of all that we know and are when we slip sideways. These go to whatever afterlife will have them, in accordance with their genuine beliefs. That's related, but it's another matter entirely."

Edmund leaned back, stroking his mustache in an absent-minded way. "But you said they—or *we*—go *back* to this ... dark ocean?"

Aedelt cast a glance toward each of them in turn. Seeing the looks of confusion on all faces save Olga's, he sighed and closed his eyes. After gathering his thoughts, he began again.

"As those who study such things understand it, we all begin in the Dark Sea of Time. All shadows come from there, and *nearly* all shadows return. When a woman kindles with child, a portion of that Dark Sea melds with the child's flesh. But it takes time. Once a child enters the world, he or she begins to learn, and, potentially at least, to rediscover things his or her shadow once knew. As we experience life—as we grow taller, wiser, and so on—so too does our shadow. When we *die*, that shadow begins its journey back to the Dark Sea, to enrich all that is, was, and shall be with its own experiences."

Edmund gave a thoughtful nod. "You said the spirit is different from the shadow... that it's like a painting of who we are and what we know. The shadow leaving us is ... like that paint *drying?* Is that what you mean to say?"

The baron gave a one-shouldered shrug, nodding for good measure. "It's a good enough simile for our purposes."

The count nodded. "And it takes the best part of a year in the womb for the shadow to fully... what, become?" He looked between Aedelt and Olga. Both gave nods of acceptance at his choice of words. "Fine. It takes most of a year's time for the shadow to become a new, living person. When we die, the forty-nine days of the soul exist to dry the paint, as it were, and draw the shadow back to this ... Dark Sea?"

"Yes, Excellency," Olga said. "That's near enough the mark. Forty-nine days to say farewell to people and places, to speak in dreams to those you love or those you hate, and to come to terms with your end. The shadow *will* go. It falls, just as rain must." She paused, considering. "Rain... that's a fair enough analogy. The shadow passes through the layers of creation like rainwater through layers of clothing until it reaches the Dark Sea."

Aedelt took up the tale again. "And now we come back to the matter at hand. The longer one lingers, the more they will feel the tidal pull toward the Dark Sea. But there's a danger. The longer one lingers, the more they will feel the *other* pull."

"The... the hells?" Edmund's eyes were half-lidded things as he tried to make sense of it. "Are you saying that's how demons are devils are formed?"

Aedelt shook his head. "No, that's another matter... one that truly *is* beside the point. I'm speaking of passion and its dark cousin—obsession. When we live, our bodies act to shield and absorb the effects of strong emotion. When we *have* no flesh, strong emotions erode our will. They pull us away from the Dark Sea, trying to winnow us down to a single, implacable concept. If we yield? If we turn toward those strong emotions? If we turn *away* from the shadowed road, as it's called? Then we obsess over one miserable moment. We become creatures of anger, rage, fear, or sorrow."

"Haunts," said Edmund. "You're saying that's how we become haunts."

Vlk stepped back, eyes wide. "That vas vhat vas happening to me!"

Hroth nodded, putting a hand on Vlk's shoulder. "Aye. S'why I pulled you back, just as the baron did for me."

Olga and Aedelt were studying him with some interest. He didn't much care for the attention, but couldn't think of a way to deflect it. Before the combined weight of their regard became too much for Vlk to bear, Edmund came to his rescue, albeit unintentionally.

The count frowned, considering. "So we can stay for a while, but by the end of the forty-nine days of the soul, we either return to the Dark Sea, or we turn into haunts. Is that the only danger?"

Olga shook her head. "Hardly. Beyond the dangers that may lurk *within* the Grey Between—where we now sit—there are dangers we ourselves court."

"As you say, Olga. The more time we spend trying to interact with the world of the living, the greater our temptation to give in to the blue becomes. Strong emotions work to change you into a haunt. Speaking with those you love, or indeed those for whom you harbor hatred, is bound to conjure up such emotions."

Both Edmund and Hroth nodded. Vlk was too busy trying to absorb it all to do more than stare.

Olga spoke up. "Even if you survive such interactions with your wits intact, the weight of understanding when you're out of time might well be enough to bring on the change. The bitterness of being forced to leave before you want to..." She shook her head. "It comes to this. The sooner we're on our way, the better. I grant you, there's more to do than we'll ever have time for, but there *is* a point at which we cease being useful to any but the enemy. For my part, I fear the longer I linger, the greater the risk that I'm forced into what they call our Third Life. I have no wish to become one of those red-skinned devils, even *if* it means seeing Radek again."

Edmund bowed his head, then turned to Aedelt. "But you told Kastan we could tie ourselves to swords and the like. Help me understand how?"

Aedelt sighed, nodding. "Everything and everyone we interact with is touched by our own shadow. Think of it like water or wet ink. It washes off easily enough, but regular use can leave a stain. That stain is the impact we have on one another, for good or ill. Think of fabrications—what the stories might call enchanted or ensorcelled items—in the same way you might a tattoo. A deliberate and largely permanent addition of the creator's shadow into the item. Do you see?"

Edmund did. "And as you told Kastan, doing that binds us to the item forever. We never move back to the Dark Sea, nor to any afterlife. We become ... finished things."

He considered for a long moment, then shook his head. "Right. We need to get Vlk on the ... shadowed road, did you call it?" The baron nodded, and Edmund went on. "Fine. We need to get him onto the shadowed road and moving toward the Dark Sea as swiftly as may be. Hroth and Olga as well."

"No!"

Vlk hadn't meant to shout. All eyes were upon him now. He drew a deep breath, forcing himself to be calm as he spoke his piece.

"I vill go, of course. I vill deliver the message. I just vant to stay and help my friends vhile I still can."

"Vlk..." Edmund shook his head.

"You told me my oath vasn't... You said I vasn't free from it. You made me svear to be brave... to be a knight and to protect Lady Kastan. Can't I do something to help? Other than race off to the seaside?"

Aedelt spoke up, sounding thoughtful. "He *is* Andrej's friend, Edmund. He was sitting squire for him, so to speak, up on the alure."

"That's true... it nearly *killed* him, but it's true." Edmund considered. "Aedelt, you'll need to train him at speed. I'm not willing to sacrifice him for my own designs."

Aedelt nodded. "I can do that. Now I think on it, I believe young Vlk might make things easier all around. You can speak with Kastan. Vlk can speak with Andrej."

"And Hroth." Once again, Vlk had spoken before he'd known he meant to.

"What about me?" Hroth sounded amused as he broke the silence.

"Maksu and his mother are here."

Edmund blinked. "Eobum's... well, Eobum's nothing when last seen. But Lashjuk? Is *that* who you mean? What in hells is she doing here?"

"She came looking for Maksu. Ebistian stole him, I think. He vas in Ebistian's coach and garden, at least."

Aedelt spoke up. "Garden?"

Hroth grinned. "Aye, well, you've been so busy I've not had time to tell you. Vlk and I saw somet you might find interesting."

Vlk stepped forward. "You see? Hroth's a scout. He goes and sees, then comes home to tell vhat he's seen. I thought *all* armies needed scouts."

Edmund snorted, then actually laughed. When the fit had subsided, he turned his gaze on Hroth. "I won't ask you to stay, Hroth. You've done all I could've asked. You and yours have done right by me for nearly a decade."

Hroth leaned back on his heels, shrugging his brows. "You used to scare me ta death the way you'd just walk into camp. Weren't about you owning it, mind. Was just that you acted like you belonged among us, or at least with Eobum and his kin." He grinned. "I doubt he'd let you walk into a fight blind. Not if he could help it, anyroad."

He cast about, then looked back at Edmund. "Mmmm. Looks as if yer one Eobum short, though."

"I am, at that. With luck, that means he yet lives. A thing we should all be glad about. I won't spar with you, Hroth—not on this, at least. If you *choose* to stay a while, I can promise you I'll put you to work."

"Aye, I'll stay." Hroth grinned. "I'm prettier than he is. Got more hair, too."

Edmund nodded, meeting each eye in turn. "Then we have work to do."

-IV-

**County Thorion
Wick**

Red rain turned the new night's air above Wick's wet cobles into a blood-burnished brume. The persistence of broad, bloated droplets was summer-storm warm, despite the early winter's wish that'd been on this morning's wind. That hardly mattered now. The Keening had indeed come. The knell of Havoc's Horn wouldn't be far behind.

Methias took silent stock of his situation. He was alright. In truth, he was feeling far better than he ought to, given the weave work he'd wielded in the last half a bell. But oh, how he would sleep when all of this was over.

He stood alone before the growing crowd of Nebelblut and their apparent mouthpiece. *I expect I'll have to do at least some fighting. They don't seem the type to offer me a cup of mulled cider to pass the time, more's the pity.*

When it came to rites of any real combat power, his remaining options were... limited. Most of the weave work he'd prepared for today had been for utility, not warfare. There was always Belen's Desperation—the idea that *any* rite could be repurposed into a bolt of concussive force in a pinch. It was effective, but difficult to aim. Such raw power took a practiced and determined hand just to *direct*, let alone to strike a specific target.

Well, at least there's a job lot of them. That's... something.

Effective use of the gambit was an art, really. He had no talent for it, which was why he always preferred the ordered road of a studied rite when it came to combat. The problem was, he'd already *used* the most destructive weave work in today's meager arsenal.

And what Waker rites I have left are only useful against one or two targets at a time. Good at range, but up close? Two more Fabricant rites, one more Sagacite rite... all useless here. I've a Caller rite still, but I can't summon enough sundekin to counter so many damned goblins. I have my Crown of Stars... That might make them blink—maybe rub their eyes? Not much of a weapon, that. If the enemy had been some form of once-man, or a foe empowered by the hells themselves...

Methias shook his head, murmuring, "Aye, and if beef were blue..."

Here and now, the Crown will be little more than a glorified weaver's lamp. Still, that instant of hesitation may buy me enough time if I use it at a critical moment. Worth remembering in a pinch. In the meantime, War Cry will serve me better than any weave work I've held in reserve.

Thinking of time, he reckoned he'd bought Pallith and Ibhroth enough to reach the conduit. He just needed to keep the enemy focused on him long enough for that conduit to go dormant. Then he could slip the noose the goblins were preparing for him. He still had the power to effect an escape. That was something. He could even bring along a handful of stragglers, if he found any.

The hunger had ebbed away, which was *also* something. Still, he had an idea this brief respite was a matter of circumstance. Other than the goblins and the thing Pallith had named Rakshasa, there was nobody near.

Nobody that wakes my hunger, at least. Oh, I can still feel it. But it's quiet for the moment. There's more to this than the physical sensations of hunger or thirst, though. There's a... a sound to it. It's as if I'm hearing the river of my own blood as it races along.

His thoughts were cast aside by an influx of new ones. He saw himself kneeling before that one-eyed goblin archer again, but this time it was as if he were a supplicant, not a criminal awaiting sentence. As the next image faded into existence, he found himself flooded with a sense of boundless well-being. This one showed him standing *beside* the goblin. Fighting beside him. It promised combat in concert, carrying with it a feeling of utter liberation. There would be no question of misunderstanding, let alone mistrust. He and the Nebelblut would act in perfect harmony.

The Rakshasa grinned, his fangs on full display. "I think it best to give you a fair presentation, Methias. You *do* prefer Methias, do you not? I shouldn't wonder. Galganus Methias Arthod? *Galganus?* This is too haughty a name for a man such as you."

Methias ignored him, though he couldn't help but wonder how the creature had known his given name. He was rewarded for his silence with another vision. Again he saw himself stood beside that same Nebelblut. An instant later, it faded, giving way to a goblin a bit taller than he himself was. Next came a massive blue creature stood in the goblin's place, followed by a slender, well-muscled being of dusky gold. Each of these had one commonality... a single blinded eye. The final image showed Methias—tall and fell—stood alone. He was bathed in a light so brilliant it defied the very *notion* of color. Figures swam somewhere behind him, but they were hidden by—*protected* by—the light.

My light, he thought and smiled.

"There. Do you see, Methias? Do you understand the path we can lay before you? All that we can accomplish together? You and I stood here at this moment? On the very evening of the Keening? It is surely a sign of providence."

He *did* understand. Or at least thought he did.

"The Nebelblut shift through these forms? They eat shadow and gain power from it." Methias knew that idea should horrify him. It *did* horrify him, albeit in a distant sort of way. "You—or perhaps just the one-eyed archer—are asking for my..." He shook his head. "What? What is it you expect me to do?"

It was a struggle to think with any sort of clarity. At first, he'd thought his mind was racing, but that wasn't accurate. His mind was *crawling.* The hunger hadn't so much quieted as *moved.* He felt it baking into his brain... numbing him... lulling him. It whispered and moaned, singing of early autumn. Of sweet rain and wicked wind, and the desperate desire to roll over, burrow beneath the blankets, and just give in.

"It is a simple enough matter. And of course I *will* explain." The Rakshasa's voice was full of reasonable, clear-headed honesty. "We want to have you *with* us, Methias. We want to take your future away from the traitor and his false King... to swell your ranks with our own... to grant you strength and knowledge in a far more tangible way than any other can hope to offer." There was anger. Yes. But that anger was directed at the king and whoever the *traitor* was. "He must be stopped. You know this already. He creates treachery, corrupts all things, and seeks to remake the world to match his own avaricious vision. I would not willingly live in a world made by one such as he. And so we are aligned, you and I." The rakshasa paused, bowing his head to underscore his next words. "Yet the road we must take to stop him is paved with sacrifices. Nothing worth accomplishing comes without sacrifice. Isn't that so?"

It *was* so. But there was something else here. It dragged at his mind, trying to get him to turn away. He had the vague sense that he'd forgotten... what? He'd no idea.

But... tears of the Mountain, he has a plan. A plan to put a stop to the King of the Dead... Zarec wept! To be a part of someone else's plan again. To have someone else—someone who knew more than he—tell him what was to be done...

His mind shifted focus to the others... those who were supposedly fighting against the King of the Dead alongside him. He'd been the only one of their original company who seemed even vaguely *interested* in learning about their foe, let alone hammering out a plan to defeat him. That was especially true of Hakim's brash brother, Hamed. He'd been their leader ever since that black day in Thassak Pass. He *knew* the man was committed to trying to free Jannon from his jailer. The entire company was, but...

But they're content with how things are, secure in the knowledge that a solution will simply present itself. We are, after all, chosen, as Hamed keeps reminding us. The dreams prove that. And if we are Chosen, then we will be presented with the means to claim victory.

"Hells be hid! Of all the self-important, lazy..." Methias scowled, but managed to resist the strong desire to clench his fists.

"He is a fool, this Hamed." The Rakshasa was nodding. "He expects to bumble into a weapon mighty enough to, what, *bludgeon* the King of the Dead and his generals to death? To hack and slash his way to victory, and kill the dead? To kill Death? The Master of the Bloody Forge?" He shook his head. "A fool is one thing. A willful and *dangerous* fool is quite another, as you know well, Methias."

He *did* know well. His anger faded, replaced by a relief so palpable he nearly laughed. *He's right. Hamed is a fool. His brother Hakim would be well shut of him. Hakim's wise, even-handed, and nearly as skilled with a blade as his loutish brother.*

The Rakshasa spoke in a warm, avuncular tone. "And this Hakim would make for a far better champion in service to *your* wisdom and honor. Would he not?"

Methias couldn't help but grin. Perhaps he would. At the least, Hakim's life wouldn't be wasted on one of Hamed's half-formed quests for glory.

Come to that, their healer, Elliata, would be far better served with Hamed gone as well.

She's somehow managed to hold on to her sense of innocence, despite everything that's happened. Yet Hamed's taken advantage of that many times in pursuit of his goals. With him dead, there's no chance she'll wake up one day as the arrogant fool's concubine.

"She and the rest of your band? They would become *your* champions. Given no need to contend with this *Hamed's* childish nature, you would be free to focus on the war. And with the rest of your company stood at your side, you would be far more likely to thwart, or at least slow the King's advance. Your fledgling realm would become a safe haven for those who suffer under... ah, but I see you have already begun such efforts." The Rakshasa paused, looking surprised and more than a little pleased.

"Methias! We're here! We're with you!" Jastar's voice, followed by a single low bark of warning.

Methias's mind was somewhere in the White Vale of Wishes, still dancing and dreaming amidst the rakshasa's words. It took him a moment to return to the here and now. *If Ire's here, then Tharus must be with him.*

"It's well you both arrived when you did," said Methias. "It's right there should be witnesses, I think."

Was he still smiling? Well, why *shouldn't* he be? For so long now, he'd been surrounded only by those who either *relied upon* him or seemed determined to *fight* him at every turn. The realization that he was *not* alone in this war had been such a relief. The Rakshasa had made things so much clearer. It was as if the past five years had been little more than a thin nightmare. And here, now—after throwing open the shudders to a promising new day—was this blessed creature smiling by his bedside. He and his Dereek khnderath *could* defeat the traitor and his king. Of *course* they could! Especially with the Rakshasa and the Nebelblut beside them.

"Hells be hid," Jastar murmured. "Look at the devil's *eyes...*"

Ire's growl was a low, dangerous sound that made even Methias feel afraid.

"It's alright, Ire. I believe I understand now." He turned his mind to the remaining two members of what he still thought of as *Jannon's* company.

Would they fall in beside him, or try to fall upon him? How would they react to Hamed's death? Would they understand why it'd been necessary?

Wois may be a fellow caster, but he's as much a fool as Hamed. He's knowledgeable, but isn't half as wise as he pretends to be. Still, he's at least controllable.

And Naeadne was the key to that control. Though Wois swore his feelings toward the half-elf were no more than close comradery, Methias had marked the way his eye followed her... the way he haunted her steps.

And he grows cold, murmuring when he thinks I don't hear him. He rankles at the power and wisdom I've gained ... worrying that Naeadne will rely less and less upon him. And he's right to worry. As for Naeadne herself? She'll be simple enough to keep on side. So long as she's given a cause to fight for, a sense of import, and room to swing Saint Hyrro's... Hyrro's...

Methias stopped. For an instant, *everything* seemed to stop. Ire's deep growl, the rain, the wind, and the false sense of well-being just ... ceased. It was as if his mind had been doused in icy water.

The rakshasa blinked its peaceful, inverted eyes at him as it waited.

I'm a fool, he thought, and bowed his head in contrition. *Ire growled and barked...at me. I felt his light and feared it... feared it! Zarec wept! Ire growled at the rakshasa itself! And yet it took Jastar actually calling the creature a devil before I began to suspect. Even then it took the memory of Hyrro's riddles... Hyrro's voice before I...*

He sighed, shaking his head. When he spoke, his voice was small and resigned.

"You almost had me."

The creature loosed an inarticulate sound of confusion through its nose. "Mmm?"

"It shames me to admit it, but yes. You almost had me. To find someone who knows the King of the Dead even *exists* is miracle enough. Haunek and Loegrem leave precious few survivors in their wake."

The Rakshasa hissed. "Do *not* speak the traitor's name, Methias. It is a blackened, curs-ed, *unworthy* word. Do not sully your mouth with it."

Methias kicked a loose stone, sending it skittering off to one side. His head was still bowed, and his voice remained small. He resembled nothing so much as a chastened child as he spoke.

"Haunek won't trouble the world forever, Rakshasa. My company will see to that."

"As you say. Do as you will with the God Eater. We wish you joy of it. The traitor, however, belongs to *us.*"

So Loegrem is their enemy. That bears recall for later. For now, though...

"Tharus? Sir Jastar?" Methias kept his voice firm, but otherwise without inflection. "Have we gotten everyone out? Are there any left in Wick other than we four and the enemy?"

"We're the last I know of, Lord," Jastar said. By the sound of it, he was adjusting the way his shield rode on his arm.

"Aye," Tharus said. "They've all gone through." His beard-stubble voice was tight in anticipation.

"Then we're leaving."

"No, Methias, no. Do not name me an enemy. We have enemies and to spare. Together, we can bring them all to heel. You *cannot* turn away from all that I offer... all that we can accomplish together."

Methias at last lifted his head to meet the creature's strange eyes. "I can. And I do. Jastar, a hand on my left shoulder. Tharus? My right. Keep your other hand tight to Ire."

As the men moved to obey, the rakshasa stepped forward. "You misunderstand me, Methias." The Nebelblut behind him were no longer milling. They were massing. Many of them were holding bows with arrows at the ready. "I did not say you *may* not turn away. I said that you *cannot* turn away. You are one of us now. I have but to stretch out my will to claim you. Yet still I would rather you see sense. Will you not reconsider? I assure you, I am only too happy to hear your concerns, and make whatever small adjustments are necessary so that when our swords are drawn, they are drawn as one."

Methias allowed a sad little smile to play across his face. His voice took on a soft, almost gentle tone. "I did *not* misunderstand, Rakshasa. It's just that..."

"What? *Tell* me, Methias. Let us come to an understanding that we may be about our shared work."

Methias found the creature's odd eyes again, resisting the urge to fall into them. "It's just that I refuse to bend my knee before the hells, no matter their harbinger."

The creature sighed. "Then you leave me little choice."

A wave of dizzying bliss crashed over Methias. He heard a low, desperate moan that spoke more of pain's end than pleasure's echo. A few beats later, he realized the voice was his own. He could feel ethereal fingers probing, questing along the surface of his mind. They were looking for the way in, he had no doubt. And for a moment, he found himself hoping they'd find it. The relief of yielding... of letting someone else take up his burdens, his responsibilities... it was a temptation beyond measure.

A life of ignorance and simple pleasure... a chance to forget every pressure, every responsibility. He understood that the choice was his. He could give in and drown in bliss, or he could turn away.

And if I yield, I forget all of it... all of them.

His mind flashed to... well, not to his *friends.* He had no friends. Every man, woman, and child in his life either looked upon him with disdain—perhaps a grudging sort of respect—or relied upon him to lead them. There were those he loved, yes. But friends?

He thought of Morakogunn Fellhammer, the realm's seneschal. Of Farin Irengar, Dereek khn's general. Of Fyken Presh. Of his Kyria, his Nybrynci, who existed more as a memory now than a woman of flesh and blood. Of Tharus, whom he and the company had rescued from flesh peddlers back when this misery had all started. And finally, he thought of Jannon.

Jannon, who saved me. Jannon, who protected me, taught me, and in the end, made a deal in trade for my very life.

As if he'd summoned it, Jannon's laughter bubbled to the surface of his mind. Its ghost was brief, soft, and gentle. But it *did* blot out that sense of bliss, and its false promise of peace, at least for the moment.

"Honesty, Lamlith. You have to be honest with me and with yourself.

Methias nodded, eyes brimming over. "Aye. Ohhh—aye." He swallowed hard, then raised his bright-fist as if to defend himself from an incoming blow.

"Rakshasa?" His voice was barely more than a rasp.

"Yes, Methias?" In contrast, the creature's voice was a contented purr.

"Ber, Rakshasa." His voice grew full and fell as he spoke. "Ber, Maveyn. Ber quer hol ponduu solek." *(Burn, Rakshasa. Burn, Un-light. Burn beneath the bless-ed stars.)*

A new brilliance burst into being around Methias's brow. Bright white stars shone out amidst a twilight-colored band of radiance. In the crown's gleam, the Rakshasa's flesh began to bubble and crack. The creature screamed with many voices, trying to withdraw from the circle's glow.

"Hyrro's light! You are tainted by Hyrro's light!" It stumbled backward, falling to the cobbles with one arm raised in feeble defense. "Go! Take your killing-light and go! I curse you and the whore whose gift you bear! Wish warden! Root-cutter! Go!"

The hunger was gone—the temptation, as well. Methias was himself again. He felt a monstrous shame at how close he'd come to giving in, but that would have to wait. Now there was this devil-thing and his Nebelblut to escape from.

I cannot contend with them all. That hasn't changed. The goblins aren't reacting to the Crown, so it won't help me there. But...

He looked down at the Rakshasa. The creature's hand... *both* of its hands were... *backwards*! How had he missed that? Had he seen it, he'd have called upon the Crown of Stars far sooner. *Wrists turned round... hands turned round. Wrists turned round... hands turned round.* His mind didn't want to let the oddity go. The sheer physical horror of it threatened to drown him.

No... no, that's for later, he reminded himself again. *I can unravel that later.*

He couldn't breathe in too deeply. The Nebelblut's stink was too omnipresent. It was stronger, somehow—clawing at his throat. He didn't *dare* close his eyes in an attempt to regain focus. Anything could happen while he looked inward. How to reclaim himself?

After what seemed like an age of indecision as the Rakshasa screamed and cursed, Methias bit down on the sides of his tongue. The combination of fresh pain and the flooding warmth in his mouth turned the trick. He would have to remember that for later. For now...

His voice once more took on that full and terrible coldness. "If your beasts attack, I will burn you until there is nothing left of you to stain Skolf's soil. Keep them at bay and I will spare you. The decision is yours."

"Curs-ed child of the—"

"Your *answer*, Rakshasa! ...While there's enough of you left to speak."

"Accord! *Accord,* cozening whore's get! A curse on your sister's head! Go!"

Methias considered, eyeing the goblins. They remained perhaps a dozen yards away, but none of them held any weapons that he could see.

"We will meet again, I've no doubt." Methias cast a glance back to confirm that Tharus was holding tight to Ire, and nodded. "Ka xu nuq ... zul puehv luukth." (*Will and power ... take me there.*)

He felt a queer slowing as his Wayfaring rite moved them back to Kowmor. There was a watchfulness he didn't much care for, but that, too, would have to wait. For now, he was just happy to have gotten them all out of that place intact. The rest would keep. It would have to.

The Keening, the King's return, and now the Nebelblut and their rakshasa masters. And, of course, the refugees—wounded or wary, they'll all need seeing to.

As Fyken and Apiné approached, he forced down the wave of fatigue that'd threatened to overwhelm him. They needed to give—needed him to hear their reports. Then he would have to give the necessary orders to keep them all as safe as may be.

Sage, strategist, diplomat, leader, or lawgiver, he thought and forced himself to smile.

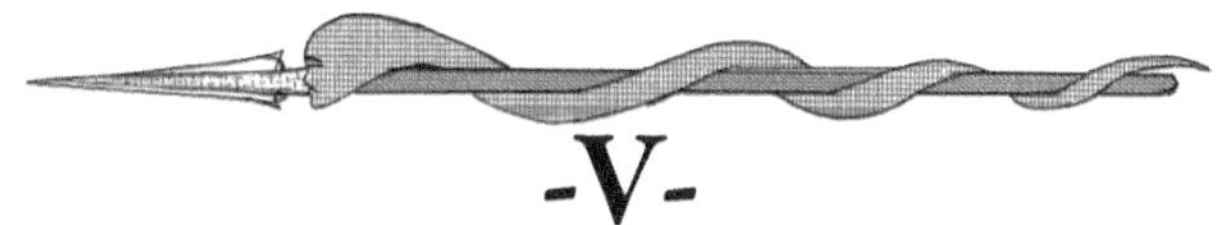

-V-

Venzene Duchy of Kovalun
County Jižní Pochod
Barony of Hartscross–Jižní Lov

"Awka... erld hshek gish gor, uthka." Lashjuk spoke in a slow, steady way as they walked. She wanted to give Kastan every chance to make sense of Grimdash Zaksh. "Ed kar el zaksh ol, Lady." *(So... you're the true crown, now. I want our conversation to be quiet.)*

Kastan paused, turning her head to meet Lashjuk's eyes, then nodded. "Erld... gar? Gar el? Is that right? You shielded us? You ... saved us?" Kastan shook her head. "I *am* sorry, Lady. I just—"

Lashjuk laughed. It was a soft chuffing noise, but it was honest. "It's fine, La—...er, Excellency. You spoke it rightly, but I wouldn't let it worry you. So long as we can be cautious in our speech, I'll take no offense if you use the Trade Tongue."

Kastan blushed and bowed her head, chuckling. "Aye, fair. And thank you ... for both the kindness and saving us all. I'd no notion how to fight living fire."

She gestured, and they resumed their walk around the central chamber. Lashjuk fought back a wince at hearing what she now accounted as *unit speech.* "Aye" was a common enough word. Certainly, it wasn't limited to Eobum and his men, but the association was difficult to shake.

She cast about for a moment to refocus herself. Her eyes marked Maksu, standing close to Andrej and the red hound. She hated to admit it, but she not only approved—she was relieved.

Andrej had suffered under the heavy burden of Ebistian's dark cloud. He *must* know at least *something* of the silver-haired devil's larger goals. To say that realization gave her pause would be underselling it. Still, he'd stood to defend her boy twice now. Gi awka glem, he'd stood to defend *her* moments ago. And, if Maksu's story was to be believed, the pair had fought against one another in a babe's lyst. While Andrej had come out the victor, he'd taken the time to help Maksu back to where Lakkrid waited with...

"...With Vlk." She bowed her head.

She felt Kastan's hand on her shoulder, offering a gentle squeeze. "I know. It's... it's awful. Would that I could kill his fool of a father a second time."

Lashjuk looked up to meet Kastan's eyes. She allowed herself a darksome grin. "Ware what you wish for, Excellency. Given today's events, you may see it come true."

Kastan paled, then nodded. She flashed her own darksome grin. "Comes down to it, Lady? That man is someone I wouldn't mind killing twice. He was misled. That's true enough. But he was *ready* to be misled. Hells, he all but begged to be misled."

She shook her head. "But never mind. Jash el zaksh?" *(What do we discuss?)*

Lashjuk widened her eyes, favoring Kastan with a genuine smile. *That was well spoken,* she thought.

"Believe me when I say I understand." She was thinking of Ebistian. She'd killed him twice today, though neither seemed to do more than slow him down. *Well, never mind. Back to it.* She gave the woman a *very well* nod and returned to the matter at hand.

"Awka... erldlg. *Hshek* wrin erldlg? Hshek wrin Edmundlg?" *(So... your son. Is he your son? Is he Edmund's son?)*

Kastan stopped short, face growing first pale, then bright red with building anger. "Fashek yashkr erld..." She shook her head, then glared at her. The force in those black dreamer's lamps augured well for her future as a leader. "De. De, erld hrek ra ol balefth edlg. De? Ed hrek dash erld, Lady. Do not doubt me." *(How dare you... No. No, you will be silent about my son. If not? I will silence you.)*

Lashjuk felt a cold smile crawl across her face. She allowed her eyes to narrow to slits, then nodded. "No fear, Excellency. I'll tell you the tale of meeting his cousin as and if we manage to escape this place. For now, know that ... ed hrek nqas erld ol. So long as you're true." *(I will keep your silence.)*

Kastan gave a slow nod, her face relaxing. "Was there more?"

Lashjuk nodded. "A bit. There is something called the Keening going on above. I know little about it, but we would do better not to venture into the open while it lasts. Is there any other way out of this place? Somewhere we can hide?"

Kastan grinned, nodding. "There is. Hajvarr? Otta? Are we as ready as may be?"

Both spoke their confirmations. Otta's was bright and clear, if fearful. Hajvarr's voice held a cold, detached tone that Lashjuk didn't much care for.

Nodding both to her captains, as it were, and to Lashjuk, Kastan reached for the scepter-thing at her belt. Striding toward the angel's statue, she lifted her chin so that her voice would carry.

"And now it is time for yet *another* of Edmund's secrets to be revealed. My Lord was always thinking of the future and how best to be ready for it. It is my hope to take those lessons forward as we—" She swallowed hard. Her face appeared to clench. Strong emotion had, it seemed, robbed her of her ability to speak. With an admirable effort, she forced herself to forge ahead. "As we leave this place behind."

She looked to Andrej, then beckoned him over. He came willingly enough, though he looked more than a touch apprehensive.

"Mm-mother?"

Kastan flashed him a sad smile, even as she flushed. Lashjuk couldn't help but grin.

It takes some getting used to, she thought. *There's great joy in hearing that word, Lady... in knowing it's directed at you. But I fear that joy will creep up and pounce on you for a while yet.*

Kastan gestured to the angel statue, even as she proffered the žezlo toward the blond boy. "Give it andělovi, Andrej. Let it be in *her* keeping for the nonce."

He took it with undeniable reverence, gave her a questioning look, then moved to obey. He had to stand on his toes in order to gain the necessary angle, but he managed it, and moved to drop his dim hand beneath the angel's fist. He was trying to catch the scepter as it slid through. To everyone's surprise, based on their murmurs and gasps at any rate, the žezlo clicked into place with a reverberant *ting*.

Kastan beamed. "Just so. Now, take it in both hands. Twist it toward your bright side."

Lashjuk walked over to stand by Maksu and the war hound. The animal looked up at her, then leaned her head back against Lashjuk's bright arm and made a noise that sounded almost like a question. Her front paws came off the stone floor for an instant before she settled back to watch Andrej.

Lashjuk followed her gaze. The statue's hand was turning under the boy's efforts. When the scepter it now held faced five of the clock, she heard a deep, reverberant *click* from somewhere in the walls.

Kastan nodded. "Excellent. If I may?"

She stepped up beside Andrej, replacing his hand on the scepter with her own. Bowing her head, Kastan pulled straight outward. The statue came sliding forward as if it weighed nothing. Behind it, a pale green light revealed a well-made stone corridor.

That light is... familiar, Lashjuk thought. *Certain climbers along the walls of caverns make light like that, but there's something else...* she was distracted by the assembled crowd. They gasped and mumbled in awe, but at least there was no fear.

Kastan looked inside, then nodded. "Hajvarr? If you would lead the way?" Once the man had nodded and stepped through, she spoke to the chamber at large again. "As soon as the initial area's been made as safe as time allows, the rest of us will follow. *This* is Edmund's long-sightedness. Here, we may find a safe place to weather this storm. We may even find..."

The man called Hajvarr returned, looking thunderstruck. "Excellency, it's... it's a *trove.*" His voice was breathy and awed. "And further on, there's a stone way. It's well lit by the lichen and goes on for ... ages."

Kastan nodded, smiling with clear relief. "Set guards at every door until we can explore the place fully. The rest of you?" She raised her face toward the roof. "Gather your things. It's time we're on our way."

Lashjuk gave Maksu's shoulder a squeeze. The boy beamed up at her, then took her hand. They walked to stand beside Kastan and Andrej, watching the survivors of this once-vibrant place stumble toward an uncertain future.

"Vrek nak dush, Og." Lashjuk allowed a smile to creep into her voice. *(A clever beginning, chieftainess.)*

Kastan eyed her, then grinned. "Aye, well... hope doesn't hunt *for* you, Lady. Best we give it a helping hand."

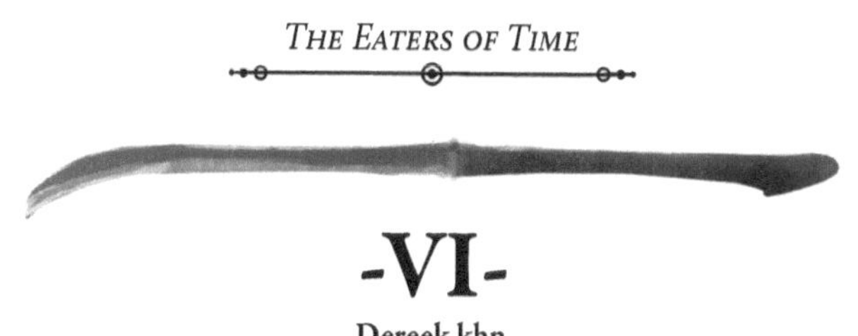

-VI-

Dereek khn
Kor Kowmor
6 Korunasykli: 23 Days after the Red Storm at Westsong

Dawn crept over the horizon amidst gaudy gold and purple clouds. The air was still and somehow heavy. The fleeting smells of impending rain and unmoving mist turned the early morning into a logy, living inducement to roll over and go back to sleep.

Yet there *was* life. The sounds coming from the northernmost portion of the ringwork made that clear. More than a dozen men and women were either stretching, sparring, or practicing strikes against wooden pells. Olshnak could see them from his place on the eastern alure.

He saw something else as well. Huron stood a lonely vigil further to the south. He was looking out over the pocket forest east of this place and singing to himself.

He heard Ricgerd's undainty voice somewhere below and had to smile. "Well," he said to no one in particular, "Nobody can question the oaf's loyalty now. So *that's* something." He snorted, then realized how hypocritical that had been.

"And what of me, then? Where does *my* loyalty lie?"

He didn't know. What he *did* know was that he was afraid. And why shouldn't he be? He'd failed in his mission. Wick was lost, and that had made completing it impossible.

"It may have been beyond my ability to stop, but the end result is the same. Wick is lost, my jailers are gone, and I think... I *think* that devil-thing—that raksasha was—"

"Rak-*sha*-sa, Nk." Methias's voice came from several feet behind him.

Olshnak winced. *This. This is why musing aloud is so dangerous. Gi awka glem but I'm a fool.*

He turned his head to look back at the man. Methias was standing still, not far away. He wore a questioning expression that, at first, Olshnak couldn't credit.

Methias gestured to the gnoerk's right. "May I? Or would you prefer to be alone?"

Olshnak considered, then shrugged. "Was about to move off toward

Huron. He's a fair enough singer."

"This has bearing on him as well. Though again, if you'd prefer to be alone…"

Olshnak shrugged again. What the hells?

"As you like, Lord."

As the man came up beside him, he tried to think of something useful to ask. The problem was, there were too damned many useful things he didn't know.

"I wouldn't let it worry you. I knew nothing about them until last night. Even then, I'd had nothing more than a name and the good sense to fear the one before us. I learned the rest from Pallith once we'd returned." Methias shook his head, smirking. "It's ironic, really. And more than a bit dangerous. My folk never thought to tell me. They assumed I already knew."

Olshnak chuckled. "Aye, well you're their leader. Their lord. Folk from Shesh in the north to the wild lands in the south are all taught not to question their rulers, aren't they." His voice made it clear this wasn't a question.

Methias sighed through a smile. "We say *better an aggressive mistake than a death while doing nothing.* Amongst one another, they hold to that rule. But I carried myself with enough surety that applying it to *me* never occurred to them. My own fault, really. In any event, it's a problem I hope I've corrected, though I'll need to be on guard against it in the future." He shook his head. "Regardless, Rakshasa are, I'm told, shapeshifters, flesh eaters, corruptors, and seducers, though not often in the carnal sense."

Olshnak was amused to see the lord was actually blushing. At first he thought it might've been the chill, but it faded as he watched. Could it really be talk of carnal seduction? If so, how had someone so un-worldly found himself in such a high position? The man had an army, after all.

These are excellent questions, he thought, *and not the kind I can come right out and ask.*

"Alright," he said. "Rak-sha-sa are shapeshifting devils out of Barghad myths, but you managed to defeat one."

Methias shook his head. "I nearly managed to defeat *myself.* I'd likely have been able to see to him last night, but with a small army of Nebelblut armed and at the ready barely a breath away…"

Olshnak gave a slow nod. "You satisfied yourself with shaming him and returning here. To what end? Are you…are *we* regrouping before we re-take Wick? Or have you done all you mean to on that score?"

Methias considered, looking out over the treeline. "I think I need to send word to Thorionden. They need to know what's happened, and better they learn it from those who were there."

"Seems sensible."

"But I don't know who to send. Lord Ricgerd would, by rank, be a fine fit. But..."

"But he's better at fighting foes than reporting on them." Olshnak grinned, nodding. "Glem, de zaksh."

Methias grinned back. "Aye. Iron, not speech. That's as good a way as any to put it. I'd send Sir Jastar, but he's parted ways with the Thorion Throne. They'll not likely be pleased to see him again, and are even less likely to listen to him. Your sergeant won't go, as he's unwilling to leave Sir Kaith in such a state. The same goes for that other armsmen... Vil... Vil-something."

"Vilmocz," said Olshnak. "He won't think much of you for spending time with the likes of me, Lord. I admit there's not much he can *do* about it, but..."

Methias rolled his eyes, making a noise that spoke of distaste. *Uhhhkh.* "But the man's another in an endless procession of the blind, deaf, and dead."

Olshnak arched his brows. Enough was enough. He had to ask, and now seemed as good a time as any.

"Ng? Fashek, jagrl awka aehe erld enjh Grimdash?" *(Chieftain? How, where, and why did you learn the gnoerkish tongue?)*

Methias bowed his head, grinning. "Hres ed de uthka enjh, Olshnak?" His tone suggested playfulness, rather than mockery. *(Should I not have learned, Olshnak?)*

"Aye, fair, but Lord... surely you take my meaning." He kept the touch of annoyance out of his voice. He didn't care for verbal sparring, at least on subjects such as this.

Methias nodded, letting his grin drop away. "My master was half-human. He was born in a gnoerkish fastness somewhere far to the north—a place called Sugi Kor. Do you know it?" His tone was hopeful, but not expectant.

"I ... do not. Stone-Blood Hold? No, Lord."

Methias accepted this with an easy nod. "It wasn't likely, but worth asking. My master was Emil Draksh. He taught it to me once I asked him to." Olshnak's surprise must've shown, for Methias gave a soft little laugh. "Aye, you're wearing the same look he did when I asked him."

They remained there in silence for a time. The soldiers went about their training behind and below them, and Huron went on singing to himself some yards away south.

Methias, at last, broke the silence. "You wanted to walk to, erm…"

"Huron, Lord." Olshnak's voice still wore its grating growl, but it had softened somewhat. *He called him a half-human, not a half-orc or a half-gnoerk. Hells, half of us don't make that effort.*

Methias made a gesture that they should walk that way. Olshnak nodded, and they went. As they neared Huron's spot atop the alure, his singing grew clearer. His voice was soft and sad, yet it carried well upon the heavy morning air.

…To tame you by and by.

Winter is a road. The danger that can lead you home.
A shadowed, shifting way of stone,
To claim your bones, and leave your loves to cry
…And leave your loves to cry.

Springtime is a prayer.
A moment's breath of gold and green,
A glimpse of how things might have been,
A hope for clearer skies,
A hope for clearer—

He cut himself off as they came near. Turning, he bowed to Methias, then flashed Olshnak a grin that made no effort to reach his eyes. Those eyes looked red and tired, as if they'd only recently heard of sleep, and weren't sure it was for them.

"Stone in sky, Huron, no need to stop on our account," said Methias. His voice was full of a warmth that seemed somehow unexpected from such a man. "You've a fair singing voice, even if the song sounds sad."

Stone in sky? So that means you're from Nausha. Olshnak tucked that information away for later use. *Given all I saw last night, I suppose that shouldn't surprise me.*

"No, Lord. The song is a rebellious thing." Huron's grin shone out again, but this time it seemed more honest. "Only the *melody* is sad. The staves are full of hope, as am I. Forgive me for being so bold, but have you come with news of Kai—of Sir Kaith?"

Methias gave a neutral nod. "I have. It isn't *good* news, but nor is it ill. His wound is too great for my healers here. Sir Kaith's wound is…" He shook his head. "It's too much for them. I'll need to move him to Koavahd

Kor. My seneschal may be able to do more."

Olshnak winced before he could stop himself. Huron, on the other hand, seemed to take the news in stride.

"I understand, Lord. That all of this trouble is taken for my friend, I thank you."

Methias offered a deep nod of respect for the man's words. "I note you call him friend, not lord."

Huron gave an embarrassed smile in reply. After a moment, he found his voice again. "We've known one another since we were boys. I was a slave, and he a page in service to the Countess's seneschal. His knighthood is a newish thing. Our friendship is," he shrugged, "much older."

Methias nodded, though his face had grown darker. "Old enough for him to buy your freedom?"

Huron blinked, then grinned. "His very first act, Lord. How did you know?"

Methias glanced to Olshnak, then back to the Sheshik man. "I didn't, but it does my heart good to hear it. We do not allow slavery in Dereek khn. The moment a slave crosses into our borders, they are free folk."

Olshnak snorted. "That won't please their masters."

Methias flashed a dark, satisfied grin at that. "No. No, it won't. But neither will the concept of having to raise an army to win their former slaves back."

Olshnak blinked, and hard. "You risk war over a single slave?"

Methias laughed. "There's little risk in it. It's less expensive to purchase new slaves elsewhere than to raise, provision, and march an army to get back the few you've lost. But if it came to it, aye. Slaves are welcome to *enter* Dereek khn. They just aren't welcome to leave it again *as slaves*. They can come and go as they please, otherwise."

Huron looked to Olshnak, then back to Methias. "Lord, did you know that Olshnak is a slave?"

Methias snapped his head around to look at the gnoerk. "Were you?"

Damnit boy, why did you have to mention that?

He paused, then shook his head. "I am, Lord. To the... to the Throne of Thorion."

Methias closed his eyes, bowing his head. "Well, then..."

"No fear, lord. I'm treated well enough. I'll return as soon as Sir Kaith is seen to."

Methias shook his head again, looking up to meet Olshnak's eyes. "Perhaps you misheard me, Nk. You were freed the moment you stepped onto my soil."

Olshnak blinked, then shook his own head. "Ng, no. I won't be the reason a war is waged. Do I *look* like a cradle tale princess?"

Methias's face grew flat and affectless. So did his voice. "I will, it seems, be speaking with the Countess of Thorion myself. We will come to some sort of understanding. If war comes of it, then war is something she was already planning. Unless you're her sometime lover, Nk, I cannot imagine she would refuse an accord with her neighbor. If she does?" He shrugged as if to say *so be it.*

"But lord, I—"

"Dash, Nk." *(Stop, brother.)* Methias's voice was short and sharp, like a distant whip crack. "I'm not going to war for you, specifically. Put that twaddle out of your head. If war comes of my talks with the Countess, then war was always an inevitability. But again, I won't go in seeking it."

He paused for a few beats, then spoke in a calmer, more animated tone. "I've been buying and freeing slaves, by and by, for months now. Slavery is a fool's bargain. It trades whatever that slave might one day bring into the world for labor in the now... labor the owners consider *beneath* them. You grow a garden by working the soil, not by paying others to work it. Doing that just means you *own* a garden. It may bring you joy, but it won't bring you pride, industry, or creativity. It won't fill the hole."

An older man called Methias's name from down in the courtyard. All three of them turned to look, and Olshnak saw the fellow raise both arms to beckon the lord. "A word?"

"If you will both excuse me. Oh, and we'll be moving your lord within the hour. You're welcome to stay here or come along as you like." With that, Methias turned and headed off.

Olshnak watched him go. He was left with mixed feelings about the man and their conversation both.

No matter what he says, if war comes, it'll be my fault. Yet if I run, he may well go speak with Ylspeth, anyway. He may go to war, anyway.

"Will you go with us, Olshnak?"

He looked up at Huron. "I don't... of course I will. If our lord—"

"*My* lord, Olshnak. Only a free man or woman can enter into such an agreement. *You* joined us as a slave. An important slave, I grant you. You did come with two guards to keep you in line. But a slave nonetheless. While I think Kaith would be pleased to have you with us, you are a free man now. The decision must be your own."

Olshnak offered a slow nod at that. "True enough. Still, I should stay with Sir Kaith until he recovers. No point making decisions before that happens."

Huron nodded. "So you're with us?"

"Aye," said Olshnak. "For now, at least, I'm with you."

Epilogue

-I-

Venzene Duchy of Kamieńalun
County Czarny Wodospad
6 Korunasykli: 23 Days after the Red Storm at Westsong

Kozioł woke with a shout already forming in his throat. He suppressed it, but it was a near thing. The air was thin and chill—the cold scraping its way up into his nose. Rubbing the back of his dim hand beneath it, he sniffled as he tried to unravel his muddled mind.

He'd been dreaming about... *something*. It'd involved him fighting. He was certain of that much... almost. Had he held a sword? A mace? He couldn't recall. All he knew for certain was that the experience had been both involved and intense. His inability to recall the dream was *odd*, though. His dreams had become lucid things that, upon waking, were in easy reach and recall... at least since beginning his lessons with Yeidil. Well, never mind. He would ask his mistress about it when next they spoke. For now, he had to face the terrible specter of life beyond the warmth of his bed.

Speaking of warmth, small streams of brief heat carved their way down his cheeks. He didn't *think* he'd been crying. His dream had left him disturbed, but it hadn't left him trembling in an imagined corner. *No,* he decided. *It's just the cold making my eyes water. Fine. What time is it?*

Looking up at the tent's ceiling, he marked the telltale paleness that meant dawn was either fast approaching or already here. Under ordinary circumstances, he might've allowed a longing, lingering gaze to rest on the furs that covered him. His boots, too, might've earned a withering, mistrustful glare. He'd learned from experience. Boots on a cold morning might *look* innocent, but that was a trap for the sleep-fogged mind. As familiar and inviting as they were, they would be stiff and cold to the touch. And an angry chill awaited the hurried and unwary feet that donned them.

There was nothing for it. Reluctant as he was, he forced himself to get on with the business of getting up and into the doings. The yellow boot leather was as warm and inviting as he'd expected. Even two layers of wool on his feet weren't enough to counter their chill. No matter. His toes were nearly numb with the cold, anyway. He'd be warm enough once he was out and in the sun.

He used the chamber pot before bundling himself up. He'd carry the thing outside to empty it in a bit. For some reason—even after he'd finished—he still felt as if he needed to make water. Rolling his eyes, he fetched a soft sigh. *Ah well. I'll be outside in half a beat. If I need to, I'll just do it there.*

Kozioł stood as ready as may be to face the day. He walked toward the room's canvas drape, catching the muted noise of their horses as he moved. The sound caused him to slow his step. Something was off. He wasn't *alarmed*, but their mounts seemed to be a touch more vocal than he'd come to expect. He'd spent his fair share of pre-dawn hours tending to several of the family's steeds. The noisy, whickered conversations were always worth looking into, but he wasn't hearing the screaming or trumpeting sounds that spoke of real danger. *I'd best see to them, though,* he thought, yawning. *Something's got them singing.*

Exiting his small portion of Azhferd's tent, he moved into the main chamber. It was darker here. The walls were covered in hanging rugs, and well-kept fur pelts of wolf, bear, and moose. There would also have been a few tapestries in the ordinary course of things, but Azhferd had asked him to leave those marks of wealth and status packed away for the time being.

"There's no reason to give Sir Dorean any more information about us than necessary, Kozioł. Is there?"

No. No there was not. He made to move outside when a thought struck him. If Azhferd was still deep enough asleep, he could empty both of their chamber pots at once, saving himself a trip. He turned and made his way to his cousin's side of the tent

At first, Azhferd's canvas drape wouldn't open. Kozioł kept grabbing at it, but it seemed determined to slip through his numb fingers. Shaking his head, he crouched down and found the place where the canvas flaps overlapped. Tracing that line upward as he stood, he finally managed to part the panels and make his way inside.

Azhferd was sitting on his bed, his back to the somewhat draft-prone entrance. The scent of steam and the tallow from his shaving soap hung heavy in the air. There was another, more metallic tang as well, but he couldn't place it.

"Azhferd... I'm sorry. I didn't realize you'd wakened before me, let alone that you'd heated fresh water. That... I should've done that." His face was growing hot with the shame of it. He fidgeted with the woodenhandle of the chamber pot he carried. "Sh... shall I empty your—"

"You've kept something *from* me." Azhferd's voice was cold and hollow, somehow. He tapped his razor against the side of his bowl, then brought it back to his face. A wet, scraping sound followed the motion, but it was off somehow. Louder? Cold *did* make sound travel further... made it easier to hear, didn't it?

"Lord?" Kozioł tried to recall what he might've kept from his cousin, but nothing came to mind. Nothing Azhferd could've uncovered, at any rate. Until this very sykli, he'd have said he never kept *anything* from Azhferd, unless it was a present, an unexpected party... something that might make him smile. Even Kozioł's studies of the weave had been relegated to the Green Lands almost since the beginning.

Again came that tapping sound—the razor being cleaned in the bowl of steaming water.

"You knew. You've known. You've heard, and you've held your treacherous tongue." Again, these words were delivered in a chilly, heartbreaking monotone. Azhferd was usually calm and matter-of-fact. Even so, he was anything but grim.

Kozioł stepped further into the chamber. His chest hitched with fear, even as his head swam with a disorienting sense of grief. "Azhferd, no! I don't know what you're speaking of, but I know I'm not—"

The bowl made an audible *click* as his lord placed it on the small bedside table. The sound was so loud in the gloom that it made Kozioł stop in mid-sentence.

Azhferd bowed his head. He was still seated on the bed with his back to the entrance. "And still you deny it. Still you deny ... *me.*"

"I would *never* deny you!" Kozioł's voice wasn't so much loud as it was sharp.

"The *Keening* has come. Can't you hear it?"

As if his words had summoned it, the sound of heavy raindrops impacted the tent's roof. They struck in an endless series of *plops* that seemed to take an age to fade. The noise built on itself until it'd become a tumult.

It's the applause of the damned... they try to appease him—Pusty Ogień, the Hungry Fiddler. They must, lest he feed on them for being an unkind audience. He shuddered, feeling his eyes prickle with fresh tears. *Not that it matters. Someone always feeds him. Someone grows too tired, or too broken to continue, and... and...* And hells be hid, what was he on about? He'd no idea. He'd have sworn he'd never *heard* of Pusty Ogień, *or* the Hungry Fiddler. Yet the imagery wouldn't leave his mind.

"Nothing to sayyyyy?" Azhferd's voice rose, overtopping the strange sound of rain. "Nothing? You still refuse to tell me the truth? Is that it?" Azhferd stood, seeming to dominate the chamber. "The Keening has come! The Keening! And *with* the Keening, the *King* returns! He returns, and will tear *alllll* the towers down! He would have forgiven me! Would have forgiven *you,* were you not such a liar! Such a traitor!"

"Azh ... ferd?" Kozioł's voice was small and full of tears. His heart was a stallion galloping in his chest.

Azhferd spun around. "*What,* traitor? What could you *possibly* say to me now?"

Kozioł took an involuntary stagger-step backward. Azhferd's face was ... *ruined.* It hadn't been his *beard* he was shaving. That still covered the lower half of his face. No, it was the bare skin he'd been shaving... *carving.* What remained was a bloody, bony horror of ragged muscle and flesh from his mustache to his hairline. His eyes were cracked and broken, as if they'd been made of glass. Yet a strange and sickly greenish light shone from behind them.

Kozioł did the only thing he could think of. He hurled his chamber pot at Azhferd's mangled face, turned, and groped for the exit.

Have to get away! I have to! Azhferd's fallen! I've failed him, and now I have to... to...

Then he felt a hand touch his shoulder, its fingers crawling—curling around the back of his neck. He drew in breath to scream...

His eyes opened. Azhferd—the real, living Azhferd was kneeling over him. His face bore an anxious look. And yes, his cousin's hand *was* cupping the back of his neck.

"Kozioł? Can you hear me? Do you *know* me?"

He felt his heart returning to its normal rhythm. Swallowing, he nodded. "I... yes, Lord."

Azhferd shook his head. "None of that, Kozioł. Not while it's just we two. Remember?"

He felt the claws of the dream loosen a notch as he smiled. "Azhferd, then. Just a bad dream. I... I'm fine. Forgive me if I wakened you."

His knight smiled and shook his head. Ruffling the blond of Kozioł's sleep-skewed mop, he spoke on in a low *all is well* tone. "Caught me up early, mały kuzyn. That's all. *(little cousin)*

Kozioł beamed at the old endearment. "All right. Still, Azhferd, I'm sorry to have caused a fuss."

"Nonsense." He grinned, further mussing the boy's already untidy hair. "You're alright now? You're sure?"

At that moment, he longed for the days when he was still small enough to be tucked into bed... when the simple act of an embrace—perhaps a goodnight kiss from someone he *knew* he could trust was enough to ward the woe away. *Gone days, now. I'm a squire. A squire and an apprentice. I need to put that part of me away once and for all.*

Kozioł drew in a deep breath, held it for a beat, then let it out as he nodded. "Fine. Truly. Just... it isn't raining, is it?"

Azhferd blinked, looked up, then back down. "No. It's been dry all night, save some snowflakes. Why?"

He shook his head. "The dream. It's nothing."

"Can you get back to sleep? Dawn's a few hours off yet. It'll be a long day in the saddle, and another short night tomorrow. Should be like that the rest of the road to tournament, truth be told. And growing boys need their sleep."

Kozioł grinned. "I'll sleep. Just don't let me sleep too long. I'm your squire. I've duties... *Syr.*"

Azhferd chuckled as he stood. "No fear on that score, good my squire. We knights are a forgetful lot. Most of us have little more than a vague memory of how horses are saddled. It's a trade-off for wearing the white belt."

He snorted as Azhferd left. *I've no idea what that dream was about, but Yeidil will want to hear as much as I can remember. Not that I want to remember any of it. I just hope she's there tomorrow night. If not...* He shook his head. He didn't know *what* he would do if she wasn't there to speak

with. *She should be, though. She said we'd next speak once I was well and truly on the way to tournament.*

He sighed and closed his eyes. Next he knew, the Twilight Sea had risen up to meet him. If he dreamed again, he had no memory of it, which was a blessing.

-II-

County Thorion
Eastshadow
9 Korunasykli: 26 Days after the Red Storm at Westsong

Barnic slowed his pace. Ready as he was to finish, the girl was close to a fourth climax. And he wanted to keep her as drunk on him as he could. She was a *good* girl, was Kelsey. A young, pretty thing—well into the march toward her seventeenth summer. She was also kind, enthusiastic, generous with her time, and ever-eager to please. If things went well...

She began to shudder and keen atop him. Grabbing hold of her hips, he rolled her onto her back. Teasing his tongue along her left nipple, he kept his hips still for a mental ten count before resuming his earlier rhythm. Now came the test.

Barnic was still learning her body—the way her passion built. As close as he was, he *wanted* them to finish at the same instant. The idea was, like as not, so much romantic twaddle. There was no special significance to that happy accident. Yet a part of him still held out hope that the old tales were true. That moment of deep and abiding connection between lovers—of sharing shadow, as it was once called—seemed a more worth-while pursuit than most.

It didn't take long. She reached up, wrapping her hands around the back of his neck. Her eyes rolled back to reveal their whites, and her lips parted in an almost feral snarl. Her body grew taut—hands sliding down to grip his shoulders as wave after wave crashed over her.

Her breath slowed. She was satisfied, as best he could tell. Given she'd been his first lover—and that only a few days agone—he supposed he ought to be pleased. He'd clearly learned a trick or two. Still, he was a touch disappointed that he'd failed to produce *that* moment yet again.

No matter. There would be other chances soon enough. His body recovered with astonishing speed these days. Yet another gift from *that night's* work.

When they'd both caught their breaths, she giggled—a sound of surprised delight that was more reflex than anything else.

"There's that laugh again. At least I amuse you." He kept his voice light. Kelsey was a servant still. She might very well *remain* a servant. Only time would tell that tale. It would be far too easy to make her feel small, or afraid. And that wouldn't do.

She shook her head, face aglow as she smiled. "Nay, mi'lord. You do many things to me, but that's n'one of them." She leaned over and kissed him before pressing herself to his side. "I s'pose... nay, near mind, Lord."

Barnic resisted the urge to roll his eyes, even though she'd be unable to see them from her vantage. Times like these brought the reality of her age home to him in full measure. It was best he keep his reactions under control. One bad habit displayed at the wrong moment and the entire game board might shift.

"Tell me, my girl." Her head rested on his chest. He stroked her hair as he spoke, allowing his tone to drop into its lowest range. He wanted her to *feel* his voice, not merely to hear it.

"I fear..." she trailed off.

"You fear..."

Again, she laughed, but this time the sound had become a nervous thing.

"I fear I'm easily thrown over, Lord. I fear ee've only to set eyes on some pretty, titled thing and ee'll have me dismissed from service." She grabbed a handful of his scant chest hair, as if she were afraid he might *physically* throw her over here and now.

Good, he thought. *Now we come to it.* He ran his finger behind her ear, then down along her jawline. She shuddered and sighed, and he spoke his answer.

"Kelsey... I'll *not* have you dismissed from service, regardless of what befalls. As for you being *thrown over,* as you put it, there's but one way that can happen."

She stiffened. "wha... what's that, mi'lord?"

"If another woman kindles before you."

She pushed herself up, using her hands to support her weight. Her brown hair spilled down over one milky shoulder, lustrous in the eerie light of the room's single candle. "Another..."

"Woman. Another woman, Kelsey." He was careful to keep his voice patient... even kindly. He'd been expecting this conversation, but he'd found himself hesitating to be the one who began it. "The first to kindle with my get will be the one I wed. I *must* have an heir, and sooner's not soon enough."

"Are... are ee' with others, then?" She sounded more shocked than angry.

He nodded. "Aye. Two, though I doubt either of them will—"

She pushed herself up to sit on her knees, eyes wide and mouth turned down. "Who?"

Barnic let her lapses in decorum pass without comment. This was the first time she'd spoken to him without adding some version of *lord*. The realization made him grin.

"Ee mustn't 'ave a go at me on it. Who? ...Please." Kelsey's voice had grown soft on that last word, wiping the smile from his face in an instant.

He had an obligation to further his line, just as Jast had said. But he hadn't meant to cause the girl pain. His reactions within his control once more, he did his best to explain.

"Whom is no matter, Kelsey. I've barely been with the others. Perhaps half-a-dozen times between them. I *want* it to be you. But what I *need* is an heir. My own desires are *nothing* set against that need."

She opened her mouth to reply, but a pounding on the door gainsaid her.

Barnic sat up, gave her a brief, soft kiss, and rose to walk naked from the bed. He opened the door wide, looking out into the hall.

Oswald... *Ossie* stood there, naked to the waist, with a blonde beauty curled against his muscular chest. "Lord, I know what this looks like, but—"

The oh-so-formal Lord Eastshadow snorted, watching the blonde woman's eye travel down the length of his own body. "It *looks* as if you mean to join us uninvited." He stepped back, grinning.

Oswald smirked, nodding. "Aye, could do. But there's a visitor in the main hall. He's come from Wick, Lord, and he's brought ee' somet."

Barnic arched his brows, then shrugged. "Someone's offered him a room, surely."

"Aye. 'ave, Lord. Ee's refused it till ee and 'is party've seen you."

"Brave, given the hour. Ah well. Give us half a heartbeat and I'll find something 'propriate to wear."

Ossie looked him up and down with the same frank interest his woman had. "Don't know much 'bout what's 'propriate, but I'd put *that* away at the least... less ee' want the fellow never to meet yer eyes."

Barnic followed his gaze, realized Oswald was speaking of his nakedness, then blushed from face to upper chest.

"Fair," said he. "Come to that, Ossie, you'd best dress and arm yourself as well."

"Oh?"

"Aye. I'm the Lord of Eastshadow. Best I have my strong bright arm in bright-arm's reach when accepting an audience like this."

Ossie blinked. "*Grantin',* ee mean. *Grantin'* an audience like this."

Barnic gave his head a single shake. "Accepting. He's refused to wait and see me on my terms. Made it a staring contest."

Ossie bobbed his head. "And ee're willing to blink first?" He sounded dubious.

"Aye. And why not?" Barnic made his smile placid, his eyes dropping to a half-lidded state. He took on the brogue of the common salt as he went on. "Ee's n'important fellow, ain't ee? Come from far afield. Wick, was it?" He saw Ossie fighting the urge to laugh, and losing bit by bit. "Well, I can't keep one such as ee *wait-in',* can I! An embassage from a storied place like Wick... ee must've seen wonders ee and me'd scarce've *dreamed* of!"

Oswald broke, cackling. "Aye, Lord. Ee're on it, ain't'ee! Ee've got the patter!" Still laughing, he took his companion—his evening's pretty exercise—and headed back toward his newly gifted room.

Turning his head back toward his bed, Barnic spoke as he dressed.

"I'll be back as soon as I can, Kelsey... once this is dealt with. Stay if you like. I'll answer what questions I can, then."

She spoke no reply but nodded.

He met her innocent-looking brown dreamer's lamps. They'd grown large, regarding him with an undisguised hunger that brought his blush back all over again. *Had I really thought her a child?* Not for the first time, he realized that yes, indeed, he had. And yes, he'd been a fool.

He forced himself to return to the task at hand—seeing to the puffed-up priss from Wick. A moment later, he'd knotted his belt about his waist, pulled his new boots on, and headed for the great hall.

Ossie fell into step beside him. He was pleased to see the man had belted on the talwar he'd gifted him after the battle. Barnic bore no weapon, much to his frustration. He hated the policy, but recognized the wisdom in it. A lord who bore his weapon within his own hall was a lord who didn't believe himself worthy to lead. There were certain commonsense exceptions, of course, but still. There were always others who would be all too happy to find a replacement for a weak, frightened ruler.

"Sh' I send f'Sir Aethan?"

Barnic shrugged. "He's other matters to look after, I'm sure. If not, he'll already be waiting for us." His squire brother had grown distant since the battle. *Since my change, really.* Barnic had grown nearly a foot in height. The rest of his frame had filled out to match, putting on muscle definition he'd never dreamt of. Ossie, too, had grown more hale and hearty, though his changes were far less stark... for now, at least. As for Aethan's unease? It was an understandable reaction. It would pass. Things between them would return to the way they were in time.

"We'll bring him on side soon enough," he continued. "Just need to give him time to adjust. We've known one another since we weren't much older than boys."

Ossie frowned for a beat, considering. Then he nodded his acceptance.

They rounded the corner. Barnic held them there as Eastshadow's Night Steward—an older fellow called Islwyn—stepped toward them. This severe-looking man offered a brief, practiced bow, then had to look up to meet Barnic's eyes.

A brief glance *past* Islwyn revealed five figures seated in the main hall. The room's only actual *chair* belonged to the lord. So they'd been relegated to rough benches set around the trestle table used for evening meals. Most of his would-be guests looked uncomfortable. Given the hour, and their insistence on an immediate audience, Barnic was having difficulty mustering up much in the way of guilt.

"Lord, the harried-looking one? The jolly-framed man in the silk tunic and wolf's fur collar?" He waited until Barnic nodded before going on. "He's presented himself as Tavin Bailifson of Wick." He paused before adding, "Of the court of Lord Aleksandr Silverson."

Sir Barnic, lord of Eastshadow, scowled at the implication as he gazed down into the steward's face. "So Ricgerd has fallen as well. More's the pity. Another skilled sword lost." He looked to Oswald, laying a hand on the man's broad shoulder. "I'm blessed to have found you when I did." Turning back to Islwyn, he offered a nod. "We'd best see what he wants, or at least what his new lord wants."

The Night Steward nodded, then sketched another brief bow before stepping into the hall proper.

"Stand now! *Stand now!!* Stand now and pay heed. Lord Barnic Eastshadow ... one of the Nineteen, Knight of the Valadin, and Defender of the Shivering March ... is come now into his hall." Islwyn spoke in dusty, rhythmic *gusts* of sound. His voice rose high, lingering in the rafters before the night swallowed it.

Benches shuffled. Two guardsmen, a boy who likely served as this *Tavin's* page, and a Barghad girl of *astonishing* beauty rose to receive him.

Both Tavin and his page watched in awe as he and Ossie walked toward the hall's high seat. They were, he had no doubt, trying to absorb the reality he and his guardsman presented. Barnic slowed his step by a small measure, wanting them to have every chance to size up the person they'd disturbed.

Tavin spoke up, chin quivering as he stammered. "M-mi-my Lord Eastshadow. What a decided pleasure it is to be graced with your presence!" His voice was nervous as he strove to control himself. "I am—"

"The lout who saw fit to interrupt me in the dark of early night." He was pleased to see the round-bellied man break out in a thin sheen of sweat, beginning to splutter. "The same *uncultured oaf* who refused my hospitality, spoke nothing of his business to my men, and yet *required* that I dress and entertain him as if he were the Countess's non-existent consort. The silk-swanned servant of an upstart, unknown lord who now controls one of the wealthiest places in all of *Thorion*—oh yes, Tavin... I know *exactly* who you are."

Tavin hunched his shoulders, bending in a kind of servile half-bow. "My lord is too shrewd by half. R-ru-rumors of your wisdom and the keenness of your mind are—"

"*Also* non-existent." Barnic's tone suggested he'd smelled, or perhaps tasted, something foul.

He eschewed his high seat. The damned thing was uncomfortable now. The new one he'd ordered to be built would be right-sized, but it was still being crafted. That was fine for this specific audience. He'd be better served by keeping his feet.

Wick hadn't been small enough to employ a bailiff in *donkey's*. It'd boasted a steward, and several counselors for at least three generations now. The idea that this man hoped to trade on such a surname was bordering on offensive.

"*Battles—even social ones—are most often won in the will,*" Valad would say. "*People are always playing games with one another... always trying to show the wide world where they believe they belong among their fellows. You must learn to read—learn to see and hear the way others see You. Then you can accept or change those views with impunity.*" And so, Valad had taught him the untold tongue in which most folk spoke... the language of stance and shoulder.

Barnic now took on the courtly aspects of disgust and disinterest in as near as no matter to equal measure. He let his arms hang limply at his sides, fingers dangling. His shoulders, too, relaxed as he peered down his nose at the sniveling fellow.

"Well? What *is* it, man? What *demands* both my servants and their lord rise from their beds to come before you?"

He heard Oswald groan from over his shoulder. It was the hunger again, he had no doubt. The man was under control, but he'd clearly realized Barnic's intent. It was very likely that Tavin would be sentenced for one of several missteps by the end of this meeting. Insulting and making demands above his station seemed the likeliest crimes, but it didn't much matter. If he was involved with the usurpation of Wick's high seat, Barnic would be only too happy to hand him off to Ossie. *His* transformation... his *ascension* had just begun, after all. And growing boys...

"I... yes, Lord. I have... I bear a message for you from Wick. Aleks, that is to say, the Lord Aleksandr of—"

Barnic allowed his fists to clench and unclench, speaking through gritted teeth. "My patience hangs by the *merest* of threads, and still you play this game? There *is* no *lord* by that name. Lord Ricgerd is the rightful heir to the house of Wick, and Ylspeth or her seneschal would've sent word had she promoted some other man to his high seat. Now—"

"There is such a one." This was the woman. She spoke in an altogether pleasing tone, though there was no shortage of fire in her. "Forgive me, great Samraja," she stepped forward and dropped to her knees before him. "I am called Shiza, Lord. And I have *seen* the man with my own eyes." She bowed her head, waiting.

"Get up, foolish girl!" Tavin's embarrassed hiss bounced off of the walls as if he'd shouted.

"*You* do not give orders in my hall, lout."

Tavin—who looked less loutish than anyone Barnic had ever seen— turned bright red, then subsided.

Barnic turned back to Shiza, though she still stared at the floor before her. "I thank you for your words, Shiza. I am Lord Barnic, not this... Rah..."

"Saum-*rah*-jah, Lord. And forgive me, but you *are*... or at the least, you have within you the right and might to *become* Samraja. Your rebirth... it has awakened you to the might of your blood... the *majesty* of your blood. You have but to reach out your hand and *claim* the—"

"Traitorous witch!," Tavin snarled. "You *lied* to me! You lied to *all* of us!"

Barnic started to turn toward Tavin, fighting the urge to backhand the ill-mannered goat. Ossie had already stepped forward, anticipating that very action.

"What are you *waiting* for? Do your duty! Now!" Tavin took several steps back. He was far lighter on his feet than his size suggested. The man was making flapping motions to his guards as if ushering them forward.

Ossie shouldered Barnic aside just in the nick. One guard had drawn a blade of some sort, and *hurled* it at Barnic's unsuspecting self. Ossie took the blow square in the chest. It hung from a place just below his right shoulder.

After a glance to confirm the man was, for the moment, alright, Barnic raised his voice to fill the hall. "Guards! Bar the exits. My *guests,* it seems, wish to entertain me!"

He heard the men moving to obey him but paid them little mind. Something about Ossie's wound had drawn his eye. The dirk, or whatever specific make of blade it was, was wrapped at the hilt with an absurd amount of leather. It swelled the way a beehive or hornet's nest did, eliminating the sleek lines such weapons were known for.

But the blade itself... it's greenish-grey. It's... He grinned, eyes growing wide. Reaching up, he yanked the weapon free from Ossie's flesh. For his part, Ossie just grunted but seemed otherwise unaffected.

"Go! What are you *waiting* for?!" Tavin's voice had grown into a whining shout.

Dagger in hand, Barnic stepped back to reset his balance, then charged the nearest of Tavin's guardsmen. He heard the other guard drawing his sword and had to laugh. He punched the first man hard at the hinge of his jaw. The fellow went down with a shout that cut off in mid-career. As the body began to fall, Barnic grabbed it and thrust it into the swordsman.

That worthy dodged his falling comrade, trying to keep his sword arm unimpeded. He had skill and was no stranger to his weapon, but it made no difference.

Barnic saw him cast his gaze down at the fallen man, which was all the opening he'd needed. Holding the dagger by its meaty hilt, he lunged, stabbing in and upward. The man's chain was almost enough to block the blow, but Barnic was *not* to be denied. He reached up with his dim hand and grabbed the fellow's shoulder.

Tavin was shouting, as were his own guards. His foe was raining pommel strikes down across his back, trying to distract or dislodge him. To no avail.

Growling a wordless battle cry, Barnic yanked the man's shoulder toward him, even as he shoved the dagger forward. There was a moment of hesitation as the linked rings of the armor resisted, but it was short-lived. As the weapon broke through, biting into the man's flesh, Barnic saw the spark wink out of his eyes.

A flash of pale light and a groan from Ossie forced him to turn. As he'd expected, his friend's wounded flesh was knitting closed bit by bit. He removed the dagger, grinning at the thing as it turned to that strange dust.

"Ossie?"

"L... lord?"

"You've more where that came from. Take the dagger from this one's belt. Anoint it with your own blood, then use it on his fool of a friend... the one still drawing breath."

Ossie's voice had grown fuller, somehow. "I will, Lord. What'll ee be doing?"

Barnic stalked toward Tavin, who looked as if he were either about to wet himself or already had done. "Oh, *Iiiii* have other business to tend to."

"Lord, no... Lord... *please!* Hear me! I only acted as I was told. It wasn't me, it was that whore over *there!* She promised me that she... that I..."

Barnic backhanded him, then punched him in his sternum for good measure. With a *whoosh* of air, Tavin collapsed to his knees, then passed out entirely.

"Islwyn?"

"Lord?" The Night Steward sounded nonplussed, as if to say *this is all very well and good, but it's no business of mine.*

"See that this plump bird neither waddles nor flies away. I may need him before long."

"Of course, Lord Eastshadow." He turned and began to make the necessary arrangements.

Another flash of pale light made Barnic turn to regard Ossie. The man shuddered, then seemed to stretch in all directions at once. It was over within seconds.

"And Islwyn? Fetch my sword. Oswald? To me."

Both men complied, the former moving off toward Barnic's bed chamber as Eastshadow's guards hauled an unconscious Tavin away.

"You are wise, great Samraja," said Shiza. She hadn't moved from her kneeling position. Even now, she appeared to contemplate the stony floor as she spoke. "You use what resources present themselves to you, have the stomach to kill in order to defend what is yours, and you do not react in haste, or out of blind rage. Tavin will live until you have learned all that you can from him. A lesser man would have taken his life, devoured his shadow, and had done."

Barnic considered her. "You know much, Shiza. Much that *I* do not."

"May I rise, Lord?"

"You may. I should have said as much already."

She unlimbered herself, seeming almost to *grow* to her full height. The woman bowed her head, then turned to face him.

Her hands! What's wrong with her... storms be swift! They've grown in ... backwards!

She followed his gaze, then flashed him a coy smile. "You now wonder not only what I may know and what I may tell, but what I may *be.* If you will offer me your protection, Samraja, I will reveal all that I know to you."

"Protection from whom or what?"

Islwyn returned with his sword belt. He moved to wrap Barnic in it, but Ossie stopped him with a hand on his shoulder. The Night steward offered a deep nod, then passed the duty on to Ossie.

Barnic could have seen to his sword and its belt on his own. In truth, he would've been all too happy to do so. *But there are times when others need to be allowed to show their own loyalty—their own desire to be of service.*

Shiza spoke in answer. "I was here when you defeated the... what does this tongue call it, the..." She shook her head. "The golden one. You know of whom and what I speak. I was also there as the place you call *Wick* fell. The firstborn of us... he is blind and foolish, but powerful. I seek your sheltering shield that I might find safety from *him*... at least until the time is right."

Barnic blinked, processing that. "Will he come after you?"

She nodded, eyes cast down for a beat. "He will, eventually. If I do nothing—tell you nothing, he will leave me be. But then he will walk unchallenged beneath the burning sky." She paused, raising her face to gaze at him again. "And I promise you, Samraja, the sky *shall* burn."

Her eyes... Their color is ... reversed.

Barnic pushed the realization aside. The woman's *hands* were backwards. Her eyes were nothing set against *that* impossibility. He nodded, holding up a hand toward her. "A moment, Shiza. I've something I must do before we go on."

He turned to Ossie. "Kneel." His voice had shifted into a cold, ringing thing, not much like his usual timbre.

Oswald blinked, stepped back a pace—he'd only just finished tightening Barnic's sword belt—and did as he'd been commanded.

"You've been well fed this evening, Oswald."

"Aye, my lord." The man sounded as if he were having an internal war. His voice gyred between two perches—amused delight and awed uncertainty.

Shiza watched everything with large, doleful black eyes.

Is it your need to leave your fellows? Your family? Is that why you mourn? Is that why your eyes are so sadful?

Islwyn cleared his throat—a soft *hmm-mm* that brought Barnic's mind back to the matter at hand. He gave the steward a nod, then flicked his eyes toward first Ossie, then the throne. Once Islwyn had given him a silent *ah* of understanding, Barnic turned his gaze on the kneeling man. Once more, he made his voice a cold, ringing thing.

"Oswald of Eastshadow... twice in the short time I have known you, you have proven your courage, your strength, your prowess, and most importantly—your loyalty. Without hesitation ... you raced to save others, putting their lives before your own. Tonight ... your instinct was to take the blow meant for me. Once again, you acted without hesitation— risking your own life to defend your lord's." He cast an eye toward Islwyn. The older man gave him a deep nod, then looked down at his clasped hands with a grin. All was in readiness.

"With deliberation, therefore, I call you to service as a knight of Eastshadow, and await your oath of fealty."

Ossie shuddered in shocked gratitude. His eyes were wet, and though his mouth worked—no sound came. It was several beats before the man had recovered enough to speak. When he did, it was in a grateful, breathy tone, not much like the fun-loving, brash guardsman of half a bell agone.

"Lord, I..." he shook his head. "I would do... I *will* do anything you ask. Ee've uplifted me from the mud and scree, given me a room in ee're very hall, treated me as a brother at every turn. Now ee'd ask me to stand as a knight? As *your* knight?" His shoulders gave a brief, silent shake as if he were laughing. "I've no idea what to say. I've not seen a knighting a'fore... 'ave no idea what words I sh'speak."

"You must speak from a place of truth, Oswald of Eastshadow." Shiza's voice rolled across the room like a silk banner catching the wind. "Your Samraja has recognized your worth. Now, he only asks that you make your oath. And it must be an oath you can and will keep. You must tell

Lord Barnic of Eastshadow—Samraja of the severed throne—what it is that you would offer him."

The room fell silent as this litany ceased. Barnic wanted to rebuke the woman for inserting herself into Oswald's moment. In the same breath, he wanted to acknowledge how right she'd been. He doubted Valad himself would've been able to put it better. That thought felt a fair bit like blasphemy, but that didn't make it any less true.

Oswald looked up, face wet, smile bright. "It's no matter what ee're called... Sir Barnic, Lord of Eastshadow, Samraja of the... the severed throne? I've no wealth or name, yet what I 'ave is yours. My arm, mi'back, mi'hand and mi'heart. Comes to it, ee've mi'life as well." He bowed his head again. "Comes woe or wealth, I swear it. If ee'll have me, ee has me."

For a moment, Barnic was speechless. He *understood* the effect he'd had on the man's life, but to hear it put so plain was ... humbling. Still, he needed to speak the words that would seal the ceremony. Drawing breath, as well as his sword, he gestured to Islwyn.

"The throne of Eastshadow hears your words, accepts your oath, and offers you its own. Fealty with love, valor with honor, oath-breaking with deadly vengeance." He nodded to Islwyn, who produced a glittering chain of station and lowered it over Oswald's head. The heavy, lozenge-shaped links of gold swung—slow and pendulous—beneath the man's bent brow.

Barnic lowered the sword he held to rest on first one, then the other of Ossie's shoulders. "Rise, Sir Oswald of Eastshadow," said he.

He did as bidden, looking around the chamber as if he'd never seen it before. As Barnic sheathed his sword, Ossie gave him a brief, fierce embrace.

Smiling as he stepped back, he cast about a final time, then met Barnic's eyes. "What now, Lord?"

Barnic grinned, looking to Shiza. "Now we must call for refreshment and hear the lady's tale. She cannot tell us everything, perhaps. At least not without my grant of protection." He lifted his chin toward her, seeking out her odd, inverted eyes. "Yet, Lady, will you tell us what you can? If I am to stand against the force that, you say, took Wick..."

Shiza gave a deep, deferential nod, then gestured to their party's page. "Come out, boy. The lord is unlikely to blame you for the men and their foolishness."

Barnic blinked, then shook his head. He'd forgotten all about the page. Well, no matter. "Quite right, Lady. For now, you may join the other pages. Islwyn will show you where they take their sleep. Tomorrow, we will speak of what comes next for you."

The dark-haired boy crept out from behind the central fire, eyes enormous and grave. He nodded, then turned as Islwyn beckoned him.

"I will tell you all that I can, great Samraja. Much of it, I think, you will find useful in contending with all that moves against you and your county."

He met Oswald's eyes, then turned back to find the woman's. "Do you mean the goblins?"

"Noooo, Lord. I speak of the monster who created us—who corrupted our captain, and exiled us to the Red Valley, beyond Skolf's own seam. My kin may indeed come for you and your own. Yet the King of the Dead walks. And where he walks, the world... time itself is scourged."

She glided back to the room's lone table, pulled out a bench that would allow her to face the men, and alighted upon it. Her eyes never left Barnic's own. When she had settled herself, she spoke again.

"Shall we begin, Lord?"

Author's Note

 nd with that, we're all caught up.

Hey Cadre,

Eaters marks a milestone for us. With this publication, all of the work I'd written as an indie author's been revised, re-edited, and re-published—not only in black and white, as it were, but in audiobook format. Incidentally, for those of you who've struggled (or just glossed over) the various tongues that have appeared over the last half-a-million words, the audiobook versions might be worth checking out. I've worked extensively with my narrators to give them the tools they need for proper pronunciation. What tools? Oh, I just went in and recorded the words myself. It was ... an involved process, but I feel the same way about the linguistics of The Cycle of Bones that I do about its music. The work and your ears are worth the effort. I'd rather you get to hear the songs and the spoken word in as close to the same way as *I* hear them.

Speaking of effort, I want to take an extra moment to again thank my research team and my translators. I know, I know, they're thanked in the acknowledgements, but honestly... From Traead's Welsh and Irish origins, to the Latin American influence on my Elven tongues, to the Timucua touch on my Dwarven (I really am *so* glad the project to document, analyze, and preserve this Native American tongue continues its important work), I owe such a *debt* of gratitude. It's more than just the linguistics, though. I've had help understanding the way wetlands work, the first recorded real-world appearances of specific technologies and social concepts... I've gotten first-hand explanations of autism, various cultural and racial experiences, sexuality, military service, and (this'll shock you, I know), what it's like not only to be handicapped, but what it means *not* to be. How else was I going to know what sort of detail you sighted people can make out clearly at X range or distance?

So yes. From the bottom of my heart, thank you, one and all, for helping me with varying degrees of research, hours and hours of conversation, and putting up with what undoubtedly seemed like my endless questions.

If you'd told me at the end of Drums that the battles of Wick, Eastshadow, and Jižní Lov would take an entire tome to tell, I'd have laughed at you. *"Surely not,"* I'd have scoffed. And yet here we are, right? I knew I needed to roll the clock and calendar back a few days. If you were going to feel anything for the folk of Jižní Lov and their plight, you needed at least a little bit of time with them. Besides, Vlk had more to say, as did Andrej. And Kastan? She was always going to have a huge role to play.

For those wondering, yes. Even before you met him as Dargory's rescuer in Drums, Methias was *Methias*. There just wasn't a compelling reason for him to give anyone his name at that point. Methias has been in the tale since before Ylspeth spoke her first words in Thorionden's throneroom.

We help to shape and are *shaped by* the lives we interact with. And we never really know the impact we may have on someone else. As far as I can see—Yes. *See*. I kinda *had* to sneak another one in. At this point, I'm contractually obligated for a certain number of blind jokes per day. Sorry-not-sorry—the best prose gives at least a nod to this idea. For me, at least, part of what makes a character feel real and alive is their impact on others, for good or ill.

You, and indeed the men and women (and children, yes. Them too.) we've been traveling with may never learn the details. But literally every person we see, hear, or meet within these books has a rich internal world—a *life*, if you wanna get right down to it. From the loutish guardsman that Jastar knocked into the dirt, to Azhferd's sergeant, Skar—from Ilimor (the pretty serving girl with the damaged teeth in Kieran Isyl), to little Jitka—everyone's as real as roses, so to speak. Do they all matter? To the broader narrative? Perhaps not. But I'd argue that without them, the broader narrative would feel empty. "Wides as an ocean and deep as a puddle" they say, right?

Okay, okay, I'll get down off my soapbox now. I don't wanna get a nose bleed, after all.

What's next? *The Echo of Tombs* looks like it'll be released in the fall of 2024. Among other things, there's the little matter of a certain tournament that I've been itching to share with you. Beyond that, I won't say.

As for the series itself, those who survive have challenges beyond the King of the Dead and his plans for Skolf. But as Jannon told a young Methias, "One horror at a time."

Thanks for all the Electricity,

~JPC

Coral Springs, FL/Newmarket, UK
September, 2023

Acknowledgements

As always, there are many, many people without whom I could not have written and released this book, all the books that will follow in The Cycle of Bones, and future series.

Jim Trice, Dawn Hart, David Shepherd, Knut Martin Fjelldal, Diane Worden, Ed & Scott Abbot, Sean Dorosinski, Nicholas Ranch, and Jancie Johnson Ter Louw, Sean Lewis—you made up the foundation upon which I stood. Without your love and support, this book would never have come to pass.

My editorial staff Joe, Laura and Gwen; your individual and collective help was (as always) invaluable and insightful.

A special thank you to Julio Chacon. You came in clutch, playing a pivotal eleventh-hour role as my seeing-eye editor when I stumbled into some major formatting errors.

Simon Vance—the narrator for the *Dawn of Unions*, and the literal embodiment of the voices in my head; you most assuredly did *not* have to offer me your services for my debut. I cannot thank you enough. I've learned so much from you. I'll do my level best to carry those lessons forward.

Jeff Brown—the man responsible for bringing the faces and places in my head to startling and stunning life; my only complaint is having to wait until the next book is ready for art before I get to work with you again.

My Research team Krista "Brekke" Capps, Warren Capps, Craig Woodward, Katherine (Fish), Cherish Erin, Jason Cole, Steve Mattox, Cameron A. Kabinoff, Aaron Dean, Dave Scheidecker, Sayf al-Dawla bin-Arslan al-Rumi, S. Chavers (Sir Brealthen De Raimes KSCA), and Jennifer Marriott (Professional Wetland Scientist, Wet.land, LLC). Along with my editors Gwen and Laura, you were often my eyes and my sounding board, and always managed to have the right information or perspective when I needed it. Thank you.

My translators Knut Martin Fjelldal (Norwegian/Havalunth), Ben Beyeresdorf (German/Gerstealunth), Inga (Polish/Kamienalunth),

Acknowledgements

Janshuro (Czech/Kovalunth), Maredudd ap Gwylim and Nik Whitehead (Welsh/much of Traeadish), Lynette Nusbacher and Ellen Rawson (Middle English), and Pegasus (Urdu/the Barghad tongue)—thank you for putting up with my endless questions and clarifications.

To my Hastati Gard—I say again, it was an honor and one of the great joys of my life to train, stand, and fight at your side. Protego Regnum.

A special and enormous thank you to my Patrons on Patreon. Your love and support make all of this madness possible in more ways than just the obvious financial one.

Thanks for all the Electricity,
~JP Corwyn

Book Club Questions

1. We follow several points of view as we work our way through the battles that ended *The Drums of Unrest*. We also meet Methias Arthod (in earnest, this time). And thanks to Jastar, we finally see what's really going on in the lands formerly owned by the Shivering Song. Who would you consider the "main" character or point of view?

2. Lashjuk spends much of the book wrestling with her own instincts as a mother. She wants to charge in to rescue her boy, but time and again she holds herself back. Was she right to do so? What do you think would've happened if she'd listened to her heart rather than her head?

3. When did you realize Andrej's true parentage?

4. Attentive readers will have recognized Skar from his appearances in *Drums*. Those who've eaten and slept since reading that book may have seen him as an entirely new character here, in *Eaters*. Given what we now know about him, and his purpose, what do you think will happen to Azhferd and company when the enemy's presence is felt in Zlaté Pole?

5. What do you suppose happened to Fetinba? For that matter, what do you hope happened to her?

6. Why do you think Kastan's pursuers simply winked out of existence before the gates of Jižní Lov?

7. When did you first suspect or realize Methias's position within Dereek khn?

8. Olshnak, Tomet, and Jek appear to be involved in something much larger than simply serving Sir Kaith. Hells, Olshnak seems concerned that he may have to let Kaith die in service to whatever he's truly been sent to Wick to do. Whom does he really serve? What do you think his actual mission is?

9. In the ordinary course, Jastar would have been the right man to infiltrate, observe, and report back to the Thorion Throne. He

was warned that there was at least some degree of magic being used in construction, so even that wasn't a surprise. The extent to which magic is being used by the realm's military? That's another matter entirely. What do you think Jast should do? Should he remain undercover? Should he hie for the hills and race back to inform the throne? Should he attempt to assassinate Methias, removing the most obvious danger to Thorion's interests?

10. Should Olshnak remain in Dereek khn and let Methias sort things with Thorion? Should he remain with Kaith, presuming Methias's people can revive him? Or should he flee the entire affair and hope to escape to a new life elsewhere?

11. What do you think happened to the little dwarven girl before Methias found her? Do you have any thoughts as to what might be done to heal or revive her?

12. The Venzene Empire doesn't strictly have a religion. The nearest thing to a priesthood is their order of scholars. Yet we now know that those scholars have a connection to, or some knowledge of, the King of the Dead. What do you think that connection is?

13. There's clearly more to Tomet and Jek than simple guardsmen. Who or what are they, really?

14. The goblins shifted after their encounters with Tomet and Jek and quite dramatically. Why do you suppose that happened? What caused it?

15. We discover at least some of the truth about Rákos, and Lashjuk rightly wonders what secrets the man told Andrej. While the boy's done nothing thus far but help, she can't help but be cautious, if not outright paranoid, about his ultimate loyalties. Is she right to worry? Do you trust Andrej's motivations and loyalties? Why or why not?

16. There's a substantial body count within these pages. Did any of the deaths come as a surprise or hit you particularly hard? If so, which ones and why?

17. Why did the battle for Eastshadow end so abruptly? There were clearly still goblins-a-plenty on the field, after all.

18. What role do you think the Rakshasa and his forces will play in the wars to come?

19. Should Methias have made a different choice at Wick? Would you have?

20. What role do you think Edmund, Vlk, and company will play

going forward?

21. Who was the woman in Jastar's dream? What do you suppose she wanted?

22. Why do you suppose Hajvarr looked so distressed when Kastan spoke to the people under Jižní Lov?

23. Aethan and Barnic appear to be growing distant from one another since the battle of Eastshadow. Do you agree with Barnic that Aethan will come around? Is Aethan just showing jealousy over Barnic's seemingly endless ascension of prominence and power, or is he right to be cautious and concerned?

24. What do you think Shiza's true motivations are? Whose side is she truly on?

THE CYCLE OF BONES WILL CONTINUE IN:

THE ECHO OF TOMBS

About the Author

How could you be so blind? You haven't heard of JP Corwyn? Haven't seen him live? Haven't heard his music? How embarrassing for you!

It's okay. You're in the right place. For JP, the rationale for the blind jokes is, well, reasonable. He is legally blind. Born with a degenerative eye condition, his genre tags of Blind Indie Rock, and now Blind Indie Prose, make more sense. Otherwise, he'd just be sort of pretentious and snarky, but not in the fun-depraved sit-com way.

Corwyn's vocal-driven indie rock style is infectious, described as "Shinedown and Angie Aparo on a tour bus ... with Stevie Wonder driving!" On vocals and acoustic guitar, Corwyn has helmed an EP, four full-length albums, and numerous single releases thus far in his career. He has taken a raw and unplugged show from Tampa up the east coast to New York, overseas to the UK, EU, and Asia, and back again.

...But Corwyn's harbored a dark, secret obsession throughout his musical career: his other driving force—writing fiction. Corwyn started work on The Cycle of Bones in early 2019. This epic multi-book series burned its way onto the literary scene with the novella The Dawn of Unions (November 2019). It has continued with the novels The Drums of Unrest (November 2020), and The Eaters of Time (September 2022). Combining his passions, JP has recorded soundtracks for the first two books, including an original cinematic score and songs appearing in the pages of the novels.

Yep, he's blind. But he's hardly unaware. So why should you be?

Find out more about JP
Linktree-
https//linktr.ee/jpcorwyn

More books from 4 Horsemen Publications

Horror, Thriller, & Suspense

Alan Berkshire
Jungle
Hell's Road

Erika Lance
Jimmy
Illusions of Happiness
No Place for Happiness
I Hunt You

Maria DeVivo
Witch of the Black Circle
Witch of the Red Thorn
Witch of the Silver Locust
Witch of the White Serpernt

Mark Tarrant
The Mighty Hook

October Kane
Nothing Will Be Left
Everything Will Burn

Steve Altier
The Camping Trip
Jimmy's Curse
The Ghost Hunter

Fantasy

D. Lambert
To Walk into the Sands
Rydan
Celebrant
Northlander
Esparan
King
Traitor
His Last Name

D.A. Spruzen
The Turkish Connection
The Witch of Tut

Danielle Orsino
Locked Out of Heaven
Thine Eyes of Mercy
From the Ashes
Kingdom Come
Fire, Ice, Acid, & Heart
A Fae is Done

J.M. Paquette
Klauden's Ring
Solyn's Body
The Inbetween
Hannah's Heart

Lou Kemp
The Violins Played Before Junstan
Music Shall Untune the Sky
The Raven and the Pig
The Pirate Danced and the Automat Died
The Wyvern, the Pirate, and the Madman

Megan Mackie
Silverblood Scion

R.J. Young
Challenges of Tawa
Witch of the Whirlwind

Sydney Wilder
Daughter of Serpents

Valerie Willis
Cedric: The Demonic Knight
Romasanta: Father of Werewolves
The Oracle: Keeper of the Gaea's Gate
Artemis: Eye of Gaea
King Incubus: A New Reign

Kyle Sorrell
Munderworld
Potarium

Discover more at
4HorsemenPublications.com